The Best Horror Stories

The Best Horror Stories

Introduction
by
Lynn Picknett

HAMLYN

Published 1977 by
Hamlyn Publishing,
a division of The Hamlyn Publishing
Group Limited,
Bridge House, London Road,
Twickenham, Middlesex

This collection and Introduction,
© The Hamlyn Publishing Group 1977
Second Impression 1984
Third impression 1985

ISBN 0 600 38244 3

Printed in Great Britain by
Hazell Watson & Viney Limited,
Member of the BPCC Group,
Aylesbury, Bucks

Contents

5

CONTENTS

Introduction

It can't happen to me. It can't *happen* . . . The moment that paralyses the soul, freezes the blood, stops the world; a few seconds of the depth of horror known only in nightmare. This is what these stories are about. But nightmares are insubstantial: they come, but they go and the friendly light switch, the first rays of dawn, the sound of the milkman – in short, a reunion with the mundane and familiar and we are back in the land of the sane. This collection is not about dreams, horrifying though they might be. It is about nightmare, true. But about nightmare becoming reality, about the sort of world where God is dead, there is no appeal, and the worst that can happen is infinitely worse than your worst imaginings.

No anthology of horror stories would be complete without Poe. His world of premature burials and morbid obsessions overlaid with guilt has never been equalled; nor the atmosphere he conjures up – an oppressive dream-like horror always on the edge of the unbearable. *The Premature Burial* seems to crystallize not only his particular obsession but underlines the fact that what tortured him *was* that obsession. The horror came from inside his own head while the real world simply took no notice of him. Madness is the key to much of the horror in this book.

The prospect of going mad; the suspicion that you are already mad; a confrontation with a madman, an idiot, or an urbane and smiling psychopath; the sudden realization that you have been living with a madman for years; the contagion of madness, these and other refinements of very basic terror find full and awful expression in these pages. It is a favourite subject for horror stories because it is one of the universal fears. *Yours Truly, Jack the Ripper* by Robert Bloch sounds predictable at first, with its obsessive's visit to a modern psychiatrist, blathering on about Jack the Ripper still being alive in the America of the mid-twentieth century. It is well told. It is amusing. You just might feel a bit superior. Anyone can see how it's going to end. I guarantee you feel a chill that can pin you to your seat for very long seconds, cold leaden heartbeats long at the end of this little tale. For, you see, it is about mad-

7

ness and madness would not be horrible if it were predictable.

It is perhaps a good thing that horror stories are so popular; they shake us, unsettle our neat world for just long enough to escape from the threat of smugness. They are, after all, fiction, aren't they? Yet two stories in this book are centred on episodes in a concentration camp. It has been said that some of the first liberators through the gates of Belsen lost their minds. Maybe those men, in going through those gates had crossed over the borderline between nightmare-sleeping and nightmare-waking, never to return. It wasn't simply man's inhumanity to man that could rob an experienced soldier of his reason. War, is, after all, just that. It was the unbelievable fact that the S.S. made an industry of it. Some people think that even the most innocent factory has a sinister air about it. How much more frightful, then, is the extermination camp with its mounds of teeth and hair, the 'sick parades' where the skeleton people pretend to be bursting with health to avoid the gas chambers for one more day. C. S. Forester gives us two stories set in one of these death factories, both concerning men caught up in the mind-destroying, soul-destroying, machinery that ran the industry. Men whose nausea, whose very humanity could not be revealed by so much as a twitch or an unusual pallor. This is the torturer tortured but none the less horrible for that.

Torture is the very stuff of nightmare; if it were not so it would not have been – and still be – such a popular form of punishment. We all know, because we have read about it, that there is physical and there is mental torture. But sometimes there is both.

The Torture of Hope expresses in its title only a fraction of the pulse-stopping horror of the last few paragraphs. The old Jew tortured by a fanatical Inquisitor; the Inquisitor's detailed description of the Jew's 'baptism by fire' *tomorrow*. And then the door someone 'forgot' to lock. That way madness lies. To be deprived of life, or under threat of execution, that is terrible enough. But to be given, then deprived of hope: that is pure refined horror.

Where you have torture, where indeed you have madness, you will have monsters. Monsters are enjoying a vogue at the moment and most of them are a lot smaller, and a lot less lovable than King Kong. I am referring to the spate of monster-children beloved of the cinema of the 1970s. But neither the Damien of *The Omen* nor Carrie, whose party-going habits are somewhat anti-social, are not alone in their pint-sized corruption. There are many small monsters in this book: in *The Veld*, *The Game*, *The Comforts of Home*, *The Web* and most horribly in *Robert* and *Corabella*. And there are the reluctant and frightened children who are forced to take swift and deadly action through passion; Cinci and the boy who refused to eat the terrapin. We have all been children and should

8

remember what it's like to be a child but we don't. Mothers are constantly amazed at the happy imaginings of their child. 'He lives in another world' they say, wonderingly. Just as no one can love quite like a child so no one has the capacity for blind, enduring hate of a child. But the essence of horror is, as Geoffrey Household says in *Taboo* 'evil . . . something that behaves as it has no right to behave'. And children, are supposed to be, if not angelic, then innocent and harmless. Rightly or wrongly that is the universal opinion of children. Faced with a child both evil and corrupt we feel the moorings of our mind fraying. Children who can torture, kill or drive you mad with horror are not of this world. They don't act like *children*, dammit. Come to think of it they don't act like humans at all.

Anything that isn't as it seems, is anyway unnatural, can be profoundly disturbing. Just as the frantic behaviour of certain species precedes an eclipse or an earthquake, so quite minute changes in the pattern of the familiar can precede moments of shattering horror. In *The Fanatic* by Arthur Porges we, in our humanitarian way, are appalled to hear the principal character outlining his life's work – to capture any animals whose behaviour is not typical of their kind and torture them *to make them speak*. His madness is all the more pointed by his own repulsion for sadism for its own sake. His is a serious task: all the world's wildlife is infiltrated with spies from another planet. If tortured they will have to drop their disguise as raccoons, say, or marmosets, and speak. His girlfriend's initial horror and subsequent fascination might be our own.

Arthur Machen's *The Terror* deals with animals, too, cleverly setting a complex scene apparently masterminded by some supernatural agency. But the supernatural has no place in this story. It is the *unnatural* we come to grips with here, the fascination of the abnormal. The climax of *The Terror* is all the more horrifying for its lack of an occult explanation. The real, solid world has been threatened by itself but a real, solid world that seems to have turned inside out, in contradiction to natural laws, betraying those who still abide by them. The anguish of one caught up in the natural world gone haywire is summed up by one of the characters: 'What had happened to it, that friendly, that familiar world?'

We can accept a ghost more easily than the familiar turned corrupt just as we can accept, in our minds and hearts, the atrocities of some psychopath in the newspapers. But we can't begin to accept the slightest sign of out-of-character behaviour of someone we know well. *The Terror* works for us as a horror story, first because it provides a sickeningly *natural* explanation for bizarre and tragic happenings; second, because it is extraordinarily well written and contains the seeds of a thumping good thriller and even the hint of a First World War spy story.

Perversely, only by the thinnest thread will the best horror stories fit into the themes which hold any good anthology together. It is not possible to place a measure on the quality of *Skeleton* by Ray Bradbury, *The Game* by Thomasina Weber, *The Fanatic* by Arthur Porges, or *A Rose for Emily* by William Faulkner. The only yardstick is success, and by that measure we were vouchsafed a classic in 1945, when John Keir Cross wrote *The Glass Eye*. Mr Bradbury excels with his skeleton-obsessed hypochondriac. Characteristically the story unfolds with grim economy. It's the last line that says it.

The Game plays up the monster-child theme. As with several stories in this volume there is no Goodie and the only real decision you can make about the Baddies is, whose side are you on?

The Fanatic I've already touched on as an example of the subtle horrors of madness and of confronting madness. When I first read it I had this vague feeling that there was going to be a nasty twist. I employed my old technique used for detecting the murderer in Agatha Christies – suspect *everybody*. That way you're always right. So I duly imagined everything I, and a background of pretty horrendous reading, could predict. I was wrong. You might not be. But if I were you I'd worry about getting it right.

We all have phobias. Some people are inexplicably terrified of cats, or more-than-usually repelled by spiders (both themes touched on in this book). Maybe not phobias in the sense that they can be clinically defined, just the old pity and terror mercilessly applied in the most cunning fashion. It's all there in *The Torture of Hope* but a personal quirk makes me single out *The Glass Eye* as a particularly shattering piece of writing. The loveless, obsessional spinster in her sordid room, falling pathetically in love with – a ventriloquist. It could easily be sob stuff, but it's not.

The reader will have noted that my comments are prompted chiefly by the modern stories. This is because of their immediacy – they occur in an instantly recognizable world. At the worst level you can wonder what could make our flesh crawl after Belsen, after Hiroshima? More superficially, after films, after television, literally after *all*. The modern cinema has acquainted us with demon-possessed children; Satanic rites and even quasi-documentary cannibalism. But cinema provides you with the pictures, channels you visually. Oddly, people still read the book of the film even after having seen the film. The images must be yours for the horror to be yours. When you read horror the images are yours, personally. They by-pass the censor. The shape they take is you, no getting away from it; words wriggle into your brain and fester. The poison is of your own manufacture.

But such is the universality of horror that one thing I can guarantee. Somewhere, something in this book will make you stare in disbelief at the page. A last line will hit you like a tidal wave. Somewhere in here you and your nightmares belong.

But take comfort. If they didn't touch you, if these stories, covering centuries and continents did not shock you, you'd be sick.

Lynn Picknett
London
March 1977.

Edgar Allan Poe

The Black Cat

For the most wild, yet most homely narrative which I am about to pen, I neither expect nor solicit belief. Mad indeed would I be to expect it, in a case where my very senses reject their own evidence. Yet, mad am I not – and very surely do I not dream. But tomorrow I die, and today I would unburden my soul. My immediate purpose is to place before the world, plainly, succinctly, and without comment, a series of mere household events. In their consequences, these events have terrified – have tortured – have destroyed me. Yet I will not attempt to expound them. To me, they have presented little but horror – to many they will seem less terrible than *baroques*. Hereafter, perhaps, some intellect may be found which will reduce my phantasm to the commonplace – some intellect more calm, more logical, and far less excitable than my own, which will perceive, in the circumstances I detail with awe, nothing more than an ordinary succession of very natural causes and effects.

From my infancy I was noted for the docility and humanity of my disposition. My tenderness of heart was even so conspicuous as to make me the jest of my companions. I was especially fond of animals, and was indulged by my parents with a great variety of pets. With these I spent most of my time, and never was so happy as when feeding and caressing them. This peculiarity of character grew with my growth, and, in my manhood, I derived from it one of my principal sources of pleasure. To those who have cherished an affection for a faithful and sagacious dog, I need hardly be at the trouble of explaining the nature or the intensity of the gratification thus derivable. There is something in the unselfish and self-sacrificing love of a brute, which goes directly to the heart of him who has had frequent occasion to test the paltry friendship and gossamer fidelity of mere *Man*.

I married early, and was happy to find in my wife a disposition not uncongenial with my own. Observing my partiality for domestic pets, she lost no opportunity of procuring those of the most agreeable kind. We had birds, goldfish, a fine dog, rabbits, a small monkey, and *a cat*.

This latter was a remarkably large and beautiful animal, entirely black, and sagacious to an astonishing degree. In speaking of his intelligence, my wife, who at heart was not a little tinctured with superstition, made frequent allusion to the ancient popular notion, which regarded all black cats as witches in disguise. Not that she was ever *serious* upon this point – and I mention the matter at all for no better reason than that it happens, just now, to be remembered.

Pluto – this was the cat's name – was my favourite pet and playmate. I alone fed him, and he attended me wherever I went about the house. It was even with difficulty that I could prevent him from following me through the streets.

Our friendship lasted, in this manner, for several years, during which my general temperament and character – through the instrumentality of the fiend Intemperance – had (I blush to confess it) experienced a radical alteration for the worse. I grew, day by day, more moody, more irritable, more regardless of the feelings of others. I suffered myself to use intemperate language to my wife. At length, I even offered her personal violence. My pets, of course, were made to feel the change in my disposition. I not only neglected, but ill-used them. For Pluto, however, I still retained sufficient regard to restrain me from maltreating him, as I made no scruple of maltreating the rabbits, the monkey, or even the dog, when by accident, or through affection, they came in my way. But my disease grew upon me – for what disease is like alcohol? – and at length even Pluto, who was now becoming old, and consequently somewhat peevish – even Pluto began to experience the effects of my ill temper.

One night, returning home, much intoxicated, from one of my haunts about town, I fancied that the cat avoided my presence. I seized him; when, in his fright at my violence, he inflicted a slight wound upon my hand with his teeth. The fury of a demon instantly possessed me. I knew myself no longer. My original soul seemed, at once, to take its flight from my body; and a more than fiendish malevolence, gin-nurtured, thrilled every fibre of my frame. I took from my waistcoat pocket a pen-knife, opened it, grasped the poor beast by the throat, and deliberately cut one of its eyes from the socket! I blush, I burn, I shudder, while I pen the damnable atrocity.

When reason returned with the morning – when I had slept off the fumes of the night's debauch – I experienced a sentiment half of horror, half of remorse, for the crime of which I had been guilty; but it was, at best, a feeble and equivocal feeling, and the soul remained untouched.

I again plunged into excess, and soon drowned in wine all memory of the deed.

In the meantime the cat slowly recovered. The socket of the lost eye presented, it is true, a frightful appearance, but he no longer appeared to suffer any pain. He went about the house as usual, but, as might be expected, fled in extreme terror at my approach. I had so much of my old heart left, as to be at first grieved by this evident dislike on the part of a creature which had once so loved me. But this feeling soon gave place to irritation. And then came, as if to my final and irrevocable overthrow, the spirit of PERVERSENESS. Of this spirit philosophy takes no account. Yet I am not more sure that my soul lives, than I am that perverseness is one of the primitive impulses of the human heart – one of the indivisible primary faculties, or sentiments, which give direction to the character of man. Who has not, a hundred times, found himself committing a vile or a silly action, for no other reason than because he knows he should *not*? Have we not a perpetual inclination, in the teeth of our best judgment, to violate that which is *Law*, merely because we understand it to be such? This spirit of perverseness, I say, came to my final overthrow. It was this unfathomable longing of the soul *to vex itself* – to offer violence to its own nature – to do wrong for the wrong's sake only – that urged me to continue and finally to consummate the injury I had inflicted upon the unoffending brute. One morning, in cool blood, I slipped a noose about its neck and hung it to the limb of a tree – hung it with the tears streaming from my eyes, and with the bitterest remorse at my heart – hung it *because* I knew that it had loved me, and *because* I felt it had give me no reason of offence – hung it *because* I knew that in so doing I was committing a sin – a deadly sin that would so jeopardise my immortal soul as to place it – if such a thing were possible – even beyond the reach of the infinite mercy of the Most Merciful and Most Terrible God.

On the night of the day on which this cruel deed was done, I was aroused from sleep by the cry of 'Fire!' The curtains of my bed were in flames. The whole house was blazing. It was with great difficulty that my wife, a servant, and myself, made our escape from the conflagration. The destruction was complete. My entire worldly wealth was swallowed up, and I resigned myself thenceforward to despair.

I am above the weakness of seeking to establish a sequence of cause and effect between the disaster and the atrocity. But I am detailing a chain of facts, and wish not to leave even a possible link imperfect. On the day succeeding the fire, I visited the ruins. The walls, with one exception, had fallen in. This exception was found in a compartment wall, not very thick, which stood about the middle of the house, and against which had rested the head of my bed. The plastering had here, in great measure, resisted the action of the fire – a fact which I attributed to its having been recently spread. About this wall a dense crowd were collected, and many persons seemed to be examining a particular portion of it with very minute and eager attention. The words 'strange!' 'singular!' and other similar expressions, excited my curiosity. I approached and saw, as if graven in bas-relief upon the white surface, the figure of a gigantic *cat*. The impression was given with an accuracy truly marvellous. There was a rope about the animal's neck.

When I first beheld this apparition – for I could scarcely regard it as less – my wonder and my terror were extreme. But at length reflection came to my aid. The cat, I remembered, had been hung in a garden adjacent to the house. Upon the alarm of fire, this garden had been immediately filled by the crowd – by some one of whom the animal must have been cut from the tree and thrown, through an open window, into my chamber. This had probably been done with the view of arousing me from sleep. The falling of other walls had compressed the victim of my cruelty into the substance of the freshly-spread plaster; the lime of which, with the flames and the *ammonia* from the carcass, had then accomplished the portraiture as I saw it.

Although I thus readily accounted to my reason, if not altogether to my conscience, for the startling fact just detailed, it did not the less fail to make a deep impression upon my fancy. For months I could not rid myself of the phantasm of the cat; and, during this period, there came back into my spirit a half-sentiment that seemed, but was not, remorse. I went so far as to regret the loss of the animal, and to look about me, among the vile haunts which I now habitually frequented, for another pet of the same species, and of somewhat similar appearance, with which to supply its place.

One night as I sat, half stupefied, in a den of more than infamy, my attention was suddenly drawn to some black object, reposing upon the head of one of the immense hogsheads of gin, or of rum, which constituted the chief furniture of the apartment. I had been looking steadily at the top of this hogshead for some minutes, and what now caused me surprise was the fact that I had not sooner perceived the object thereupon. I approached it, and touched it with my hand. It was a black cat – a very large one – fully as large as Pluto, and closely resembling him in every respect but one. Pluto had not a white hair upon any portion of his body; but this cat had a large, although indefinite, splotch of white, covering nearly the whole region of the breast.

Upon my touching him, he immediately arose, purred loudly, rubbed against my hand, and appeared delighted with my notice. This, then, was the very creature of which I was in search. I at once offered to purchase it of the landlord; but this person made no claim to it – knew nothing of it – had never seen it before.

I continued my caresses, and when I prepared to go home, the animal evinced a disposition to accompany me. I permitted it to do so; occasionally stooping and patting it as I proceeded. When it reached the house it domesticated itself at once, and became immediately a great favourite with my wife.

For my own part, I soon found a dislike to it arising within me. This was just the reverse of what I had anticipated; but – I know not how or why it was – its evident fondness for myself rather disgusted and annoyed me. By slow degrees, these feelings of disgust and annoyance rose into the bitterness of hatred. I avoided the creature; a certain sense of shame, and the remembrance of my former deed of cruelty, preventing me from physically abusing it. I did not, for some weeks, strike, or otherwise violently ill-use it; but gradually – very gradually – I came to look upon it with unutterable loathing, and to flee silently from its odious presence, as from the breath of a pestilence.

What added, no doubt, to my hatred of the beast, was the discovery, on the morning after I brought it home, that, like Pluto, it also had been deprived of one of its eyes. The circumstance, however, only endeared it to my wife, who, as I have already said, possessed, in a high degree, that humanity of feeling which had once been my distinguishing trait, and the source of many of my simplest and purest pleasures.

With my aversion to this cat, however, its partiality for myself seemed to increase. It followed my footsteps with a pertinacity which it would be difficult to make the reader comprehend. Whenever I sat, it would crouch beneath my chair, or spring upon my knees, covering me with its loathsome caresses. If I arose to walk, it would get between my feet, and thus nearly throw me down, or, fastening its long and sharp claws in my dress, clamber, in this manner, to my breast. At such times, although I longed to destroy it with a blow, I was yet withheld from so doing, partly by a memory of my former crime, but chiefly – let me confess it at once – by absolute *dread* of the beast.

This dread was not exactly a dread of physical evil – and yet I should be at a loss how otherwise to define it. I am almost ashamed to own – yes, even in this felon's cell, I am almost ashamed to own – that the terror and horror with which the animal inspired me, had been heightened by one of the merest chimeras it would be possible to conceive. My wife had called my attention, more than once, to the character of the mark of white hair, of which I have spoken, and which constituted the sole visible difference between the strange beast and the one I had destroyed. The reader will remember that this mark, although large, had been originally very indefinite; but, by slow degrees – degrees nearly imperceptible, and which for a long time my reason struggled to reject as fanciful – it had, at length, assumed a rigorous distinctness of outline. It was now the representation of an object that I shudder to name – and for this, above all, I loathed, and dreaded, and would have rid myself of the monster *had I dared* – it was now, I say, the image of a hideous – of a ghastly thing – of the GALLOWS! – oh, mournful and terrible engine of horror and of crime – of agony and of death!

And now was I indeed wretched beyond the wretchedness of mere humanity. And *a brute beast* – whose fellow I had contemptuously destroyed – *a brute beast* to work out for *me* – for me, a man, fashioned in the image of the High God – so much of insufferable woe! Alas! neither by day nor by night knew I the blessing of rest any more! During the former the creature left me no moment alone; and, in the latter, I started, hourly, from dreams of unutterable fear, to find the hot breath of *the thing* upon my face, and its vast weight – an incarnate nightmare that I had no power to shake off – incumbent eternally upon my *heart*!

Beneath the pressure of torments such as these, the feeble remnant of the good within me succumbed. Evil thoughts became my sole intimates – the darkest and most evil of thoughts. The moodiness of my usual temper increased to hatred of all things and of all mankind; while, from the sudden, frequent, and ungovernable outbursts of a fury to which I now blindly abandoned myself, my uncomplaining wife, alas! was the most usual and the most patient of sufferers.

One day she accompanied me, upon some household errand, into the cellar of the old building which our poverty compelled us to inhabit. The cat followed me down the steep stairs, and, nearly throwing me headlong, exasperated me to madness. Uplifting an axe, and forgetting, in my wrath, the childish dread which had hitherto stayed my hand, I aimed a blow at the animal which, of course, would have proved instantly fatal had it descended as I wished. But this blow was arrested by the hand of my wife. Goaded, by the interference, into a rage more than demoniacal, I withdrew my arm from her grasp, and buried the axe in her brain. She fell dead upon the spot, without a groan.

This hideous murder accomplished, I set myself forthwith, and with entire deliberation, to the task of concealing the body. I knew that I could not remove it from the house, either by day or by night, without the risk of being observed by the neighbours. Many projects entered my mind. At one period I thought of cutting the corpse into minute fragments, and destroying them by fire. At another, I resolved to dig a grave for it in the floor of the cellar. Again, I deliberated about casting it into the well in the yard – about packing it in a box, as if merchandise, with the usual arrangements, and so getting a porter to take it from the house. Finally I hit upon what I considered a far better expedient than either of these. I determined to wall it up in the cellar – as the monks of the

Middle Ages are recorded to have walled up their victims.

For a purpose such as this the cellar was well adapted. Its walls were loosely constructed, and had lately been plastered throughout with a rough plaster, which the dampness of the atmosphere had prevented from hardening. Moreover, in one of the walls was a projection, caused by a false chimney, or fireplace, that had been filled up, and made to resemble the rest of the cellar. I made no doubt that I could readily displace the bricks at this point, insert the corpse, and wall the whole up as before, so that no eye could detect anything suspicious.

And in this calculation I was not deceived. By means of a crowbar I easily dislodged the bricks, and, having carefully deposited the body against the inner wall, I propped it in that position, while, with little trouble, I relaid the whole structure as it originally stood. Having procured mortar, sand, and hair, with every possible precaution, I prepared a plaster which could not be distinguished from the old, and with this I very carefully went over the new brickwork. When I had finished, I felt satisfied that all was right. The wall did not present the slightest appearance of having been disturbed. The rubbish on the floor was picked up with the minutest care. I looked around triumphantly, and said to myself, 'Here at least, then, my labour has not been in vain.'

My next step was to look for the beast which had been the cause of so much wretchedness; for I had, at length, firmly resolved to put it to death. Had I been able to meet with it, at the moment, there could have been no doubt of its fate; but it appeared that the crafty animal had been alarmed at the violence of my previous anger, and forebore to present itself in my present mood. It is impossible to describe, or to imagine, the deep, the blissful sense of relief which the absence of the detested creature occasioned in my bosom. It did not make its appearance during the night – and thus for one night at least, since its introduction into the house, I soundly and tranquilly slept; aye, *slept* even with the burden of murder upon my soul!

The second and the third day passed, and still my tormentor came not. Once again I breathed as a free man. The monster, in terror, had fled the premises for ever! I should behold it no more! My happiness was supreme! The guilt of my dark deed disturbed me but little. Some few inquiries had been made, but these had been readily answered. Even a search had been instituted – but of course nothing was to be discovered. I looked upon my future felicity as secured.

Upon the fourth day of the assassination, a party of the police came, very unexpectedly, into the house, and proceeded again to make rigorous investigation of the premises. Secure, however, in the inscrutability of my place of concealment, I felt no embarrassment whatever. The officers bade me accompany them in their search. They left no nook or corner unexplored. At length, for the third or fourth time, they descended into the cellar. I quivered not in a muscle. My heart beat calmly as that of one who slumbers in innocence. I walked the cellar from end to end. I folded my arms upon my bosom, and roamed easily to and fro. The police were thoroughly satisfied, and prepared to depart. The glee at my heart was too strong to be restrained. I burned to say if but one word, by way of triumph, and to render doubly sure their assurance of my guiltlessness.

'Gentlemen,' I said at last, as the party ascended the steps, 'I delight to have allayed your suspicions. I wish you all health, and a little more courtesy. By-the-bye, gentlemen, this – this is a very well-constructed house.' (In the rabid desire to say something easily, I scarcely knew what I uttered at all.) 'I may say an *excellently* well-constructed house. These walls – are you going, gentlemen? – these walls are solidly put together;' and here, through the mere frenzy of bravado, I rapped heavily, with a cane which I held in my hand, upon that very portion of the brickwork behind which stood the corpse of the wife of my bosom.

But may God shield and deliver me from the fangs of the Arch-Fiend! No sooner had the reverberation of my blows sunk into silence, than I was answered by a voice from within the tomb! – by a cry, at first muffled and broken, like the sobbing of a child, and then quickly swelling into one long, loud, and continuous scream, utterly anomalous and in-human – a howl – a wailing shriek, half of horror and half of triumph, such as might have arisen only out of hell, conjointly from the throats of the damned in their agony and of the demons that exult in the damnation.

Of my own thoughts it is folly to speak. Swooning, I staggered to the opposite wall. For one instant the party upon the stairs remained motion-less, through extremity of terror and of awe. In the next, a dozen stout arms were toiling at the wall. It fell bodily. The corpse, already greatly decayed and clotted with gore, stood erect before the eyes of the specta-tors. Upon its head, with red extended mouth and solitary eye of fire, sat the hideous beast whose craft had seduced me into murder, and whose informing voice had consigned me to the hangman. I had walled the monster up within the tomb!

Edgar Allan Poe

The Tell-Tale Heart

True! – nervous – very, very dreadfully nervous I had been and am; but why *will* you say that I am mad? The disease had sharpened my senses – not destroyed – not dulled them. Above all was the sense of hearing acute. I heard all things in the heaven and in the earth. I heard many things in hell. How, then, am I mad? Hearken! and observe how healthily – how calmly I can tell you the whole story.

It is impossible to say how first the idea entered my brain; but onec conceived, it haunted me day and night. Object there was none. Passion there was none. I loved the old man. He had never wronged me. He had never given me insult. For his gold I had no desire. I think it was his eye! yes, it was this! One of his eyes resembled that of a vulture – a pale blue eye, with a film over it. Whenever it fell upon me, my blood ran cold; and so by degrees – very gradually – I made up my mind to take the life of the old man, and thus rid myself of the eye for ever.

Now this is the point. You fancy me mad. Madmen know nothing. But you should have seen *me*. You should have seen how wisely I proceeded – with what caution – with what foresight – with what dissimulation I went to work! I was never kinder to the old man than during the whole week before I killed him. And every night, about midnight, I turned the latch of his door and opened it – oh, so gently! And then, when I had made an opening sufficient for my head, I put in a dark lantern, all closed, closed, so that no light shone out, and then I thrust in my head. Oh, you would have laughed to see how cunningly I thrust it in! I moved it slowly – very, very slowly, so that I might not disturb the old man's sleep. It took me an hour to place my whole head within the opening so far that I could see him as he lay upon his bed. Ha! – would a madman have been so wise as this? And then, when my head was well in the room, I undid the lantern, cautiously – oh, so cautiously – cautiously (for the hinges creaked) I undid it just so much that a single thin ray fell upon the vulture eye. And this I did for seven long nights – every night just at midnight – but I found the eye always closed; and so it was impossible to do the work; for it was not the old man who vexed me, but his Evil Eye. And every morning, when the day broke, I went boldly into the chamber, and spoke courageously to him, calling him by name in a hearty tone, and inquiring how he had passed the night. So you see he would have been a very profound old man, indeed, to suspect that every night, just at twelve, I looked in upon him while he slept.

Upon the eighth night I was more than usually cautious in opening the door. A watch's minute hand moves more quickly than did mine. Never before that night had I *felt* the extent of my own powers – of my sagacity. I could scarcely contain my feelings of triumph. To think that there I was, opening the door, little by little, and he not even to dream of my secret deeds or thoughts. I fairly chuckled at the idea; and perhaps he heard me – for he moved on the bed suddenly, as if startled. Now you may think that I drew back – but no. His room was as black as pitch with the thick darkness (for the shutters were close-fastened, through fear of robbers), and so I knew that he could not see the opening of the door, and I kept pushing it on steadily, steadily.

I had my head in, and was about to open the lantern, when my thumb slipped upon the tin fastening, and the old man sprang up in the bed, crying out, 'Who's there?'

I kept quite still and said nothing. For a whole hour I did not move a muscle, and in the meantime I did not hear him lie down. He was sitting up in the bed, listening – just as I have done, night after night, hearkening to the death-watches in the wall.

Presently I heard a groan, and I knew it was the groan of mortal terror. It was not a groan of pain or grief – oh, no! – it was the low stifled sound that arises from the bottom of the soul when overcharged with awe. I knew the sound well. Many a night, just at midnight, when all the world slept, it has welled up from my own bosom, deepening, with its dreadful echo, the terrors that distracted me. I say I knew it well. I knew what the old man felt, and pitied him, although I chuckled at heart. I knew that he had been lying awake ever since the first slight noise, when he had turned in the bed. His fears had been ever since growing upon him. He had been trying to fancy them causeless, but could not. He had been saying to himself, 'It is nothing but the wind in the chimney – it is only a mouse crossing the floor,' or, 'It is merely a cricket which has made a single chirp.' Yes, he had been trying to comfort himself with these suppositions; but he had found all in vain. *All in vain;* because Death, in approaching him, had stalked with his black shadow before him, and enveloped the victim. And it was the mournful influence of the unperceived shadow that caused him to feel – although he neither saw nor heard – to *feel* the presence of my head within the room.

When I had waited a long time, very patiently, without hearing him lie down, I resolved to open a little – a very, very little crevice in the lantern. So I opened it – you cannot imagine how stealthily, stealthily – until, at length, a single dim ray, like the thread of the spider, shot from out the crevice and fell upon the vulture eye.

It was open – wide, wide open – and I grew furious as I gazed upon it. I saw it with perfect distinctness – all a dull blue, with a hideous veil over it that chilled the very marrow in my bones; but I could see nothing else of the old man's face or person, for I had directed the ray, as if by instinct, precisely upon the damned spot.

And now have I not told you what you mistake for madness is but over-acuteness of the senses? – now, I say, there came to my ears a low, dull, quick sound, such as a watch makes when enveloped in cotton. I knew *that* sound well, too. It was the beating of the old man's heart. It increased my fury, as the beating of a drum stimulates the soldier into courage.

But even yet I refrained and kept still. I scarcely breathed. I held the lantern motionless. I tried how steadily I could maintain the ray upon the eye. Meantime the hellish tattoo of the heart increased. It grew quicker and quicker, and louder and louder every instant. The old man's terror *must* have been extreme! It grew louder, I say, louder every moment! – do you mark me well? I have told you that I am nervous: so I am. And now, at the dead hour of the night, amid the dreadful silence of that old house, so strange a noise as this excited me to uncontrollable terror. Yet, for some minutes longer, I refrained and stood still. But the beating grew louder, louder! I thought the heart must burst. And now a new anxiety seized me – the sound would be heard by a neighbour! The old man's hour had come! With a loud yell I threw open the lantern and leaped into the room. He shrieked once – once only. In an instant I dragged him to the floor, and pulled the heavy bed over him. I then smiled gaily, to find the deed so far done. But, for many minutes, the heart beat on with a muffled sound. This, however, did not vex me; it would not be heard through the wall. At length it ceased. The old man was dead. I removed the bed and examined the corpse. Yes, he was stone, stone dead. I placed my hand upon the heart and held it there many minutes. There was no pulsation. He was stone dead. His eye would trouble me no more.

If you still think me mad, you will think so no longer when I describe the wise precautions I took for the concealment of the body. The night waned, and I worked hastily, but in silence. First of all I dismembered the corpse. I cut off the head and the arms and the legs.

I then took up three planks from the flooring of the chamber and deposited all between the scantlings. I then replaced the boards so cleverly, so cunningly, that no human eye – not even *his* – could have detected anything wrong. There was nothing to wash out – no stain of any kind – no blood-spot whatever. I had been too wary for that. A tub had caught all – ha! ha!

When I had made an end of these labours, it was four o'clock – still dark as midnight. As the bell sounded the hour, there came a knocking at the street door. I went down to open it with a light heart – for what had I *now* to fear? There entered three men, who introduced themselves, with perfect suavity, as officers of the police. A shriek had been heard by a neighbour during the night; suspicion of foul play had been aroused; information had been lodged at the police office, and they (the officers) had been deputed to search the premises.

I smiled – for *what* had I to fear? I bade the gentlemen welcome. The shriek, I said, was my own in a dream. The old man, I mentioned, was absent in the country. I took my visitors all over the house. I bade them search – search *well*. I led them, at length, to *his* chamber. I showed them his treasures, secure, undisturbed. In the enthusiasm of my confidence, I brought chairs into the room, and desired them *here* to rest from their fatigues, while I myself, in the wild audacity of my perfect triumph, placed my own seat upon the very spot beneath which reposed the corpse of the victim.

The officers were satisfied. My manner had convinced them. I was singularly at ease. They sat, and while I answered cheerily, they chatted of familiar things. But, ere long, I felt myself getting pale and wished them gone. My head ached, and I fancied a ringing in my ears; but still they sat and chatted. The ringing became more distinct – it continued and became more distinct. I talked more freely to get rid of the feeling; but it continued and gained definitiveness – until, at length, I found that the noise was *not* within my ears.

No doubt I now grew very pale; but I talked more fluently, and with a heightened voice. Yet the sound increased – and what could I do? It was *a low, dull, quick sound – much such a sound as a watch makes when enveloped in cotton*. I gasped for breath – and yet the officers heard it not. I talked more quickly – more vehemently; but the noise steadily increased. I arose and argued about trifles, in a high key and with violent gesticulations; but the noise steadily increased. Why *would* they not be gone? I paced the floor to and fro with heavy strides, as if excited to fury by the observations of the men – but the noise steadily increased. O God! what *could* I do? I foamed – I raved – I swore! I swung the chair upon which I had been sitting, and grated it upon the boards, but the noise

arose over all and continually increased. It grew louder – louder –
louder! And still the men chatted pleasantly, and smiled. Was it possible
they heard not? Almighty God! – no, no! They heard! – they suspected!
– they *knew!* – they were making a mockery of my horror! – this I thought
and this I think. But anything was better than this agony! Anything
was more tolerable than this derision! I could bear those hypocritical
smiles no longer! I felt that I must scream or die! – and now – again!
hark! louder! louder! louder! *louder!*——

   'Villains!' I shrieked, 'dissemble no more! I admit the deed! – tear
up the planks! – here, here! – it is the beating of his hideous heart!'

Edgar Allan Poe

The Premature Burial

There are certain themes of which the interest is all-absorbing, but which are too entirely horrible for the purposes of legitimate fiction. These the mere romanticist must eschew, if he do not wish to offend, or to disgust. They are with propriety handled only when the severity and majesty of truth sanctify and sustain them. We thrill, for example, with the most intense of 'pleasurable pain', over the accounts of the Passage of the Beresina, of the Earthquake at Lisbon, of the Plague at London, of the Massacre of St Bartholomew, or of the stifling of the hundred and twenty-three prisoners in the Black Hole at Calcutta. But, in these accounts, it is the fact – it is the reality – it is the history which excites. As inventions, we should regard them with simple abhorrence.

I have mentioned some few of the more prominent and august calamities on record; but in these it is the extent, not less than the character of the calamity, which so vividly impresses the fancy. I need not remind the reader that, from the long and weird catalogue of human miseries, I might have selected many individual instances more replete with essential suffering than any of these vast generalities of disaster. The true wretchedness, indeed – the ultimate woe – is particular, not diffuse. That the ghastly extremes of agony are endured by man the unit, and never by man the mass – for this let us thank a merciful God!

To be buried while alive is, beyond question, the most terrific of these extremes which has ever fallen to the lot of mere mortality. That it has frequently, very frequently, so fallen, will scarcely be denied by those who think. The boundaries which divide Life from Death are at best shadowy and vague. Who shall say where the one ends, and where the other begins? We know that there are diseases in which occur total cessations of all the apparent functions of vitality, and yet in which these

26

cessations are merely suspensions, properly so called. They are only temporary pauses in the incomprehensible mechanism. A certain period elapses, and some unseen mysterious principle again sets in motion the magic pinions and the wizard wheels. The silver cord was not for ever loosed, nor the golden bowl irreparably broken. But where, meantime, was the soil?

Apart, however, from the inevitable conclusion, *a priori*, that such causes must produce such effects – that the well-known occurrence of such cases of suspended animation must naturally give rise, now and then, to premature interments – apart from this consideration, we have the direct testimony of medical and ordinary experience, to prove that a vast number of such interments have actually taken place. I might refer at once, if necessary, to a hundred well-authenticated instances. One of very remarkable character, and of which the circumstances may be fresh in the memory of some of my readers, occurred, not very long ago, in the neighbouring city of Baltimore, where it occasioned a painful, intense, and widely extended excitement. The wife of one of the most respectable citizens – a lawyer of eminence and a member of Congress – was seized with a sudden and unaccountable illness, which completely baffled the skill of her physicians. After much suffering, she died, or was supposed to die. No one suspected, indeed, or had reason to suspect, that she was not actually dead. She presented all the ordinary appearances of death. The face assumed the usual pinched and sunken outline. The lips were of the usual marble pallor. The eyes were lustreless. There was no warmth. Pulsation had ceased. For three days the body was preserved unburied, during which it had acquired a stony rigidity. The funeral, in short, was hastened, on account of the rapid advance of what was supposed to be decomposition.

The lady was deposited in her family vault, which, for three subsequent years, was undisturbed. At the expiration of this term, it was opened for the reception of a sarcophagus – but, alas! how fearful a shock awaited the husband, who, personally, threw open the door. As its portals swung outwardly back, some white-apparelled object fell rattling within his arms. It was the skeleton of his wife in her yet unmouldered shroud.

A careful investigation rendered it evident that she had revived within two days after her entombment – that her struggles within the coffin had caused it to fall from a ledge, or shelf, to the floor, where it was so broken as to permit her escape. A lamp which had been accidentally left, full of oil, within the tomb, was found empty; it might have been exhausted, however, by evaporation. On the uppermost of the steps which led down into the dread chamber, was a large fragment of the coffin, with which it seemed that she had endeavoured to arrest attention, by striking the iron door. While thus occupied, she probably swooned, or possibly died, through sheer terror; and, in falling, her shroud became entangled in some ironwork which projected interiorly. Thus she remained, and thus she rotted, erect.

In the year 1810, a case of living inhumation happened in France, attended with circumstances which go far to warrant the assertion that truth is, indeed, stranger than fiction. The heroine of the story was a Mademoiselle Victorine Lafourcade, a young girl of illustrious family, of wealth, and of great personal beauty. Among her numerous suitors was Julien Bossuet, a poor *litterateur*, or journalist, of Paris. His talents and general amiability had recommended him to the notice of the heiress, by whom he seems to have been truly beloved; but her pride of birth decided her, finally, to reject him, and to wed a Monsieur Renelle, banker, and a diplomatist of some eminence. After marriage, however, this gentleman neglected, and, perhaps, even more positively ill-treated her. Having passed with him some wretched years, she died – at least her condition so closely resembled death as to deceive every one who saw her. She was buried – not in a vault – but in an ordinary grave in the village of her nativity. Filled with despair, and still inflamed by the memory of a profound attachment, the lover journeys from the capital to the remote province in which the village lies, with the romantic purpose of disinterring the corpse, and possessing himself of its luxuriant tresses. He reaches the grave. At midnight he unearths the coffin, opens it, and is in the act of detaching the hair, when he is arrested by the unclosing of the beloved eyes. In fact, the lady had been buried alive. Vitality had not altogether departed; and she was aroused, by the caresses of her lover, from the lethargy which had been mistaken for death. He bore her frantically to his lodgings in the village. He employed certain powerful restoratives suggested by no little medical learning. In fine, she revived. She recognised her preserver. She remained with him until, by slow degrees, she fully recovered her original health. Her woman's heart was not adamant, and this last lesson of love sufficed to soften it. She bestowed it upon Bossuet. She returned no more to her husband, but concealing from him her resurrection, fled with her lover to America. Twenty years afterwards, the two returned to France, in the persuasion that time had so greatly altered the lady's appearance, that her friends would be unable to recognise her. They were mistaken, however; for, at the first meeting, Monsieur Renelle did actually recognise and make claim to his wife. This claim she resisted; and a judicial tribunal sustained her in her resistance; deciding that the peculiar circumstances, with the long lapse of years, had extinguished, not only equitably, but legally, the authority of the husband.

The *Chirurgical Journal* of Leipsic – a periodical of high authority and merit, which some American bookseller would do well to translate and republish – records, in a late number, a very distressing event of the character in question.

An officer of artillery, a man of gigantic stature and of robust health, being thrown from an unmanageable horse, received a very severe contusion upon the head, which rendered him insensible at once; the skull was slightly fractured; but no immediate danger was apprehended. Trepanning was accomplished successfully. He was bled, and many other of the ordinary means of relief were adopted. Gradually, however, he fell into a more and more hopeless state of stupor; and, finally, it was thought that he died.

The weather was warm; and he was buried, with indecent haste, in one of the public cemeteries. His funeral took place on Thursday. On the Sunday following, the grounds of the cemetery were, as usual, much thronged with visitors; and about noon, an intense excitement was created by the declaration of a peasant, that, while sitting upon the grave of the officer, he had distinctly felt a commotion of the earth, as if occasioned by some one struggling beneath. At first, little attention was paid to the man's asseveration; but his evident terror, and the dogged obstinacy with which he persisted in his story, had at length their natural effect upon the crowd. Spades were hurriedly procured, and the grave, which was shamefully shallow, was, in a few minutes, so far thrown open that the head of its occupant appeared. He was then, seemingly, dead; but he sat nearly erect within his coffin, the lid of which, in his furious struggles, he had partially uplifted.

He was forthwith conveyed to the nearest hospital and, there pronounced to be still living, although in an asphytic condition. After some hours he revived, recognised individuals of his acquaintance, and, in broken sentences, spoke of his agonies in the grave.

From what he related, it was clear that he must have been conscious of life for more than an hour, while inhumed, before lapsing into insensibility. The grave was carelessly and loosely filled with an exceedingly porous soil; and thus some air was necessarily admitted. He heard the footsteps of the crowd overhead, and endeavoured to make himself heard in turn. It was the tumult within the grounds of the cemetery, he said, which appeared to awaken him from a deep sleep – but no sooner was he awake than he became fully aware of the awful horrors of his position.

This patient, it is recorded, was doing well, and seemed to be in a fair way of ultimate recovery, but fell a victim to the quackeries of medical experiment. The galvanic battery was applied, and he suddenly expired in one of those ecstatic paroxysms which, occasionally, it superinduces.

The mention of the galvanic battery, nevertheless, recalls to my memory a well-known and very extraordinary case in point, where its action proved the means of restoring to animation a young attorney of London, who had been interred for two days. This occurred in 1831, and created, at the time, a very profound sensation wherever it was made the subject of converse.

The patient, Mr Edward Stapleton, had died, apparently, of typhus fever, accompanied with some anomalous symptoms which had excited the curiosity of his medical attendants. Upon his seeming decease, his friends were requested to sanction a *post-mortem* examination, but declined to permit it. As often happens, when such refusals are made, the practitioners resolved to disinter the body and dissect it at leisure, in private. Arrangements were easily effected with some of the numerous corps of body-snatchers with which London abounds; and, upon the third night after the funeral, the supposed corpse was unearthed from a grave eight feet deep, and deposited in the operating chamber of one of the private hospitals.

An incision of some extent had been actually made in the abdomen, when the fresh and undecayed appearance of the subject suggested an application of the battery. One experiment succeeded another, and the customary effects supervened, with nothing to characterise them in any respect, except, upon one or two occasions, a more than ordinary degree of life-likeness in the convulsive action.

It grew late. The day was about to dawn; and it was thought expedient, at length, to proceed at once to the dissection. A student, however, was especially desirous of testing a theory of his own, and insisted upon applying the battery to one of the pectoral muscles. A rough gash was made, and a wire hastily brought in contact; when the patient, with a hurried, but quite unconvulsive movement, arose from the table, stepped into the middle of the floor, gazed about him uneasily for a few seconds, and then – spoke. What he said was unintelligible; but the words were uttered; the syllabification was distinct. Having spoken, he fell heavily to the floor.

For some moments all were paralysed with awe – but the urgency of the case soon restored them their presence of mind. It was seen that Mr Stapleton was alive, although in a swoon. Upon exhibition of ether he revived and was rapidly restored to health, and to the society of his friends – from whom, however, all knowledge of his resuscitation was withheld, until a relapse was no longer to be apprehended. Their wonder – their rapturous astonishment – may be conceived.

The most thrilling peculiarity of this incident, nevertheless, is involved in what Mr S. himself asserts. He declares that at no period was he altogether insensible – that, dully and confusedly, he was aware of everything which happened to him, from the moment in which he was pronounced *dead* by his physicians, to that in which he fell swooning to the floor of the hospital. 'I am alive,' were the uncomprehended words which, upon recognising the locality of the dissecting-room, he had endeavoured, in his extremity, to utter.

It were an easy matter to multiply such histories as these – but I forbear – for, indeed, we have no need of such to establish the fact that premature interments occur. When we reflect how very rarely, from the nature of the case, we have it in our power to detect them, we must admit that they may *frequently* occur without our cognisance. Scarcely, in truth, is a graveyard ever encroached upon, for any purpose, to any great extent, that skeletons are not found in postures which suggest the most fearful of suspicions.

Fearful indeed the suspicion – but more fearful the doom! It may be asserted, without hesitation, that *no* event is so terribly well adapted to inspire the supremeness of bodily and of mental distress, as is burial before death. The unendurable oppression of the lungs – the stifling fumes of the damp earth – the clinging to the death garments – the rigid embrace of the narrow house – the blackness of the absolute Night – the silence like a sea that overwhelms – the unseen but palpable presence of the Conqueror Worm – these things, with thoughts of the air and grass above, with memory of dear friends who would fly to save us if but informed of our fate, and with consciousness that of this fate they can *never* be informed – that our hopeless portion is that of the really dead – these considerations, I say, carry into the heart, which still palpitates, a degree of appalling and intolerable horror from which the most daring imagination must recoil. We know of nothing so agonising upon Earth – we can dream of nothing half so hideous in the realms of the nethermost Hell. And thus all narratives upon this topic have an interest profound; an interest, nevertheless, which, through the sacred awe of the topic itself, very properly and very peculiarly depends upon our conviction of the *truth* of the matter narrated. What I have now to tell, is of my own actual knowledge – of my own positive and personal experience.

For several years I had been subject to attacks of the singular disorder which physicians have agreed to term catalepsy, in default of a more definite title. Although both the immediate and the predisposing causes, and even the actual diagnosis of this disease, are still mysteries, its obvious and apparent character is sufficiently well understood. Its variations seem to be chiefly of degree. Sometimes the patient lies, for a day only, or even for a shorter period, in a species of exaggerated lethargy. He is senseless and externally motionless; but the pulsation of the heart is still faintly perceptible; some traces of warmth remain; a slight colour lingers within the centre of the cheek; and, upon application of a mirror to the lips, we can detect a torpid, unequal, and vacillating action of the lungs. Then, again, the duration of the trance is for weeks – even for months; while the closest scrutiny, and the most rigorous medical tests, fail to establish any material distinction between the state of the sufferer and what we conceive of absolute death. Very usually, he is saved from premature interment solely by the knowledge of his friends that he has been previously subject to catalepsy, by the consequent suspicion excited, and, above all, by the non-appearance of decay. The advances of the malady are, luckily, gradual. The first manifestations, although marked, are unequivocal. The fits grow successively more and more distinctive, and endure each for a longer term than the preceding. In this lies the principal security from inhumation. The unfortunate whose *first* attack should be of the extreme character which is occasionally seen, would almost inevitably be consigned alive to the tomb.

My own case differed in no important particular from those mentioned in medical books. Sometimes, without any apparent cause, I sank, little by little, into a condition of semi-syncope, or half swoon; and, in this condition, without pain, without ability to stir, or strictly speaking, to think, but with a dull lethargic consciousness of life and of the presence of those who surrounded my bed, I remained, until the crisis of the disease restored me, suddenly, to perfect sensation. At other times I was quickly and impetuously smitten. I grew sick, and numb, and chilly, and dizzy, and so fell prostate at once. Then, for weeks, all was void, and black, and silent, and Nothing became the universe. Total annihilation could be no more. From these latter attacks I awoke, however, with a gradation slow in proportion to the suddenness of the seizure. Just as the day dawns to the friendless and houseless beggar who roams the streets throughout the long desolate winter night – just so tardily – just so wearily – just so cheerily came back the light of the Soul to me.

Apart from the tendency to trance, however, my general health appeared to be good; nor could I perceive that it was at all affected by the one prevalent malady – unless, indeed, an idiosyncrasy in an ordinary *sleep* may be looked upon as superinduced. Upon awaking from slumber, I could never gain, at once, thorough possession of my senses, and always remained, for many minutes, in much bewilderment and perplexity – the mental faculties in general, but the memory in especial, being in a condition of absolute abeyance.

In all that I endured there was no physical suffering, but of moral distress an infinitude. My fancy grew charnel. I talked 'of worms, of tombs and epitaphs'. I was lost in reveries of death, and the idea of premature burial held continual possession of my brain. The ghastly danger to which I was subjected haunted me day and night. In the former, the torture of meditation was excessive – in the latter, supreme. When the grim darkness overspread the earth, then, with very horror of thought, I shook – shook as the quivering plumes upon the hearse. When nature could endure wakefulness no longer, it was with a struggle that I consented to sleep – for I shuddered to reflect that, upon awaking, I might find myself the tenant of a grave. And when, finally, I sank into slumber, it was only to rush at once into a world of phantasms, above which, with vast, sable, overshadowing wings, however, predominant, the one sepulchral Idea.

From the innumerable images of gloom which thus oppressed me in dreams, I select for record but a solitary vision. Methought I was immersed in a cataleptic trance of more than usual duration and profundity. Suddenly there came an icy hand upon my forehead, and an impatient, gibbering voice whispered the word 'Arise!' within my ear.

I sat erect. The darkness was total. I could not see the figure of him who had aroused me. I could call to mind neither the period at which I had fallen into the trance, nor the locality in which I then lay. While I remained motionless, and busied in endeavours to collect my thoughts, the cold hand grasped me fiercely by the wrist, shaking it petulantly, while the gibbering voice said again –

'Arise! did I not bid thee arise?'

'And who,' I demanded, 'art thou?'

'I have no name in the regions which I inhabit,' replied the voice mournfully; 'I was mortal, but am fiend. I was merciless, but am pitiful. Thou dost feel that I shudder. My teeth chatter as I speak, yet it is not with the chilliness of the night – of the night without end. But this hideousness is insufferable. How canst *thou* tranquilly sleep? I cannot rest for the cry of these great agonies. These sights are more than I can bear. Get thee up! Come with me into the outer Night, and let me unfold to thee the graves. Is not this a spectacle of woe? Behold!'

I looked; and the unseen figure, which still grasped me by the wrist, had caused to be thrown open the graves of all mankind; and from each issued the faint phosphoric radiance of decay, so that I could see into the innermost recesses, and there view the shrouded bodies in their sad and solemn slumbers with the worm. But, alas! the real sleepers were fewer, by many millions, than those who slumbered not at all; and there was a feeble struggling; and there was a general sad unrest; and from out the depths of the countless pits there came a melancholy rustling from the garments of the buried. And, of those who seemed tranquilly to repose I saw that a vast number had changed, in a greater or less degree, the rigid and uneasy position in which they had originally been entombed. And the voice again said to me, as I gazed –

'Is it not – oh, is it *not* a pitiful sight?' But, before I could find words to reply, the figure had ceased to grasp my wrist, the phosphoric lights expired, and the graves were closed with a sudden violence, while from out them arose a tumult of despairing cries, saying again, 'Is it not – O

God! is it *not* a very pitiful sight?'

Phantasies such as these, presenting themselves at night, extended their terrific influence far into my waking hours. My nerves became thoroughly unstrung, and I fell a prey to perpetual horror. I hesitated to ride, or to walk, or to indulge in any exercise that would carry me from home. In fact, I no longer dared trust myself out of the immediate presence of those who were aware of my proneness to catalepsy, lest, falling into one of my usual fits, I should be buried before my real condition could be ascertained. I doubted the care, the fidelity of my dearest friends. I dreaded that, in some trance of more than customary duration, they might be prevailed upon to regard me as irrecoverable. I even went so far as to fear that, as I occasioned much trouble, they might be glad to consider any very protracted attack as sufficient excuse for getting rid of me altogether. It was in vain they endeavoured to reassure me by the most solemn promises. I exacted the most sacred oaths, that under no circumstances they would bury me until decomposition had so materially advanced as to render further preservation impossible. And, even then, my mortal terrors would listen to no reason – would accept no consolation. I entered into a series of elaborate precautions. Among other things, I had the family vault so remodelled as to admit of being readily opened from within. The slightest pressure upon a long lever that extended far into the tomb would cause the iron portals to fly back. There were arrangements also for the free admission of air and light, and convenient receptacles for food and water, within immediate reach of the coffin intended for my reception. This coffin was warmly and softly padded, and was provided with a lid, fashioned upon the principle of the vault-door, with the addition of springs so contrived that the feeblest movement of the body would be sufficient to set it at liberty. Besides all this, there was suspended from the roof of the tomb a large bell, the rope of which, it was designed, should extend through a hole in the coffin, and so be fastened to one of the hands of the corpse. But, alas! what avails the vigilance against the Destiny of man? Not even these well-contrived securities sufficed to save from the uttermost agonies of living inhumation a wretch to these agonies foredoomed!

There arrived an epoch – as often before there had arrived – in which I found myself emerging from total unconsciousness into the first feeble and indefinite sense of existence. Slowly – with a tortoise gradation – approached the faint grey dawn of the psychal day. A torpid uneasiness. An apathetic endurance of dull pain. No care – no hope – no effort. Then, after long interval, a ringing in the ears; then, after a lapse still longer, a prickling or tingling sensation in the extremities; then a seemingly eternal period of pleasurable quiescence, during which the awakening feelings are struggling into thought; then a brief resinking into non-entity; then a sudden recovery. At length the slight quivering of an eyelid, and immediately thereupon an electric shock of a terror, deadly and indefinite, which sends the blood in torrents from the temples to the heart. And now the first positive effort to think. And now the first endeavour to remember. And now a partial and evanescent success. And now the memory has so far regained its dominion, that, in some measure, I am cognisant of my state. I feel that I am not awaking from ordinary sleep. I recollect that I have been subject to catalepsy. And now, at last, as if by the rush of an ocean, my shuddering spirit is overwhelmed by the one grim Danger – by the one spectral and ever-prevalent Idea.

For some minutes after this fancy possessed me, I remained without motion. And why? I could not summon courage to move. I dared not make the effort which was to satisfy me of my fate – and yet there was something at my heart which whispered me *it was sure*. Despair – such as no other species of wretchedness ever calls into being – despair alone urged me, after long irresolution, to uplift the heavy lids of my eyes. I uplifted them. It was dark – all dark. I knew that the fit was over. I knew that the crisis of my disorder had long passed. I knew that I had now fully recovered the use of my visual faculties – and yet it was dark – all dark – the intense and utter raylessness of the Night that endureth for evermore.

I endeavoured to shriek; and my lips and my parched tongue moved convulsively together in the attempt – but no voice issued from the cavernous lungs, which, oppressed as if by the weight of some incumbent mountain, gasped and palpitated, with the heart, at every elaborate and struggling inspiration.

The movement of the jaws, in this effort to cry aloud, showed me that they were bound up, as is usual with the dead. I felt, too, that I lay upon some hard substance; and by something similar my sides were, also, closely compressed. So far, I had not ventured to stir any of my limbs – but now I violently threw up my arms, which had been lying at length, with the wrists crossed. They struck a solid wooden substance, which extended above my person at an elevation of not more than six inches from my face. I could no longer doubt that I reposed within a coffin at last.

And now, amid all my infinite miseries, came sweetly the cherub Hope – for I thought of my precautions. I writhed, and made spasmodic exertions to force open the lid; it would not move. I felt my wrists for the bell-rope; it was not to be found. And now the Comforter fled for ever, and a still sterner Despair reigned triumphant; for I could not help perceiving the absence of the paddings which I had so carefully prepared – and then, too, there came suddenly to my nostrils the strong peculiar odour of moist earth. The conclusion was irresistible. I was *not* within the vault. I had fallen into a trance while absent from home – while among strangers – when, or how, I could not remember – and it was they who had buried me as a dog – nailed up in some common coffin – and thrust, deep, deep, and for ever, into some ordinary and nameless *grave*.

As this awful conviction forced itself, thus, into the innermost chambers of my soul, I once again struggled to cry aloud. And in this second endeavour I succeeded. A long, wild, and continuous shriek, or yell, of agony, resounded through the realms of the subterrene Night.

'Hillo! hillo, there!' said a gruff voice, in reply.

'What the devil's the matter now?' said a second.

'Get out o' that!' said a third.

'What do you mean by yowling in that ere kind of style, like a cattymount?' said a fourth; and hereupon I was seized and shaken without ceremony, for several minutes, by a junto of very rough-looking individuals. They did not arouse me from my slumber – for I was wide awake when I screamed – but they restored me to full possession of my memory.

This adventure occurred near Richmond, in Virginia. Accompanied by a friend, I had proceeded, upon a gunning expedition, some miles down the banks of James River. Night approached, and we were overtaken by a storm. The cabin of a small sloop lying at anchor in the stream, and laden with garden mould, afforded us the only available shelter. We made the best of it, and passed the night on board. I slept in one of the only two berths in the vessel – and the berths of a sloop of sixty or seventy tons need scarcely be described. That which I occupied had no bedding of any kind. Its extreme width was eighteen inches. The distance of its bottom from the deck overhead was precisely the same. I found it a matter of exceeding difficulty to squeeze myself in. Nevertheless, I slept soundly; and the whole of my vision – for it was no dream, and no nightmare – arose naturally from the circumstances of my position – from my ordinary bias of thought – and from the difficulty, to which I have alluded, of collecting my senses, and especially of regaining my memory, for a long time after awaking from slumber. The men who shook me were the crew of the sloop, and some labourers engaged to unload it. From the load itself came the earthy smell. The bandage about the jaws was a silk handkerchief in which I bound up my head, in default of my customary nightcap.

The tortures endured, however, were indubitably quite equal, for the time, to those of actual sepulture. They were fearfully – they were inconceivably hideous; but out of evil proceeded good; for their very excess wrought in my spirit an inevitable revulsion. My soul acquired tone – acquired temper. I went abroad. I took vigorous exercise. I breathed the free air of heaven. I thought upon other subjects than death. I discarded my medical books. 'Buchan' I burned. I read no

THE PREMATURE BURIAL

'Night Thoughts' – no fustian about churchyards – no bugaboo tales – *such as this*. In short I became a new man, and lived a man's life. From that memorable night I dismissed for ever my charnel apprehensions, and with them vanished the cataleptic disorder, of which, perhaps, they had been less the consequence than the cause.

There are moments when, even to the sober eye of Reason, the world of our sad Humanity may assume the semblance of a Hell – but the imagination of man is no Carathis, to explore with impunity its every cavern. Alas! the grim legion of sepulchral terrors cannot be regarded as altogether fanciful – but, like the Demons in whose company Afrasiab made his voyage down the Oxus, they must sleep, or they will devour us – they must be suffered to slumber, or we perish.

Villiers de l'Isle Adam

The Torture of Hope

Many years ago, as evening was closing in, the venerable Pedro Arbuez d'Espila, sixth prior of the Dominicans of Segovia, and third Grand Inquisitor of Spain, followed by a *fra redemptor*, and preceded by two familiars of the Holy Office, the latter carrying lanterns, made their way to a subterranean dungeon. The bolt of a massive door creaked, and they entered a mephitic *in pace*, where the dim light revealed between rings fastened to the wall a bloodstained rack, a brazier and a jug. On a pile of straw, loaded with fetters and his neck encircled by an iron carcan, sat a haggard man, of uncertain age, clothed in rags.

This prisoner was no other than Rabbi Aser Abarbanel, a Jew of Aragon, who – accused of usury and pitiless scorn for the poor – had been daily subjected to torture for more than a year. Yet 'his blindness was as dense as his hide', and he had refused to abjure his faith.

Proud of a filiation dating back thousands of years, proud of his ancestors – for all Jews worthy of the name are vain of their blood – he descended Talmudically from Othoniel and consequently from Ipsiboa, the wife of the last judge of Israel, a circumstance which had sustained his courage amid incessant torture. With tears in his eyes at the thought of this resolute soul rejecting salvation, the venerable Pedro Arbuez d'Espila, approaching the shuddering rabbi, addressed him as follows:

'My son, rejoice: your trials here below are about to end. If in the presence of such obstinacy I was forced to permit, with deep regret, the use of great severity, my task of fraternal correction has its limits. You are the fig tree which, having failed so many times to bear fruit, at last withered, but God alone can judge your soul. Perhaps Infinite Mercy will shine upon you at the last moment! We must hope so. There are examples. So sleep in peace tonight. Tomorrow you will be included in

38

the *auto da fé*: that is, you will be exposed to the *quémadero*, the symbolical flames of the Everlasting Fire: it burns, as you know, only at a distance, my son; and Death is at least two hours (often three) in coming, on account of the wet, iced bandages with which we protect the heads and hearts of the condemned. There will be forty-three of you. Placed in the last row, you will have time to invoke God and offer to Him this baptism of fire, which is of the Holy Spirit. Hope in the Light, and rest.'

With these words, having signed to his companions to unchain the prisoner, the prior tenderly embraced him. Then came the turn of the *fra redemptor*, who, in a low tone, entreated the Jew's forgiveness for what he had made him suffer for the purpose of redeeming him; then the two familiars silently kissed him. This ceremony over, the captive was left, solitary and bewildered, in the darkness.

Rabbi Aser Abarbanel, with parched lips and visage worn by suffering, at first gazed at the closed door with vacant eyes. Closed? The word unconsciously roused a vague fancy in his mind, the fancy that he had seen for an instant the light of the lanterns through a chink between the door and the wall. A morbid idea of hope, due to the weakness of his brain, stirred his whole being. He dragged himself toward the strange *appearance*. Then, very gently and cautiously, slipping one finger into the crevice, he drew the door toward him. Marvellous! By an extraordinary accident the familiar who closed it had turned the huge key an instant before it struck the stone casing, so that the rusty bolt not having entered the hole, the door again rolled on its hinges.

The rabbi ventured to glance outside. By the aid of a sort of luminous dusk he distinguished at first a semicircle of walls indented by winding stairs; and opposite to him, at the top of five or six stone steps, a sort of black portal, opening into an immense corridor, whose first arches only were visible from below.

Stretching himself flat he crept to the threshold. Yes, it was really a corridor, but endless in length. A wan light illumined it: lamps suspended from the vaulted ceiling lightened at intervals the dull hue of the atmosphere – the distance was veiled in shadow. Not a single door appeared in the whole extent! Only on one side, the left, heavily grated loopholes, sunk in the walls, admitted a light which must be that of evening, for crimson bars at intervals rested on the flags of the pavement. What a terrible silence! Yet, yonder, at the far end of that passage there might be a doorway of escape! The Jew's vacillating hope was tenacious, for it was *the last*.

Without hesitating, he ventured on the flags, keeping close under the loopholes, trying to make himself part of the blackness of the long walls. He advanced slowly, dragging himself along on his breast, forcing back the cry of pain when some raw wound sent a keen pang through his whole body.

Suddenly the sound of a sandalled foot approaching reached his ears. He trembled violently, fear stifled him, his sight grew dim. Well, it was over, no doubt. He pressed himself into a niche and, half lifeless with terror, waited.

It was a familiar hurrying along. He passed swiftly by, holding in his clenched hand an instrument of torture – a frightful figure – and vanished. The suspense which the rabbi had endured seemed to have suspended the functions of life, and he lay nearly an hour unable to move. Fearing an increase of tortures if he were captured, he thought of returning to his dungeon. But the old hope whispered in his soul that divine *perhaps*, which comforts us in our sorest trials. A miracle had happened. He could doubt no longer. He began to crawl toward the chance of escape. Exhausted by suffering and hunger, trembling with pain, he pressed onward. The sepulchral corridor seemed to lengthen mysteriously, while he, still advancing, gazed into the gloom where there *must* be some avenue of escape.

Oh! oh! He again heard footsteps, but this time they were slower, more heavy. The white and black forms of two inquisitors appeared, emerging from the obscurity beyond. They were conversing in low tones, and seemed to be discussing some important subject, for they were gesticulating vehemently.

At this spectacle Rabbi Aser Abarbanel closed his eyes: his heart beat so violently that it almost suffocated him; his rags were damp with the cold sweat of agony; he lay motionless by the wall, his mouth wide open, under the rays of a lamp, praying to the God of David.

Just opposite to him the two inquisitors paused under the light of the lamp – doubtless owing to some accident due to the course of their argument. One, while listening to his companion, gazed at the rabbi! And, beneath the look – whose absence of expression the hapless man did not at first notice – he fancied he again felt the burning pincers scorch his flesh, he was to be once more a living wound. Fainting, breathless, with fluttering eyelids, he shivered at the touch of the monk's floating robe. But – strange yet natural fact – the inquisitor's gaze was evidently that of a man deeply absorbed in his intended reply, engrossed by what he was hearing; his eyes were fixed – and seemed to look at the Jew *without seeing him*.

In fact, after the lapse of a few minutes, the two gloomy figures slowly pursued their way, still conversing in low tones, toward the place whence the prisoner had come; HE HAD NOT BEEN SEEN! Amid the horrible confusion of the rabbi's thoughts, the idea darted through his brain: 'Can I be already dead that they did not see me?' A hideous impression roused him from his lethargy: in looking at the wall against which his face was pressed, he imagined he beheld two fierce eyes watching him! He flung his head back in a sudden frenzy of fright, his hair fairly bristling! Yet, no! No. His hand groped over the stones: it was the *reflection* of the inquisitor's eyes, still retained in his own, which had been refracted from two spots on the wall.

Forward! He must hasten toward that goal which he fancied (absurdly, no doubt) to be deliverance, toward the darkness from which he was now barely thirty paces distant. He pressed forward faster on his knees, his hands, at full length, dragging himself painfully along, and soon entered the dark portion of this terrible corridor.

Suddenly the poor wretch felt a gust of cold air on the hands resting upon the flags; it came from under the little door to which the two walls led.

Oh, Heaven, if that door should open outward. Every nerve in the miserable fugitive's body thrilled with hope. He examined it from top to bottom, though scarcely able to distinguish its outlines in the surrounding darkness. He passed his hand over it: no bolt, no lock! A latch! He started up, the latch yielded to the pressure of his thumb: the door silently swung open before him.

'Halleluia!' murmured the rabbi in a transport of gratitude as, standing on the threshold, he beheld the scene before him.

The door had opened into the gardens, above which arched a starlit sky, into spring, liberty, life! It revealed the neighbouring fields, stretching toward the sierras, whose sinuous blue lines were relieved against the horizon. Yonder lay freedom! Oh, to escape! He would journey all night through the lemon groves, whose fragrance reached him. Once in the mountains and he was safe! He inhaled the delicious air; the breeze revived him, his lungs expanded! He felt in his swelling heart the *Veni foràs* of Lazarus! And to thank once more the God who had bestowed this mercy upon him, he extended his arms, raising his eyes toward Heaven. It was an ecstasy of joy!

Then he fancied he saw the shadow of his arms approach him – fancied that he felt those shadowy arms inclose, embrace him – and that he was pressed tenderly to someone's breast. A tall figure actually did stand directly before him. He lowered his eyes – and remained motionless, gasping for breath, dazed, with fixed eyes, fairly drivelling with terror.

Horror! He was in the clasp of the Grand Inquisitor himself, the venerable Pedro Arbuez d'Espila, who gazed at him with tearful eyes, like a good shepherd who had found his stray lamb.

The dark-robed priest pressed the hapless Jew to his heart with so fervent an outburst of love, that the edges of the monachal haircloth

41

rubbed the Dominican's breast. And while Aser Abarbanel with protruding eyes gasped in agony in the ascetic's embrace, vaguely comprehending that *all the phases of this fatal evening were only a prearranged torture, that of* Hope, the Grand Inquisitor, with an accent of touching reproach and a look of consternation, murmured in his ear, his breath parched and burning from long fasting:

'What, my son! On the eve, perchance, of salvation – you wished to leave us?'

Honoré de Balzac

An Episode of the Terror

On the 22nd of January, 1793, toward eight o'clock in the evening, an old lady came down the steep street that comes to an end opposite the Church of Saint Laurent in the Faubourg Saint Martin. It had snowed so heavily all day long that the lady's footsteps were scarcely audible; the streets were deserted, and a feeling of dread, not unnatural amid the silence, was further increased by the whole extent of the Terror beneath which France was groaning in those days; what was more, the old lady so far had met no one by the way. Her sight had long been failing, so that the few foot passengers dispersed like shadows in the distance over the wide thoroughfare through the faubourg were quite invisible to her by the light of the lanterns.

She passed the end of the Rue des Morts, when she fancied that she could hear the firm, heavy tread of a man walking behind her. Then it seemed to her that she had heard that sound before, and dismayed by the idea of being followed, she tried to walk faster toward a brightly lit shop window, in the hope of verifying the suspicions which had taken hold of her mind.

So soon as she stood in the shaft of light that streamed out across the road, she turned her head suddenly, and caught sight of a human figure looming through the fog. The dim vision was enough for her. For one moment she reeled beneath an overpowering weight of dread, for she could not doubt any longer that the man had followed her the whole way from her own door; then the desire to escape from the spy gave her strength. Unable to think clearly, she walked twice as fast as before, as if it were possible to escape from a man who of course could move much faster; and for some minutes she fled on, till, reaching a pastry-cook's shop, she entered and sank rather than sat down upon a chair by the counter.

A young woman busy with embroidery looked up from her work at the rattling of the door-latch, and looked out through the square window panes. She seemed to recognize the old-fashioned violet silk mantle, for she went at once to a drawer as if in search of something put aside for the newcomer. Not only did this movement and the expression of the woman's face show a very evident desire to be rid as soon as possible of an unwelcome visitor, but she even permitted herself an impatient exclamation when the drawer proved to be empty. Without looking at the lady, she hurried from her desk into the back shop and called to her husband who appeared at once.

'Wherever have you put . . . ?' she began mysteriously, glancing at the customer by way of finishing her question.

The pastry-cook could only see the old lady's head-dress, a huge black-silk bonnet with knots of violet ribbon around it, but he looked at his wife as who should say, 'Did you think I should leave such a thing as that lying about in your drawer?' and then vanished.

The old lady kept so still and silent that the shopkeeper's wife was surprised. She went back to her, and on a nearer view a sudden impulse of pity, blended perhaps with curiosity, got the better of her. The old lady's face was naturally pale; she looked as though she secretly practiced austerities; but it was easy to see that she was paler than usual from recent agitation of some kind. Her head-dress was so arranged as almost to hide hair that was white, no doubt with age, for there was not a trace of powder on the collar of her dress. The extreme plainness of her dress lent an air of austerity to her face, and her features were proud and grave. The manner and habits of people of condition were so different from those of other classes in former times that a noble was easily known, and the shopkeeper's wife felt persuaded that her customer was a *ci-devant*, and that she had been about the Court.

'Madame?' she began with involuntary respect, forgetting that the title was proscribed.

But the old lady made no answer. She was staring fixedly at the shop window as though some dreadful thing had taken shape against the panes. The pastry-cook came at that moment, and drew the lady from her musings, by holding out a little cardboard box wrapped in blue paper.

'What is the matter, *citoyenne?*' he asked.

'Nothing, nothing, my friends,' she answered, in a gentle voice. She looked up at the man as she spoke, as if to thank him by a glance; but she saw the red cap on his head, and a cry broke from her. 'Ah! *You* have betrayed me!'

The man and his young wife replied by an indignant gesture that brought the colour to the old lady's face; perhaps she felt relief, she blushed for her suspicions.

'Forgive me!' she said, with a childlike sweetness in her tones. Then, drawing a gold louis from her pocket, she held it out to the pastry-cook. 'That is the price agreed upon,' she added.

There is a kind of want that is felt instinctively by those who know want. The man and his wife looked at one another, then at the elderly woman before them, and read the same thoughts in each other's eyes. That bit of gold was so plainly the last. Her hands shook a little as she held it out, looking at it sadly but ungrudgingly, as one who knows the full extent of the sacrifice. Hunger and penury had carved lines as easy to read in her face as the traces of asceticism and fear. There were vestiges of by-gone splendour in her clothes. She was dressed in thread-bare silk, a neat but well-worn mantle, and daintily mended lace – in the rags of former grandeur, in short. The shopkeeper and his wife, drawn two ways by pity and self-interest, began by lulling their consciences with words.

'You seem very poorly, *citoyenne* . . .'

'Perhaps Madame might like to take something,' the wife broke in.

'We have some very nice broth,' added the pastry-cook.

'And it is so cold,' continued his wife. 'Perhaps you have caught a chill, Madame, on your way here. But you can rest and warm yourself a bit.'

'We are not so black as the devil!' cried the man.

The kindly intention in the words and tones of the charitable couple won the old lady's confidence. She said that a strange man had been following her, and she was afraid to go home alone.

'Is that all?' returned he of the red bonnet. 'Wait for me, *citoyenne*.'

He handed the gold coin to his wife, and then went out to put on his National Guard's uniform, impelled, thereto, by the idea of making some adequate return for the money; an idea that sometimes slips into a tradesman's head when he has been prodigiously overpaid for goods of no great value. He took up his cap, buckled on his sabre, and came out in full dress. But his wife had had time to reflect, and reflection, as not unfrequently happens, closed the hand that kindly intentions had opened. Feeling frightened and uneasy lest her husband might be drawn into something unpleasant, she tried to catch the skirt of his coat, to hold him back, but he, good soul, obeying his charitable first thought, brought out his offer to see the lady home, before his wife could stop him.

'The man of whom the *citoyenne* is afraid is still prowling about the shop, it seems,' she said sharply.

'I am afraid so,' the lady said innocently.

'How if it is a spy? A plot? Don't go. And take the box away from her . . .'

The words whispered in the pastry-cook's ear cooled his hot fit of courage down to zero.

'Oh! I will just go out and say a word or two. I will rid you of him soon enough,' he exclaimed, as he bounced out of the shop.

The old lady meanwhile, passive as a child and almost dazed, sat down on her chair again. But the honest pastry-cook came back directly. A countenance red enough to begin with, and further flushed by the bake-house fire, was suddenly blanched; such terror perturbed him that he reeled as he walked, and stared about him like a drunken man.

'Miserable aristocrat! Do you want to have our heads cut off?' he shouted furiously. 'You just take to your heels and never show yourself here again. Don't come to me for materials for your plots.'

He tried, as he spoke, to take away the little box which she had slipped into one of her pockets. But at the touch of a profane hand on her clothes, the stranger recovered youth and activity for a moment, preferring to face the dangers of the street with no protector save God, to the loss of the thing that she had just paid for. She sprang to the door, flung it open, and disappeared, leaving the husband and wife dumfounded and quaking with fright.

Once outside in the street, she started away at a quick walk; but her strength soon failed her. She heard the sound of the snow crunching under a heavy step, and knew that the pitiless spy was on her track. She was obliged to stop. He stopped likewise. From sheer terror, or lack of intelligence, she did not dare to speak or to look at him. She went slowly on; the man slackened his pace and fell behind so that he could still keep her in sight. He might have been her very shadow.

Nine o'clock struck as the silent man and woman passed again by the Church of Saint Laurent. It is in the nature of things that calm must succeed to violent agitation, even in the weakest soul; for if feeling is infinite, our capacity to feel is limited. So, as the strange lady met with no harm from her supposed persecutor, she tried to look upon him as an unknown friend anxious to protect her. She thought of all the circumstances in which the stranger had appeared, and put them together, as if to find some ground for this comforting theory, and felt inclined to credit him with good intentions rather than bad. Forgetting the fright that he had given the pastry-cook, she walked on with a firmer step through the upper end of the Faubourg Saint Martin; and another half hour's walk brought her to a house at the corner where the road to the Barrière de Pantin turns off from the main thoroughfare. Even at this day, the place is one of the least frequented parts of Paris. The north wind sweeps over the Buttes-Chaumont and Belleville, and whistles through the houses (the hovels rather) scattered over an almost uninhabited low-lying waste, where the fences are heaps of earth and bones.

It was a desolate-looking place, a fitting refuge for despair and misery.

The sight of it appeared to make an impression upon the relentless pursuer of a poor creature so daring as to walk alone at night through the silent streets. He stood in thought, and seemed by his attitude to hesitate. She could see him dimly now, under the street lamp that sent a faint, flickering light through the fog. Fear gave her eyes. She saw, or thought she saw, something sinister about the stranger's features. Her old terrors awoke; she took advantage of a kind of hesitation on his part, slipped through the shadows to the door of the solitary house, pressed a spring, and vanished swiftly as a phantom.

For a while the stranger stood motionless, gazing up at the house. It was in some sort a type of the wretched dwellings in the suburb; a tumble-down hovel, built of rough stones, daubed over with a coat of yellowish stucco, and so riven with great cracks that there seemed to be danger lest the slightest puff of wind might blow it down. The roof, covered with brown moss-grown tiles, had given way in several places, and looked as though it might break down altogether under the weight of the snow. The frames of the three windows on each story were rotten with damp and warped by the sun; evidently the cold must find its way inside. The house standing thus quite by itself looked like some old tower that Time had forgotten to destroy. A faint light shone from the attic windows pierced at irregular distances in the roof; otherwise the whole building was in total darkness.

Meanwhile the old lady climbed not without difficulty up the rough, clumsily built staircase, with a rope by way of a hand-rail. At the door of the lodging in the attic she stopped and tapped mysteriously; an old man brought forward a chair for her. She dropped into it at once.

'Hide! Hide!' she exclaimed, looking up at him. 'Seldom as we leave the house everything that we do is known, and every step is watched ...'

'What is it now?' asked another elderly woman, sitting by the fire.

'The man that has been prowling about the house yesterday and today, followed me tonight ...'

At those words all three dwellers in the wretched den looked in each other's faces and did not try to dissimulate the profound dread that they felt. The old priest was the least overcome, probably because he ran the greatest danger. If a brave man is weighed down by great calamities or the yoke of persecution, he begins, as it were, by making the sacrifice of himself; and thereafter every day of his life becomes one more victory snatched from fate. But from the way in which the women looked at him it was easy to see that their intense anxiety was on his account.

'Why should our faith in God fail us, my sisters?' he said, in low but fervent tones. 'We sang His praises through the shrieks of murderers and their victims at the Carmelites. If it was His will that I should come

47

alive out of that butchery, it was, no doubt, because I was reserved for some fate which I am bound to endure without murmuring. God will protect His own; He can do with them according to His will. It is for you, not for me that we must think.'

'No,' answered one of the women. 'What is our life compared with a priest's life?'

'Once outside the Abbaye de Chelles, I look upon myself as dead,' added the nun who had not left the house, while the Sister that had just returned held out the little box to the priest.

'Here are the wafers . . . But I can hear someone coming up the stairs!' At this, the three began to listen. The sound ceased.

'Do not be alarmed if somebody tries to come in,' said the priest. 'Somebody on whom we could depend was to make all necessary arrangements for crossing the frontier. He is to come for the letters that I have written to the Duc de Langeais and the Marquis de Beauséant, asking them to find some way of taking you out of this dreadful country, and away from the death or the misery that waits for you here.'

'But you are not going to follow us?' the nuns cried under their breath, almost despairingly.

'My post is here where the sufferers are,' the priest said simply, and the women said no more, but looked at their guest in reverent admiration. He turned to the nun with the wafers.

'Sister Marthe,' he said, 'the messenger will say *Fiat Voluntas* in answer to the word *Hosanna.*'

'There is someone on the stairs!' cried the other nun, opening a hiding-place contrived in the roof.

This time it was easy to hear, amid the deepest silence, a sound echoing up the staircase: it was a man's tread on the steps covered with dried lumps of mud. With some difficulty the priest slipped into a kind of cupboard, and the nun flung some clothes over him.

'You can shut the door, Sister Agathe,' he said in a muffled voice.

He was scarcely hidden before three raps sounded on the door. The holy women looked into each other's eyes for counsel, and dared not say a single word.

They seemed to be about sixty years of age. They had lived out of the world for forty years, and had grown so accustomed to the life of the convent that they could scarcely imagine any other. To them, as to plants kept in a hot-house, a change of air meant death. And so, when the grating was broken down one morning, they knew with a shudder that they were free. The effect produced by the Revolution upon their simple souls is easy to imagine; it produced a temporary imbecility not natural to them. They could not bring the ideas learned in the convent into harmony with life and its difficulties; they could not even understand their own position. They were like children whom others have always cared for, deserted by their maternal providence. And as a child cries, they betook themselves to prayer. Now, in the presence of imminent danger, they were mute and passive, knowing no defence save Christian resignation.

The man at the door, taking silence for consent, presented himself, and the women shuddered. This was the prowler that had been making inquiries about them for some time past. But they looked at him with frightened curiosity, much as shy children stare silently at a stranger; and neither of them moved.

The newcomer was a tall, burly man. Nothing in his behaviour, bearing or expression suggested malignity as, following the example set by the nuns, he stood motionless, while his eyes travelled around the room.

Two straw mats laid upon planks did duty as beds. On the one table, placed in the middle of the room, stood a brass candlestick, several plates, three knives and a round loaf. A small fire burned in the grate. A few bits of wood in a heap in a corner bore further witness to the poverty of the recluses. You had only to look at the coating of paint on the walls to discover the bad condition of the roof, and the ceiling was a perfect network of brown stains made by rain water. A relic, saved no doubt from the wreck of the Abbaye de Chelles, stood like an ornament on the chimney piece. Three chairs, two boxes, and a rickety chest of drawers completed the list of the furniture, but a door beside the fireplace suggested an inner room beyond.

The brief inventory was soon made by the personage introduced into their midst under such terrible auspices. It was with a compassionate expression that he turned to the two women; he looked benevolently at them, and seemed, at least, as much embarrassed as they. But the strange silence did not last long, for presently the stranger began to understand. He saw how inexperienced, how helpless (mentally speaking), the two poor creatures were, and he tried to speak gently.

'I am far from coming as an enemy, *citoyennes* . . .' he began. Then he suddenly broke off and went on, 'Sisters, if anything should happen to you, believe me, I shall have no share in it. I have come to ask a favour of you.'

Still the women were silent.

'If I am annoying you – if – if I am intruding, speak freely, and I will go; but you must understand that I am entirely at your service; that if I can do anything for you, you need not fear to make use of me. I, and I only, perhaps, am above the law, since there is no King now.'

There was such a ring of sincerity in the words that Sister Agathe hastily pointed to a chair as if to bid their guest be seated. Sister Agathe came of the house of Langeais; her manner seemed to indicate that once she had been familiar with brilliant scenes, and had breathed the air of courts. The stranger seemed half pleased, half distressed when he understood her invitation; he waited to sit down until the women were seated.

'You are giving shelter to a reverend father who refused to take the oath, and escaped the massacres at the Carmelites by a miracle . . .'

'*Hosanna!*' Sister Agathe exclaimed eagerly, interrupting the stranger, while she watched him with curious eyes.

'That is not the name, I think,' he said.

'But, Monsieur,' Sister Marthe broke in quickly, 'we have no priest here, and . . .'

'In that case you should be more careful and on your guard,' he answered gently, stretching out his hand for a breviary that lay on the table. 'I do not think that you know Latin, and . . .'

He stopped; for, at the sight of the great emotion in the faces of the two poor nuns, he was afraid that he had gone too far. They were trembling, and the tears stood in their eyes.

'Do not fear,' he said frankly. 'I know your names and the name of your guest. Three days ago I heard of your distress and devotion to the venerable Abbé de—'

'Hush!' Sister Agathe cried, in the simplicity of her heart, as she laid her finger on her lips.

'You see, Sisters, that if I had conceived the horrible idea of betraying you, I could have given you up already, more than once . . .'

At the words the priest came out of his hiding-place and stood in their midst.

'I cannot believe, Monsieur, that you can be one of our persecutors,' he said, addressing the stranger, 'and I trust you. What do you want with me?'

The priest's holy confidence, the nobleness expressed in every line in his face, would have disarmed a murderer. For a moment the mysterious stranger, who had brought an element of excitement into lives of misery and resignation, gazed at the little group; then he turned to the priest and said, as if making a confidence, 'Father, I came to beg you to celebrate a mass for the repose of – of – of an august personage whose body will never rest in consecrated earth . . .'

Involuntarily the abbé shivered. As yet, neither of the Sisters understood of whom the stranger was speaking; they sat with their heads stretched out and faces turned toward the speaker, curiosity in their whole attitude. The priest, meanwhile, was scrutinizing the stranger; there was no mistaking the anxiety in the man's face, the ardent entreaty in his eyes.

'Very well,' returned the abbé. 'Come back at midnight. I shall be ready to celebrate the only funeral service that it is in our power to offer in expiation of the crime of which you speak.'

A quiver ran through the stranger, but a sweet yet sober satisfaction seemed to prevail over a hidden anguish. He took his leave respectfully, and the three generous souls felt his unspoken gratitude.

Two hours later, he came back and tapped at the garret door. Mademoiselle de Beauséant showed the way into the second room in their humble lodging. Everything had been made ready. The Sisters had moved the old chest of drawers between the two chimneys, and covered its quaint outlines over with a splendid altar cloth of green watered silk.

The bare walls looked all the barer, because the one thing that hung there was the great ivory and ebony crucifix, which of necessity attracted the eyes. Four slender little altar candles, which the Sisters had contrived to fasten into their places with sealing-wax, gave a faint pale light, almost absorbed by the walls; the rest of the room lay well-nigh in the dark. But the dim brightness, concentrated upon the holy things, looked like a ray from Heaven shining down upon the unadorned shrine. The floor was reeking with damp. An icy wind swept in through the chinks here and there, in a roof that rose sharply on either side, after the fashion of attic roofs. Nothing could be less imposing; yet perhaps, too, nothing could be more solemn than this mournful ceremony. A silence so deep that they could have heard the faintest sound of a voice on the Route d'Allemagne, invested the night-piece with a kind of sombre majesty; while the grandeur of the service – all the grander for the strong contrast with the poor surroundings – produced a feeling of reverent awe.

The Sisters kneeling on either side of the altar, regardless of the deadly chill from the wet brick floor, were engaged in prayer, while the priest, arrayed in pontifical vestments, brought out a golden chalice set with gems; doubtless one of the sacred vessels saved from the pillage of the Abbaye de Chelles. Beside a ciborium, the gift of royal munificence, the wine and water for the holy sacrifice of the mass, stood ready in two glasses such as could scarcely be found in the meanest tavern. For want of a missal, the priest had laid his breviary on the altar, and a common earthenware plate was set for the washing of hands that were pure and undefiled with blood. It was all so infinitely great, yet so little, poverty-stricken yet noble, a mingling of sacred and profane.

The stranger came forward reverently to kneel between the two nuns. But the priest had tied crape around the chalice of the crucifix, having no other way of marking the mass as a funeral service; it was as if God himself had been in mourning. The man suddenly noticed this, and the sight appeared to call up some overwhelming memory, for great drops of sweat stood out on his broad forehead.

Then the four silent actors in the scene looked mysteriously at one another; and their souls in emulation seemed to stir and communicate the thoughts within them until all were melted into one feeling of awe and pity. It seemed to them that the royal martyr whose remains had been consumed with quicklime, had been called up by their yearning and now stood, a shadow in their midst, in all the majesty of a king. They were celebrating an anniversary service for the dead whose body lay elsewhere. Under the disjointed laths and tiles, four Christians were holding a funeral service without a coffin, and putting up prayers to God for the soul of a King of France. No devotion could be purer than this. It was a wonderful act of faith achieved without an afterthought. Surely in the sight of God it was like the cup of cold water which counter-balances the loftiest virtues. The prayers put up by two feeble nuns and a priest representing the whole Monarchy, and possibly at the same time, the Revolution found expression in the stranger, for the remorse in his face was so great that it was impossible not to think that he was fulfilling the vows of a boundless repentance.

When the priest came to the Latin words, *Introibo ad altare Dei* a sudden divine inspiration flashed upon him; he looked at the three kneeling figures, the representatives of Christian France, and said in-stead, as though to blot out the poverty of the garret, 'We are about to enter the Sanctuary of God!'

Those words, uttered with thrilling earnestness, struck reverent awe into the nuns and the stranger. Under the vaulted roof of St Peter's in Rome, God would not have revealed Himself in greater majesty than here for the eyes of the Christians in that poor refuge; so true is it that all intermediaries between God and the soul of man are superfluous and all the grandeur of God proceeds from Himself alone.

The stranger's fervour was sincere. One emotion blended the prayers of the four servants of God and the King in a single supplication. The holy words rang like the music of heaven through the silence. At one moment, tears gathered in the stranger's eyes. This was during the *Pater Noster;* for the priest added a petition in Latin, and his audience doubtless understood him when he said: '*Et remitte scelus regicidis sicut Ludovicus eis remisit semetipse . . .*' Forgive the regicides as Louis himself forgave them.

The Sisters saw two great tears trace a channel down the stranger's manly cheeks and fall to the floor. Then the office for the dead was recited; the *Domine salvum fac regem* chanted in an undertone that went to the hearts of the faithful Royalists, for they thought how the child-King for whom they were praying was even then a captive in the hands of his enemies; and a shudder ran through the stranger, as he thought that a new crime might be committed, and that he could not choose but take his part in it.

The service came to an end. The priest made a sign to the Sisters, and they withdrew. As soon as he was left alone with the stranger, he went toward him with a grave, gentle face, and said, in fatherly tones: 'My son, if your hands are stained with the blood of the royal martyr, confide in me. There is no sin may not be blotted out in the sight of God by penitence as sincere and touching as yours appears to be.'

At the first words, the man stared with terror, in spite of himself. Then he recovered composure, and looked quietly at the astonished priest.

'Father,' he said, and the other could not miss the tremor in his voice, 'no one is more guiltless than I of the blood shed . . .'

'I am bound to believe you,' said the priest. He paused a moment, and again he scrutinized his penitent. But, persisting in the idea that the man before him was one of the members of the Convention, one of the timorous voters who betrayed an inviolable and anointed head to save their own, he began again gravely:

'Remember, my son, that it is not enough to have taken no active part in the great crime; that fact does not absolve you. The men who might have defended the King and left their swords in their scabbards will have a very heavy account to render to the King of Heaven . . . Ah! yes,' he added, with an eloquent shake of the head, 'heavy indeed! For by doing nothing they became accomplices in the awful wickedness . . .'

'But do you think that an indirect participation will be punished?' the stranger asked with a bewildered look. 'There is the private soldier commanded to fall into line – is he actually responsible?'

The priest hesitated. The stranger was glad; he had put the Royalist precisian in a dilemma, between the dogma of passive obedience on the one hand (for the upholders of the Monarchy maintained that obedience was the first principle of military law), and the equally important dogma which turns respect for the person of a king into a matter of religion. In the priest's indecision he was eager to see a favourable solution of the doubts which seemed to torment him. To prevent too prolonged reflection on the part of the reverend Jansenist, he added:

'I should blush to offer remuneration of any kind for the funeral service which you have just performed for the repose of the King's soul and the relief of my conscience. The only possible return for something of inestimable value is an offering likewise beyond price. Will you deign, Monsieur, to take my gift of a holy relic? A day will perhaps come when you will understand its value.'

As he spoke the stranger held out a box; it was very small and exceedingly light. The priest took it mechanically, as it were, so astonished was he by the man's solemn words, the tones of his voice, and the reverence with which he held out the gift.

The two men went back together into the first room. The Sisters were waiting for them.

'This house that you are living in belongs to Mucius Scaevola, the plasterer on the first floor,' he said. 'He is well known in the section for his patriotism, but in reality he is an adherent of the Bourbons. He used to be a huntsman in the service of His Highness, the Prince de Conti, and he owes everything to him. So long as you stay in the house, you are safer here than anywhere else in France. Do not go out. Pious souls will minister your necessities, and you can wait in safety for better times. Next year, on the 21st of January' – he could not hide an involuntary shudder as he spoke – 'next year, if you are still in this dreary refuge, I will come back again to celebrate the expiatory mass with you . . .'

He broke off, bowed to the three, who answered not a word, gave a last look at the garret with its signs of poverty, and vanished.

Such an adventure possessed all the interest of a romance in the lives of the innocent nuns. So, as soon as the venerable abbé told them the story of the mysterious gift, it was placed upon the table, and by the feeble light of the tallow dip an indescribable curiosity appeared in the three anxious faces. Mademoiselle de Langeais opened the box, and found a very fine lawn handkerchief, soiled with sweat; darker stains appeared as they unfolded it.

'That is blood!' exclaimed the priest.

'It is marked with a royal crown!' cried Sister Agathe.

The women, aghast, allowed the precious relic to fall. For their simple souls the mystery that hung about the stranger grew inexplicable: as for the priest, from that day forth he did not even try to understand it,

Before very long the prisoners knew that, in spite of the Terror, some powerful hand was extended over them. It began when they received firewood and provisions; and next the Sisters knew that a woman had lent counsel to their protector, for linen was sent to them, and clothes in which they could leave the house without causing remark upon the aristocrat's dress that they had been forced to wear. After a while Mucius Scaevola gave them two civic cards; and often tidings necessary for the priest's safety came to them in roundabout ways. Warnings and advice reached them so opportunely that they could only have been sent by some person in the possession of state secrets. And, at a time when famine threatened Paris, invisible hands brought rations of white bread for the proscribed women in the wretched garret. Still they fancied that Citizen Mucius Scaevola was only the mysterious instrument of a kindness always ingenious, and no less intelligent.

The noble ladies in the garret could no longer doubt that their protector was the stranger of the expiatory mass on the night of the 22nd of January, 1793; and a kind of cult of him sprang up among them. Their one hope was in him; they lived through him. They added special petitions for him to their prayers; night and morning the pious souls prayed for his happiness, his prosperity, his safety; entreating God to remove all snares far from his path; to deliver him from his enemies, to grant him a long and peaceful life. And with this daily renewed gratitude, as it may be called, there blended a feeling of curiosity which grew more lively day by day. They talked over the circumstances of his first sudden appearance, their conjectures were endless; the stranger had conferred one more benefit upon them by diverting their minds. Again, and again, they said, when he next came to see them as he promised, to celebrate the sad anniversary of the death of Louis XVI, he should not escape their friendship.

The night so impatiently awaited came at last. At midnight the old wooden staircase echoed with the stranger's heavy footsteps. They had made the best of their room for his coming; the altar was ready, and this time the door stood open, and the two Sisters were out at the stairhead, eager to light the way. Mademoiselle de Langeais even came down a few steps, to meet their benefactor the sooner.

'Come,' she said, with a quaver in the affectionate tones. 'Come in, we are expecting you.'

He raised his face, gave her a dark look, and made no answer. The Sister felt as if an icy mantle had fallen over her, and said no more. At the sight of him, the glow of gratitude and curiosity died away in their hearts. Perhaps he was not so cold, not so taciturn, not so stern as he seemed to them, for in their highly wrought mood they were ready to pour out their feeling of friendship. But the three poor prisoners understood that he wished to be a stranger to them – and submitted. The priest fancied that he saw a smile on the man's lips as he saw their preparations for his visit, but it was at once repressed. He heard mass, said his prayer, and then disappeared, declining, with a few polite words, Mademoiselle de Langeais's invitation to partake of the little collation made ready for him.

After the 9th Thermidor, the Sisters and the Abbé de Marolles could go about Paris without the least danger. The first time that the abbé went out he walked to a perfumer's shop at the sign of the Queen of Roses, kept by the Citizen Ragon and his wife, court perfumers. The Ragons had been faithful adherents of the Royalist cause; it was through their means that the Vendéen leaders kept up a correspondence with the Princes and the Royalist Committee in Paris. The abbé, in the ordinary dress of the time, was standing on the threshold of the shop, which stood between Saint Roch and the Rue des Frondeurs, when he saw that the Rue Saint Honoré was filled with a crowd and he could not go out.

'What is the matter?' he asked Madame Ragon.

'Nothing,' she said. 'It is only the tumbril cart and the executioner going to the Place Louis XV. Ah! We used to see it often enough last year; but today, four days after the anniversary of the 21st of January, one does not feel sorry to see the ghastly procession.'

'Why not?' asked the abbé. 'That is not said like a Christian.'

'Eh! But it is the execution of Robespierre's accomplices. They defended themselves as long as they could, but now it is their turn to go where they sent so many innocent people.'

The crowd poured by like a flood. The abbé, yielding to an impulse of curiosity, looked up above the heads, and there in the tumbril stood the man who had heard mass in the garret three days ago.

'Who is it?' he asked. 'Who is the man with . . . ?'

'That is the headsman,' answered M. Ragon, calling the executioner – the *exécuteur des hautes oeuvres* – by the name he had borne under the Monarchy.

'Oh! My dear, my dear! M. l'abbé is dying!' cried out old Madame Ragon. She caught up a flask of vinegar, and tried to restore the old priest to consciousness.

'He must have given me the handkerchief that the King used to wipe his brow on the way to his martyrdom,' murmured he. 'Poor man! There was a heart in the steel blade, when none was found in all France . . .'

The perfumers thought that the poor abbé was raving.

Guy de Maupassant

The Hand

We were all seated round Monsieur Bermutier, the magistrate, who was giving us his opinion on the affair at St Cloud. The inexplicable crime had convulsed Paris for a whole month, yet no single being had solved the mystery.

Upright, with his back to the fireplace, Monsieur Bermutier held forth, marshalled proofs, and discussed divers opinions, but he came to no conclusion.

Several of the women present had risen from their seats to be nearer to him; and they remained standing, their eyes fixed on the clean-shaven lips whence issued such words of grave import. They thrilled and shuddered, devoured with curiosity and with that avid and insatiable love of the horrible that haunts their souls and tortures them like hunger.

One, paler than the others, broke the silence:

'It is terrible! It is almost supernatural! We shall never know anything about it.'

The magistrate turned to her:

'You are right, madame; it is quite probable we shall never know anything about it. But the word "supernatural" that you used a moment ago has no meaning in this case. We have before us a crime very ably conceived and very ably carried out, so wrapped in mystery that we are unable to dissociate it from the impenetrable circumstances surrounding it. But in times gone by I had to follow up a case where the fantastic element was really intermingled. We had to abandon it, however, as no one was able to throw any light on it.'

Breathlessly, and as if with one voice, several of the ladies exclaimed:

'Oh, do tell us about it!'

Monsieur Bermutier smiled gravely, as befits a magistrate, and continued:

You must not think for a moment that I fancied there was any element of the supernatural in this case. I am no believer in the abnormal. But if, instead of using the word 'supernatural' to explain what we do not understand, we were to use the word 'inexplicable', it would be far better. At any rate, in the tale I am about to relate to you it was mainly the surrounding circumstances, the preparatory circumstances, so to speak, which affected me. Briefly, these are the facts:

In those days I was resident magistrate at Ajaccio, a little white town nestled on the borders of a beautiful gulf, and surrounded by high mountains.

What I had principally to deal with were cases of vendetta. There were some that were really magnificent, others excessively dramatic, savage, and again heroic. The most splendid subjects of revenge that a man may dream of – time-honoured hatreds momentarily appeased, perhaps, but never really extinguished – abominably cunning tricks, murder swelling into massacre, and actions almost noble.

For two years I heard of nothing but the price of blood, of the terrible Corsican law which enforces vengeance on the evil-doer to be borne by his descendents and near relations. I had seen old men, children, and cousins with their throats cut. My brain teemed with such happenings.

One day I heard that an Englishman had rented a little villa on the edge of the gulf for several years. He had brought a French manservant with him, picked up on the way at Marseilles. Soon everyone was talking of this queer foreigner, who lived alone in his house; leaving it only to hunt and fish. He never spoke to anyone, never entered the town, and practised shooting every morning for two or three hours with pistol and rifle.

Stories were rife about him. Some made out he was a great personage who had fled his country for political reasons, others affirmed that he was in hiding for having committed a terrible crime. They even cited the particularly horrible details.

In my position as magistrate I wanted to gain some information about this man, but I failed to learn anything at all. He gave his name as Sir John Rowell.

So I had to be content to watch him closely, but, to speak candidly, my attention was called to nothing suspicious about him. However, as the rumours about him continued, swelled, and became common talk, I resolved to see him for myself; and I set about shooting regularly in his neighbourhood.

For a long while I awaited an opportunity. At last it came, in the

shape of a partridge which I shot and killed under the Englishman's nose.
My dog brought it to me. Taking the bird, I went and excused myself for
my want of manners, and begged Sir John Rowell to accept the dead
bird.

He was a huge man, red-haired and red-bearded, very tall, very big,
a placid and polite Hercules. He had none of that so-called British stiffness; and he thanked me warmly for my small civility in French with an
accent from over the water. After a month had gone by we had spoken
five or six times together.

At length one evening as I passed his door and I saw him sitting in his
garden, astride a chair, smoking a pipe. I bowed, and he invited me to
come in and drink a glass of beer. I did not wait to be asked twice.

He received me with the meticulous courtesy of an Englishman, spoke
warmly of France and Corsica, declaring that he liked both country and
seashore extremely.

Then cautiously I put to him some leading questions under the guise of
a lively interest in his life and doings. He answered without any embarrassment, told me that he had travelled much in Africa, India, and
America, and added, laughing:

'Oh, I had many adventures!'

Then I talked sport, and he gave me some exceedingly curious details
gathered in pursuit of the hippopotamus, the tiger, the elephant, and
even the gorilla.

'Those are all formidable beasts?' said I.

He smiled and replied:

'Oh, no; man was the worst!'

And he laughed outright, with the hearty laugh of a satisfied Englishman.

'Man was often my game,' he added.

Then he spoke of arms, and invited me to come in and look at some
rifles of different makes. His sitting-room was hung with black – black
silk embroidered with gold. Large yellow flowers sprawled over the dark
stuff, and shone like fire. The stuff was Japanese, he told me.

In the centre of the largest panel something extraordinary caught my
eye. A black object stood out in relief against a square of red velvet. I
went up to it. It was a hand – a man's hand! No bleached and well-
cleaned skeleton hand, but a dried-up black hand, with its yellow nails,
its bared muscles, and traces of dried blood – blood smeared like mud
on the bones – cut off cleanly as if by a hatchet in the middle of the forearm.

Round the wrist a heavy iron chain was riveted, welded to this unclean
member, and holding it fast to the wall with a ring strong enough to hold
an elephant in leash.

'What is that?' I asked.

'He was my deadliest foe,' replied the Englishman quietly. 'It came from America. It was cut off with a sword, the skin torn away with a flint, and then dried in the sun for a week. A good stroke of work on my part.'

I touched this remnant of humanity; it must have belonged to a colossus. The exaggeratedly long fingers were attached by tremendous tendons, which bore scraps of skin here and there. The hand was horrible to look at, skinned thus; it made one's thoughts turn instinctively to some savage and ferocious form of revenge.

'He must have been a very strong man,' said I.

'Yes,' answered the Englishman calmly; 'but I proved the stronger. I put on that chain to hold him fast.'

Thinking he was speaking in fun, I said:

'But that chain is of no use now: the hand will not try and escape.'

'It has always wanted to go; that chain was necessary,' gravely replied Sir John Rowell.

I looked at him with a rapid glance. Had I to deal with a madman, or did he but joke in very bad taste?

His face remained impenetrable, tranquil, and good-natured. I spoke of other things. I admired his guns. I observed, however, that three loaded revolvers lay about the room, as if this man lived in constant dread of being attacked.

I went to see him several times again; then I went no more. We had become used to his presence; he had become a matter of indifference to all.

A whole year slipped by. Then one morning towards the end of November my servant woke me, telling me that Sir John Rowell had been murdered during the night.

Half an hour later I entered the Englishman's house, accompanied by the Commissioner and the Chief Inspector of Police. Overcome with grief, and half distracted, the manservant stood crying in the doorway. At first I suspected the man, but he was innocent. We were never able to find the murderer.

The first thing I saw on entering Sir John's sitting-room was the body lying on its back in the middle of the room. The waistcoat was torn; one sleeve hung in ribbons; there was every sign that a terrible struggle had taken place.

The Englishman had died of strangulation. His black and swollen face, terrifying, seemed to wear an expression of awful fear. He held something between his clenched teeth; and the throat, pierced with five holes that might have been made with fangs of iron, was covered with blood.

A doctor had joined us. Lengthily he examined the marks of fingers on the flesh, and then queerly remarked:

'One might think he had been strangled by a skeleton.'

A shudder ran down my spine, and I looked towards the wall at the spot where I had seen the horrible skinned hand. It was no longer there. The chain hung down, broken.

Then I stooped over the dead man, and found between the tense jaws a finger from the hand that had disappeared, cut, or rather sawn, by the teeth just at the second joint.

Inquiries were instituted. Nothing was discovered. Neither door, window, nor furniture had been tampered with. The two watchdogs had not been aroused.

Here, briefly, is the manservant's testimony. For a month past his master had appeared restless. He had received many letters, burnt as soon as received.

In a rage which approached madness he would often take up his whip and furiously beat the shrivelled hand chained to the wall, and which had been removed, no one knew how, at the hour of the crime.

He went to bed very late, and locked himself in with care. He always had firearms within reach of his hand. Often in the night he was heard speaking with raised voice, as if he were quarrelling with someone.

That night, by chance, he had made no sound; and it was only on coming to open the windows that the servant had discovered Sir John lying murdered. He suspected no one.

I told the officers of the law all I knew of the dead man, and a minute inquiry was instituted all over the island. They discovered nothing.

Now, it happened one night three months after the crime had taken place I had a most horrible nightmare. I thought I saw the hand, the sinister hand, run like a scorpion or a spider along my curtains and walls. Three times did I wake, three times did I fall asleep; three times did I see the hideous thing gallop round my room, moving its fingers like feet.

The following day they brought it to me, found in the cemetery on the grave of Sir John Rowell, who had been laid there as we failed to discover his family. The first finger was missing. That, ladies, is my story. I know no more.

The women were all shuddering, terror-struck, and pale.

'But,' exclaimed one, 'that cannot be the end; that is no explanation! We shall none of us close our eyes tonight if you do not tell us what you think occurred.'

The magistrate smiled as he answered reprovingly:

'For my part, madame, I shall certainly spoil your horror-filled dreams, for I merely think that the rightful owner of the hand was not dead, and that he came to seek it with the one left to him. But I was unable to find out how he went about it. That was a kind of vendetta.'

One of the women murmured:

'No; it could not have been that!'

'I told you my explanation would not satisfy you,' said the magistrate, still smiling.

Thomas Hardy

The Withered Arm

I. *A Lorn Milkmaid*

It was an eighty-cow dairy, and the troop of milkers, regular and super-numerary, were all at work; for, though the time of year was as yet but early April, the feed lay entirely in water-meadows, and the cows were 'in full pail'. The hour was about six in the evening, and three-fourths of the large, red, rectangular animals having been finished off, there was opportunity for a little conversation.

'He do bring home his bride tomorrow, I hear. They've come as far as Anglebury today.'

The voice seemed to proceed from the belly of the cow called Cherry, but the speaker was a milking-woman, whose face was buried in the flank of that motionless beast.

'Hav' anybody seen her?' said another.

There was a negative response from the first. 'Though they say she's a rosy-cheeked, tisty-tosty little body enough,' she added; and as the milkmaid spoke she turned her face so that she could glance past her cow's tail to the other side of the barton, where a thin, fading woman of thirty milked somewhat apart from the rest.

'Years younger than he, they say,' continued the second, with also a glance of reflectiveness in the same direction.

'How old do you call him, then?'

'Thirty or so.'

'More like forty,' broke in an old milkman near, in a long white pina-fore or 'wropper', and with the brim of his hat tied down, so that he looked like a woman. ''A was born before our Great Weir was builded, and I hadn't man's wages when I laved water there.'

63

The discussion waxed so warm that the purr of the milk streams became jerky, till a voice from another cow's belly cried with authority, 'Now then, what the Turk do it matter to us about Farmer Lodge's age, or Farmer Lodge's new mis'ess? I shall have to pay him nine pound a year for the rent of every one of these milchers, whatever his age or hers. Get on with your work, or 'twill be dark afore we have done. The evening is pinking in a'ready.' This speaker was the dairyman himself, by whom the milkmaids and men were employed.

Nothing more was said publicly about Farmer Lodge's wedding, but the first woman murmured under her cow to her next neighbour, ' 'Tis hard for *she*,' signifying the thin worn milkmaid aforesaid.

'O no,' said the second. 'He ha'n't spoke to Rhoda Brook for years.'

When the milking was done they washed their pails and hung them on a many-forked stand made as usual of the peeled limb of an oak-tree, set upright in the earth, and resembling a colossal antlered horn. The majority then dispersed in various directions homeward. The thin woman who had not spoken was joined by a boy of twelve or thereabout, and the twain went away up the field also.

Their course lay apart from that of the others, to a lonely spot high above the water-meads, and not far from the border of Egdon Heath, whose dark countenance was visible in the distance as they drew nigh to their home.

'They've just been saying down in barton that your father brings his young wife home from Anglebury tomorrow,' the woman observed. 'I shall want to send you for a few things to market, and you'll be pretty sure to meet 'em.'

'Yes, mother,' said the boy. 'Is father married then?'

'Yes. . . . You can give her a look, and tell me what she's like, if you do see her.'

'Yes, mother.'

'If she's dark or fair, and if she's tall – as tall as I. And if she seems like a woman who has ever worked for a living, or one that has been always well off, and has never done anything, and shows marks of the lady on her, as I expect she do.'

'Yes.'

They crept up the hill in the twilight and entered the cottage. It was built of mud-walls, the surface of which had been washed by many rains into channels and depressions that left none of the original flat face visible; while here and there in the thatch above a rafter showed like a bone protruding through the skin.

She was kneeling down in the chimney-corner, before two pieces of turf laid together with the heather inwards, blowing at the red-hot ashes with her breath till the turves flamed. The radiance lit her pale cheek, and made her dark eyes, that had once been handsome, seem handsome anew. 'Yes,' she resumed, 'see if she is dark or fair, and if you can, notice if her hands be white; if not, see if they look as though she had ever done housework, or are milker's hands like mine.'

The boy again promised, inattentively this time, his mother not observing that he was cutting a notch with his pocket-knife in the beech-backed chair.

II. *The Young Wife*

The road from Anglebury to Holmstoke is in general level; but there is one place where a sharp ascent breaks its monotony. Farmers homeward-bound from the former market-town, who trot all the rest of the way, walk their horses up this short incline.

The next evening while the sun was yet bright a handsome new gig, with a lemon-coloured body and red wheels, was spinning westward along the level highway at the heels of a powerful mare. The driver was a yeoman in the prime of life, cleanly shaven like an actor, his face being toned to that bluish-vermilion hue which so often graces a thriving farmer's features when returning home after successful dealings in the town. Beside him sat a woman, many years his junior – almost, indeed, a girl. Her face too was fresh in colour, but it was of a totally different quality – soft and evanescent, like the light under a heap of rose-petals.

Few people travelled this way, for it was not a main road; and the long white riband of gravel that stretched before them was empty, save of one small scarce-moving speck, which presently resolved itself into the figure of a boy, who was creeping on at a snail's pace, and continually looking behind him – the heavy bundle he carried being some excuse for, if not the reason of, his dilatoriness. When the bouncing gig-party slowed at the bottom of the incline above mentioned, the pedestrian was only a few yards in front. Supporting the large bundle by putting one hand on his hip, he turned and looked straight at the farmer's wife as though he would read her through and through, pacing along abreast of the horse.

The low sun was full in her face, rendering every feature, shade, and contour distinct, from the curve of her little nostril to the colour of her eyes. The farmer, though he seemed annoyed at the boy's persistent presence, did not order him to get out of the way; and thus the lad pre-ceded them, his hard gaze never leaving her, till they reached the top of the ascent, when the farmer trotted on with relief in his lineaments – having taken no outward notice of the boy whatever.

'How that poor lad stared at me!' said the young wife.

'Yes, dear; I saw that he did.'

'He is one of the village, I suppose?'

'One of the neighbourhood. I think he lives with his mother a mile or two off.'

'He knows who we are, no doubt?'

'O yes. You must expect to be stared at just at first, my pretty Gertrude.'

'I do – though I think the poor boy may have looked at us in the hope we might relieve him of his heavy load, rather than from curiosity.'

'O no,' said her husband off-handedly. 'These country lads will carry a hundredweight once they get it on their backs; besides his pack had more size than weight in it. Now, then, another mile and I shall be able to show you our house in the distance – if it is not too dark before we get there.' The wheels spun round, and particles flew from their periphery as before, till a white house of ample dimensions revealed itself, with farm-buildings and ricks at the back.

Meanwhile the boy had quickened his pace, and turning up a by-lane some mile and half short of the white farmstead, ascended towards the leaner pastures, and so on to the cottage of his mother.

She had reached home after her day's milking at the outlying dairy, and was washing cabbage at the doorway in the declining light. 'Hold up the net a moment,' she said, without preface, as the boy came up.

He flung down his bundle, held the edge of the cabbage-net, and as she filled its meshes with the dripping leaves she went on, 'Well, did you see her?'

'Yes; quite plain.'

'Is she ladylike?'

'Yes; and more. A lady complete.'

'Is she young?'

'Well, she's growed up, and her ways be quite a woman's.'

'Of course. What colour is her hair and face?'

'Her hair is lightish, and her face as comely as a live doll's.'

'Her eyes, then, are not dark like mine?'

'No – of a bluish turn, and her mouth is very nice and red; and when she smiles, her teeth show white.'

'Is she tall?' said the woman sharply.

'I couldn't see. She was sitting down.'

'Then do you go to Holmstoke church tomorrow morning: she's sure to be there. Go early and notice her walking in, and come home and tell me if she's taller than I.'

'Very well, mother. But why don't you go and see for yourself?'

'*I* go to see her! I wouldn't look up at her if she were to pass my window this instant. She was with Mr Lodge, of course. What did he say or do?'

'Just the same as usual.'

'Took no notice of you?'

'None.'

Next day the mother put a clean shirt on the boy, and started him off for Holmstoke church. He reached the ancient little pile when the door was just being opened, and he was the first to enter. Taking his seat by the font, he watched all the parishioners file in. The well-to-do Farmer Lodge came nearly last; and his young wife, who accompanied him, walked up the aisle with the shyness natural to a modest woman who had appeared thus for the first time. As all other eyes were fixed upon her, the youth's stare was not noticed now.

When he reached home his mother said, 'Well?' before he had entered the room.

'She is not tall. She is rather short,' he replied.

'Ah!' said his mother, with satisfaction.

'But she's very pretty – very. In fact, she's lovely.' The youthful freshness of the yeoman's wife had evidently made an impression even on the somewhat hard nature of the boy.

'That's all I want to hear,' said his mother quickly. 'Now, spread the table-cloth. The hare you wired is very tender; but mind that nobody catches you. – You've never told me what sort of hands she had.'

'I have never seen 'em. She never took off her gloves.'

'What did she wear this morning?'

'A white bonnet and a silver-coloured gownd. It whewed and whistled so loud when it rubbed against the pews that the lady coloured up more than ever for very shame at the noise, and pulled it in to keep it from touching; but when she pushed into her seat, it whewed more than ever. Mr Lodge, he seemed pleased, and his waistcoat stuck out, and his great golden seals hung like a lord's; but she seemed to wish her noisy gownd anywhere but on her.'

'Not she! However, that will do now.'

These descriptions of the newly-married couple were continued from time to time by the boy at his mother's request, after any chance encounter he had had with them. But Rhoda Brook, though she might easily have seen young Mrs Lodge for herself by walking a couple of miles, would never attempt an excursion towards the quarter where the farmhouse lay. Neither did she, at the daily milking in the dairyman's yard on Lodge's outlying second farm, ever speak on the subject of the recent marriage. The dairyman, who rented the cows of Lodge, and knew perfectly the tall milkmaid's history, with manly kindliness always kept the gossip in the cow-barton from annoying Rhoda. But the atmosphere thereabout was full of the subject during the first days of Mrs Lodge's arrival; and from her boy's description and the casual words of the other milkers, Rhoda Brook could raise a mental image of the unconscious Mrs Lodge that was realistic as a photograph.

THOMAS HARDY

III. *A Vision*

One night, two or three weeks after the bridal return, when the boy was gone to bed, Rhoda sat a long time over the turf ashes that she had raked out in front of her to extinguish them. She contemplated so intently the new wife, as presented to her in her mind's eye over the embers, that she forgot the lapse of time. At last, wearied with her day's work, she too retired.

But the figure which had occupied her so much during this and the previous days was not to be banished at night. For the first time Gertrude Lodge visited the supplanted woman in her dreams. Rhoda Brook dreamed – since her assertion that she really saw, before falling asleep, was not to be believed – that the young wife, in the pale silk dress and white bonnet, but with features shockingly distorted, and wrinkled as by age, was sitting upon her chest as she lay. The pressure of Mrs Lodge's person grew heavier; the blue eyes peered cruelly into her face; and then the figure thrust forward its left hand mockingly, so as to make the wedding-ring it wore glitter in Rhoda's eyes. Maddened mentally, and nearly suffocated by pressure, the sleeper struggled; the incubus, still regarding her, withdrew to the foot of the bed, only, however, to come forward by degrees, resume her seat, and flash her left hand as before.

Gasping for breath, Rhoda, in a last desperate effort, swung out her right hand, seized the confronting spectre by its obtrusive left arm, and whirled it backward to the floor, starting up herself as she did so with a low cry.

'O, merciful heaven!' she cried, sitting on the edge of the bed in a cold sweat; 'that was not a dream – she was here!'

She could feel her antagonist's arm within her grasp even now – the very flesh and bone of it, as it seemed. She looked on the floor whither she had whirled the spectre, but there was nothing to be seen.

Rhoda Brook slept no more that night, and when she went milking at the next dawn they noticed how pale and haggard she looked. The milk that she drew quivered into the pail; her hand not calmed even yet, and still retained the feel of the arm. She came home to breakfast as wearily as if it had been supper-time.

'What was that noise in your chimmer, mother, last night?' said her son. 'You fell off the bed, surely?'

'Did you hear anything fall? At what time?'

'Just when the clock struck two.'

She could not explain, and when the meal was done went silently about her household work, the boy assisting her, for he hated going afield on the farms, and she indulged his reluctance. Between eleven and twelve the garden-gate clicked, and she lifted her eyes to the window. At the

68

bottom of the garden, within the gate, stood the woman of her vision. Rhoda seemed transfixed.

'Ah, she said she would come!' exclaimed the boy, also observing her.

'Said so – when? How does she know us?'

'I have seen and spoken to her. I talked to her yesterday.'

'I told you,' said the mother, flushing indignantly, 'never to speak to anybody in that house, or go near the place.'

'I did not speak to her till she spoke to me. And I did not go near the place. I met her in the road.'

'What did you tell her?'

'Nothing. She said, "Are you the poor boy who had to bring the heavy load from market?" And she looked at my boots, and said they would not keep my feet dry if it came on wet, because they were so cracked. I told her I lived with my mother, and we had enough to do to keep ourselves, and that's how it was; and she said then, "I'll come and bring you some better boots, and see your mother." She gives away things to other folks in the meads besides us.'

Mrs Lodge was by this time close to the door – not in her silk, as Rhoda had dreamt of in the bed-chamber, but in a morning hat, and gown of common light material, which became her better than silk. On her arm she carried a basket.

The impression remaining from the night's experience was still strong. Brook had almost expected to see the wrinkles, the scorn, and the cruelty on her visitor's face. She would have escaped an interview, had escape been possible. There was, however, no backdoor to the cottage, and in an instant the boy had lifted the latch to Mrs Lodge's gentle knock.

'I see I have come to the right house,' said she, glancing at the lad, and smiling. 'But I was not sure till you opened the door.'

The figure and action were those of the phantom; but her voice was so indescribably sweet, her glance so winning, her smile so tender, so unlike that of Rhoda's midnight visitant, that the latter could hardly believe the evidence of her senses. She was truly glad that she had not hidden away in sheer aversion, as she had been inclined to do. In her basket Mrs Lodge brought the pair of boots that she had promised to the boy, and other useful articles.

At these proofs of a kindly feeling towards her and hers Rhoda's heart reproached her bitterly. This innocent young thing should have her blessing and not her curse. When she left them a light seemed gone from the dwelling. Two days later she came again to know if the boots fitted; and less than a fortnight after that paid Rhoda another call. On this occasion the boy was absent.

'I walk a good deal,' said Mrs Lodge, 'and your house is the nearest outside our own parish. I hope you are well. You don't look quite well.'

Rhoda said she was well enough; and, indeed, though the paler of the two, there was more of the strength that endures in her well-defined features and large frame than in the soft-cheeked young woman before her. The conversation became quite confidential as regarded their powers and weaknesses; and when Mrs Lodge was leaving, Rhoda said, 'I hope you will find this air agree with you, ma'am, and not suffer from the damp of the water meads.'

The younger one replied that there was not much doubt of it, her general health being usually good. 'Though, now you remind me,' she added, 'I have one little ailment which puzzles me. It is nothing serious, but I cannot make it out.'

She uncovered her left hand and arm; and their outline confronted Rhoda's gaze as the exact original of the limb she had beheld and seized in her dream. Upon the pink round surface of the arm were faint marks of an unhealthy colour, as if produced by a rough grasp. Rhoda's eyes became riveted on the discolorations; she fancied that she discerned in them the shape of her own four fingers.

'How did it happen?' she said mechanically.

'I cannot tell,' replied Mrs Lodge, shaking her head. 'One night when I was sound asleep, dreaming I was away in some strange place, a pain suddenly shot into my arm there, and was so keen as to awaken me. I must have struck it in the daytime, I suppose, though I don't remember doing so.' She added, laughing, 'I tell my dear husband that it looks just as if he had flown into a rage and struck me there. O, I daresay it will soon disappear.'

'Ha, ha! Yes. . . . On what night did it come?'

Mrs Lodge considered, and said it would be a fortnight ago on the morrow. 'When I awoke I could not remember where I was,' she added, 'till the clock striking two reminded me.'

She had named the night and the hour of Rhoda's spectral encounter, and Brook felt like a guilty thing. The artless disclosure startled her; she did not reason on the freaks of coincidence; and all the scenery of that ghastly night returned with double vividness to her mind.

'O, can it be,' she said to herself, when her visitor had departed, 'that I exercise a malignant power over people against my own will?' She knew that she had been slyly called a witch since her fall; but never having understood why that particular stigma had been attached to her, it had passed disregarded. Could this be the explanation, and had such things as this ever happened before?

IV. *A Suggestion*

The summer drew on, and Rhoda Brook almost dreaded to meet Mrs Lodge again, notwithstanding that her feeling for the young wife amounted well-nigh to affection. Something in her own individuality seemed to convict Rhoda of crime. Yet a fatality sometimes would direct the steps of the latter to the outskirts of Holmstoke whenever she left her house for any other purpose than her daily work; and hence it happened that their next encounter was out of doors. Rhoda could not avoid the subject which had so mystified her, and after the first few words she stammered, 'I hope your – arm is well again, ma'am?' She had perceived with consternation that Gertrude Lodge carried her left arm stiffly.

'No; it is not quite well. Indeed it is no better at all; it is rather worse. It pains me dreadfully sometimes.'

'Perhaps you had better go to a doctor, ma'am.'

She replied that she had already seen a doctor. Her husband had insisted upon her going to one. But the surgeon had not seemed to understand the afflicted limb at all; he had told her to bathe it in hot water, and she had bathed it, but the treatment had done no good.

'Will you let me see it?' said the milkwoman.

Mrs Lodge pushed up her sleeve and disclosed the place, which was a few inches above the wrist. As soon as Rhoda Brook saw it, she could hardly preserve her composure. There was nothing of the nature of a wound, but the arm at that point had a shrivelled look, and the outline of the four fingers appeared more distinct than at the former time. Moreover, she fancied that they were imprinted in precisely the relative position of her clutch upon the arm in the trance; the first finger towards Gertrude's wrist, and the fourth towards her elbow.

What the impress resembled seemed to have struck Gertrude herself since their last meeting. 'It looks almost like finger-marks,' she said; adding with a faint laugh, 'my husband says it is as if some witch, or the devil himself, had taken hold of me there, and blasted the flesh.'

Rhoda shivered. 'That's fancy,' she said hurriedly. 'I wouldn't mind it, if I were you.'

'I shouldn't so much mind it,' said the younger, with hesitation, 'if – if I hadn't a notion that it makes my husband – dislike me – no, love me less. Men think so much of personal appearance.'

'Some do – he for one.'

'Yes; and he was very proud of mine, at first.'

'Keep your arm covered from his sight.'

'Ah – he knows the disfigurement is there!' She tried to hide the tears that filled her eyes.

'Well, ma'am, I earnestly hope it will go away soon.'

And so the milkwoman's mind was chained anew to the subject by a horrid sort of spell as she returned home. The sense of having been guilty of an act of malignity increased, affect as she might to ridicule her superstition. In her secret heart Rhoda did not altogether object to a slight diminution of her successor's beauty, by whatever means it had come about; but she did not wish to inflict upon her physical pain. For though this pretty young woman had rendered impossible any reparation which Lodge might have made Rhoda for his past conduct, everything like resentment at the unconscious usurpation had quite passed away from the elder's mind.

If the sweet and kindly Gertrude Lodge only knew of the dream-scene in the bed-chamber, what would she think? Not to inform her of it seemed treachery in the presence of her friendliness; but tell she could not of her own accord – neither could she devise a remedy.

She mused upon the matter the greater part of the night; and the next day, after the morning milking, set out to obtain another glimpse of Gertrude Lodge if she could, being held to her by a gruesome fascination. By watching the house from a distance the milkmaid was presently able to discern the farmer's wife in a ride she was taking alone – probably to join her husband in some distant field. Mrs Lodge perceived her, and cantered in her direction.

'Good morning, Rhoda!' Gertrude said, when she had come up. 'I was going to call.'

Rhoda noticed that Mrs Lodge held the reins with some difficulty.

'I hope – the bad arm,' said Rhoda.

'They tell me there is possibly one way by which I might be able to find out the cause, and so perhaps the cure, of it,' replied the other anxiously. 'It is by going to some clever man over in Egdon Heath. They did not know if he was still alive – and I cannot remember his name at this moment; but they said that you knew more of his movements than anybody else hereabout, and could tell me if he were still to be consulted. Dear me – what was his name? But you know.'

'Not Conjuror Trendle?' said her thin companion, turning pale.

'Trendle – yes. Is he alive?'

'I believe so,' said Rhoda, with reluctance.

'Why do you call him conjuror?'

'Well – they say – they used to say he was a – he had powers other folks have not.'

'O, how could my people be so superstitious as to recommend a man of that sort! I thought they meant some medical man. I shall think no more of him.'

Rhoda looked relieved, and Mrs Lodge rode on. The milkwoman had inwardly seen, from the moment she heard of her having been mentioned as a reference for this man, that there must exist a sarcastic feeling among the work-folk that a sorceress would know the whereabouts of the exorcist. They suspected her, then. A short time ago this would have given no concern to a woman of her common-sense. But she had a haunting reason to be superstitious now; and she had been seized with sudden dread that this Conjuror Trendle might name her as the malignant influence which was blasting the fair person of Gertrude, and so lead her friend to hate her for ever, and to treat her as some fiend in human shape.

But all was not over. Two days after, a shadow intruded into the window-pattern thrown on Rhoda Brook's floor by the afternoon sun. The woman opened the door at once, almost breathlessly.

'Are you alone?' said Gertrude. She seemed to be no less harassed and anxious than Brook herself.

'Yes,' said Rhoda.

'The place on my arm seems worse, and troubles me!' the young farmer's wife went on. 'It is so mysterious! I do hope it will not be an incurable wound. I have again been thinking of what they said about Conjuror Trendle. I don't really believe in such men, but I should not mind just visiting him, from curiosity – though on no account must my husband know. Is it far to where he lives?'

'Yes – five miles,' said Rhoda backwardly. 'In the heart of Egdon.'

'Well, I should have to walk. Could not you go with me to show me the way – say to-morrow afternoon?'

'O, not I; that is——,' the milkwoman murmured, with a start of dismay. Again the dread seized her that something to do with her fierce act in the dream might be revealed, and her character in the eyes of the most useful friend she had ever had be ruined irretrievably.

Mrs Lodge urged, and Rhoda finally assented, though with much misgiving. Sad as the journey would be to her, she could not conscientiously stand in the way of a possible remedy for her patron's strange affliction. It was agreed that, to escape suspicion of their mystic intent, they should meet at the edge of the heath at the corner of a plantation which was visible from the spot where they now stood.

V. *Conjuror Trendle*

By the next afternoon Rhoda would have done anything to escape this inquiry. But she had promised to go. Moreover, there was a horrid fascination at times in becoming instrumental in throwing such possible light on her own character as would reveal her to be something greater in the occult world than she had ever herself suspected.

She started just before the time of day mentioned between them, and half-an-hour's brisk walking brought her to the south-eastern extension of the Egdon tract of country, where the fir plantation was. A slight figure, cloaked and veiled, was already there. Rhoda recognized, almost with a shudder, that Mrs Lodge bore her left arm in a sling.

They hardly spoke to each other, and immediately set out on their climb into the interior of this solemn country, which stood high above the rich alluvial soil they had left half-an-hour before. It was a long walk; thick clouds made the atmosphere dark, though it was as yet only early afternoon; and the wind howled dismally over the slopes of the heath – not improbably the same heath which had witnessed the agony of the Wessex King Ina, presented to after-ages as Lear. Gertrude Lodge talked most, Rhoda replying with monosyllabic preoccupation. She had a strange dislike to walking on the side of her companion where hung the afflicted arm, moving round to the other when inadvertently near it. Much heather had been brushed by their feet when they descended upon a cart-track, beside which stood the house of the man they sought.

He did not profess his remedial practices openly, or care anything about their continuance, his direct interests being those of a dealer in furze, turf, 'sharp sand', and other local products. Indeed, he affected not to believe largely in his own powers, and when warts that had been shown him for cure miraculously disappeared – which it must be owned they infallibly did – he would say lightly, 'O, I only drink a glass of grog upon 'em at your expense – perhaps it's all chance,' and immediately turn the subject.

He was at home when they arrived, having in fact seen them descending into his valley. He was a grey-bearded man, with a reddish face, and he looked singularly at Rhoda the first moment he beheld her. Mrs Lodge told him her errand; and then with words of self-disparagement he examined her arm.

'Medicine can't cure it,' he said promptly. ' 'Tis the work of an enemy.'

Rhoda shrank into herself, and drew back.

'An enemy? What enemy?' asked Mrs Lodge.

He shook his head. 'That's best known to yourself,' he said. 'If you like, I can show the person to you, though I shall not myself know who it is. I can do no more; and don't wish to do that.'

She pressed him; on which he told Rhoda to wait outside where she stood, and took Mrs Lodge into the room. It opened immediately from the door; and, as the latter remained ajar, Rhoda Brook could see the proceedings without taking part in them. He brought a tumbler from the dresser, nearly filled it with water, and fetching an egg, prepared it in some private way; after which he broke it on the edge of the glass, so that the white went in and the yolk remained. As it was getting gloomy, he took the glass and its contents to the window, and told Gertrude to watch the mixture closely. They leant over the table together, and the milkwoman could see the opaline hue of the egg-fluid changing form as it sank in the water, but she was not near enough to define the shape that it assumed.

'Do you catch the likeness of any face or figure as you look?' demanded the conjuror of the young woman.

She murmured a reply, in tones so low as to be inaudible to Rhoda, and continued to gaze intently into the glass. Rhoda turned, and walked a few steps away.

When Mrs Lodge came out, and her face was met by the light, it appeared exceedingly pale – as pale as Rhoda's – against the sad dun shades of the upland's garniture. Trendle shut the door behind her, and they at once started homeward together. But Rhoda perceived that her companion had quite changed.

'Did he charge much?' she asked tentatively.

'O no – nothing. He would not take a farthing,' said Gertrude.

'And what did you see?' inquired Rhoda.

'Nothing I – care to speak of.' The constraint in her manner was remarkable; her face was so rigid as to wear an oldened aspect, faintly suggestive of the face in Rhoda's bed-chamber.

'Was it you who first proposed coming here?' Mrs Lodge suddenly inquired, after a long pause. 'How very odd, if you did!'

'No. But I am not sorry we have come, all things considered,' she replied. For the first time a sense of triumph possessed her, and she did not altogether deplore that the young thing at her side should learn that their lives had been antagonized by other influences than their own.

The subject was no more alluded to during the long and dreary walk home. But in some way or other a story was whispered about the many-dairied lowland that winter that Mrs Lodge's gradual loss of the use of her left arm was owing to her being 'overlooked' by Rhoda Brook. The latter kept her own counsel about the incubus, but her face grew sadder and thinner; and in the spring she and her boy disappeared from the neighbourhood of Holmstoke.

VI. *A Second Attempt*

Half a dozen years passed away, and Mr and Mrs Lodge's married experience sank into prosiness, and worse. The farmer was usually gloomy and silent: the woman whom he had wooed for her grace and beauty was contorted and disfigured in the left limb; moreover, she had brought him no child, which rendered it likely that he would be the last of a family who had occupied that valley for some two hundred years. He thought of Rhoda Brook and her son; and feared this might be a judgment from heaven upon him.

The once blithe-hearted and enlightened Gertrude was changing into an irritable, superstitious woman, whose whole time was given to experimenting upon her ailment with every quack remedy she came across. She was honestly attached to her husband, and was ever secretly hoping against hope to win back his heart again by regaining some at least of her personal beauty. Hence it arose that her closet was lined with bottles, packets, and ointment-pots of every description – nay, bunches of mystic herbs, charms, and books of necromancy, which in her schoolgirl time she would have ridiculed as folly.

'Damned if you won't poison yourself with these apothecary messes and witch mixtures some time or other,' said her husband, when his eye chanced to fall upon the multitudinous array.

She did not reply, but turned her sad, soft glance upon him in such heart-swollen reproach that he looked sorry for his words, and added, 'I only meant it for your good, you know, Gertrude.'

'I'll clear out the whole lot, and destroy them,' said she huskily, 'and try such remedies no more!'

'You want somebody to cheer you,' he observed. 'I once thought of adopting a boy; but he is too old now. And he is gone away I don't know where.'

She guessed to whom he alluded; for Rhoda Brook's story had in the course of years become known to her; though not a word had ever passed between her husband and herself on the subject. Neither had she ever spoken to him of her visit to Conjuror Trendle, and of what was revealed to her, or she thought was revealed to her, by that solitary heathman.

She was now five-and-twenty; but she seemed older. 'Six years of marriage, and only a few months of love,' she sometimes whispered to herself. And then she thought of the apparent cause, and said, with a tragic glance at her withering limb, 'If I could only again be as I was when he first saw me!'

She obediently destroyed her nostrums and charms; but there remained a hankering wish to try something else – some other sort of cure altogether. She had never revisited Trendle since she had been conducted to the house of the solitary by Rhoda against her will; but it now suddenly occurred to Gertrude that she would, in a last desperate effort at deliverance from this seeming curse, again seek out the man, if he yet lived. He was entitled to a certain credence, for the indistinct form he had raised in the glass had undoubtedly resembled the only woman in the world who – as she now knew, though not then – could have a reason for bearing her ill-will. The visit should be paid.

This time she went alone, though she nearly got lost on the heath, and roamed a considerable distance out of her way. Trendle's house was reached at last, however: he was not indoors, and instead of waiting at the cottage, she went to where his bent figure was pointed out to her at work a long way off. Trendle remembered her, and laying down the handful of furze-roots which he was gathering and throwing into a heap, he offered to accompany her in her homeward direction, as the distance was considerable and the days were short. So they walked together, his head bowed nearly to the earth, and his form of a colour with it.

'You can send away warts and other excrescences, I know,' she said; 'why can't you send away this?' And the arm was uncovered.

'You think too much of my powers!' said Trendle; 'and I am old and weak now, too. No, no; it is too much for me to attempt in my own person. What have ye tried?'

She named to him some of the hundred medicaments and counter-spells which she had adopted from time to time. He shook his head.

'Some were good enough,' he said approvingly; 'but not many of them for such as this. This is of the nature of a blight, not of the nature of a wound; and if you ever do throw it off, it will be all at once.'

'If I only could!'

'There is only one chance of doing it known to me. It has never failed in kindred afflictions – that I can declare. But it is hard to carry out, and especially for a woman.'

'Tell me!' said she.

'You must touch with the limb the neck of a man who's been hanged.'

She started a little at the image he had raised.

'Before he's cold – just after he's cut down,' continued the conjuror impassively.

'How can that do good?'

'It will turn the blood and change the constitution. But, as I say, to do it is hard. You must go to the jail when there's a hanging, and wait for him when he's brought off the gallows. Lots have done it, though per-haps not such pretty women as you. I used to send dozens for skin complaints. But that was in former times. The last I sent was in '13 – near twelve years ago.'

He had no more to tell her; and, when he had put her into a straight track homeward, turned and left her, refusing all money as at first.

VII. *A Ride*

The communication sank deep into Gertrude's mind. Her nature was rather a timid one; and probably of all remedies that the white wizard could have suggested there was not one which would have filled her with so much aversion as this, not to speak of the immense obstacles in the way of its adoption.

Casterbridge, the county-town, was a dozen or fifteen miles off; and though in those days, when men were executed for horse-stealing, arson, and burglary, an assize seldom passed without a hanging, it was not likely that she could get access to the body of the criminal unaided. And the fear of her husband's anger made her reluctant to breathe a word of Trendle's suggestion to him or to anybody about him.

She did nothing for months, and patiently bore her disfigurement as before. But her woman's nature, craving for renewed love, through the medium of renewed beauty (she was but twenty-five), was ever stimulating her to try what, at any rate, could hardly do her any harm. 'What came by a spell will go by a spell surely,' she would say. Whenever her imagination pictured the act she shrank in terror from the possibility of it: then the words of the conjuror, 'It will turn your blood,' were seen to be capable of a scientific no less than a ghastly interpretation; the mastering desire returned, and urged her on again.

There was at this time but one county paper, and that her husband only occasionally borrowed. But old-fashioned days had old-fashioned means, and news was extensively conveyed by word of mouth from market to market, or from fair to fair, so that, whenever such an event as an execution was about to take place, few within a radius of twenty miles were ignorant of the coming sight; and, so far as Holmstoke was concerned, some enthusiasts had been known to walk all the way to Casterbridge and back in one day, solely to witness the spectacle. The next assizes were in March; and when Gertrude Lodge heard that they had been held, she inquired stealthily at the inn as to the result, as soon as she could find opportunity.

She was, however, too late. The time at which the sentences were to be carried out had arrived, and to make the journey and obtain admission at such short notice required at least her husband's assistance. She dared not tell him, for she had found by delicate experiment that these smouldering village beliefs made him furious if mentioned, partly because he half entertained them himself. It was therefore necessary to wait for another opportunity.

Her determination received a fillip from learning that two epileptic children had attended from this very village of Holmstoke many years before with beneficial results, though the experiment had been strongly condemned by the neighbouring clergy. April, May, June, passed; and it is no overstatement to say that by the end of the last-named month Gertrude well-nigh longed for the death of a fellow-creature. Instead of her formal prayers each night, her unconscious prayer was, 'O Lord, hang some guilty or innocent person soon!'

This time she made earlier inquiries, and was altogether more systematic in her proceedings. Moreover, the season was summer, between the haymaking and the harvest, and in the leisure thus afforded him her husband had been holiday-taking away from home.

The assizes were in July, and she went to the inn as before. There was to be one execution – only one – for arson.

Her greatest problem was not how to get to Casterbridge, but what means she should adopt for obtaining admission to the jail. Though access for such purposes had formerly never been denied, the custom had fallen into desuetude; and in contemplating her possible difficulties, she was again almost driven to fall back upon her husband. But, on sounding him about the assizes, he was so uncommunicative, so more than usually cold, that she did not proceed, and decided that whatever she did she would do alone.

Fortune, obdurate hitherto, showed her unexpected favour. On the Thursday before the Saturday fixed for the execution, Lodge remarked to her that he was going away from home for another day or two on business at a fair, and that he was sorry he could not take her with him.

She exhibited on this occasion so much readiness to stay at home that he looked at her in surprise. Time had been when she would have shown deep disappointment at the loss of such a jaunt. However, he lapsed into his usual taciturnity, and on the day named left Holmstoke.

It was now her turn. She at first had thought of driving, but on reflection held that driving would not do, since it would necessitate her keeping to the turnpike-road, and so increase by tenfold the risk of her ghastly errand being found out. She decided to ride, and avoid the beaten track, notwithstanding that in her husband's stables there was no animal just at present which by any stretch of imagination could be considered a lady's mount, in spite of his promise before marriage to always keep a mare for her. He had, however, many cart-horses, fine ones of their kind; and among the rest was a serviceable creature, an equine Amazon, with a back as broad as a sofa, on which Gertrude had occasionally taken an airing when unwell. This horse she chose.

On Friday afternoon one of the men brought it round. She was dressed, and before going down looked at her shrivelled arm. 'Ah!' she said to it, 'if it had not been for you this terrible ordeal would have been saved me!'

When strapping up the bundle in which she carried a few articles of clothing, she took occasion to say to the servant, 'I take these in case I should not get back tonight from the person I am going to visit. Don't be alarmed if I am not in by ten, and close up the house as usual. I shall be at home tomorrow for certain.' She meant then to tell her husband privately: the deed accomplished was not like the deed projected. He would almost certainly forgive her.

And then the pretty palpitating Gertrude Lodge went from her husband's homestead; but though her goal was Casterbridge she did not take the direct route thither through Stickleford. Her cunning course at first was in precisely the opposite direction. As soon as she was out of sight, however, she turned to the left, by a road which led into Egdon, and on entering the heath wheeled round, and set out in the true course, due westerly. A more private way down the county could not be imagined; and as to direction, she had merely to keep her horse's head to a point a little to the right of the sun. She knew that she would light upon a furze-cutter or cottager of some sort from time to time, from whom she might correct her bearing.

Though the date was comparatively recent, Egdon was much less fragmentary in character than now. The attempts – successful and otherwise – at cultivation on the lower slopes, which intrude and break up the original heath into small detached heaths, had not been carried far; Enclosure Acts had not taken effect, and the banks and fences which now exclude the cattle of those villagers who formerly enjoyed rights of commonage thereon, and the carts of those who had turbary privileges which kept them in firing all the year round, were not erected. Gertrude, therefore, rode along with no other obstacles than the prickly furze-bushes, the mats of heather, the white water-courses, and the natural steeps and declivities of the ground.

Her horse was sure, if heavy-footed and slow, and though a draught animal, was easy-paced; had it been otherwise, she was not a woman who could have ventured to ride over such a bit of country with a half-dead arm. It was therefore nearly eight o'clock when she drew rein to breathe her bearer on the last outlying high point of heath-land towards Casterbridge, previous to leaving Egdon for the cultivated valleys.

She halted before a pool called Rushy-pond, flanked by the ends of two hedges; a railing ran through the centre of the pond, dividing it in half. Over the railing she saw the low green country; over the green trees the roofs of the town; over the roofs a white flat façade, denoting the entrance to the county jail. On the roof of this front specks were moving about; they seemed to be workmen erecting something. Her flesh crept. She descended slowly, and was soon amid corn-fields and pastures. In another half-hour, when it was almost dusk, Gertrude reached the White Hart, the first inn of the town on that side.

Little surprise was excited by her arrival; farmers' wives rode on horseback then more than they do now; though, for that matter, Mrs Lodge was not imagined to be a wife at all; the innkeeper supposed her some harum-skarum young woman who had come to attend 'hang-fair' next day. Neither her husband nor herself ever dealt in Casterbridge market, so that she was unknown. While dismounting she beheld a crowd of boys standing at the door of a harness-maker's shop just above the inn, looking inside it with deep interest.

'What is going on there?' she asked of the ostler.

'Making the rope for tomorrow.'

She throbbed responsively, and contracted her arm.

' 'Tis sold by the inch afterwards,' the man continued. 'I could get you a bit, miss, for nothing, if you'd like?'

She hastily repudiated any such wish, all the more from a curious creeping feeling that the condemned wretch's destiny was becoming interwoven with her own; and having engaged a room for the night, sat down to think.

Up to this time she had formed but the vaguest notions about her means of obtaining access to the prison. The words of the cunning-man returned to her mind. He had implied that she should use her beauty, impaired though it was, as a pass-key. In her inexperience she knew little about jail functionaries; she had heard of a high-sheriff and an under-sheriff, but dimly only. She knew, however, that there must be a hangman, and to the hangman she determined to apply.

VIII. *A Water-side Hermit*

At this date, and for several years after, there was a hangman to almost every jail. Gertrude found, on inquiry, that the Casterbridge official dwelt in a lonely cottage by a deep slow river flowing under the cliff on which the prison buildings were situate – the stream being the self-same one, though she did not know it, which watered the Stickleford and Holmstoke meads lower down in its course.

Having changed her dress, and before she had eaten or drunk – for she could not take her ease till she had ascertained some particulars – Gertrude pursued her way by a path along the water-side to the cottage indicated. Passing thus the outskirts of the jail, she discerned on the level roof over the gateway three rectangular lines against the sky, where the specks had been moving in her distant view; she recognized what the erection was, and passed quickly on. Another hundred yards brought her to the executioner's house, which a boy pointed out. It stood close to the same stream, and was hard by a weir, the waters of which emitted a steady roar.

While she stood hesitating the door opened, and an old man came forth shading a candle with one hand. Locking the door on the outside, he turned to a flight of wooden steps fixed against the end of the cottage, and began to ascend them, this being evidently the staircase to his bed-room. Gertrude hastened forward, but by the time she reached the foot of the ladder he was at the top. She called to him loudly enough to be heard above the roar of the weir; he looked down and said, 'What d'ye want here?'

'To speak to you a minute.'

The candle-light, such as it was, fell upon her imploring, pale, up-turned face, and Davies (as the hangman was called) backed down the ladder. 'I was just going to bed,' he said; ' "Early to bed and early to rise," but I don't mind stopping a minute for such a one as you. Come into the house.' He reopened the door, and preceded her to the room within.

The implements of his daily work, which was that of a jobbing gardener, stood in a corner, and seeing probably that she looked rural, he said, 'If you want me to undertake country work I can't come, for I never leave Casterbridge for gentle nor simple – not I. My real calling is officer of justice,' he added formally.

'Yes, yes! That's it. Tomorrow!'

'Ah! I thought so. Well, what's the matter about that? 'Tis no use to come here about the knot – folks do come continually, but I tell 'em one knot is as merciful as another if ye keep it under the ear. Is the unfortunate man a relation; or, I should say, perhaps' (looking at her dress) 'a person who's been in your employ?'

'No. What time is the execution?'

'The same as usual – twelve o'clock, or as soon after as the London mail-coach gets in. We always wait for that, in case of a reprieve.'

'O – a reprieve – I hope not!' she said involuntarily.

'Well – hee, hee! – as a matter of business, so do I! But still if ever a young fellow deserved to be let off, this one does; only just turned eighteen, and only present by chance when the rick was fired. Howsomever, there's not much risk of it, as they are obliged to make an example of him, there having been so much destruction of property that way lately.'

'I mean,' she explained, 'that I want to touch him for a charm, a cure of an affliction, by the advice of a man who has proved the virtue of the remedy.'

'O yes, miss! Now I understand. I've had such people come in past years. But it didn't strike me that you looked of a sort to require blood-turning. What's the complaint? The wrong kind for this, I'll be bound.'

'My arm.' She reluctantly showed the withered skin.

'Ah! – 'tis all a-scram!' said the hangman, examining it.

'Yes,' said she.

'Well,' he continued, with interest, 'that *is* the class o' subject, I'm bound to admit! I like the look of the wownd; it is truly as suitable for the cure as any I ever saw. 'Twas a knowing-man that sent 'ee, whoever he was.'

'You can contrive for me all that's necessary?' she said breathlessly.

'You should really have gone to the governor of the jail, and your doctor with 'ee, and given your name and address – that's how it used to be done, if I recollect. Still, perhaps, I can manage it for a trifling fee.'

'O, thank you! I would rather do it this way, as I should like it kept private.'

'Lover not to know, eh?'

'No – husband.'

'Aha! Very well. I'll get 'ee a touch of the corpse.'

'Where is it now?' she said, shuddering.

'It? – *he*, you mean; he's living yet. Just inside that little small winder up there in the glum.' He signified the jail on the cliff above.

She thought of her husband and her friends. 'Yes, of course,' she said; 'and how am I to proceed?'

He took her to the door. 'Now, do you be waiting at the little wicket in the wall, that you'll find up there in the lane, not later than one o'clock. I will open it from the inside, as I shan't come home to dinner till he's cut down. Good-night. Be punctual; and if you don't want anybody to know 'ee, wear a veil. Ah – once I had such a daughter as you!'

She went away, and climbed the path above, to assure herself that she would be able to find the wicket next day. Its outline was soon visible to her – a narrow opening in the outer wall of the prison precincts. The steep was so great that, having reached the wicket, she stopped a moment to breathe; and, looking back upon the water-side cot, saw the hangman again ascending his outdoor staircase. He entered the loft or chamber to which it led, and in a few minutes extinguished his light.

The town clock struck ten, and she returned to the White Hart as she had come.

IX. *A Rencounter*

It was one o'clock on Saturday. Gertrude Lodge, having been admitted to the jail as above described, was sitting in a waiting-room within the second gate, which stood under a classic archway of ashlar, then comparatively modern, and bearing the inscription, 'COVNTY JAIL: 1793'. This had been the façade she saw from the heath the day before. Near at hand was a passage to the roof on which the gallows stood.

The town was thronged, and the market suspended; but Gertrude had seen scarcely a soul. Having kept her room till the hour of the appointment, she had proceeded to the spot by a way which avoided the open space below the cliff where the spectators had gathered; but she could, even now, hear the multitudinous babble of their voices, out of which rose at intervals the hoarse croak of a single voice uttering the words, 'Last dying speech and confession!' There had been no reprieve, and the execution was over; but the crowd still waited to see the body taken down.

Soon the persistent woman heard a trampling overhead, then a hand beckoned to her, and, following directions, she went out and crossed the inner paved court beyond the gatehouse, her knees trembling so that she could scarcely walk. One of her arms was out of its sleeve, and only covered by her shawl.

On the spot at which she had now arrived were two trestles, and before she could think of their purpose she heard heavy feet descending stairs somewhere at her back. Turn her head she would not, or could not, and, rigid in this position, she was conscious of a rough coffin passing her shoulder, borne by four men. It was open, and in it lay the body of a young man, wearing the smockfrock of a rustic, and fustian breeches. The corpse had been thrown into the coffin so hastily that the skirt of the smockfrock was hanging over. The burden was temporarily deposited on the trestles.

By this time the young woman's state was such that a grey mist seemed to float before her eyes, on account of which, and the veil she wore, she could scarcely discern anything: it was as though she had nearly died, but was held up by a sort of galvanism.

'Now!' said a voice close at hand, and she was just conscious that the word had been addressed to her.

By a last strenuous effort she advanced, at the same time hearing persons approaching behind her. She bared her poor curst arm; and Davies, uncovering the face of the corpse, took Gertrude's hand, and held it so that her arm lay across the dead man's neck, upon a line the colour of an unripe blackberry, which surrounded it.

Gertrude shrieked: 'the turn o' the blood,' predicted by the conjuror, had taken place. But at that moment a second shriek rent the air of the enclosure: it was not Gertrude's, and its effect upon her was to make her start round.

Immediately behind her stood Rhoda Brook, her face drawn, and her eyes red with weeping. Behind Rhoda stood Gertrude's own husband; his countenance lined, his eyes dim, but without a tear.

'D—n you! what are you doing here?' he said hoarsely.

'Hussy – to come between us and our child now!' cried Rhoda. 'This is the meaning of what Satan showed me in the vision! You are like her at last!' And clutching the bare arm of the younger woman, she pulled her unresistingly back against the wall. Immediately Brook had loosened her hold the fragile young Gertrude slid down against the feet of her husband. When he lifted her up she was unconscious.

The mere sight of the twain had been enough to suggest to her that the dead young man was Rhoda's son. At that time the relatives of an executed convict had the privilege of claiming the body for burial, if they chose to do so; and it was for this purpose that Lodge was awaiting the inquest with Rhoda. He had been summoned by her as soon as the young man was taken in the crime, and at different times since; and he had attended in court during the trial. This was the 'holiday' he had been indulging in of late. The two wretched parents had wished to avoid exposure; and hence had come themselves for the body, a waggon and sheet for its conveyance and covering being in waiting outside.

Gertrude's case was so serious that it was deemed advisable to call to her the surgeon who was at hand. She was taken out of the jail into the town; but she never reached home alive. Her delicate vitality, sapped perhaps by the paralyzed arm, collapsed under the double shock that followed the severe strain, physical and mental, to which she had subjected herself during the previous twenty-four hours. Her blood had been 'turned' indeed – too far. Her death took place in the town three days after.

Her husband was never seen in Casterbridge again; once only in the old market-place at Anglebury, which he had so much frequented, and very seldom in public anywhere. Burdened at first with moodiness and remorse, he eventually changed for the better, and appeared as a chastened and thoughtful man. Soon after attending the funeral of his poor young wife he took steps towards giving up the farms in Holmstoke and the adjoining parish, and, having sold every head of his stock, he went away to Port-Bredy, at the other end of the county, living there in solitary lodgings till his death two years later of a painless decline. It was then found that he had bequeathed the whole of his not inconsiderable property to a reformatory for boys, subject to the payment of a small annuity to Rhoda Brook, if she could be found to claim it.

For some time she could not be found; but eventually she reappeared in her old parish – absolutely refusing, however, to have anything to do with the provision made for her. Her monotonous milking at the dairy was resumed, and followed for many long years, till her form became bent, and her once abundant dark hair white and worn away at the forehead – perhaps by long pressure against the cows. Here, sometimes, those who knew her experiences would stand and observe her, and wonder what sombre thoughts were beating inside that impassive, wrinkled brow, to the rhythm of the alternating milk-streams.

'Blackwood's Magazine,'
  January 1888.

Joseph Conrad

The Idiots

We were driving along the road from Treguier to Kervanda. We passed at a smart trot between the hedges topping an earth wall on each side of the road; then at the foot of the steep ascent before Ploumar the horse dropped into a walk, and the driver jumped down heavily from the box. He flicked his whip and climbed the incline, stepping clumsily uphill by the side of the carriage, one hand on the footboard, his eyes on the ground. After a while he lifted his head, pointed up the road with the end of the whip, and said—

'The idiot!'

The sun was shining violently upon the undulating surface of the land. The rises were topped by clumps of meagre trees, with their branches showing high on the sky as if they had been perched upon stilts. The small fields, cut up by hedges and stone walls that zigzagged over the slopes, lay in rectangular patches of vivid greens and yellows, resembling the unskilful daubs of a naive picture. And the landscape was divided in two by the white streak of a road stretching in long loops far away, like a river of dust crawling out of the hills on its way to the sea.

'Here he is,' said the driver, again.

In the long grass bordering the road a face glided past the carriage at the level of the wheels as we drove slowly by. The imbecile face was red, and the bullet head with close-cropped hair seemed to lie alone, its chin in the dust. The body was lost in the bushes growing thick along the bottom of the deep ditch.

It was a boy's face. He might have been sixteen, judging from the size – perhaps less, perhaps more. Such creatures are forgotten by time, and live untouched by years till death gathers them up into its compassionate bosom; the faithful death that never forgets in the press of work

86

the most insignificant of its children.

'Ah! there's another,' said the man; with a certain satisfaction in his tone, as if he had caught sight of something expected.

There was another. That one stood nearly in the middle of the road in the blaze of sunshine at the end of his own short shadow. And he stood with his hands pushed into the opposite sleeves of his long coat, his head sunk between the shoulders, all hunched up in the flood of heat. From a distance he had the aspect of one suffering from intense cold.

'Those are twins,' explained the driver.

The idiot shuffled two paces out of the way and looked at us over his shoulder when we brushed past him. The glance was unseeing and staring, a fascinated glance; but he did not turn to look after us. Probably the image passed before the eyes without leaving any trace on the misshapen brain of the creature. When we had topped the ascent I looked over the hood. He stood in the road just where we had left him.

The driver clambered into his seat, clicked his tongue, and we went down hill. The brake squeaked horribly from time to time. At the foot he eased off the noisy mechanism and said, turning half round on his box—

'We shall see some more of them by-and-by.'

'More idiots? How many of them are there, then?' I asked.

'There's four of them – children of a farmer near Ploumar here ... The parents are dead now,' he added, after a while. 'The grandmother lives on the farm. In the daytime they knock about on this road, and they come home at dusk along with the cattle ... It's a good farm.'

We saw the other two: a boy and a girl, as the driver said. They were dressed exactly alike, in shapeless garments with petticoat-like skirts. The imperfect thing that lived within them moved those beings to howl at us from the top of the bank, where they sprawled amongst the tough stalks of furze. Their cropped black heads stuck out from the bright yellow wall of countless small blossoms. The faces were purple with the strain of yelling; the voices sounded blank and cracked like a mechanical imitation of old people's voices; and suddenly ceased when we turned into a lane.

I saw them many times in my wandering about the country. They lived on that road, drifting along its length here and there, according to the inexplicable impulses of their monstrous darkness. They were an offence to the sunshine, a reproach to empty heaven, a blight on the concentrated and purposeful vigour of the wild landscape. In time the story of their parents shaped itself before me out of the listless answers to my questions, out of the indifferent words heard in wayside inns or on the very road those idiots haunted. Some of it was told by an emaciated and sceptical old fellow with a tremendous whip, while we trudged together over the sands by the side of a two-wheeled cart loaded with dripping seaweed. Then at other times other people confirmed and completed the story: till it stood at last before me, a tale formidable and simple, as they always are, those disclosures of obscure trials endured by ignorant hearts.

When he returned from his military service Jean-Pierre Bacadou found the old people very much aged. He remarked with pain that the work of the farm was not satisfactorily done. The father had not the energy of old days. The hands did not feel over them the eye of the master. Jean-Pierre noted with sorrow that the heap of manure in the courtyard before the only entrance to the house was not so large as it should have been. The fences were out of repair, and the cattle suffered from neglect. At home the mother was practically bedridden, and the girls chattered loudly in the big kitchen, unrebuked, from morning to night. He said to himself: 'We must change all this.' He talked the matter over with his father one evening when the rays of the setting sun entering the yard between the outhouses ruled the heavy shadows with luminous streaks. Over the manure heap floated a mist, opal-tinted and odorous, and the marauding hens would stop in their scratching to examine with a sudden glance of their round eye the two men, both lean and tall, talking in hoarse tones. The old man, all twisted with rheumatism and bowed with years of work, the younger bony and straight, spoke without gestures in the indifferent manner of peasants, grave and slow. But before the sun had set the father had submitted to the sensible arguments of the son. 'It is not for me that I am speaking,' insisted Jean-Pierre. 'It is for the land. It's a pity to see it badly used. I am not impatient for myself.' The old fellow nodded over his stick. 'I dare say; I dare say,' he muttered. 'You may be right. Do what you like. It's the mother that will be pleased.'

The mother was pleased with her daughter-in-law. Jean-Pierre brought the two-wheeled spring-cart with a rush into the yard. The grey horse galloped clumsily, and the bride and bridegroom, sitting side by side, were jerked backwards and forwards by the up and down motion of the shafts, in a manner regular and brusque. On the road the distanced wedding guests straggled in pairs and groups. The men advanced with heavy steps, swinging their idle arms. They were clad in town clothes: jackets cut with clumsy smartness, hard black hats, immense boots polished highly. Their women all in simple black, with white caps and shawls of faded tints folded triangularly on the back, strolled lightly by their side. In front the violin sang a strident tune, and the biniou snored and hummed, while the player capered solemnly, lifting high his heavy clogs. The sombre procession drifted in and out of the narrow lanes, through sunshine and through shade, between fields and hedgerows, scaring the little birds that darted away in troops right and left. In the yard of Bacadou's farm the dark ribbon wound itself up into a mass of men and women pushing at the door with cries and greetings. The wedding dinner was remembered for months. It was a splendid feast in the orchard. Farmers of considerable means and excellent repute were to be found sleeping in ditches, all along the road to Treguier, even as late as the afternoon of the next day. All the countryside participated in the happiness of Jean-Pierre. He remained sober, and, together with his quiet wife, kept out of the way, letting father and mother reap their due of honour and thanks. But the next day he took hold strongly, and the old folks felt a shadow – precursor of the grave – fall upon them finally. The world is to the young.

When the twins were born there was plenty of room in the house, for the mother of Jean-Pierre had gone away to dwell under a heavy stone in the cemetery of Ploumar. On that day, for the first time since his son's marriage, the elder Bacadou, neglected by the cackling lot of strange women who thronged the kitchen, left in the morning his seat under the mantel of the fireplace, and went into the empty cow-house, shaking his white locks dismally. Grandsons were all very well, but he wanted his soup at midday. When shown the babies, he stared at them with a fixed gaze, and muttered something like: 'It's too much.' Whether he meant too much happiness, or simply commented upon the number of his descendants, it is impossible to say. He looked offended – as far as his old wooden face could express anything; and for days afterwards could be seen, almost any time of the day, sitting at the gate, with his nose over his knees, a pipe between his gums, and gathered up into a kind of raging concentrated sulkiness. Once he spoke to his son, alluding to the newcomers with a groan: 'They will quarrel over the land.' 'Don't bother about that, father,' answered Jean-Pierre, stolidly, and passed, bent double, towing a recalcitrant cow over his shoulder.

He was happy, and so was Susan, his wife. It was not an ethereal joy welcoming new souls to struggle, perchance to victory. In fourteen years both boys would be a help; and, later on, Jean-Pierre pictured two big sons striding over the land from patch to patch, wringing tribute from the earth beloved and fruitful. Susan was happy too, for she did not want to be spoken of as the unfortunate woman, and now she had children no one could call her that. Both herself and her husband had seen something of the larger world – he during the time of his service; while she had spent a year or so in Paris with a Breton family; but had been too home-sick to remain longer away from the hilly and green country, set in a barren circle of rocks and sands, where she had been born. She thought that one of the boys ought perhaps to be a priest, but said nothing to her husband, who was a republican, and hated the 'crows,' as he called the ministers of religion. The christening was a splendid affair. All the commune came to it, for the Bacadous were rich and influential, and, now and then, did not mind the expense. The grandfather had a new coat.

Some months afterwards, one evening when the kitchen had been swept, and the door locked, Jean-Pierre, looking at the cot, asked his wife: 'What's the matter with those children?' And, as if these words, spoken calmly, had been the portent of misfortune, she answered with a loud wail that must have been heard across the yard in the pig-sty; for the pigs (the Bacadous had the finest pigs in the country) stirred and grunted complainingly in the night. The husband went on grinding his bread and butter slowly, gazing at the wall, the soup-plate smoking under his chin. He had returned late from the market, where he had overheard (not for the first time) whispers behind his back. He revolved the words in his mind as he drove back. 'Simple! Both of them . . . Never any use! . . . Well! May be, may be. One must see. Would ask his wife.' This was her answer. He felt like a blow on his chest, but said only: 'Go, draw me some cider. I am thirsty!'

She went out moaning, an empty jug in her hand. Then he arose, took up the light, and moved slowly towards the cradle. They slept. He looked at them sideways, finished his mouthful there, went back, heavily, and sat down before his plate. When his wife returned he never looked up, but swallowed a couple of spoonfuls noisily, and remarked, in a dull manner—

'When they sleep they are like other people's children.'

She sat down suddenly on a stool near by, and shook with a silent tempest of sobs, unable to speak. He finished his meal, and remained idly thrown back in his chair, his eyes lost amongst the black rafters of the ceiling. Before him the tallow candle flared red and straight, sending up a slender thread of smoke. The light lay on the rough, sunburnt skin of his throat; the sunk cheeks were like patches of darkness, and his aspect was mournfully stolid, as if he had ruminated with difficulty endless ideas. Then he said, deliberately—

'We must see . . . consult people. Don't cry . . . They won't be all like that . . . surely! We must sleep now.'

After the third child, also a boy, was born, Jean-Pierre went about his work with tense hopefulness. His lips seemed more narrow, more tightly compressed than before; as if for fear of letting the earth he tilled hear the voice of hope that murmured within his breast. He watched the child, stepping up to the cot with a heavy clang of sabots on the stone floor, and glanced in, along his shoulder, with that indifference which is like a deformity of peasant humanity. Like the earth they master and serve, those men, slow of eye and speech, do not show the inner fire;

so that, at last, it becomes a question with them as with the earth, what there is in the core: heat, violence, a force mysterious and terrible – or nothing but a clod, a mass fertile and inert, cold and unfeeling, ready to bear a crop of plants that sustain life or give death.

The mother watched with other eyes; listened with otherwise expectant ears. Under the high hanging shelves supporting great sides of bacon overhead, her body was busy by the great fireplace, attentive to the pot swinging on iron gallows, scrubbing the long table where the field hands would sit down directly to their evening meal. Her mind remained by the cradle, night and day on the watch, to hope and suffer. That child, like the other two, never smiled, never stretched its hands to her, never spoke; never had a glance of recognition for her in its big black eyes, which could only stare fixedly at any glitter, but failed hopelessly to follow the brilliance of a sun-ray slipping slowly along the floor. When the men were at work she spent long days between her three idiot children and the childish grandfather, who sat grim, angular, and immovable, with his feet near the warm ashes of the fire. The feeble old fellow seemed to suspect that there was something wrong with his grandsons. Only once, moved either by affection or by the sense of proprieties, he attempted to nurse the youngest. He took the boy up from the floor, clicked his tongue at him, and essayed a shaky gallop of his bony knees. Then he looked closely with his misty eyes at the child's face and deposited him down gently on the floor again. And he sat, his lean shanks crossed, nodding at the steam escaping from the cooking-pot with a gaze senile and worried.

Then mute affliction dwelt in Bacadou's farmhouse, sharing the breath and the bread of its inhabitants; and the priest of the Ploumar parish had great cause for congratulation. He called upon the rich landowner, the Marquis de Chavanes, on purpose to deliver himself with joyful unction of solemn platitudes about the inscrutable ways of Providence. In the vast dimness of the curtained drawing-room, the little man, resembling a black bolster, leaned towards a couch, his hat on his knees, and gesticulated with a fat hand at the elongated, gracefully-flowing lines of the clear Parisian toilette from within which the half-amused, half-bored marquise listened with gracious languor. He was exulting and humble, proud and awed. The impossible had come to pass. Jean-Pierre Bacadou, the enraged republican farmer, had been to mass last Sunday – had proposed to entertain the visiting priests at the next festival of Ploumar! It was a triumph for the Church and for the good cause. 'I thought I would come at once to tell Monsieur le Marquis. I know how anxious he is for the welfare of our country,' declared the priest, wiping his face. He was asked to stay to dinner.

The Chavanes returning that evening, after seeing their guest to the main gate of the park, discussed the matter while they strolled in the moonlight, trailing their long shadows up the straight avenue of chestnuts. The marquis, a royalist of course, had been mayor of the commune which includes Ploumar, the scattered hamlets of the coast, and the stony islands that fringe the yellow flatness of the sands. He had felt his position insecure, for there was a strong republican element in that part of the country; but now the conversion of Jean-Pierre made him safe. He was very pleased 'You have no idea how influential those people are,' he explained to his wife. 'Now, I am sure, the next communal election will go all right. I shall be re-elected,' 'Your ambition is perfectly insatiable, Charles,' exclaimed the marquise, gaily. 'But, ma chère amie,' argued the husband, seriously, 'it's most important that the right man should be mayor this year, because of the elections to the Chamber. If you think it amuses me . . .'

Jean-Pierre had surrendered to his wife's mother. Madame Levaille was a woman of business, known and respected within a radius of at least fifteen miles. Thick-set and stout, she was seen about the country, on foot or in an acquaintance's cart, perpetually moving, in spite of her fifty-eight years, in steady pursuit of business. She had houses in all the hamlets, she worked quarries of granite, she freighted coasters with stone – even traded with the Channel Islands. She was broad-cheeked, wide-eyed, persuasive in speech: carrying her point with the placid and invincible obstinacy of an old woman who knows her own mind. She very seldom slept for two nights together in the same house; and the wayside inns were the best places to inquire in as to her whereabouts. She had either passed, or was expected to pass there at six; or somebody, coming in, had seen her in the morning, or expected to meet her that evening. After the inns that command the roads, the churches were the buildings she frequented most. Men of liberal opinions would induce small children to run into sacred edifices to see whether Madame Levaille was there, and to tell her that so-and-so was in the road waiting to speak to her – about potatoes, or flour, or stones, or houses; and she would curtail her devotions, come out blinking and crossing herself into the sunshine; ready to discuss business matters in a calm, sensible way across the table in the kitchen of the inn opposite. Latterly she had stayed for a few days several times with her son-in-law, arguing against sorrow and misfortune with composed face and gentle tones. Jean-Pierre felt the convictions imbibed in the regiment torn out of his breast – not by arguments, but by facts. Striding over his fields he thought it over. There were three of them. Three! All alike! Why? Such things did not happen to everybody – to nobody he ever heard of. One yet – it might pass. But three! All three. For ever useless, to be fed while he lived and . . . What would become of the land when he died? This must be

seen to. He would sacrifice his convictions. One day he told his wife—
'See what your God will do for us. Pay for some masses.'

Susan embraced her man. He stood unbending, then turned on his
heels and went out. But afterwards, when a black *soutane* darkened his
doorway, he did not object; even offered some cider himself to the priest.
He listened to the talk meekly; went to mass between the two women;
accomplished what the priest called 'his religious duties' at Easter. That
morning he felt like a man who had sold his soul. In the afternoon he
fought ferociously with an old friend and neighbour who had remarked
that the priests had the best of it and were now going to eat the priest-
eater. He came home dishevelled and bleeding, and happening to catch
sight of his children (they were kept generally out of the way), cursed
and swore incoherently, banging the table. Susan wept. Madame
Levaille sat serenely unmoved. She assured her daughter that 'It will
pass'; and taking up her thick umbrella, departed in haste to see after a
schooner she was going to load with granite from her quarry.

A year or so afterwards the girl was born. A girl. Jean-Pierre heard
of it in the fields, and was so upset by the news that he sat down on the
boundary wall and remained there till the evening, instead of going home
as he was urged to do. A girl! He felt half cheated. However, when he
got home he was partly reconciled to his fate. One could marry her to
a good fellow – not to a good for nothing, but to a fellow with some understanding and a good pair of arms. Besides, the next may be a boy, he
thought. Of course they would be all right. His new credulity knew of
no doubt. The ill luck was broken. He spoke cheerily to his wife. She
was also hopeful. Three priests came to that christening, and Madame
Levaille was godmother. The child turned out an idiot too.

Then on market days Jean-Pierre was seen bargaining bitterly, quarrel-
some and greedy; then getting drunk with taciturn earnestness; then
driving home in the dusk at a rate fit for a wedding, but with a face
gloomy enough for a funeral. Sometimes he would insist for his wife to
come with him; and they would drive in the early morning, shaking
side by side on the narrow seat above the helpless pig, that, with tied
legs, grunted a melancholy sigh at every rut. The morning drives were
silent; but in the evening, coming home, Jean-Pierre, tipsy, was viciously
muttering, and growled at the confounded woman who could not rear
children that were like anybody else's. Susan, holding on against the
erratic swayings of the cart, pretended not to hear. Once, as they were
driving through Ploumar, some obscure and drunken impulse caused
him to pull up sharply opposite the church. The moon swam amongst
light white clouds. The tombstones gleamed pale under the fretted
shadows of the trees in the churchyard. Even the village dogs slept.
Only the nightingales, awake, spun out the thrill of their song above the

silence of graves. Jean-Pierre said thickly to his wife—

'What do you think is there?'

He pointed his whip at the tower – in which the big dial of the clock appeared high in the moonlight like a pallid face without eyes – and getting out carefully, fell down at once by the wheel. He picked himself up and climbed one by one the few steps to the iron gate of the church-yard. He put his face to the bars and called out indistinctly—

'Hey there! Come out!'

'Jean! Return! Return!' entreated his wife in low tones.

He took no notice, and seemed to wait there. The song of nightingales beat on all sides against the high walls of the church, and flowed back between stone crosses and flat grey slabs, engraved with words of hope and sorrow.

'Hey! Come out!' shouted Jean-Pierre loudly.

The nightingales ceased to sing.

'Nobody?' went on Jean-Pierre. 'Nobody there. A swindle of the crows. That's what this is. Nobody anywhere. I despise it. Allez! Houp!'

He shook the gate with all his strength, and the iron bars rattled with a frightful clanging, like a chain dragged over stone steps. A dog near-by barked hurriedly. Jean-Pierre staggered back, and after three successive dashes got into his cart. Susan sat very quiet and still. He said to her with drunken severity—

'See? Nobody. I've been made a fool! Malheur! Somebody will pay for it. The next one I see near the house I will lay my whip on ... on the black spine ... I will. I don't want him in there ... he only helps the carrion crows to rob poor folk. I am a man ... We will see if I can't have children like anybody else ... now you mind ... They won't be all ... all ... we see ...'

She burst out through the fingers that hid her face—

'Don't say that, Jean; don't say that, my man!'

He struck her a swinging blow on the head with the back of his hand and knocked her into the bottom of the cart, where she crouched, thrown about lamentably by every jolt. He drove furiously, standing up, brandishing his whip, shaking the reins over the grey horse that galloped ponderously, making the heavy harness leap upon his broad quarters. The country rang clamorous in the night with the irritated barking of farm dogs, that followed the rattle of wheels all along the road. A couple of belated wayfarers had only just time to step into the ditch. At his own gate he caught the post and was shot out of the cart head first. The horse went on slowly to the door. At Susan's piercing cries the farm hands rushed out. She thought him dead, but he was only sleeping where he fell, and cursed his men, who hastened to him, for disturbing his slumbers.

Autumn came. The clouded sky descended low upon the black contours of the hills; and the dead leaves danced in spiral whirls under naked trees, till the wind, sighing profoundly, laid them to rest in the hollows of bare valleys. And from morning till night one could see all over the land black denuded boughs, the boughs gnarled and twisted, as if contorted with pain, swaying sadly between the wet clouds and the soaked earth. The clear and gentle streams of summer days rushed discoloured and raging at the stones that barred the way to the sea, with the fury of madness bent upon suicide. From horizon to horizon the great road to the sands lay between the hills in a dull glitter of empty curves, resembling an unnavigable river of mud.

Jean-Pierre went from field to field, moving blurred and tall in the drizzle, or striding on the crests of rises, lonely and high upon the grey curtain of drifting clouds, as if he had been pacing along the very edge of the universe. He looked at the black earth, at the earth mute and promising, at the mysterious earth doing its work of life in death-like stillness under the veiled sorrow of the sky. And it seemed to him that to a man worse than childless there was no promise in the fertility of fields, that from him the earth escaped, defied him, frowned at him like the clouds, sombre and hurried above his head. Having to face alone his own fields, he felt the inferiority of man who passes away before the clod that remains. Must he give up the hope of having by his side a son who would look at the turned-up sods with a master's eye? A man that would think as he thought, that would feel as he felt; a man who would be part of himself, and yet remain to trample masterfully on that earth when he was gone! He thought of some distant relations, and felt savage enough to curse them aloud. They! Never! He turned homewards, going straight at the roof of his dwelling visible between the enlaced skeletons of trees. As he swung his legs over the stile a cawing flock of birds settled slowly on the field; dropped down behind his back, noiseless and fluttering, like flakes of soot.

That day Madame Levaille had gone early in the afternoon to the house she had near Kervanion. She had to pay some of the men who worked in her granite quarry there, and she went in good time because her little house contained a shop where the workmen could spend their wages without the trouble of going to town. The house stood alone amongst rocks. A lane of mud and stones ended at the door. The sea-winds coming ashore on Stonecutter's point, fresh from the fierce turmoil of the waves, howled violently at the unmoved heaps of black boulders holding up steadily short-armed, high crosses against the tremendous rush of the invisible. In the sweep of gales the sheltered dwelling stood in a calm resonant and disquieting, like the calm in the centre of a hurricane. On stormy nights, when the tide was out, the bay of Fougère, fifty feet below the house, resembled an immense black pit, from which ascended mutterings and sighs as if the sands down there had been alive and complaining. At high tide the returning water assaulted the ledges of rock in short rushes, ending in bursts of livid light and columns of spray, that flew inland, stinging to death the grass of pastures.

The darkness came from the hills, flowed over the coast, put out the red fires of sunset, and went on to seaward pursuing the retiring tide. The wind dropped with the sun, leaving a maddened sea and a devastated sky. The heavens above the house seemed to be draped in black rags, held up here and there by pins of fire. Madame Levaille, for this evening the servant of her own workmen, tried to induce them to depart. 'An old woman like me ought to be in bed at this late hour,' she good-humouredly repeated. The quarrymen drank, asked for more. They shouted over the table as if they had been talking across a field. At one end four of them played cards, banging the wood with their hard knuckles, and swearing at every lead. One sat with a lost gaze, humming a bar of some song, which he repeated endlessly. Two others, in a corner, were quarrelling confidentially and fiercely over some woman, looking close into one another's eyes as if they had wanted to tear them out, but speaking in whispers that promised violence and murder discreetly, in a venomous sibillation of subdued words. The atmosphere in there was thick enough to slice with a knife. Three candles burning about the long room glowed red and dull like sparks expiring in ashes.

The slight click of the iron latch was at that late hour as unexpected and startling as a thunder-clap. Madame Levaille put down a bottle she held above a liqueur glass; the players turned their heads; the whispered quarrel ceased; only the singer, after darting a glance at the door, went on humming with a stolid face. Susan appeared in the doorway, stepped in, flung the door to, and put her back against it, saying, half aloud—

'Mother!'

Madame Levaille, taking up the bottle again, said calmly: 'Here you are, my girl. What a state you are in!' The neck of the bottle rang on the rim of the glass, for the old woman was startled, and the idea that the farm had caught fire had entered her head. She could think of no other cause for her daughter's appearance.

Susan, soaked and muddy, stared the whole length of the room towards the men at the far end. Her mother asked—

'What has happened? God guard us from misfortune!'

Susan moved her lips. No sound came. Madame Levaille stepped up to her daughter, took her by the arm, looked into her face.

'In God's name,' she said shakily, 'what's the matter? You have been rolling in mud . . . Why did you come? . . . Where's Jean?'

The men had all got up and approached slowly, staring with dull surprise. Madame Levaille jerked her daughter away from the door, swung her round upon a seat close to the wall. Then she turned fiercely to the men—

'Enough of this! Out you go – you others! I close.'

One of them observed, looking down at Susan collapsed on the seat: 'She is – one may say – half dead.'

Madame Levaille flung the door open.

'Get out! March!' she cried, shaking nervously.

They dropped out into the night, laughing stupidly. Outside, the two Lotharios broke out into loud shouts. The others tried to soothe them, all talking at once. The noise went away up the lane with the men, who staggered together in a tight knot, remonstrating with one another foolishly.

'Speak, Susan. What is it? Speak!' entreated Madame Levaille, as soon as the door was shut.

Susan pronounced some incomprehensible words, glaring at the table. The old woman clapped her hands above her head, let them drop, and stood looking at her daughter with disconsolate eyes. Her husband had been 'deranged in his head' for a few years before he died, and now she began to suspect her daughter was going mad. She asked, pressingly—

'Does Jean know where you are? Where is Jean?'

Susan pronounced with difficulty—

'He knows . . . he is dead.'

'What!' cried the old woman. She came up near, and peering at her daughter, repeated three times: 'What do you say? What do you say? What do you say?'

Susan sat dry-eyed and stony before Madame Levaille, who contemplated her, feeling a strange sense of inexplicable horror creep into the silence of the house. She had hardly realised the news, further than to understand that she had been brought in one short moment face to face with something unexpected and final. It did not even occur to her to ask for any explanation. She thought: accident – terrible accident – blood to the head – fell down a trap door in the loft . . . She remained there, distracted and mute, blinking her old eyes.

Suddenly, Susan said—

'I have killed him.'

For a moment the mother stood still, almost unbreathing, but with composed face. The next second she burst out into a shout—

'You miserable madwoman . . . they will cut your neck . . .'

She fancied the gendarmes entering the house, saying to her: 'We want your daughter; give her up:' the gendarmes with the severe, hard faces of men on duty. She knew the brigadier well – an old friend, familiar and respectful, saying heartily, 'To your good health, madame!'

before lifting to his lips the small glass of cognac – out of the special bottle she kept for friends. And now! ... She was losing her head. She rushed here and there, as if looking for something urgently needed – gave that up, stood stock still in the middle of the room, and screamed at her daughter—

'Why? Say! Say! Why?'

The other seemed to leap out of her strange apathy.

'Do you think I am made of stone?' she shouted back, striding towards her mother.

'No! It's impossible ...' said Madame Levaille, in a convinced tone.

'You go and see, mother,' retorted Susan, looking at her with blazing eyes. 'There's no mercy in heaven – no justice. No! ... I did not know ... Do you think I have no heart? Do you think I have never heard people jeering at me, pitying me, wondering at me? Do you know how some of them were calling me? The mother of idiots – that was my nickname! And my children never would know me, never speak to me. They would know nothing; neither men – nor God. Haven't I prayed! But the Mother of God herself would not hear me. A mother! ... Who is accursed – I, or the man who is dead? Eh? Tell me. I took care of myself. Do you think I would defy the anger of God and have my house full of those things – that are worse than animals who know the hand that feeds them? Who blasphemed in the night at the very church door? Was it I? ... I only wept and prayed for mercy ... and I feel the curse at every moment of the day – I see it round me from morning to night ... I've got to keep them alive – to take care of my misfortune and shame. And he would come. I begged him and Heaven for mercy ... No! ... Then we shall see ... He came this evening. I thought to myself: 'Ah! again!' ... I had my long scissors. I heard him shouting ... I saw him near ... I must – must I? ... Then take! ... And I struck him in the throat above the breastbone. ... I never heard him even sigh. ... I left him standing. ... It was a minute ago. How did I come here?'

Madame Levaille shivered. A wave of cold ran down her back, down her fat arms under her tight sleeves, made her stamp gently where she stood. Quivers ran over the broad cheeks, across the thin lips, ran amongst the wrinkles at the corners of her steady old eyes. She stammered—

'You wicked woman – you disgrace me. But there! You always resembled your father. What do you think will become of you ... in the other world? In this ... Oh misery!'

She was very hot now. She felt burning inside. She wrung her perspiring hands – and suddenly, starting in great haste, began to look for her big shawl and umbrella, feverishly, never once glancing at her daughter, who stood in the middle of the room following her with a gaze distracted and cold.

'Nothing worse than in this,' said Susan.

Her mother, umbrella in hand and trailing the shawl over the floor, groaned profoundly.

'I must go to the priest,' she burst out passionately. 'I do not know whether you even speak the truth! You are a horrible woman. They will find you anywhere. You may stay here – or go. There is no room for you in this world.'

Ready now to depart, she yet wandered aimlessly about the room, putting the bottles on the shelf, trying to fit with trembling hands the covers on cardboard boxes. Whenever the real sense of what she had heard emerged for a second from the haze of her thoughts she would fancy that something had exploded in her brain without, unfortunately, bursting her head to pieces – which would have been a relief. She blew the candles out one by one without knowing it, and was horribly startled by the darkness. She fell on a bench and began to whimper. After a while she ceased, and sat listening to the breathing of her daughter, whom she could hardly see, still and upright, giving no other sign of life. She was becoming old rapidly at last, during those minutes. She spoke in tones unsteady, cut about by the rattle of teeth, like one shaken by a deadly cold fit of ague.

'I wish you had died little. I will never dare to show my old head in the sunshine again. There are worse misfortunes than idiot children. I wish you had been born to me simple – like your own . . .'

She saw the figure of her daughter pass before the faint and livid clearness of a window. Then it appeared in the doorway for a second, and the door swung to with a clang. Madame Levaille, as if awakened by the noise from a long nightmare, rushed out.

'Susan!' she shouted from the doorstep.

She heard a stone roll a long time down the declivity of the rocky beach above the sands. She stepped forward cautiously, one hand on the wall of the house, and peered down into the smooth darkness of the empty bay. Once again she cried—

'Susan! You will kill yourself there.'

The stone had taken its last leap in the dark, and she heard nothing now. A sudden thought seemed to strangle her, and she called no more. She turned her back upon the black silence of the pit and went up the lane towards Ploumar, stumbling along with sombre determination, as if she had started on a desperate journey that would last, perhaps, to the end of her life. A sullen and periodic clamour of waves rolling over reefs followed her far inland between the high hedges sheltering the gloomy solitude of the fields.

Susan had run out, swerving sharp to the left at the door, and on the edge of the slope crouched down behind a boulder. A dislodged stone went on downwards, rattling as it leaped. When Madame Levaille called out, Susan could have, by stretching her hand, touched her mother's skirt, had she had the courage to move a limb. She saw the old woman go away, and she remained still, closing her eyes and pressing her side to the hard and rugged surface of the rock. After a while a familiar face with fixed eyes and an open mouth became visible in the intense obscurity amongst the boulders. She uttered a low cry and stood up. The face vanished, leaving her to gasp and shiver alone in the wilderness of stone heaps. But as soon as she had crouched down again to rest, with her head against the rock, the face returned, came very near, appeared eager to finish the speech that had been cut short by death, only a moment ago. She scrambled quickly to her feet and said: 'Go away, or I will do it again.' The thing wavered, swung to the right, to the left. She moved this way and that, stepped back, fancied herself screaming at it, and was appalled by the unbroken stillness of the night. She tottered on the brink, felt the steep declivity under her feet, and rushed down blindly to save herself from a headlong fall. The shingle seemed to wake up; the pebbles began to roll before her, pursued her from above, raced down with her on both sides, rolling past with an increasing clatter. In the peace of the night the noise grew, deepening to a rumour, continuous and violent, as if the whole semicircle of the stony beach had started to tumble down into the bay. Susan's feet hardly touched the slope that seemed to run down with her. At the bottom she stumbled, shot forward, throwing her arms out, and fell heavily. She jumped up at once and turned swiftly to look back, her clenched hands full of sand she had clutched in her fall. The face was there, keeping its distance, visible in its own sheen that made a pale stain in the night. She shouted, 'Go away' – she shouted at it with pain, with fear, with all the rage of that useless stab that could not keep him quiet, keep him out of her sight. What did he want now? He was dead. Dead men have no children. Would he never leave her alone? She shrieked at it – waved her outstretched hands. She seemed to feel the breath of parted lips, and, with a long cry of discouragement, fled across the level bottom of the bay.

She ran lightly, unaware of any effort of her body. High sharp rocks that, when the bay is full, show above the glittering plain of blue water like pointed towers of submerged churches, glided past her, rushing to the land at tremendous pace. To the left, in the distance, she could see something shining: a broad disc of light in which narrow shadows pivoted round the centre like the spokes of a wheel. She heard a voice calling, 'Hey! There!' and answered with a wild scream. So, he could call yet! He was calling after her to stop. Never! ... She tore through the night, past the startled group of seaweed-gatherers who stood round their lantern paralysed with fear at the unearthly screech coming from that fleeing shadow. The men leaned on their pitchforks staring fearfully. A woman fell on her knees, and, crossing herself, began to pray aloud. A little girl with her ragged skirt full of slimy seaweed began to sob despairingly, lugging her soaked burden close to the man who carried the light. Somebody said: 'The thing ran out towards the sea.' Another voice exclaimed: 'And the sea is coming back! Look at the spreading puddles. Do you hear – you woman – there! Get up!' Several voices cried together. 'Yes, let us be off! Let the accursed thing go to the sea!' They moved on, keeping close round the light. Suddenly a man swore loudly. He would go and see what was the matter. It had been a woman's voice. He would go. There were shrill protests from women – but his high form detached itself from the group and went off running. They sent a unanimous call of scared voices after him. A word, insulting and mocking, came back, thrown at them through darkness. A woman moaned. An old man said gravely: 'Such things ought to be left alone.' They went on slower, shuffling in the yielding sand and whispering to one another that Millot feared nothing, having no religion, but that it would end badly some day.

Susan met the incoming tide by the Raven islet and stopped, panting, with her feet in the water. She heard the murmur and felt the cold caress of the sea, and, calmer now, could see the sombre and confused mass of the Raven on one side and on the other the long white streak of Molène sands that are left high above the dry bottom of Fougère Bay at every ebb. She turned round and saw far away, along the starred background of the sky, the ragged outline of the coast. Above it, nearly facing her, appeared the tower of Ploumar church; a slender and tall pyramid shooting up dark and pointed into the clustered glitter of the stars. She felt strangely calm. She knew where she was, and began to remember how she came there – and why. She peered into the smooth obscurity near her. She was alone. There was nothing there; nothing near her, either living or dead.

The tide was creeping in quietly, putting out long impatient arms of strange rivulets that ran towards the land between ridges of sand. Under the night the pools grew bigger with mysterious rapidity, while the great sea, yet far off, thundered in a regular rhythm along the indistinct line of the horizon. Susan splashed her way back for a few yards without being able to get clear of the water that murmured tenderly all around and, suddenly, with a spiteful gurgle, nearly took her off her feet. Her heart thumped with fear. This place was too big and too empty to die in. To-morrow they would do with her what they liked. But before she died she must tell them – tell the gentlemen in black clothes that there are things no woman can bear. She must explain how it happened . . .

She splashed through a pool, getting wet to the waist, too pre-occupied to care ... She must explain. 'He came in the same way as ever and said, just so: "Do you think I am going to leave the land to those people from Morbihan that I do not know? Do you? We shall see! Come along, you creature of mischance!" And he put his arms out. Then, Messieurs, I said: "Before God – never!" And he said, striding at me with open palms: "There is no God to hold me! Do you understand, you useless carcass. I will do what I like." And he took me by the shoulders. Then I, Messieurs, called to God for help, and next minute, while he was shaking me, I felt my long scissors in my hand. His shirt was unbuttoned, and, by the candle-light, I saw the hollow of his throat. I cried: "Let go!" He was crushing my shoulders. He was strong, my man was! Then I thought: No! ... Must I? ... Then take! – and I struck in the hollow place. I never saw him fall. Never! Never! ... Never saw him fall ... The old father never turned his head. He is deaf and childish, gentlemen ... Nobody saw him fall. I ran out ... Nobody saw ...'

She had been scrambling amongst the boulders of the Raven and now found herself, all out of breath, standing amongst the heavy shadows of the rocky islet. The Raven is connected with the main land by a natural pier of immense and slippery stones. She intended to return home that way. Was he still standing there? At home. Home! Four idiots and a corpse. She must go back and explain. Anybody would understand ...

Below her the night or the sea seemed to pronounce distinctly —

'Aha! I see you at last!'

She started, slipped, fell; and without attempting to rise, listened, terrified. She heard heavy breathing, a clatter of wooden clogs. It stopped.

'Where the devil did you pass?' said an invisible man, hoarsely.

She held her breath. She recognised the voice. She had not seen him fall. Was he pursuing her there dead, or perhaps ... alive?

She lost her head. She cried from the crevice where she lay huddled, 'Never, never!'

'Ah! You are still there. You led me a fine dance. Wait, my beauty, I must see how you look after all this. You wait ...'

Millot was stumbling, laughing, swearing meaninglessly out of pure satisfaction, pleased with himself for having run down that fly-by-night. 'As if there were such things as ghosts! Bah! It took an old African soldier to show those clodhoppers ... But it was curious. Who the devil was she?'

Susan listened, crouching. He was coming for her, this dead man. There was no escape. What a noise he made amongst the stones ... She saw his head rise up, then the shoulders. He was tall – her own man! His long arms waved about, and it was his own voice sounding a little strange . . . because of the scissors. She scrambled out quickly, rushed to the edge of the causeway, and turned round. The man stood still on a high stone, detaching himself in dead black on the glitter of the sky.

'Where are you going to?' he called roughly.

She answered, 'Home!' and watched him intensely. He made a striding, clumsy leap on to another boulder, and stopped again, balancing himself, then said—

'Ha! ha! Well, I am going with you. It's the least I can do. Ha! ha! ha!'

She stared at him till her eyes seemed to become glowing coals that burned deep into her brain, and yet she was in mortal fear of making out the well-known features. Below her the sea lapped softly against the rock with a splash, continuous and gentle.

The man said, advancing another step—

'I am coming for you. What do you think?'

She trembled. Coming for her! There was no escape, no peace, no hope. She looked round despairingly. Suddenly the whole shadowy coast, the blurred islets, the heaven itself, swayed about twice, then came to a rest. She closed her eyes and shouted—

'Can't you wait till I am dead!'

She was shaken by a furious hate for that shade that pursued her in this world, unappeased even by death in its longing for an heir that would be like other people's children.

'Hey! What?' said Millot, keeping his distance prudently. He was saying to himself: 'Look out! Some lunatic. An accident happens soon.'

She went on, wildly—

'I want to live. To live alone – for a week – for a day. I must explain to them . . . I would tear you to pieces, I would kill you twenty times over rather than let you touch me while I live. How many times must I kill you – you blasphemer! Satan sends you here. I am damned too!'

'Come,' said Millot, alarmed and conciliating. 'I am perfectly alive! .. Oh, my God!'

She had screamed, 'Alive!' and at once vanished before his eyes, as if the islet itself had swerved aside from under her feet. Millot rushed forward, and fell flat with his chin over the edge. Far below he saw the water whitened by her struggles, and heard one shrill cry for help that seemed to dart upwards along the perpendicular face of the rock, and soar past, straight into the high and impassive heaven.

Madame Levaille sat, dry-eyed, on the short grass of the hill side, with her thick legs stretched out, and her old feet turned up in their black cloth shoes. Her clogs stood near by, and further off the umbrella lay on the withered sward like a weapon dropped from the grasp of a vanquished warrior. The Marquis of Chavanes, on horseback, one gloved hand on thigh, looked down at her as she got up laboriously, with groans. On the narrow track of the seaweed-carts four men were carrying inland Susan's body on a hand barrow, while several others straggled listlessly behind. Madame Levaille looked after the procession. 'Yes, Monsieur le Marquis,' she said dispassionately, in her usual calm tone of a reasonable old woman. 'There are unfortunate people on this earth. I had only one child. Only one! And they won't bury her in consecrated ground!'

Her eyes filled suddenly, and a short shower of tears rolled down the broad cheeks. She pulled the shawl close about her. The Marquis leaned slightly over in his saddle, and said—

'It is very sad. You have all my sympathy. I shall speak to the Curé. She was unquestionably insane, and the fall was accidental. Millot says so distinctly. Good-day, Madame.'

And he trotted off, thinking to himself: I must get this old woman appointed guardian of those idiots, and administrator of the farm. It would be much better than having here one of those other Bacadous, probably a red republican, corrupting my commune.

Thomas Burke

The Bird

It is a tale that they tell softly in Pennyfields, when the curtains are drawn and the shapes of the night are shut out. . . .

Those who held that Captain Chudder, s.s. *Peacock*, owners, Peter Dubbin & Co., had a devil in him, were justified. But they were nearer the truth who held that his devil was not within him, but at his side, perching at his elbow, dropping sardonic utterance in his ear; moving with him day and night and prompting him – so it was held – to frightful excesses. His devil wore the shape of a white parrot, a bird of lusty wings and the cruellest of beaks. There were those who whispered that the old man had not always been the man that his crew knew him to be: that he had been a normal, kindly fellow until he acquired his strange companion from a native dealer in the malevolent Solomons. Certainly his maniac moods dated from its purchase; and there was truth in the dark hints of his men that there was something wrong with that damned bird . . . a kind of . . . something you sort of felt when it looked at you or answered you back. For one thing, it had a diabolical knack of mimicry, and many a chap would cry: 'Yes, George!' or 'Right, sir!' in answer to a commanding voice which chuckled with glee as he came smartly to order. They invariably referred to it as 'that bloody bird', though actually it had done nothing to merit such opprobrium. When they thought it over calmly, they could think of no harm that it had done to them: nothing to arouse such loathing as every man on the boat felt towards it. It was not spiteful; it was not bad-tempered. Mostly, it was in cheery mood and would chuckle deep in the throat, like the Captain, and echo or answer, quite pleasantly, such remarks, usually rude, as were addressed to it.

And yet . . . Somehow. . . .

There it was. It was always there – everywhere; and in its speech they seemed to find a sinister tone which left them guessing at the meaning of its words. On one occasion, the cook, in the seclusion of the fo'c'sle, had remarked that he would like to wring its neck if he could get hold of it; but old grizzled Snorter had replied that that bird couldn't be killed. There was something about that bird that . . . well, he betted no one wouldn't touch that bird without trouble. And a moment of panic stabbed the crowd as a voice leapt from the sombre shadows of the corner.

'That's the style, me old brown son. Don't try to come it with me – what?' and ceased in a spasmodic flutter of wicked white wings.

That night, as the cook was ascending the companion, he was caught by a huge sea, which swept across the boat from nowhere and dashed him, head-on, below. For a week he was sick with a broken head, and throughout that week the bird would thrust its beak to the berth where he lay, and chortle to him:

'Yep, me old brown son. Wring his bleeding neck – what? Waltz me around again, Willie, round and round and round!'

That is the seamen's story and, as the air of Limehouse is thick with seamen's stories, it is not always good to believe them. But it is a widely known fact that on the last voyage the Captain did have a devil with him, the foulest of all devils that possess mortal men, not the devil of slaughter, but the devil of cruelty. They were from Swatow to London, and it was noted that he was drinking heavily ashore, and he continued the game throughout the voyage. He came aboard from Swatow, drunk, bringing with him a Chinese boy, also drunk. The greaser, being a big man, kicked him below, otherwise, the boat in his charge would have gone there, and so he sat or sprawled in his cabin, with a rum-bottle before him and, on the corner of his chair, the white parrot, which conversed with him and sometimes fluttered on deck to shout orders in the frightful voice of his master and chuckle to see them momentarily obeyed.

'Yes,' repeated old man Snorter, sententiously, 'I'd run a hundred miles 'fore I'd try to monkey with the old man or his bloody bird. There's something about that bird . . . I said so before. I 'eard a story once about a bird. Out in T'ai-ping I 'eard it. It'll make yeh sick if I tell it. . . .'

Now while the Captain remained drunk in his cabin, he kept with him for company the miserable, half-starved Chinky boy whom he had brought aboard. And it would make others sick if the full dark tale were told here of what the master of the *Peacock* did to that boy. You may read of monstrosities in police reports of cruelty cases, you may read old records of the Middle Ages, but the bestialities of Captain Chudder could not be told in words.

His orgy of drink and delicious torture lasted till they were berthed in the Thames, and the details remain sharp and clear in the memories of those who witnessed it. At all the ceremonial horrors which were wrought in that wretched cabin, the parrot was present. It jabbered to the old man, the old man jabbered back, and gave it an occasional sip of rum from his glass, and the parrot would mimic the Chink's entreaties, and wag a grave claw at him as he writhed under the ritual of punishment, and when that day's ceremony was finished it would flutter from bow to stern of the boat, its cadaverous figure stinging the shadows with shapes of fear for all aboard, perching here, perching there, simpering and whining in tune with the Chink's placid moaning.

Placid; yes, outwardly. But the old man's wickedness had lighted a flame beneath that yellow skin which nothing could quench, nothing but the floods of vengeance. Had the old man been a little more cute and a little less drunk, he might have remembered that a Chinaman does not forget. He would have read danger in the face that was so submissive under his devilries. Perhaps he did see it, but, because of the rum that was in him, felt himself secure from the hate of any outcast Chink; knew that his victim would never once get the chance to repay him, Captain Chudder, master of the *Peacock*, and one of the very smartest. The Chink was alone and weaponless, and dare not come aft without orders. He was master of the boat, he had a crew to help him, and knives and guns, and he had his faithful white bird to warn him. Too, as soon as they docked at Limehouse, he would sling him off or arrange quick transfer to an outward boat, since he had no further use for him.

But it happened that he made no attempt to transfer. He had forgotten that idea. He just sat below, finished his last two bottles, paid off his men, and then, after a sleep, went ashore to report. Having done that, he forgot all trivial affairs, such as business, and set himself seriously to search for amusement. He climbed St George's, planning a real good booze-up, and the prospect that spread itself before his mind was so compelling that he did not notice a lurking yellow phantom that hung on his shadow. He visited the Baltic on the chance of finding an old pal or so, and, meeting none, he called at a shipping office in Fenchurch Street, where he picked up an acquaintance, and the two returned eastward to Poplar, and the Phantom feet *sup-supped* after them. Through the maze and glamour of the London streets and traffic the shadow slid; it dodged and danced about the Captain's little cottage in Gill Street, and when he, and others, came out and strolled to a bar, and, later, to a music-hall, it flitted, moth-like, around them.

Surely since there is no step in the world that has just the obvious stealth of the Chinaman's, he must have heard those whispering feet?

Surely his path was darkened by that shadow? But no. After the music-hall he drifted to a water-side wine-shop and then, with a bunch of the others, went wandering.

It was late. Eleven notes straggled across the waters from many grey towers. Sirens were screeching their derisive song, and names of various Scotch whiskies spelt themselves in letters of yellow flame along the night. Far in the darkness a voice was giving the chanty:

'What shall we do with a drunken sailor?'

The Captain braced himself up and promised himself a real glittering night of good-fellowship, and from gin-warmed bar to gin-warmed bar he roved, meeting the lurid girls of the places and taking one of them upstairs. At the last bar his friends, too, went upstairs with their ladies, and, it being then one o'clock in the morning, he brought a pleasant evening to a close at a certain house in Poplar High Street, where he took an hour's amusement by flinging half-crowns over the fan-tan table.

But always the yellow moth was near, and when, at half past two, he came, with uncertain steps, into the sad street, now darkened and loud only with the drunken, who found unfamiliar turnings in familiar streets, and the old landmarks many yards away from their rightful places, the moth buzzed closer and closer.

The Captain talked as he went. He talked of the night he had had, and the girls his hands had touched. His hard face was cracked to a meaningless smile, and he spat words at obstructive lamp posts and kerbstones, and swears dropped like toads from his lips. But at last he found his haven in Gill Street, and his hefty brother, with whom he lived when ashore, shoved him upstairs to his bedroom. He fell across the bed, and the sleep of the swinish held him fast.

The grey towers were rolling three o'clock, and the thick darkness of the water-side covered the night like a blanket. The lamps were pale and few. The waters sucked miserably at the staples of the wharves. One heard the measured beat of a constable's boot, sometimes the rattle of chains and blocks, mournful hooters, shudders of noise as engines butted lines of trucks at the shunting station.

Captain Chudder slept, breathing stertorously, mouth open, limbs heavy and nerveless. His room was deeply dark, and so little light shone on the back reaches of the Gill Street cottages that the soft raising of the window made no visible aperture. Into this blank space something rose from below, and soon it took the shape of a flat, yellow face which hung motionless, peering into the room. Then a yellow hand came through, the aperture was widened, and swiftly and silently a lithe, yellow body hauled itself up and slipped over the sill.

It glided, with outstretched hand, from the window and, the moment it touched the bed, its feeling fingers went here and there, and it stood still, gazing upon the sleep of drunkenness. Calmly and methodically a yellow hand moved to its waist and withdrew a kris. The same hand raised the kris and held it poised. It was long, keen, and beautifully curved, but not a ray of light was in the room to fall upon it, and the yellow hand had to feel its bright blade to find whether the curve ran from or towards it.

Then, with terrific force and speed, it came down, one – two – three. The last breath rushed from the open lips. Captain Chudder was out.

The strong yellow hand withdrew the kris for the last time, wiped it on the coverlet of the bed, and replaced it in its home. The figure turned, like a wraith, for the window, turned for the window and found, in a moment of panic, that it knew not which way to turn. It hesitated for a moment. It thought it heard a sound at the bed. It touched the coverlet and the boots of the Captain; all was still. Stretching a hand to the wall, Sung Dee began to creep and to feel his way along. Dark as the room was, he had found his way in, without matches or illuminant. Why could he not find his way out? Why was he afraid of something?

Blank wall was all he found at first. Then his hand touched what seemed to be a picture frame. It swung and clicked and the noise seemed to echo through the still house. He moved farther, and a sharp rattle told him that he had struck the loose handle of the door. But that was of little help. He could not use the door, he knew not what perils lay behind it. It was the window he wanted – the window.

Again he heard that sound from the bed. He stepped boldly and judged that he was standing in the middle of the room. Momentarily a sharp shock surged over him. He prayed for matches, and something in his throat was almost crying, 'The window! The window!' He seemed like an island in a sea of darkness, one man surrounded by legions of immortal intangible enemies. His cold Chinese heart went hot with fear.

The middle of the room he judged, and took another step forward, a step which landed his chin sharply against the jutting edge of the mantel-shelf over the fireplace. He jumped like a cat and his limbs shook, for now he had lost the door and the bed, as well as the window, and had made terrible noises which might bring disaster. All sense of direction was gone. He knew not whether to go forward or backwards, to right or left. He heard the tinkle of the shunting trains, and he heard a rich voice crying something in his own tongue. But he was lapped around by darkness and terror, and a cruel fancy came to him that he was imprisoned here for ever and for ever, and that he would never escape from this enveloping, suffocating room. He began to think that—

And then a hot iron of agony rushed down his back as, sharp and clear, at his elbow came the Captain's voice:

'Get forrard, you damn lousy Chink – get forrard. Lively there! Get out of my room!'

He sprang madly aside from the voice that had been the terror of his life for so many weeks, and collided with the door; realised that he had made further fearful noises; dashed away from it and crashed into the bed; fell across it and across the warm, wet body that lay there. Every nerve in every limb of him was seared with horror at the contact, and he leapt off, kicking, biting, writhing. He leapt off, and fell against a table, which tottered, and at last fell with a stupendous crash into the fender.

'Lively, you damn Chink!' said the Captain. 'Lively, I tell yeh. Dance, d'yeh hear? I'll have yeh for this. I'll learn you something. I'll give you something with a sharp knife and bit of hot iron, my cocky. I'll make yer yellow skin crackle, yeh damn lousy chopstick. I'll have yeh in a minute. And when I get yeh, orf with yeh clothes. I'll cut yeh to pieces I will.'

Sung Dee shrieked. He ran round and round, beating the wall with his hands, laughing, crying, jumping, while all manner of shapes arose in his path, lit by the grey light of fear. He realised that it was all up now. He cared not how much noise he made. He hadn't killed the old man; only wounded him. And now all he desired was to find the door and any human creatures who might save him from the Captain. He met the bed again, suddenly, and the tormentor who lay there. He met the upturned table and fell upon it, and he met the fireplace and the blank wall; but never, never the window or the door. They had vanished. There was no way out. He was caught in that dark room, and the Captain would do as he liked with him. . . . He heard footsteps in the passage and sounds of menace and alarm below. But to him they were friendly sounds, and he screamed loudly towards them.

He cried to the Captain, in his pidgin, for mercy.

'Oh, Captain – no burn me today, Captain. Sung Dee be heap good sailor, heap good servant, all same slave. Sung Dee heap plenty solly hurt Captain. Sung Dee be good boy. No do feller bad lings no feller more. O Captain. Let Sung Dee go lis time. Let Sung Dee go. O Captain!'

But 'Oh, my Gawd!' answered the Captain. 'Bless your yellow heart. Wait till I get you trussed up. Wait till I get you below. I'll learn yeh.'

And now those below came upstairs, and they listened in the passage, and for the space of a minute they were hesitant. For they heard all manner of terrible noises, and by the noises there might have been half a dozen fellows in the Captain's room. But very soon the screaming and the pattering feet were still, and they heard nothing but low moans; and at last the bravest of them, the Captain's brother, swung the door open and flashed a large lantern.

And those who were with him fell back in dumb horror, while the brother cried harshly: 'Oh! . . . my . . . God!' For the lantern shone on a Chinaman seated on the edge of the bed. Across his knees lay the dead body of the Captain, and the Chink was fondling his damp, dead face, talking baby talk to him, dancing him on his knee, and now and then making idiot moans. But what sent the crowd back in horror was that a great death-white Thing was flapping about the yellow face of the Chink, cackling: 'I'll learn yeh! I'll learn yeh!' and dragging strips of flesh away with every movement of the beak.

Arthur Machen

The Terror

I. *The Coming of the Terror*

After two years we are turning once more to the morning's news with a sense of appetite and glad expectation. There were thrills at the beginning of the war; the thrill of horror and of a doom that seemed at once incredible and certain; this was when Namur fell and the German host swelled like a flood over the French fields, and drew very near to the walls of Paris. Then we felt the thrill of exultation when the good news came that the awful tide had been turned back, that Paris and the world were safe; for awhile at all events.

Then for days we hoped for more news as good as this or better. Has von Kluck been surrounded? Not today, but perhaps he will be surrounded tomorrow. But the days became weeks, the weeks drew out to months; the battle in the west seemed frozen. Now and again things were done that seemed hopeful, with promise of events still better. But Neuve Chapelle and Loos dwindled into disappointments as their tale was told fully; the lines in the west remained, for all practical purposes of victory, immobile. Nothing seemed to happen, there was nothing to read save the record of operations that were clearly trifling and insignificant. People speculated as to the reason of this inaction; the hopeful said that Joffre had a plan, that he was 'nibbling', others declared that we were short of munitions, others again that the new levies were not yet ripe for battle. So the months went by, and almost two years of war had been completed before the motionless English line began to stir and quiver as if it awoke from a long sleep, and began to roll onward, overwhelming the enemy.

The secret of the long inaction of the British armies has been well kept.

On the one hand it was rigorously protected by the censorship, which severe, and sometimes severe to the point of absurdity – 'the captains and the . . . depart', for instance – became in this particular matter ferocious. As soon as the real significance of that which was happening, or beginning to happen, was perceived by the authorities, an underlined circular was issued to the newspaper proprietors of Great Britain and Ireland. It warned each proprietor that he might impart the contents of this circular to one other person only, such person being the responsible editor of his paper, who was to keep the communication secret under the severest penalties. The circular forbade any mention of certain events that had taken place, that might take place; it forbade any kind of allusion to these events or any hint of their existence, or of the possibility of their existence, not only in the press, but in any form whatever. The subject was not to be alluded to in conversation, it was not to be hinted at, however obscurely, in letters; the very existence of the circular, its subject apart, was to be a dead secret.

These measures were successful. A wealthy newspaper proprietor of the north, warmed a little at the end of the Throwsters' Feast (which was held as usual, it will be remembered), ventured to say to the man next to him: 'How awful it would be, wouldn't it, if. . . .' His words were repeated, as proof, one regrets to say, that it was time for 'old Arnold' to 'pull himself together'; and he was fined a thousand pounds. Then, there was the case of an obscure weekly paper published in the county town of an agricultural district in Wales. The *Meiros Observer* (we will call it) was issued from a stationer's back premises, and filled its four pages with accounts of local flower shows, fancy fairs at vicarages, reports of parish councils, and rare bathing fatalities. It also issued a visitors' list, which has been known to contain six names.

This enlightened organ printed a paragraph, which nobody noticed, which was very like paragraphs that small country newspapers have long been in the habit of printing, which could hardly give so much as a hint to any one – to any one, that is, who was not fully instructed in the secret. As a matter of fact, this piece of intelligence got into the paper because the proprietor, who was also the editor, incautiously left the last processes of this particular issue to the staff, who was the Lord-High-Everything-Else of the establishment; and the staff put in a bit of gossip he had heard in the market to fill up two inches on the back page. But the result was that the *Meiros Observer* ceased to appear, owing to 'untoward circumstances,' as the proprietor said; and he would say no more. No more, that is, by way of explanation, but a great deal more by way of execration of 'damned, prying busybodies'.

Now a censorship that is sufficiently minute and utterly remorseless can do amazing things in the way of hiding . . . what it wants to hide. Before the war, one would have thought otherwise; one would have said that, censor or no censor, the fact of the murder at X or the fact of the bank robbery at Y would certainly become known; if not through the press, at all events through rumour and the passage of the news from mouth to mouth. And this would be true – of England three hundred years ago, and of savage tribelands of today. But we have grown of late to such a reverence for the printed word and such a reliance on it, that the old faculty of disseminating news by word of mouth has become atrophied. Forbid the press to mention the fact that Jones has been murdered, and it is marvellous how few people will hear of it, and of those who hear how few will credit the story that they have heard. You meet a man in the train who remarks that he has been told something about a murder in Southwark; there is all the difference in the world between the impression you receive from such a chance communication and that given by half a dozen lines of print with name, and street and date and all the facts of the case. People in trains repeat all sorts of tales, many of them false; newspapers do not print accounts of murders that have not been committed.

Then another consideration that has been made for secrecy. I may have seemed to say that the old office of rumour no longer exists; I shall be reminded of the strange legend of the Russians and the mythology of the angels of Mons. But let me point out, in the first place, that both these absurdities depended on the papers for their wide dissemination. If there had been no newspapers or magazines Russians and angels would have made but a brief, vague appearance of the most shadowy kind – a few would have heard of them, fewer still would have believed in them, they would have been gossiped about for a bare week or two, and so they would have vanished away.

And, then, again, the very fact of these vain rumours and fantastic tales having been so widely believed for a time was fatal to the credit of any stray mutterings that may have got abroad. People had been taken in twice; they had seen how grave persons, men of credit, had preached and lectured about the shining forms that had saved the British army at Mons, or had testified to the trains, packed with grey-coated Muscovites, rushing through the land at dead of night: and now there was a hint of something more amazing than either of the discredited legends. But this time there was no word of confirmation to be found in daily papers, or weekly review, or parish magazine, and so the few that heard either laughed, or, being serious, went home and jotted down notes for essays on 'War-time Psychology: Collective Delusions'.

I followed neither of these courses. For before the secret circular had been issued my curiosity had somehow been aroused by certain paragraphs concerning a 'Fatal Accident to Well-known Airman'. The propeller of the aeroplane had been shattered, apparently by a collision with a flight of pigeons; the blades had been broken and the machine had fallen like lead to the earth. And soon after I had seen this account, I heard some very odd circumstances relating to an explosion in a great munition factory in the Midlands. I thought I saw the possibility of a connection between two very different events.

It has been pointed out to me by friends who have been good enough to read this record, that certain phrases I have used may give the impression that I ascribe all the delays of the war on the western front to the extraordinary circumstances which occasioned the issue of the secret circular. Of course this is not the case, there were many reasons for the immobility of our lines from October 1914 to July 1916. These causes have been evident enough and have been openly discussed and deplored. But behind them was something of infinitely greater moment. We lacked men, but men were pouring into the new army; we were short of shells, but when the shortage was proclaimed the nation set itself to mend this matter with all its energy. We could undertake to supply the defects of our army both in men and munitions – *if* the new and incredible danger could be overcome. It has been overcome; rather, perhaps, it has ceased to exist; and the secret may now be told.

I have said my attention was attracted by an account of the death of a well-known airman. I have not the habit of preserving cuttings, I am sorry to say, so that I cannot be precise as to the date of this event. To the best of my belief it was either towards the end of May or the beginning of June 1915. The newspaper paragraph announcing the death of Flight-Lieutenant Western-Reynolds was brief enough; accidents, and fatal accidents, to the men who are storming the air for us are, unfortunately, by no means so rare as to demand an elaborated notice. But the manner in which Western-Reynolds met his death struck me as extraordinary, inasmuch as it revealed a new danger in the element that we have lately conquered. He was brought down, as I said, by a flight of birds; of pigeons, as appeared by what was found on the blood-stained and shattered blades of the propeller. An eye-witness of the accident, a fellow officer, described how Western-Reynolds set out from the aerodrome on a fine afternoon, there being hardly any wind. He was going to France; he had made the journey to and fro half a dozen times or more, and felt perfectly secure and at ease.

' "Wester" rose to a great height at once, and we could scarcely see the machine. I was turning to go when one of the fellows called out: "I say! What's this?" He pointed up, and we saw what looked like a black cloud coming from the south at a tremendous rate. I saw at once it wasn't a cloud; it came with a swirl and a rush quite different from any cloud I've ever seen. But for a second I couldn't make out exactly what it was. It altered its shape and turned into a great crescent, and wheeled and veered about as if it was looking for something. The man who had called out had got his glasses, and was staring for all he was worth. Then he shouted that it was a tremendous flight of birds, "thousands of them". They went on wheeling and beating about high up in the air, and we were watching them, thinking it was interesting, but not supposing that they would make any difference to Wester, who was just about out of sight. His machine was just a speck. Then the two arms of the crescent drew in as quick as lightning, and these thousands of birds shot in a solid mass right up there across the sky, and flew away somewhere about nor'-nor'-by-west. Then Henley, the man with the glasses, called out: "He's down!" and started running, and I went after him. We got a car and as we were going along Henley told me that he'd seen the machine drop dead, as if it came out of that cloud of birds. He thought then that they must have mucked up the propeller somehow. That turned out to be the case. We found the propeller blades all broken and covered with blood and pigeon feathers, and carcasses of the birds had got wedged in between the blades, and were sticking to them.'

This was the story that the young airman told one evening in a small company. He did not speak 'in confidence', so I have no hesitation in reproducing what he said. Naturally, I did not take a verbatim note of his conversation, but I have something of a knack of remembering talk that interests me, and I think my reproduction is very near to the tale that I heard. And let it be noted that the flying man told his story without any sense or indication of a sense that the incredible, or all but the incredible, had happened. So far as he knew, he said, it was the first accident of the kind. Airmen in France had been bothered once or twice by birds – he thought they were eagles – flying viciously at them, but poor old Wester had been the first man to come up against a flight of some thousands of pigeons.

'And perhaps I shall be the next,' he added, 'but why look for trouble? Anyhow, I'm going to see *Toodle-oo* tomorrow afternoon.'

Well, I heard the story, as one hears all the varied marvels and terrors of the air; as one heard some years ago of 'air pockets', strange gulfs or voids in the atmosphere into which airmen fell with great peril; or as one heard of the experience of the airman who flew over the Cumberland Mountains in the burning summer of 1911, and as he swam far above the heights was suddenly and vehemently blown upwards, the hot air from the rocks striking his plane as if it had been a blast from a furnace chimney. We have just begun to navigate a strange region; we must expect to encounter strange adventures, strange perils. And here a new chapter in the chronicles of these perils and adventures had been opened by the death of Western-Reynolds; and no doubt invention and contrivance would presently hit on some way of countering the new danger.

It was, I think, about a week or ten days after the airman's death that my business called me to a northern town, the name of which, perhaps, had better remain unknown. My mission was to inquire into certain charges of extravagance which had been laid against the working people, that is, the munition workers of this especial town. It was said that the men who used to earn £2 10s. a week were now getting from seven to eight pounds, that 'bits of girls' were being paid two pounds instead of seven or eight shillings, and that, in consequence, there was an orgy of foolish extravagance. The girls, I was told, were eating chocolates at four, five, and six shillings a pound, the women were ordering thirty-pound pianos which they couldn't play, and the men bought gold chains at ten and twenty guineas apiece.

I dived into the town in question and found, as usual, that there was a mixture of truth and exaggeration in the stories that I had heard. Gramophones, for example: they cannot be called in strictness necessaries, but they were undoubtedly finding a ready sale, even in the more expensive brands. And I thought that there were a great many very spick-and-span perambulators to be seen on the pavement; smart perambulators, painted in tender shades of colour and expensively fitted.

'And how can you be surprised if people will have a bit of a fling?' a worker said to me. 'We're seeing money for the first time in our lives, and it's bright. And we work hard for it, and we risk our lives to get it. You've heard of explosion yonder?'

He mentioned certain works on the outskirts of the town. Of course, neither the name of the works nor of the town had been printed; there had been a brief notice of 'Explosion at Munition Works in the Northern District: Many Fatalities'. The working man told me about it, and added some dreadful details.

'They wouldn't let their folks see bodies; screwed them up in coffins as they found them in shop. The gas had done it.'

'Turned their faces black, you mean?'

'Nay. They were all as if they had been bitten to pieces.'

This was a strange gas.

I asked the man in the northern town all sorts of questions about the extraordinary explosion of which he had spoken to me. But he had very little more to say. As I have noted already, secrets that may not be printed are often deeply kept; last summer there were very few people outside high official circles who knew anything about the 'tanks', of which we have all been talking lately, though these strange instruments of war were being exercised and tested in a park not far from London. So the man who told me of the explosion in the munition factory was most likely genuine in his profession that he knew nothing more of the disaster. I found out that he was a smelter employed at a furnace on the other side of the town to the ruined factory; he didn't know even what they had been making there; some very dangerous high explosive, he supposed. His information was really nothing more than a bit of gruesome gossip, which he had heard probably at third or fourth or fifth hand. The horrible detail of faces 'as if they had been bitten to pieces' had made its violent impression on him, that was all.

I gave him up and took a tram to the district of the disaster; a sort of industrial suburb, five miles from the centre of the town. When I asked for the factory, I was told that it was no good my going to it as there was nobody there. But I found it; a raw and hideous shed with a walled yard about it, and a shut gate. I looked for signs of destruction, but there was nothing. The roof was quite undamaged; and again it struck me that this had been a strange accident. There had been an explosion of sufficient violence to kill work-people in the building, but the building itself showed no wounds or scars.

A man came out of the gate and locked it behind him. I began to ask him some sort of question, or rather, I began to 'open' for a question with 'A terrible business here, they tell me,' or some such phrase of convention. I got no farther. The man asked me if I saw a policeman walking down the street. I said I did, and I was given the choice of getting about my business forthwith or of being instantly given in charge as a spy. 'Th'ast better be gone and quick about it,' was, I think, his final advice, and I took it.

Well, I had come literally up against a brick wall. Thinking the problem over, I could only suppose that the smelter or his informant had twisted the phrases of the story. The smelter had said the dead men's faces were 'bitten to pieces'; this might be an unconscious perversion of 'eaten away'. That phrase might describe well enough the effect of strong acids, and, for all I knew of the processes of munition-making, such acids might be used and might explode with horrible results in some perilous stage of their admixture.

It was a day or two later that the accident to the airman, Western-Reynolds, came into my mind. For one of those instants which are far shorter than any measure of time there flashed out the possibility of a link between the two disasters. But here was a wild impossibility, and I drove it away. And yet I think that the thought, mad as it seemed, never left me; it was the secret light that at last guided me through a sombre grove of enigmas.

It was about this time, so far as the date can be fixed, that a whole district, one might say a whole county, was visited by a series of extraordinary and terrible calamities, which were the more terrible inasmuch as they continued for some time to be inscrutable mysteries. It is, indeed, doubtful whether these awful events do not still remain mysteries to many of those concerned; for before the inhabitants of this part of the country had time to join one link of evidence to another the circular was issued, and thenceforth no one knew how to distinguish undoubted fact from wild and extravagant surmise.

The district in question is in the far west of Wales; I shall call it, for convenience, Meirion. In it there is one seaside town of some repute with holiday-makers for five or six weeks in the summer, and dotted about the county there are three or four small old towns that seem drooping in a slow decay, sleepy and grey with age and forgetfulness. They remind me of what I have read of towns in the west of Ireland. Grass grows between the uneven stones of the pavements, the signs above the shop windows decline, half the letters of these signs are missing, here and there a house has been pulled down, or has been allowed to slide into ruin, and wild greenery springs up through the fallen stones, and there is silence in all the streets. And it is to be noted, these are not places that were once magnificent. The Celts have never had the art of building, and so far as I can see, such towns as Towy and Merthyr Tegveth and Meiros must have been always much as they are now, clusters of poorish, meanly built houses, ill kept and down at heel.

And these few towns are thinly scattered over a wild country where north is divided from south by a wilder mountain range. One of these places is sixteen miles from any station; the others are doubtfully and deviously connected by single-line railways served by rare trains that pause and stagger and hesitate on their slow journey up mountain passes, or stop for half an hour or more at lonely sheds called stations, situated in the midst of desolate marshes. A few years ago I travelled with an Irishman on one of these queer lines, and he looked to right and saw the bog with its yellow and blue grasses and stagnant pools, and he looked to left and saw a ragged hill-side, set with grey stone walls. 'I can hardly believe,' he said, 'that I'm not still in the wilds of Ireland.'

Here, then, one sees a wild and divided and scattered region, a land of outland hills and secret and hidden valleys. I know white farms on this coast which must be separate by two hours of hard, rough walking from any other habitation, which are invisible from any other house. And inland, again, the farms are often ringed about by thick groves of ash, planted by men of old days to shelter their roof-trees from rude winds of the mountain and stormy winds of the sea; so that these places, too, are hidden away, to be surmised only by the wood smoke that rises from the green surrounding leaves. A Londoner must see them to believe in them; and even then he can scarcely credit their utter isolation.

Such, then, in the main is Meirion, and on this land in the early summer of last year terror descended – a terror without shape, such as no man there had ever known.

It began with the tale of a little child who wandered out into the lanes to pick flowers one sunny afternoon, and never came back to the cottage on the hill.

II. *Death in the Village*

The child who was lost came from a lonely cottage that stands on the slope of a steep hill-side called the Allt, or the height. The land about it is wild and ragged; here the growth of gorse and bracken, here a marshy hollow of reeds and rushes, marking the course of the stream from some hidden well, here thickets of dense and tangled undergrowth, the outposts of the wood. Down through this broken and uneven ground a path leads to the lane at the bottom of the valley; then the land rises again and swells up to the cliffs over the sea, about a quarter of a mile away. The little girl, Gertrude Morgan, asked her mother if she might go down to the lane and pick the purple flowers – these were orchids – that grew there, and her mother gave her leave, telling her she must be sure to be back by tea time, as there was apple tart for tea.

She never came back. It was supposed that she must have crossed the road and gone to the cliff's edge, possibly in order to pick the sea pinks that were then in full blossom. She must have slipped, they said, and fallen into the sea, two hundred feet below. And, it may be said at once, that there was no doubt some truth in this conjecture, though it stopped very far short of the whole truth. The child's body must have been carried out by the tide, for it was never found.

The conjecture of a false step or of a fatal slide on the slippery turf that slopes down to the rocks was accepted as being the only explanation possible. People thought the accident a strange one because, as a rule, country children living by the cliffs and the sea become wary at an early age, and Gertrude Morgan was almost ten years old. Still, as the neighbours said, 'That's how it must have happened, and it's a great pity, to be sure.' But this would not do when in a week's time a strong young labourer failed to come to his cottage after the day's work. His body was found on the rocks six or seven miles from the cliffs where the child was supposed to have fallen; he was going home by a path that he had used every night of his life for eight or nine years, that he used of dark nights in perfect security, knowing every inch of it. The police asked if he drank, but he was a teetotaller; if he were subject to fits, but he wasn't. And he was not murdered for his wealth, since agricultural labourers are not wealthy. It was only possible again to talk of slippery turf and a false step; but people began to be frightened. Then a woman was found with her neck broken at the bottom of a disused quarry near Llanfihangel, in the middle of the county. The 'false step' theory was eliminated here, for the quarry was guarded with a natural hedge of gorse bushes. One would have to struggle and fight through sharp thorns to destruction in such a place as this; and indeed the gorse bushes were broken as if some one had rushed furiously through them, just above the place where the woman's body was found. And this was strange: there was a dead sheep lying beside her in the pit, as if the woman and the sheep together had been chased over the brim of the quarry. But chased by whom, or by what? And then there was a new form of terror.

This was in the region of the marshes under the mountain. A man and his son, a lad of fourteen or fifteen, set out early one morning to work and never reached the farm where they were bound. Their way skirted the marsh, but it was broad, firm and well metalled, and it had been raised about two feet above the bog. But when search was made in the evening of the same day Phillips and his son were found dead in the marsh, covered with black slime and pondweed. And they lay some ten yards from the path, which, it would seem, they must have left deliberately. It was useless, of course, to look for tracks in the black ooze, for if one threw a big stone into it a few seconds removed all marks of the disturbance. The men who found the two bodies beat about the verges and purlieus of the marsh in hope of finding some trace of the murderers; they went to and fro over the rising ground where the black cattle were grazing, they searched the alder thickets by the brook; but they discovered nothing.

Most horrible of all these horrors, perhaps, was the affair of the Highway, a lonely and unfrequented by-road that winds for many miles on high and lonely land. Here, a mile from any other dwelling, stands a cottage on the edge of a dark wood. It was inhabited by a labourer named Williams, his wife, and their three children. One hot summer's evening, a man who had been doing a day's gardening at a rectory three or four miles away, passed the cottage, and stopped for a few minutes to chat with Williams, the labourer, who was pottering about his garden, while the children were playing on the path by the door. The two talked of their neighbours and of the potatoes till Mrs Williams appeared at the doorway and said supper was ready, and Williams turned to go into the house. This was about eight o'clock, and in the ordinary course the family would have their supper and be in bed by nine, or by half past nine at latest. At ten o'clock that night the local doctor was driving home along the Highway. His horse shied violently and then stopped dead just opposite the gate to the cottage. The doctor got down, frightened at what he saw; and there on the roadway lay Williams, his wife, and the three children, stone dead, all of them. Their skulls were battered in as if by some heavy iron instrument; their faces were beaten into a pulp.

III. *The Doctor's Theory*

It is not easy to make any picture of the horror that lay dark on the hearts of the people of Meirion. It was no longer possible to believe or to pretend to believe that these men and women and children had met their deaths through strange accidents. The little girl and the young labourer might have slipped and fallen over the cliffs, but the woman who lay dead with the dead sheep at the bottom of the quarry, the two men who had been lured into the ooze of the marsh, the family who were found murdered on the Highway before their own cottage door; in these cases there could be no room for the supposition of accident. It seemed as if it were impossible to frame any conjecture or outline of a conjecture that would account for these hideous and, as it seemed, utterly purposeless crimes. For a time people said that there must be a madman at large, a sort of country variant of Jack the Ripper, some horrible pervert who was possessed by the passion of death, who prowled darkling about that lonely land, hiding in woods and in wild places, always watching and seeking for the victims of his desire.

Indeed, Dr Lewis, who found poor Williams, his wife, and children miserably slaughtered on the Highway, was convinced at first that the presence of a concealed madman in the countryside offered the only possible solution to the difficulty.

'I felt sure,' he said to me afterwards, 'that the Williamses had been killed by a homicidal maniac. It was the nature of the poor creatures' injuries that convinced me that this was the case. Some years ago – thirty-seven or thirty-eight years ago as a matter of fact – I had something to do with a case which on the face of it had a strong likeness to the Highway murder. At that time I had a practice at Usk, in Monmouthshire. A whole family living in a cottage by the roadside were murdered one evening; it was called, I think, the Llangibby murder; the cottage was near the village of that name. The murderer was caught in Newport; he was a Spanish sailor, named Garcia, and it appeared that he had killed father, mother, and the three children for the sake of the brass works of an old Dutch clock, which were found on him when he was arrested.

'Garcia had been serving a month's imprisonment in Usk gaol for some small theft, and on his release he set out to walk to Newport, nine or ten miles away; no doubt to get another ship. He passed the cottage and saw the man working in his garden. Garcia stabbed him with his sailor's knife. The wife rushed out; he stabbed her. Then he went into the cottage and stabbed the three children, tried to set the place on fire, and made off with the clock-works. That looked like the deed of a madman, but Garcia wasn't mad – they hanged him, I may say – he was merely a man of a very low type, a degenerate who hadn't the slightest value for human life. I am not sure, but I think he came from one of the Spanish islands, where the people are said to be degenerates, very likely from too much interbreeding.

'But my point is that Garcia stabbed to kill and did kill, with one blow in each case. There was no senseless hacking and slashing. Now those poor people on the Highway had their heads smashed to pieces by what must have been a storm of blows. Any one of them would have been fatal, but the murderer must have gone on raining blows with his iron hammer on people who were already stone dead. And *that* sort of thing is the work of a madman, and nothing but a madman. That's how I argued the matter out to myself just after the event.

'I was utterly wrong, monstrously wrong. But who could have suspected the truth?'

Thus Dr Lewis, and I quote him, or the substance of him, as representative of most of the educated opinion of the district at the beginnings of the terror. People seized on this theory largely because it offered at least the comfort of an explanation, and any explanation, even the poorest, is better than an intolerable and terrible mystery. Besides, Dr Lewis's theory was plausible; it explained the lack of purpose that seemed to characterize the murders. And yet – there were difficulties even from the first. It was hardly possible that a strange madman should be able to keep hidden in a countryside where any stranger is instantly noted and noticed; sooner or later he would be seen as he prowled along the lanes or across the wild places. Indeed, a drunken, cheerful, and altogether harmless tramp was arrested by a farmer and his man in the fact and act of sleeping off beer under a hedge; but the vagrant was able to prove complete and undoubted alibis, and was soon allowed to go on his wandering way.

Then another theory, or rather a variant of Dr Lewis's theory, was started. This was to the effect that the person responsible for the outrages was, indeed, a madman; but a madman only at intervals. It was one of the members of the Porth Club, a certain Mr Remnant, who was supposed to have originated this more subtle explanation. Mr Remnant was a middle-aged man, who, having nothing particular to do, read a great many books by way of conquering the hours. He talked to the club – doctors, retired colonels, parsons, lawyers – about 'personality', quoted various psychological text-books in support of his contention that personality was sometimes fluid and unstable, went back to *Dr Jekyll and Mr Hyde* as good evidence of this proposition, and laid stress on Dr

Jekyll's speculation that the human soul, so far from being one and indivisible, might possibly turn out to be a mere polity, a state in which dwelt many strange and incongruous citizens, whose characters were not merely unknown but altogether unsurmised by that form of consciousness which so rashly assumed that it was not only the president of the republic but also its sole citizen.

'The long and the short of it is,' Mr Remnant concluded, 'that any one of us may be the murderer, though he hasn't the faintest notion of the fact. Take Llewelyn there.'

Mr Payne Llewelyn was an elderly lawyer, a rural Tulkinghorn. He was the hereditary solicitor to the Morgans of Pentwyn. This does not sound anything tremendous to the Saxons of London; but the style is far more than noble to the Celts of west Wales; it is immemorial; Teilo Sant was of the collaterals of the first known chief of the race. And Mr Payne Llewelyn did his best to look like the legal adviser of this ancient house. He was weighty, he was cautious, he was sound, he was secure. I have compared him to Mr Tulkinghorn of Lincoln's Inn Fields; but Mr Llewelyn would most certainly never have dreamed of employing his leisure in peering into the cupboards where the family skeletons were hidden. Supposing such cupboards to have existed, Mr Payne Llewelyn would have risked large out-of-pocket expenses to furnish them with double, triple, impregnable locks. He was a new man, an *advena*, certainly; for he was partly of the Conquest, being descended on one side from Sir Payne Turberville; but he meant to stand by the old stock.

'Take Llewelyn now,' said Mr Remnant. 'Look here, Llewelyn, can you produce evidence to show where you were on the night those people were murdered on the Highway? I thought not.'

Mr Llewelyn, an elderly man, as I have said, hesitated before speaking.

'I thought not,' Remnant went on. 'Now I say that it is perfectly possible that Llewelyn may be dealing death throughout Meirion, although in his present personality he may not have the faintest suspicion that there is another Llewelyn within him, a Llewelyn who follows murder as a fine art.'

Mr Payne Llewelyn did not at all relish Mr Remnant's suggestion that he might well be a secret murderer, ravening for blood, remorseless as a wild beast. He thought the phrase about his following murder as a fine art was both nonsensical and in the worst taste, and his opinion was not changed when Remnant pointed out that it was used by De Quincey in the title of one of his most famous essays.

'If you had allowed me to speak,' he said with some coldness of manner, 'I would have told you that on Tuesday last, the night on which those unfortunate people were murdered on the Highway I was staying at the Angel Hotel, Cardiff. I had business in Cardiff, and I was detained till Wednesday afternoon.'

Having given this satisfactory alibi, Mr Payne Llewelyn left the club, and did not go near it for the rest of the week.

Remnant explained to those who stayed in the smoking-room that, of course, he had merely used Mr Llewelyn as a concrete example of his theory, which, he persisted, had the support of a considerable body of evidence.

'There are several cases of double personality on record,' he declared. 'And I say again that it is quite possible that these murders may have been committed by one of us in his secondary personality. Why, I may be the murderer in my Remnant B state, though Remnant A knows nothing whatever about it, and is perfectly convinced that he could not kill a fowl, much less a whole family. Isn't it so, Lewis?'

Dr Lewis said it was so, in theory, but he thought not in fact.

'Most of the cases of double or multiple personality that have been investigated,' he said, 'have been in connection with the very dubious experiments of hypnotism, or the still more dubious experiments of spiritualism. All that sort of thing, in my opinion, is like tinkering with the works of a clock – amateur tinkering, I mean. You fumble about with the wheels and cogs and bits of mechanism that you don't really know anything about; and then you find your clock going backwards or striking 240 at tea time. And I believe it's just the same thing with these psychical research experiments; the secondary personality is very likely the result of the tinkering and fumbling with a very delicate apparatus that we know nothing about. Mind, I can't say that it's impossible for one of us to be the Highway murderer in his B state, as Remnant puts it. But I think it's extremely improbable. Probability is the guide of life, you know, Remnant,' said Dr Lewis, smiling at that gentleman, as if to say that he also had done a little reading in his day. 'And it follows, therefore, that improbability is also the guide of life. When you get a very high degree of probability, that is, you are justified in taking it as a certainty; and on the other hand, if a supposition is highly improbable, you are justified in treating it as an impossible one. That is, in nine hundred and ninety-nine cases out of a thousand.'

'How about the thousandth case?' said Remnant. 'Supposing these extraordinary crimes constitute the thousandth case?'

The doctor smiled and shrugged his shoulders, being tired of the subject. But for some little time highly respectable members of Porth society would look suspiciously at one another wondering whether, after all, there mightn't be 'something in it'. However, both Mr Remnant's somewhat crazy theory and Dr Lewis's plausible theory became untenable when two more victims of an awful and mysterious death were offered up in sacrifice, for a man was found dead in the Llanfihangel quarry, where the woman had been discovered. And on the same day a girl of fifteen was found broken on the jagged rocks under the cliffs near Porth. Now, it appeared that these two deaths must have occurred at about the same time, within an hour of one another, certainly; and the distance between the quarry and the cliffs by Black Rock is certainly twenty miles.

'A motor could do it,' one man said.

But it was pointed out that there was no high road between the two places; indeed, it might be said that there was no road at all between them. There was a network of deep, narrow, and tortuous lanes that wandered into one another at all manner of queer angles for, say, seventeen miles; this in the middle, as it were, between Black Rock and the quarry at Llanfihangel. But to get to the high land of the cliffs one had to take a path that went through two miles of fields; and the quarry lay a mile away from the nearest by-road in the midst of gorse and bracken and broken land. And, finally, there was no track of motor-car or motor bicycle in the lanes which must have been followed to pass from one place to the other.

'What about an aeroplane, then?' said the man of the motor-car theory. Well, there was certainly an aerodrome not far from one of the two places of death; but somehow, nobody believed that the Flying Corps harboured a homicidal maniac. It seemed clear, therefore, that there must be more than one person concerned in the terror of Meirion. And Dr Lewis himself abandoned his own theory.

'As I said to Remnant at the club,' he remarked, 'improbability is the guide of life. I can't believe that there are a pack of madmen or even two madmen at large in the country. I give it up.'

And now a fresh circumstance or set of circumstances became manifest to confound judgement and to awaken new and wild surmises. For at about this time people realized that none of the dreadful events that were happening all about them was so much as mentioned in the press. I have already spoken of the fate of the *Meiros Observer*. This paper was suppressed by the authorities because it had inserted a brief paragraph about some person who had been 'found dead under mysterious circumstances'; I think that paragraph referred to the first death of Llanfihangel quarry. Thenceforth, horror followed on horror, but no word was printed in any of the local journals. The curious went to the newspaper offices – there were two left in the county – but found nothing save a firm refusal to discuss the matter. And the Cardiff papers were drawn and found blank; and the London press was apparently ignorant of the fact that crimes that had no parallel were terrorizing a whole countryside. Everybody wondered what could have happened, what was happening; and then it was whispered that the coroner would allow no inquiry to be made as to these deaths of darkness.

'In consequence of instructions received from the Home Office,' one coroner was understood to have said, 'I have to tell the jury that their business will be to hear the medical evidence and to bring in a verdict immediately in accordance with that evidence. I shall disallow all questions.'

One jury protested. The foreman refused to bring in any verdict at all.

'Very good,' said the coroner. 'Then I beg to inform you, Mr Foreman and gentlemen of the jury, that under the Defence of the Realm Act, I have power to supersede your functions, and to enter a verdict according to the evidence which has been laid before the court as if it had been the verdict of you all.'

The foreman and jury collapsed and accepted what they could not avoid. But the rumours that got abroad of all this, added to the known fact that the terror was ignored in the press, no doubt by official command, increased the panic that was now arising, and gave it a new direction. Clearly, people reasoned, these government restrictions and prohibitions could only refer to the war, to some great danger in connection with the war. And that being so, it followed that the outrages which must be kept so secret were the work of the enemy; that is, of concealed German agents.

IV. *The Spread of the Terror*

It is time, I think, for me to make one point clear. I began this history with certain references to an extraordinary accident to an airman whose machine fell to the ground after collision with a huge flock of pigeons; and then to an explosion in a northern munition factory, an explosion, as I noted, of a very singular kind. Then I deserted the neighbourhood of London, and the northern district, and dwelt on a mysterious and terrible series of events which occurred in the summer of 1915 in a Welsh county, which I have named, for convenience, Meirion.

Well, let it be understood at once that all this detail that I have given about the occurrences in Meirion does not imply that the county in the far west was alone or especially afflicted by the terror that was over the land. They tell me that in the villages about Dartmoor the stout Devonshire hearts sank as men's hearts used to sink in the time of plague and pestilence. There was horror, too, about the Norfolk Broads, and far up by Perth no one would venture on the path that leads by Scone to the wooded heights above the Tay. And in the industrial districts: I met a man by chance one day in an odd London corner who spoke with horror of what a friend had told him.

' "Ask no questions, Ned," he says to me, "but I tell yow a' was in Bairnigan t'other day, and a' met a pal who'd seen three hundred coffins going out of a works not far from there." '

And then the ship that hovered outside the mouth of the Thames with all sails set and beat to and fro in the wind, and never answered any hail, and showed no light! The forts shot at her and brought down one of the masts, but she went suddenly about with a change of wind under what sail still stood, and then veered down Channel, and drove ashore at last on the sandbanks and pinewoods of Arcachon, and not a man alive on her, but only rattling heaps of bones! That last voyage of the *Semiramis* would be something horribly worth telling; but I only heard it at a distance as a yarn, and only believed it because it squared with other things that I knew for certain.

This, then, is my point; I have written of the terror as it fell on Meirion, simply because I have had opportunities of getting close there to what really happened. Third of fourth or fifth hand in the other places; but round about Porth and Merthyr Tegveth I have spoken with people who have seen the tracks of the terror with their own eyes.

Well, I have said that the people of that far-western county realized, not only that death was abroad in their quiet lanes and on their peaceful hills, but that for some reason it was to be kept all secret. Newspapers might not print any news of it, the very juries summoned to investigate it were allowed to investigate nothing. And so they concluded that this veil of secrecy must somehow be connected with the war; and from this position it was not a long way to a further inference: that the murderers of innocent men and women and children were either Germans or agents of Germany. It would be just like the Huns, everybody agreed, to think out such a devilish scheme as this; and they always thought out their schemes beforehand. They hoped to seize Paris in a few weeks, but when they were beaten on the Marne they had their trenches on the Aisne ready to fall back on: it had all been prepared years before the war. And so, no doubt, they had devised this terrible plan against England in case they could not beat us in open fight: there were people ready, very likely, all over the country, who were prepared to murder and destroy everywhere as soon as they got the word. In this way the Germans intended to sow terror throughout England and fill our hearts with panic and dismay, hoping so to weaken their enemy at home that he would lose all heart over the war abroad. It was the Zeppelin notion, in another form; they were committing these horrible and mysterious outrages thinking that we should be frightened out of our wits.

It all seemed plausible enough; Germany had by this time perpetrated so many horrors and had so excelled in devilish ingenuities that no abomination seemed too abominable to be probable, or too ingeniously wicked to be beyond the tortuous malice of the Hun. But then came the questions as to who the agents of this terrible design were, as to where they lived, as to how they contrived to move unseen from field to field, from lane to lane. All sorts of fantastic attempts were made to answer these questions; but it was felt that they remained unanswered. Some suggested that the murderers landed from submarines, or flew from hiding places on the west coast of Ireland, coming and going by night; but there were seen to be flagrant impossibilities in both these suggestions. Everybody agreed that the evil work was no doubt the work of Germany; but nobody could begin to guess how it was done. Somebody at the club asked Remnant for his theory.

'My theory,' said that ingenious person, 'is that human progress is simply a long march from one inconceivable to another. Look at that airship of ours that came over Porth yesterday: ten years ago that would have been an inconceivable sight. Take the steam engine, take printing, take the theory of gravitation: they were all inconceivable till somebody thought of them. So it is, no doubt, with this infernal dodgery that we're talking about: the Huns have found it out, and we haven't; and there you are. We can't conceive how these poor people have been murdered, because the method's inconceivable to us.'

The club listened with some awe to this high argument. After Remnant had gone, one member said:

'Wonderful man, that.' 'Yes,' said Dr Lewis. 'He was asked whether he knew something. And his reply really amounted to "No, I don't." But I have never heard it better put.'

It was, I suppose, at about this time when the people were puzzling their heads as to the ecret methods used by the Germans or their agents to accomplish their crimes that a very singular circumstance became known to a few of the Porth people. It related to the murder of the Williams family on the Highway in front of their cottage door. I do not know that I have made it plain that the old Roman road called the Highway follows the course of a long, steep hill that goes steadily westward till it slants down and droops towards the sea. On either side of the road the ground falls away, here into deep shadowy woods, here to high pastures, now and again into a field of corn, but for the most part into the wild and broken land that is characteristic of Arfon. The fields are long and narrow, stretching up the steep hill-side; they fall into sudden dips and hollows, a well springs up in the midst of one and a grove of ash and thorn bends over it, shading it; and beneath it the ground is thick with reeds and rushes. And then may come on either side of such a field territories glistening with the deep growth of bracken, and rough with gorse and rugged with thickets of blackthorn, green lichen hanging strangely from the branches; such are the lands on either side of the Highway.

Now on the lower slopes of it, beneath the Williams's cottage, some three or four fields down the hill, there is a military camp. The place has been used as a camp for many years, and lately the site has been extended and huts have been erected. But a considerable number of the men were under canvas here in the summer of 1915.

On the night of the Highway murder this camp, as it appeared afterwards, was the scene of the extraordinary panic of the horses.

A good many men in the camp were asleep in their tents soon after 9.30, when the last post was sounded. They woke up in panic. There was a thundering sound on the steep hill-side above them, and down upon the tents came half a dozen horses, mad with fright, trampling the canvas, trampling the men, bruising dozens of them and killing two.

Everything was in wild confusion, men groaning and screaming in the darkness, struggling with the canvas and the twisted ropes, shouting out, some of them, raw lads enough, that the Germans had landed, others wiping the blood from their eyes, a few, roused suddenly from heavy sleep, hitting out at one another, officers coming up at the double roaring out orders to the sergeants, a party of soldiers who were just returning to camp from the village seized with fright at what they could scarcely see or distinguish, at the wildness of the shouting and cursing and groaning that they could not understand, bolting out of the camp again and racing for their lives back to the village: everything in the maddest confusion of wild disorder.

Some of the men had seen the horses galloping down the hill as if terror itself was driving them. They scattered off into the darkness, and somehow or another found their way back in the night to their pasture above the camp. They were grazing there peacefully in the morning, and the only sign of the panic of the night before was the mud they had scattered all over themselves as they pelted through a patch of wet ground. The farmer said they were as quiet a lot as any in Meirion; he could make nothing of it.

'Indeed,' he said, 'I believe they must have seen the devil himself to be in such a fright as that: save the people!'

Now all this was kept as quiet as might be at the time when it happened; it became known to the men of the Porth Club in the days when they were discussing the difficult question of the German outrages, as the murders were commonly called. And this wild stampede of the farm horses was held by some to be evidence of the extraordinary and unheard-of character of the dreadful agency that was at work. One of the members of the club had been told by an officer who was in the camp at the time of the panic that the horses that came charging down were in a perfect fury of fright, that he had never seen horses in such a state, and so there was endless speculation as to the nature of the sight or the sound that had driven half a dozen quiet beasts into raging madness.

Then, in the middle of this talk, two or three other incidents, quite as odd and incomprehensible, came to be known, borne on chance trickles of gossip that came into the towns from outland farms, or were carried by cottagers tramping into Porth on market-day with a fowl or two and eggs and garden stuff; scraps and fragments of talk gathered by servants from the country folk and repeated to their mistresses. And in such ways it came out that up at Plas Newydd there had been a terrible business over swarming the bees; they had turned as wild as wasps and much more savage. They had come about the people who were taking the swarms like a cloud. They settled on one man's face so that you could not see the flesh for the bees crawling all over it, and they had stung him so badly that the doctor did not know whether he would get over it, and they had chased a girl who had come out to see the swarming, and settled on her and stung her to death. Then they had gone off to a brake below the farm and got into a hollow tree there, and it was not safe to go near it, for they would come out at you by day or by night.

And much the same thing had happened, it seemed, at three or four farms and cottages where bees were kept. And there were stories, hardly so clear or so credible, of sheep-dogs, mild and trusted beasts, turning as savage as wolves and injuring the farm boys in a horrible manner – in one case it was said with fatal results. It was certainly true that old Mrs Owen's favourite Brahma-Dorking cock had gone mad; she came into Porth one Saturday morning with her face and her neck all bound up and plastered. She had gone out to her bit of a field to feed the poultry the night before, and the bird had flown at her and attacked her most savagely, inflicting some very nasty wounds before she could beat it off.

'There was a stake handy, lucky for me,' she said, 'and I did beat him and beat him till the life was out of him. But what is come to the world, whatever?'

Now Remnant, the man of theories, was also a man of extreme leisure. It was understood that he had succeeded to ample means when he was quite a young man, and after tasting the savours of the law, as it were, for half a dozen terms at the board of the Middle Temple, he had decided that it would be senseless to bother himself with passing examinations for a profession which he had not the faintest intention of practising. So he turned a deaf ear to the call of 'Manger' ringing through the Temple Courts, and set himself out to potter amiably through the world. He had pottered all over Europe, he had looked at Africa, and had even put his head in at the door of the East, on a trip which included the Greek isles and Constantinople. Now, getting into the middle fifties, he had settled at Porth for the sake, as he said, of the Gulf Stream and the fuchsia hedges, and pottered over his books and his theories and the local gossip. He was no more brutal than the general public, which revels in the details of mysterious crime; but it must be said that the terror, black though it was, was a boon to him. He peered and investigated and poked about with the relish of a man to whose life a new zest has been added. He listened attentively to the strange tales of bees and dogs and poultry that came into Porth with the country baskets of butter, rabbits, and green peas; and he evolved at last a most extraordinary theory.

Full of this discovery, as he thought it, he went one night to see Dr Lewis and take his view of the matter.

'I want to talk to you,' said Remnant to the doctor, 'about what I have called, provisionally, the Z Ray.'

V. *The Incident of the Unknown Tree*

Dr Lewis, smiling indulgently, and quite prepared for some monstrous piece of theorizing, led Remnant into the room that overlooked the terraced garden and the sea.

The doctor's house, though it was only a ten minutes' walk from the centre of the town, seemed remote from all other habitations. The drive to it from the road came through a deep grove of trees and a dense shrubbery, trees were about the house on either side, mingling with neighbouring groves, and below, the garden fell down, terrace by green terrace, to wild growth, a twisted path amongst red rocks, and at last to the yellow sand of a little cove. The room to which the doctor took Remnant looked over these terraces and across the water to the dim boundaries of the bay. It had french windows that were thrown wide open, and the two men sat in the soft light of the lamp – this was before the days of severe lighting regulations in the far west – and enjoyed the sweet odours and the sweet vision of the summer evening. Then Remnant began:

'I suppose, Lewis, you've heard these extraordinary stories of bees and dogs and things that have been going about lately?'

'Certainly I have heard them. I was called in at Plas Newydd, and treated Thomas Trevor, who's only just out of danger, by the way. I certified for the poor child, Mary Trevor. She was dying when I got to the place. There was no doubt she was stung to death by bees, and I believe there were other very similar cases at Llantarnam and Morwen; none fatal, I think. What about them?'

'Well: then there are the stories of good-tempered old sheep-dogs turning wicked and "savaging" children?'

'Quite so. I haven't seen any of these cases professionally; but I believe the stories are accurate enough.'

'And the old woman assaulted by her own poultry?'

'That's perfectly true. Her daughter put some stuff of their own concoction on her face and neck, and then she came to me. The wounds seemed going all right, so I told her to continue the treatment, whatever it might be.'

'Very good,' said Mr Remnant. He spoke now with an italic impressiveness. '*Don't you see the link between all this and the horrible things that have been happening about here for the last month?*'

Lewis stared at Remnant in amazement. He lifted his red eyebrows and lowered them in a kind of scowl. His speech showed traces of his native accent.

'Great burning!' he exclaimed. 'What on earth are you getting at now? It is madness. Do you mean to tell me that you think there is some connection between a swarm or two of bees that have turned nasty, a cross dog, and a wicked old barn-door cock and these poor people that have been pitched over the cliffs and hammered to death on the road? There's no sense in it, you know.'

'I am strongly inclined to believe that there is a great deal of sense in it,' replied Remnant with extreme calmness. 'Look here, Lewis, I saw you grinning the other day at the club when I was telling the fellows that in my opinion all these outrages had been committed, certainly by the Germans, but by some method of which we have no conception. But what I meant to say when I talked about inconceivables was just this: that the Williamses and the rest of them have been killed in some way that's not in theory at all, not in our theory, at all events, some way we've not contemplated, not thought of for an instant. Do you see my point?'

'Well, in a sort of way. You mean there's an absolute originality in the method? I suppose that is so. But what next?'

Remnant seemed to hesitate, partly from a sense of the portentous nature of what he was about to say, partly from a sort of half unwillingness to part with so profound a secret.

'Well,' he said, 'you will allow that we have two sets of phenomena of a very extraordinary kind occurring at the same time. Don't you think that it's only reasonable to connect the two sets with one another.'

'So the philosopher of Tenterden steeple and the Goodwin Sands thought, certainly,' said Lewis. 'But what is the connection? Those poor folks on the Highway weren't stung by bees or worried by a dog. And horses don't throw people over cliffs or stifle them in marshes.'

'No; I never meant to suggest anything so absurd. It is evident to me that in all these cases of animals turning suddenly savage the cause has been terror, panic, fear. The horses that went charging into the camp were mad with fright, we know. And I say that in the other instances we have been discussing the cause was the same. The creatures were exposed to an infection of fear, and a frightened beast or bird or insect uses its weapons, whatever they may be. If, for example, there had been anybody with those horses when they took their panic they would have lashed out at him with their heels.'

'Yes, I dare say that that is so. Well.'

'Well; my belief is that the Germans have made an extraordinary discovery. I have called it the Z ray. You know that the ether is merely an hypothesis; we have to suppose that it's there to account for the passage of the Marconi current from one place to another. Now, suppose that there is a psychic ether as well as a material ether, suppose that it is possible to direct irresistible impulses across this medium, suppose that these impulses are towards murder or suicide; then I think that you have an explanation of the terrible series of events that have been happening in Meirion for the last few weeks. And it is quite clear to my mind that the horses and the other creatures have been exposed to this Z ray, and that it has produced on them the effect of terror, with ferocity as the result of terror. Now what do you say to that? Telepathy, you know, is well established; so is hypnotic suggestion. You have only to look in the *Encyclopædia Britannica* to see that, and suggestion is so strong in some cases as to be an irresistible imperative. Now don't you feel that putting telepathy and suggestion together, as it were, you have more than the elements of what I call the Z ray? I feel myself that I have more to go on in making my hypothesis than the inventor of the steam-engine had in making his hypothesis when he saw the lid of the kettle bobbing up and down. What do you say?'

Dr Lewis made no answer. He was watching the growth of a new, unknown tree in his garden.

The doctor made no answer to Remnant's question. For one thing, Remnant was profuse in his eloquence – he has been rigidly condensed in this history – and Lewis was tired of the sound of his voice. For another thing, he found the Z-ray theory almost too extravagant to be bearable, wild enough to tear patience to tatters. And then as the tedious argument continued Lewis became conscious that there was something strange about the night.

It was a dark summer night. The moon was old and faint, above the Dragon's Head across the bay, and the air was very still. It was so still that Lewis had noted that not a leaf stirred on the very tip of a high tree that stood out against the sky; and yet he knew that he was listening to some sound that he could not determine or define. It was not the wind in the leaves, it was not the gentle wash of the water of the sea against the rocks; that latter sound he could distinguish quite easily. But there was something else. It was scarcely a sound; it was as if the air itself trembled and fluttered, as the air trembles in a church when they open the great pedal pipes of the organ.

The doctor listened intently. It was not an illusion, the sound was not in his own head, as he had suspected for a moment; but for the life of him he could not make out whence it came or what it was. He gazed down into the night over the terraces of his garden, now sweet with the scent of the flowers of the night; tried to peer over the tree-tops across the sea towards the Dragon's Head. It struck him suddenly that this strange fluttering vibration of the air might be the noise of a distant aeroplane or airship; there was not the usual droning hum, but this sound might be caused by a new type of engine. A new type of engine? Possibly it was an enemy airship; their range, it had been said, was getting longer; and Lewis was just going to call Remnant's attention to the sound, to its possible cause, and to the possible danger that might be hovering over them, when he saw something that caught his breath and his heart with wild amazement and a touch of terror.

He had been staring upward into the sky, and, about to speak to Remnant, he had let his eyes drop for an instant. He looked down towards the trees in the garden, and saw with utter astonishment that one had changed its shape in the few hours that had passed since the setting of the sun. There was a thick grove of ilexes bordering the lowest terrace, and above them rose one tall pine, spreading its head of sparse, dark branches dark against the sky.

As Lewis glanced down over the terraces he saw that the tall pine tree was no longer there. In its place there rose above the ilexes what might have been a greater ilex; there was the blackness of a dense growth of foliage rising like a broad and far-spreading and rounded cloud over the lesser trees.

Here, then, was a sight wholly incredible, impossible. It is doubtful whether the process of the human mind in such a case has ever been analysed and registered; it is doubtful whether it ever can be registered. It is hardly fair to bring in the mathematician, since he deals with absolute truth (so far as mortality can conceive absolute truth); but how would a mathematician feel if he were suddenly confronted with a two-sided triangle? I suppose he would instantly become a raging madman; and Lewis, staring wide-eyed and wild-eyed at a dark and spreading tree which his own experience informed him was not there, felt for an instant that shock which should affront us all when we first realize the intolerable antinomy of Achilles and the tortoise. Common sense tells us that Achilles will flash past the tortoise almost with the speed of the lightning;

the inflexible truth of mathematics assures us that till the earth boils and the heavens cease to endure, the tortoise must still be in advance; and thereupon we should, in common decency, go mad. We do not go mad, because, by special grace, we are certified that, in the final court of appeal, all science is a lie, even the highest science of all; and so we simply grin at Achilles and the tortoise, as we grin at Darwin, deride Huxley, and laugh at Herbert Spencer.

Dr Lewis did not grin. He glared into the dimness of the night, at the great spreading tree that he knew could not be there. And as he gazed he saw that what at first appeared the dense blackness of foliage was fretted and starred with wonderful appearances of lights and colours.

Afterwards he said to me: 'I remember thinking to myself: "Look here, I am not delirious; my temperature is perfectly normal. I am not drunk; I only had a pint of Graves with my dinner, over three hours ago. I have not eaten any poisonous fungus; I have not taken *Anhelonium Lewinii* experimentally. So, now then! What is happening?" '

The night had gloomed over; clouds obscured the faint moon and the misty stars. Lewis rose, with some kind of warning and inhibiting gesture to Remnant, who, he was conscious was gaping at him in astonishment. He walked to the open french window, and took a pace forward on to the path outside, and looked, very intently, at the dark shape of the tree, down below the sloping garden, above the washing of the waves. He shaded the light of the lamp behind him by holding his hands on each side of his eyes.

The mass of the tree – the tree that couldn't be there – stood out against the sky, but not so clearly, now that the clouds had rolled up. Its edges, the limits of its leafage, were not so distinct. Lewis thought that he could detect some sort of quivering movement in it; though the air was at a dead calm. It was a night on which one might hold up a lighted match and watch it burn without any wavering or inclination of the flame.

'You know,' said Lewis, 'how a bit of burnt paper will sometimes hang over the coals before it goes up the chimney, and little worms of fire will shoot through it. It was like that, if you should be standing some distance away. Just threads and hairs of yellow light I saw, and specks and sparks of fire, and then a twinkling of a ruby no bigger than a pin point, and a green wandering in the black, as if an emerald were crawling, and then little veins of deep blue. "Woe is me!" I said to myself in Welsh, "What is all this colour and burning?"

'And, then, at that very moment there came a thundering rap at the door of the room inside, and there was my man telling me that I was wanted directly up at the Garth, as old Mr Trevor Williams had been taken very bad. I knew his heart was not worth much, so I had to go off directly and leave Remnant to make what he could of it all.'

VI. *Mr Remnant's Z Ray*

Dr Lewis was kept some time at the Garth. It was past twelve when he got back to his house. He went quickly to the room that overlooked the garden and the sea and threw open the french window and peered into the darkness. There, dim indeed against the dim sky but unmistakable, was the tall pine with its sparse branches, high above the dense growth of the ilex-trees. The strange boughs which had amazed him had vanished; there was no appearance now of colours or of fires.

He drew his chair up to the open window and sat there gazing and wondering far into the night, till brightness came upon the sea and sky, and the forms of the trees in the garden grew clear and evident. He went up to his bed at last filled with a great perplexity, still asking questions to which there was no answer.

The doctor did not say anything about the strange tree to Remnant. When they next met, Lewis said that he had thought there was a man hiding amongst the bushes – this in explanation of that warning gesture he had used, and of his going out into the garden and staring into the night. He concealed the truth because he dreaded the Remnant doctrine that would undoubtedly be produced; indeed, he hoped that he had heard the last of the theory of the Z ray. But Remnant firmly reopened this subject.

'We were interrupted just as I was putting my case to you,' he said. 'And to sum it all up, it amounts to this: that the Huns have made one of the great leaps of science. They are sending "suggestions" (which amount to irresistible commands) over here, and the persons affected are seized with suicidal or homicidal mania. The people who were killed by falling over the cliffs or into the quarry probably committed suicide; and so with the man and boy who were found in the bog. As to the Highway case, you remember that Thomas Evans said that he stopped ¬nd talked to Williams on the night of the murder. In my opinion Evans was the murderer. He came under the influence of the ray, became a homicidal maniac in an instant, snatched Williams's spade from his hand and killed him and the others.'

'The bodies were found by me on the road.'

'It is possible that the first impact of the ray produces violent nervous excitement, which would manifest itself externally. Williams might have called to his wife to come and see what was the matter with Evans. The children would naturally follow their mother. It seems to me simple. And as for the animals—the horses, dogs, and so forth, they as I say, were no doubt panic-stricken by the ray, and hence driven to frenzy.'

'Why should Evans have murdered Williams instead of Williams murdering Evans? Why should the impact of the ray affect one and not the other?'

'Why does one man react violently to a certain drug, while it makes no impression on another man? Why is A able to drink a bottle of whisky and remain sober, while B is turned into something very like a lunatic after he has drunk three glasses?'

'It is a question of idiosyncrasy,' said the doctor.

'Is "idiosyncrasy" Greek for "I don't know"?' asked Remnant.

'Not at all,' said Lewis, smiling blandly. 'I mean that in some diatheses whisky – as you have mentioned whisky – appears not to be pathogenic, or at all events not immediately pathogenic. In other cases, as you very justly observed, there seems to be a very marked cachexia associated with the exhibition of the spirit in question, even in comparatively small doses.'

Under this cloud of professional verbiage Lewis escaped from the club and from Remnant. He did not want to hear any more about that dreadful ray, because he felt sure that the ray was all nonsense. But asking himself why he felt this certitude in the matter, he had to confess that he didn't know. An aeroplane, he reflected, was all nonsense before it was made; and he remembered talking in the early nineties to a friend of his about the newly discovered X rays. The friend laughed incredulously, evidently didn't believe a word of it, till Lewis told him that there was an article on the subject in the current number of the *Saturday Review*; whereupon the unbeliever said, 'Oh, is that so? Oh, really. I *see*,' and was converted to the X ray faith on the spot. Lewis, remembering this talk, marvelled at the strange processes of the human mind, its illogical and yet all-compelling *ergos*, and wondered whether he himself was only waiting for an article on the Z ray in the *Saturday Review* to become a devout believer in the doctrine of Remnant.

But he wondered with far more fervour as to the extraordinary thing he had seen in his own garden with his own eyes. The tree that changed all its shape for an hour or two of the night, the growth of strange boughs, the apparition of secret fires among them, the sparkling of emerald and ruby lights: how could one fail to be afraid with great amazement at the thought of such a mystery?

Dr Lewis's thoughts were distracted from the incredible adventure of the tree by the visit of his sister and her husband. Mr and Mrs Merritt lived in a well-known manufacturing town of the Midlands, which was now, of course, a centre of munition work. On the day of their arrival at Porth, Mrs Merritt, who was tired after the long, hot journey, went to bed early, and Merritt and Lewis went into the room by the garden for their talk and tobacco. They spoke of the year that had passed since their last meeting, of the weary dragging of the war, of friends that had perished in it, of the hopelessness of an early ending of all this misery. Lewis said nothing of the terror that was on the land. One does not greet a tired man who is come to a quiet, sunny place for relief from black smoke and work and worry with a tale of horror. Indeed, the doctor saw that his brother-in-law looked far from well. And he seemed 'jumpy'; there was an occasional twitch of his mouth that Lewis did not like at all.

'Well,' said the doctor, after an interval of silence and port wine, 'I am glad to see you here again. Porth always suits you. I don't think you're looking quite up to your usual form. But three weeks of Meirion air will do wonders.'

'Well, I hope it will,' said the other. 'I am not up to the mark. Things are not going well at Midlingham.'

'Business is all right, isn't it?'

'Yes. Business is all right. But there are other things that are all wrong. We are living under a reign of terror. It comes to that.'

'What on earth do you mean?'

'Well, I suppose I may tell you what I know. It's not much. I didn't dare write it. But do you know that at every one of the munition works in Midlingham and all about it there's a guard of soldiers with drawn bayonets and loaded rifles day and night? Men with bombs, too. And machine-guns at the big factories.'

'German spies?'

'You don't want Lewis guns to fight spies with. Nor bombs. Nor a platoon of men. I woke up last night. It was the machine-gun at Benington's Army Motor Works. Firing like fury. And then bang! bang! bang! That was the hand bombs.'

'But what against?'

'Nobody knows.'

'Nobody knows what is happening,' Merritt repeated, and he went on to describe the bewilderment and terror that hung like a cloud over the great industrial city in the Midlands, how the feeling of concealment, of some intolerable secret danger that must not be named, was worst of all.

'A young fellow I know,' he said, 'was on short leave the other day from the front, and he spent it with his people at Belmont – that's about four miles out of Midlingham, you know. "Thank God," he said to me, "I am going back tomorrow. It's no good saying that the Wipers salient is nice, because it isn't. But it's a damned sight better than this. At the front you know what you're up against anyhow." At Midlingham everybody has the feeling that we're up against something awful and we don't know what; it's that that makes people inclined to whisper. There's terror in the air.'

Merritt made a sort of picture of the great town cowering in its fear of an unknown danger.

'People are afraid to go about alone at nights in the outskirts. They make up parties at the stations to go home together if it's anything like dark, or if there are any lonely bits on their way.'

'But why? I don't understand. What are they afraid of?'

'Well, I told you about my being awakened up the other night with the machine-guns at the motor works rattling away, and the bombs exploding and making the most terrible noise. That sort of thing alarms one, you know. It's only natural.'

'Indeed, it must be very terrifying. You mean, then, there is a general nervousness about, a vague sort of apprehension that makes people inclined to herd together?'

'There's that, and there's more. People have gone out that have never come back. There were a couple of men in the train to Holme, arguing about the quickest way to get to Northend, a sort of outlying part of Holme where they both lived. They argued all the way out of Midlingham, one saying that the high road was the quickest though it was the longest way. "It's the quickest going because it's the cleanest going," he said.

'The other chap fancied a short cut across the fields, by the canal. "It's half the distance," he kept on. "Yes, if you don't lose your way," said the other. Well, it appears they put an even halfcrown on it, and each was to try his own way when they got out of the train. It was arranged that they were to meet at the Wagon in Northend. "I shall be at the Wagon first," said the man who believed in the short cut, and with that he climbed over the stile and made off across the fields. It wasn't late enough to be really dark, and a lot of them thought he might win the stakes. But he never turned up at the Wagon – or anywhere else for the matter of that.'

'What happened to him?'

'He was found lying on his back in the middle of a field – some way from the path. He was dead. The doctors said he'd been suffocated. Nobody knows how. Then there have been other cases. We whisper about them at Midlingham, but we're afraid to speak out.'

Lewis was ruminating all this profoundly. Terror in Meirion and terror far away in the heart of England; but at Midlingham, so far as he could gather from these stories of soldiers on guard, of crackling machine-guns, it was a case of an organized attack on the munitioning of the army. He felt that he did not know enough to warrant his deciding that the terror of Meirion and of Stratfordshire were one.

Then Merritt began again:

'There's a queer story going about, when the door's shut and the curtain's drawn, that is, as to a place right out in the country over the other side of Midlingham; on the opposite side to Dunwich. They've built one of the new factories out there, a great red-brick town of sheds they tell me it is, with a tremendous chimney. It's not been finished more than a month or six weeks. They plumped it down right in the middle of the fields, by the line, and they're building huts for the workers as fast as they can but up to the present the men are billeted all about, up and down the line.

'About two hundred yards from this place there's an old footpath, leading from the station and the main road up to a small hamlet on the hill-side. Part of the way this path goes by a pretty large wood, most of it thick undergrowth. I should think there must be twenty acres of wood, more or less. As it happens, I used this path once long ago; and I can tell you it's a black place of nights.

'A man had to go this way one night. He got along all right till he came to the wood. And then he said his heart dropped out of his body. It was awful to hear the noises in that wood. Thousands of men were in it, he swears that. It was full of rustling, and pattering of feet trying to go dainty, and the crack of dead boughs lying on the ground as some one trod on them, and swishing of the grass, and some sort of chattering speech going on, that sounded, so he said, as if the dead sat in their bones and talked! He ran for his life, anyhow; across fields, over hedges, through brooks. He must have run, by his tale, ten miles out of his way before he got home to his wife, and beat at the door, and broke in, and bolted it behind him.'

'There is something rather alarming about any wood at night,' said Dr Lewis.

Merritt shrugged his shoulders.

'People say that the Germans have landed, and that they are hiding in underground places all over the country.'

VII. *The Case of the Hidden Germans*

Lewis gasped for a moment, silent in contemplation of the magnificence of rumour. The Germans already landed, hiding underground, striking by night, secretly, terribly, at the power of England! Here was a conception which made the myth of the Russians a paltry fable; before which the legend of Mons was an ineffectual thing.

It was monstrous. And yet –

He looked steadily at Merritt; a square-headed, black-haired, solid sort of man. He had symptoms of nerves about him for the moment, certainly, but one could not wonder at that, whether the tales he told were true, or whether he merely believed them to be true. Lewis had known his brother-in-law for twenty years or more, and had always found him a sure man in his own small world. 'But then,' said the doctor to himself, 'those men, if they once get out of the ring of that little world of theirs, they are lost. Those are the men that believed in Madame Blavatsky.'

'Well,' he said, 'what do you think yourself? The Germans landed and hiding somewhere about the country: there's something extravagant in the notion, isn't there?'

'I don't know what to think. You can't get over the facts. There are the soldiers with their rifles and their guns at the works all over Stratford-shire, and those guns go off. I told you I'd heard them. Then who are the soldiers shooting at? That's what we ask ourselves at Midlingham.'

'Quite so; I quite understand. It's an extraordinary state of things.'

'It's more than extraordinary; it's an awful state of things. It's terror in the dark, and there's nothing worse than that. As that young fellow I was telling you about said, "At the front you do know what you're up against." '

'And people really believe that a number of Germans have somehow got over to England and have hid themselves underground?'

'People say they've got a new kind of poison gas. Some think that they dig underground places and make the gas there, and lead it by secret pipes into the shops; others say that they throw gas bombs into the factories. It must be worse than anything they've used in France, from what the authorities say.'

'The authorities? Do *they* admit that there are Germans in hiding about Midlingham?'

'No. They call it "explosions". But we know it isn't explosions. We know in the Midlands what an explosion sounds like and looks like. And we know that the people killed in these "explosions" are put into their coffins in the works. Their own relations are not allowed to see them.'

'And so you believe in the German theory?'

'If I do, it's because one must believe in something. Some say they've seen the gas. I heard that a man living in Dunwich saw it one night like a black cloud with sparks of fire in it floating over the tops of the trees by Dunwich Common.'

The light of an ineffable amazement came into Lewis's eyes. The night of Remnant's visit, the trembling vibration of the air, the dark tree that had grown in his garden since the setting of the sun, the strange leafage that was starred with burning, with emerald and ruby fires, and all vanished away when he returned from his visit to the Garth; and such a leafage had appeared as a burning cloud far in the heart of England: what intolerable mystery, what tremendous doom was signified in this? But one thing was clear and certain: that the terror of Meirion was also the terror of the Midlands.

Lewis made up his mind most firmly that if possible all this should be kept from his brother-in-law. Merritt had come to Porth as to a city of refuge from the horrors of Midlingham; if it could be managed he should be spared the knowledge that the cloud of terror had gone before him and hung black over the western land. Lewis passed the port and said in an even voice:

'Very strange, indeed; a black cloud with sparks of fire?'

'I can't answer for it, you know; it's only a rumour.'

'Just so; and you think, or you're inclined to think, that this and all the rest you've told me is to be put down to the hidden Germans?'

'As I say; because one must think something.'

'I quite see your point. No doubt, if it's true, it's the most awful blow that has ever been dealt at any nation in the whole history of man. The enemy established in our vitals! But is it possible, after all? How could it have been worked?'

Merritt told Lewis how it had been worked, or rather, how people said it had been worked. The idea, he said, was that this was a part, and a most important part, of the great German plot to destroy England and the British Empire.

The scheme had been prepared years ago, some thought soon after the Franco–Prussian War. Moltke had seen that the invasion of England (in the ordinary sense of the term 'invasion') presented very great difficulties. The matter was constantly in discussion in the inner military and high political circles, and the general trend of opinion in these quarters was that at the best, the invasion of England would involve Germany in the gravest difficulties, and leave France in the position of the *tertius gaudens*. This was the state of affairs when a very high Prussian personage was approached by the Swedish professor, Huvelius.

Thus Merritt, and here I would say in parenthesis that this Huvelius was by all accounts an extraordinary man. Considered personally and apart from his writings he would appear to have been a most amiable individual. He was richer than the generality of Swedes, certainly far richer than the average university professor in Sweden. But his shabby, green frock-coat, and his battered, furry hat were notorious in the university town where he lived. No one laughed, because it was well known that Professor Huvelius spent every penny of his private means and a large portion of his official stipend on works of kindness and charity. He hid his head in a garret, some one said, in order that others might be able to swell on the first floor. It was told of him that he restricted himself to a diet of dry bread and coffee for a month in order that a poor woman of the streets, dying of consumption, might enjoy luxuries in hospital.

And this was the man who wrote the treatise *De Facinore Humano*; to prove the infinite corruption of the human race.

Oddly enough, Professor Huvelius wrote the most cynical book in the world – Hobbes preaches rosy sentimentalism in comparison – with the very highest motives. He held that a very large part of human misery, misadventure, and sorrow was due to the false convention that the heart of man was naturally and in the main well disposed and kindly, if not exactly righteous. 'Murderers, thieves, assassins, violators, and all the host of the abominable,' he says in one passage, 'are created by the false pretence and foolish credence of human virtue. A lion in a cage is a fierce beast, indeed; but what will he be if we declare him to be a lamb and open the doors of his den? Who will be guilty of the deaths of the men, women and children whom he will surely devour, save those who unlocked the cage?' And he goes on to show that kings and the rulers of the peoples could decrease the sum of human misery to a vast extent by acting on the doctrine of human wickedness. 'War,' he declares, 'which is one of the worst of evils, will always continue to exist. But a wise king will desire a brief war rather than a lengthy one, a short evil rather than a long evil. And this not from the benignity of his heart towards his enemies, for we have seen that the human heart is naturally malignant, but because he desires to conquer, and to conquer easily, without a great expenditure of men or of treasure, knowing that if he can accomplish this feat his people will love him and his crown will be secure. So he will wage brief victorious wars, and not only spare his own nation, but the nation of the enemy, since in a short war the loss is less on both sides than in a long war. And so from evil will come good.'

And how, asks Huvelius, are such wars to be waged? The wise prince, he replies, will begin by assuming the enemy to be infinitely corruptible and infinitely stupid, since stupidity and corruption are the chief characteristics of man. So the prince will make himself friends in the very councils of his enemy, and also amongst the populace, bribing the wealthy by proffering to them the opportunity of still greater wealth, and winning the poor by swelling words. 'For, contrary to the common opinion, it is the wealthy who are greedy of wealth; while the populace are to be gained by talking to them about liberty, their unknown god. And so much are they enchanted by the words liberty, freedom, and such like, that the wise can go to the poor, rob them of what little they have, dismiss them with a hearty kick, and win their hearts and their votes for ever, if only they will assure them that the treatment which they have received is called liberty.'

Guided by these principles, says Huvelius, the wise prince will entrench himself in the country that he desires to conquer; 'nay, with but little trouble, he may actually and literally throw his garrisons into the heart of the enemy country before war has begun.'

This is a long and tiresome parenthesis; but it is necessary as explaining the long tale which Merritt told his brother-in-law, he having received it from some magnate of the Midlands, who had travelled in Germany. It is probable that the story was suggested in the first place by the passage from Huvelius which I have just quoted.

Merritt knew nothing of the real Huvelius, who was all but a saint; he thought of the Swedish professor as a monster of iniquity, 'worse', as he said, 'than Neech' – meaning, no doubt, Nietzsche.

So he told the story of how Huvelius had sold his plan to the Germans; a plan for filling England with German soldiers. Land was to be bought in certain suitable and well-considered places, Englishmen were to be bought as the apparent owners of such land, and secret excavations were to be made, till the country was literally undermined. A subterranean Germany, in fact, was to be dug under selected districts of England; there were to be great caverns, underground cities, well drained, well ventilated, supplied with water, and in these places vast stores both of food and of munitions were to be accumulated, year after year, till 'the day' dawned. And then, warned in time, the secret garrison would leave shops, hotels, offices, villas, and vanish underground, ready to begin their work of bleeding England at the heart.

'That's what Henson told me,' said Merritt at the end of his long story. 'Henson, head of the Buckley Iron and Steel Syndicate. He has been a lot in Germany.'

'Well,' said Lewis, 'of course, it may be so. If it is so, it is terrible beyond words.'

Indeed, he found something horribly plausible in the story. It was an extraordinary plan, of course; an unheard-of scheme; but it did not seem impossible. It was the Trojan horse on a gigantic scale; indeed, he reflected, the story of the horse with the warriors concealed within it which was dragged into the heart of Troy by the deluded Trojans themselves might be taken as a prophetic parable of what had happened to England – if Henson's theory were well founded. And this theory certainly squared with what one had heard of German preparations in Belgium and in France: emplacements for guns ready for the invader, German manufactories which were really German forts on Belgian soil, the caverns by the Aisne made ready for the cannon; indeed, Lewis thought he remembered something about suspicious concrete tennis-courts on the heights commanding London. But a German army hidden under English ground! It was a thought to chill the stoutest heart.

And it seemed from that wonder of the burning tree, that the enemy mysteriously and terribly present at Midlingham, was present also in Meirion. Lewis, thinking of the country as he knew it, of its wild and desolate hillsides, its deep woods, its wastes and solitary places, could not

but confess that no more fit region could be found for the deadly enterprise of secret men. Yet, he thought again, there was but little harm to be
done in Meirion to the armies of England or to their munitionment.
They were working for panic terror? Possibly that might be so; but the
camp under the Highway? That should be their first object, and no
harm had been done there.

Lewis did not know that since the panic of the horses men had died
terribly in that camp; that it was now a fortified place, with a deep,
broad trench, a thick tangle of savage barbed wire about it, and a
machine-gun planted at each corner.

VIII. *What Mr Merritt Found*

Mr Merritt began to pick up his health and spirits a good deal. For the
first morning or two of his stay at the doctor's he contented himself with
a very comfortable deck chair close to the house, where he sat under the
shade of an old mulberry-tree beside his wife and watched the bright
sunshine on the green lawns, on the creamy crests of the waves, on the
headlands of that glorious coast, purple even from afar with the imperial
glow of the heather, on the white farmhouses gleaming in the sunlight,
high over the sea, far from any turmoil, from any troubling of men.

The sun was hot, but the wind breathed all the while gently, incessantly, from the east, and Merritt, who had come to this quiet place, not
only from dismay, but from the stifling and oily airs of the smoky Midland town, said that that east wind, pure and clear and like well-water
from the rock, was new life to him. He ate a capital dinner at the end of
his first day at Porth and took rosy views. As to what they had been
talking about the night before, he said to Lewis, no doubt there must be
trouble of some sort, and perhaps bad trouble; still, Kitchener would
soon put it all right.

So things went on very well. Merritt began to stroll about the garden,
which was full of the comfortable spaces, groves, and surprises that only
country gardens know. To the right of one of the terraces he found an
arbor or summer-house covered with white roses, and he was as pleased
as if he had discovered the pole. He spent a whole day there, smoking
and lounging and reading a rubbishy sensational story, and declared that
the Devonshire roses had taken many years off his age. Then on the other
side of the garden there was a filbert grove that he had never explored
on any of his former visits; and again there was a find. Deep in the shadow
of the filberts was a bubbling well, issuing from rocks, and all manner of
green, dewy ferns growing about it and above it, and an angelica spring-
ing beside it. Merritt knelt on his knees, and hollowed his hand and
drank the well-water. He said (over his port) that night that if all water
were like the water of the filbert well the world would turn to teetotal-

ism. It takes a townsman to relish the manifold and exquisite joys of the country.

It was not till he began to venture abroad that Merritt found that something was lacking of the old rich peace that used to dwell in Meirion. He had a favourite walk which he never neglected, year after year. This walk led along the cliffs towards Meiros, and then one could turn inland and return to Porth by deep winding lanes that went over the Allt. So Merritt set out early one morning and got as far as a sentry-box at the foot of the path that led up to the cliff. There was a sentry pacing up and down in front of the box, and he called on Merritt to produce his pass, or to turn back to the main road. Merritt was a good deal put out, and asked the doctor about this strict guard. And the doctor was surprised.

'I didn't know they had put their bar up there,' he said. 'I suppose it's wise. We are certainly in the far west here; still, the Germans might slip round and raid us and do a lot of damage just because Meirion is the last place we should expect them to go for.'

'But there are no fortifications, surely, on the cliff?'

'Oh, no; I never heard of anything of the kind there.'

'Well, what's the point of forbidding the public to go on the cliff, then? I can quite understand putting a sentry on the top to keep a look-out for the enemy. What I don't understand is a sentry at the bottom who can't keep a look-out for anything, as he can't see the sea. And why warn the public off the cliffs? I couldn't facilitate a German landing by standing on Pengareg, even if I wanted to.'

'It is curious,' the doctor agreed. 'Some military reasons, I suppose.'

He let the matter drop, perhaps because the matter did not affect him. People who live in the country all the year round, country doctors certainly, are little given to desultory walking in search of the picturesque.

Lewis had no suspicion that sentries whose object was equally obscure were being dotted all over the country. There was a sentry, for example, by the quarry at Llanfihangel, where the dead woman and the dead sheep had been found some weeks before. The path by the quarry was used a good deal, and its closing would have inconvenienced the people of the neighbourhood very considerably. But the sentry had his box by the side of the track and had his orders to keep everybody strictly to the path, as if the quarry were a secret fort.

It was not known till a month or two ago that one of these sentries was himself a victim of the terror. The men on duty at this place were given certain very strict orders, which from the nature of the case, must have seemed to them unreasonable. For old soldiers, orders are orders; but here was a young bank clerk, scarcely in training for a couple of months, who had not begun to appreciate the necessity of hard, literal obedience to an order which seemed to him meaningless. He found himself on a remote and lonely hill-side, he had not the faintest notion that his every movement was watched; and he disobeyed a certain instruction that had been given him. The post was found deserted by the relief; the sentry's dead body was found at the bottom of the quarry.

This by the way; but Mr Merritt discovered again and again that things happened to hamper his walks and his wanderings. Two or three miles from Porth there is a great marsh made by the Afon River before it falls into the sea, and here Merritt had been accustomed to botanize mildly. He had learned pretty accurately the causeways of solid ground that lead through the sea of swamp and ooze and soft yielding soil, and he set out one hot afternoon determined to make a thorough exploration of the marsh, and this time to find that rare bog bean, that he felt sure, must grow somewhere in its wide extent.

He got into the by-road that skirts the marsh, and to the gate which he had always used for entrance.

There was the scene as he had known it always, the rich growth of reeds and flags and rushes, the mild black cattle grazing on the 'islands' of firm turf, the scented procession of the meadow-sweet, the royal glory of the loosestrife, flaming pennons, crimson and golden, of the giant dock.

But they were bringing out a dead man's body through the gate.

A labouring man was holding open the gate on the marsh. Merritt, horrified spoke to him and asked who it was, and how it had happened.

'They do say he was a visitor at Porth. Somehow he has been drowned in the marsh, whatever.'

'But it's perfectly safe. I've been all over it a dozen times.'

'Well, indeed, we did always think so. If you did slip by accident, like, and fall into the water, it was not so deep; it was easy enough to climb out again. And this gentleman was quite young, to look at him, poor man; and he has come to Meirion for his pleasure and holiday and found his death in it!'

'Did he do it on purpose? Is it suicide?'

'They say he had no reasons to do that.'

Here the sergeant of police in charge of the party interposed, according to orders, which he himself did not understand.

'A terrible thing, sir, to be sure, and a sad pity; and I am sure this is not the sort of sight you have come to see down in Meirion this beautiful summer. So don't you think, sir, that it would be more pleasantlike, if you would leave us to this sad business of ours? I have heard many gentlemen staying in Porth say that there is nothing to beat the view from the hill over there, not in the whole of Wales.'

Every one is polite in Meirion, but somehow Merritt understood that, in English, this speech meant 'move on'.

Merritt moved back to Porth – he was not in the humour for any idle, pleasurable strolling after so dreadful a meeting with death. He made some inquiries in the town about the dead man, but nothing seemed known of him. It was said that he had been on his honeymoon, that he had been staying at the Porth Castle Hotel; but the people of the hotel declared that they had never heard of such a person. Merritt got the local paper at the end of the week; there was not a word in it of any fatal accident in the marsh. He met the sergeant of police in the street. That officer touched his helmet with the utmost politeness and a 'hope you are enjoying yourself, sir; indeed you do look a lot better already'; but as to the poor man who was found drowned or stifled in the marsh, he knew nothing.

The next day Merritt made up his mind to go to the marsh to see whether he could find anything to account for so strange a death. What he found was a man with an armlet standing by the gate. The armlet had the letters 'C. W.' on it, which are understood to mean 'Coast Watcher'. The watcher said he had strict instructions to keep everybody away from the marsh. Why? He didn't know, but some said that the river was changing its course since the new railway embankment was built, and the marsh had become dangerous to people who didn't know it thoroughly.

'Indeed, sir,' he added, 'it is part of my orders not to set foot on the other side of that gate myself, not for one scrag-end of a minute.'

Merritt glanced over the gate incredulously. The marsh looked as it had always looked; there was plenty of sound, hard ground to walk on; he could see the track that he used to follow as firm as ever. He did not believe in the story of the changing course of the river, and Lewis said he had never heard of anything of the kind. But Merritt had put the question in the middle of general conversation; he had not led up to it from any discussion of the death in the marsh, and so the doctor was taken unawares. If he had known of the connection in Merritt's mind between the alleged changing of the Afon's course and the tragical event in the marsh, no doubt he would have confirmed the official explanation. He was, above all things, anxious to prevent his sister and her husband from finding out that the invisible hand of terror that ruled at Midlingham was ruling also in Meirion.

Lewis himself had little doubt that the man who was found dead in the marsh had been struck down by the secret agency, whatever it was, that had already accomplished so much of evil; but it was a chief part of the terror that no one knew for certain that this or that particular event was to be ascribed to it. People do occasionally fall over cliffs through their own carelessness, and as the case of Garcia, the Spanish sailor, showed, cottagers and their wives and children are now and then the victims of savage and purposeless violence. Lewis had never wandered about the marsh himself; but Remnant had pottered round it and about it, and declared that the man who met his death there – his name was never known, in Porth at all events – must either have committed suicide by deliberately lying prone in the ooze and stifling himself, or else must have been held down in it. There were no details available, so it was clear that the authorities had classified this death with the others; still, the man might have committed suicide, or he might have had a sudden seizure and fallen in the slimy water face downwards. And so on: it was possible to believe that case A *or* B *or* C was in the category of ordinary accidents or ordinary crimes. But it was not possible to believe that A *and* B *and* C were all in that category. And thus it was to the end, and thus it is now. We know that the terror reigned, and how it reigned, but there were many dreadful events ascribed to its rule about which there must always be room for doubt.

For example, there was the case of the *Mary Ann*, the rowing-boat which came to grief in so strange a manner, almost under Merritt's eyes. In my opinion he was quite wrong in associating the sorry fate of the boat and her occupants with a system of signalling by flash-lights which he detected, or thought that he detected, on the afternoon in which the *Mary Ann* was capsized. I believe his signalling theory to be all nonsense, in spite of the naturalized German governess who was lodging with her employers in the suspected house. But, on the other hand, there is no doubt in my own mind that the boat was overturned and those in it drowned by the work of the terror.

IX. *The Light on the Water*

Let it be noted carefully that so far Merritt had not the slightest suspicion that the terror of Midlingham was quick over Meirion. Lewis had watched and shepherded him carefully. He had let out no suspicion of what had happened in Meirion, and before taking his brother-in-law to the club he had passed round a hint among the members. He did not tell the truth about Midlingham – and here again is a point of interest, that as the terror deepened the general public co-operated voluntarily, and, one would say, almost subconsciously, with the authorities in concealing what they knew from one another – but he gave out a desirable portion of the truth: that his brother-in-law was 'nervy', not by any means up to the mark, and that it was therefore desirable that he should be spared the knowledge of the intolerable and tragic mysteries which were being enacted all about them.

'He knows about that poor fellow who was found in the marsh,' said Lewis, 'and he has a kind of vague suspicion that there is something out of the common about the case; but no more than that.'

'A clear case of suggested, or rather commanded suicide,' said Remnant. 'I regard it as a strong confirmation of my theory.'

'Perhaps so,' said the doctor, dreading lest he might have to hear about the Z ray all over again. 'But please don't let anything out to him; I want him to get built up thoroughly before he goes back to Midlingham.'

Then, on the other hand, Merritt was as still as death about the doings of the Midlands; he hated to think of them, much more to speak of them and thus, as I say, he and the men at the Porth Club kept their secrets from one another; and thus, from the beginning to the end of the terror, the links were not drawn together. In many cases, no doubt, A and B met every day and talked familiarly, it may be confidentially, on other matters of all sorts, each having in his possession half of the truth, which he concealed from the other. So the two halves were never put together to make a whole.

Merritt, as the doctor guessed had a kind of uneasy feeling – it scarcely amounted to a suspicion – as to the business of the marsh; chiefly because he thought the official talk about the railway embankment and the course of the river rank nonsense. But finding that nothing more happened, he let the matter drop from his mind, and settled himself down to enjoy his holiday.

He found to his delight that there were no sentries or watchers to hinder him from the approach to Larnac Bay, a delicious cove, a place where the ash-grove and the green meadow and the glistening bracken sloped gently down to red rocks and firm yellow sands. Merritt remembered a rock that formed a comfortable seat, and here he established himself of a golden afternoon, and gazed at the blue of the sea and the crimson bastions and bays of the coast as it bent inward to Sarnau and swept out again southward to the odd-shaped promontory called the Dragon's Head. Merritt gazed on, amused by the antics of the porpoises who were tumbling and splashing and gambolling a little way out at sea, charmed by the pure and radiant air that was so different from the oily smoke that often stood for heaven at Midlingham, and charmed, too, by the white farmhouses dotted here and there on the heights of the curving coast.

Then he noticed a little row-boat at about two hundred yards from the shore. There were two or three people aboard, he could not quite make out how many, and they seemed to be doing something with a line; they were no doubt fishing, and Merritt (who disliked fish) wondered how people could spoil such an afternoon, such a sea, such pellucid and radiant air by trying to catch white, flabby, offensive, evil-smelling creatures that would be excessively nasty when cooked. He puzzled over this problem and turned away from it to the contemplation of the crimson headlands. And then he says that he noticed that signalling was going on. Flashing lights of intense brilliance, he declares, were coming from one of those farms on the heights of the coast; it was as if white fire was spouting from it. Merritt was certain, as the light appeared and disappeared, that some message was being sent, and he regretted that he knew nothing of heliography. Three short flashes, a long and very brilliant flash, then two short flashes. Merritt fumbled in his pocket for pencil and paper so that he might record these signals, and, bringing his eyes down to the sea level, he became aware, with amazement and horror, that the boat had disappeared. All that he could see was some vague, dark object far to westward, running out with the tide.

Now it is certain, unfortunately, that the *Mary Ann* was capsized and that two school-boys and the sailor in charge were drowned. The bones of the boat were found amongst the rocks far along the coast, and the three bodies were also washed ashore. The sailor could not swim at all, the boys only a little, and it needs an exceptionally fine swimmer to fight against the outward suck of the tide as it rushes past Pengareg Point.

But I have no belief whatever in Merritt's theory. He held (and still holds, for all I know), that the flashes of light which he saw coming from Penyrhaul, the farmhouse on the height, had some connection with the disaster to the *Mary Ann*. When it was ascertained that a family were spending their summer at the farm, and that the governess was a German, though a long-naturalized German, Merritt could not see that there was anything left to argue about, though there might be many details to discover. But, in my opinion, all this was a mere mare's nest; the flashes of brilliant light were caused, no doubt, by the sun lighting up one window of the farmhouse after the other.

Still, Merritt was convinced from the very first, even before the damning circumstance of the German governess was brought to light; and on the evening of the disaster, as Lewis and he sat together after dinner, he was endeavouring to put what he called the common sense of the matter to the doctor.

'If you hear a shot,' said Merritt, 'and you see a man fall, you know pretty well what killed him.'

There was a flutter of wild wings in the room. A great moth beat to and fro and dashed itself madly against the ceiling, the walls, the glass bookcase. Then a sputtering sound, a momentary dimming of the lamp. The moth had succeeded in its mysterious quest.

'Can you tell me,' said Lewis as if he were answering Merritt, 'why moths rush into the flame?'

Lewis had put his question as to the strange habits of the common moth to Merritt with the deliberate intent of closing the debate on death by heliograph. The query was suggested, of course, by the incident of the moth in the lamp, and Lewis thought that he had said: 'Oh, shut up!' in a somewhat elegant manner. And, in fact Merritt looked dignified, remained silent, and helped himself to port.

That was the end that the doctor had desired. He had no doubt in his own mind that the affair of the *Mary Ann* was but one more item in a long account of horrors that grew larger almost with every day; and he was in no humour to listen to wild and futile theories as to the manner in which the disaster had been accomplished. Here was a proof that the terror that was upon them was mighty not only on the land but on the waters; for Lewis could not see that the boat could have been attacked by any ordinary means of destruction. From Merritt's story, it must have been in shallow water. The shore of Larnac Bay shelves very gradually, and the Admiralty charts showed the depth of water two hundred yards out to be only two fathoms; this would be too shallow for a submarine. And it could not have been shelled, and it could not have been torpedoed; there was no explosion. The disaster might have been due to carelessness; boys, he considered, will play the fool anywhere, even in a boat; but he did not think so; the sailor would have stopped them. And, it may be mentioned, that the two boys were as a matter of fact extremely steady, sensible young fellows, not in the least likely to play foolish tricks of any kind.

Lewis was immersed in these reflections, having successfully silenced his brother-in-law; he was trying in vain to find some clue to the horrible enigma. The Midlingham theory of a concealed German force, hiding in places under the earth, was extravagant enough, and yet it seemed the only solution that approached plausibility; but then again even a subterranean German host would hardly account for this wreckage of a boat, floating on a calm sea. And then what of the tree with the burning in it that had appeared in the garden there a few weeks ago, and the cloud with a burning in it that had shown over the trees of the Midland village?

I think I have already written something of the probable emotions of the mathematician confronted suddenly with an undoubted two-sided triangle. I said, if I remember, that he would be forced, in decency, to go mad; and I believe that Lewis was very near to this point. He felt himself confronted with an intolerable problem that most instantly demanded solution, and yet, with the same breath, as it were, denied the possibility of there being any solution. People were being killed in an inscrutable manner by some inscrutable means, day after day, and one asked why and how; and there seemed no answer. In the Midlands where every kind of munitionment was manufactured, the explanation of German agency was plausible; and even if the subterranean notion was to be rejected as savouring altogether too much of the fairy-tale, or rather of the sensational romance, yet it was possible that the backbone of the theory was true; the Germans might have planted their agents in some way or another in the midst of our factories. But here in Meirion, what serious effect could be produced by the casual and indiscriminate slaughter of a couple of school-boys in a boat, of a harmless holiday-maker in a marsh? The creation of an atmosphere of terror and dismay? It was possible, of course, but it hardly seemed tolerable, in spite of the enormities of Louvain and of the *Lusitania*.

Into these meditations, and into the still dignified silence of Merritt broke the rap on the door of Lewis's man, and those words which harass the ease of the country doctor when he tries to take any ease: 'You're wanted in the surgery, if you please, sir.' Lewis bustled out, and appeared no more that night.

The doctor had been summoned to a little hamlet on the outskirts of Porth, separated from it by half a mile or three quarters of road. One dignifies, indeed, this settlement without a name in calling it a hamlet; it was a mere row of four cottages, built about a hundred years ago for the accommodation of the workers in a quarry long since disused. In one of these cottages the doctor found a father and mother weeping and crying out to 'doctor *bach*, doctor *bach*', and two frightened children, and one little body, still and dead. It was the youngest of the three, little Johnnie, and he was dead.

The doctor found that the child had been asphyxiated. He felt the clothes; they were dry; it was not a case of drowning. He looked at the neck; there was no mark of strangling. He asked the father how it had happened, and father and mother, weeping most lamentably, declared they had no knowledge of how their child had been killed: 'unless it was the People that had done it.' The Celtic fairies are still malignant. Lewis asked what had happened that evening; where had the child been?

'Was he with his brother and sister? Don't they know anything about it?'

Reduced into some sort of order from its original piteous confusion, this is the story that the doctor gathered.

All three children had been well and happy through the day. They had walked in with the mother, Mrs Roberts, to Porth on a marketing expedition in the afternoon; they had returned to the cottage, had had their tea, and afterwards played about on the road in front of the house. John Roberts had come home somewhat late from his work, and it was after dusk when the family sat down to supper. Supper over, the three children went out again to play with other children from the cottage

154

next door, Mrs Roberts telling them that they might have half an hour before going to bed.

The two mothers came to the cottage gates at the same moment and called out to their children to come along and be quick about it. The two small families had been playing on the strip of turf across the road, just by the stile into the fields. The children ran across the road; all of them except Johnnie Roberts. His brother Willie said that just as their mother called them he heard Johnnie cry out:

'Oh, what is that beautiful shiny thing over the stile?'

X. *The Child and the Moth*

The little Robertses ran across the road, up the path, and into the lighted room. Then they noticed that Johnnie had not followed them. Mrs Roberts was doing something in the back kitchen, and Mr Roberts had gone out to the shed to bring in some sticks for the next morning's fire. Mrs Roberts heard the children run in and went on with her work. The children whispered to one another that Johnnie would 'catch it' when their mother came out of the back room and found him missing; but they expected he would run in through the open door any minute. But six or seven, perhaps ten, minutes passed, and there was no Johnnie. Then the father and mother came into the kitchen together, and saw that their little boy was not there.

They thought it was some small piece of mischief – that the two other children had hidden the boy somewhere in the room: in the big cupboard perhaps.

'What have you done with him then?' said Mrs Roberts. 'Come out, you little rascal, directly in a minute.'

There was no little rascal to come out, and Margaret Roberts, the girl, said that Johnnie had not come across the road with them: he must be still playing all by himself by the hedge.

'What did you let him stay like that for?' said Mrs Roberts. 'Can't I trust you for two minutes together? Indeed to goodness, you are all of you more trouble than you are worth.' She went to the open door.

'Johnnie! Come in directly, or you will be sorry for it. Johnnie!'

The poor woman called at the door. She went out to the gate and called there:

'Come you, little Johnnie. Come you, *bachgen*, there's a good boy. I do see you hiding there.'

She thought he must be hiding in the shadow of the hedge, and that he would come running and laughing – 'He was always such a happy little fellow' – to her across the road. But no little merry figure danced out of the gloom of the still, dark night; it was all silence.

It was then, as the mother's heart began to chill, though she still called cheerfully to the missing child, that the elder boy told how Johnnie had said there was something beautiful by the stile: 'And perhaps he did climb over, and he is running now about the meadow, and has lost his way.'

The father got his lantern then, and the whole family went crying and calling about the meadow, promising cakes and sweets and a fine toy to poor Johnnie if he would come to them.

They found the little body, under the ash-grove in the middle of the field. He was quite still and dead, so still that a great moth had settled on his forehead, fluttering away when they lifted him up.

Dr Lewis heard this story. There was nothing to be done; little to be said to these most unhappy people.

'Take care of the two that you have left to you,' said the doctor as he went away. 'Don't let them out of your sight if you can help it. It is dreadful times that we are living in.'

It is curious to record that all through these dreadful times the simple little 'season' went through its accustomed course at Porth. The war and its consequences had somewhat thinned the numbers of the summer visitors; still a very fair contingent of them occupied the hotels and boarding-houses and lodging-houses and bathed from the old-fashioned machines on one beach, or from the new-fashioned tents on the other, and sauntered in the sun, or lay stretched out in the shade under the trees that grow down almost to the water's edge. Porth never tolerated Ethiopians or shows of any kind on its sands, but the Rockets did very well during that summer in their garden entertainment, given in the castle grounds, and the fit-up companies that came to the Assembly Rooms are said to have paid their bills to a woman and to a man.

Porth depends very largely on its Midland and northern custom, custom of a prosperous, well-established sort. People who think Llandudno overcrowded and Colwyn Bay too raw and red and new come year after year to the placid old town in the south-west and delight in its peace; and as I say, they enjoyed themselves much as usual there in the summer of 1915. Now and then they became conscious, as Mr Merritt became conscious, that they could not wander about quite in the old way; but they accepted sentries and coast watchers and people who politely pointed out the advantages of seeing the view from this point rather than from that as very necessary consequences of the dreadful war that was being waged; nay, as a Manchester man said, after having been turned back from his favourite walk to Castell Coch, it was gratifying to think that they were so well looked after.

'So far as I can see,' he added, 'there's nothing to prevent a submarine from standing out there by Ynys Sant and landing half a dozen men in a collapsible boat in any of these little coves. And pretty fools we should look, shouldn't we, with our throats cut on the sands; or carried back to Germany in the submarine?' He tipped the coast watcher half a crown.

'That's right, lad,' he said, 'you give us the tip.'

Now here was a strange thing. The North-countryman had his thoughts on elusive submarines and German raiders; the watcher had simply received instructions to keep people off the Castell Coch fields, without reason assigned. And there can be no doubt that the authorities themselves, while they marked out the fields as in the 'terror zone', gave their orders in the dark and were themselves profoundly in the dark as to the manner of the slaughter that had been done there; for if they had understood what had happened, they would have understood also that their restrictions were useless.

The Manchester man was warned off his walk about ten days after Johnnie Robert's death. The watcher had been placed at his post because, the night before, a young farmer had been found by his wife lying in the grass close to the castle, with no scar on him, nor any mark of violence, but stone dead.

The wife of the dead man, Joseph Cradock, finding her husband lying motionless on the dewy turf, went white and stricken up the path to the village and got two men who bore the body to the farm. Lewis was sent for, and knew at once when he saw the dead man that he had perished in the way that the little Roberts boy had perished – whatever that awful way might be. Cradock had been asphyxiated; and here again there was no mark of a grip on the throat. It might have been a piece of work by Burke and Hare, the doctor reflected; a pitch plaster might have been clapped over the man's mouth and nostrils and held there.

Then a thought struck him; his brother-in-law had talked of a new kind of poison gas that was said to be used against the munition workers in the Midlands: was it possible that the deaths of the man and the boy were due to some such instrument? He applied his tests but could find no trace of any gas having been employed. Carbonic acid gas? A man could not be killed with that in the open air; to be fatal that required a confined space, such a position as the bottom of a huge vat or of a well.

He did not know how Cradock had been killed; he confessed it to himself. He had been suffocated; that was all he could say.

It seemed that the man had gone out at about half past nine to look after some beasts. The field in which they were was about five minutes' walk from the house. He told his wife he would be back in a quarter of an hour or twenty minutes. He did not return, and when he had gone for three quarters of an hour Mrs Cradock went out to look for him. She went into the field where the beasts were, and everything seemed all right, but there was no trace of Cradock. She called out; there was no answer.

Now the meadow in which the cattle were pastured is high ground; a hedge divides it from the fields which fall gently down to the castle and the sea. Mrs Cradock hardly seemed able to say why, having failed to find her husband among his beasts, she turned to the path which led to Castell Coch. She said at first that she had thought that one of the oxen might have broken through the hedge and strayed, and that Cradock had perhaps gone after it. And then, correcting herself, she said:

'There was that; and then there was something else that I could not make out at all. It seemed to me that the hedge did look different from usual. To be sure, things do look different at night, and there was a bit of sea mist about, but somehow it did look odd to me, and I said to my-self: "Have I lost my way, then?" '

She declared that the shape of the trees in the hedge appeared to have changed, and besides, it had a look 'as if it was lighted up, somehow', and so she went on towards the stile to see what all this could be, and when she came near everything was as usual. She looked over the stile and called and hoped to see her husband coming towards her or to hear his voice; but there was no answer, and glancing down the path she saw, or thought she saw, some sort of brightness on the ground, 'a dim sort of light like a bunch of glow-worms in a hedge-bank.

'And so I climbed over the stile and went down the path, and the light seemed to melt away; and there was my poor husband lying on his back, saying not a word to me when I spoke to him and touched him.'

So for Lewis the terror blackened and became altogether intolerable, and others, he perceived, felt as he did. He did not know, he never asked whether the men at the club had heard of these deaths of the child and the young farmer; but no one spoke of them. Indeed, the change was evident; at the beginning of the terror men spoke of nothing else; now it had become all too awful for ingenious chatter or laboured and grotesque theories. And Lewis had received a letter from his brother-in-law at Midlingham; it contained the sentence, 'I am afraid Fanny's health has not greatly benefited by her visit to Porth; there are still several symp-toms I don't at all like.' And this told him, in a phraseology that the doctor and Merritt had agreed upon, that the terror remained heavy in the Midland town.

It was soon after the death of Cradock that people began to tell strange tales of a sound that was to be heard of nights about the hills and valleys to the northward of Porth. A man who had missed the last train from Meiros and had been forced to tramp the ten miles between Meiros and Porth seems to have been the first to hear it. He said he had got to the top of the hill by Tredonoc, somewhere between half past ten and eleven, when he first noticed an odd noise that he could not make out at all; it was like a shout, a long, drawn-out, dismal wail coming from a great way off, faint with distance. He stopped to listen, thinking at first that it might be owls hooting in the woods; but it was different, he said, from that: it was a long cry, and then there was silence and then it began over again. He could make nothing of it, and feeling frightened, he did not quite know of what, he walked on briskly and was glad to see the lights of Porth station.

He told his wife of this dismal sound that night, and she told the neighbours, and most of them thought that it was 'all fancy' – or drink, or the owls after all. But the night after, two or three people, who had been to some small merry-making in a cottage just off the Meiros road, heard the sound as they were going home, soon after ten. They, too, described it as a long, wailing cry, indescribably dismal in the stillness of the autumn night; 'Like the ghost of a voice,' said one; 'As if it came up from the bottom of the earth,' said another.

XI. *At Treff Loyne Farm*

Let it be remembered, again and again, that, all the while that the terror lasted, there was no common stock of information as to the dreadful things that were being done. The press had not said one word upon it, there was no criterion by which the mass of the people could separate fact from mere vague rumour, no test by which ordinary misadventure or disaster could be distinguished from the achievements of the secret and awful force that was at work.

And so with every event of the passing day. A harmless commercial traveller might show himself in the course of his business in the tumble-down main street of Meiros and find himself regarded with looks of fear and suspicion as a possible worker of murder, while it is likely enough that the true agents of the terror went quite unnoticed. And since the real nature of all this mystery of death was unknown, it followed easily that the signs and warnings and omens of it were all the more unknown. Here was horror, there was horror; but there was no link to join one horror with another; no common basis of knowledge from which the connection between this horror and that horror might be inferred.

So there was no one who suspected at all that this dismal and hollow sound that was now heard of nights in the region to the north of Porth, had any relation at all to the case of the little girl who went out one afternoon to pick purple flowers and never returned, or to the case of the man whose body was taken out of the peaty slime of the marsh, or to the case of Cradock, dead in his fields, with a strange glimmering of light about his body, as his wife reported. And it is a question as to how far the rumour of this melancholy, nocturnal summons got abroad at all. Lewis heard of it, as a country doctor hears of most things, driving up

and down the lanes, but he heard of it without much interest, with no
sense that it was in any sort of relation to the terror. Remnant had been
given the story of the hollow and echoing voice of the darkness in a
coloured and picturesque form; he employed a Tredonoc man to work
in his garden once a week. The gardener had not heard the summons
himself, but he knew a man who had done so.

'Thomas Jenkins, Pentoppin, he did put his head out late last night to
see what the weather was like, as he was cutting a field of corn the next
day, and he did tell me that when he was with the Methodists in Cardigan he did never hear no singing eloquence in the chapels that was like
to it. He did declare it was like a wailing of Judgement Day.'

Remnant considered the matter, and was inclined to think that the
sound must be caused by a subterranean inlet of the sea; there might be,
he supposed, an imperfect or half-opened or tortuous blowhole in the
Tredonoc woods, and the noise of the tide, surging up below, might very
well produce that effect of a hollow wailing, far away. But neither he nor
any one else paid much attention to the matter; save the few who heard
the call at dead of night, as it echoed awfully over the black hills.

The sound had been heard for three or perhaps four nights, when the
people coming out of Tredonoc church after morning service on Sunday
noticed that there was a big yellow sheep-dog in the churchyard. The
dog, it appeared, had been waiting for the congregation; for it at once
attached itself to them, at first to the whole body, and then to a group of
half a dozen who took the turning to the right. Two of these presently
went off over the fields to their respective houses, and four strolled on in
the leisurely Sunday-morning manner of the country, and these the dog
followed, keeping to heel all the time. The men were talking hay, corn,
and markets and paid no attention to the animal, and so they strolled
along the autumn lane till they came to a gate in the hedge, whence a
roughly made farm road went through the fields, and dipped down into
the woods and to Treff Loyne farm.

Then the dog became like a possessed creature. He barked furiously.
He ran up to one of the men and looked up at him, 'as if he were begging
for his life,' as the man said, and then rushed to the gate and stood by it,
wagging his tail and barking at intervals. The men stared and laughed.

'Whose dog will that be?' said one of them.

'It will be Thomas Griffith's, Treff Loyne,' said another.

'Well, then, why doesn't he go home? Go home then!' He went
through the gesture of picking up a stone from the road and throwing it
at the dog. 'Go home, then! Over the gate with you.'

But the dog never stirred. He barked and whined and ran up to the
men and then back to the gate. At last he came to one of them, and
crawled and abased himself on the ground and then took hold of the

man's coat and tried to pull him in the direction of the gate. The farmer shook the dog off, and the four went on their way; and the dog stood in the road and watched them and then put up its head and uttered a long and dismal howl that was despair.

The four farmers thought nothing of it; sheep-dogs in the country are dogs to look after sheep, and their whims and fancies are not studied. But the yellow dog – he was a kind of degenerate collie – haunted the Tredonoc lanes from that day. He came to a cottage door one night and scratched at it, and when it was opened lay down, and then, barking, ran to the garden gate and waited, entreating, as it seemed, the cottager to follow him. They drove him away and again he gave that long howl of anguish. It was almost as bad, they said, as the noise that they had heard a few nights before. And then it occurred to somebody, so far as I can make out with no particular reference to the odd conduct of the Treff Loyne sheep-dog, that Thomas Griffith had not been seen for some time past. He had missed market-day at Porth, he had not been at Tredonoc church, where he was a pretty regular attendant on Sunday; and then, as heads were put together, it appeared that nobody had seen any of the Griffith family for days and days.

Now in a town, even in a small town, this process of putting heads together is a pretty quick business. In the country, especially in a countryside of wild lands and scattered and lonely farms and cottages, the affair takes time. Harvest was going on, everybody was busy in his own fields, and after the long day's hard work neither the farmer nor his men felt inclined to stroll about in search of news or gossip. A harvester at the day's end is ready for supper and sleep and for nothing else.

And so it was late in that week when it was discovered that Thomas Griffith and all his house had vanished from this world.

I have often been reproached for my curiosity over questions which are apparently of slight importance, or of no importance at all. I love to inquire, for instance, into the question of the visibility of a lighted candle at a distance. Suppose, that is, a candle lighted on a still, dark night in the country; what is the greatest distance at which you can see that there is a light at all? And then as to the human voice; what is its carrying distance, under good conditions, as a mere sound, apart from any matter of making out words that may be uttered?

They are trivial questions, no doubt, but they have always interested me, and the latter point has its application to the strange business of Treff Loyne. That melancholy and hollow sound, that wailing summons that appalled the hearts of those who heard it was, indeed, a human voice, produced in a very exceptional manner; and it seems to have been heard at points varying from a mile and a half to two miles from the farm. I do not know whether this is anything extraordinary; I do not know whether the peculiar method of production was calculated to increase or to diminish the carrying power of the sound.

Again and again I have laid emphasis in this story of the terror on the strange isolation of many of the farms and cottages in Meirion. I have done so in the effort to convince the townsman of something that he has never known. To the Londoner a house a quarter of a mile from the outlying suburban lamp, with no other dwelling within two hundred yards, is a lonely house, a place to fit with ghosts and mysteries and terrors. How can he understand then, the true loneliness of the white farmhouses of Meirion, dotted here and there, for the most part not even on the little lanes and deep winding by-ways, but set in the very heart of the fields, or alone on huge bastioned headlands facing the sea, and whether on the high verge of the sea or on the hills or in the hollows of the inner country, hidden from the sight of men, far from the sound of any common call. There is Penyrhaul, for example, the farm from which the foolish Merritt thought he saw signals of light being made: from seaward it is, of course, widely visible; but from landward, owing partly to the curving and indented configuration of the bay, I doubt whether any other habitation views it from a nearer distance than three miles.

And of all these hidden and remote places, I doubt if any is so deeply buried as Treff Loyne. I have little or no Welsh, I am sorry to say, but I suppose that the name is corrupted from Trellwyn, or Tref-y-llwyn, 'the place in the grove', and, indeed, it lies in the very heart of the dark, overhanging woods. A deep, narrow valley runs down from the high lands of the Allt, through these woods, through steep hill-sides of bracken and gorse, right down to the great marsh, whence Merritt saw the dead man being carried. The valley lies away from any road, even from that byroad, little better than a bridle-path, where the four farmers, returning from church were perplexed by the strange antics of the sheep-dog. One cannot say that the valley is overlooked, even from a distance, for so narrow is it that the ash-groves that rim it on either side seem to meet and shut it in. I, at all events, have never found any high place from which Treff Loyne is visible; though, looking down from the Allt, I have seen blue wood-smoke rising from its hidden chimneys.

Such was the place, then, to which one September afternoon a party went up to discover what had happened to Griffith and his family. There were half a dozen farmers, a couple of policemen, and four soldiers, carrying their arms; those last had been lent by the officer commanding at the camp. Lewis, too, was of the party; he had heard by chance that no one knew what had become of Griffith and his family; and he was anxious about a young fellow, a painter, of his acquaintance, who had been lodging at Treff Loyne all the summer.

They all met by the gate of Tredonoc churchyard, and tramped solemnly along the narrow lane; all of them, I think, with some vague discomfort of mind, with a certain shadowy fear, as of men who do not quite know what they may encounter. Lewis heard the corporal and the three soldiers arguing over their orders.

'The captain says to me,' muttered the corporal, ' "Don't hesitate to shoot if there's any trouble." "Shoot what, sir," I says. "The trouble," says he, and that's all I could get out of him.'

The men grumbled in reply; Lewis thought he heard some obscure reference to rat-poison, and wondered what they were talking about.

They came to the gate in the hedge, where the farm road led down to Treff Loyne. They followed this track, roughly made, with grass growing up between its loosely laid stones, down by the hedge from field to wood, till at last they came to the sudden walls of the valley, and the sheltering groves of the ash-trees. Here the way curved down the steep hill-side, and bent southward, and followed henceforward the hidden hollow of the valley, under the shadow of the trees.

Here was the farm enclosure; the outlying walls of the yard and the barns and sheds and outhouses. One of the farmers threw open the gate and walked into the yard, and forthwith began bellowing at the top of his voice:

'Thomas Griffith! Thomas Griffith! Where be you, Thomas Griffith?'

The rest followed him. The corporal snapped out an order over his shoulder, and there was a rattling metallic noise as the men fixed their bayonets and became in an instant dreadful dealers out of death, in place of harmless fellows with a feeling for beer.

'Thomas Griffith!' again bellowed the farmer.

There was no answer to this summons. But they found poor Griffith lying on his face at the edge of the pond in the middle of the yard. There was a ghastly wound in his side, as if a sharp stake had been driven into his body.

XII. *The Letter of Wrath*

It was a still September afternoon. No wind stirred in the hanging woods that were dark all about the ancient house of Treff Loyne; the only sound in the dim air was the lowing of the cattle; they had wandered, it seemed, from the fields and had come in by the gate of the farmyard and stood there melancholy, as if they mourned for their dead master. And the horses; four great, heavy, patient-looking beasts they were there too, and in the lower field the sheep were standing, as if they waited to be fed.

'You would think they all knew there was something wrong,' one of the soldiers muttered to another. A pale sun showed for a moment and glittered on their bayonets. They were standing about the body of poor, dead Griffith, with a certain grimness growing on their faces and hardening there. Their corporal snapped something at them again; they were quite ready. Lewis knelt down by the dead man and looked closely at the great gaping wound in his side.

'He's been dead a long time,' he said. 'A week, two weeks, perhaps. He was killed by some sharp pointed weapon. How about the family? How many are there of them? I never attended them.'

'There was Griffith, and his wife, and his son Thomas and Mary Griffith, his daughter. And I do think there was a gentleman lodging with them this summer.'

That was from one of the farmers. They all looked at one another, this party of rescue, who knew nothing of the danger that had smitten this house of quiet people, nothing of the peril which had brought them to this pass of a farmyard with a dead man in it, and his beasts standing patiently about him, as if they waited for the farmer to rise up and give them their food. Then the party turned to the house. It was an old, sixteenth-century building, with the singular round, Flemish chimney that is characteristic of Meirion. The walls were snowy with whitewash, the windows were deeply set and stone-mullioned, and a solid, stone-tiled porch sheltered the doorway from any winds that might penetrate to the hollow of that hidden valley. The windows were shut tight. There was no sign of any life or movement about the place. The party of men looked at one another, and the churchwarden amongst the farmers, the sergeant of police, Lewis, and the corporal drew together.

'What is it to goodness, doctor?' said the churchwarden.

'I can tell you nothing at all – except that that poor man there has been pierced to the heart,' said Lewis.

'Do you think they are inside and they will shoot us?' said another farmer. He had no notion of what he meant by 'they', and no one of them knew better than he. They did not know what the danger was, or where it might strike them, or whether it was from without or from within. They stared at the murdered man, and gazed dismally at one another.

'Come!' said Lewis, 'we must do something. We must get into the house and see what is wrong.'

'Yes, but suppose they are at us while we are getting in,' said the sergeant. 'Where shall we be then, Doctor Lewis?'

The corporal put one of his men by the gate at the top of the farmyard, another at the gate by the bottom of the farmyard, and told them to challenge and shoot. The doctor and the rest opened the little gate of the front garden and went up to the porch and stood listening by the door. It was all dead silence. Lewis took an ash stick from one of the farmers and beat heavily three times on the old, black, oaken door studded with antique nails.

He struck three thundering blows, and then they all waited. There was no answer from within. He beat again, and still silence. He shouted to the people within, but there was no answer. They all turned and looked at one another, that party of quest and rescue who knew not what they sought, what enemy they were to encounter. There was an iron ring on the door. Lewis turned it but the door stood fast; it was evidently barred and bolted. The sergeant of police called out to open, but again there was no answer.

They consulted together. There was nothing for it but to blow the door open, and some one of them called in a loud voice to anybody that might be within to stand away from the door, or they would be killed. And at this very moment the yellow sheep-dog came bounding up the yard from the woods and licked their hands and fawned on them and barked joyfully.

'Indeed now,' said one of the farmers, 'he did know that there was something amiss. A pity it was, Thomas Williams, that we did not follow him when he implored us last Sunday.'

The corporal motioned the rest of the party back, and they stood looking fearfully about them at the entrance to the porch. The corporal disengaged his bayonet and shot into the keyhole, calling out once more before he fired. He shot and shot again; so heavy and firm was the ancient door, so stout its bolts and fastenings. At last he had to fire at the massive hinges, and then they all pushed together and the door lurched open and fell forward. The corporal raised his left hand and stepped back a few paces. He hailed his two men at the top and bottom of the farmyard. They were all right, they said. And so the party climbed and struggled over the fallen door into the passage, and into the kitchen of the farmhouse.

Young Griffith was lying dead before the hearth, before a dead fire of white wood ashes. They went on towards the parlour, and in the doorway of the room was the body of the artist, Secretan, as if he had fallen in trying to get to the kitchen. Upstairs the two women, Mrs Griffith and her daughter, a girl of eighteen, were lying together on the bed in the big bedroom, clasped in each other's arms.

They went about the house, searched the pantries, the back kitchen and the cellars; there was no life in it.

'Look!' said Dr Lewis, when they came back to the big kitchen. 'Look! It is as if they had been besieged. Do you see that piece of bacon, half gnawed through?'

Then they found these pieces of bacon, cut from the sides on the kitchen wall, here and there about the house. There was no bread in the place, no milk, no water.

'And,' said one of the farmers, 'they had the best water here in all Meirion. The well is down there in the wood; it is most famous water. The old people did use to call it Ffynnon Teilo; it was Saint Teilo's Well, they did say.'

'They must have died of thirst,' said Lewis. 'They have been dead for days and days.'

The group of men stood in the big kitchen and stared at one another, a dreadful perplexity in their eyes. The dead were all about them, within the house and without it; and it was in vain to ask why they had died thus. The old man had been killed with the piercing thrust of some sharp weapon; the rest had perished, it seemed probable, of thirst; but what possible enemy was this that besieged the farm and shut in its inhabitants? There was no answer.

The sergeant of police spoke of getting a cart and taking the bodies into Porth, and Dr Lewis went into the parlour that Secretan had used as a sitting-room, intending to gather any possessions or effects of the dead artist that he might find there. Half a dozen portfolios were piled up in one corner, there were some books on a side table, a fishing-rod and basket behind the door – that seemed all. No doubt there would be clothes and such matters upstairs, and Lewis was about to rejoin the rest of the party in the kitchen, when he looked down at some scattered papers lying with the books on the side table. On one of the sheets he read to his astonishment the words: 'Dr. James Lewis, Porth'. This was written in a staggering trembling scrawl, and examining the other leaves he saw that they were covered with writing.

The table stood in a dark corner of the room, and Lewis gathered up the sheets of paper and took them to the window-ledge and began to read, amazed at certain phrases that had caught his eye. But the manuscript was in disorder; as if the dead man who had written it had not been equal to the task of gathering the leaves into their proper sequence; it was some time before the doctor had each page in its place. This was the statement that he read, with ever-growing wonder, while a couple of the farmers were harnessing one of the horses in the yard to a cart, and the others were bringing down the dead women.

I do not think that I can last much longer. We shared out the last drops of water a long time ago. I do not know how many days ago. We fall asleep and dream and walk about the house in our dreams, and I am often not sure whether I am awake or still dreaming, and so the days and nights are confused in my mind. I awoke not long ago, at least I suppose I awoke and found I was lying in the passage. I had a confused feeling that I had had an awful dream which seemed horribly real, and I thought for a moment what a relief it was to know that it wasn't true, whatever it might have been. I made up my mind to have a good long walk to freshen myself up, and then I looked round and found that I had been lying on the stones of the passage; and it all came back to me. There was no walk for me.

I have not seen Mrs. Griffith or her daughter for a long while. They said they were going upstairs to have a rest. I heard them moving about the room at first, now I can hear nothing. Young Griffith is lying in the kitchen, before the hearth. He was talking to himself about the harvest and the weather when I last went into the kitchen. He didn't seem to know I was there, as he went gabbling on in a low voice very fast, and then he began to call the dog, Tiger.

There seems no hope for any of us. We are in the dream of death. . . .

Here the manuscript became unintelligible for half a dozen lines. Secretan had written the words 'dream of death' three or four times over. He had begun a fresh word and had scratched it out and then followed strange, unmeaning characters, the script, as Lewis thought, of a terrible language. And then the writing became clear, clearer than it was at the beginning of the manuscript, and the sentences flowed more easily, as if the cloud on Secretan's mind had lifted for a while. There was a fresh start, as it were, and the writer began again, in ordinary letter form:

Dear Lewis,

I hope you will excuse all this confusion and wandering. I intended to begin a proper letter to you, and now I find all that stuff that you have been reading – if this ever gets into your hands. I have not the energy even to tear it up. If you read it you will know to what a sad pass I had come even when it was written. It looks like delirium or a bad dream, and even now, though my mind seems to have cleared up a good deal, I have to hold myself in tightly to be sure that the experiences of the last days in this awful place are true, real things, not a long nightmare from which I shall wake up presently and find myself in my rooms at Chelsea.

I have said of what I am writing, 'if it ever gets into your hands', and I am not at all sure that it ever will. If what is happening here is happening everywhere else, then I suppose, the world is coming to an end. I cannot understand it, even now I can hardly believe it. I know that I dream such wild dreams and walk in such mad fancies that I have to look out and look about me to make sure that I am not still dreaming.

Do you remember that talk we had about two months ago when I dined with you? We got on, somehow or other, to space and time, and I think we agreed that as soon as one tried to reason about space and time one was landed in a maze of contradictions. You said something to the effect that it was very curious but this was just like a dream. 'A man will sometimes wake himself from his crazy dream,' you said, 'by realising that he is thinking nonsense.' And we both wondered whether these contradictions that one can't avoid if one begins to think of time and space may not really be proofs that the whole of life is a dream, and the moon and the stars bits of nightmare. I have often thought over that lately. I kick at the walls as Dr Johnson kicked at the stone, to make sure that the things about me are there. And then that other question gets into my mind – is the world really coming to an end, the world as we have always known it; and what on earth will this new world be like? I can't imagine it; it's a story like Noah's Ark and the Flood. People used to talk about the end of the world and fire, but no one ever thought of anything like this.

And then there's another thing that bothers me. Now and then I wonder whether we are not all mad together in this house. In spite of what I see and know, or, perhaps, I should say, because what I see and know is so impossible, I wonder whether we are not all suffering from a delusion. Perhaps we are our own gaolers, and we are really free to go out and live. Perhaps what we think we see is not there at all. I believe I have heard of whole families going mad together, and I may have come under the influence of the house, having lived in it for the last four months. I know there have been people who have been kept alive by their keepers forcing food down their throats, because they are quite sure that their throats are closed, so that they feel they are unable to swallow a morsel. I wonder now and then whether we are all like this in Treff Loyne; yet in my heart I feel sure that it is not so.

Still, I do not want to leave a madman's letter behind me, and so I will not tell you the full story of what I have seen, or believe I have seen. If I am a sane man you will be able to fill in the blanks for yourself from your own knowledge. If I am mad, burn the letter and say nothing about it. Or perhaps – and indeed, I am not quite sure – I may wake up and hear Mary Griffith calling to me in her cheerful sing-song that breakfast will be ready 'directly, in a minute,' and I shall enjoy it and walk over to Porth and tell you the queerest, most horrible dream that a man ever had, and ask what I had better take.

I think that it was on a Tuesday that we first noticed that there was something queer about, only at the time we didn't know that there was anything really queer in what we noticed. I had been out since nine o'clock in the morning trying to paint the marsh, and I found it a very tough job. I came home about five or six o'clock and found the family at Treff Loyne laughing at old Tiger, the sheepdog. He was making short runs from the farmyard to the door of the house, barking, with quick, short yelps. Mrs Griffith and Miss Griffith were standing by the porch, and the dog would go to them, look in their faces, and then run up the farmyard to the gate, and then look back with that eager yelping bark, as if he were waiting for the women to follow him. Then, again and again, he ran up to them and tugged at their skirts as if he would pull them by main force away from the house.

Then the men came home from the fields and he repeated this performance. The dog was running all up and down the farmyard, in and out of the barn and sheds yelping, barking; and always with that eager run to the person he addressed, and running away directly, and looking back as if to see whether we were following him. When the house-door was shut and they all sat down to supper, he would give them no peace, till at last they turned him out of doors. And then he sat in the porch and scratched at the door with his claws, barking all the while. When the daughter brought in my meal, she said: 'We can't think what is come to old Tiger, and indeed, he has always been a good dog, too.'

The dog barked and yelped and whined and scratched at the door all through the evening. They let him in once, but he seemed to have become quite frantic. He ran up to one member of the family after another; his eyes were bloodshot and his mouth was foaming, and he tore at their clothes till they drove him out again into the darkness. Then he broke into a long, lamentable howl of anguish, and we heard no more of him.

XIII. *The Last Words of Mr Secretan*

I slept ill that night. I awoke again and again from uneasy dreams, and I seemed in my sleep to hear strange calls and noises and a sound of murmurs and beatings on the door. There were deep, hollow voices, too, that echoed in my sleep, and when I woke I could hear the autumn wind, mournful, on the hills above us. I started up once with a dreadful scream in my ears; but then the house was all still, and I fell again into uneasy sleep.

It was soon after dawn when I finally roused myself. The people in the house were talking to each other in high voices, arguing about something that I did not understand.

'It is those damned gipsies, I tell you,' said old Griffith.

'What would they do a thing like that for?' asked Mrs Griffith. 'If it was stealing now –'

'It is more likely that John Jenkins has done it out of spite,' said the son. 'He said that he would remember you when we did catch him poaching.

They seemed puzzled and angry, so far as I could make out, but not at all frightened. I got up and began to dress. I don't think I looked out of the window. The glass on my dressing-table is high and broad, and the window is small; one would have to poke one's head round the glass to see anything.

The voices were still arguing downstairs. I heard the old man say, 'Well, here's for a beginning anyhow,' and then the door slammed.

A minute later the old man shouted, I think, to his son. Then there was a great noise which I will not describe more particularly, and a dreadful screaming and crying inside the house and a sound of rushing feet. They all cried out at once to each other. I heard the daughter crying, 'it is no good, mother, he is dead, indeed they have killed him,' and Mrs Griffith screaming to the girl to let her go. And then one of them rushed out of the kitchen and shot the great bolts of oak across the door, just as something beat against it with a thundering crash.

I ran downstairs. I found them all in wild confusion, in an agony of grief and horror and amazement. They were like people who had seen something so awful that they had gone mad.

I went to the window looking out on the farmyard. I won't tell you all that I saw. But I saw poor old Griffith lying by the pond, with blood pouring out of his side.

I wanted to go out to him and bring him in. But they told me that he must be stone dead, and such things also that it was quite plain that any one who went out of the house would not live more than a moment. We could not believe it, even as we gazed at the body of the dead man; but it was there. I used to wonder sometimes what one would feel like if one saw an apple drop from the tree and shoot up into the air and disappear. I think I know now how one would feel.

Even then we couldn't believe that it would last. We were not seriously afraid for ourselves. We spoke of getting out in an hour or two, before dinner anyhow. It couldn't last, because it was impossible. Indeed, at twelve o'clock young Griffith said he would go down to the well by the back way and draw another pail of water. I went to the door and stood by it. He had not gone a dozen yards before they were on him. He ran for his life, and we had all we could do to bar the door in time. And then I began to get frightened.

Still we could not believe in it. Somebody would come along shouting in an hour or two and it would all melt away and vanish. There could not be any real danger. There was plenty of bacon in the house, and half the weekly baking of loaves and some beer in the cellar and a pound or so of tea, and a whole pitcher of water that had been drawn from the well the night before. We could do all right for the day and in the morning it would have all gone away.

But day followed day and it was still there. I knew Treff Loyne was a lonely place – that was why I had gone there, to have a long rest from all the jangle and rattle and turmoil of London, that makes a man alive and kills him too. I went to Treff Loyne because it was buried in the narrow valley under the ash trees, far away from any track. There was not so much as a footpath that was near it; no one ever came that way. Young Griffith had told me that it was a mile and a half to the nearest house, and the thought of the silent peace and retirement of the farm used to be a delight to me.

And now this thought came back without delight, with terror. Griffith thought that a shout might be heard on a still night up away on the Allt, 'if a man was listening for it,' he added, doubtfully. My voice was clearer and stronger than his, and on the second night I said I would go up to my bedroom and call for help through the open window. I waited till it was all dark and still, and looked out through the window before opening it. And when I saw over the ridge of the long barn across the yard what looked like a tree, though I knew there was no tree there. It was a dark mass against the sky, with wide-spread boughs, a tree of thick, dense growth. I wondered what this could be, and I threw open the window, not only because I was going to call for help, but because I wanted to see more clearly what the dark growth over the barn really was.

I saw in the depth of the dark of it points of fire, and colours in light, all glowing and moving, and the air trembled. I stared out into the night, and the dark tree lifted over the roof of the barn and rose up in the air and floated towards me. I did not move till at the last moment when it was close to the house; and then I saw what it was and banged the window down only just in time. I had to fight, and I saw the tree that was like a burning cloud rise up in the night and sink again and settle over the barn.

I told them downstairs of this. They sat with white faces, and Mrs Griffith said that ancient devils were let loose and had come out of the trees and out of the old hills because of the wickedness that was on the earth. She began to murmur something to herself, something that sounded to me like broken-down Latin.

I went up to my room again an hour later, but the dark tree swelled over the barn. Another day went by, and at dusk I looked out, but the eyes of fire were watching me. I dared not open the window.

And then I thought of another plan. There was the great old fireplace, with the round Flemish chimney going high above the house. If I stood beneath it and shouted I thought perhaps the sound might be carried better than if I called out of the window; for all I knew the round chimney might act as a sort of megaphone. Night after night, then, I stood in the hearth and called for help from nine o'clock to eleven. I thought of the lonely place, deep in the valley of the ash trees, of the lonely hills and lands about it. I thought of the little cottages far away and hoped that my voice might reach to those within them. I thought of the winding lane high on the Allt, and of the few men that came there of nights; but I hoped that my cry might come to one of them.

But we had drunk up the beer, and we would only let ourselves have water by little drops, and on the fourth night my throat was dry, and I began to feel strange and weak; I knew that all the voice I had in my lungs would hardly reach the length of the field by the farm.

It was then we began to dream of wells and fountains, and water coming very cold, in little drops, out of rocky places in the middle of a cool wood. We had given up all meals; now and then one would cut a lump from the sides of bacon on the kitchen wall and chew a bit of it, but the saltness was like fire.

There was a great shower of rain one night. The girl said we might open a window and hold out bowls and basins and catch the rain. I spoke of the cloud with burning eyes. She said, 'we will go to the window in the dairy at the back, and one of us can get some water at all events.' She stood up with her basin on the stone slab in the dairy and looked out and heard the plashing of the rain, falling very fast. And she unfastened the catch of the window and had just opened it gently with one hand, for about an inch, and had her basin in the other hand. 'And then,' she said, 'there was something that began to tremble and shudder and shake as it did when we went to the Choral Festival at St Teilo's, and the organ played, and there was the cloud and the burning close before me.'

And then we began to dream, as I say. I woke up in my sitting-room one hot afternoon when the sun was shining, and I had been looking and searching in my dream all through the house, and I had gone down to the old cellar that wasn't used, the cellar with the pillars and the vaulted room, with an iron pike in my hand. Something said to me that there was water there, and in my dream I went to a heavy stone by the middle pillar and raised it up, and there beneath was a bubbling well of cold, clear water, and I had just hollowed my hand to drink it when I woke. I went into the kitchen and told young Griffith. I said I was sure there was water there. He shook his head, but he took up the great kitchen poker and we went down to the old cellar. I showed him the stone by the pillar, and he raised it up. But there was no well.

Do you know, I reminded myself of many people whom I have met in life? I would not be convinced. I was sure that, after all, there was a well there. They had a butcher's cleaver in the kitchen and I took it down to the old cellar and hacked at the ground with it. The others didn't interfere with me. We were getting past that. We hardly ever spoke to one another. Each one would be wandering about the house, upstairs and downstairs, each one of us, I suppose, bent on his own foolish plan and mad design, but we hardly ever spoke. Years ago, I was an actor for a bit, and I remember how it was on first nights; the actors treading softly up and down the wings, by their entrance, their lips moving and muttering over the words of their parts, but without a word for one another. So it was with us. I came upon young Griffith one evening evidently trying to make a subterranean passage under one of the walls of the house. I knew he was mad, as he knew I was mad when he saw me digging for a well in the cellar; but neither said anything to the other.

Now we are past all this. We are too weak. We dream when we are awake and when we dream we think we wake. Night and day come and go and we mistake one for another; I hear Griffith murmuring to himself about the stars when the sun is high at noonday, and at midnight I have found myself thinking that I walked in bright sunlit meadows beside cold, rushing streams that flowed from high rocks.

Then at the dawn figures in black robes, carrying lighted tapers in their hands pass slowly about and about; and I hear great rolling organ music that sounds as if some tremendous rite were to begin, and voices crying in an ancient song shrill from the depths of the earth.

Only a little while ago I heard a voice which sounded as if it were at my very ears, but rang and echoed and resounded as if it were rolling and reverberating from the vault of some cathedral, chanting in terrible modulations. I heard the words quite clearly.

Incipit liber iræ Domini Dei nostri. (Here beginneth The Book of the Wrath of the Lord our God.)

And then the voice sang the word *Aleph*, prolonging it, it seemed through ages, and a light was extinguished as it began the chapter:

In that day, saith the Lord, there shall be a cloud over the land, and in the cloud a burning and a shape of fire, and out of the cloud shall issue forth my messengers; they shall run all together, they shall not turn aside; this shall be a day of exceeding bitterness, without salvation. And on every high hill, saith the Lord of Hosts, I will set my sentinels, and my armies shall encamp in the place of every valley; in the house that is amongst rushes I will execute judgment, and in vain shall they fly for refuge to the munitions of the rocks. In the groves of the woods, in the places where the leaves are as a tent above them, they shall find the sword of the slayer; and they that put their trust in walled cities shall be con-

founded. Woe unto the armed man, woe unto him that taketh pleasure in the strength of his artillery, for a little thing shall smite him, and by one that hath no might shall he be brought down into the dust. That which is low shall be set on high; I will make the lamb and the young sheep to be as the lion from the swellings of Jordan; they shall not spare, saith the Lord, and the doves shall be as eagles on the hill Engedi; none shall be found that may abide the onset of their battle.

Even now I can hear the voice rolling far away, as if it came from the altar of a great church and I stood at the door. There are lights very far away in the hollow of a vast darkness, and one by one they are put out. I hear a voice chanting again with that endless modulation that climbs and aspires to the stars, and shines there, and rushes down to the dark depths of the earth, again to ascend; the word is *Zain*.

Here the manuscript lapsed again, and finally into utter, lamentable confusion. There were scrawled lines wavering across the page on which Secretan seemed to have been trying to note the unearthly music that swelled in his dying ears. As the scrapes and scratches of ink showed, he had tried hard to begin a new sentence. The pen had dropped at last out of his hand upon the paper, leaving a blot and a smear upon it.

Lewis heard the tramp of feet along the passage; they were carrying out the dead to the cart.

XIV. *The End of the Terror*

Dr Lewis maintained that we should never begin to understand the real significance of life until we began to study just those aspects of it which we now dismiss and overlook as utterly inexplicable, and therefore, unimportant.

We were discussing a few months ago the awful shadow of the terror which at length had passed away from the land. I had formed my opinion, partly from observation, partly from certain facts which had been communicated to me, and the passwords having been exchanged, I found that Lewis had come by very different ways to the same end.

'And yet,' he said, 'it is not a true end, or rather, it is like all the ends of human inquiry, it leads one to a great mystery. We must confess that what has happened might have happened at any time in the history of the world. It did not happen till a year ago as a matter of fact, and therefore we made up our minds that it never could happen; or, one would better say, it was outside the range even of imagination. But this is our way. Most people are quite sure that the Black Death – otherwise the plague – will never invade Europe again . They have made up their complacent minds that it was due to dirt and bad drainage. As a matter of fact the plague had nothing to do with dirt or with drains; and there is nothing to prevent its ravaging England tomorrow. But if you tell people so, they won't believe you. They won't believe in anything that isn't there at the particular moment when you are talking to them. As with the plague, so with the terror. We could not believe that such a thing could ever happen. Remnant said, truly enough, that whatever it was, it was outside theory, outside our theory. Flatland cannot believe in the cube or the sphere.'

I agreed with all this. I added that sometimes the world was incapable of seeing, much less believing, that which was before its own eyes.

'Look,' I said, 'at any eighteenth-century print of a Gothic cathedral. You will find that the trained artistic eye even could not behold in any true sense the building that was before it. I have seen an old print of Peterborough Cathedral that looks as if the artist had drawn it from a clumsy model, constructed of bent wire and children's bricks.

'Exactly; because Gothic was outside the æsthetic theory (and therefore vision) of the time. You can't believe what you don't see: rather, you can't see what you don't believe. It was so during the time of the terror. All this bears out what Coleridge said as to the necessity of having the idea before the facts could be of any service to one. Of course, he was right; mere facts, without the correlating idea, are nothing and lead to no conclusion. We had plenty of facts, but we could make nothing of them. I went home at the tail of that dreadful procession from Treff Loyne in a state of mind very near to madness. I heard one of the soldiers saying to the other: "There's no rat that'll spike a man to the heart, Bill." I don't know why, but I felt that if I heard any more of such talk as that I should go crazy; it seemed to me that the anchors of reason were parting. I left the party and took the short cut across the fields into Porth. I looked up Davies in the High Street and arranged with him that he should take on any cases I might have that evening, and then I went home and gave my man his instructions to send people on. And then I shut myself up to think it all out – if I could.

'You must not suppose that my experiences of that afternoon had afforded me the slightest illumination. Indeed, if it had not been that I had seen poor old Griffith's body lying pierced in his own farmyard, I think I should have been inclined to accept one of Secretan's hints, and to believe that the whole family had fallen a victim to a collective delusion or hallucination, and had shut themselves up and died of thirst through sheer madness. I think there have been such cases. It's the insanity of inhibition, the belief that you can't do something which you are really perfectly capable of doing. But; I had seen the body of the murdered man and the wound that had killed him.

'Did the manuscript left by Secretan give me no hint? Well, it seemed to me to make confusion worse confounded. You have seen it; you know that in certain places it is evidently mere delirium, the wanderings of a dying mind. How was I to separate the facts from the phantasms – lacking the key to the whole enigma. Delirium is often a sort of cloud-castle, a sort of magnified and distorted shadow of actualities, but it is a very difficult thing, almost an impossible thing, to reconstruct the real house from the distortion of it, thrown on the clouds of the patient's brain. You see, Secretan in writing that extraordinary document almost insisted on the fact that he was not in his proper sense; that for days he had been part asleep, part awake, part delirious. How was one to judge his statement, to separate delirium from fact? In one thing he stood confirmed; you remember he speaks of calling for help up the old chimney of Treff Loyne; that did seem to fit in with the tales of a hollow, moaning cry that had been heard upon the Allt: so far one could take him as a recorder of actual experiences. And I looked in the old cellars of the farm and found a frantic sort of rabbit-hole dug by one of the pillars; again he was confirmed. But what was one to make of that story of the chanting voice, and the letters of the Hebrew alphabet, and the chapter out of some unknown minor prophet? When one has the key it is easy enough to sort out the facts, or the hints of facts from the delusions; but I hadn't the key on that September evening. I was forgetting the 'tree' with lights and fires in it; that, I think, impressed me more than anything with the feeling that Secretan's story was, in the main, a true story. I had seen a like appearance down there in my own garden; but what was it?

'Now, I was saying that, paradoxically, it is only by the inexplicable things that life can be explained. We are apt to say, you know, "a very odd coincidence" and pass the matter by, as if there were no more to be said, or as if that were the end of it. Well, I believe that the only real path lies through the blind alleys.'

'How do you mean?'

'Well, this is an instance of what I mean. I told you about Merritt, my brother-in-law, and the capsizing of that boat, the *Mary Ann*. He had seen, he said, signal lights flashing from one of the farms on the coast, and he was quite certain that the two things were intimately connected as cause and effect. I thought it all nonsense, and I was wondering how I was going to shut him up when a big moth flew into the room through that window, fluttered about, and succeeded in burning itself alive in the lamp. That gave me my cue; I asked Merritt if he knew why moths made for lamps or something of the kind; I thought it would be a hint to him that I was sick of his flash-lights and his half-baked theories. So it was – he looked sulky and held his tongue.

'But a few minutes later I was called out by a man who had found his little boy dead in a field near his cottage about an hour before. The child was so still, they said, that a great moth had settled on his forehead and only fluttered away when they lifted up the body. It was absolutely illogical; but it was this odd "coincidence" of the moth in my lamp and the moth on the dead boy's forehead that first set me on the track. I can't say that it guided me in any real sense; it was more like a great flare of red paint on a wall; it rang up my attention, if I may say so; it was a sort of shock like a bang on the big drum. No doubt Merritt was talking great nonsense that evening so far as his particular instance went; the flashes of light from the farm had nothing to do with the wreck of the boat. But his general principle was sound; when you hear a gun go off and see a man fall it is idle to talk of "a mere coincidence". I think a very interesting book might be written on this question: I would call it *A Grammar of Coincidence*.

'But as you will remember, from having read my notes on the matter, I was called in about ten days later to see a man named Cradock, who had been found in a field near his farm quite dead. This also was at night. His wife found him, and there were some very queer things in her story. She said that the hedge of the field looked as if it were changed; she began to be afraid that she had lost her way and got into the wrong field. Then she said the hedge was lighted up as if there were a lot of glow worms in it, and when she peered over the stile there seemed to be some kind of glimmering upon the ground, and then the glimmering melted away, and she found her husband's body near where this light had been. Now this man Cradock had been suffocated just as the little boy Roberts had been suffocated, and as that man in the Midlands who took a short cut one night had been suffocated. Then I remembered that poor Johnnie Roberts had called out about "something shiny" over the stile just before he played truant. Then, on my part, I had to contribute the very remarkable sight I witnessed here, as I looked down over the garden; the appearance as of a spreading tree where I knew there was no such tree, and then the shining and burning of lights and moving colours. Like the poor child and Mrs Cradock, I had seen something shiny, just as some man in Stratfordshire had seen a dark cloud with points of fire in it floating over the trees. And Mrs Cradock thought that the shape of the trees in the hedge had changed.

'My mind almost uttered the word that was wanted; but you see the difficulties. This set of circumstances could not, so far as I could see, have any relation with the other circumstances of the terror. How could I connect all this with the bombs and machine-guns of the Midlands, with the armed men who kept watch about the munition shops by day and night. Then there was the long list of people here who had fallen over the cliffs or into the quarry; there were the cases of the men stifled in the slime of the marshes; there was the affair of the family murdered in front of their cottage on the Highway; there was the capsized *Mary Ann*. I could not see any thread that could bring all these incidents together; they seemed to me to be hopelessly disconnected. I could not make out any relation between the agency that beat out the brains of the Williamses and the agency that overturned the boat. I don't know, but I think it's very likely if nothing more had happened that I should have put the whole thing down as an unaccountable series of crimes and accidents which chanced to occur in Meirion in the summer of 1915. Well, of course, that would have been an impossible standpoint in view of certain incidents in Merritt's story. Still, if one is confronted by the insoluble, one lets it go at last. If the mystery is inexplicable, one pretends that there isn't any mystery. That is the justification for what is called free thinking.

'Then came that extraordinary business of Treff Loyne. I couldn't put that on one side. I couldn't pretend that nothing strange or out of the way had happened. There was no getting over it or getting round it. I had seen with my eyes that there was a mystery, and a most horrible mystery. I have forgotten my logic, but one might say that Treff Loyne demonstrated the existence of a mystery in the figure of death.

'I took it all home, as I have told you, and sat down for the evening before it. It appalled me, not only by its horror, but here again by the discrepancy between its terms. Old Griffith, so far as I could judge, had been killed by the thrust of a pike or perhaps of a sharpened stake: how could one relate this to the burning tree that had floated over the ridge of the barn. It was as if I said to you: "Here is a man drowned, and here is a man burned alive: show that each death was caused by the same agency!" And the moment that I left this particular case of Treff Loyne, and tried to get some light on it from other instances of the terror, I would think of the man in the Midlands who heard the feet of a thousand men rustling in the wood, and their voices as if dead men sat up in their bones and talked. And then I would say to myself: "And how about that boat overturned in a calm sea?" There seemed no end to it, no hope oj any solution.

'It was, I believe, a sudden leap of the mind that liberated me from the tangle. It was quite beyond logic. I went back to that evening when Merritt was boring me with his flash-lights, to the moth in the candle, and to the moth on the forehead of poor Johnnie Roberts. There was no sense in it; but I suddenly determined that the child and Joseph Cradock the farmer, and that unnamed Stratfordshire man, all found at night, all asphyxiated, had been choked by vast swarms of moths. I don't pretend even now that this is demonstrated, but I'm sure it's true.

'Now suppose you encounter a swarm of these creatures in the dark.

Suppose the smaller ones fly up your nostrils. You will gasp for breath and open your mouth. Then, suppose some hundreds of them fly into your mouth, into your gullet, into your windpipe, what will happen to you? You will be dead in a very short time, choked, asphyxiated.'

'But the moths would be dead too. They would be found in the bodies.'

'The moths? Do you know that it is extremely difficult to kill a moth with cyanide of potassium? Take a frog, kill it, open its stomach. There you will find its dinner of moths and small beetles, and the "dinner" will shake itself and walk off cheerily, to resume an entirely active existence. No; that is no difficulty.

'Well, now I came to this. I was shutting out all the other cases. I was confining myself to those that came under the one formula. I got to the assumption or conclusion, whichever you like, that certain people had been asphyxiated by the action of moths. I had accounted for that extraordinary appearance of burning or coloured lights that I had witnessed myself, when I saw the growth of that strange tree in my garden. That was clearly the cloud with points of fire in it that the Stratfordshire man took for a new and terrible kind of poison gas, that was the shiny something that poor little Johnnie Roberts had seen over the stile, that was the glimmering light that had led Mrs Cradock to her husband's dead body, that was the assemblage of terrible eyes that had watched over Treff Loyne by night. Once on the right track I understood all this, for coming into this room in the dark, I have been amazed by the wonderful burning and the strange fiery colours of the eyes of a single moth, as it crept up the pane of glass, outside. Imagine the effect of myriads of such eyes, of the movement of these lights and fires in a vast swarm of moths, each insect being in constant motion while it kept its place in the mass: I felt that all this was clear and certain.

'Then the next step. Of course, we know nothing really about moths; rather, we know nothing of moth reality. For all I know there may be hundreds of books which treat of moth and nothing but moth. But these are scientific books, and science only deals with surfaces; it has nothing to do with realities – it is impertinent if it attempts to do with realities. To take a very minor matter, we don't even know why the moth desires the flame. But we do know what the moth does not do; it does not gather itself into swarms with the object of destroying human life. But here, by the hypothesis, were cases in which the moth had done this very thing; the moth race had entered, it seemed, into a malignant conspiracy against the human race. It was quite impossible, no doubt – that is to say, it had never happened before – but I could see no escape from this conclusion.

'These insects, then, were definitely hostile to man; and then I stopped, for I could not see the next step, obvious though it seems to me now. I believe that the soldiers' scraps of talk on the way to Treff Loyne and back flung the next plank over the gulf. They had spoken of "rat-poison", of no rat being able to spike a man through the heart; and then, suddenly, I saw my way clear. If the moths were infected with hatred of men, and possessed the design and the power of combining against him, why not suppose this hatred, this design, this power shared by other non-human creatures?

'The secret of the terror might be condensed into a sentence: the animals had revolted against men.

'Now, the puzzle became easy enough; one had only to classify. Take the cases of the people who met their deaths by falling over cliffs or over the edge of quarries. We think of sheep as timid creatures, who always ran away. But suppose sheep that don't run away; and, after all, in reason why should they run away? Quarry or no quarry, cliff or no cliff; what would happen to you if a hundred sheep ran after you instead of running from you? There would be no help for it; they would have you down and beat you to death or stifle you. Then suppose man, woman, or child near a cliff's edge or a quarry-side, and a sudden rush of sheep. Clearly there is no help; there is nothing for it but to go over. There can be no doubt that that is what happened in all these cases.

'And again; you know the country and you know how a herd of cattle will sometimes pursue people through the fields in a solemn, stolid sort of way. They behave as if they wanted to close in on you. Townspeople sometimes get frightened and scream and run; you or I would take no notice, or at the utmost, wave our sticks at the herd, which will stop dead or lumber off. But suppose they don't lumber off. The mildest old cow, remember, is stronger than any man. What can one man or half a dozen men do against half a hundred of these beasts no longer restrained by that mysterious inhibition, which has made for ages the strong the humble slaves of the weak? But if you are botanizing in the marsh, like that poor fellow who was staying at Porth, and forty or fifty young cattle gradually close round you, and refuse to move when you shout and wave your stick, but get closer and closer instead, and get you into the slime. Again, where is your help? If you haven't got an automatic pistol, you must go down and stay down, while the beasts lie quietly on you for five minutes. It was a quicker death for poor Griffith of Treff Loyne – one of his own beasts gored him to death with one sharp thrust of its horn into his heart. And from that morning those within the house were closely besieged by their own cattle and horses and sheep; and when those un-happy people within opened a window to call for help or to catch a few drops of rain water to relieve their burning thirst, the cloud waited for them with its myriad eyes of fire. Can you wonder that Secretan's statement reads in places like mania? You perceive the horrible position of those people in Treff Loyne; not only did they see death advancing on them, but advancing with incredible steps, as if one were to die not only in nightmare but by nightmare. But no one in his wildest, most fiery dreams had ever imagined such a fate. I am not astonished that Secretan at one moment suspected the evidence of his own senses, at another surmised that the world's end had come.'

'And how about the Williamses who were murdered on the Highway near here?'

'The horses were the murderers; the horses that afterwards stampeded the camp below. By some means which is still obscure to me they lured that family into the road and beat their brains out; their shod hoofs were the instruments of execution. And, as for the *Mary Ann*, the boat that was capsized, I have no doubt that it was overturned by a sudden rush of the porpoises that were gambolling about in the water of Larnac Bay. A porpoise is a heavy beast – half a dozen of them could easily upset a light rowing-boat. The munition works? Their enemy was rats. I believe that it has been calculated that in greater London the number of rats is about equal to the number of human beings, that is, there are about seven millions of them. The proportion would be about the same in all the great centres of population; and the rat, moreover, is, on occasion, migratory in its habits. You can understand now that story of the *Semiramis*, beating about the mouth of the Thames, and at last cast away by Arcachon, her only crew dry heaps of bones. The rat is an expert boarder of ships. And so one can understand the tale told by the frightened man who took the path by the wood that led up from the new munition works. He thought he heard a thousand men treading softly through the wood and chattering to one another in some horrible tongue; what he did hear was the marshalling of an army of rats – their array before the battle.

'And conceive the terror of such an attack. Even one rat in a fury is said to be an ugly customer to meet; conceive then, the irruption of these terrible, swarming myriads, rushing upon the helpless, unprepared, astonished workers in the munition shops.'

There can be no doubt, I think, that Dr Lewis was entirely justified in these extraordinary conclusions. As I say, I had arrived at pretty much the same end, by different ways; but this rather as to the general situation, while Lewis had made his own particular study of those circumstances of the terror that were within his immediate purview, as a physician in large practice in the southern part of Meirion. Of some of the cases which he reviewed he had, no doubt, no immediate or first-hand knowledge; but he judged these instances by their similarity to the facts which had come under his personal notice. He spoke of the affairs of the quarry at Llanfihangel on the analogy of the people who were found dead at the bottom of the cliffs near Porth, and he was no doubt justified in doing so. He told me that, thinking the whole matter over, he was hardly more astonished by the terror in itself than by the strange way in which he had arrived at his conclusions.

'You know,' he said, 'those certain evidences of animal malevolence which we knew of, the bees that stung the child to death, the trusted sheep-dog's turning savage, and so forth. Well, I got no light whatever from all this; it suggested nothing to me – simply because I had not got that "idea" which Coleridge rightly holds necessary in all inquiry; facts *qua* facts, as we said, mean nothing and, come to nothing. You do not believe, therefore you cannot see.

'And then, when the truth at last appeared it was through the whimsical "coincidence", as we call such signs, of the moth in my lamp and the moth on the dead child's forehead. This, I think, is very extraordinary.'

'And there seems to have been one beast that remained faithful; the dog at Treff Loyne. That is strange.'

'That remains a mystery.'

It would not be wise, even now, to describe too closely the terrible scenes that were to be seen in the munition areas of the north and the Midlands during the black months of the terror. Out of the factories issued at black midnight the shrouded dead in their coffins, and their very kinsfolk did not know how they had come by their deaths. All the towns were full of houses of mourning, were full of dark and terrible rumours; incredible, as the incredible reality. There were things done and suffered that perhaps never will be brought to light, memories and secret traditions of these things will be whispered in families, delivered from father to son, growing wilder with the passage of the years, but never growing wilder than the truth.

It is enough to say that the cause of the Allies was for awhile in deadly peril. The men at the front called in their extremity for guns and shells. No one told them what was happening in the places where these munitions were made.

At first the position was nothing less than desperate; men in high places were almost ready to cry mercy to the enemy. But, after the first panic, measures were taken such as those described by Merritt in his account of the matter. The workers were armed with special weapons, guards were mounted, machine-guns were placed in position, bombs and liquid flame were ready against the obscene hordes of the enemy, and the 'burning clouds' found a fire fiercer than their own. Many deaths occurred amongst the airmen; but they, too, were given special guns, arms that scattered shot broadcast, and so drove away the dark flights that threatened the airplanes.

And, then, in the winter of 1915–16, the terror ended suddenly as it had begun. Once more a sheep was a frightened beast that ran instinctively from a little child; the cattle were again solemn, stupid creatures, void of harm; the spirit and the convention of malignant design passed out of the hearts of all the animals. The chains that they had cast off for a while were thrown again about them.

And, finally, there comes the inevitable 'why'? Why did the beasts who had been humbly and patiently subject to man, or affrighted by his presence, suddenly know their strength and learn how to league together, and declare bitter war against their ancient master?

It is a most difficult and obscure question. I give what explanation I have to give with very great diffidence, and an eminent disposition to be corrected, if a clearer light can be found.

Some friends of mine, for whose judgment I have very great respect, are inclined to think that there was a certain contagion of hate. They hold that the fury of the whole world at war, the great passion of death that seems driving all humanity to destruction, infected at last these lower creatures, and in place of their native instinct of submission, gave them rage and wrath and ravening.

This may be the explanation. I cannot say that it is not so, because I do not profess to understand the working of the universe. But I confess that the theory strikes me as fanciful. There may be a contagion of hate as there is a contagion of smallpox; I do not know, but I hardly believe it.

In my opinion, and it is only an opinion, the source of the great revolt of the beasts is to be sought in a much subtler region of inquiry. I believe that the subjects revolted because the king abdicated. Man has dominated the beasts throughout the ages, the spiritual has reigned over the rational through the peculiar quality and grace of spirituality that men possess, that makes a man to be that which he is. And when he maintained this power and grace, I think it is pretty clear that between him and the animals there was a certain treaty and alliance. There was supremacy on the one hand, and submission on the other; but at the same time there was between the two that cordiality which exists between lords and subjects in a well-organized state. I know a socialist who maintains that Chaucer's *Canterbury Tales* give a picture of true democracy. I do not know about that, but I see that knight and miller were able to get on quite pleasantly together, just because the knight knew that he was a knight and the miller knew that he was a miller. If the knight had had conscientious objections to his knightly grade, while the miller saw no reason why he should not be a knight, I am sure that their intercourse would have been difficult, unpleasant, and perhaps murderous.

So with man. I believe in the strength and truth of tradition. A learned man said to me a few weeks ago: 'When I have to choose between the evidence of tradition and the evidence of a document, I always believe the evidence of tradition. Documents may be falsified, and often are falsified; tradition is never falsified.' This is true; and, therefore, I think, one may put trust in the vast body of folk-lore which asserts that there was once a worthy and friendly alliance between man and the beasts. Our popular tale of Dick Whittington and his cat no doubt represents the adaptation of a very ancient legend to a comparatively modern personage, but we may go back into the ages and find the popular tradition asserting that not only are the animals the subjects, but also the friends of man.

All that was in virtue of that singular spiritual element in man which the rational animals do not possess. 'Spiritual' does not mean 'respectable', it does not even mean 'moral', it does not mean 'good' in the ordinary acceptation of the word. It signifies the royal prerogative of man, differentiating him from the beasts.

For long ages he has been putting off this royal robe, he has been wiping the balm of consecration from his own breast. He has declared, again and again, that he is not spiritual, but rational, that is, the equal of the beasts over whom he was once sovereign. He has vowed that he is not Orpheus but Caliban.

But the beasts also have within them something which corresponds to the spiritual quality in men – we are content to call it instinct. They perceived that the throne was vacant – not even friendship was possible between them and the self-deposed monarch. If he were not king he was a sham, an impostor, a thing to be destroyed.

Hence, I think, the terror. They have risen once – they may rise again.

Arthur Conan Doyle

Lot No. 249

Of the dealings of Edward Bellingham with William Monkhouse Lee, and of the cause of the great terror of Abercrombie Smith, it may be that no absolute and final judgment will ever be delivered. It is true that we have the full and clear narrative of Smith himself, and such corroboration as he could look for from Thomas Styles the servant, from the Reverend Plumptree Peterson, Fellow of Old's, and from such other people as chanced to gain some passing glance at this or that incident in a singular chain of events. Yet, in the main, the story must rest upon Smith alone, and the most will think that it is more likely that one brain, however outwardly sane, has some subtle warp in its texture, some strange flaw in its workings, than that the path of Nature has been over-stepped in open day in so famed a centre of learning and light as the University of Oxford. Yet when we think how narrow and how devious this path of Nature is, how dimly we can trace it, for all our lamps of science, and how from the darkness which girds it round great and terrible possibilities loom ever shadowly upwards, it is a bold and confident man who will put a limit to the strange by-paths into which the human spirit may wander.

In a certain wing of what we will call Old College in Oxford there is a corner turret of an exceeding great age. The heavy arch which spans the open door has bent downwards in the centre under the weight of its years, and the grey, lichen-blotched blocks of stone are bound and knitted together with withes and strands of ivy, as though the old mother had set herself to brace them up against wind and weather. From the door a stone stair curves upward spirally, passing two landings, and terminating in a third one, its steps all shapeless and hollowed by the tread of so many generations of the seekers after knowledge. Life has flowed like water down this winding stair, and, waterlike, has left these smooth-worn grooves behind it. From the long-gowned, pedantic scholars of Plantagenet days down to the young bloods of a later age, how full and strong had been that tide of young, English life. And what was left now of all those hopes, those strivings, those fiery energies, save here and there in some old-world churchyard a few scratches upon a stone, and perchance a handful of dust in a mouldering coffin? Yet here were the silent stair and the grey, old wall, with bend and saltire and many another heraldic device still to be read upon its surface, like grotesque shadows thrown back from the days that had passed.

In the month of May, in the year 1884, three young men occupied the sets of rooms which opened on to the separate landings of the old stair. Each set consisted simply of a sitting-room and of a bedroom, while the two corresponding rooms upon the ground-floor were used, the one as a coal-cellar, and the other as the living-room of the servant, or scout, Thomas Styles, whose duty it was to wait upon the three men above him. To right and to left was a line of lecture-rooms and of offices, so that the dwellers in the old turret enjoyed a certain seclusion, which made the chambers popular among the more studious undergraduates. Such were the three who occupied them now – Abercombie Smith above, Edward Bellingham beneath him, and William Monkhouse Lee upon the lowest storey.

It was ten o'clock on a bright, spring night, and Abercombie Smith lay back in his arm-chair, his feet upon the fender, and his briar-root pipe between his lips. In a similar chair, and equally at his ease, there lounged on the other side of the fireplace his old school friend Jephro Hastie. Both men were in flannels, for they had spent their evening upon the river, but apart from their dress no one could look at their hard-cut, alert faces without seeing that they were open-air men – men whose minds and tastes turned naturally to all that was manly and robust. Hastie, indeed, was stroke of his college boat, and Smith was an even better oar, but a coming examination had already cast its shadow over him and held him to his work, save for the few hours a week which health demanded. A litter of medical books upon the table, with scattered bones, models, and anatomical plates, pointed to the extent as well as the nature of his studies, while a couple of single-sticks and a set of boxing-gloves above the mantelpiece hinted at the means by which, with Hastie's help, he might take his exercise in its most compressed and least-distant form. They knew each other very well – so well that they could sit now in that soothing silence which is the very highest development of companionship.

'Have some whisky,' said Abercombie Smith at last between two cloudbursts. 'Scotch in the jug and Irish in the bottle.'

'No, thanks. I'm in for the sculls. I don't liquor when I'm training.

How about you?'

'I'm reading hard. I think it best to leave it alone.'

Hastie nodded, and they relapsed into a contented silence.

'By the way, Smith,' asked Hastie, presently, 'have you made the acquaintance of either of the fellows on your stair yet?'

'Just a nod when we pass. Nothing more.'

'Hum! I should be inclined to let it stand at that. I know something of them both. Not much, but as much as I want. I don't think I should take them to my bosom if I were you. Not that there's much amiss with Monkhouse Lee.'

'Meaning the thin one?'

'Precisely. He is a gentlemanly little fellow. I don't think there is any vice in him. But then you can't know him without knowing Bellingham.'

'Meaning the fat one?'

'Yes, the fat one. And he's a man whom I, for one, would rather not know.'

Abercombie Smith raised his eyebrows and glanced across at his companion.

'What's up, then?' he asked. 'Drink? Cards? Cad? You used not to be censorious.'

'Ah! you evidently don't know the man, or you wouldn't ask. There's something damnable about him – something reptilian. My gorge always rises at him. I should put him down as a man with secret vices – an evil liver. He's no fool, though. They say that he is one of the best men in his line that they have ever had in the college.'

'Medicine or classics?'

'Eastern languages. He's demon at them. Chillingworth met him somewhere above the second cataract last long, and he told me that he just prattled to the Arabs as if he had been born and nursed and weaned among them. He talked Coptic to the Copts, and Hebrew to the Jews, and Arabic to the Bedouins, and they were all ready to kiss the hem of his frock-coat. There are some old hermit Johnnies up in those parts who sit on rocks and scowl and spit at the casual stranger. Well, when they saw this chap Bellingham, before he had said five words they just lay down on their bellies and wriggled. Chillingworth said that he never saw anything like it. Bellingham seemed to take it as his right, too, and strutted about among them and talked down to them like a Dutch uncle. Pretty good for an undergrad. of Old's, wasn't it?'

'Why do you say you can't know Lee without knowing Bellingham?'

'Because Bellingham is engaged to his sister Eveline. Such a bright little girl, Smith! I know the whole family well. It's disgusting to see that brute with her. A toad and a dove, that's what they always remind me of.'

Abercombie Smith grinned and knocked his ashes out against the side of the grate.

'You show every card in your hand, old chap,' said he. 'What a prejudiced, green-eyed, evil-thinking old man it is! You have really nothing against the fellow except that.'

'Well, I've known her ever since she was as long as that cherry-wood pipe, and I don't like to see her taking risks. And it is a risk. He looks beastly. And he has a beastly temper, a venomous temper. You remember his row with Long Norton?'

'No; you always forget that I am a freshman.'

'Ah, it was last winter. Of course. Well, you know the towpath along by the river. There were several fellows going along it, Bellingham in front, when they came on an old market-woman coming the other way. It had been raining – you know what those fields are like when it has rained – and the path ran between the river and a great puddle that was nearly as broad. Well, what does this swine do but keep the path, and push the old girl into the mud, where she and her marketings came to terrible grief. It was a blackguard thing to do, and Long Norton, who is as gentle a fellow as ever stepped, told him what he thought of it. One word led to another, and it ended in Norton laying his stick across the fellow's shoulders. There was the deuce of a fuss about it, and it's a treat to see the way in which Bellingham looks at Norton when they meet now. By Jove, Smith, it's nearly eleven o'clock!'

'No hurry. Light your pipe again.'

'Not I. I'm supposed to be in training. Here I've been sitting gossiping when I ought to have been safely tucked up. I'll borrow your skull, if you can spare it. Williams has had mine for a month. I'll take the little bones of your ear, too, if you are sure you won't need them. Thanks very much. Never mind a bag, I can carry them very well under my arm. Good night, my son, and take my tip as to your neighbour.'

When Hastie, bearing his anatomical plunder, had clattered off down the winding stair, Abercombie Smith hurled his pipe into the wastepaper basket, and drawing his chair nearer to the lamp, plunged into a formidable, green-covered volume, adorned with great, coloured maps of that strange, internal kingdom of which we are the hapless and helpless monarchs. Though a freshman at Oxford, the student was not so in medicine, for he had worked for four years at Glasgow and at Berlin, and this coming examination would place him finally as a member of his profession. With his firm mouth, broad forehead, and clear-cut, somewhat hard-featured face, he was a man who, if he had no brilliant talent, was yet so dogged, so patient, and so strong that he might in the end overtop a more showy genius. A man who can hold his own among Scotchmen and North Germans is not a man to be easily set back. Smith had left a name at Glasgow and at Berlin, and he was bent now upon doing as much at Oxford, if hard work and devotion could accomplish it.

He had sat reading for about an hour, and the hands of the noisy carriage clock upon the side-table were rapidly closing together upon the twelve, when a sudden sound fell upon the student's ear – a sharp, rather shrill sound, like the hissing intake of a man's breath who gasps under some strong emotion. Smith laid down his book and slanted his ear to listen. There was no one on either side or above him, so that the interruption came certainly from the neighbour beneath – the same neighbour of whom Hastie had given so unsavoury an account. Smith knew him only as a flabby, pale-faced man of silent and studious habits, a man whose lamp threw a golden bar from the old turret even after he had extinguished his own. This community in lateness had formed a certain silent bond between them. It was soothing to Smith when the hours stole on towards dawning to feel that there was another so close who set as small a value upon his sleep as he did. Even now, as his thoughts turned towards him, Smith's feelings were kindly. Hastie was a good fellow, but he was rough, strong-fibred, with no imagination or sympathy. He could not tolerate departures from what he looked upon as the model type of manliness. If a man could not be measured by a public-school standard, then he was beyond the pale with Hastie. Like so many who are themselves robust, he was apt to confuse the constitution with the character, to ascribe to want of principle what was really a want of circulation. Smith, with his stronger mind, knew his friend's habit, and made allowance for it now as his thoughts turned towards the man beneath him.

There was no return of the singular sound, and Smith was about to turn to his work once more, when suddenly there broke out in the silence of the night a hoarse cry, a positive scream – the call of a man who is moved and shaken beyond all control. Smith sprang out of his chair and dropped his book. He was a man of fairly firm fibre, but there was something in this sudden, uncontrollable shriek of horror which chilled his blood and pringled in his skin. Coming in such a place and at such an hour, it brought a thousand fantastic possibilities into his head. Should he rush down, or was it better to wait? He had all the national hatred of making a scene, and he knew so little of his neighbour that he would not lightly intrude upon his affairs. For a moment he stood in doubt and even as he balanced the matter there was a quick rattle of footsteps upon the stairs, and young Monkhouse Lee, half-dressed and as white as ashes, burst into his room.

'Come down!' he gasped. 'Bellingham's ill.'

Abercrombie Smith followed him closely downstairs into the sitting-room which was beneath his own, and intent as he was upon the matter in hand, he could not but take an amazed glance around him as he crossed the threshold. It was such a chamber as he had never seen before – a museum rather than a study. Walls and ceiling were thickly covered with a thousand strange relics from Egypt and the East. Tall, angular figures bearing burdens or weapons stalked in an uncouth frieze round the apartments. Above were bull-headed, stork-headed, cat-headed, owl-headed statues, with viper-crowned, almond-eyed monarchs, and strange, beetle-like deities cut out of the blue Egyptian lapis lazuli. Horus and Isis and Osiris peeped down from every niche and shelf, while across the ceiling a true son of Old Nile, a great, hanging-jawed crocodile, was slung in a double noose.

In the centre of this singular chamber was a large, square table, littered with papers, bottles, and the dried leaves of some graceful, palm-like plant. These varied objects had all been heaped together in order to make room for a mummy case, which had been conveyed from the wall, as was evident from the gap there, and laid across the front of the table. The mummy itself, a horrid, black, withered thing, like a charred head on a gnarled bush, was lying half out of the case, with its claw-like hand and bony forearm resting upon the table. Propped up against the sarcophagus was an old, yellow scroll of papyrus, and in front of it, in a wooden arm-chair, sat the owner of the room, his head thrown back, his widely opened eyes directed in a horrified stare to the crocodile above him, and his blue, thick lips puffing loudly with every expiration.

'My God! he's dying!' cried Monkhouse Lee, distractedly.

He was a slim, handsome young fellow, olive-skinned and dark-eyed, of a Spanish rather than of an English type, with a Celtic intensity of manner which contrasted with the Saxon phlegm of Abercrombie Smith.

'Only a faint, I think,' said the medical student. 'Just give me a hand with him. You take his feet. Now on to the sofa. Can you kick all those little wooden devils off? What a litter it is! Now he will be all right if we undo his collar and give him some water. What has he been up to at all?'

'I don't know. I heard him cry out. I ran up. I know him pretty well, you know. It is very good of you to come down.'

'His heart is going like a pair of castanets,' said Smith, laying his hand on the breast of the unconscious man. 'He seems to me to be frightened all to pieces. Chuck the water over him! What a face he has got on him!'

It was indeed a strange and most repellent face, for colour and outline were equally unnatural. It was white, not with the ordinary pallor of fear, but with an absolutely bloodless white, like the under side of a sole. He was very fat, but gave the impression of having at some time been considerably fatter, for his skin hung loosely in creases and folds, and was shot with a meshwork of wrinkles. Short, stubbly brown hair bristled up from his scalp, with a pair of thick, wrinkled ears protruding at the sides. His light-grey eyes were still open, the pupils dilated and the balls projecting in a fixed and horrid stare. It seemed to Smith as he looked down upon him that he had never seen Nature's danger signals flying so plainly upon a man's countenance, and his thoughts turned more seriously to the warning which Hastie had given him an hour before.

'What the deuce can have frightened him so?' he asked.

'It's the mummy.'

'The mummy? How, then?'

'I don't know. It's beastly and morbid. I wish he would drop it. It's the second fright he has given me. It was the same last winter. I found him just like this, with that horrid thing in front of him.'

'What does he want with the mummy, then?'

'Oh, he's a crank, you know. It's his hobby. He knows more about these things than any man in England. But I wish he wouldn't! Ah, he's beginning to come to.'

A faint tinge of colour had begun to steal back into Bellingham's ghastly cheeks, and his eyelids shivered like a sail after a calm. He clasped and unclasped his hands, drew a long, thin breath between his teeth, and suddenly jerking up his head, threw a glance of recognition around him. As his eyes fell upon the mummy, he sprang off the sofa, seized the roll of papyrus, thrust it into a drawer, turned the key, and then staggered back on to the sofa.

'What's up?' he asked. 'What do you chaps want?'

'You've been shrieking out and making no end of a fuss,' said Monkhouse Lee. 'If our neighbour here from above hadn't come down, I'm sure I don't know what I should have done with you.'

'Ah, it's Abercrombie Smith,' said Bellingham, glancing up at him. 'How very good of you to come in! What a fool I am! Oh, my God, what a fool I am!'

He sank his head on to his hands, and burst into peal after peal of hysterical laughter.

'Look here! Drop it!' cried Smith, shaking him roughly by the shoulder.

'Your nerves are all in a jangle. You must drop these little midnight games with mummies, or you'll be going off your chump. You're all on wires now.'

'I wonder,' said Bellingham, 'whether you would be as cool as I am if you had seen——'

'What then?'

'Oh, nothing. I meant that I wonder if you could sit up at night with a mummy without trying your nerves. I have no doubt that you are quite right. I dare say that I have been taking it out of myself too much lately.

But I am all right now. Please don't go, though. Just wait for a few minutes until I am quite myself.'

'The room is very close,' remarked Lee, throwing open the window and letting in the cool night air.

'It's balsamic resin,' said Bellingham. He lifted up one of the dried palmate leaves from the table and frizzled it over the chimney of the lamp. It broke away into heavy smoke wreaths, and a pungent, biting odour filled the chamber. 'It's the sacred plant – the plant of the priests,' he remarked. 'Do you know anything of Eastern languages, Smith?'

'Nothing at all. Not a word.'

The answer seemed to lift a weight from the Egyptologist's mind.

'By the way,' he continued, 'how long was it from the time that you ran down, until I came to my senses?'

'Not long. Some four or five minutes.'

'I thought it could not be very long,' said he, drawing a long breath. 'But what a strange thing unconsciousness is! There is no measurement to it. I could not tell from my own sensations if it were seconds or weeks. Now that gentleman on the table was packed up in the days of the eleventh dynasty, some forty centuries ago, and yet if he could find his tongue, he would tell us that this lapse of time has been but a closing of the eyes and a reopening of them. He is a singularly fine mummy, Smith.'

Smith stepped over to the table and looked down with a professional eye at the black and twisted form in front of him. The features, though horribly discoloured, were perfect, and two little nut-like eyes still lurked in the depths of the black, hollow sockets. The blotched skin was drawn tightly from bone to bone, and a tangled wrap of black, coarse hair fell over the ears. Two thin teeth, like those a of rat, overlay the shrivelled lower lip. In its crouching position, with bent joints and craned head, there was a suggestion of energy about the horrid thing which made Smith's gorge rise. The gaunt ribs, with their parchment-like covering, were exposed, and the sunken, leaden-hued abdomen, with the long slit where the embalmer had left his mark; but the lower limbs were wrapped round with coarse, yellow bandages. A number of little clove-like pieces of myrrh and of cassia were sprinkled over the body, and lay scattered on the inside of the case.

'I don't know his name,' said Bellingham, passing his hand over the shrivelled head. 'You see the outer sarcophagus with the inscriptions is missing. Lot 249 is all the title he has now. You see it printed on his case. That was his number in the auction at which I picked him up.'

'He has been a very pretty sort of fellow in his day,' remarked Abercrombie Smith.

'He has been a giant. His mummy is six feet seven in length, and that would be a giant over there, for they were never a very robust race. Feel these great, knotted bones, too. He would be a nasty fellow to tackle.'

'Perhaps these very hands helped to build the stones into the pyramids,' suggested Monkhouse Lee, looking down with disgust in his eyes at the crooked, unclean talons.

'No fear. This fellow has been pickled in natron, and looked after in the most approved style. They did not serve hodsmen in that fashion. Salt or bitumen was enough for them. It has been calculated that this sort of thing cost about seven hundred and thirty pounds in our money. Our friend was a noble at the least. What do you make of that small inscription near his feet, Smith?'

'I told you that I know no Eastern tongue.'

'Ah, so you did. It is the name of the embalmer, I take it. A very conscientious worker he must have been. I wonder how many modern works will survive four thousand years?'

He kept on speaking lightly and rapidly, but it was evident to Abercrombie Smith that he was still palpitating with fear. His hands shook, his lower lip trembled, and look where he would, his eye always came sliding round to his gruesome companion. Through all his fear, however, there was a suspicion of triumph in his tone and manner. His eyes shone, and his footstep, as he paced the room, was brisk and jaunty. He gave the impression of a man who has gone through an ordeal, the marks of which he still bears upon him, but which has helped him to his end.

'You're not going yet?' he cried, as Smith rose from the sofa.

At the prospect of solitude, his fears seemed to crowd back upon him, and he stretched out a hand to detain him.

'Yes, I must go. I have my work to do. You are all right now. I think that with your nervous system you should take up some less morbid study.'

'Oh, I am not nervous as a rule; and I have unwrapped mummies before.'

'You fainted last time,' observed Monkhouse Lee.

'Ah, yes, so I did. Well, I must have a nerve tonic or a course of electricity. You are not going, Lee?'

'I'll do whatever you wish, Ned.'

'Then I'll come down with you and have a shakedown on your sofa. Good night, Smith. I am so sorry to have disturbed you with my foolishness.'

They shook hands, and as the medical student stumbled up the spiral and irregular stair he heard a key turn in a door, and the steps of his two new acquaintances as they descended to the lower floor.

In this strange way began the acquaintance between Edward Bellingham and Abercrombie Smith, an acquaintance which the latter, at least, had no desire to push further. Bellingham, however, appeared to have taken a fancy to his rough-spoken neighbour, and made his advances in such a way that he could hardly be repulsed without absolute brutality. Twice he called to thank Smith for his assistance, and many times afterwards he looked in with books, papers and such other civilities as two bachelor neighbours can offer each other. He was, as Smith soon found, a man of wide reading, with catholic tastes and an extraordinary memory. His manner, too, was so pleasing and suave that one came, after a time, to overlook his repellent appearance. For a jaded and wearied man he was no unpleasant companion, and Smith found himself, after a time, looking forward to his visits, and even returning them.

Clever as he undoubtedly was, however, the medical student seemed to detect a dash of insanity in the man. He broke out at times into a high, inflated style of talk which was in contrast with the simplicity of his life.

'It is a wonderful thing,' he cried, 'to feel that one can command powers of good and of evil – a ministering angel or a demon of vengeance.' And again, of Monkhouse Lee, he said, – 'Lee is a good fellow, an honest fellow, but he is without strength or ambition. He would not make a fit partner for a man with a great enterprise. He would not make a fit partner for me.'

At such hints and innuendoes stolid Smith, puffing solemnly at his pipe, would simply raise his eyebrows and shake his head, with little interjections of medical wisdom as to earlier hours and fresher air.

One habit Bellingham had developed of late which Smith knew to be a frequent herald of a weakening mind. He appeared to be for ever talking to himself. At late hours of the night, when there could be no visitor with him, Smith could still hear his voice beneath him in a low, muffled monologue, sunk almost to a whisper, and yet very audible in the silence. This solitary babbling annoyed and distracted the student, so that he spoke more than once to his neighbour about it. Bellingham, however, flushed up at the charge, and denied curtly that he had uttered a sound; indeed, he showed more annoyance over the matter than the occasion seemed to demand.

Had Abercrombie Smith had any doubts as to his own ears he had not to go far to find corroboration. Tom Styles, the little wrinkled man-servant who had attended to the wants of the lodgers in the turret for a longer time than any man's memory could carry him, was sorely put to it over the same matter.

'If you please, sir,' said he, as he tidied down the top chamber one morning, 'do you think Mr Bellingham is all right, sir?'

'All right, Styles?'

'Yes, sir. Right in his head, sir.'

'Why should he not be, then?'

'Well, I don't know, sir. His habits has changed of late. He's not the same man he used to be, though I make free to say that he was never quite one of my gentlemen, like Mr Hastie or yourself, sir. He's took to talkin' to himself something awful. I wonder it don't disturb you. I don't know what to make of him, sir.'

'I don't know what business it is of yours, Styles.'

'Well, I takes an interest, Mr Smith. It may be forward of me, but I can't help it. I feel sometimes as if I was mother and father to my young gentlemen. It all falls on me when things go wrong and the relations come. But Mr Bellingham, sir. I want to know what it is that walks about his room sometimes when he's out and when the door's locked on the outside.'

'Eh? you're talking nonsense, Styles.'

'Maybe so, sir; but I heard it more'n once with my own ears.'

'Rubbish, Styles.'

'Very good, sir. You'll ring the bell if you want me.'

Abercrombie Smith gave little heed to the gossip of the old man-servant, but a small incident occurred a few days later which left an unpleasant effect upon his mind, and brought the words of Styles forcibly to his memory.

Bellingham had come up to see him late one night, and was entertaining him with an interesting account of the rock tombs of Beni Hassan in Upper Egypt, when Smith, whose hearing was remarkably acute, distinctly heard the sound of a door opening on the landing below.

'There's some fellow gone in or out of your room,' he remarked.

Bellingham sprang up and stood helpless for a moment, with the expression of a man who is half-incredulous and half-afraid.

'I surely locked it. I am almost positive that I locked it,' he stammered. 'No one could have opened it.'

'Why, I hear someone coming up the steps now,' said Smith.

Bellingham rushed out through the door, slammed it loudly behind him, and hurried down the stairs. About half-way down Smith heard him stop, and thought he caught the sound of whispering. A moment later the door beneath him shut, a key creaked in a lock, and Bellingham, with beads of moisture upon his pale face, ascended the stairs once more, and re-entered the room.

'It's all right,' he said, throwing himself down in a chair. 'It was that fool of a dog. He had pushed the door open. I don't know how I came to forget to lock it.'

'I didn't know you kept a dog,' said Smith, looking very thoughtfully at the disturbed face of his companion.

'Yes, I haven't had him long. I must get rid of him. He's a great nuisance.'

'He must be, if you find it so hard to shut him up. I should have thought that shutting the door would have been enough, without locking it.'

'I want to prevent old Styles from letting him out. He's of some value, you know, and it would be awkward to lose him.'

'I am a bit of a dog-fancier myself,' said Smith, still gazing hard at his companion from the corner of his eyes. 'Perhaps you'll let me have a look at it.'

'Certainly. But I am afraid it cannot be to-night; I have an appointment. Is that clock right? Then I am a quarter of an hour late already. You'll excuse me, I am sure.'

He picked up his cap and hurried from the room. In spite of his appointment, Smith heard him re-enter his own chamber and lock his door upon the inside.

This interview left a disagreeable impression upon the medical student's mind. Bellingham had lied to him, and lied so clumsily that it looked as if he had desperate reasons for concealing the truth. Smith knew that his neighbour had no dog. He knew, also, that the step which he had heard upon the stairs was not the step of an animal. But if it were not, then what could it be? There was old Style's statement about the something which used to pace the room at times when the owner was absent. Could it be a woman? Smith rather inclined to the view. If so, it would mean disgrace and expulsion to Bellingham if it were discovered by the authorities, so that his anxiety and falsehoods might be accounted for. And yet it was inconceivable that an undergraduate could keep a woman in his rooms without being instantly detected. Be the explanation what it might, there was something ugly about it, and Smith determined, as he turned to his books, to discourage all further attempts at intimacy on the part of his soft-spoken and ill-favoured neighbour.

But his work was destined to interruption that night. He had hardly caught up the broken threads when a firm, heavy footfall came three steps at a time from below, and Hastie, in blazer and flannels, burst into the room.

'Still at it!' said he, plumping down into his wonted arm-chair. 'What a chap you are to stew! I believe an earthquake might come and knock Oxford into a cocked hat, and you would sit perfectly placid with your books among the ruins. However, I won't bore you long. Three whiffs of baccy, and I am off.'

'What's the news, then?' asked Smith, cramming a plug of bird's-eye into his briar with his forefinger.

'Nothing very much. Wilson made 70 for the freshmen against the eleven. They say that they will play him instead of Buddicomb, for Buddicomb is clean off colour. He used to be able to bowl a little, but it's nothing but half-volleys and long hops now.'

'Medium right,' suggested Smith, with the intense gravity which comes upon a 'varsity man when he speaks of athletics.

'Inclining to fast, with a work from leg. Comes with the arm about three inches or so. He used to be nasty on a wet wicket. Oh, by the way, have you heard about Long Norton?'

'What's that?'

'He's been attacked.'

'Attacked?'

'Yes, just as he was turning out of the High Street, and within a hundred yards of the gate of Old's.'

'But who——'

'Ah, that's the rub! If you said "what," you would be more grammatical. Norton swears that it was not human, and, indeed, from the scratches on his throat, I should be inclined to agree with him.'

'What, then? Have we come down to spooks?'

Abercrombie Smith puffed his scientific contempt.

'Well, no; I don't think that is quite the idea, either. I am inclined to think that if any showman has lost a great ape lately, and the brute is in these parts, a jury would find a true bill against it. Norton passes that way every night, you know, about the same hour. There's a tree that hangs low over the path – the big elm from Rainy's garden. Norton thinks the thing dropped on him out of the tree. Anyhow, he was nearly strangled by two arms, which, he says, were as strong and as thin as steel bands. He saw nothing; only those beastly arms that tightened and tightened on him. He yelled his head nearly off, and a couple of chaps came running, and the thing went over the wall like a cat. He never got a fair sight of it the whole time. It gave Norton a shake up, I can tell you. I tell him it has been as good as a change at the seaside for him.'

'A garrotter, most likely,' said Smith.

'Very possibly. Norton says not; but we don't mind what he says. The garrotter had long nails, and was pretty smart at swinging himself over walls. By the way, your beautiful neighbour would be pleased if he heard about it. He had a grudge against Norton, and he's not a man, from what I know of him, to forget his little debts. But hallo, old chap, what have you got in your noddle?'

'Nothing,' Smith answered curtly.

He had started in his chair, and the look had flashed over his face which comes upon a man who is struck suddenly by some unpleasant idea.

'You looked as if something I had said had taken you on the raw. By the way, you have made the acquaintance of Master B. since I looked in last, have you not? Young Monkhouse Lee told me something to that effect.'

'Yes; I know him slightly. He has been up here once or twice.'

'Well, you're big enough and ugly enough to take care of yourself. He's not what I should call exactly a healthy sort of Johnny, though, no doubt, he's very clever, and all that. But you'll soon find out for yourself. Lee is all right; he's a very decent little fellow. Well, so long, old chap! I row Mullins for the Vice-Chancellor's pot on Wednesday week, so mind you come down, in case I don't see you before.'

Bovine Smith laid down his pipe and turned stolidly to his books once more. But with all the will in the world, he found it very hard to keep his mind upon his work. It would slip away to brood upon the man beneath him, and upon the little mystery which hung round his chambers. Then his thoughts turned to this singular attack of which Hastie had spoken, and to the grudge which Bellingham was said to owe the object of it. The two ideas would persist in rising together in his mind, as though there were some close and intimate connection between them. And yet the suspicion was so dim and vague that it could not be put down in words.

'Confound the chap!' cried Smith, as he shied his book on pathology across the room. 'He has spoiled my night's reading, and that's reason enough, if there were no other, why I should steer clear of him in the future.'

For ten days the medical student confined himself so closely to his studies that he neither saw nor heard anything of either of the men beneath him. At the hours when Bellingham had been accustomed to visit him, he took care to sport his oak, and though he more than once heard a knocking at his outer door, he resolutely refused to answer it. One afternoon, however, he was descending the stairs when, just as he was passing it, Bellingham's door flew open, and young Monkhouse Lee came out with his eyes sparkling and a dark flush of anger upon his olive cheeks. Close at his heels followed Bellingham, his fat, unhealthy face all quivering with malignant passion.

'You fool!' he hissed. 'You'll be sorry.'

'Very likely,' cried the other. 'Mind what I say. It's off! I won't hear of it!'

'You've promised, anyhow.'

'Oh, I'll keep that! I won't speak. But I'd rather little Eva was in her grave. Once for all, it's off. She'll do what I say. We don't want to see you again.'

So much Smith could not avoid hearing, but he hurried on, for he had no wish to be involved in their dispute. There had been a serious breach between them, that was clear enough, and Lee was going to cause the engagement with his sister to be broken off. Smith thought of Hastie's comparison of the toad and the dove, and was glad to think that the matter was at an end. Bellingham's face when he was in a passion was not pleasant to look upon. He was not a man to whom an innocent girl could be trusted for life. As he walked, Smith wondered languidly what could have caused the quarrel, and what the promise might be which Bellingham had been so anxious that Monkhouse Lee should keep.

It was the day of the sculling match between Hastie and Mullins, and a stream of men were making their way down to the banks of the Isis. A May sun was shining brightly, and the yellow path was barred with the black shadows of the tall elm-trees. On either side the grey colleges lay back from the road, and hoary old mothers of minds looking out from their high, mullioned windows at the tide of young life which swept so merrily past them. Black-clad tutors, prim officials, pale, reading men, brown-faced, straw-hatted young athletes in white sweaters or many-coloured blazers, all were hurrying towards the blue, winding river which curves through the Oxford meadows.

Abercrombie Smith, with the intuition of an old oarsman, chose his position at the point where he knew that the struggle, if there were a struggle, would come. Far off he heard the hum which announced the start, the gathering roar of the approach, the thunder of running feet, and the shouts of the men in the boats beneath him. A spray of half-clad, deep-breathing runners shot past him, and craning over their shoulders, he saw Hastie pulling a steady thirty-six, while his opponent, with a jerky forty, was a good boat's length behind him. Smith gave a cheer for his friend, and pulling out his watch, was starting off again for his chambers, when he felt a touch upon his shoulder, and found that young Monkhouse Lee was beside him.

'I saw you there,' he said, in a timid, deprecating way. 'I wanted to speak to you, if you could spare me a half-hour. This cottage is mine. I share it with Harrington of King's. Come in and have a cup of tea.'

'I must be back presently,' said Smith. 'I am hard on the grind at present. But I'll come in for a few minutes with pleasure. I wouldn't have come out only Hastie is a friend of mine.'

'So he is of mine. Hasn't he a beautiful style? Mullins wasn't in it. But come into the cottage. It's a little den of a place, but it is pleasant to work in during the summer months.'

It was a small, square, white building, with green doors and shutters, and a rustic trellis-work porch, standing back some fifty yards from the river's bank. Inside, the main room was roughly fitted up as a study – deal table, unpainted shelves with books, and a few cheap oleographs upon the wall. A kettle sang upon a spirit-stove, and there were tea things upon a tray on the table.

'Try that chair and have a cigarette,' said Lee. 'Let me pour you out a cup of tea. It's so good of you to come in, for I know that your time if a good deal taken up. I wanted to say to you that, if I were you, I should change my rooms at once.'

'Eh?'

Smith sat staring with a lighted match in one hand and his unlit cigarette in the other.

'Yes; it must seem very extraordinary, and the worst of it is that I cannot give any reasons, for I am under a solemn promise – a very solemn promise. But I may go so far as to say that I don't think Bellingham is a very safe man to live near. I intend to camp out here as much as I can for a time.'

'Not safe! What do you mean?'

'Ah, that's what I mustn't say. But do take my advice and move your rooms. We had a grand row to-day. You must have heard us, for you came down the stairs.'

'I saw that you had fallen out.'

'He's a horrible chap, Smith. That is the only word for him. I have had doubts about him ever since that night when he fainted – you remember, when you came down. I taxed him to-day, and he told me things that made my hair rise, and wanted me to stand in with him. I'm not straight-laced, but I am a clergyman's son, you know, and I think there are some things which are quite beyond the pale. I only thank God that I found him out before it was too late, for he was to have married into my family.'

'This is all very fine, Lee,' said Abercrombie Smith curtly. 'But either you are saying a great deal too much or a great deal too little.'

'I give you a warning.'

'If there is real reason for warning, no promise can bind you. If I see a rascal about to blow a place up with dynamite no pledge will stand in my way of preventing him.'

'Ah, but I cannot prevent him, and I can do nothing but warn you.'

'Without saying what you warn me against.'

'Against Bellingham.'

'But that is childish. Why should I fear him, or any man?'

'I can't tell you. I can only entreat you to change your rooms. You are in danger where you are. I don't even say that Bellingham would wish to injure you. But it might happen, for he is a dangerous neighbour just now.'

'Perhaps I know more than you think,' said Smith, looking keenly at the young man's boyish, earnest face. 'Suppose I tell you that someone else shares Bellingham's rooms.'

Monkhouse Lee sprang from his chair in uncontrollable excitement.
'You know, then?' he gasped.

'A woman.'

Lee dropped back again with a groan.

'My lips are sealed,' he said. 'I must not speak.'

'Well, anyhow,' said Smith, rising, 'it is not likely that I should allow myself to be frightened out of rooms which suit me very nicely. It would be a little too feeble for me to move out all my goods and chattels because you say that Bellingham might in some unexplained way do me an injury. I think that I'll just take my chance, and stay where I am, and as I see that it's nearly five o'clock, I must ask you to excuse me.'

He bade the young student adieu in a few curt words, and made his way homeward through the sweet spring evening, feeling half-ruffled, half-amused, as any other strong, unimaginative man might who has been menaced by a vague and shadowy danger.

There was one little indulgence which Abercrombie Smith always allowed himself, however closely his work might press upon him. Twice a week, on the Tuesday and the Friday, it was his invariable custom to walk over to Farlingford, the residence of Doctor Plumptree Peterson, situated about a mile and a half out of Oxford. Peterson had been a close friend of Smith's elder brother, Francis, and as he was a bachelor, fairly well-to-do, with a good cellar and a better library, his house was a pleasant goal for a man who was in need of a brisk walk. Twice a week, then, the medical student would swing out there along the dark country roads and spend a pleasant hour in Peterson's comfortable study, discussing, over a glass of old port, the gossip of the 'varsity or the latest developments of medicine or of surgery.

On the day which followed his interview with Monkhouse Lee, Smith shut up his books at a quarter past eight, the hour when he usually started for his friend's house. As he was leaving his room, however, his eyes chanced to fall upon one of the books which Bellingham had lent him, and his conscience pricked him for not having returned it. However repellent the man might be, he should not be treated with discourtesy. Taking the book, he walked downstairs and knocked at his neighbour's door. There was no answer; but on turning the handle he found that it was unlocked. Pleased at the thought of avoiding an interview, he stepped inside, and placed the book with his card upon the table.

The lamp was turned half down, but Smith could see the details of the room plainly enough. It was all much as he had seen it before – the frieze, and animal-headed gods, the hanging crocodile, and the table littered over with papers and dried leaves. The mummy case stood upright against the wall, but the mummy itself was missing. There was no sign of any second occupant of the room, and he felt as he withdrew that he had probably done Bellingham an injustice. Had he a guilty secret to preserve, he would hardly leave his door open so that all the world might enter.

The spiral stair was a black as pitch, and Smith was slowly making his way down its irregular steps, when he was suddenly conscious that something had passed him in the darkness. There was a faint sound, a whiff of air, a light brushing past his elbow, but so slight that he could scarcely be certain of it. He stopped and listened, but the wind was rustling among the ivy outside, and he could hear nothing else.

'Is that you, Styles?' he shouted.

There was no answer, and all was still behind him. It must have been a sudden gust of air, for there were crannies and cracks in the old turret. And yet he could almost have sworn that he heard a footfall by his very side. He had emerged into the quadrangle, still turning the matter over in his head, when a man came running swiftly across the smooth-cropped lawn.

'Is that you, Smith?'

'Hullo, Hastie!'

'For God's sake come at once! Young Lee is drowned! Here's Harrington of King's with the news. The doctor is out. You'll do, but come along at once. There may be life in him.'

'Have you brandy?'

'No.'

'I'll bring some. There's a flask on my table.'

Smith bounded up the stairs, taking three at a time, seized the flask, and was rushing down with it, when, as he passed Bellingham's room, his eyes fell upon something which left him gasping and staring upon the landing.

The door, which he had closed behind him, was now open, and right in front of him, with the lamp-light shining upon it, was the mummy case. Three minutes ago it had been empty. He could swear to that. Now it framed the lank body of its horrible occupant, who stood, grim and stark, with his black, shrivelled face towards the door. The form was lifeless and inert, but it seemed to Smith as he gazed that there still lingered a lurid spark of vitality, some faint sign of consciousness in the little eyes which lurked in the depths of the hollow sockets. So astounded and shaken was he that he had forgotten his errand, and was still staring at the lean, sunken figure when the voice of his friend below recalled him to himself.

'Come on, Smith!' he shouted. 'It's life and death, you know. Hurry up! Now, then,' he added, as the medical student reappeared, 'let us do a sprint. It is well under a mile, and we should do it in five minutes. A human life is better worth running for than a pot.'

Neck and neck they dashed through the darkness, and did not pull up until panting and spent, they had reached the little cottage by the river. Young Lee, limp and dripping like a broken water-plant, was stretched upon the sofa, the green scum of the river upon his black hair, and a fringe of white foam upon his leaden-hued lips. Beside him knelt his fellow-student, Harrington, endeavouring to chafe some warmth back into his rigid limbs.

'I think there's life in him,' said Smith, with his hand to the lad's side. 'Put your watch glass to his lips. Yes, there's dimming on it. You take one arm, Hastie. Now work it as I do, and we'll soon pull him round.'

For ten minutes they worked in silence, inflating and depressing the chest of the unconscious man. At the end of that time a shiver ran through his body, his lips trembled, and he opened his eyes. The three students burst out into an irrepressible cheer.

'Wake up, old chap. You've frightened us quite enough.'

'Have some brandy. Take a sip from the flask.'

'He's all right now,' said his companion Harrington. 'Heavens, what a fright I got! I was reading here, and he had gone out for a stroll as far as the river, when I heard a scream and a splash. Out I ran, and by the time I could find him and fish him out, all life seemed to have gone. Then Simpson couldn't get a doctor, for he has a game-leg, and I had to run, and I don't know what I'd have done without you fellows. That's right, old chap. Sit up.'

Monkhouse Lee had raised himself on his hands, and looked wildly about him.

'What's up?' he asked. 'I've been in the water. Ah, yes; I remember.'

A look of fear came into his eyes, and he sank his face into his hands.

'How did you fall in?'

'I didn't fall in.'

'How then?'

'I was thrown in. I was standing by the bank, and something from behind picked me up like a feather and hurled me in. I heard nothing, and I saw nothing. But I know what it was, for all that.'

'And so do I,' whispered Smith.

Lee looked up with a quick glance of surprise.

'You've learned, then?' he said. 'You remember the advice I gave you?'

'Yes, and I begin to think that I shall take it.'

'I don't know what the deuce you fellows are talking about,' said Hastie, 'but I think, if I were you, Harrington, I should get Lee to bed at once. It will be time enough to discuss the why and the wherefore when he is a little stronger. I think, Smith, you and I can leave him alone now. I am walking back to college; if you are coming in that direction, we can have a chat.'

But it was little chat that they had upon their homeward path. Smith's mind was too full of the incidents of the evening, the absence of the mummy from his neighbour's rooms, the step that passed him on the stair, the reappearance – the extraordinary, inexplicable reappearance of the grisly thing – and then this attack upon Lee, corresponding so closely to the previous outrage upon another man against whom Bellingham bore a grudge. All this settled in his thoughts, together with the many little incidents which had previously turned him against his neighbour, and the singular circumstances under which he was first called in to him. What had been a dim suspicion, a vague, fantastic conjecture, had suddenly taken form, and stood out in his mind as a grim fact, a thing not to be denied. And yet, how monstrous it was! how unheard of! how entirely beyond all bounds of human experience. An impartial judge, or even the friend who walked by his side, would simply tell him that his eyes had deceived him, that the mummy had been there all the time, that young Lee had tumbled into the river as any other man tumbles into a river, and the blue pill was the best thing for a disordered liver. He felt that he would have said as much if the positions had been reversed. And yet he could swear that Bellingham was a murderer at heart, and that he wielded a weapon such as no man had ever used in all the grim history of crime.

Hastie had branched off to his rooms with a few crisp and emphatic comments upon his friend's unsociability, and Abercrombie Smith crossed the quadrangle to his corner turret with a strong feeling of repulsion for his chambers and their associations. He would take Lee's advice, and move his quarters as soon as possible, for how could a man study when his ear was ever straining for every murmur or footstep in the room below? He observed, as he crossed over the lawn, that the light was still shining in Bellingham's window, and as he passed up the staircase the door opened, and the man himself looked out at him. With his fat, evil face he was like some bloated spider fresh from the weaving of his poisonous web.

'Good evening,' said he. 'Won't you come in?'

'No,' cried Smith fiercely.

'No? You are as busy as ever? I wanted to ask you about Lee. I was sorry to hear that there was a rumour that something was amiss with him.'

His features were grave, but there was the gleam of a hidden laugh in his eyes as he spoke. Smith saw it, and he could have knocked him down for it.

'You'll be sorrier still to hear that Monkhouse Lee is doing very well, and is out of all danger,' he answered. 'Your hellish tricks have not come off this time. Oh, you needn't try to brazen it out. I know all about it.'

Bellingham took a step back from the angry student, and half-closed the door as if to protect himself.

'You are mad,' he said. 'What do you mean? Do you assert that I had anything to do with Lee's accident?'

'Yes,' thundered Smith. 'You and that bag of bones behind you; you worked it between you. I tell you what it is, Master B., they have given up burning folk like you, but we still keep a hangman, and, by George! if any man in this college meets his death while you are here, I'll have you up, and if you don't swing for it, it won't be my fault. You'll find that your filthy Egyptian tricks won't answer in England.'

'You're a raving lunatic,' said Bellingham.

'All right. You just remember what I say, for you'll find that I'll be better than my word.'

The door slammed, and Smith went fuming up to his chamber, where he locked the door upon the inside, and spent half the night in smoking his old briar and brooding over the strange events of the evening.

Next morning Abercrombie Smith heard nothing of his neighbour, but Harrington called upon him in the afternoon to say that Lee was almost himself again. All day Smith stuck fast to his work, but in the evening he determined to pay the visit to his friend Doctor Peterson upon which he had started the night before. A good walk and a friendly chat would be welcome to his jangled nerves.

Bellingham's door was shut as he passed, but glancing back when he was some distance from the turret, he saw his neighbour's head at the window outlined against the lamp-light, his face pressed apparently against the glass as he gazed out into the darkness. It was a blessing to be away from all contact with him, if but for a few hours, and Smith stepped out briskly, and breathed the soft spring air into his lungs. The half-moon lay in the west between two Gothic pinnacles, and threw upon the silvered street a dark tracery from the stonework above. There was a brisk breeze, and light, fleecy clouds drifted swiftly across the sky. Old's was on the very border of the town, and in five minutes Smith found himself beyond the houses and between the hedges of a May-scented, Oxfordshire lane.

It was a lonely and little-frequented road which led to his friend's house. Early as it was, Smith did not meet a single soul upon his way. He walked briskly along until he came to the avenue gate, which opened into the long, gravel drive leading up to Farlingford. In front of him he could see the cosy, red light of the windows glimmering through the foliage. He stood with his hand upon the iron latch of the swinging gate, and he glanced back at the road along which he had come. Something was coming swiftly down it.

It moved in the shadow of the hedge, silently and furtively, a dark, crouching figure, dimly visible against the black background. Even as he gazed back at it, it had lessened its distance by twenty paces, and was fast closing upon him. Out of the darkness he had a glimpse of a scraggy neck, and of two eyes that will ever haunt him in his dreams. He turned, and with a cry of terror he ran for his life up the avenue. There were the red lights, the signals of safety, almost within a stone's-throw of him. He was a famous runner, but never had he run as he ran that night.

The heavy gate had swung into the place behind him but he heard it dash open again before his pursuer. As he rushed madly and wildly through the night, he could hear a swift, dry patter behind him, and could see, as he threw back a glance, that this horror was bounding like a tiger at his heels, with blazing eyes and one stringy arm out-thrown. Thank God, the door was ajar. He could see the thin bar of light which shot from the lamp in the hall. Nearer yet sounded the clatter from behind. He heard a hoarse gurgling at his very shoulder. With a shriek he flung himself against the door, slammed and bolted it behind him, and sank half-fainting on to the hall chair.

'My goodness, Smith, what's the matter?' asked Peterson, appearing at the door of his study.

'Give me some brandy.'

Peterson disappeared, and came rushing out again with a glass and a decanter.

'You need it,' he said, as his visitor drank off what he poured out for him. 'Why, man, you are as white as a cheese.'

Smith laid down his glass, rose up, and took a deep breath.

'I am my own man again now,' said he. 'I was never so unmanned before. But, with your leave, Peterson, I will sleep here to-night, for I don't think I could face that road again except by daylight. It's weak, I know, but I can't help it.'

Peterson looked at his visitor with a very questioning eye.

'Of course you shall sleep here if you wish. I'll tell Mrs Burney to make up the spare bed. Where are you off to now?'

'Come up with me to the window that overlooks the door. I want you to see what I have seen.'

They went up to the window of the upper hall whence they could look upon the approach to the house. The drive and the fields on either side lay quiet and still, bathed in the peaceful moonlight.

'Well, really, Smith,' remarked Peterson, 'it is well that I know you to be an abstemious man. What in the world can have frightened you?'

'I'll tell you presently. But where can it have gone? Ah, now, look,

look! See the curve of the road just beyond your gate.'

'Yes, I see; you needn't pinch my arm off. I saw someone pass. I should say a man, rather thin, apparently, and tall, very tall. But what of him? And what of yourself? You are still shaking like an aspen leaf.'

'I have been within hand-grip of the devil, that's all. But come down to your study, and I shall tell you the whole story.'

He did so. Under the cheery lamp-light with a glass of wine on the table beside him, and the portly form and florid face of his friend in front, he narrated, in their order, all the events, great and small, which had formed so singular a chain, from the night on which he had found Bellingham fainting in front of the mummy case until this horrid experience of an hour ago.

'There now,' he said as he concluded, 'that's the whole, black business. It is monstrous and incredible, but it is true.'

Doctor Plumptree Peterson sat for some time in silence with a very puzzled expression upon his face.

'I never heard of such a thing in my life, never!' he said at last. 'You have told me the facts. Now tell me your inferences.'

'You can draw your own.'

'But I should like to hear yours. You have thought over the matter, and I have not.'

'Well, it must be a little vague in detail, but the main points seem to me to be clear enough. This fellow Bellingham, in his Eastern studies, has got hold of some infernal secret by which a mummy – or possibly only this particular mummy – can be temporarily brought to life. He was trying this disgusting business on the night when he fainted. No doubt the sight of the creature moving had shaken his nerve, even though he had expected it. You remember that almost the first words he said were to call out upon himself as a fool. Well, he got more hardened afterwards, and carried the matter through without fainting. The vitality which he could put into it was evidently only a passing thing, for I have seen it continually in its case as dead as this table. He has some elaborate process, I fancy, by which he brings the thing to pass. Having done it, he naturally bethought him that he might use the creature as an agent. It has intelligence and it has strength. For some purpose he took Lee into his confidence; but Lee, like a decent Christian, would have nothing to do with such a business. Then they had a row, and Lee vowed that he would tell his sister of Bellingham's true character. Bellingham's game was to prevent him, and he nearly managed it, by setting this creature of his on his track. He had already tried its powers upon another man – Norton – towards whom he had a grudge. It is the merest chance that he has not two murders upon his soul. Then, when I taxed him with the matter, he had the strongest reasons for wishing to get me out of the way before I could convey my knowledge to anyone else. He got his chance when I went out, for he knew my habits and where I was bound for. I have had a narrow shave, Peterson, and it is mere luck you didn't find me on your doorstep in the morning. I'm not a nervous man as a rule, and I never thought to have the fear of death put upon me as it was to-night.'

'My dear boy, you take the matter too seriously,' said his companion. 'Your nerves are out of order with your work, and you make too much of it. How could such a thing as this stride about the streets of Oxford, even at night, without being seen?'

'It has been seen. There is quite a scare in the town about an escaped ape, as they imagine the creature to be. It is the talk of the place.'

'Well, it's a striking chain of events. And yet, my dear fellow, you must allow that each incident in itself is capable of a more natural explanation.'

'What! even my adventure of to-night?'

'Certainly. You come out with your nerves all unstrung, and your head full of this theory of yours. Some gaunt, half-famished tramp steals after you, and seeing you run, is emboldened to pursue you. Your fears and imagination do the rest.'

'It won't do, Peterson; it won't do.'

'And again, in the instance of your finding the mummy case empty, and then a few moments later with an occupant, you know that it was lamp-light, that the lamp was half turned down, and that you had no special reason to look hard at the case. It is quite possible that you may have overlooked the creature in the first instance.'

'No, no; it is out of the question.'

'And then Lee may have fallen into the river, and Norton been garrotted. It is certainly a formidable indictment that you have against Bellingham; but if you were to place it before a police magistrate, he would simply laugh in your face.'

'I know he would. That is why I mean to take the matter into my own hands.'

'Eh?'

'Yes; I feel that a public duty rests upon me, and, besides, I must do it for my own safety, unless I choose to allow myself to be hunted by this beast out of the college, and that would be a little too feeble. I have quite made up my mind what I shall do. And first of all, may I use your paper and pens for an hour?'

'Most certainly. You will find all that you want upon that side-table.'

Abercrombie Smith sat down before a sheet of foolscap, and for an hour, and then for a second hour his pen travelled swiftly over it. Page after page was finished and tossed aside while his friend leaned back in his arm-chair, looking across at him with patient curiosity. At last, with an exclamation of satisfaction, Smith sprang to his feet, gathered his papers up into order, and laid the last one upon Peterson's desk.

'Kindly sign this as a witness,' he said.

'A witness? Of what?'

'Of my signature, and of the date. The date is the most important. Why, Peterson, my life might hang upon it.'

'My dear Smith, you are talking wildly. Let me beg you to go to bed.'

'On the contrary, I never spoke so deliberately in my life. And I will promise to go to bed the moment you have signed it.'

'But what is it?'

'It is a statement of all that I have been telling you to-night. I wish you to witness it.'

'Certainly,' said Peterson, signing his name under that of his companion. 'There you are! But what is the idea?'

'You will kindly retain it, and produce it in case I am arrested.'

'Arrested? For what?'

'For murder. It is quite on the cards. I wish to be ready for every event. There is only one course open to me, and I am determined to take it.'

'For Heaven's sake, don't do anything rash!'

'Believe me, it would be far more rash to adopt any other course. I hope that we won't need to bother you, but it will ease my mind to know that you have this statement of my motives. And now I am ready to take your advice and to go to roost, for I want be to at my best in the morning.'

Abercrombie Smith was not an entirely pleasant man to have as an enemy. Slow and easy-tempered, he was formidable when driven to action. He brought to every purpose in life the same deliberate resoluteness which had distinguished him as a scientific student. He had laid his studies aside for a day, but he intended that the day should not be wasted. Not a word did he say to his host as to his plans, but by nine o'clock he was well on his way to Oxford.

In the High Street he stopped at Clifford's, the gunmaker's, and bought a heavy revolver, with a box of central-fire cartridges. Six of them he slipped into the chambers, and half-cocking the weapon, placed it in the pocket of his coat. He then made his way to Hastie's rooms, where the big oarsman was lounging over his breakfast, with the *Sporting Times* propped up against the coffee-pot.

'Hullo! What's up?' he asked. 'Have some coffee?'

'No thank you. I want you to come with me, Hastie, and do what I ask you.'

'Certainly, my boy.'

ARTHUR CONAN DOYLE

'And bring a heavy stick with you.'

'Hullo!' Hastie stared. 'Here's a hunting crop that would fell an ox.'

'One other thing. You have a box of amputating knives. Give me the longest of them.'

'There you are. You seem to be fairly on the war trail. Anything else?'

'No; that will do.' Smith placed the knife inside his coat, and led the way to the quadrangle. 'We are neither of us chickens, Hastie,' said he. 'I think I can do this job alone, but I take you as a precaution. I am going to have a little talk with Bellingham. If I have only him to deal with, I won't, of course, need you. If I shout, however, up you come, and lam out with your whip as hard as you can lick. Do you understand?'

'All right. I'll come if I hear you bellow.'

'Stay here, then. I may be a little time, but don't budge until I come down.'

'I'm a fixture.'

Smith ascended the stairs, opened Bellingham's door and stepped in. Bellingham was seated behind his table, writing. Beside him, among his litter of strange possessions, towered the mummy case, with its sale number 249 still stuck upon its front, and its hideous occupant stiff and stark within it. Smith looked very deliberately round him, closed the door, and then, stepping across to the fireplace, struck a match and set the fire alight. Bellingham sat staring, with amazement and rage upon his bloated face.

'Well, really now, you make yourself at home,' he gasped.

Smith sat himself deliberately down, placing his watch upon the table, drew out his pistol, cocked it, and laid it in his lap. Then he took the long amputating knife from his bosom, and threw it down in front of Bellingham.

'Now, then,' said he, 'just get to work and cut up that mummy.'

'Oh, is that it?' said Bellingham with a sneer.

'Yes, that is it. They tell me that the law can't touch you. But I have a law that will set matters straight. If in five minutes you have not set to work, I swear by the God who made me that I will put a bullet through your brain!'

'You would murder me?'

Bellingham had half-risen, and his face was the colour of putty.

'Yes.'

'And for what?'

'To stop your mischief. One minute has gone.'

'But what have I done?'

'I know and you know.'

'This is mere bullying.'

'Two minutes are gone.'

'But you must give reasons. You are a madman – a dangerous madman. Why should I destroy my own property? It is a valuable mummy.'

'You must cut it up, and you must burn it.'

'I will do no such thing.'

'Four minutes are gone.'

Smith took up the pistol and he looked towards Bellingham with an inexorable face. As the secondhand stole round, he raised his hand, and the finger twitched upon the trigger.

'There! there! I'll do it!' screamed Bellingham.

In frantic haste he caught up the knife and hacked at the figure of the mummy, ever glancing round to see the eye and the weapon of his terrible visitor bent upon him. The creature crackled and snapped under every stab of the keen blade. A thick, yellow dust rose up from it. Spices and dried essences rained down upon the floor. Suddenly, with a rending crack, its backbone snapped asunder, and it fell, a brown heap of sprawling limbs, upon the floor.

'Now into the fire!' said Smith.

The flames leaped and roared as the dried and tinder-like debris was piled upon it. The little room was like the stoke-hole of a steamer and the sweat ran down the faces of the two men; but still the one stooped and worked, while the other sat watching him with a set face. A thick, fat smoke oozed out from the fire, and a heavy smell of burned resin and singed hair filled the air. In a quarter of an hour a few charred and brittle sticks were all that was left of Lot No. 249.

'Perhaps that will satisfy you,' snarled Bellingham, with hate and fear in his little grey eyes as he glanced back at his tormentor.

'No; I must make a clean sweep of all your materials. We must have no more devil's tricks. In with all these leaves! They may have something to do with it.'

'And what now?' asked Bellingham, when the leaves also had been added to the blaze.

'Now the roll of papyrus which you had on the table that night. It is in that drawer, I think.'

'No, no,' shouted Bellingham. 'Don't burn that! Why, man, you don't know what you do. It is unique; it contains wisdom which is nowhere else to be found.'

'Out with it!'

'But look here, Smith, you can't really mean it. I'll share the knowledge with you. I'll teach you all that is in it. Or, stay, let me only copy it before you burn it!'

Smith stepped forward and turned the key in the drawer. Taking out the yellow, curled roll of paper, he threw it into the fire, and pressed it down with his heel. Bellingham screamed, and grabbed at it; but Smith pushed him back and stood over it until it was reduced to a formless, grey ash.

'Now, Master B.,' said he, 'I think I have pretty well drawn your teeth. You'll hear from me again, if you return to your old tricks. And now good morning, for I must go back to my studies.'

And such is the narrative of Abercrombie Smith as to the singular events which occurred in Old College, Oxford, in the spring of '84. As Bellingham left the university immediately afterwards, and was last heard of in the Soudan, there is no one who can contradict his statement. But the wisdom of men is small, and the ways of Nature are strange, and who shall put a bound to the dark things which may be found by those who seek for them?

Hilaire Belloc

The Apprentice

29th January (or, as we should say, 10th February) 1649

Charles I was executed on this day, upon a scaffold outside the second window on the north of Whitehall Banqueting Hall, at four in the afternoon.

Men were well into the working week; it was a Tuesday and apprentices were under the hard eyes of their masters throughout the City of London and in the rarer business places that elbowed the great palaces along the Strand. The sky was overcast and the air distastefully cold, nor did anything in the landscape seem colder than the dark band of the river under those colourless and lifeless January clouds.

Whether it were an illusion or a reality, one could have sworn that there was a sort of silence over the houses and on the families of the people; one could have sworn that men spoke in lower tones than was their custom, and that the streets were emptier. The trial and the sentence of the King had put all that great concourse of men into the very presence of Death.

The day wore on; the noise of the workmen could be heard at the scaffold by Whitehall; one hour was guessed at and then another; rumours and flat assertions were busy everywhere, especially among the young, and an apprentice to a harness-maker in the Water Lane, near Essex House, knew not what to believe. But he was determined to choose his moment and to slip away lest he should miss so great a sight. The tyranny of the army kept all the city in doubt all day long, and allowed no news; none the less, from before noon there had begun a little gathering of people in Whitehall, round the scaffold at which men were still giving the last strokes of the hammer. Somewhat after noon a horseshoe of cavalry assembled in their long cloaks and curious tall civilian hats; they stood ranked, with swords drawn, all round the platform. Their horses shifted uneasily in the cold.

The harness-maker's apprentice found his opportunity; his master was called to the door for an order from Arundel House, and the lad left his bench quickly, just as he was, without hat or coat, in the bitter weather, and darting through the side door ran down through the Water Gate and down its steps to the river. The tide was at the flood and his master's boat lay moored. He cast her off and pulled rapidly up the line of gardens, backing water when he came to the public stairs just beyond Whitehall. Here he quickly tied the painter and ran up breathless to Whitehall Gate, fearing he might have missed his great expectation. He was in ample time.

It was perhaps half-past three o'clock when he got through the gate and found himself in the press of people. Far off to the left, among the soldiery that lined the avenue from the park to the Mall, and so to St James's, a continuous roll of drums burdened the still air.

The crowd was not very large, but it filled the space from the gate to the scaffold and a little beyond, save where it was pressed ouward by the ring of cavalry. It did not overflow into the wide spaces of the park, though these lay open to Whitehall, nor did it run up towards Charing Cross beyond the Banqueting Hall.

The apprentice was not so tall as the men about him; he strained and elbowed a little to see, and he was sworn at. He could make out the low scaffold, a large platform all draped in black, with iron staples, and a railing round it; it covered the last three blank windows of Whitehall, running from the central casement until it met the brick house at the north end of the stonework; there the brickwork beneath one of the windows had been taken out so as to give access through it from the floor within to the scaffold on the same level without; and whispers round told the apprentice, though he did not know how much to trust them, that it was through this hasty egress that the King would appear. Upon the scaffold itself stood a group of men, two of them masked, and one of the masked ones, of great stature and strong, leant upon the axe with his arms crossed upon the haft of it. A little block, barely raised above the floor of the platform, he could only see by leaping on tiptoe, catching it by glimpses between the heads of his neighbours or the shoulders of the cavalry guard; but he noticed in those glimpses how very low it was, and saw, ominous upon it, two staples driven as though to contain the struggler. Before it, so that one kneeling would have his face toward the palace and away from the crowd, was a broad footstool covered with red velvet, and making a startling patch upon all that expanse of black baize.

THE APPRENTICE

It was cold waiting; the motionless twigs of the small bare trees in the park made it seem colder still. The three-quarters struck in the new clock behind him upon Whitehall Gate, but as yet no one had appeared.

In a few moments, however, there was a movement in the crowd, heads turning to the right, and a corresponding backing of the mounted men to contain the first beginnings of a rush, for the commanders of the army feared, while they despised, the popular majority of London; and the wealthy merchants, the allies of the army, had not joined this common lot. This turning of faces towards the great blank stone wall of the palace was caused by a sound of many footsteps within. The only window not masked with stone, the middle window, was that upon which their gaze universally turned. They saw, passing it very rapidly, a group of men within; they were walking very sharply along the floor (which was here raised above the level of the window itself and cut the lower panes of it); they were hurrying towards the northern end of the great Banqueting Hall. It was but a moment's vision, and again they appeared in the open air through the broken brickwork at the far end of the stone façade.

For a moment the apprentice saw clearly the tall King, his face grown old, his pointed beard left full, his long features not moved. The great cloak that covered him, with the Great Star of the Garter upon the left shoulder, he drew off quickly and let fall into the hands of Herbert. He wore no hat, he stepped forward with precision towards the group of executioners, and a little murmur ran through the crowd.

The old bishop, moving his limbs with difficulty, but suppliant and attendant upon his friend, stood by in an agony. He helped the King to pull off his inner coat until he stood conspicuous in the sky-blue vest beneath it, and round his neck a ribbon and one ornament upon it, a George carved in onyx. This also he removed and gave to the bishop, while he took from his hands a little white silken cap and fixed it firmly upon his long and beautiful hair. From beneath the sky-blue of his garment, at the neck and at the wrists, appeared frills of exquisite linen and the adornment of lace. He stood for a few moments praying, then turned and spoke as though he were addressing them all. But the apprentice, though he held his breath, and strained to hear, as did all others about him, could catch no separate word, but only the general sound of the King's voice speaking. The movement of the horses, the occasional striking of a hoof upon the setts of the street, the distance, covered that voice. Next, Charles was saying something to the masked man, and a moment later he was kneeling upon the footstool. The apprentice saw him turn a moment and spread his arms out as an example of what he next should do; he bent him toward the block – it was too low; he lay at full length, and the crowd lifted and craned to see him in this posture.

The four heavy strokes of the hour struck and boomed in the silence. The hands of the lying figure were stretched out again, this time as a final signal, and right up in the air above them all the axe swung, white against the grey sky, flashed and fell.

In a moment the group upon the scaffold had closed round, a cloth was thrown, the body was raised, and among the hands stretched out to it were the eager and enfeebled hands of the bishop, trembling and still grasping the George.

A long moan or wail, very strange and dreadful, not very loud, rose from the people now that their tension was slackened by the accomplishment of the deed. And at once from the north and from the south, with such ceremony as is used to the conquered, the cavalry charged right through, hacking and dispersing these Londoners and driving them every way.

The apprentice dodged and ran, his head full of the tragedy and bewildered, his body in active fear of the horses that pursued flying packets of the crowd down the alley-ways of the offices and palace buildings.

He went off by a circuitous way to find, not his master's house after such an escapade, but his mother's, where she lived beyond St Martin's.

The dusk did not long tarry; as it gathered and turned to night small flakes of snow began to fall and lie upon the frozen ground.

J. Kaden-Bandrowski

The Sentence

'Yakób . . . Yakób . . . Yakób!'

The old man was repeating his name to himself, or rather he was inwardly listening to the sound of it which he had been accustomed to hear for so many years. He had heard it in the stable, in the fields, and on the grazing-ground, on the steps of the manor-house and at the Jew's, but never like this. It seemed to issue from unknown depths, summoning sounds never heard before, sights never yet seen, producing a confusion which he had never experienced. He saw it, felt it everywhere; it was itself the cause of a hopeless despair.

This despair crept silently into Yakób's fatalistic and submissive soul. He felt it under his hand, as though he were holding another hand. He was as conscious of it as of his hairy chest, his cold and starved body. This despair, moreover, was blended with a kind of patient expectancy which was expressed by the whispering of his pale, trembling lips, the tepid sweat under his armpits, the saliva running into his throat and making his tongue feel rigid like a piece of wood.

This is what happened: he tried to remember how it had all happened.

They had come swarming in from everywhere; they had taken the men away; it was firearms everywhere . . . everywhere firearms, noise and hubbub. The whole world was pushing, running, sweating or freezing. They arrived from this side or from that; they asked questions, they hunted people down, they followed up a trail, they fought. Of course, one must not betray one's brothers, but then . . . who are one's brothers?

They placed watches in the mountains, in the forests, on the fields; they even drove people into the mountain-passes and told them to hold out at any cost.

217

Yakób had been sitting in the chimney-corner in the straw and dust, covered with his frozen rags. The wind swept over the mountains and penetrated into the cottage, bringing with it a white covering of hoar-frost; it was sighing eerily in the fields; the fields themselves seemed to flee from it, and to be alive, running away into the distance. The earth in white convulsions besieged the sky, and and sky got entangled in the mountain-forests.

Yakób was looking at the snow which was falling thickly, and tried to penetrate the veil with his eyes. Stronger and faster raged the blizzard. Yakób's stare became vacant under the rumbling of the storm and the driving of the snow; one could not have told whether he was looking with eyes or with lumps of ice.

Shadows were flitting across the snowdrifts. They were the outlines of objects lit by the fire; they trembled on the window-frames; the fire flickered, and the shadows treacherously caressed the images of saints on the walls. The beam played on the window, threw a red light on the short posts of the railing, and disappeared in pursuit of the wind in the fields.

'Yakób . . . Yakób . . . Yakób!'

And he had really had nothing to do with it! It had all gone against him continuously, pertinaciously, and to no purpose. It had attached itself to him, clung to the dry flour that flew about in atoms in the tin where the bit of cheese also was kept. It had bewitched the creaking of the windows on their hinges; it had stared from the empty seats along the walls.

But he kept on beating his breast. His forehead was wrinkled in dried-up folds, his brows bristled fantastically into shaggy, dirty tufts. His heavy, blunt nose, powdered with hairs at the tip, stood out obstinately between two deep folds on either side. These folds overhung the corners of his mouth, and were joined below the chin by a network of pallid veins. A noise, light as a beetle's wing, came in puffs from the half-open lips; they were swollen and purple like an overgrown bean.

Yakób had been sitting in Turkish fashion, his hands crossed over his chest, breathing forth his misery so quietly that it covered him, together with the hoar-frost, stopped his ears and made the tufts of hair on his chest glitter. He was hugging his sorrow to himself, abandoning the last remnant of hope, and longing for deliverance. Behind the wrinkles of his forehead there swarmed a multitude not so much of pictures as of ghosts of the past, yet vividly present.

At last he got up and sat down on the bench in the chimney-corner, drew a pipe from his trouser-pocket and put it between his teeth, forgetting to light it. He laid his heavy hands round the stem. Beyond the blizzard and the shadow-play of the flame, there appeared to him the scene of his wife and daughters' flight. He had given up everything he possessed, had taken off his sheepskin, had himself loosened the cow from the post. For a short moment he had caught sight of his wife and daughters again in the distance, tramping through the snow as they passed the cross-roads, then they had been swallowed up in a mass of people, horses, guns, carts, shouts and curses. Since then he had constantly fancied that he was being called, yet he knew that there was no one to call him. His thoughts were entirely absorbed in what he had seen then. With his wife all his possessions had gone. Now there was nothing but silence, surrounding him with a sharp breath of pain and death.

By day and by night Yakób had listened to the shots that struck his cottage and his pear-trees. He chewed a bit of cheese from time to time, and gulped down with it the bitter fear that his cottage might be set on fire.

For here and there, like large red poppies on the snow, the glare of burning homesteads leapt up into the sky.

'Here I am . . . watching,' he said to himself, when he looked at these blood-red graves. He smiled at the sticks of firewood on his hearth, which was the dearest thing on earth to him. The walls of his cottage were one with his inmost being, and every moment when he saw them standing, seemed to him like precious savings which he was putting away. So he watched for several days; the vermin were over-running the place, and he was becoming desperate. Since mid-day the silence had deepened; the day declined, and there was nothing in the world but solitude and snow.

Yakób went over to the window. The snow was lying deep on the fields, like a shimmering coat of varnish; the world was bathed in the light of a pale, wan moon. The forest-trees stood out here and there in blue points, like teeth. Large and brilliant the stars looked down, and above the milky way, veiled in vapours, hung the sickle of the moon.

While in the immensity of the night cold and glittering worlds were bowing down before the eternal, Yakób looked, and noticed something approaching from the mountains. Along the heights and slopes there was a long chain of lights; it was opening out from the centre into two lines on either side, which looked as though they were lost in the forest. Below them there were confused gleams in the fields, and behind, in the distance, the glow of the burning homesteads.

'They have burned the vicarage,' thought Yakób, and his heart answered: 'and here am I . . . watching.'

He pressed against the window-frame, glued his grey face to the panes and, trembling with cold, sent out an obstinate and hostile glance into space, as though determined to obtain permission to keep his own heritage.

Suddenly he pricked up his ears. Something was approaching from the distance across the forest very cautiously. The snow was creaking under the advancing steps. In the great silence it sounded like the forging of iron. Those were horses' hoofs stamping the snow.

This sound, suppressed as it was, produced in him a peculiar sensation which starts in the head and grips you in the nape of the neck, the consciousness that someone is hiding close to you.

Yakób stood quite still at the window, not even moving his pipe from one corner of his mouth to the other. Not he himself seemed to be trembling, only his rags.

The door was suddenly thrown open and a soldier appeared on the threshold. The light of a lantern which was suspended on his chest, filled the room.

Yakób's blood was freezing. Cossacks, hairy like bears, were standing in the opening of the door, the snow which covered them was shining like a white flame. In the courtyard there were steaming horses; lanceheads were glittering like reliquaries.

Yakób understood that they were calling him 'old man', and asking him questions. He extended his hands to express that he knew nothing. Some of the Cossacks entered, and made signs to him to make up the fire.

He noticed that they were bringing more horses into the yard, small, shaggy ponies like wolves.

He became calmer, and his fear disappeared; he only remained cautious and observant; everything that happened seemed to take hours, yet he saw it with precision.

'It is cold . . . it is cold!'

He made up the fire for these bandits who stretched themselves on the benches; he felt they were talking and laughing about him, and he turned to them and nodded; he thought it would please them if he showed that he approved of them.

They asked him about God knows what, where they were, and where they were not.

As though he knew!

Then they started all over again, while they swung their booted legs under the seats. One of them came up to the hearth, and clapped the crouching Yakób on his back for fun, but it hurt. It was a resounding smack. Yakób scratched himself and rumpled his hair, unable to understand.

They boiled water and made tea; a smell of sausages spread about the room. Yakób bit his jaws together and looked at the fire. He sat in his place as though he had been glued to it.

His ears were tingling when he heard the soldiers grinding their teeth on their food, tearing the skin off the sausages and smacking their lips.

A large and painful void was gaping in his inside.

They devoured their food fast and noisily, and an odour of brandy began to fill the room, and contracted Yakób's throat.

He understood that they were inviting him to share the meal, but he felt uneasy about that, and though his stomach seemed to have shrunk, and the sausage-skins and bones which they had thrown away lay quite close to him, he could not make up his mind to move and pick them up.

'Come on!'

The soldier beckoned to him. 'Come here!'

The old man felt that he was weakening, the savoury smell took possession of him.

But, 'I shan't go,' he thought. The soldier, gnawing a bone, repeated, 'Come on!'

'I shan't go,' thought Yakób, and spat into the fire, to assure himself that he was not going. All the same . . . the terribly tempting smell made him more and more feeble.

At last two of them got up, took him under the arms, and sat him down between them.

They made signs to him, they held the sausage under his nose; the tea was steaming, the brandy smelt delicious.

Yakób put his hands on the table, then put them behind him. Black shadows were gesticulating on the walls. He felt unhappy about sharing a meal with people without knowing what they were, never having seen or known them before. They were Russians, thus much he knew. He had a vision of something that happened long ago, he could not distinctly remember what it was, for it happened so very long ago; his grandfather had come home from the fair that was held in the town, shivering and groaning. There had been outcries and curses.

'They are going to poison me like a dog,' he thought.

The wind was changing and moaning under the roof. The fire flickered up and went down; the red flame and the darkness were dancing together on the walls. The wan moon was looking in at the window. Yakób was sitting on the bench among the soldiers like his own ghost.

'They are surely going to poison me,' he kept repeating to himself. He was still racking his memory as to what it was that had happened so long ago to his grandfather during the fair, at the inn. God knows what it was . . . who could know anything?

'They are going to poison me!'

His sides were heaving with his breath, he was trying to breathe carefully, so as not to smell the repast.

The shadows on the walls seemed to jeer at him. The soldiers were beginning to talk thickly; their mouths, their fingers were shining with grease. They took off their belts and laid their swords aside. The one next to Yakób put his arm round his neck and whispered in his ear; his red mouth was quite close; he passed his hand over Yakób's head, and brought his arm right round his throat. He was young and he was talking of his father.

'Daddy,' he said, and put the sausage between his teeth.

Yakób tried to clench his teeth; but he bit the sausage at the same time.

'Daddy,' said the young soldier again, holding out the sausage for another bite; he stroked his head, looked into his eyes, and laughed. Yakób was sorry for himself. Was he to be fed like a half-blind old man? Couldn't he eat by himself?

When the soldiers saw that Yokób was eating, they burst into shouts of laughter, and stamped their feet, rattling their spurs.

He knew they were laughing at him, and it made him easier in his mind to see that he was affording them pleasure. He purposely made himself ridiculous with the vague idea that he must do something for them in payment of what they were giving him; they struck him on the shoulder-blades to see him gasp with his beanlike mouth, and to see the frightened smile run over his face like a flash of lightning.

He ate as though from bravado, but he ate well. They started drinking again. Yakób looked at them with eagerness, his arms folded over his stomach, his head bent forward; the hairy hand of the captain put the bottle to his mouth.

Now he could laugh his own natural laugh again, and not only from bravado, for he felt quite happy. His frozen body was getting warmed through.

He felt as if a great danger had irrevocably passed.

Gradually he became garrulous, although they hardly understood what he was talking about: 'Yes, the sausage was good . . . to be sure!' He nodded his head and clicked his tongue; he also approved of the huge chunks of bread, and whenever the bottle was passed round, he put his head on one side and folded his hands, as if he were listening to a sermon. From his neighbour's encircling black sleeve the old face peeped out with equanimity, looking like a withering poppy.

'Daddy,' the loquacious Cossack would say from time to time, and point in the direction of the mountains; tears were standing in his eyes.

Yakób put his swollen hand on his, and waited for him to say more.

The soldier held his hand, pointed in the direction of the mountains again, and sniffled.

'He respects old age . . . they are human, there's no denying it,' thought Yakób, and got up to put more wood on the fire.

They seized hold of him, they would not allow him to do it. A young soldier jumped up: 'Sit down, you are old.'

Yakób held out his empty pipe, and the captain himself filled it.

So there he sat, among these armed bandits. They were dressed in sheepskins and warm materials, had sheepskin caps on their heads; there was he with his bare arms, in well-worn grey trousers, his shirt fastened together at the neck with a piece of wood. Sitting among them, defenceless as a centipede, without anyone belonging to him, puffing clouds of smoke, he inwardly blessed this adventure, in which everything had turned out so well. The Cossacks looked at the fire and they too said; 'This is very nice, very nice.'

To whom would not a blazing fire on a cold winter's night appeal?

They got more and more talkative and asked: 'Where are your wife and children?' They probably too had wives and children!

'My wife,' he said, 'has gone down to the village, she was afraid.' They laughed and tapped their chests: 'War is a bad thing, who would not be afraid?' Yakób assented all the more readily as he felt that for him the worst was over.

'Do you know the way to the village?' suddenly asked the captain. He was almost hidden in clouds of tobacco-smoke, but in his eyes there was a gleam, hard and sinister, like a bullet in a puff of smoke.

Yakób did not answer. How should he not know the way?

They started getting up, buckled on their belts and swords.

Yakób jumped up to give them the rest of the sausages and food which had been left on the plates. But they would only take the brandy, and left the tobacco and the broken meat.

'That will be for you . . . afterwards,' said the young Cossack, took a red muffler off his neck and put it round Yakób's shoulder.

'That will keep you warm.'

Yakób laughed back at him, and submitted to having the muffler knotted tightly round his throat. The young soldier drew a pair of trousers from his kitbag: 'Those will keep you warm, you are old.' He told him a long story about the trousers; they had belonged to his brother who had been killed.

'You know, it's lucky to wear things like that. Poor old fellow!'

Yakób stood and looked at the breeches. In the fire-light they seemed to be trembling like feeble and stricken legs. He laid his hand on them and smiled, a little defiant and a little touched.

'You may have them, you may have them,' grunted the captain, and insisted on his putting them on at once.

When he had put them on in the chimney-corner and showed himself, they were all doubled up with laughter. He looked appalling in the black trousers which were much too large for him, a grey hood and the red muffler. His head wobbled above the red line as if it had been fixed on a bleeding neck. The rags on his chest showed the thin, hairy body, the stiff folds of the breeches produced an effect as if he were not walking on the ground but floating above it.

The captain gave the command, the soldiers jumped up and looked once more round the cottage; the young Cossack put the sausage and meat in a heap and covered it with a piece of bread. 'For you,' he said once more, and they turned to leave.

Yakób went out with them to bid them God-speed. A vague presentiment seized him on the threshold, when he looked out at the frozen world, the stars, like nails fixed into the sky, and the light of the moon on everything. He was afraid.

The men went up to their horses, and he saw that there were others outside. The wind ruffled the shaggy little ponies' manes and threw snow upon them. The horses, restless, began to bite each other, and the Cossacks, scattered on the snow like juniper-bushes, reined them in.

The cottage-door remained open. The lucky horseshoe, nailed to the threshold, glittered in the light of the hearth, which threw blood-red streaks between the legs of the table, across the door and beyond it on to the snow.

'I wonder whether they will ever return to their families?' he thought, and: 'How queer it is that one should meet people like that.'

He was sorry for them.

The captain touched his arm and asked the way.

'Straight on.'

'Far?'

'No, not far, not at all far.'

'Where is it?'

The little group stood in front of him by the side of their wolf-like ponies. He drew back into the cottage.

The thought confusedly crossed his mind: 'After all, we did sit together and ate together, two and two, like friends.'

He began hurriedly, 'Turn to the left at the cross-roads, then across the fields as far as Gregor's cottage . . .'

The captain made a sign that he did not understand.

He thought: 'Perhaps they will lose their way and make a fuss; then they will come back to the cottage and eat the meat. I will go with them as far as the cross-roads.'

They crept down the road, passed the clump of pine-trees which came out in a point beside the brook, and went along the valley on the slippery stones. A large block of ice lay across the brook, shaped like a silver plough; the waves surrounded it as with golden crescents. The snow creaked under the soldiers' feet. Yakób walked beside them on his sandals, like a silent ghost.

'Now keep straight on as far as the cross,' he said, pointing to a dark object with a long shadow.

'I can't see anything,' said the captain.

He accompanied them as far as the cross, by the side of which stood a little shrine; the wan saint was wearing a crown of icicles.

From that point the village could be seen across the fields. Yakób discovered that the chain of lights which he had observed earlier in the evening, had come down from the mountains, for it now seemed to be close to the village.

Silence reigned in the sleeping world, every step could be heard.

This silence filled Yakób's heart with a wild fear; he turned round with a feeling of helplessness and looked back at his cottage. Probably the fire was now going out; a red glow appeared and disappeared on the windows.

Beyond the cross the road lay through low-lying ground, and was crossed by another road which led abruptly downwards into fields.

Yakób hesitated.

'Come on, old man, come on,' they called to him, and walked on without waiting for his answer.

The Cossacks dug their heels into the rugged ice of the road, and tumbled about in all directions. They had left their horses at the cross-roads. Each one kept a close hold on his gun, so that there should be no noise. They were whispering to each other; it sounded as if a congregation were murmuring their prayers. Yakób led them, and mentally he held fast to every bush, every lump of ice, saying to himself at every step that now he was going to leave them, they could not miss the road now. But he was afraid.

They no longer whispered, they had become taciturn as they pushed onwards, stumbling, breathing hard.

'As far as Gregor's cottage, and then no more!'

The effect of the drink was passing off. He rubbed his eyes, drew his rags across his chest. 'What was he doing, leading these people about on this night?'

He suddenly stopped where the field-road crossed theirs; the soldiers in front and behind threw themselves down. It was as if the ground had swallowed them.

A black horse was standing in the middle of the road, with extended nostrils. Its black mane, covered with hoar-frost, was tossed about its head; the saddle-bags, which were fur-lined, swung in the breeze; large dark drops were falling from its leg to the ground.

'Damn it!' cursed the captain.

The horse looked meekly at them, and stretched its head forward submissively. Yakób was sorry for the creature; perhaps one could do something for it. He stood still beside it, and again pointed out the road.

'I have done enough, I shan't go any further!' He scratched his head and smiled, thinking that this was a good opportunity for escape.

'Come on,' hissed the captain so venomously in his ear that he marched forward without delay; they followed.

A dull fear mixed with resentment gripped him with terrible force. He now ran at the head like a sheep worried by watch-dogs.

They stopped in front of the cottage, silent, breathless, expectant.

Yakób looked at his companions with boundless astonishment. Their faces under their fur-caps had a tense, cruel look, their brows were wrinkled, their eyes glittered.

From all sides other Cossacks were advancing.

He noticed only now that there were some lying concealed behind the fence on the straw in a confused mass.

He shuddered; thick drops of perspiration stood on his forehead. The beating of his heart filled his head like the noise of a hammer, it seemed to fill everything. In spite of the feeling that he was being forced to do this thing, he again heard the voice calling: 'Yakób, Yakób!'

Up the hillock where Gregor's cottage stood, they advanced on all fours.

He clambered upwards, thinking of his wife, and of the cow he had loosed. Fear veiled his eyes, he saw black spots dancing.

Gregor's cottage was empty as a graveyard. It had been abandoned; the open doors creaked on their hinges. Under the window stood a cradle, covered with snow.

Silently the soldiers surrounded the cottage, and Yakób went with them, as though mesmerized by terror, mute and miserable.

They had hardly got round, when a red glow shot up from the other side of the village. The soldiers threw themselves down in the snow.

The thundering of guns began on all sides; blood-red lights came flying overhead. An appalling noise broke out, reinforced by the echo from the mountains, as though the whole world were going to perish. The Cossacks advanced, trembling.

Yakób advanced with them, for the captain had hit him across the head. He saw stars when he received the blow, gesticulated wildly, and staggered along the road.

He could distinguish the road running out from the forest like a silver thread. As they advanced, they came under a diabolically heavy rifle fire; bullets were raining upon them from all sides.

Here and there he heard moans already, when one of the soldiers fell bleeding on the snow. Close to him fell the young Cossack who had given him the muffler and breeches. He held out his hand, groaning. Yakób wanted to stop, but the captain would not let him, but rapped him over the head again with his knuckles.

The soldiers lay in heaps. The rest wavered, fell back, hid in the ditch or threw themselves down. The rifle-fire came nearer, the outlines and the faces of the advancing enemy could already be distinguished. Another blow on the head stretched Yakób to the ground, and he feigned death. The Cossacks retreated, the others advanced, and he understood that they belonged to his friends.

When he got up, he was immediately surrounded by them, taken by the scruff of the neck and so violently shaken, that he tumbled on his knees.

Gunfire was roaring from the mountains, shadows of soldiers flitted past him, the wounded Cossacks groaned in the snow. Young, well-nourished looking men were bending over him. Looking up into their faces, he crossed his hands over his chest and laughed joyfully.

'Ah, those Russians, those Russians . . . the villains!' he croaked, 'aho, aho, ho hurlai!' He rolled his tear-filled eyes.

Things were happening thick and fast. From where the chimney stood close to the water, near the manor-house, the village was burning. He could feel the heat and soot and hear the shouting of the crowd through the noise of the gunfire. Now he would see his wife and children again, the friendly soldiers surely had saved them. The young Cossack was still struggling on the ground; now he stretched himself out for his eternal sleep.

'Ah, the villains!' Yakób repeated; the great happiness which filled his heart rushed to his lips in incoherent babblings. 'The villains, they have served me nicely!'

He felt his bleeding head, crouched on his heels and got up. The fleshy red faces were still passing close to him, breathing harder and harder. Fear rose and fell in him like the flames of the burning village; again everything was swallowed up in indescribable noise.

Suddenly Yakób began to sob; he threw himself down at the soldiers' feet and wept bitterly, as though he would weep out his soul and the marrow of his bones.

They lifted him up, almost unconscious, and took him along the high road, under escort with fixed bayonets. His tears fell fast upon the snow, and thus he came into his own village, among his own people, pale as a corpse, with poison in his heart.

He looked dully at the blazing wooden church-spire where it stood enveloped in flames as though wrapped in an inflated glittering cloak. Dully he let his eyes wander over the hedges and fences; everything seemed unreal, as things seen across a distant wave or a downpour of rain, out of reach and strange.

He was standing where the field-path joined the high road. The soldiers sat down on a heap of stones and lighted their cigarettes.

Yakób, trembling all over, looked at his own black shadow; fugitives arrived from the burning village and swarmed past him; the rifle fire now sounded from the direction of the mountains.

Suddenly Gregor's cottage burst into flames. A blood-red glow inflated the clouds of smoke, trembled on the snow and ran over the pine-trees like gold.

Soldiers were arriving from that direction, streaming with blood, supported by their comrades.

Yakób stood motionless, looking at his shadow; fear was burning within him. He looked at the sky above the awful chaos on the earth, and became calmer. He tried to remember how it had all happened.

They had come, had given him food. His wife and children were probably safe in the manor-house. Blinking his swollen eyelids, he tried to deceive himself, crouched down near the guard who was smoking, and asked him for fire. His fear miraculously disappeared.

He began to talk rapidly to the soldier: 'I was sitting . . . the wind was moaning . . .' he told him circumstantially how he was sitting, what he had been thinking, how the shots had struck his cottage.

The soldier put his rifle between his knees, crossed his hands over his sleeves, spat out and sighed.

'But you have had underhand dealings with the Russians.'

'No . . . no.'

'Tell that to another.'

'I shall,' replied Yakób calmly.

'And who showed them the way?'

'Who?' said Yakób.

'Who showed them the way over here? Or did they find it on the map?'

'Yes, on the map,' assented Yakób, as though he were quite convinced.

'Well, who did?' said the soldier, wagging his head.

'Who?' repeated Yakób like an echo.

'I suppose it wasn't I?' said the soldier.

'I?' asked Yakób.

The other three soldiers approached inquisitively to where Yakób was crouching.

'A nice mess you've made,' one of them said, pointing to the wounded who were arriving across the fields. 'Do you understand?'

Yakób fixed his eyes on the soldiers' boots, and would not look in that direction. But he could not understand what it all meant . . . all this noise, and the firing that ran from hill to hill.

'Nice mess this you've made, old man.'

'Yes.'

'You!'

Yakób looked up at them, and had the sensation of being deep down at the bottom of a well instead of crouching at their feet.

'That is a lie, a lie, a lie!' he cried, beating his chest; his hair stood on end. The soldiers sat down in a row on the stones. They were young, cold, tired.

'But now they'll play the deuce with you.'

'Why?' said Yakób softly, glancing sideways at them.

'You're an old ass,' remarked one of them.

'But,' he began again, 'I was sitting, looking at the snow. . . .'

He had a great longing to talk to them, they looked as if they would understand, although they were so young.

'I was sitting . . . give me some fire . . . do you come from these parts yourselves?'

They did not answer.

He thought of his cottage, the bread and sausage, the black horse at the cross-roads.

'They beat me,' he sobbed, covering his face with his rags.

The soldiers shrugged their shoulders: 'Why did you let them?'

'O . . . o . . . o!' cried the old man. But tears would no longer wash away a conviction which was taking possession of him, searing his soul as the flames seared the pines.

'Why did you let them? Aren't you ashamed of yourself?'

No, he was not ashamed of himself for that. But that he had shown them the way . . . the way they had come by . . . what did it all mean? All his tears would not wash away this conviction: that he had shown them the way . . . the way they had come by.

Guns were thundering from the hills, the village was burning, the mill was burning . . . a black mass of people was surrounding him. More and more wounded came in from the fields, covered with grey mud. The flying sparks from the mill fell at his feet.

A detachment of soldiers was returning.

'Get up, old man,' cried his guard; 'we're off!'

Yakób jumped to his feet, hitched up his trousers, and went off perplexed, under cover of four bayonets that seemed to carry a piece of sky between them like a starred canopy.

His fear grew as he approached the village. He did not see the familiar cottages and hedges; he felt as though he were moving onwards without a goal. Moving onwards and yet not getting any farther. Moving onwards and yet hoping not to get to the end of the journey.

He sucked his pipe and paid no attention to anything; but the village was on his conscience.

The fear which filled his heart was not like that which he had felt when the Cossacks arrived, but a senseless fear, depriving him of sight and hearing . . . as though there were no place for him in the world.

'Are we going too fast?' asked the guard hearing Yakób's heavy breathing.

'All right, all right,' he answered cheerfully. The friendly words had taken his fear away.

'Take it easy,' said the soldier. 'We will go more slowly. Here's a dry cigarette, smoke.'

Without turning round, he offered Yakób a cigarette, which he put behind his ear.

They entered the village. It smelt of burning, like a gipsy camp. The road seemed to waver in the flickering of the flames, the wind howled in the timber.

Yakób looked at the sky. Darkness and stars melted into one.

He would not look at the village. He knew there were only women and children in the cottages, the men had all gone. This thought was a relief to him, he hardly knew why.

Meanwhile the detachment of soldiers, instead of going to the manor-house, had turned down a narrow road which led to the mill. They stopped and formed fours. Every stone here was familiar to Yakób, and yet, standing in the snow up to his knees, he was puzzled as to where he was. If he could only sleep off this nightmare . . . he did not recognize the road . . . the night was far advanced, and the village not asleep as usual . . . if they would only let him go home!

He would return to-morrow.

The mill was burning out. Cinders were flying across from the granaries; the smoke bit into the eyes of the people who were standing about looking upwards, with their arms crossed.

Everything showed up brilliantly in the glare; the water was dripping from rung to rung of the silent wheel, and mixed its sound with that of the fire.

The adjoining buildings were fenced round with a small running fire; smoke whirled round the tumbling roof like a shock of hair shot through with flames. The faces of the bystanders assumed a metallic glow.

The wails of the miller and his family could be heard through the noise of battle, of water, and of fire.

It was as if the crumbling walls, the melting joints, the smoke, the cries were dripping down the wheel, transformed into blood, and were carried down by the black waves and swallowed up in the infinite abyss of the night.

'They beat me. . . .' Yakób justified himself to himself, when the tears rose to his eyes again. No tears could wash away the conviction that it was he who had shown them the way by which they had come.

The first detachment was waiting for the arrival of the second. It arrived, bringing in prisoners, Cossacks. A large number of them were being marched along; they did not walk in order but irregularly, like tired peasants. They were laughing, smoking cigarettes, and pushing against each other. Among them were those who had come to his cottage; he recognized the captain and others.

When they saw Yakób they waved their hands cordially and called out to him, 'Old man, old man!'

Yakób did not reply; he shrunk into himself. Shame filled his soul. He looked at them vacantly. His forehead was wrinkled as with a great effort to remember something, but he could think of nothing but a huge millwheel turning under red, smooth waves. Suddenly he remembered: it was the young Cossack who had given him his brother's clothes.

'The other one,' he shouted, pointing to his muffler, 'where did you leave him?'

Soldiers came between them and pushed the crowd away.

There was a terrific crash in the mill; a thick red cloud rushed upwards, dotted with sparks. Under this cloud an ever-increasing mass of people was flocking towards the spot where Yakób was; they were murmuring, pulling the soldiers by their cloaks. Women, children, and old men pressed in a circle round him, gesticulating, shouting: 'It was he . . . he . . . he!'

Words were lost in the chaos of sounds, faces became merely a dense mass, above which fists were flung upwards like stones.

Yakób tripped about among the soldiers like a fawn in a cage, raised and lowered his head, and clutched his rags; he could not shut his quivering mouth, and from his breast came a cry like the sob of a child.

The crowd turned upon him with fists and nails; he hid his face in his rags, stopped his ears with his fingers, and shook his head.

The prisoners had been dispatched, and it was Yakób's turn to be taken before the officer in command of the battalion.

'Say that I . . . that I . . .' Yakób entreated his guard.

'What are you in such a hurry for?'

'Say that I . . .'

The soldiers were sitting round a camp-fire, piling up the faggots. Soup was boiling in a cauldron.

'Say that I . . .' he begged again, standing in the thick smoke.

At last he was taken into the school-house.

The officer in command stood in the middle of the room with a cigarette between his fingers.

'I . . . I . . .' groaned Yakób, already in the door. His dishevelled hair made him look like a sea-urchin; his face was quite disfigured with black marks of violence; behind his bleeding left ear still stuck the cigarette. His swollen upper lip was drawn sideways and gave him the expression of a ghastly smile. His eyes looked out helpless, dispirited, from his swollen lids.

'What do you want to say?' asked the officer, without looking at him. Something suddenly came over him.

'It was I,' he said hoarsely.

The soldier made his report.

'They gave me food,' Yakób said, 'and this muffler and breeches, and they beat me.'

'It was you who showed them the way?'

'It was.'

'You did show them the way?'

He nodded.

'Did they beat you in the cottage?'

Yakób hesitated. 'In the cottage we were having supper.'

'They beat you afterwards, on the way?'

He again hesitated, and looked into the officer's eyes. They were clear, calm eyes. The guard came a step nearer.

The officer looked down, turned towards the window and asked more gently: 'You had supper together in the cottage. Then you went out with them. Did they beat you on the way?'

He turned suddenly and looked at Yakób. The peasant stood, looked at the grey snowflakes outside the window, and his face, partly black, partly pallid, wrinkled in deep folds.

'Well, what have you got to say?'

'It was I . . .' This interrogation made him alternately hot and cold.

'You who beat them, and not they who beat you?' laughed the officer.

'The meat is still there in the cottage, and here is what they gave me,' he said, holding up the muffler and tobacco.

The officer threw his cigarette away and turned on his heel. Yakób's eyes became dull, his arm with the muffler dropped.

The officer wrote an order. 'Take him away.'

They passed the schoolmaster and some women and soldiers in the passage.

'Well . . . well . . .' they whispered, leaning against the wall.

The guard made a sign with his hand. Yakób, behind him, looked dully into the startled faces of the bystanders.

'How frightened he looks . . . how they have beaten him . . . how frightened he looks!' they murmured.

He put the muffler round his neck again, for he felt cold.

'That's him, that's him,' growled the crowd outside.

The manor-house was reached. The light from the numerous windows fell upon horses and gun-carriages drawn up in the yard.

'What do you want?' cried the sentry to the crowd, pushing them back.

He nodded towards Yakób. 'Where is he to go?'

'That sort . . .' murmured the crowd. Yakób's guard delivered his order. They stopped in the porch. The pillars threw long shadows which lost themselves towards the fence and across the waves of the stream beyond, in the darkness of the night.

The heat in the waiting-room was overpowering. This was the room where the bailiff had so often given him his pay. The office no longer existed. Soldiers were lying asleep everywhere.

They passed on into a brilliantly lighted room. The staff was quartered there. The general took a few steps across the room, murmured something and stood still in front of Yakób.

'Ah, that is the man?' he turned and looked at Yakób with his blue eyes that shot glances quick as lightning from under bushy grey eyebrows.

'It was I,' ejaculated Yakób hoarsely.

'It was you who showed them the way?'

Yakób became calmer. He felt he would be able to make himself more quickly understood here. 'It was.'

'You brought them here?'

'Yes.'

He passed his hand over his hair and shrank into himself again. He looked at the brilliant lights.

'Do you know what is the punishment for that?'

The general came a step nearer; Yakób felt overawed by the feeling of strength and power that emanated from him. He was choking. Yes, he understood and yet did not understand.

'What have you got to say for yourself?'

'We had supper together . . .' he began, but stopped, for the general frowned and eyed him coldly. Yakób looked towards the window and listened to hear the sound of wind and waves. The general was still looking at him, and so they stood for a moment which seemed an eternity to Yakób, the man in the field-grey uniform who looked as if he had been sculptured in stone, and the quailing, shrunken, shivering form, covered with dirt and rags. Yakób felt as though a heavy weight were resting on him. Then both silently looked down.

'Take him back to the battalion.'

The steely sound of the command moved something in the souls of the soldiers, and took the enjoyment of their sleep from them.

They returned to the school-house. The crowd, as though following a thief caught in the act, ran by their side again.

They found room for the old man in a shed, some one threw him a blanket. Soldiers were sleeping in serried ranks. Their heavy breathing mixed with the sound of wind and waves, and the cold blue light of the moon embraced everything.

Yakób buried himself in the straw, looked out through a hole in the boarding and wept bitterly.

'What are you crying for?' asked the sentry outside, and tapped his shoulder with his gun.

Yakób did not answer.

'Thinking of your wife?' the soldier gossiped, walking up and down outside the shed. 'You're old, what good is your wife to you?' The soldier stopped and stretched his arms till the joints cracked.

'Or your children? Never mind, they'll get on in the world without a helpless old man like you.'

Yakób was silent, and the soldier crouched down near him.

'Old man, you ought . . .'

'No . . .' tremblingly came from the inside.

'You see,' the soldier paced up and down again, 'you are thinking of your cottage. I can understand that. But do you think the cottage will be any worse off for your death?'

The soldier's simple and dour words outside in the blue night, his talk of Yakób's death, of his own death which might come at any moment, slowly brought sleep to Yakób.

In the morning he woke with a start. The sun was shining on the snow, the mountains glittered like glass. The trees on the slopes were covered with millions of shining crystals; freshness floated between heaven and earth. Yakób stepped out of the shed, greeted the sentry and sat down on the boards, blinking his eyes.

The air was fresh and cold, tiny atoms of hoar-frost were flying about. Yakób felt the sun's warmth thawing his limbs, caressing him. He let himself be absorbed into the pure, rosy morning.

Doors creaked, and voices rang out clear and fresh. Opposite to him a squadron of Uhlans were waiting at the farrier's, who came out, black as a charcoal-burner, and chatted with them. They were laughing, their eyes shone. From inside the forge the hammer rang out like a bell. Yakób held his head in his hand and listened. At each stroke he shut his eyes. The soldiers brought him a cup of hot coffee; he drank it and lighted his pipe.

The murmuring of the brook, punctuated by the hammer-strokes, stimulated his thoughts till they became clearer, limpid as the stream.

'It was I . . . it was I . . .' he silently confided to all the fresh voices of the morning.

The guard again took him away with fixed bayonets. He knew where he was going. They would go through the village and stop at the wall of the cemetery.

The sky was becoming overcast, the beauty of the morning was waning. They called at the school-house for orders. Yakób remained outside the open window.

'I won't . . .' he heard a voice.

'Nor I . . .' another.

Yakób leant against the fence, supported his temples on his fists and watched the snow-clouds and mists.

A feeling of immense, heavy weariness came over him, and made him limp. He could see the ruins of the mill, the tumbled-down granaries, the broken doors. The water trickled down the wheel; smoke and soot were floating on the water, yet the water flowed on.

Guilty . . . not guilty. . . . What did it all matter?

'Do you hear?' he asked of the water. 'Do you hear?' he asked of his wife and children and his little property.

They took him here and they took him there. They made him wait outside houses, and he sat down on the steps as if he had never been used to anything else. He picked up a dry branch and gently tapped the snow with it and waited. He waited as in a dream, going round and round the wish that it might all be over soon.

While he was waiting, the crowd amused themselves with shaking their fists at him; he was thankful that his wife seemed to have gone away to the town and did not see him.

At last his guard went off in a bad temper. A soldier on horseback remained with him.

'Come on, old man,' he said, 'no one will have anything to do with it.'

Yakób glanced at him; the soldier and his horse seemed to be towering above the cottages, above the trees of the park with their flocks of circling crows. He looked into the far distance.

'It was I.'

'You're going begging, old man.'

Again they began their round, and behind them followed the miller's wife and other women. His legs were giving way, as though they were rushes. He took off his cap and gave a tired look in the direction of his cottage.

At last they joined a detachment which was starting off on the old road. They went as far as Gregor's cottage, then to the cross-roads, and in single file down the path. From time to time isolated gunshots rang out.

They sat down by the side of a ditch.

'We've got to finish this business,' said the sergeant, and scratched his head. 'No one would come forward voluntarily . . . I have been ordered. . . .'

The soldiers looked embarrassed and drew away, looking at Yakób.

He hid his head between his knees, and his thoughts dwelt on everything, sky, water, mountains, fire.

His heart was breaking; a terrible sweat stood on his brows.

Shots rang out.

A deep groan escaped from Yakób's breast, a groan like a winter-wind. He sprang up, stood on the edge of the ditch, sighed with all the strength of his old breast and fell like a branch.

Puffs of smoke rose from the ditch and from the forests.

Ernest Hemingway

The Killers

The door of Henry's lunch-room opened and two men came in. They sat down at the counter.

'What's yours?' George asked them.

'I don't know,' one of the men said. 'What do you want to eat, Al?'

'I don't know,' said Al. 'I don't know what I want to eat.'

Outside it was getting dark. The street light came on outside the window. The two men at the counter read the menu. From the other end of the counter Nick Adams watched them. He had been talking to George when they came in.

'I'll have a roast pork tenderloin with apple sauce and mashed potatoes,' the first man said.

'It isn't ready yet.'

'What the hell do you put it on the card for?'

'That's the dinner,' George explained. 'You can get that at six o'clock.'

George looked at the clock on the wall behind the counter.

'It's five o'clock.'

'The clock says twenty minutes past five,' the second man said.

'It's twenty minutes fast.'

'Oh, to hell with the clock,' the first man said. 'What have you got to eat?'

'I can give you any kind of sandwiches,' George said. 'You can have ham and eggs, bacon and eggs, liver and bacon, or a steak.'

'Give me chicken croquettes with green peas and cream sauce and mashed potatoes.'

'That's the dinner.'

'Everything we want's the dinner, eh? That's the way you work it.'

'I can give you ham and eggs, bacon and eggs, liver——'

'I'll take ham and eggs,' the man called Al said. He wore a derby hat and a black overcoat buttoned across the chest. His face was small and white and he had tight lips. He wore a silk muffler and gloves.

'Give me bacon and eggs,' said the other man. He was about the same size as Al. Their faces were different, but they were dressed like twins. Both wore overcoats too tight for them. They sat leaning forward, their elbows on the counter.

'Got anything to drink?' Al asked.

'Silver beer, bevo, ginger ale,' George said.

'I mean you got anything to *drink*?'

'Just those I said.'

'This is a hot town,' said the other. 'What do they call it?'

'Summit.'

'Ever hear of it?' Al asked his friend.

'No,' said the friend.

'What do you do here nights?' Al asked.

'They eat the dinner,' his friend said. 'They all come here and eat the big dinner.'

'That's right,' George said.

'So you think that's right?' Al asked George.

'Sure.'

'You're a pretty bright boy, aren't you?'

'Sure,' said George.

'Well, you're not,' said the other little man. 'Is he, Al?'

'He's dumb,' said Al. He turned to Nick. 'What's your name?'

'Adams.'

'Another bright boy,' Al said. 'Ain't he a bright boy, Max?'

'The town's full of bright boys,' Max said.

George put the two platters, one of ham and eggs, the other of bacon and eggs, on the counter. He set down two side-dishes of fried potatoes and closed the wicket into the kitchen.

'Which is yours?' he asked Al.

'Don't you remember?'

'Ham and eggs.'

'Just a bright boy,' Max said. He leaned forward and took the ham and eggs. Both men ate with their gloves on. George watched them eat.

'What are *you* looking at?' Max looked at George.

'Nothing.'

'The hell you were. You were looking at me.'

'Maybe the boy meant it for a joke, Max,' Al said.

George laughed.

'*You* don't have to laugh,' Max said to him. '*You* don't have to laugh at all, see?'

'All right,' said George.

'So he thinks it's all right.' Max turned to Al. 'He thinks it's all right. That's a good one.'

'Oh, he's a thinker,' Al said. They went on eating.

'What's the bright boy's name down the counter?' Al asked Max.

'Hey, bright boy,' Max said to Nick. 'You go around on the other side of the counter with your boy friend.'

'What's the idea?' Nick asked.

'There isn't any idea.'

'You better go around, bright boy,' Al said. Nick went around behind the counter.

'What's the idea?' George asked.

'None of your damn business,' Al said. 'Who's out in the kitchen?'

'The nigger.'

'What do you mean, the nigger?'

'The nigger that cooks.'

'Tell him to come in.'

'What's the idea?'

'Tell him to come in.'

'Where do you think you are?'

'We know damn well where we are,' the man called Max said. 'Do we look silly?'

'You talk silly,' Al said to him. 'What the hell do you argue with this kid for? Listen,' he said to George, 'tell the nigger to come out here.'

'What are you going to do to him?'

'Nothing. Use your head, bright boy. What would we do to a nigger?'

George opened the slit that opened back into the kitchen. 'Sam,' he called. 'Come in here a minute.'

The door to the kitchen opened and the nigger came in. 'What was it?' he asked. The two men at the counter took a look at him.

'All right, nigger. You stand right there,' Al said.

Sam, the nigger, standing in his apron, looked at the two men sitting at the counter. 'Yes, sir,' he said. Al got down from his stool.

'I'm going back to the kitchen with the nigger and bright boy,' he said. 'Go on back to the kitchen, nigger. You go with him, bright boy.' The little man walked after Nick and Sam, the cook, back into the kitchen. The door shut after them. The man called Max sat at the counter opposite George. He didn't look at George but looked in the mirror that ran along back of the counter. Henry's had been made over from a saloon into a lunch-counter.

'Well, bright boy,' Max said, looking into the mirror, 'why don't you say something?'

'What's it all about?'

'Why don't you tell him?' Al's voice came from the kitchen.

'What do you think it's all about?'

'I don't know.'

'What do you think?'

Max looked into the mirror all the time he was talking.

'I wouldn't say.'

'Hey, Al, bright boy says he wouldn't say what he thinks it's all about.'

'I can hear you, all right,' Al said from the kitchen. He had propped open the slit that dishes passed through into the kitchen with a catsup bottle. 'Listen, bright boy,' he said from the kitchen to George, 'Stand a little farther along the bar. You move a little to the left, Max.' He was like a photographer arranging for a group picture.

'Talk to me, bright boy,' Max said. 'What do you think's going to happen?'

George did not say anything.

'I'll tell you,' Max said. 'We're going to kill a Swede. Do you know a big Swede named Ole Andreson?'

'Yes.'

'He comes here to eat every night, don't he?'

'Sometimes he comes here.'

'He comes here at six o'clock, don't he?'

'If he comes.'

'We know all that, bright boy,' Max said. 'Talk about something else. Ever go to the movies?'

'Once in a while.'

'You ought to go to the movies more. The movies are fine for a bright boy like you.'

'What are you going to kill Ole Andreson for? What did he ever do to you?'

'He never had a chance to do anything to us. He never even seen us.'

'And he's only going to see us once,' Al said from the kitchen.

'What are you going to kill him for, then?' George asked.

'We're killing him for a friend. Just to oblige a friend, bright boy.'

'Shut up,' said Al from the kitchen. 'You talk too goddam much.'

'Well, I got to keep bright boy amused. Don't I, bright boy?'

'You talk too damn much,' Al said. 'The nigger and my bright boy are amused by themselves. I got them tied up like a couple of girl friends in the convent.'

'I suppose you were in a convent.'

'You never know.'

'You were in a kosher convent. That's where you were.'

George looked up at the clock.

'If anybody comes in you tell them the cook is off, and if they keep after it, you tell them you'll go back and cook yourself. Do you get that, bright boy?'

'All right,' George said. 'What you going to do with us afterwards?'

'That'll depend,' Max said. 'That's one of those things you never know at the time.'

George looked up at the clock. It was a quarter past six. The door from the street opened. A street-car motorman came in.

'Hello, George,' he said. 'Can I get supper?'

'Sam's gone out,' George said. 'He'll be back in about half an hour.'

'I'd better go up the street,' the motorman said. George looked at the clock. It was twenty minutes past six.

'That was nice, bright boy,' Max said. 'You're a regular little gentleman.'

'He knew I'd blow his head off,' Al said from the kitchen.

'No,' said Max. 'It ain't that. Bright boy is nice. He's a nice boy. I like him.'

At six-fifty-five George said: 'He's not coming.'

Two other people had been in the lunch-room. Once George had gone out to the kitchen and made a ham-and-egg sandwich 'to go' that a man wanted to take with him. Inside the kitchen he saw Al, his derby hat tipped back, sitting on a stool beside the wicket with the muzzle of a sawed-off shotgun resting on the ledge. Nick and the cook were back to back in the corner, a towel tied in each of their mouths. George had cooked the sandwich, wrapped it up in oiled paper, put it in a bag, brought it in, and the man had paid for it and gone out.

'Bright boy can do anything,' Max said. 'He can cook and everything. You'd make some girl a nice wife, bright boy.'

'Yes?' George said. 'Your friend, Ole Andreson, isn't going to come.'

'We'll give him ten minutes,' Max said.

Max watched the mirror and the clock. The hands of the clock marked seven o'clock, and then five minutes past seven.

'Come on, Al,' said Max. 'We better go. He's not coming.'

'Better give him five minutes,' Al said from the kitchen.

In the five minutes a man came in, and George explained that the cook was sick.

'Why the hell don't you get another cook?' the man asked. 'Aren't you running a lunch-counter?' He went out.

'Come on, Al,' Max said.

'What about the two bright boys and the nigger?'

'They're all right.'

'You think so?'

'Sure. We're through with it.'

'I don't like it,' said Al. 'It's sloppy. You talk too much.'

'Oh, what the hell,' said Max. 'We got to keep amused, haven't we?'

'You talk too much, all the same,' Al said. He came out from the kitchen. The cut-off barrels of the shotgun made a slight bulge under the waist of his too tight-fitting overcoat. He straightened his coat with his gloved hands.

'So long, bright boy,' he said to George. 'You got a lot of luck.'

'That's the truth,' Max said. 'You ought to play the races, bright boy.'

The two of them went out the door. George watched them, through the window, pass under the arc-light and cross the street. In their tight overcoats and derby hats they looked like a vaudeville team. George went back through the swinging door into the kitchen and untied Nick and the cook.

'I don't want any more of that,' said Sam, the cook. 'I don't want any more of that.'

Nick stood up. He had never had a towel in his mouth before.

'Say,' he said. 'What the hell?' He was trying to swagger it off.

'They were going to kill Ole Andreson,' George said. 'They were going to shoot him when he came in to eat.'

'Ole Andreson?'

'Sure.'

The cook felt the corners of his mouth with his thumbs.

'They all gone?' he asked.

'Yeah,' said George. 'They're gone now.'

'I don't like it,' said the cook. 'I don't like any of it at all.'

'Listen,' George said to Nick. 'You better go see Ole Andreson.'

'All right.'

'You better not have anything to do with it at all,' Sam, the cook, said. 'You better stay way out of it.'

'Don't go if you don't want to,' George said.

'Mixing up in this ain't going to get you anywhere,' the cook said. 'You stay out of it.'

'I'll go see him,' Nick said to George. 'Where does he live?'

The cook turned away.

'Little boys always know what they want to do,' he said.

'He lives up at Hirsch's rooming house,' George said to Nick.

'I'll go up there.'

Outside the arc-light shone through the bare branches of a tree. Nick walked up the street beside the car-tracks and turned at the next arc-light down a side-street. Three houses up the street was Hirsch's rooming house. Nick walked up the two steps and pushed the bell. A woman came to the door.

'Is Ole Andreson here?'

'Do you want to see him?'

'Yes, if he's in.'

Nick followed the woman up a flight of stairs and back to the end of a corridor. She knocked on the door.

'Who is it?'

'It's somebody to see you, Mr Andreson,' the woman said.

'It's Nick Adams.'

'Come in.'

Nick opened the door and went into the room. Ole Andreson was lying on the bed with all his clothes on. He had been a heavy-weight prize-fighter and he was too long for the bed. He lay with his head on two pillows. He did not look at Nick.

'What was it?' he asked.

'I was up at Henry's,' Nick said, 'and two fellows came in and tied up me and the cook, and they said they were going to kill you.'

It sounded silly when he said it. Ole Andreson said nothing.

'They put us out in the kitchen,' Nick went on. 'They were going to shoot you when you came in to supper.'

Ole Andreson looked at the wall and did not say anything.

'George thought I better come and tell you about it.'

'There isn't anything I can do about it,' Ole Andreson said.

'I'll tell you what they were like.'

'I don't want to know what they were like,' Ole Andreson said. He looked at the wall. 'Thanks for coming to tell me about it.'

'That's all right.'

Nick looked at the big man lying on the bed.

'Don't you want me to go and see the police?'

'No,' Ole Andreson said. 'That wouldn't do any good.'

'Isn't there something I could do?'

'No. There ain't anything to do.'

'Maybe it was just a bluff.'

'No. It ain't just a bluff.'

Ole Andreson rolled over towards the wall.

'The only thing is,' he said, talking towards the wall, 'I just can't make up my mind to go out. I been in here all day.'

'Couldn't you get out of town?'

'No,' Ole Andreson said. 'I'm through with all that running around.'

He looked at the wall.

'There ain't anything to do now.'

'Couldn't you fix it up some way?'

'No. I got in wrong.' He talked in the same flat voice. 'There ain't anything to do. After a while I'll make up my mind to go out.'

'I better go back and see George,' Nick said.

'So long,' said Ole Andreson. He did not look towards Nick. 'Thanks for coming around.'

Nick went out. As he shut the door he saw Ole Andreson with all his clothes on, lying on the bed looking at the wall.

'He's been in his room all day,' the landlady said downstairs. 'I guess he don't feel well. I said to him: "Mr Andreson, you ought to go out and take a walk on a nice fall day like this," but he didn't feel like it.'

'He doesn't want to go out.'

'I'm sorry he don't feel well,' the woman said. 'He's an awfully nice man. He was in the ring, you know.'

'I know it.'

'You'd never know it except from the way his face is,' the woman said. They stood talking just inside the street door. 'He's just as gentle.'

'Well, good-night, Mrs Hirsch,' Nick said.

'I'm not Mrs Hirsch,' the woman said. 'She owns the place. I just look after it for her. I'm Mrs Bell.'

'Well, good-night, Mrs Bell,' Nick said.

'Good-night,' the woman said.

Nick walked up the dark street to the corner under the arc-light, and then along the car-tracks to Henry's eating-house. George was inside, back of the counter.

'Did you see Ole?'

'Yes,' said Nick. 'He's in his room and he won't go out.'

The cook opened the door from the kitchen when he heard Nick's voice.

'I don't even listen to it,' he said and shut the door.

'Did you tell him about it?' George asked.

'Sure. I told him but he knows what it's all about.'

'What's he going to do?'

'Nothing.'

'They'll kill him.'

'I guess they will.'

'He must have got mixed up in something in Chicago.'

'I guess so,' said Nick.

'It's a hell of a thing.'

'It's an awful thing,' Nick said.

They did not say anything. George reached down for a towel and wiped the counter.

'I wonder what he did?' Nick said.

'Double-crossed somebody. That's what they kill them for.'

'I'm going to get out of this town,' Nick said.

'Yes,' said George. 'That's a good thing to do.'

'I can't stand to think about him waiting in the room and knowing he's going to get it. It's too damned awful.'

'Well,' said George, 'you better not think about it.'

A. E. Coppard

Arabesque: the Mouse

In the main street amongst tall establishments of mart and worship was a high narrow house pressed between a coffee factory and a bootmaker's. It had four flights of long dim echoing stairs, and at the top, in a room that was full of the smell of dried apples and mice, a man in the middle age of life had sat reading Russian novels until he thought he was mad. Late was the hour, the night outside black and freezing, the pavements below empty and undistinguishable when he closed his book and sat motionless in front of the glowing but flameless fire. He felt he was very tired, yet he could not rest. He stared at a picture on the wall until he wanted to cry; it was a colour-print by Utamaro of a suckling child caressing its mother's breasts as she sits in front of a black-bound mirror. Very chaste and decorative it was, in spite of its curious anatomy. The man gazed, empty of sight though not of mind, until the sighing of the gas-jet maddened him. He got up, put out the light, and sat down again in the darkness trying to compose his mind before the comfort of the fire. And he was just about to begin a conversation with himself when a mouse crept from a hole in the skirting near the fireplace and scurried into the fender. The man had the crude dislike for such sly nocturnal things, but this mouse was so small and bright, its antics so pretty, that he drew his feet carefully from the fender and sat watching it almost with amusement. The mouse moved along the shadows of the fender, out upon the hearth, and sat before the glow, rubbing its head, ears and tiny belly with its paws, as if it were bathing itself with the warmth, until, sharp and sudden, the fire sank, an ember fell, and the mouse flashed into its hole.

The man reached forward to the mantelpiece and put his hand upon a pocket lamp. Turning on the beam, he opened the door of a cupboard beside the fireplace. Upon one of the shelves there was a small trap baited with cheese, a trap made with a wire spring, one of those that smashed down to break the back of ingenuous and unwary mice.

'Mean – so mean,' he mused, 'to appeal to the hunger of any living thing just in order to destroy it.'

He picked up the empty trap as if to throw it in the fire.

'I suppose I had better leave it, though – the place swarms with them.' He still hesitated. 'I hope that little beastie won't go and do anything foolish.' He put the trap back quite carefully, closed the door of the cupboard, sat down again and extinguished the lamp.

Was there anyone else in the world so squeamish and foolish about such things! Even his mother, mother so bright and beautiful, even she had laughed at his childish horrors. He recalled how once in his child-hood, not long after his sister Yosine was born, a friendly neighbour had sent him home with a bundle of dead larks tied by the feet 'for supper'. The pitiful inanimity of the birds had brought a gush of tears; he had run weeping home and into the kitchen, and there he had found the strange thing doing. It was dusk; mother was kneeling before the fire. He dropped the larks.

'Mother!' he exclaimed softly.

She looked at his tearful face.

'What's the matter, Filip?' she asked, smiling too, at his astonishment.

'Mother! What are you doing?'

Her bodice was open and she was squeezing her breasts; long thin streams of milk spurted into the fire with a plunging noise.

'Weaning your little sister,' laughed mother. She took his inquisitive face and pressed it against the delicate warmth of her bosom, and he forgot the dead birds behind him.

'Let me do it, Mother,' he cried, and doing so he discovered the throb of the heart in his mother's breast. Wonderful it was for him to experience it, although she could not explain it to him.

'Why does it do that?'

'If it did not beat, little son, I should die and the Holy Father would take me from you.'

'God?'

She nodded. He put his hand upon his own breast. 'Oh feel it, Mother!' he cried. Mother unbuttoned his little coat and felt the gentle *tick tick* with her warm palm.

'Beautiful!' she said.

'Is it a good one?'

She kissed his smiling lips. 'It is good if it beats truly. Let it always beat truly, Filip; let it always beat truly.'

There was the echo of a sigh in her voice, and he had divined some grief, for he was very wise. He kissed her bosom in his tiny ecstasy and whispered soothingly: 'Little Mother! Little Mother!' In such joys he forgot his horror of the dead larks; indeed he helped mother to pluck them and spit them for supper.

It was a black day that succeeded, and full of tragedy for the child. A great bay horse with a tawny mane had knocked down his mother in the lane, and a heavy cart had passed over her, crushing both her hands. She was borne away moaning with anguish to the surgeon who cut off the two hands. She died in the night. For years the child's dreams were filled with the horror of the stumps of arms bleeding unendingly. Yet he had never seen them, for he was sleeping when she died.

While this old woe was come vividly before him he again became aware of the mouse. His nerves stretched upon him in repulsion, but he soon relaxed to a tolerant interest, for it was really a most engaging little mouse. It moved with curious staccato scurries, stopping to rub its head or flicker with its ears; they seemed almost transparent ears. It spied a red cinder and skipped innocently up to it . . . sniffing . . . sniffing . . . until it jumped back scorched. It would crouch as a cat does, blinking in the warmth, or scamper madly as if dancing, and then roll upon its side rubbing its head with those pliant paws. The melancholy man watched it until it came at last to rest and squatted meditatively upon its haunches, hunched up, looking curiously wise, a pennyworth of philosophy; then once more the coals sank with a rattle and again the mouse was gone.

The man sat on before the fire and his mind filled again with unaccountable sadness. He had grown into manhood with a burning generosity of spirit and rifts of rebellion in him that proved too exacting for his fellows and seemed mere wantonness to men of casual rectitudes. 'Justice and Sin,' he would cry, 'Property and Virtue – incompatibilities! There can be no sin in a world of justice, no property in a world of virtue!' With an engaging extravagance and a certain clear-eyed honesty of mind he had put his two and two together and seemed then to rejoice, as in some topsy-turvy dream, in having rendered unto Caesar, as you might say, the things that were due to Napoleon! But this kind of thing could not pass unexpiated in a world of men having an infinite regard to Property and a pride in their traditions of Virtue and Justice. They could indeed forgive him his sins, but they could not forgive him his compassions. So he had to go seek for more melodious-minded men and fair unambiguous women. But rebuffs can deal more deadly blows than daggers; he became timid – a timidity not of fear but of pride – and grew with the years into misanthropy, susceptible to trivial griefs and despairs, a vessel of emotion that emptied as easily as it filled, until he came at last to know that his griefs were half deliberate, his despairs half unreal, and to live but for beauty – which is tranquillity – to put her wooing hand upon him.

Now, while the mouse hunts in the cupboard, one fair recollection stirs in the man's mind – of Cassia and the harmony of their only meeting, Cassia who had such rich red hair, and eyes, yes, her eyes were full of starry inquiry like the eyes of mice. It was so long ago that he had forgotten how he came to be in it, that unaccustomed orbit of vain vivid things – a village festival, all oranges and hoop-la. He could not remember how he came to be there, but at night, in the court hall, he had danced with Cassia – fair and unambiguous indeed – who had come like the wind from among the roses and swept into his heart.

'It is easy to guess,' he had said to her, 'what you like most in the world.'

She laughed. 'To dance? Yes, and you . . . ?'

'To find a friend.'

'I know, I know,' she cried, caressing him with recognitions. 'Ah, at times I quite love my friends – until I begin to wonder how much they hate me!'

He had loved at once that cool pale face, the abundance of her strange hair as light as the autumn's clustered bronze, her lilac dress and all the sweetness about her like a bush of lilies. How they had laughed at the two old peasants whom they had overheard gabbling of trifles like sickness and appetite!

'There's a lot of nature in a parsnip,' said one, a fat person of the kind that swells grossly when stung by a bee, 'a lot of nature when it's young, but when it's old it's like everything else.'

'True it is.'

'And I'm very fond of vegetables, yes, and I'm very fond of bread.'

'Come out with me,' whispered Cassia to Filip, and they walked out in the blackness of midnight into what must have been a garden.

'Cool it is here,' she said, 'and quiet, but too dark even to see your face – can you see mine?'

'The moon will not rise until after dawn,' said he, 'it will be white in the sky when the starlings whistle in your chimney.'

They walked silently and warily about until they felt the chill of the air. A dull echo of the music came to them through the walls, then stopped, and they heard the bark of a fox away in the woods.

'You are cold,' he whispered, touching her bare neck with timid fingers. 'Quite, quite cold,' drawing his hand tenderly over the curves of her chin and face. 'Let us go in,' he said, moving with discretion from the rapture he desired.

'We will come out again,' said Cassia.

But within the room the ball was just at an end, the musicians were packing up their instruments and the dancers were flocking out and homewards, or to the buffet which was on a platform at one end of the room. The two old peasants were there, munching hugely.

'I tell you,' said one of them, 'there's nothing in the world for it but the grease of an owl's liver. That's it, that's it! Take something on your stomach now, just to offset the chill of the dawn!'

Filip and Cassia were beside them, but there were so many people crowding the platform that Filip had to jump down. He stood then looking up adoringly at Cassia, who had pulled a purple cloak around her.

'For Filip, Filip, Filip,' she said, pushing the last bite of her sandwich into his mouth, and pressing upon him her glass of Loupiac. Quickly he drank it with a great gesture, and, flinging the glass to the wall, took Cassia into his arms, shouting, 'I'll carry you home, the whole way home, yes, I'll carry you!'

'Put me down!' she cried, beating his head and pulling his ear, as they passed among the departing dancers. 'Put me down, you wild thing!'

Dark, dark was the lane outside, and the night an obsidian net, into which he walked carrying the girl. But her arms were looped around him; she discovered paths for him, clinging more tightly as he staggered against a wall, stumbled upon a gulley, or when her sweet hair was caught in the boughs of a little lime tree.

'Do not loose me, Filip, will you? Do not loose me,' Cassia said, putting her lips against his temple.

His brain seemed bursting, his heart rocked within him, but he adored the rich grace of her limbs against his breast. 'Here it is,' she murmured, and he carried her into a path that led to her home in a little lawned garden where the smell of ripe apples upon the branches and the heavy lustre of roses stole upon the air. Roses and apples! Roses and apples! He carried her right into the porch before she slid down and stood close to him with her hands still upon his shoulders. He could breathe happily at the release, standing silent and looking round at the sky sprayed with wondrous stars but without a moon.

'You are stronger than I thought you, stronger than you look; you are really very strong,' she whispered, nodding her head to him. Opening the buttons of his coat, she put her palm against his breast.

'Oh, how your heart does beat! Does it beat truly – and for whom?'

He had seized her wrists in a little fury of love, crying, 'Little mother, little mother!'

'What are you saying?' asked the girl; but before he could continue there came a footstep sounding behind the door, and the clack of a bolt. . .

What was that? Was that really a bolt or was it . . . was it . . . the snap of the trap? The man sat up in his room intently listening, with nerves quivering again, waiting for the trap to kill the little philosopher. When he felt it was all over he reached guardedly in the darkness for the lantern, turned on the beam, and opened the door of the cupboard. Focusing the light upon the trap, he was amazed to see the mouse sitting on its haunches before it, uncaught. Its head was bowed, but its bead-like eyes were full of brightness, and it sat blinking, it did not flee.

'Shoosh!' said the man, but the mouse did not move.

'Why doesn't it go? Shoosh!' he said again, and suddenly the reason of the mouse's strange behaviour was made clear. The trap had not caught it completely, but it had broken off both its forefeet, and the thing crouched there holding out its two bleeding stumps humanely, too stricken to stir.

Horror flooded the man, and conquering his repugnance he plucked the mouse up quickly by the neck. Immediately the little thing fastened its teeth in his finger; the touch was no more than the slight prick of a pin. The man's impulse then exhausted itself. What should he do with it? He put his hand behind him, he dared not look, but there was nothing to be done except kill it at once, quickly, quickly. Oh, how should he do it? He bent towards the fire as if to drop the mouse into its quenching glow; but he paused and shuddered, he would hear its cries, he would have to listen. Should he crush it with finger and thumb? A glance towards the window decided him. He opened the sash with one hand and flung the wounded mouse far into the dark street. Closing the window with a crash, he sank into a chair, limp with pity too deep for tears.

So he sat for two minutes, five minutes, ten minutes. Anxiety and shame filled him with heat. He opened the window again, and the freezing air poured in and cooled him. Seizing his lantern, he ran down the echoing stairs, into the dark empty street, searching long and vainly for the little philosopher until he had to desist and return to his room, shivering, frozen to his very bones.

When he had recovered some warmth he took the trap from its shelf. The two feet dropped into his hand; he cast them into the fire. Then he once more set the trap and put it back carefully into the cupboard.

F. Tennyson Jesse

Treasure Trove

Summer stayed late that year, and it was not until the last day of October that Brandon realized it had gone. Then a storm sprang up which went sweeping over the marshes, ruffling the still, grey waters of the meres and inlets, and rending the leaves from the twisted trees. After it had passed, the warmth had gone from the air and only a pale, wintry sunshine lay pure and chill over the fen land. A few leaves still clung to the elms that grew about the farm place, and, as he pushed open the gate of the farmyard, he heard the cawing of the rooks about their nests, which showed black amid the bare branches.

Brandon felt for the moment the classic melancholy appropriate to the dying year, annual reminder of the Autumn that approaches to every man. But the next moment, turning his head to look back the way he had come, he saw that between the pale brown masses of the reeds the waters were a cold, bright blue, and the crystalline notes of the robin, practising for its winter song, came to his ear. Beauty still lived in this fenny country and his heart responded gratefully.

He went across the muddy yard and met his friend Miles in the doorway of the farmhouse. Dear, good Miles – sun or rain, summer or winter, held very little message for him that was not strictly utilitarian. But Miles's ruddy, outdoor face seemed somehow to have lost its usual cheerfulness of outlook, though it would certainly not be because of anything to do with some allegorical message of the dying summer.

'Have you seen Tom and Jack?' asked Miles. 'They were supposed to be ploughing in the five-acre today, and they're not to be found. They're so dependable as a rule.'

'Tom and Jack? No. It doesn't matter, does it? I suppose they're harrowing or mulching or marling or sowing or some other of the many processes that you indulge in.'

The strange expression on his host's face had not lightened.

'They've been queer,' he said, 'darn queer, for two days now, ever since they found that cursed treasure while ploughing the reclaimed piece of wasteland over by the big dyke. This morning they looked so queerly at each other I didn't quite like them going out together. There's something odd about it, Bill. I don't like it.'

Brandon smiled and began to stuff his pipe.

'Nonsense, what could be wrong with your men?' he said. 'It won't be the first time a little bit of money has gone to a man's head. They'll get over it, you'll see.'

But to himself he was thinking that it was a bit queer all the same. Everyone knew Tom and Jack, they were the famous friends of the village. Damon and Pythias weren't in it when it came to friendship. They had been to the same Council school as boys, been in the same footer team in the winter, same cricket team in the summer, skated together, gone duck-shooting together, gone fishing together, fought in the same regiment through the war and had even married twin sisters, and as far as anyone knew there had never been a wry word between them. They were not men of any special ability which would have caused them to grow away from the class of life into which they had been born, but in that class they were easily first in their district. Honest, decent, intelligent men, a little slow in the process of their thoughts, perhaps, but none the less shrewd and sound for that. Tom a year younger, slightly built and active, Jack heavy compared with his friend but strong as a bull. Tom might be quick in his temper, but it was soon over. Jack had the serenity that often goes with men of his large build. It seemed sad and a little odd that a few dirty antique coins should have been able to come between them.

'Why don't you tell them,' he suggested to Miles, 'that their old coins are probably worth very little?'

'I have,' said Miles. 'But you know what these people are, they always imagine anything they dig up must be of immense value and that the British Museum would buy it for a large sum. I can understand that part of it, what I can't understand is that they should begin to quarrel over it. I should have thought they'd have been only too glad to share it, however much or little it's worth. Besides, their working hours are not over yet, and I've never known them to down tools until the right hour, generally not till after it. They're the real old-fashioned kind that doesn't like to leave a job half done.'

Scarcely had he said this when one of the maid-servants came running from the passage at his back, calling to him in a loud and frightened voice:

'Come quick, sir, Tom and Jack be fighting in the barn, they're killing each other . . .'

Miles turned and ran through the house, out into the front garden and across it, Brandon at his heels.

The big barn stood on the slope of the field beyond, a wooden building, black with pitch, with a red fluted roof. Beside it the straw ricks gleamed golden in the late sunshine. The two men ran up the slope of the field where the trodden turf was heavy and greasy to their feet and Brandon, outstepping his more elderly host, burst through the door into the barn.

For the first moment it all seemed very dark to him, a darkness filled with dust motes that wreathed like steam in the rays shining through the doorway. The smell of cattle and trodden earth, and of the sweet stored hay, filled the dimness; rafters and rough wooden pillars stood out in the gloom. Then, as sight grew clear, his ears became aware of a horrible sound of sobbing that rose and fell, and the thud of blows. Two men were fighting, backward and forward, on the earthy floor. As Miles and Brandon sprang forward, the bigger man, who was winning, rained blows upon either side of his opponent's head, and the smaller man, from whom came the noise of sobbing, suddenly crumpled up and fell to the floor, where he lay still.

'Good God, man!' cried Miles, hanging on to the big fellow's arm. 'You must be mad, you might kill him.'

The man turned a ravaged face to his master.

'I shouldn't care if I had, the dirty hound!' he said. 'He's a thief, that's what he is.'

'Tom a thief! Nonsense. Why, you'd have fought anybody else who said as much.'

'Aye, I *would* have,' said the man. 'But not now . . . He's stolen all the money we'd dug up in the new field. He's hidden it away somewhere and won't say where. He's just lying and saying he hasn't got it.'

Brandon had knelt down beside the unconscious Tom, whose face was running with blood; now he looked up and said:

'Well, you've nearly killed him. Even if it's true, you ought to be ashamed of yourself, and I don't believe it *is* true. Tom wouldn't do a thing like that. By God, Miles, look at his fists. Open your fists.'

And he got up and advanced on Jack, who stood staring sullenly at him, his clenched fists still held before him. Jack offered no resistance as his master and Brandon pulled his fingers apart and discovered, clenched in each hand, a ragged flint stone, their ends dripping with Tom's blood. Brandon, looking at Jack's glazed eyes, said nothing; it would be little use saying anything, he felt, to a man as changed from the self they all knew, as this man was. Instead, he said to Miles:

'We must get Tom out of this. You and Jack pick him up while I have a look around.'

With surprising docility Jack bent down and picked up gently the head he had ill-treated, and he and Miles between them carried the unconscious man out through the ray of sunlight into the air.

Brandon sat down on an upturned bucket near at hand. He felt sick and ill at the sight of the blood, an idiosyncrasy of his so unconquerable that he had ceased to be ashamed of it. It seemed to him that the dim air of the barn was laden still with the violent passions that had been released there, that the element of strangeness in this sudden hatred sickened the very sunlight that slanted in upon the spot trodden by the men's struggling feet.

Brandon was not normally a super-sensitive man, but all his life he had been the prey of moments which had taken and shaken him oddly, moments when he had seemed not through any superior gifts of his own, but because of some outer compulsion, to be aware of more than most men, of more than, ordinarily, he would have been aware of himself. Usually these strange spaces of clarity were prefaced by an unaccountable aspect of external things; a familiar tree or bookshelf would take on a look that he could only describe himself as 'tilted', as though the angle of the visible world had started off in a new direction, pointing towards an unknown dimension; as though the tree or bookshelf had lost, all of a sudden, its treeness or furniturehood, and become a wedge thrust into space. At the time this would seem all right to him; only afterwards, looking back, his senses still giddy, he would realize the different tilt. And, cutting across this new space, there would come a wedge of light, tilted at the same new angle, which for the moment was the right angle, and in it he would be aware of, rather than see, a new and more complete aspect of something he had only imperfectly known before. A friend's motive for doing what had to him previously seemed inexplicable; the solution to some riddle in the history lecture he was working out; of sometimes even a fresh light upon a matter which had no earthly connection, as far as he knew, with himself.

He was almost hypnotized into this feeling now, as he sat there in the barn, but he shook off the dizzying sensations, like the familiar pins and needles of the children, that were stealing over him, and told himself it was due to the upset of his nerves and to the angle of the shaft of light that streamed in at the door. He got to his feet and as he did so he caught sight of a battered felt hat lying against the wall of the barn. He went over to it to take it up. He recognized it as Tom's by its peculiar light-grey colour and by the blue jay's feather stuck in the band. He bent to pick it up, but to his surprise it was so unexpectedly heavy in his hand that he almost dropped it. He ran his fingers behind the head lining of the crown; wrapped in a thin piece of stuff he felt the uneven surfaces of coins. So Tom had lied after all . . . he had concealed the coins. Brandon felt as when he had seen the flints concealed in Jack's fists.

He picked up the hat, and went heavily out of the barn with the hat carried between his two hands. He crossed the garden and went into the little room outside the front door which Miles used as his office.

Brandon closed the door and sat down at the table, pushing away papers and ledgers to make a clear space in front of him. Then he turned the hat up, and pulled out the pack of coins which lay, snakelike, circled around the crown. He unfolded the strip of soiled silk handkerchief and poured the coins out on the table before him. There they lay, the source of all the trouble between Tom and Jack, a mere handful of dirty, almost shapeless coins. Brandon looked at them curiously. They were so old and battered he could only just make out the head of a Caesar – which, he knew not, but the Roman look of it was unmistakable. It seemed incredible that through these coins, the passion of envy, mounting murder high, had come into being . . . He scraped the coins together in his two hands.

And then, as he sat there, the strange sensation came flooding over him, drenching him, as it were, to the tips of his fingers and toes, so that he felt he could not move if the house caught fire about him. He felt very cold, in spite of the tingling that pervaded him, and he knew – how, he could not have told – that he was holding in his palms things so evil that his very flesh revolted, things so evil that whenever they were discovered and rediscovered by men they brought evil in their train. He knew, with a dreadful clearness in the midst of this dark red mist, that these things had been turned up by the ploughshare, or dragged from the sea, or cast upon beaches throughout the years, and whosoever found them knew desolation and decay of everything that had been his until then. There beat at him persistently the knowledge that he must take these things out and throw them away in the place where it was least likely they would be found for generations to come. He must weight them heavily and cast them out to sea, or throw them into the still waters of some disused pit.

He struggled violently against the feeling of horror that held him, because he wished to see about this business as soon as might be, and by a violent effort of the will he pulled himself back into the present. The evening sun was still shining into the little room. Shaking, but with the tingling slowly growing less all over his body, he drew his hands away from the clustering coins and let them fall upon the table. He passed his palm across his wet forehead and told himself that in another moment or so he would be able to do what he had to do, and quite soon he stood up, his steady self again, although not denying he had been shaken.

It was suddenly that the dreadful idea took him. Putting out his hands he began to count the coins; he counted three times, always hoping that in his hurry he might have erred, but count as he would, the battered pieces of silver numbered thirty. Brandon leaped up, and drew away from the table, his hands shaking. He found himself saying in a dreadful whisper: 'Thirty pieces of silver . . . thirty pieces . . . of silver.'

Luigi Pirandello

Cinci

The dog squatted there patiently on its hind legs, in front of the closed
door, waiting for someone to open it and let him in. The nearest he came
to protesting was to let out an occasional low whine, as he lifted a paw
and scratched himself.

He was a dog, so he knew there was nothing more he could do.

When Cinci got back from afternoon school, with his textbooks and
his exercise books all strapped together and tucked under his arm, he
found the dog stuck there outside the door. It irritated him to see it
waiting there, patiently like that, so he gave it a kick. Then he gave the
door a good kicking, too, even though he knew it was locked and there
was nobody at home. Finally, if only because he felt they were the worst
of his burdens, he flung his bundle of books furiously against the door –
just to get rid of them – as if he had some daft idea that they'd pass
straight through the woodwork and land up in the house. Contrary to
any such expectation, however, the door flung them straight back at his
chest with the same force with which he'd hurled them originally. Cinci
was quite surprised: it was as if this were some wonderful game that the
door was suggesting they might play. So he threw the bundle back at the
door. Then, since there were already three of them playing this game –
Cinci, the bundle of books, and the door – the dog thought he'd join in
as well. Every time Cinci slung the books at the door and every time they
bounced back, he'd leap in the air, barking away. Several passers-by
stopped to watch. A few of them smiled, almost ashamed of themselves,
of course, because of the utter silliness of the game and because of the
equal silliness of the dog, who was having such a riotous time. Others
waxed highly indignant, because of the way those poor books were being
treated. Books cost money, you know. People oughtn't to be allowed to

treat them like that, with so little regard. Cinci brought the show to an end, dropped his bundle of books on the ground, and slumped to a sitting position by sliding his backbone down the wall. It had been his intention to sit on the books, but the bundle slid from under him and he landed on the ground with a sudden jolt. He gave a wry, comic grin and looked around, while the dog bounded back and eyed him speculatively.

All the devilment that passed through Cinci's mind was – well, you could almost see it written all over that untidy thatch of straw-coloured hair of his, and in those sharp green eyes, which seemed almost to be wriggling with life. He was at the awkward age, all gawky and sallow. He'd left his handkerchief at home when he'd gone back to school that afternoon. Now, as a consequence, he'd every so often give a snuffle, as he sat there on the ground. He drew his enormous knees up until they almost reached his chin. His huge legs were bare, because he was still wearing short trousers – and shouldn't have been. When he ran, his legs splayed out sideways. There wasn't a pair of shoes that could stand up to the treatment he meted out to them; the ones he had on then were right through already. He was bored stiff. He folded his arms round his knees, gave a huge, puffing sigh, and then dragged his spine up the wall again until he was standing upright once more. The dog got up too, and it was just as if he was asking, 'Well, where are we off to now?' Yes, where were we going? Out into the country, to have a snack? Knock off the odd fig or apple? It was an idea. He hadn't quite made up his mind, though.

The paved road ended at their house, and the cinder-path took over, and if you went on and on through their suburb you landed in the country. What a wonderful sensation it must be – if you were riding in a carriage, that is – when the horses' hooves and the carriage-wheels passed from the hard surface of the stridently noisy paving, to the soft, silent cinder-road. It's probably like what happens when the teacher who's been busy shouting your head off – oh, you've made him so angry! – starts talking to you gently, kindly, with a sort of resigned melancholy. You find it so much more agreeable, because it puts a safe distance between you and the punishment you were afraid you were in for. Yes, it would be a good idea to go into the country, to get away, out along the narrow stretch of road flanked by the last houses of this stinking suburb, down to where the road widened out into the little square that marked the end of the town. The new hospital was down there now, the walls of which were so freshly white-washed that when the sun was shining on them you had to shut your eyes, or you got blinded. In the last few days they'd been busy bringing down all the patients from the old hospital – ambulances and stretchers galore there'd been. It had been as good as a procession, as they all filed along. The ambulances in front, with all their curtains fluttering away at the windows, and then, for the more seriously ill patients, those lovely hammock-trolley things, bouncing along on their springs, like a lot of spiders' webs. It was pretty late now, though, and the sun was just about to set, so there wouldn't be the occasional convalescent patient up at one or other of the huge windows, wearing his grey nightshirt and his white nightcap, and sadly looking at the little old church opposite, as it stood there among a cluster of houses as old as itself and the odd tree or two. Once you'd left that little square, the road became a country-lane and went on up the side of the little hill.

Cinci stopped and gave another huge puffing sigh. Ought he to go? Really? He set off again in a resentful sort of way, because he was beginning to feel boiling away in his guts all the horrible feelings that kept welling up inside him because of so many things that he couldn't explain to himself. His mother, now: how did she live and what did she live on? Never at home, still stubbornly insisting on sending him to that damned school. Yes, that *damned* school – miles away from home it was! Every day he went there – and you had to run like hell for at least three-quarters of an hour to get there in time, from where they lived, out there on the outskirts, that is. Then another three-quarters of an hour sprint to get back home at midday; then another three-quarters of an hour to get back again, after he'd managed to bolt down a couple of mouthfuls – how the hell was he supposed to do it in the time? And his mother busy telling him that he wasted all his time playing with the dog, that he was an idle layabout. And, oh bloody hell! Always throwing the same old muck in his face: he didn't study, he always looked dirty, and if she sent him out to buy something at the shop, they always fobbed him off with any old rubbish.

Where was Fox?

There he was, trotting along behind him, poor little beast. Huh, at least he knew what he had to do: just follow his master. To do something. That's what all the frenzy of life's about – not knowing *what* to do. She could leave him the key, couldn't she – his mother, he meant – when she went off, as she did every day, to sew in gentlemen's houses? (That's what she told him she did.) Oh, no! She said he wasn't to be trusted, and that if she wasn't back by the time he got in from school, she couldn't possibly be long, and that he was to wait. Where? Outside the door, like a lemon? There'd been times when he'd waited for two whole hours, out in the cold – out in the rain, even. As a matter of fact, on *that* particular occasion, he'd deliberately not taken shelter, but had gone and stood under the overflow, so that when she came in she'd find him all sopping wet. Finally she'd appeared, all out of breath, her face flushed, and carrying a borrowed umbrella, her eyes bright, unable to meet his, and so nervy that she couldn't even find the key in her purse.

'Are you soaked? Shan't be a moment now. I had to stay late.'

Cinci frowned. There were certain things he preferred not to think about. He'd never known his father. They'd told him he was dead, that he'd died even before he was born. But they didn't tell him who he'd been. And now he no longer had any desire to know, or to ask any more questions. He might even have been that cripple, the one who was paralysed down one side, but who still managed to drag himself along to the pub, stout fellow. Fox used to rush up to him and bark at him. It was probably the crutch he didn't like. And look at those women standing around in a huddle – all that belly and not one of them pregnant. No, maybe one of them was. The one with her skirt hoicked up a good six inches at the front and sweeping the street behind. And that other one with the baby in her arms, fishing out a breast to—— *Ugh*! What a horrible blubbery mass of flesh! His mother was beautiful, and still very young, and when he'd been a baby, she'd given him milk from her breast, just like that. And perhaps it had been in a house in the country, or out in the sun, in the yard where they did the threshing. Cinci had a vague recollection of a house in the country. Perhaps it was there – always supposing he hadn't dreamt it – that he'd lived when he was a tiny child. Or perhaps he'd seen it somewhere when he was small. Heaven only knows where, though. Certainly now when, from a distance, he saw houses in the country, he felt that same sort of melancholy which you feel *must* come into those houses when it begins to get evening. When the lamps are lit – the sort you fill with paraffin and carry about in your hand from one room to another – and you see the light disappearing from one window and reappearing at another.

He'd reached the little square by this time. And now he could see the whole vast expanse of the sky. The last rays of the setting sun had disappeared and, over the now darkened hill, the sky was the tenderest of clear blues. The shadow of evening was already upon the earth, and the great white wall of the hospital was muted to a dull grey. The occasional old woman hurried along to the little church, late for Vespers. Cinci suddenly felt a desire to go in himself. Fox stood and looked at him. He knew perfectly well that he wasn't allowed into churches. In the church doorway the old woman who was late was panting and moaning away as she struggled with the leather curtain. It was far too heavy for her to cope with. Cinci helped her to hold it to one side but, instead of thanking him, she only gave him a nasty look. She'd realized only too clearly, of course, that he hadn't gone into that church for devotional reasons. The little church was freezing; cold as a cave. On the main altar two candles burned fitfully, while scattered here and there about the church there were a few dismayed-looking little oil-lamps. The dust of ages lay thick on everything in that little old church and, there in the crude dampness, the very dust itself had a smell of decay about it. And it was for all the world as if the shadow-filled silence were lying in ambush for the slightest noise, so that it could go crashing off into echo upon echo upon echo. Cinci felt a terrible temptation to let out a mighty yell, just to start all those echoes bounding about the place. The pious old dears had already filed into their pews. No, it wouldn't be a good idea to give a yell. But why not throw that bundle of books on to the ground? Well, they were awfully heavy, and they might quite well have dropped from his arm by sheer accident. . . . Why not? He hurled them to the ground, and instantly, the moment they hit the ground, the echoes came raining down upon him, thundering in his ears, crushing him beneath their weight – almost contemptuously. Cinci had often (and with very great relish) tried this experiment of raising echoes. He liked to feel the echo pouncing on a noise and crushing it to the ground, just like a dog that's been irked by something while he's asleep. There was no need for him to tempt the patience of those scandalized and pious old bodies any further, so he mooched out of the church, where he found Fox all ready to follow him, and off he set again along the road leading to the little hill. He felt the need to lay his hands on some fruit somewhere – something he could get his teeth into. Over the low wall he went, and hurled himself among the trees. He felt an enormous sense of tormented longing. But whether it was simply because of that frenzy which was biting into his guts, the frenzy to do something, he just couldn't say.

It was a country road, steep and lonely, strewn with pebbles that got caught by the hooves of passing donkeys, got sent rolling for a little way, and then – where they stopped, there they stayed. Look, there was one of them! He gave it a kick with the toe of his shoe. Go on, stone, enjoy yourself! Oh, it flies through the air with the greatest of ease . . . ! Grass was growing by the roadside and, at the foot of the low walls, long plumed stalks of oats which were very pleasant to chew on – when you'd stripped off the little plumes. They came off like a bouquet when you ran them through your fingers. Then you threw them at somebody, and the number of them that stuck on her (assuming she was a woman), was the number of husbands she was going to have – or, if it was a man, the number of wives. Cinci thought he'd try it out on Fox. Seven wives! No less than seven wives was his ration! It didn't really count, though, because they all stuck on Fox's black coat, the whole lot of them. And Fox, the silly old stupid, just stood there with his eyes shut! He didn't get the joke! There he was, with seven wives on his back.

Cinci didn't feel like going any farther. He was tired and he was bored. He swerved to the left and sat down on the low wall beside the road. And as he sat there he began to study the new moon, whose pale gold crescent was just beginning to gleam brightly through the green light that filled the sky in those last moments of sunset. He saw the moon and yet somehow he didn't see it – it was like so many things that were wandering through his mind, one thing merging into another, and every single one of them receding farther and farther away from that young body of his as it sat there, so motionless that he was no longer aware of it. If he'd caught sight then of his own hand on his knee, it would have seemed like a stranger's to him – just as his own leg would have done, as it dangled there, with his dirty, broken-down shoe at the end of it. He was no longer in his body. He was in all those things which he saw and didn't see: the sky that grew darker as the day died; the moon that was getting brighter and brighter; he was there in those gloomy clumps of trees, which stood so sharply in the empty air, and in the earth over there – the fresh, black, recently hoed earth, from which there still breathed that smell of damp, rotting vegetation, so characteristic of the sultry tedium of the end of October, when the days are still very warm and sunny.

While he was sitting there, completely absorbed, an extraordinary and unidentifiable *something* suddenly ran through his body, distracting him. Instinctively he raised his hand to his ear. A shrill little laugh came from behind the wall. A boy of about his own age, a well-built peasant lad, had been hiding behind it, on the field side. He too had plucked and stripped a long blade of oats for himself. He'd made a little noose at the top of it, and then, very, very quietly, he'd raised his arm and tried to hitch the noose over Cinci's ear. This annoyed Cinci, but the moment he turned round, the boy immediately gestured to him to shush, and held the blade of oats along the wall, towards where the head of a lizard was popping out from between a couple of stones. He'd been trying for the last hour to snare that lizard with his noose. Cinci leant backwards and down, anxiously trying to see what happened. Without realizing what it was doing, the little creature had popped its head into the noose which had been put there in the hope that it would be just so obliging. There was a long way to go yet, however. You had to wait till it stuck its head out a little farther. And it might well be that, instead of doing so, it would withdraw, especially if the hand which was holding the blade of oats trembled and so gave it warning of the ambush. At that very moment it might be on the point of darting out like an arrow, in order to escape from that refuge which had become a prison. Yes! Oh, yes! But you had to stand by, ready to give the jerk that would put the noose round its neck, just at the right moment. It was the work of an instant! There, he'd got it! The lizard was squirming like a fish at the end of that blade of oats. Cinci couldn't resist! He jumped down from the wall. But the other boy, afraid, perhaps, that he was planning to take over the little creature, whirled his arm round several times in the air, and smashed the lizard ferociously down again and again on a huge slab of stone that lay there among the weeds.

'No!' screamed Cinci, but it was too late. The lizard lay motionless on the slab of stone, with the white of its belly gleaming in the light of the moon. Cinci flew into a rage. Yes, he too had wanted that poor little creature to get caught, because he himself had for the moment been overpowered by that instinct to hunt which lurks insidiously in every single one of us. But to kill it like that, without even taking a close look at it; without looking into those eyes – those sharp, almost frantically sharp little eyes; without studying the steady rhythm of its sides as it breathed, and the whole trembling mass of its tiny green body. No, that had been stupid and utterly shameful! Cinci hurled himself at the boy, and punched him in the chest with all his might, sending him sprawling on the ground. He landed a little farther away than he might have done, because he'd been a bit off-balance when Cinci had hit him, and he'd tried and tried to prevent himself from falling. But, no sooner had he hit the ground, than he leapt up again, livid with fury, dug a clod of earth out of the ground and hurled it in Cinci's face. Cinci stood there for a moment, blinded by the dirt. The damp taste in his mouth only gave him a worse sense of outrage. He became like an animal in his fury. Now he grabbed a clod of earth, and hurled it back. The fight immediately became desperate. It was a duel now. The other boy was quicker on his feet, however, and a much more skilled fighter. He never missed. He moved in steadily, getting closer and closer, keeping up a bombardment with those clods of earth, which, even if they didn't actually injure Cinci still hit him pretty hard, as they rained down on him. It was like a hailstorm as they disintegrated with a thud on his chest or in his face. The dirt got in his hair, and in his eyes – even into his shoes. Choked with dirt, and completely at a loss to know how to defend himself or shield his body, Cinci, now quite beside himself with rage, leapt in the air, stretched out his arm, and snatched a stone from the top of the wall. He was vaguely aware that something scurried away – Fox, probably. He hurled the stone, and all of a sudden— How did it happen? Everything had been spinning round before. Sort of upside-down. Dancing in front of his eyes. Those clumps of trees. The moon, like a sliver of light in the sky. And now, nothing was moving any more. Almost as if Time itself, and everything else in the world too, were standing still in amazement and stupefaction at the sight of that boy stretched out there, face downwards on the ground.

Cinci, still panting, and with his heart in his mouth, gazed at it all in utter terror. His back against the wall, he gazed at the incredible, silent stillness of the countryside, with the moon high above. He gazed at that boy, lying there with his face half-hidden in the ground, and he felt growing within him, as a formidable reality, the sensation of an eternal solitude, from which he must immediately run away. It wasn't him! He hadn't wanted it to happen! He didn't know anything about it! And then, just as if he really hadn't done it, just as if he were simply going over to him out of curiosity, he took a step forward. Then another, and leant over him to have a look. The boy's head was bashed in, and his mouth was black where blood had dripped through it and on to the ground. You could see part of one of his legs, where his trousers had ridden up above the top of his cotton sock. He was dead, just as if he'd always been dead. Everything lay there, as if it were in a dream. He really must wake up, if he was to get away in time. Over there – just as if it were in a dream – that lizard, lying on its back on the stone, belly upwards to the moon, and with the blade of oats still hanging round its neck. Off he went, with his bundle of books under his arm once again, and Fox trotting along behind him. He didn't know anything about it either.

Gradually, as he went down the slope and moved farther and farther away from the spot, he got more and more the – yes, a strange feeling of being safe. So he didn't even bother to hurry. He reached the little square – it was quite deserted by this time. The moon was shining there too. It was another moon, though. One that didn't know anything at all about – things. It was busy lighting up the white façade of the hospital. He'd reached the road for their part of the suburb by this time, just like before. He reached home. His mother still hadn't got back. So he wouldn't even have to tell her where he'd been. He'd been there all the time, waiting for her. And this statement, which immediately became true as far as his mother was concerned, immediately became true as far as he himself was concerned. Yes, as a matter of fact, there he was, with his shoulders resting against the wall by the door.

It would be quite sufficient for all concerned, if he let her find him like that.

Dorothy L. Sayers

Suspicion

As the atmosphere of the railway carriage thickened with tobacco smoke, Mr Mummery became increasingly aware that his breakfast had not agreed with him.

There could have been nothing wrong with the breakfast itself. Brown bread, rich in vitamin content, as advised by the *Morning Star's* health expert; bacon fried to a delicious crispness; eggs just nicely set; coffee made as only Mrs Sutton knew how to make it. Mrs Sutton had been a real find, and that was something to be thankful for. For Ethel, since her nervous breakdown in the summer, had really not been fit to wrestle with the untrained girls who had come and gone in tempestuous succession. It took very little to upset Ethel nowadays, poor child. Mr Mummery, trying hard to ignore his growing internal discomfort, hoped he was not in for an illness. Apart from the trouble it would cause at the office, it would worry Ethel terribly, and Mr Mummery would cheerfully have laid down his rather uninteresting little life to spare Ethel a moment's uneasiness.

He slipped a digestive tablet into his mouth – he had taken lately to carrying a few tablets about with him – and opened his paper. There did not seem to be very much news. A question had been asked in the House about Government typewriters. The Prince of Wales had smilingly opened an all-British exhibition of footwear. A further split had occurred in the Liberal party. The police were still looking for the woman who was supposed to have poisoned a family in Lincoln. Two girls had been trapped in a burning factory. A film star had obtained her fourth decree nisi.

At Paragon Station, Mr Mummery descended and took a tram. The internal discomfort was taking the form of a definite nausea. Happily he contrived to reach his office before the worst occurred. He was seated at his desk, pale but in control of himself, when his partner came breezing in.

' 'Morning, Mummery,' said Mr Brookes in his loud tones, adding inevitably, 'cold enough for you?'

'Quite,' replied Mr Mummery. 'Unpleasantly raw, in fact.'

'Beastly, beastly,' said Mr Brookes. 'Your bulbs all in?'

'Not quite all,' confessed Mr Mummery. 'As a matter of fact I haven't been feeling—'

'Pity,' interrupted his partner. 'Great pity. Ought to get 'em in early. Mine were in last week. My little place will be a picture in the spring. For a town garden, that is. You're lucky, living in the country. Find it better than Hull, I expect, eh? Though we get plenty of fresh air up in the Avenues. How's the missus?'

'Thank you, she's very much better.'

'Glad to hear that, very glad. Hope we shall have her about again this winter as usual. Can't do without her in the Drama Society, you know. By Jove I shan't forget her acting last year in *Romance*. She and young Welbeck positively brought the house down, didn't they? The Welbecks were asking after her only yesterday.'

'Thank you, yes. I hope she will soon be able to take up her social activities again. But the doctor says she mustn't overdo it. No worry, he says – that's the important thing. She is to go easy and not rush about or undertake too much.'

'Quite right, quite right. Worry's the devil and all. I cut out worrying years ago and look at me! Fit as a fiddle, for all I shan't see fifty again. *You're* not looking altogether the thing, by the way.'

'A touch of dyspepsia,' said Mr Mummery. 'Nothing much. Chill on the liver, that's what I put it down to.'

'That's what it is,' said Mr Brookes, seizing his opportunity. 'Is life worth living? It depends upon the liver. Ha, ha! Well now, well now – we must do a spot of work, I suppose. Where's that lease of Ferraby's?'

Mr Mummery, who did not feel at his conversational best that morning, rather welcomed this suggestion, and for half an hour was allowed to proceed in peace with the duties of an estate agent. Presently, however, Mr Brookes burst into speech again.

'By the way,' he said abruptly, 'I suppose your wife doesn't know of a good cook, does she?'

'Well, no,' replied Mr Mummery. 'They aren't so easy to find nowadays. In fact, we've only just got suited ourselves. But why? Surely your old Cookie isn't leaving you?'

'Good lord, no!' Mr Brookes laughed heartily. 'It would take an earthquake to shake off old Cookie. No. It's for the Philipsons. Their girl's getting married. That's the worst of girls. I said to Philipson, "You mind what you're doing," I said. "Get somebody you know something about, or you may find yourself landed with this poisoning woman – what's her name – Andrews. Don't want to be sending wreaths to your funeral yet awhile," I said. He laughed, but it's no laughing matter and so I told him. What we pay the police for I simply don't know. Nearly a month now, and they can't seem to lay hands on the woman. All they say is, they think she's hanging about the neighbourhood and "may seek a situation as cook." As cook! Now I ask you!'

'You don't think she committed suicide, then?' suggested Mr Mummery.

'Suicide my foot!' retorted Mr Brookes coarsely. 'Don't you believe it, my boy. That coat found in the river was all eyewash. *They* don't commit suicide, that sort don't.'

'What sort?'

'Those arsenic maniacs. They're too damned careful of their own skins. Cunning as weasels, that's what they are. It's only to be hoped they'll manage to catch her before she tries her hand on anybody else. As I told Philipson—'

'You think Mrs Andrews did it, then?'

'Did it? Of course she did it. It's plain as the nose on your face. Looked after her old father, and he died suddenly – left her a bit of money, too. Then she keeps house for an elderly gentleman, and *he* dies suddenly. Now there's this husband and wife – man dies and woman taken very ill, of arsenic poisoning. Cook runs away, and you ask, did she do it? I don't mind betting that when they dig up the father and the other old bird they'll find *them* bung full of arsenic, too. Once that sort gets started, they don't stop. Grows on 'em, as you might say.'

'I suppose it does,' said Mr Mummery. He picked up his paper again and studied the photograph of the missing woman. 'She looks harmless enough,' he remarked. 'Rather a nice, motherly-looking kind of woman.'

'She's got a bad mouth,' pronounced Mr Brookes. He had a theory that character showed in the mouth. 'I wouldn't trust that woman an inch.'

As the day went on, Mr Mummery felt better. He was rather nervous about his lunch, choosing carefully a little boiled fish and custard pudding and being particular not to rush about immediately after the meal. To his great relief, the fish and custard remained where they were put, and he was not visited by that tiresome pain which had become almost habitual in the last fortnight. By the end of the day he became quite light-hearted. The bogey of illness and doctor's bills ceased to haunt him. He brought a bunch of bronze chrysanthemums to carry home to Ethel, and it was with a feeling of pleasant anticipation that he left the train and walked up the garden path of *Mon Abri*.

He was a little dashed by not finding his wife in the sitting-room. Still clutching the bunch of chrysanthemums he pattered down the passage and pushed open the kitchen door.

Nobody was there but the cook. She was sitting at the table with her back to him, and started up almost guiltily as he approached.

'Lor,' sir,' she said, 'you give me quite a start. I didn't hear the front door go.'

'Where is Mrs Mummery? Not feeling bad again, is she?'

'Well, sir, she's got a bit of a headache, poor lamb. I made her lay down and took her up a nice cup o' tea at half-past four. I think she's dozing nicely now.'

'Dear, dear,' said Mr Mummery.

'It was turning out the dining-room done it, if you ask me,' said Mrs Sutton. ' "Now, don't you overdo yourself, ma'am," I says to her, but you know how she is, sir. She gets that restless, she can't abear to be doing nothing.'

'I know,' said Mr Mummery. 'It's not your fault, Mrs Sutton. I'm sure you look after us both admirably. I'll just run up and have a peep at her. I won't disturb her if she's asleep. By the way, what are we having for dinner?'

'Well, I *had* made a nice steak-and-kidney pie,' said Mrs Sutton, in accents suggesting that she would readily turn it into a pumpkin or a coach and four if it was not approved of.

'Oh!' said Mr Mummery. 'Pastry? Well, I—'

'You'll find it beautiful and light,' protested the cook, whisking open the oven door for Mr Mummery to see. 'And it's made with butter, sir, you having said that you found lard indigestible.'

'Thank you, thank you,' said Mr Mummery. 'I'm sure it will be most excellent. I haven't been feeling altogether the thing just lately, and lard does not seem to suit me nowadays.'

'Well, it don't suit some people, and that's a fact,' agreed Mrs Sutton. 'I shouldn't wonder if you've got a bit of a chill on the liver. I'm sure this weather is enough to upset anybody.'

She bustled to the table and cleared away the picture paper which she had been reading.

'Perhaps the mistress would like her dinner sent up to her?' she suggested.

Mr Mummery said he would go and see, and tiptoed his way upstairs. Ethel was lying snuggled under the eiderdown and looked very small and fragile in the big double bed. She stirred as he came in and smiled up at him.

'Hullo, darling!' said Mr Mummery.

'Hullo! You back? I must have been asleep. I got tired and headachy, and Mrs Sutton packed me off upstairs.'

'You've been doing too much, sweetheart,' said her husband, taking her hand in his and sitting down on the edge of the bed.

'Yes – it was naughty of me. What lovely flowers, Harold. All for me?'

'All for you, Tiddleywinks,' said Mr Mummery tenderly. 'Don't I deserve something for that?'

Mrs Mummery smiled, and Mr Mummery took his reward several times over.

'That's quite enough, you sentimental old thing,' said Mrs Mummery. 'Run away, now, I'm going to get up.'

'Much better go to bed, my precious, and let Mrs Sutton send your dinner up,' said her husband.

Ethel protested, but he was firm with her. If she didn't take care of herself, she wouldn't be allowed to go to the Drama Society meetings. And everybody was so anxious to have her back. The Welbecks had been asking after her and saying that they really couldn't get on without her.

'Did they?' said Ethel with some animation. 'It's very sweet of them to want me. Well, perhaps I'll go to bed after all. And how has my old Hubby been all day?'

'Not too bad, not too bad.'

'No more tummyaches?'

'Well, just a *little* tummyache. But it's quite gone now. Nothing for Tiddleywinks to worry about.'

Mr Mummery experienced no more distressing symptoms the next day or the next. Following the advice of the newspaper expert, he took to drinking orange juice, and was delighted with the results of the treatment. On Thursday, however, he was taken so ill in the night that Ethel was alarmed and insisted on sending for the doctor. The doctor felt his pulse and looked at his tongue and appeared to take the matter lightly. An inquiry into what he had been eating elicited the fact that dinner had consisted of pig's trotters, followed by a milk pudding, and that, before retiring, Mr Mummery had consumed a large glass of orange juice, according to his new régime.

'There's your trouble,' said Dr Griffith cheerfully. 'Orange juice is an excellent thing, and so are trotters, but not in combination. Pig and oranges together are extraordinarily bad for the liver. I don't know why they should be, but there's no doubt that they are. Now I'll send you round a little prescription and you stick to slops for a day or two and keep off pork. And don't you worry about him, Mrs Mummery, he's as sound as a trout. *You're* the one we've got to look after. I don't want to see those black rings under the eyes, you know. Disturbed night, of course – yes. Taking your tonic regularly? That's right. Well, don't be alarmed about your hubby. We'll soon have him out and about again.'

The prophecy was fulfilled, but not immediately. Mr Mummery, though confining his diet to Benger's food, bread and milk, and beef tea skilfully prepared by Mrs Sutton and brought to his bedside by Ethel, remained very seedy all through Friday, and was only able to stagger rather shakily downstairs on Saturday afternoon. He had evidently suffered a 'thorough upset.' However, he was able to attend to a few papers which Brookes had sent down from the office for his signature, and to deal with the household books. Ethel was not a business woman, and Mr Mummery always ran over the accounts with her. Having settled up with the butcher, the baker, the dairy, and the coal merchant, Mr Mummery looked up inquiringly.

'Anything more, darling?'

'Well, there's Mrs Sutton. This is the end of her month, you know.'

'So it is. Well, you're quite satisfied with her, aren't you, darling?'

'Yes, rather – aren't you? She's a good cook, and a sweet, motherly old thing, too. Don't you think it was a real brain wave of mine, engaging her like that, on the spot?'

'I do, indeed,' said Mr Mummery.

'It was a perfect providence, her turning up like that, just after that wretched Jane had gone off without even giving notice. I was in absolute *despair*. It was a little bit of a gamble, of course, taking her without any references, but naturally, if she's been looking after a widowed mother, you couldn't expect her to give references.'

'N-no,' said Mr Mummery. At the time he had felt uneasy about the matter, though he had not liked to say much because, of course, they simply had to have somebody. And the experiment had justified itself so triumphantly in practice that one couldn't say much about it now. He had once rather tentatively suggested writing to the clergyman of Mrs Sutton's parish but, as Ethel had said, the clergyman wouldn't have been able to tell them anything about cooking, and cooking, after all, was the chief point.

Mr Mummery counted out the month's money.

'And by the way, my dear,' he said, 'you might just mention to Mrs Sutton that if she must *read* the morning paper before I come down, I should be obliged if she would fold it neatly afterwards.'

'What an old fuss-box you are, darling,' said his wife.

Mr Mummery sighed. He could not explain that it was somehow important that the morning paper should come to him fresh and prim, like a virgin. Women did not feel these things.

On Sunday, Mr Mummery felt very much better – quite his old self, in fact. He enjoyed the *News of the World* over breakfast in bed, reading the murders rather carefully. Mr Mummery got quite a lot of pleasure out of murders – they gave him an agreeable thrill of vicarious adventure, for, naturally, they were matters quite remote from daily life in the outskirts of Hull.

He noticed that Brookes had been perfectly right. Mrs Andrews' father and former employer had been 'dug up' and had, indeed, proved to be 'bung full' of arsenic.

He came downstairs for dinner – roast sirloin, with the potatoes done under the meat, and Yorkshire pudding of delicious lightness, and an apple tart to follow. After three days of invalid diet, it was delightful to savour the crisp fat and underdone lean. He ate moderately, but with a sensuous enjoyment. Ethel, on the other hand, seemed a little lacking in appetite, but then, she had never been a great meat eater. She was fastidious and, besides, she was (quite unnecessarily) afraid of getting fat.

It was a fine afternoon, and at three o'clock, when he was quite certain that the roast beef was 'settling' properly, it occurred to Mr Mummery that it would be a good thing to put the rest of those bulbs in. He slipped on his old gardening coat and wandered out to the potting-shed. Here he picked up a bag of tulips and a trowel, and then, remembering that he was wearing his good trousers, decided that it would be wise to take a mat to kneel on. When had he had the mat last? He could not recollect, but he rather fancied he had put it away in the corner under the potting-shelf. Stooping down, he felt about in the dark among the flower pots. Yes, there it was, but there was a tin of something in the way. He lifted the tin carefully out. Of course – yes – the remains of the weed-killer.

Mr Mummery glanced at the pink label, printed in staring letters with the legend: 'ARSENICAL WEED-KILLER. *Poison*,' and observed, with a mild feeling of excitement, that it was the same brand of stuff that had been associated with Mrs Andrews' latest victim. He was rather pleased about it. It gave him a sensation of being remotely but definitely in touch with important events. Then he noticed, with surprise and a little annoyance, that the stopper had been put in quite loosely.

'However'd I come to leave it like that?' he grunted. 'Shouldn't wonder if all the goodness has gone off.' He removed the stopper and squinted into the can, which appeared to be half-full. Then he rammed the thing home again, giving it a sharp thump with the handle of the trowel for better security. After that he washed his hands carefully at the scullery tap, for he did not believe in taking risks.

He was a trifle disconcerted, when he came in after planting the tulips, to find visitors in the sitting-room. He was always pleased to see Mrs Welbeck and her son, but he would rather have had warning, so that he could have scrubbed the garden mould out of his nails more thoroughly. Not that Mrs Welbeck appeared to notice. She was a talkative woman and paid little attention to anything but her own conversation. Much to Mr Mummery's annoyance, she chose to prattle about the Lincoln Poisoning Case. A most unsuitable subject for the tea-table, thought Mr Mummery, at the best of times. His own 'upset' was vivid enough in his memory to make him queasy over the discussion of medical symptoms, and besides, this kind of talk was not good for Ethel. After all, the poisoner was still supposed to be in the neighbourhood. It was enough to make even a strong-nerved woman uneasy. A glance at Ethel showed him that she was looking quite white and tremulous. He must stop Mrs Welbeck somehow, or there would be a repetition of one of the old, dreadful, hysterical scenes.

He broke into the conversation with violent abruptness.

'Those forsythia cuttings, Mrs Welbeck,' he said. 'Now is just about the time to take them. If you care to come down the garden I will get them for you.'

He saw a relieved glance pass between Ethel and young Welbeck. Evidently the boy understood the situation and was chafing at his mother's tactlessness. Mrs Welbeck, brought up all standing, gasped slightly and then veered off with obliging readiness on the new tack. She accompanied her host down the garden and chattered cheerfully about horticulture while he selected and trimmed the cuttings. She complimented Mr Mummery on the immaculacy of his gravel paths. 'I simply *cannot* keep the weeds down,' she said.

Mr Mummery mentioned the weed-killer and praised its efficacy.

'That stuff!' Mrs Welbeck stared at him. Then she shuddered. 'I wouldn't have it in my place for a thousand pounds,' she said, with emphasis.

Mr Mummery smiled. 'Oh, we keep it well away from the house,' he said. 'Even if I were a careless sort of person—'

He broke off. The recollection of the loosened stopper had come to him suddenly, and it was as though, deep down in his mind, some obscure assembling of ideas had taken place. He left it at that, and went into the kitchen to fetch a newspaper to wrap up the cuttings.

Their approach to the house had evidently been seen from the sitting-room window, for when they entered, young Welbeck was already on his feet and holding Ethel's hand in the act of saying good-bye. He manoeuvred his mother out of the house with tactful promptness, and Mr Mummery returned to the kitchen to clear up the newspapers he had fished out of the drawer. To clear them up and to examine them more closely. Something had struck him about them, which he wanted to verify. He turned them over very carefully, sheet by sheet. Yes – he had been right. Every portrait of Mrs Andrews, every paragraph and line about the Lincoln Poisoning Case, had been carefully cut out.

Mr Mummery sat down by the kitchen fire. He felt as though he needed warmth. There seemed to be a curious cold lump of something at the pit of his stomach – something that he was chary of investigating.

He tried to recall the appearance of Mrs Andrews as shown in the newspaper photographs, but he had not a good visual memory. He remembered having remarked to Brookes that it was a 'motherly' face. then he tried counting up the time since the disappearance. Nearly a month, Brookes had said – and that was a week ago. Must be over a month now. A month. He has just paid Mrs Sutton her month's money.

'Ethel!' was the thought that hammered at the door of his brain. At all costs, he must cope with this monstrous suspicion on his own. He must spare her any shock or anxiety. And he must be sure of his ground. To dismiss the only decent cook they had ever had out of sheer, unfounded panic, would be wanton cruelty to both women. If he did it at all, it would have to be done arbitrarily, preposterously – he could not suggest horrors to Ethel. However it was done, there would be trouble. Ethel would not understand and he dared not tell her.

But if by any chance there was anything in this ghastly doubt – how could he expose Ethel to the appalling danger of having the woman in the house a moment longer? He thought of the family at Lincoln – the husband dead, the wife escaped by a miracle with her life. Was not any shock, any risk, better than that?

Mr Mummery felt suddenly very lonely and tired. His illness had taken it out of him.

Those illnesses – they had begun, when? Three weeks ago he had had the first attack. Yes, but then he had always been rather subject to gastric troubles. Bilious attacks. Not so violent, perhaps, as these last, but undoubted bilious attacks.

He pulled himself together and went, rather heavily, into the sitting-room. Ethel was tucked up in a corner of the chesterfield.

'Tired, darling?'

'Yes, a little.'

'That woman has worn you out with talking. She oughtn't to talk so much.'

'No.' Her head shifted wearily in the cushions. 'All about that horrible case. I don't like hearing about such things.'

'Of course not. Still, when a thing like that happens in the neighbourhood, people will gossip and talk. It would be a relief if they caught the woman. One doesn't like to think—'

'I don't want to think of anything so hateful. She must be a horrible creature.'

. 'Horrible. Brookes was saying the other day—'

'I don't want to hear what he said. I don't want to hear about it at all. I want to be quiet. I want to be quiet!'

He recognized the note of rising hysteria.

'Tiddleywinks shall be quiet. Don't worry, darling. We won't talk about horrors.'

No. It would not do to talk about them.

Ethel went to bed early. It was understood that on Sundays Mr Mummery should sit up till Mrs Sutton came in. Ethel was a little anxious about this, but he assured her that he felt quite strong enough. In body, indeed, he did; it was his mind that felt weak and confused. He had decided to make a casual remark about the mutilated newspapers – just to see what Mrs Sutton would say.

He allowed himself the usual indulgence of a whisky and soda as he sat waiting. At a quarter to ten he heard the familiar click of the garden gate. Footsteps passed up the gravel – squeak, squeak, to the back door. Then the sound of the latch, the shutting of the door, the rattle of the bolts being shot home. Then a pause. Mrs Sutton would be taking off her hat. The moment was coming.

The step sounded in the passage. The door opened. Mrs Sutton in her neat black dress stood on the threshold. He was aware of a reluctance to face her. Then he looked up. A plump-faced woman, her eyes obscured by thick horn-rimmed spectacles. Was there, perhaps, something hard about the mouth? Or was it just that she had lost most of her front teeth?

'Would you be requiring anything to-night, sir, before I go up?'

'No, thank you, Mrs Sutton.'

'I hope you are feeling better, sir.' Her eager interest in his health seemed to him almost sinister, but the eyes, behind the thick glasses, were inscrutable.

'Quite better, thank you, Mrs Sutton.'

'Mrs Mummery is not indisposed, is she, sir? Should I take her up a glass of hot milk or anything?'

'No, thank you, no.' He spoke hurriedly, and fancied that she looked disappointed.

'Very well, sir. Good night, sir.'

'Good night. Oh! by the way, Mrs Sutton—'

'Yes, sir?'

'Oh, nothing,' said Mr Mummery, 'nothing.'

Next morning, Mr Mummery opened his paper eagerly. He would have been glad to learn that an arrest had been made over the week-end. But there was no news for him. The chairman of a trust company had blown out his brains, and the headlines were all occupied with tales about lost millions and ruined shareholders. Both in his own paper and in those he purchased on the way to the office, the Lincoln Poisoning Tragedy had been relegated to an obscure paragraph on a back page, which informed him that the police were still baffled.

The next few days were the most uncomfortable that Mr Mummery had ever spent. He developed a habit of coming down early in the morning and prowling about the kitchen. This made Ethel nervous, but Mrs Sutton offered no remark. She watched him tolerantly, even, he thought, with something like amusement. After all, it was ridiculous. What was the use of supervising the breakfast, when he had to be out of the house every day between half-past nine and six?

At the office, Brookes rallied him on the frequency with which he rang up Ethel. Mr Mummery paid no attention. It was reassuring to hear her voice and to know that she was safe and well.

Nothing happened, and by the following Thursday he began to think that he had been a fool. He came home late that night. Brookes had persuaded him to go with him to a little bachelor dinner for a friend who was about to get married. He left the others at eleven o'clock, however, refusing to make a night of it. The household was in bed when he got back but a note from Mrs Sutton lay on the table, informing him that there was cocoa for him in the kitchen, ready for hotting up. He hotted it up accordingly in the little saucepan where it stood. There was just one good cupful.

He sipped it thoughtfully, standing by the kitchen stove. After the first sip, he put the cup down. Was it his fancy, or was there something queer about the taste? He sipped it again, rolling it upon his tongue. It seemed to him to have a faint tang, metallic and unpleasant. In a sudden dread he ran out to the scullery and spat the mouthful into the sink.

After this, he stood quite still for a moment or two. Then, with a curious deliberation, as though his movements had been dictated to him, he fetched an empty medicine bottle from the pantry shelf, rinsed it under the tap and tipped the contents of the cup carefully into it. He slipped the bottle into his coat pocket and moved on tiptoe to the back door. The bolts were difficult to draw without noise, but he managed it at last. Still on tiptoe, he stole across the garden to the potting-shed. stooping down, he struck a match. He knew exactly where he had left the tin of weed-killer, under the shelf behind the pots at the back. Cautiously he lifted it out. The match flared up and burnt his fingers,

276

but before he could light another his sense of touch had told him what he wanted to know. The stopper was loose again.

Panic seized Mr Mummery, standing there in the earthy-smelling shed, in his dress suit and overcoat, holding the tin in one hand and the match box in the other. He wanted very badly to run and tell somebody what he had discovered.

Instead, he replaced the tin exactly where he had found it and went back to the house. As he crossed the garden again, he noticed a light in Mrs Sutton's bedroom window. This terrified him more than anything which had gone before. Was she watching him? Ethel's window was dark. If she had drunk anything deadly there would be lights everywhere, movements, calls for the doctor, just as when he himself had been attacked. Attacked – that was the right word, he thought.

Still, with the same odd presence of mind and precision, he went in, washed out the utensils and made a second brew of cocoa, which he left standing in the saucepan. He crept quietly to his bedroom. Ethel's voice greeted him on the threshold.

'How late you are, Harold. Naughty old boy! Have a good time?'

'Not bad. You all right, darling?'

'Quite all right. Did Mrs Sutton leave something hot for you? She said she would.'

'Yes, but I wasn't thirsty.'

Ethel laughed. 'Oh! it was *that* sort of party, was it?'

Mr Mummery did not attempt any denials. He undressed and got into bed and clutched his wife to him as though defying death and hell to take her from him. Next morning he would act. He thanked God that he was not too late.

Mr Dimthorpe, the chemist, was a great friend of Mr Mummery's. They had often sat together in the untidy little shop on Spring Bank and exchanged views on green-fly and club-root. Mr Mummery told his story frankly to Mr Dimthorpe and handed over the bottle of cocoa. Mr Dimthorpe congratulated him on his prudence and intelligence.

'I will have it ready for you by this evening,' he said, 'and if it's what you think it is, then we shall have a clear case on which to take action.'

Mr Mummery thanked him, and was extremely vague and inattentive at business all day. But that hardly mattered, for Mr Brookes, who had seen the party through to a riotous end in the small hours, was in no very observant mood. At half-past four, Mr Mummery shut up his desk decisively and announced that he was off early, he had a call to make.

Mr Dimthorpe was ready for him.

'No doubt about it,' he said. 'I used Marsh's test. It's a heavy dose – no wonder you tasted it. There must be four or five grains of pure arsenic in that bottle. Look, here's the mirror. You can see it for yourself.'

Mr Mummery gazed at the little glass tube with its ominous purple-black stain.

'Will you ring up the police from here?' asked the chemist.

'No,' said Mr Mummery. 'No – I want to get home. God knows what's happening there. And I've only just time to catch my train.'

'All right,' said Mr Dimthorpe. 'Leave it to me. I'll ring them up for you.'

The local train did not go fast enough for Mr Mummery. Ethel – poisoned – dying – dead – Ethel – poisoned – dying – dead – the wheels drummed in his ears. He almost ran out of the station and along the road. A car was standing at his door. He saw it from the end of the street and broke into a gallop. It had happened already. The doctor was there. Fool, murderer that he was to have left things so late.

Then, while he was still a hundred and fifty yards off, he saw the front door open. A man came out followed by Ethel herself. The visitor got into his car and was driven away. Ethel went in again. She was safe – safe!

He could hardly control himself to hang up his hat and coat and go in looking reasonably calm. His wife had returned to the arm-chair by the fire and greeted him in some surprise. There were tea things on the table.

'Back early, aren't you?'

'Yes – business was slack. Somebody been to tea?'

'Yes, young Welbeck. About the arrangements for the Drama Society.' She spoke briefly but with an undertone of excitement.

A qualm came over Mr Mummery. Would a guest be any protection? His face must have shown his feelings, for Ethel stared at him in amazement.

'What's the matter, Harold, you look so queer?'

'Darling,' said Mr Mummery, 'there's something I want to tell you about.' He sat down and took her hand in his. 'Something a little unpleasant, I'm afraid—'

'Oh, ma'am!'

The cook was in the doorway.

'I beg your pardon, sir – I didn't know you was in. Will you be taking tea or can I clear away? And, oh, ma'am, there was a young man at the fishmonger's and he's just come from Grimsby and they've caught that dreadful woman – that Mrs Andrews. Isn't it a good thing? It's worritted me dreadful to think she was going about like that, but they've caught her. Taken a job as housekeeper she had to two elderly ladies and they found the wicked poison on her. Girl as spotted her will get a reward. I been keeping my eyes open for her, but it's at Grimsby she was all the time.'

Mr Mummery clutched at the arm of his chair. It had all been a mad mistake then. He wanted to shout or cry. He wanted to apologize to this foolish, pleasant, excited woman. All a mistake.

But there had been the cocoa. Mr Dimthorpe. Marsh's test. Five grains of arsenic, Who, then—?

He glanced around at his wife, and in her eyes he saw something that he had never seen before. . . .

Alec Waugh

The Last Chukka

'And they are not allowed, you say, to marry?'

The missionary doctor shook his head.

'We permit,' he said, 'no marriage in our hospital.'

'Although leprosy is not hereditary, although it is the least contagious of all diseases, although a woman may live for years with a man without contamination?'

He spoke in a breathless, agitated voice, so that Padre Martin looked up quickly and curiously at the young 'teak wallah' who had asked a few evenings back to be shown over the hospital. It was a request that had surprised the Padre considerably. It must have been a good ten years since Butterman had come out to work as an assistant on the Siamese workings of the Moulmein-Madras Timber Company, and in the course of those ten years the Padre could not recollect a single occasion on which Butterman had displayed the slightest interest in any phase of the mission's work. He had been an ambitious and conscientious worker, for whom from the very first speedy promotion had been foreseen. 'He'll step into Curwen's shoes, you wait!' people had said of him. And now that Curwen's retirement had become a matter of little more than weeks, that prophecy seemed to possess every likelihood of fulfilment. Butterman was, everyone agreed, the obvious man for station manager. He was steady, trustworthy, unemotional, keeping his temper and his head. 'He's the sort of man that you can feel safe with,' somebody had said of him. 'He won't do anything unexpected.' Martin had been genuinely surprised when Butterman had arrived three days back unheralded in the station, for no very obvious reason, to make on his first evening at the Club the curious request that he might be shown round the leper hospital.

And here he was now, with his odd, agitated questions.

'You don't let them marry!' he cried. 'But is there really all that danger? Leprosy isn't the contagious thing it was once taken for. With proper precautions a husband and wife needn't infect each other; their children could be protected. And it must be lonely, so terribly lonely for them here.'

As he spoke he swung his arm in a graphic inclusive gesture. They were in the men's part of the hospital; and in that part of it which had been set out at the plan on which, ultimately, the rest of the hospital was to be rebuilt. It had been arranged like a garden suburb, in a series of small crescents; with neat, brightly painted bungalows, each with its carefully ordered plot of ground in front of it. The gravel paths were trim, and closely weeded; in the centre of each crescent blazed gorgeously an immense bed of flowers. And on the steps and on the verandas of the bungalows the patients lounged lazily in the heavy sunlight, gossiping and chewing betel-nut.

'Lonely, terribly lonely,' repeated Butterman. 'All the appearance of a home, and none of the reality, none of the sweetness of the home. Just these men herded here together. Is the danger really great enough to warrant that?'

He spoke softly, wooingly, as though he were the pleader of a cause, and with a change of tone that only increased the Padre's perplexity.

He hesitated before he answered.

'The danger,' he said at length, 'that is a thing which we can scarcely measure. Leprosy is a disease of which we still know extremely little. But our limitations in a place like this, in Pangrai, so far from what we term civilization, with so few friends, with so many obstacles – of those we can be judges. Once at the very beginning we made the experiment of allowing marriage. But it involved us in too many complications. If we were to carry on at all, it was essential, we found, to separate the men and women.'

Butterman nodded his head slowly as he listened. 'I see,' he said, 'I see.' And in silence he followed the Padre across the waste patch of ground dividing the men's quarters from the women's, that a collection of patients, in whose system the disease had made inconsiderable progress, were converting into a further series of paths and gardens.

Midway between the two sections was the chapel. And as they drew close to it, the Padre's pace slackened. It had been built only a couple of years back, and he could never pass it without a feeling of profound thankfulness that life should have been granted him along enough to see the completion of it. He was an old man now, past sixty, weakened by fever and overwork. And to build such a chapel had been his life's ambition.

For thirty-seven years he had had to wait.

When he had come to Siam as a young man from Washington, there had been nothing at Pangrai; nothing; no mission, no school, no hospital. There had not even been a railway beyond Bangkok, and with funds scanty and supplies five weeks away, he had realized that till the schools and hospital were established every consideration but those of the most bare necessities must be denied. He had waited for thirty-seven years, till the time had come when he could build according to his dream. And there it stood now, a high, white building, very bare and open, as was inevitable from the conditions of the place, but possessed of genuine beauty, in its austere dignity of naked line.

'We have two services a week,' he said, 'and though there is no compulsion, there are very few of the patients who do not attend. They are all Christians; within a week of their joining us, they come of their own accord to be baptized. It is only natural after all. They were brought up as Buddhists, but Buddhism, for all its beauties, is not a religion that holds its hand out to the pariah. When the Buddha saw a leper he was filled with disgust and turned away, and the Buddhists have allowed their lepers to lie unwanted about their streets. But Jesus when He saw a leper was moved with compassion, and stretching out His hand He touched him and to His disciples He gave orders that they should have care for lepers and succour them. So that the leper who all his life has held himself to be an outcast discovers that after all there is a God who cares for him and who bade His servants shelter him. And he turns naturally in simple faith to the God whose heart is so great that it has room in it even for the poor leper. For the power of religion is the power of love, and we can only love where we are loved.'

He spoke softly, quietly, as though he were speaking to himself, indifferent to Butterman's presence at his side, who in his turn indeed seemed scarcely listening; at any rate, as soon as the Padre had ceased speaking, he reverted to his original argument.

'Don't you have trouble with them now and again?' he asked.

'Trouble?'

'About not marrying.'

The Padre nodded. 'Sometimes,' he said, 'with the very young particularly, and with those who are not very ill, whom the disease has no more than touched.'

'And then?'

'There is no compulsion. They are free to go.'

'But they return?'

'Sometimes. More often not.'

'More often not. Because they are ashamed, I suppose; because they are afraid they will be blamed. But they shouldn't be, Padre. It's so easy for them to yield, when they are young, when the disease has no more than touched them; so easy to yield here, when on all sides of them nature is so facile, and so fertile, where life grows so easily towards the sun. You can understand, surely, Padre, you can understand.'

'Oh, yes, I can understand.'

'Then . . . then . . .'

'To understand a thing, is not to approve it.'

They had turned away from the chapel, and were nearing the women's quarters, which had been arranged for the most part in long dormitories divided off into deep but narrow rooms, with seven to ten mattresses in each.

'It seems to work better this way with women,' explained the Padre. 'We once tried putting them in bungalows like the men, but the moment they get in couples they start quarrelling.'

And turning to the bunch of women who were seated in the shady corner of the veranda, he began to joke with one of them about the bamboo basket she was plaiting. He pretended that she was a saleswoman, and he a customer.

'I will give you,' he began, 'thirty satangs for your basket.'

And she, in the true Lao spirit, began to bargain with him.

'Oh, no, master. It is worth eighty at the very least.'

'Perhaps then I might give you forty.'

'But I would not take less than sixty-five.'

And as they haggled the other women joined merrily in their laughter, relishing this travesty of a scene that had been so familiar in the life they had abandoned. Of the little group Butterman alone remained unsmiling. With intent, eager, unhealthily bright eyes he stood gazing at a woman in whom the disease was reaching its last stages. Her nose, as though the heel of a fist had been pressed ruthlessly upon it, was flattened back upon her face. The hands with which she was preparing her dish of curry were almost fingerless. While her feet, one of which was wrapped round with bandages, were no more than slabs of flesh marked here and there with certain irregular projections.

'The hands and feet,' muttered Butterman, 'the hands and feet, it's there always, isn't it, that the thing begins?'

'At the extremities, yes; there are other signs, other earlier signs, but it's at the extremities that the attack begins.'

'The hands and feet,' Butterman repeated. His eyes were still fixed upon the huddled object. For a full two minutes he turned away, gave a quick sigh, and with a smile held out his hand towards the Padre.

'It's been very good of you,' he said. 'It's been most interesting. It's a magnificent work . . . no idea it was anything like this. Well, good-bye, Padre, good-bye.'

The sudden change of tone was as curious as it was embarrassing, and the Padre's endeavour to laugh it off was not too successful.

'We needn't surely say good-bye,' he said. 'I shall be seeing you at the Club to-night.'

'Afraid not. Going back to the jungle this afternoon.'

'What! after only three days here!' It was a surprising announcement. For Butterman's camp was a good week's march distant.

'Yes, only just came to have a look round. Good-bye, ever so many thanks, and,' he hesitated, then drawing close to the Padre he touched him on the shoulder, and lowering his voice to the tone which one employs for the communication of a shady confidence . . . 'and about that other business,' he said, 'you're quite right, you know, quite right. There are some people who aren't fit to marry.'

It was a leave-taking as astonishing as it was abrupt.

And all day long the disturbing impression of that odd interview remained with Martin, so that when he happened to find himself that evening at the Club alone for a moment, beside Curwen, Butterman's manager, at the large round table on which after sundown drinks and glasses were set out, he returned instantly to the subject.

'I'm a little worried,' he said, 'about one of your fellows. Do you mind if I talk to you about him?'

Curwen looked up quickly. He was a tall, heavily built, clean-looking man, whose small imperial and moustache scarcely concealed the thickening and sagging of his chinline. He was, in point of years, little more than youthfully middle-aged, but the tropics had begun to take their toll of him. One thought of him as old.

'One of my fellows,' he said, 'who?'

'Butterman.'

'Butterman?' he echoed the name incredulously. 'But there's nothing wrong with him. He was fit enough a few hours ago when I saw him off!'

The Padre didn't reply directly.

'Wasn't his coming all the way down from Bahang-Kong for a three days' visit rather curious?'

Curwen shrugged his shoulders.

'I don't know,' he said. 'I give my lads a pretty free hand in the way of breathers. One has to. The jungle's a curious place. For month after month you'll be working along quite happily, everything seems all right, and then suddenly one morning something snaps, your nerves are gone, and you know that if you stay another hour there you'll be off your head. A queer place the jungle. The size of it, the loneliness, the never seeing of a white man for weeks on end, the bouts of fever, and all that hidden life of the jungle crowding so closely round you. Sometimes it's like a hand throttling you.'

And sitting back in the calm of his last weeks, he mused on the number of men that he had known during his twenty-five years of whom the jungle in one way or another had got the better. The loneliness, the fever, the privation, the autumn rains, and the summer heat, one by one they had gone down before them, with broken health or broken nerves.

'I don't think there's much wrong with Butterman,' he said. 'He just felt that it was time he had a rest.'

The Padre was unconvinced, however.

'He behaved,' he said, 'very cautiously at my place this morning. I was wondering if there might not be something worrying him. I don't want to interfere, but he hasn't got himself mixed up with any girl here, has he?'

Curwen laughed, a rather coarse, brutal laugh.

'I'm afraid as far as a sleeping dictionary's concerned, Butterman's Lao's going to remain as inadequate as it's always been. He's never had any use for that sort of thing.'

'Exactly. And it was just because of that that I was wondering whether he mightn't have started now. Wasn't there some talk about his getting married during his last leave?'

'There was talk, but when it came to the point he decided that it wasn't fair to bring out a white woman to a place like this. I dare say he was right, it's no place to bring up children, what with the heat and the monotony. It's a dog's life for a young girl. There's only one woman in a hundred that could manage it. He didn't say much to me about it. He just muttered something as far as I can remember about some fellows being not fit to marry.'

The Padre started. It was the same oddly arresting phrase that Butterman had applied to the celibate lepers at the hospital. Not fit to marry. . . .

'I wish, Curwen,' he said, 'that you'd have rather a careful look at him next time you're in the jungle. I can't help being worried about him. I'm not at all sure that he doesn't want more than a three days' rest.'

I

'What'll you have – a gin and bitters?'

'No, thanks. I'll stick to *stengahs*.'

'Right. Will you mix your own?'

It was the hour when life for the 'teak-wallah' is at its sweetest, the hour just after sundown, when the air is cooling after the long day's heat, when the body, after the long day's work, is refreshed by the evening's bath, and by the afternoon's 'lie off'; when *pahits* and *stengahs* are set out on the small camp-table, and tired limbs lie slackly along the deep canvas chairs. It is the hour that consoles and cancels everything that the day had known of thirst and exposure and fatigue. And Curwen sipped at his whisky, tranquillized by the profound content of physical exhaustion, while Butterman with minute care set himself about the preparation of a *pahit*.

It had been a long hard day. They had been up at five while it was still dark and, sending their carriers ahead of them, had marched two hours before breakfast. There had been no rain for several weeks and in consequence the paths across the paddy-fields were dry, but even so the going had been extremely hard; they had marched seventeen kilometres, the greater part of it had been over rugged hilly passes, and they had come into camp a full three hours ahead of the elephants. A hard day. But it was worth it now. At no other price could you purchase this exquisite sensation of utter languor.

Out of the corner of his eye Curwen watched Butterman sip critically, then appreciatively, at his gin and bitters. They had been together for three days now, and as far as he could see there was nothing wrong with the chap. His accounts and his reports were in perfect order. His comments on the working of the teak had been extremely lucid, extremely practical. He was right enough. There had been nothing but a momentary touch of nerves that Padre Martin had magnified out of all proportion. A touch of nerves, and who should know better than he how common that was, after twenty-five years of it out here.

Twenty-five years, a long chunk out of a man's life. Not that he was regretting it. At the beginning he had been sick enough. That morning when his father had taken him into his study to explain. Yes, that had been bitter enough tasting medicine. 'I'm very sorry, my boy,' his father had said to him, 'but things have not been going too well with me of late. And I cannot afford to send both you and your brother up to Oxford. You are the elder and you have the right to first consideration. At the same time to a man such as your brother who's an intellectual pure and simple, whose career will probably be one of scholarship, a university education is a far more important thing than it can ever be for you. It seems to me, indeed, essential to his future. Whereas I feel that while you would be handicapped you would not be crippled by its absence. If you insist, of course, on what is, after all, your right, I will never refer to the matter again. I must say I hope, though. . . .'

Yes, it had been bitter medicine, but he had swallowed it. And here he was now going back to London in the middle forties, retiring on a capital of forty thousand, which was more than that brother of his would be able to do if he lived to eighty. He had swallowed the medicine to the last drop. He had played the game through to the last chukka. All down the course he had kept his head. He had not flung his money about on expensive leaves. He had not married his Lao woman like the others had, and when he had come back to Pangrai as station master he had not allowed himself to become fettered by those bonds of propinquity and habit which others had found hard when it came to the last to break. He had built Cheam a little bungalow beside the river, and when the children had grown up he had sent them to be educated in Malay. And he would play the game by them, he would leave enough when he went away for them to have a start in life. They should have their bread and butter, and if they wanted the jam to spread on it, well, they must find that for themselves. And as for Cheam, she would be happy enough with her bungalow and a paddy-field or two. She would not feel she had been ill-treated. She was unwesternized. She believed, as all Laos did believe, that the mere fact of a man and a woman living together constituted marriage, and that marriage meant simply the observances of certain practical obligations, and he had observed those obligations. He would leave a clean record here. He was getting the best of both worlds, getting it both ways.

His last jungle trip. In a few weeks now Butterman would be coming down to Pangrai, to take over. A good fellow, Butterman, sound, steady, practical. It had been ridiculous of Padre Martin to imagine that there was anything wrong with him. He was getting old, the Padre, old and fanciful and fussy. A good fellow, but getting old, had seemed old even in those distant days when he himself had been a junior assistant.

As he lay back in the long comfort of his chair, living over the days of stress and struggle, his eyes began to close, and his mouth to sag. A hard life, a good life, and now London at the end of it. The best of both worlds, he had had the thing both ways.

A good life, a hard life. His head began to nod. . . . In another minute he would have been asleep had not a shriek at his elbow abruptly disturbed his reverie, a wild, uncanny shriek it was, like that of an animal maddened by fear and anger. 'Heavens!' was his first thought, 'a tiger.' But before he had time to blink his eyes, he had realized that this was no occasion for alarm.

'Good heavens, man,' Butterman was shrieking. 'What on earth are you doing with those socks.'

He had risen to his feet, his whole body, for all that he was trying to support himself against the table, was shivering as though with ague, nor could he keep steady the arm with which he was pointing at the astonished 'boy', who stood gaping in the doorway of the tent, a pair of white socks dangling from his hand.

'What are you doing?' Butterman shrieked. 'Who told you that you could touch them?'

The boy was so frightened that he could scarcely speak.

'The socks master wear to-day,' he stammered, 'they dirty. I go wash.'

'And who told you that you could wash them?' Butterman bellowed. 'How dare you touch my things without permission? I'll tell you when I want things washed. You put them back.'

The boy hesitated.

'They dirty, master,' he explained. 'Master no can wear.'

For answer Butterman beat madly with his fist upon the flimsy table, making the glasses and the bottles shake on their tin tray.

'You put them back,' he shrieked. 'You put them back.' And as the boy hurried back into the hut, he sank into his chair with a slow gasp. His eyes were blazing and his cheeks were pale, his lips trembled and there was a circlet of sweat along his forehead. He lay back breathing heavily as though he had completed some immense effort, as though he had been preserved from some immense danger.

'They spy on me,' he said. And he pronounced each word separately and distinctly, as a child does when it repeats a lesson. 'You can't trust them. All the time you have to be on your guard against them. Spies. Every one of them. Spies!'

Curwen made no reply. He nodded his head and sipped slowly at his emptying glass. But he knew in that instant that it was over no fancy that the Padre was worrying.

'I was wondering,' he said some ninety minutes later, as the boy was clearing away the dinner, 'whether it wouldn't be a good idea for you to come back to Pangrai with me to-morrow. You'll be taking over in a month or so, and it wouldn't be a bad idea if we were to work side by side for a little, so that you can see how things fit in.'

Butterman, who since his recovery from the outburst had been exchanging in a perfectly normal manner the mixture of personalities and business that are the basis of conversation, eagerly welcomed the suggestion.

'I can't say,' he said, 'how grateful I should be to you if I might. There are one or two things that I'm not any too certain about.' And he began to discuss certain points of routine and policy in a fashion so lucid that Curwen began to wonder whether after all he and the Padre were not simply imagining things.

'There can't be anything wrong,' he thought, 'with a man whose brain's as clear and collected as this man's is.'

Before the night had passed, however, there had occurred another slight but, following on what had occurred previously, strangely disquieting incident.

For some reason or another, Curwen had found that he could not sleep. And in order to compose his thoughts he had decided to read for a few moments. He had been unable, however, to find the matches and walking to the opening of his tent was just about to call his boy when he saw that Butterman still had a light burning. To avoid disturbing the camp he walked across the few yards of ground that divided the two tents.

'Sleepless too?' he began. 'I was wondering . . .' then stopped abruptly before the unexpected sight that confronted him.

Cross-legged upon his haunches. Butterman was seated on the small rubber ground-sheet beside the bed, with the wide black silk Chinese trousers in which it is the fashion for Europeans in Siam to sleep rolled back over his knees, and with a large powerful electric torch he was examining his naked feet.

'Good Lord,' said Curwen, 'what's the matter? Have you got mud-sores or something?'

Butterman had given a start at the first sound of his friend's voice, but the expression of surprise changed quickly to one that Curwen found impossible to diagnose. It was a mixture of knowingness, and suspicion, and furtive cunning, a look that was at the same time a shield against detection and an invitation to share in a conspiracy. There was triumph in it, and fear, hatred and distrust and friendship. And when Butterman spoke his voice had a peculiar intonation that should have been the key to the mystery, but was at the same time an added veil across it.

'Not yet,' he said, 'not yet. Nothing that you can see as yet.'

And Curwen as he heard it shuddered as though he had been brought face to face with something that was uncanny and unhealthy, something that was outside the experience of practical mortality.

II

There was an odd smell of burning about the house. For a week ever since their return from the jungle, it had clung fugitive and intermittent to the wide-windowed, wide-verandaed bungalow. For half a day or so you would think it had disappeared, and then suddenly, as you came into a room or went on to a veranda, you would meet it, vague, sinister, repellent. And for hours, although it was so slight that a stranger coming into the house would not have noticed it, the smell would follow you. You would taste it in your food and in your wine. It would be upon the soap with which you washed your face and in the flowers which were upon your table. You waited for it, sought for it, in the same way that during a sleepless night you will listen with a straining ear for the faint rattle of a window pane in a distant corridor.

'For God's sake, man,' muttered Curwen irritably to his boy, 'can't you find where that smell comes from? It must be something that the boys are doing in the kitchen.'

But the boy lifted his clasped hands before his face.

'No, no, master,' he pleaded. 'Boys worried by it as much as master. No can find, master, no can find?'

It was in the liveliest of ill-tempers that Curwen went in to breakfast. In the doorway of the room he paused.

Butterman, as usual, was down already. He was seated in a wicker chair on the veranda manicuring his nails. It was a habit to which he was becoming increasingly addicted. The hours of idleness that most men devote to pipes and cigarettes he would spend drawing a long steel file slowly round the oval of his nails, lifting his fingers to the light to examine his handiwork, then once again remitting the supple metal to its task. A testy comment rose to Curwen's lips, but he bit it back; the fellow was his guest here after all. And walking over to the table he took his seat at it.

The laundry account had been placed on a slip of paper beside his plate, and as the meal had not yet been served, he picked the thing up and glanced at it. It had been arranged in two columns; down one side of it was a list of the various articles, shirts, collars, singlets, handkerchiefs. And against each article was set in the first column the number of pieces that he had sent, in the second those that had been sent by Butterman. He amused himself for a moment by comparison of the number. Shirts, collars, handkerchiefs, the same number identically. Then suddenly he gave a whistle.

'Good Lord, man!' he said. 'You're pretty economical in socks.'

Butterman looked up quickly.

'Economical? Socks? What do you mean?'

'Do you know that you haven't sent a single pair to be washed this week?'

Butterman did not answer. Instead he rose to his feet and walking to the table leant forward over it.

'Don't you think,' he said, and he spoke slowly, articulating each word carefully; 'don't you think it would be better if I were to go back to my own house now? It was extremely kind of you to offer me the hospitality of yours. But I must not trespass on it too long. The alterations that were being made to mine are practically completed. Don't you think it would be better if I were to go?'

Curwen watched him closely. There was nothing unusual or unexpected in Butterman's suggestion. A man preferred to be among his own things. But behind the intonation of the words, 'Don't you think it would be better', it was almost as though he had heard a threat. It was absurd, of course. Butterman and he were old and proven friends. It was absurd, utterly absurd. He would have to watch himself. A man was in a bad way when he began to imagine things.

'Oh, don't you worry about that, my dear fellow,' he said. 'It's only for another day or two. It's so jolly having you. Life gets a little lonely sometimes for an old bachelor like myself.'

'Old bachelor,' he repeated, and the pitch of Butterman's voice rose suddenly to a laugh. 'Why didn't you marry, then? What was to stop you marrying? And now you are finding yourself lonely!'

'Well, sometimes, naturally.'

Again Butterman laughed, a high-pitched laugh, that was a cackle almost.

'Lonely! Those homes that are not homes, that have all the appearance, but none of the reality, none of the sweetness of a home! Lonely, yes. I think I'd better be going Curwen.'

'It's as you choose, of course. But if you go I shall be extremely sorry. It's nice having you.'

'Nice having me? But why, why, why should you like having me?' He did not wait, however, for a reply. 'Well, if you want me, I suppose I might as well. Here, or another place, it comes to the same thing.'

And pulling back a chair he sat down hurriedly at the table. At that moment the boy arrived with breakfast.

It was the usual two-course meal. Eggs and bacon, preceded by a sardine fish-cake. But though Curwen doused his plate in tomato ketchup, and stirred three lumps of sugar into his tea, through every mouthful that he took he was conscious of that acrid, persistant taste of burning. 'No wonder,' he thought, 'we get nervy with this smell about the place.'

'By the way,' he said, 'Padre Martin will be dropping in to-day for tiffin.'

Butterman grunted.

'Good fellow, Martin,' Curwen added.

Butterman made no comment. He finished his fish-cake, helped himself to three of the four eggs upon the dish and consumed them resolutely. 'Whatever else there may be wrong with him, the fellow's appetite's all right,' thought Curwen. It was not till he had finished his fourth piece of toast and marmalade that Butterman spoke again.

'Do you often,' he asked, 'have Martin here to tiffin?'

'Not too often; now and again.'

'Once every four months or so, for example?'

'About that.'

'And when did you ask him last?'

'I forget, some while back at least. It seemed about time to be asking him again.'

Butterman grunted.

'Tiffin isn't a very usual meal to be asked to. It isn't like dinner, is it? One doesn't usually,' he went on, 'ask a man to tiffin unless it's for some special reason. I wonder why you asked Martin here to-day.'

'My dear fellow. . . .'

But Butterman, once he had set the question, appeared to have lost all interest in the subject.

'Here, or another place,' he said cryptically, 'it comes to the same thing.'

And rising from the table he walked over to the wicker chair by the veranda, drew from his pocket the long steel file and set himself once again to smooth the curved surface of his nails.

Curwen drew a perplexed hand across his forehead. Where was he? What was happening to him? Was this the friendly, familiar world in which he had lived so long? As he walked out of his bungalow, he felt himself to be escaping from the poisoned atmosphere of some prison-house.

He had left the house earlier than usual, but the car was already waiting for him.

'Straight to the office, master?' asked the syce.

Curwen shook his head. He had need before the day's work started of a few moments of fresh air, and the arrival of the laundry account had reminded him that there were several articles of which he stood in need.

'Drive to Yem-Sing's,' he said.

It was nine o'clock, the heat of the day was still some hours distant, and the main street of Pangrai was crowded with men and women hurrying by in their brightly coloured singlets, many of them carrying slung across their shoulders deep tins of water and baskets of fruits and vegetables. They drove slowly, for the motor-car was as new a visitant as the railway to North Siam, and neither had the Laos acquired the habit of avoiding danger, nor had the drivers learnt to resist the thrill of speed, incapacities so regrettable in their consequences that the authorities had marked at either end of the main street a series of artificial bumps in the centre of the roadway to enforce a slackening of pace. After a speed of little more than five miles an hour Curwen's car drew up before a Chinese store.

'I want quite a lot of things, Yem-Sing,' he said.

The merchant passed his hands across each other; and his lips parted gratefully over teeth blackened by many passages of lime-tinged betel-nut, as Curwen hurried through his list.

'Six shirts,' he repeated, 'six singlets, two dozen handkerchiefs, a dozen pairs of socks, white socks. Ah, but that is the one thing I cannot manage. I have not in my shop a single pair of white socks left.'

'What?'

'I am sorry, master, extremely sorry.' And in the Lao fashion he lifted his clasped hands before his face. 'But only a week back the naï Butterman came in here and bought every pair of white socks I had.'

'The naï Butterman?'

'Yes, master, truthfully. "How many pair have you of white socks,"
he asks. Forty of fifty pairs, I tell him. "Very well," he answers, "I will
take the lot." '

'Forty or fifty pairs?'

'To be exact there were forty-seven.'

For the second time that day Curwen rested a perplexed hand upon
his forehead. Forty-seven pairs, and not one pair sent to the laundry;
and in the jungle that curious outburst against his servant; and that
strangely intonated phrase: 'Wouldn't it be better if I went?' Those
questions about Martin; the odd expression of his eyes when he had come
that evening into his tent. Where was it, what had happened to it, that
friendly, that familiar world?

As he came out into the sun-drenched street he noticed Martin's car
passing on the other side of it.

'You're coming to tiffin to-day, aren't you?' he called out.

For an answer the Padre drew his car up beside the pavement. 'Tell
me,' he said, 'how is Butterman?'

Curwen shook his head helplessly. 'I don't know,' he said. 'It's something I don't understand. Something I don't begin to understand. At
times he seems perfectly all right, so perfectly all right that I begin to
wonder whether it isn't just myself imagining things. It's a hopeless
situation.'

'I know,' said the Padre, 'I know. And we're so far here from everything. If we could only get him down to Singapore or Bangkok even. If
only a specialist in these things could look at him. It's outside my scope.
I can only guess at things. Ah well, at any rate, we shall have some
common ground to compare notes on after tiffin.'

It was a tiffin of which Curwen was able subsequently to remember
little. He could not recall what they ate or what they drank, or of what
they spoke. There remained only the recollection of vague constraint: of
himself talking loudly and incessantly on topics that were of no interest
to him: of Martin's thin, high-pitched voice breaking in with an occasional comment: of Butterman taciturn and glowering, eating prodigiously of every dish: a vague impression. Everything that was said and
thought during the early stages of the meal was muffled and obliterated
by the one unforgettable moment of dramatic action. The rest was dim.
He could not even remember how that moment had come about. Suddenly it had been there upon them. One minute it had not been, the
next it was. One minute he had been talking in quick, querulous, excited
sentences, the next for some obscure reason unknown to him he had
ceased; had realized suddenly that Butterman in a trance almost of
detachment was leaning on his elbows across the table, the hands lifted
before his face, examining his fingers with the minutest care; had realized

that the Padre in a trance also was gazing at them as in moments of hypnotic influence the subject will gaze at some bright object, a shilling, a crystal, a metal disc; found himself, as his voice trickled into silence, gazing in his own turn, fascinated, spellbound, at those thin, tapered fingers that slowly one by one Butterman was revolving under his inspection.

Of how long they sat there Curwen had no idea. It was one of those instants that, belonging as they do to eternity, are timeless. There was the dateless interval of silent gazing, then the sudden shattering of that instant; the lifted head, Butterman's glance passing from one to the other, and the coming into his face, as he realized he was being watched, of an incredibly sinister expression.

'Ah!' he said. 'Ah!' And he laughed, leaning further forward across the table, so that his hands were held almost beneath their faces. 'Look at them, look closely – they're interesting hands. They're firm, strong hands; feel the bones, how strong they are. Such strong hands, it wouldn't be difficult for them to kill a man. They'd go round his throat so quietly: they'd just tighten, tighten, tighten, so firm and strong: such firm strong fingers, right to the finger-tips, to the very extremities: the extreme extremities.'

Coldly, regularly, inexorably, like the chill, persistent rain of a northern twilight, the words followed one another. Then suddenly, with a laugh, he flung himself back in his chair.

'By the way, Padre,' he said jovially, 'I know what I wanted to ask you, you're the very man to help me. I wonder if you could find a new boy for me?'

The change of attitude was so startling that the Padre could do no more than stammer feebly:

'New boy? But what's wrong with the one you've got?'

'What's wrong?' and into the voice had returned the note of menace. 'He spies, that's what's wrong with him, he spies. And I've no use for people who spy on me. I should remember that, Padre, if I were you. I get rid of them . . . one way or another. You'll get me a new boy, won't you?'

'By the way, Curwen,' he went on. 'I've thought of rather a good scheme for stabilizing the value of tical round Be-koy.' And for the next twenty minutes he discussed that very real problem of jungle life, the fluctuating value of exchange, with admirable clearness.

'I can't make it out,' said Curwen afterwards. 'There are times when he seems the sanest man I've ever come across. At others . . . well, you saw what he was like . . . and one can't place it, that's the trouble. One doesn't know what one's up against.'

It was at that moment that the boy who had been moving for some seconds at Curwen's side came forward. On his face was a peculiar smile of triumph.

'I have found out, master,' he announced, 'whence comes that smell.'

'Ah!'

'It is the naï Butterman.'

'What?'

'Yes, master, the sweeper discovered it. Every morning the naï Butterman burns in his bathroom the pair of socks that he had worn the day before.'

III.

Although there had been no creak of a lifted latch, no sound of a footfall in the passage, Curwen was conscious as he bent forward among the papers on his desk that someone was standing beside him in the room, someone who stood watching him with intent, malicious eyes. And for a moment he felt so terrified that he did not dare to move, did not dare to disturb that silent watching, did not dare to face the menace that was waiting him. Then with a quick jerk of resolution he looked up.

'Well, Butterman,' he said, 'and what is it I can do for you?'

By an immense effort of will he kept his voice natural and level-toned. But he felt the palms of his hands go moist as he met that glazed, uncannily bright stare.

'I'm rather busy at the moment,' he went on, 'but if you'd care to sit down and wait a little. . . .'

Butterman laughed. He was not wearing a topee, and the hair that fell dankly along his forehead was dishevelled. There was no collar stud at his throat and the silk tie that held his shirt was knotted loosely. His sleeves were rolled backwards above his elbow. In his eyes there was that same expression of hunted and desperate cunning with which he had leant forward an hour back across the tiffin table, and his laugh had that false unnatural note which one associates with the villains of melodrama. In his hand he was holding a heavy Colt revolver.

'Wait!' he cried. 'Oh, I don't mind waiting for a little. I'm in no hurry. Padre Martin will be at the hospital another two hours yet.'

'So you're going to see Padre Martin?'

'Yes, when I've done with you,' and stepping forward he seated himself on the edge of the table, without lowering for an instant the revolver that he had levelled at Curwen's head. 'So you thought you could spy on me,' he said, 'that you could bring me down from the jungle, and keep me in your house and spy on me, that you could have Padre Martin to tiffin with you, waiting and watching till the moment came. You thought you were very clever, didn't you, that I shouldn't see through you as easily as I saw through that boy of mine. You weren't quite clever enough, were you?'

'Now, my dear fellow,' Curwen expostulated, 'do be sensible. What on earth is there that we could be spying on you for?'

'Spying on me, what for? Ah, but my good fellow, there's no need for me to pretend things any longer. We know well enough, we three, you and Martin and I. My boy may suspect, but he doesn't know. There's just we three, and there's no need for us to hide things from each other. We can be open now, can't we? It's so easy to be open now. Nothing's any longer at stake. It doesn't matter what we say or what we reveal, because in such a little while now there'll be only one of us who'll know. Only one left by . . . well . . . shall we say by three o'clock?'

And as he leant back laughing heartily, with the revolver held unwaveringly before him, the nature of his plan grew plain.

'So you're going,' said Curwen quietly, 'to shoot me first, then you're going up to the hospital to shoot Martin.'

Butterman nodded.

'At the same time I don't quite see how you'll manage to get both of us.'

'No?'

'How could you hope to, my dear fellow? Think! A revolver's a noisy thing. You'll have no difficulty in doing me in, we'll admit that, but how will you ever get out of here when you have? There's only one way out of this room, the way you've come, through the main office, and there are three clerks there, to say nothing of a porter at the gate. What'll you do when you've finished me?'

'I shall walk straight out through your office to the car that is waiting for me in the porch.'

'With all those clerks there?'

'They won't stop me. They'll be too astonished. People always are when something unusual happens. They'll be stunned into inaction. Suppose, for instance, you were to stand up on a table in the Ritz, shout "Silence" and then recite at the top of your voice an indecent limerick. What, do you imagine, would happen? That you'd be flung out? Nothing of the sort. People would just sit and gape at you, the waiters, the band, the diners, and you'd get down from the table, walk straight out of the room, and no one would say a word to you. Which is exactly what I shall do when I've shot you, Curwen. I shall fire twice to make quite certain, then I shall walk out and no one will say a word to me. Long before the hue and cry has started I'll have settled my account with Martin.'

He spoke calmly, quietly, with the acute, clear sanity that during the last days had characterized his discussion of every topic. It was as though, by some law of compensation, the sickness that had warped one side of

his intelligence had intensified his perceptions in every other. And as
Curwen sat back in his chair a sensation of utter helplessness possessed
him. Through the window of his office he could hear the hooting of a
car. In the office beyond two of his clerks were softly chattering together.
Above his head the punkah was flapping lazily; the boy who worked it,
the string of it tied round his toe, was rocking, half asleep, with slow,
measured rhythm, only six feet away behind that partition of thin match-
board. All round him was the friendly, familiar world, pursuing its
friendly, familiar course. And here he was trapped and weaponless.

'I should doubt,' continued Butterman, 'whether it was worth while
prolonging the discussion.'

And on the butt of the revolver his finger tightened.

Curwen braced himself together. He was not the man to meet death
unprotestingly. His desk, which was flanked with two narrow sets of
drawers, was cut away in the centre to ease his legs, and he wondered
whether he might not be able by slipping downwards suddenly, and
pushing upwards, to overturn the desk and Butterman simultaneously.
Anyhow it was worth trying. Even if he did not save his own life, he
might create sufficient disturbance or delay to rescue Martin. Slackening
the muscles of his legs and gripping tightly the seat of his chair so as to
ensure strong leverage, he steadied himself to drive. ONE – TWO – he
began to count, but just as he was about to spring, he noticed a sudden
change in his assistant. A perplexed look had come into his face, the
muzzle of the revolver had begun to waver, he lifted his left hand
towards his head, his lips quivered. He staggered to his feet, to stand
swaying stupidly. His fingers loosened their hold on the revolver, letting
it fall clattering upon the floor. 'My head,' he sobbed, 'my head.' And
his face pressed tightly in his hands, he began to sway like a drunken
man across the room.

'Sunstroke!' gasped Curwen. 'Sunstroke! He had no topee!' And
leaping to his feet, he caught the reeling body into his arms.

IV.

An hour later in the small hospital ward that is reserved for American
and European patients, Curwen and the Padre were standing at the foot
of Butterman's bed. He was less restless now, packed as he was in ice, but
still he tossed occasionally from side to side, and from his lips fell cease-
lessly a delirious muttering.

'Those little painted bungalows up there . . .' that was the gist of his
tortured rambling. 'Shut away up there by oneself, all the sweetness of
one's life denied one, the softness of a woman's arms, the softness of a
woman's smile, not fit for them, not fit . . . too great a danger . . . the
hands and feet . . . the bones eaten away, perishing . . . the scorn, the

helplessness . . . not fit . . . not fit . . . they take one and they shut one away up there. They spy on you and watch you, wait till they are quite certain, then they take you . . . take you . . . and shut you away in a little bungalow . . . leave you there to rot and perish . . . fingerless, toeless, featureless, they wait and watch and wait for you . . .'

'Then in heaven's name . . .'

'So he thought,' murmured Curwen, 'that he was a leper, that we were spying on him. But he hasn't a symptom, has he, of leprosy?'

'Not a symptom.'

'Then in heaven's name . . .'

But the Padre lifted his hand. 'Wait a moment,' he said. 'I think I see.'

And as they stood there listening, gradually, through the labyrinth of repetitions and inaudibilities, the meaning of his trouble wound its way into the daylight, so that they came to see through what association of ideas the fever of an uneased longing had worked through that distracted brain till its owner had come to believe himself the victim of that dread disease.

'Not fit to marry,' the voice went on, 'the loneliness – the monotony – the fever – for eight months of the year living by herself . . . no dancing, no theatres, the treachery of the climate . . . and if she were to go out to the jungle, the squalor of a narrow tent . . . not fit to marry . . . the fellow who would dare to ask a woman to share that life . . . not fit to marry. . . . You're right, Padre, not to let them marry . . . to shut them away in those little painted houses . . . danger's too great . . . the softness and sweetness of a woman, the way she smiles, the way she speaks, the way she opens her arms to you, . . . the swooning sweetness of a woman . . . no, no, Padre, you're quite right . . . they'd only degrade it, spoil it, tarnish it, out in the jungle . . . too squalid, too narrow . . . lights and music and laughter . . . must give it them . . . they must have it . . . not fit to marry . . . shut them away in those bungalows . . . leave them to rot there in their sickness . . . not fit to marry, Padre . . . you're quite right . . . shut us away, the lot of us . . . not fit to marry, not fit . . .'

So the voice babbled on, and across that bed of suffering, Curwen's eyes met the Padre's in a look that absolved them of any need of words. They understood. There was nothing further to be said.

Another white man had been beaten by the jungle.

V.

They got him back.

A fellow in the Sarawak Company had his leave hastened by several weeks, and Butterman, his suspicions momentarily stifled by the weakness that followed his recovery, allowed himself to be persuaded by one of the junior assistants to accompany him. He would never come back, of course. Letters had been sent ahead to the London Office. The facts had been set out. Arrangements would be made for the proper medical treatment on the ship. There would be a pension waiting, and efforts would be made to find him a suitable job at home. In eighteen months probably he would be all right. Siam was finished though. Never again would he see the steaming, luxuriant greenery of the jungle, nor the little attar huts beside the river, nor watch the grey logs swinging slowly on their long road south to Bangkok.

Another white man beaten.

It was wistfully, with a heavy heart, that Curwen walked down to the Pangrai Club on the evening of the day on which they said good-bye to Butterman. One less among them, and how few there were left now of his contemporaries. Martin and the Consul and Atkinson who ran the Sarawak Company. New faces otherwise, new faces that came and went, fellows that came out for a year on trial and flung their hands in after seven months, fellows who signed on as permanents, whom everyone liked and trusted, for whom everyone prophesied quick promotion, and of whom the jungle sooner or later got the better, who were brought in as Farquharson had been on a stretcher, broken by malaria, or were sent back on a liner, their nerves gone, like Butterman. A hard life, too hard possibly for the white man. Not many came through as he had done to the last chukka. And in a few weeks he'd be going.

Only a few weeks now. And for the first time in the course of those twenty-five years, those seven chukkas, he experienced a feeling of regret, almost of nostalgia at the thought of saying good-bye to these familiar scenes. Twenty-five years. A large chunk out of a man's life. His youth and his early manhood, his first grey hairs, and he began to wonder whether he would find life in London so good a thing as he had expected. What would there be after all for him to do? His contemporaries would be strangers to him now, and it was not easy to start making friends at forty-five. His father was dead, his brother settled down in Chichester. There were no open doors waiting for him. And he remembered with misgiving the life that is led in London by the majority of pensioned Englishmen, the aimless empty days, the hanging about the Sports Club, the waiting for some fellow to drop in with whom you may exchange gossip of the far places you will not see again. Long empty days, and the drab, furtive romances with which one endeavoured to enliven them.

He hardly spoke during his game of golf. And afterwards when the sun had set, and the brief tropic twilight had darkened into night, he did not join the others at the large round table where the bottles and glasses were set out. Instead, he walked slowly homewards at Martin's side, and as they turned through the gate of the Club, for the first time in his life he passed his arm beneath the Padre's. For a little way they walked in silence, in a silence that was, however, peculiarly intimate. The Butterman incident had drawn them very close together.

'We shall miss you,' the Padre said at length. 'I sometimes wonder what we shall do without you. It isn't so much that we shall be losing a friend, though that will be bad enough, for we've become accustomed to the loss of friends. It's, if you'll forgive my saying so, what you've stood for here. Life isn't easy, in a small society like ours. There are many temptations, many difficulties. I don't think we shall realize till you've gone how much you've meant in . . . well . . . the keeping of things clean and straight.'

It was the first time that the Padre had ever spoken intimately to Curwen, but there was no sign of embarrassment in his speech.

'We shall miss you,' he said, 'more than I can say.'

'Yet I've not been what you'd call a good man, Padre.'

The Padre hesitated a moment before he answered. Not out of any embarrassment, but because he was searching for the exact words with which to convey his meaning. He knew well enough to what Curwen was referring, the small bungalow beside the river, and the unbaptized children who were growing into manhood in Malay.

'A good man,' he echoed. 'I suppose by our Western ideas you wouldn't be. And I don't mind admitting that when I left America I came here in the belief that there would be two main evils for me to fight against. Alcohol was one, and the second, and greater one, the white man's attitude to the brown woman. But that's forty years ago. And in the course of forty years one's viewpoint alters. I don't mean that I think right the things I once thought wrong, it isn't that, but that those things which I once looked on as mortal sins seem now, well, how shall I put it, just rather a pity. There are other things that are very much more important than a standard of chastity that can never be more than relative, Courage, forbearance, kindliness, above all things kindliness, those seem to me now the most truly Christian qualities. We are so few here and so far. It is so terribly important that we should be patient with one another. We shall miss you more than I can say.'

They had reached the bridge over the river, the point where their roads separated, and there were tears in Curwen's eyes as he said good night to Martin, and it was slowly that he strolled on in the warm darkness, under the tropic stars, watching the muddy waters of the Be-kang swirl past him. Twenty-five years. And it was a strange world that waited him, a world where he would have no certain habitat, where no one needed him, where no one perhaps would miss him when he went. He had talked of getting things both ways, but might it be that it was to end in his getting them in neither? Something like a sob rose in his throat as he faced the prospect of his uprooting. He was loved after all and needed here. For a long while he lingered, beside the river, and when finally he hastened his pace it was not in the direction of his own house, but in that of the small bungalow where he had spent increasingly little time of late.

To his surprise he found Cheam alone. She was dressed, for he had never made any attempt to Westernize her, in a short, blue, silk jacket that fell shapelily over a gold and scarlet sinn, her feet were bare, her hair, that was bright with coconut oil, was drawn back tightly into the clutch of a high tortoiseshell-and-enamel comb. Her teeth, for from the betel habit he had discouraged her, were unfashionably clean. But from the corner of her mouth she was puffing slowly at a large white cheroot. As he came into the room she lifted her head in the calm, unemotional manner that had from the first characterized their meetings. There had never been at any time between them what Europe would have admitted as passionate relations.

She looked at him steadily and incuriously. But as their eyes met he was conscious, on this evening of self-discovery, of a curious sense of kinship with her. They were in the same boat after all, exiles both of them, exiles from their youth and their ambitions. This life of theirs together had not been by any means the thing they had dreamed of for themselves. It was something quite other that they had planned. He had had his dream of Oxford, of English life and English shires and she, no doubt, of such a mating and such a life as had their roots in the dateless annals of her race. But for each of them fate had intervened, on each had been laid the duty of obligation to a family. He had come here that his brother might go to Oxford, and she in her turn had come to him because her parents could not afford to refuse the three hundred rupees that were her purchase. They were both in the same boat. And that same curious sense of belonging to this woman and to this country of his exile, that earlier in the evening had made him forsake the round table and the laughter and the drinks, returned with redoubled force upon him. England had grown a foreign country to him. He had taken root here, by Babel's waters.

Softly across the night came the tinkle of a temple bell: the symbol of that Eastern doctrine which preaches subservience to one's fate, the acceptance unprotestingly of one's dharma.

'I shall be retiring, you know, Cheam,' he said, 'in a few weeks from now.'

She bent her head slowly forward and he knew well enough what was passing behind that inscrutable masked face. 'How much of paddy-field was he to offer her and how many ticals.'

'Very likely,' he said, 'I shall be staying on in Pangrai. I am thinking of building myself a house across the river. It would be easier probably if you were to leave this bungalow and come and live there with me.'

Again she bent her head. Her face showed neither pleasure nor surprise. Child of Buddha, she was subservient to her dharma, to her fate, as to his ardour, passive and irresponsive.

'In which case,' he went on, 'it would probably be simpler if we were to be married according to English law.'

'It is as the Naï wishes,' she replied.

Cornell Woolrich

Dead on Her Feet

'And another thing I've got against these non-stop shindigs,' orated the chief to his slightly bored listeners, 'is they let minors get in 'em and dance for days until they wind up in a hospital with the D. T.'s, when the whole thing's been fixed ahead of time and they haven't a chance of copping the prize anyway. Here's a Missus Mollie McGuire been calling up every hour on the half-hour all day long, and bawling the eardrums off me because her daughter Toodles ain't been home in over a week and she wants this guy Pasternack arrested. So you go over there and tell Joe Pasternack I'll give him until tomorrow morning to fold up his contest and send his entries home. And tell him for me he can shove all his big and little silver loving-cups—'

For the first time his audience looked interested, even expectant, as they waited to hear what it was Mr P. could do with his loving-cups, hoping for the best.

'—back in their packing-cases,' concluded the chief chastely, if somewhat disappointingly. 'He ain't going to need 'em any more. He has promoted his last marathon in this neck of the woods.'

There was a pause while nobody stirred. 'Well, what are you all standing there looking at me for?' demanded the chief testily. 'You, Donnelly, you're nearest the door. Get going.'

Donnelly gave him an injured look. 'Me, Chief? Why, I've got a red-hot lead on that payroll thing you were so hipped about. If I don't keep after it it'll cool off on me.'

'All right, then you Stevens!'

'Why, I'm due in Yonkers right now,' protested Stevens virtuously. 'Machine-gun Rosie has been seen around again and I want to have a little talk with her—'

303

'That leaves you, Doyle,' snapped the merciless chief.

'Gee, Chief,' whined Doyle plaintively, 'gimme a break, can't you? My wife is expecting—' Very much under his breath he added: '—me home early tonight.'

'Congratulations,' scowled the chief, who had missed hearing the last part of it. He glowered at them. 'I get it!' he roared. 'It's below your dignity, ain't it! It's too petty-larceny for you! Anything less than the St Valentine's Day massacre ain't worth going out after, is that it? You figure it's a detail for a bluecoat, don't you?' His open palm hit the desk-top with a sound like a firecracker going off. Purple became the dominant colour of his complexion. 'I'll put you all back where you started, watching pickpockets in the subway! I'll take some of the high-falutin-ness out of you! I'll – I'll—' The only surprising thing about it was that foam did not appear at his mouth.

It may have been that the chief's bark was worse than his bite. At any rate no great amount of apprehension was shown by the culprits before him. One of them cleared his throat inoffensively. 'By the way, Chief, I understand that rookie, Smith, has been swiping bananas from Tony on the corner again, and getting the squad a bad name after you told him to pay for them.'

The chief took pause and considered this point.

The others seemed to get the idea at once. 'They tell me he darned near wrecked a Chinese laundry because the Chinks tried to pass him somebody else's shirts. You could hear the screeching for miles.'

Doyle put the artistic finishing touch. 'I overheard him say he wouldn't be seen dead wearing the kind of socks you do. He was asking me did I think you had lost an election bet or just didn't know any better.'

The chief had become dangerously quiet all at once. A faint drumming sound from somewhere under the desk told what he was doing with his fingers. 'Oh he did, did he?' he remarked, very slowly and very ominously.

At this most unfortunate of all possible moments the door blew open and in breezed the maligned one in person. He looked very tired and at the same time enthusiastic, if the combination can be imagined. Red rimmed his eyes, blue shadowed his jaws, but he had a triumphant look on his face, the look of a man who has done his job well and expects a kind word. 'Well, Chief,' he burst out, 'it's over! I got both of 'em. Just brought 'em in. They're in the back room right now—'

An oppressive silence greeted him. Frost seemed to be in the air. He blinked and glanced at his three pals for enlightenment.

The silence didn't last long, however. The chief cleared his throat. '*Hrrrmph.* Zat so?' he said with deceptive mildness. 'Well now, Smitty, as long as your engine's warm and you're hitting on all six, just run over to Joe Pasternack's marathon dance and put the skids under it. It's been going on in that old armoury on the west side—'

Smitty's face had become a picture of despair. He glanced mutely at the clock on the wall. The clock said four – A.M., not P.M. The chief, not being a naturally hard-hearted man, took time off to glance down at his own socks, as if to steel himself for this bit of cruelty. It seemed to work beautifully. 'An election bet!' he muttered cryptically to himself, and came up redder than ever.

'Gee, Chief,' pleaded the rookie, 'I haven't even had time to shave since yesterday morning.' In the background unseen nudgings and silent strangulation were rampant.

'You ain't taking part in it, you're putting the lid on it,' the chief reminded him morosely. 'First you buy your way in just like anyone else and size it up good and plenty, see if there's anything against it on moral grounds. Then you dig out one Toodles McGuire from under, and don't let her stall you she's of age either. Her old lady says she's sixteen and she ought to know. Smack her and send her home. You seal everything up tight and tell Pasternack and whoever else is backing this thing with him it's all off. And don't go 'way. You stay with him and make sure he refunds any money that's coming to anybody and shuts up shop good and proper. If he tries to squawk about there ain't no ordinance against marathons just lemme know. We can find an ordinance against anything if we go back far enough in the books—'

Smitty shifted his hat from northeast to southwest and started reluctantly towards the great outdoors once more. 'Anything screwy like this that comes up, I'm always It,' he was heard to mutter rebelliously. 'Nice job, shooing a dancing contest. I'll probably get bombarded with powder-puffs—'

The chief reached suddenly for the heavy brass inkwell on his desk, whether to sign some report or to let Smitty have it, Smitty didn't wait to find out. He ducked hurriedly out the door.

'Ah me,' sighed the chief profoundly, 'what a bunch of crumbs. Why didn't I listen to me old man and join the fire department instead!'

Young Mr Smith, muttering bad language all the way, had himself driven over to the unused armoury where the peculiar enterprise was taking place.

'Sixty cents,' said the taxi-driver.

Smitty took out a little pocket account-book and wrote down – *Taxi-fare* – $*1.20*. 'Send me out after nothing at four in the morning, will he!' he commented. After which he felt a lot better.

There was a box-office outside the entrance but now it was dark and untenanted. Smitty pushed through the unlocked doors and found a combination porter and doorman, a gentleman of colour, seated on the inside, who gave him a stub of pink pasteboard in exchange for fifty-five cents, then promptly took the stub back again and tore it in half. 'Boy,' he remarked affably, 'you is either up pow'ful early or up awful late.'

'I just is plain up,' remarked Smitty, and looked around him.

It was an hour before daylight and there were a dozen people left in the armoury, which was built to hold two thousand. Six of them were dancing, but you wouldn't have known it by looking at them. It had been going on nine days. There was no one watching them any more. The last of the paid admissions had gone home hours ago, even the drunks and the Park Avenue stay-outs. All the big snow-white arc lights hanging from the rafters had been put out, except one in the middle, to save expenses. Pasternack wasn't in this for his health. The one remaining light, spitting and sizzling way up overhead, and sending down violet and white rays that you could see with the naked eye, made everything look ghostly, unreal. A phonograph fitted with an amplifier was grinding away at one end of the big hall, tearing a dance-tune to pieces, giving it the beating of its life. Each time the needle got to the end of the record it was swept back to the beginning by a sort of stencil fitted over the turn-table.

Six scarecrows, three men and three girls, clung ludicrously together in pairs out in the middle of the floor. They were not dancing and they were not walking, they were tottering by now, barely moving enough to keep from standing still. Each of the men bore a number on his back. *3, 8,* and *14* the numbers were. They were the 'lucky' couples who had outlasted all the others, the scores who had started with them at the bang of a gun a week and two days ago. There wasn't a coat or vest left among the three men – or a necktie. Two of them had replaced their shoes with carpet-slippers to ease their aching feet. The third had on a pair of canvas sneakers.

One of the girls had a wet handkerchief plastered across her forehead. Another had changed into a chorus-girl's practice outfit – shorts and a blouse. The third was a slip of a thing, a mere child, her head hanging limply down over her partner's shoulder, her eyes glazed with exhaustion.

Smitty watched her for a moment. There wasn't a curve in her whole body. If there was anyone here under age, it was she. She must be Toodles McGuire, killing herself for a plated loving-cup, a line in the newspapers, a contract to dance in some cheap honky-tonk, and a thousand dollars that she wasn't going to get anyway – according to the chief. He was probably right, reflected Smitty. There wasn't a thousand dollars in the whole set-up, much less three prizes on a sliding scale. Pasternack would probably pocket whatever profits there were and blow, letting the fame-struck suckers whistle. Corner-lizards and dance-hall belles like these couldn't even scrape together enough to bring suit. Now was as good a time as any to stop the lousy racket.

Smitty sauntered over to the bleachers where four of the remaining six the armoury housed just then were seated and sprawled in various attitudes. He looked them over. One was an aged crone who acted as matron to the female participants during the brief five-minute rest-periods that came every half-hour. She had come out of her retirement for the time being, a towel of dubious cleanliness slung over her arm, and was absorbed in the working-out of a crossword puzzle, mumbling to herself all the while. She had climbed halfway up the reviewing stand to secure privacy for her occupation.

Two or three rows below her lounged a greasy-looking counterman from some one-arm lunchroom, guarding a tray that held a covered tin pail of steaming coffee and a stack of wax-paper cups. One of the rest periods was evidently approaching and he was ready to cash in on it.

The third spectator was a girl in a dance dress, her face twisted with pain. Judging by her unkempt appearance and the scornful bitter look in her eyes as she watched the remaining dancers, she had only just recently disqualified herself. She had one stockingless foot up before her and was rubbing the swollen instep with alcohol and cursing softly under her breath.

The fourth and last of the onlookers (the fifth being the darky at the door) was too busy with his arithmetic even to look up when Smitty parked before him. He was in his shirt-sleeves and wore blue elastic armbands and a green celluloid eye-shade. A soggy-looking stogie protruded from his mouth. A watch, a megaphone, a whistle, and a blank-cartridge pistol lay beside him on the bench. He appeared to be computing the day's receipts in a pocket notebook, making them up out of his head as he went along. 'Get out of my light,' he remarked ungraciously as Smitty's shadow fell athwart him.

'You Pasternack?' Smitty wanted to know, not moving an inch.

'Naw, he's in his office taking a nap.'

'Well, get him out here, I've got news for him.'

'He don't wanna hear it,' said the pleasant party on the bench.

Smitty turned over his lapel, then let it curl back again. 'Oh, the lor,' commented the auditor, and two tens left the day's receipts and were left high and dry in Smitty's right hand. 'Buy yourself a drop of schnapps,' he said without even looking up. 'Stop in and ask for me tomorrow when there's more in the kitty—'

Smitty plucked the nearest armband, stretched it out until it would have gone around a piano, then let it snap back again. The business manager let out a yip. Smitty's palm with the two sawbucks came up flat against his face, clamped itself there by the chin and bridge of the nose, and executed a rotary motion, grinding them in. 'Wrong guy,' he said and followed the financial wizard into the sanctum where Pasternack lay in repose, mouth fixed to catch flies.

'Joe,' said the humbled side-kick, spitting out pieces of ten-dollar-bill, 'the lor.'

Pasternack got vertical as though he worked by a spring. 'Where's your warrant?' he said before his eyes were even open. 'Quick, get me my mouth on the phone, Moe!'

'You go out there and blow your whistle,' said Smitty, 'and call the bally off – or do I have to throw this place out in the street?' He turned suddenly, tripped over something unseen, and went staggering halfway across the room. The telephone went flying out of Moe's hand at one end and the sound-box came ripping off the baseboard of the wall at the other. '*Tch, tch,* excuse it please,' apologized Smitty insincerely. 'Just when you needed it most, too!'

He turned back to the one called Moe and sent him headlong out into the auditorium with a hearty shove at the back of the neck. 'Now do like I told you,' he said, 'while we're waiting for the telephone repairman to get here. And when their dogs have cooled, send them all in here to me. That goes for the cannibal and the washroom dame, too.' He motioned towards the desk. 'Get out your little tin box, Pasternack. How much you got on hand to pay these people?'

It wasn't in a tin box but in a briefcase. 'Close the door,' said Pasternack in an insinuating voice. 'There's plenty here, and plenty more will be coming in. How big a cut will square you? Write your own ticket.'

Smitty sighed wearily. 'Do I have to knock your front teeth down the back of your throat before I can convince you I'm one of these old-fashioned guys that likes to work for my money?'

Outside a gun boomed hollowly and the squawking of the phonograph stopped. Moe could be heard making an announcement through the megaphone. 'You can't get away with this!' stormed Pasternack. 'Where's your warrant?'

'Where's your licence,' countered Smitty, 'if you're going to get technical? C'mon, don't waste any more time, you're keeping me up! Get the dough ready for the pay-off.' He stepped to the door and called out into the auditorium: 'Everybody in here. Get your things and line up.' Two of the three couples separated slowly like sleepwalkers and began to trudge painfully over towards him, walking zig-zag as though their metabolism was all shot.

The third pair, Number 14, still clung together out on the floor, the man facing towards Smitty. They didn't seem to realize it was over. They seemed to be holding each other up. They were in the shape of a human tent, their feet about three feet apart on the floor, their faces and shoulders pressed closely together. The girl was that clothes-pin, that stringbean of a kid he had already figured for Toodles McGuire. So she was going to be stubborn about it, was she? He went over to the pair bellicosely. 'C'mon, you heard me, break it up!'

The man gave him a frightened look over her shoulder. 'Will you take her off me please, Mac? She's passed out or something, and if I let her go she'll crack her conk on the floor.' He blew out his breath. 'I can't hold her up much longer!'

Smitty hooked an arm about her middle. She didn't weigh any more than a discarded topcoat. The poor devil who had been bearing her weight, more or less, for nine days and nights on end, let go and folded up into a squatting position at her feet like a shrivelled Buddha. 'Just lemme stay like this,' he moaned, 'it feels so good.' The girl, meanwhile, had begun to bend slowly double over Smitty's supporting arm, closing up like a jackknife. But she did it with a jerkiness, a deliberateness, that was almost grisly, slipping stiffly down a notch at a time, until her upside-down head had met her knees. She was like a walking doll whose spring has run down.

Smitty turned and barked over one shoulder at the washroom hag. 'Hey you! C'mere and gimme a hand with this girl! Can't you see she needs attention? Take her in there with you and see what you can do for her—'

The old crone edged fearfully nearer, but when Smitty tried to pass the inanimate form to her she drew hurriedly back. 'I – I ain't got the stren'th to lift her,' she mumbled stubbornly. 'You're strong, you carry her in and set her down—'

'I can't go in there,' he snarled disgustedly. 'That's no place for me! What're you here for if you can't—'

The girl who had been sitting on the sidelines suddenly got up and came limping over on one stockingless foot. 'Give her to me,' she said. 'I'll take her in for you.' She gave the old woman a long hard look before which the latter quailed and dropped her eyes. 'Take hold of her feet,' she ordered in a low voice. The hag hurriedly stooped to obey. They sidled off with her between them, and disappeared around the side of the orchestra-stand, towards the washroom. Their burden sagged low, until it almost touched the floor.

'Hang onto her,' Smitty thought he heard the younger woman say. 'She won't bite you!' The washroom door banged closed on the weird little procession. Smitty turned and hoisted the deflated Number 14 to his feet. 'C'mon,' he said. 'In you go, with the rest!'

They were all lined up against the wall in Pasternack's 'office', so played-out that if the wall had suddenly been taken away they would have all toppled flat like a pack of cards. Pasternack and his shill had gone into a huddle in the opposite corner, buzzing like a hive of bees.

'Would you two like to be alone?' Smitty wanted to know, parking Number 14 with the rest of the droops.

Pasternack evidently believed in the old adage, 'He who fights and runs away lives to fight, etc.' The game, he seemed to think, was no longer worth the candle. He unlatched the briefcase he had been guarding under his arm, walked back to the desk with it, and prepared to ease his conscience. 'Well folks,' he remarked genially, 'on the advice of this gentleman here' (big pally smile for Smitty) 'my partner and I are calling off the contest. While we are under no legal obligation to any of you' (business of clearing his throat and hitching up his necktie) 'we have decided to do the square thing, just so there won't be any trouble, and split the prize money among all the remaining entries. Deducting the rental for the armoury, the light bill, and the cost of printing tickets and handbills, that would leave—'

'No you don't!' said Smitty, 'That comes out of your first nine-days profits. What's on hand now gets divvied without any deductions. Do it your way and they'd all be owing you money!' He turned to the doorman. 'You been paid, sunburnt?'

'Nossuh! I'se got five dolluhs a night coming at me—'

'Forty-five for you,' said Smitty.

Pasternack suddenly blew up and advanced menacingly upon his partner. 'That's what I get for listening to you, know-it-all! So New York was a sucker town, was it! So there was easy pickings here, was there! Yah!'

'Boys, boys,' remonstrated Smitty, elbowing them apart.

'Throw them a piece of cheese, the rats,' remarked the girl in shorts. There was a scuffling sound in the doorway and Smitty turned in time to see the lamed girl and the washroom matron each trying to get in ahead of the other.

'You don't leave me in there!'

'Well I'm not staying in there alone with her. It ain't my job! I resign!'

The one with the limp got to him first. 'Listen, mister, you better go in there yourself,' she panted. 'We can't do anything with her. I think she's dead.'

'She's cold as ice and all stiff-like,' corroborated the old woman.

'Oh my God, I've killed her!' someone groaned. Number 14 sagged to his knees and went out like a light. Those on either side of him eased him down to the floor by his arms, too weak themselves to support him.

'Hold everything!' barked Smitty. He gripped the pop-eyed doorman by the shoulder. 'Scram out front and get a cop. Tell him to put in a call for an ambulance, and then have him report in here to me. And if you try lighting out, you lose your forty-five bucks and get the electric chair.'

'I'se pracktilly back inside again,' sobbed the terrified darky as he fled.

'The rest of you stay right where you are. I'll hold you responsible, Pasternack, if anybody ducks.'

'As though we could move an inch on these howling dogs,' muttered the girl in shorts.

Smitty pushed the girl with one shoe ahead of him. 'You come and show me,' he grunted. He was what might be termed a moral coward at the moment; he was going where he'd never gone before.

'Straight ahead of you,' she scowled, halting outside the door. 'Do you need a road-map?'

'C'mon, I'm not going in there alone,' he said and gave her a shove through the forbidden portal.

She was stretched out on the floor where they'd left her, a bottle of rubbing alcohol that hadn't worked uncorked beside her. His face was flaming as he squatted down and examined her. She was gone all right. She was as cold as they'd said and getting more rigid by the minute. 'Overtaxed her heart most likely,' he growled. 'That guy Pasternack ought to be hauled up for this. He's morally responsible.'

The cop, less well-brought-up than Smitty, stuck his head in the door without compunction.

'Stay by the entrance,' Smitty instructed him, 'Nobody leaves.' Then, 'This was the McGuire kid, wasn't it?' he asked his feminine companion.

'Can't prove it by me,' she said sulkily. 'Pasternack kept calling her Rose Lamont all through the contest. Why don't-cha ask the guy that was dancing with her? Maybe they got around to swapping names after nine days. Personally,' she said as she moved towards the door, 'I don't know who she was and I don't give a damn!'

'You'll make a swell mother for some guy's children,' commented Smitty following her out. 'In there,' he said to the ambulance doctor who had just arrived, 'but it's the morgue now, and not first-aid. Take a look.'

Number 14, when he got back to where they all were, was taking it hard and self-accusing. 'I didn't mean to do it, I didn't mean to!' he kept moaning.

'Shut up, you sap, you're making it tough for yourself,' someone hissed.

'Lemme see a list of your entries,' Smitty told Pasternack.

The impresario fished a ledger out of the desk drawer and held it out to him. 'All I got out of this enterprise was kicks in the pants! Why didn't I stick to the sticks where they don't drop dead from a little dancing? Ask me, why didn't I!'

'Fourteen,' read Smitty. 'Rose Lamont and Gene Monahan. That your real name, guy? Back it up.' 14 jerked off the coat that someone had slipped around his shoulders and turned the inner pocket inside out. The name was inked onto the label. The address checked too. 'What about her, was that her real tag?'

'McGuire was her real name,' admitted Monahan, 'Toodles McGuire She was going to change it anyway, pretty soon, if we'dda won that thousand' – he hung his head – 'so it didn't matter.'

'Why'd you say you did it? Why do you keep saying you didn't mean to?'

'Because I could feel there was something the matter with her in my arms. I knew she oughtta quit, and I wouldn't let her. I kept begging her to stick it out a little longer, even when she didn't answer me. I went crazy, I guess, thinking of that thousand dollars. We needed it to get married on. I kept expecting the others to drop out any minute, there were only two other couples left, and no one was watching us any more. When the rest-periods came, I carried her in my arms to the washroom door, so no one would notice she couldn't make it herself, and turned her over to the old lady in there. She couldn't do anything with her either, but I begged her not to let on, and each time the whistle blew I picked her up and started out from there with her—'

'Well, you've danced her into her grave,' said Smitty bitterly. 'If I was you I'd go out and stick both my feet under the first trolley-car that came along and hold them there until it went by. It might make a man of you!'

He went out and found the ambulance doctor in the act of leaving. 'What was it, her heart?'

The A.D. favoured him with a peculiar look, starting at the floor and ending at the top of his head. 'Why wouldn't it be? Nobody's heart keeps going with a seven- or eight-inch metal pencil jammed into it.'

He unfolded a handkerchief to reveal a slim coppery cylinder, tapering to needle-like sharpness at the writing end, where the case was pointed over the lead to protect it. It was aluminium – encrusted blood was what gave it its copper sheen. Smitty nearly dropped it in consternation – not because of what it had done but because he had missed seeing it.

'And another thing,' went on the A.D. 'You're new to this sort of thing, aren't you? Well, just a friendly tip. No offence, but you don't call an ambulance that long after they've gone, our time is too val—'

'I don't getcha,' said Smitty impatiently. 'She needed help; who am

I supposed to ring in, potter's field, and have her buried before she's quit breathing?'

This time the look he got was withering. 'She was past help hours ago.' The doctor scanned his wrist. 'It's five now. She's been dead since three, easily. I can't tell you when exactly, but your friend the medical examiner'll tell you whether I'm right or not. I've seen too many of 'em in my time. She's been gone two hours anyhow.'

Smitty had taken a step back, as though he were afraid of the guy. 'I came in here at four thirty,' he stammered excitedly, 'and she was dancing on that floor there – I saw her with my own eyes – fifteen, twenty minutes ago!' His face was slightly sallow.

'I don't care whether you saw her dancin' or saw her doin' double-hand-springs on her left ear, she was dead!' roared the ambulance man testily. 'She was celebrating her own wake then, if you insist!' He took a look at Smitty's horrified face, quieted down, spit emphatically out of one corner of his mouth, and remarked: 'Somebody was dancing with her dead body, that's all. Pleasant dreams, kid!'

Smitty started to burn slowly. 'Somebody was,' he agreed, gritting his teeth. 'I know who Somebody is, too. His number was Fourteen until a little while ago; well, it's Thirteen from now on!'

He went in to look at her again, the doctor whose time was so valuable trailing along. 'From the back, eh? That's how I missed it. She was lying on it the first time I came in and looked.'

'I nearly missed it myself,' the interne told him. 'I thought it was a boil at first. See this little pad of gauze? It had been soaked in alcohol and laid over it. There was absolutely no external flow of blood, and the pencil didn't protrude, it was in up to the hilt. In fact I had to use forceps to get it out. You can see for yourself, the clip that fastens to the wearer's pocket, which would have stopped it halfway, is missing. Probably broken off long before.'

'I can't figure it,' said Smitty. 'If it went in up to the hilt, what room was there left for the grip that sent it home?'

'Must have just gone in an inch or two at first and stayed there,' suggested the interne. 'She probably killed herself on it by keeling over backwards and hitting the floor or the wall, driving it the rest of the way in.' He got to his feet. 'Well, the pleasure's all yours.' He flipped a careless salute, and left.

'Send the old crow in that had charge in here,' Smitty told the cop.

The old woman came in fumbling with her hands, as though she had the seven-day itch.

'What's your name?'

'Josephine Falvey – Mrs Josephine Falvey.' She couldn't keep her eyes off what lay on the floor.

'It don't matter after you're forty,' Smitty assured her drily. 'What'd you bandage that wound up for? D'you know that makes you an accessory to a crime?'

'I didn't do no such a—' she started to deny whitely.

He suddenly thrust the postage-stamp of folded gauze, rusty on one side, under her nose. She cawed and jumped back. He followed her retreat. 'You didn't stick this on? C'mon, answer me!'

'Yeah, I did!' she cackled, almost jumping up and down, 'I did, I did – but I didn't mean no harm. Honest, mister, I—'

'When'd you do it?'

'The last time, when you made me and the girl bring her in here. Up to then I kept rubbing her face with alcohol each time he brought her back to the door, but it didn't seem to help her any. I knew I should of gone out and reported it to Pasternack, but he – that feller you know – begged me not to. He begged me to give them a break and not get them ruled out. He said it didn't matter if she acted all limp that way, that she was just dazed. And anyway, there wasn't so much difference between her and the rest any more, they were all acting dopy like that. Then after you told me to bring her in the last time, I stuck my hand down the back of her dress and I felt something hard and round, like a carbuncle or berl, so I put a little gauze application over it. And then me and her decided, as long as the contest was over anyway, we better go out and tell you—'

'Yeah,' he scoffed, 'and I s'pose if I hadn't shown up she'd still be dancing around out there, until the place needed disinfecting! When was the first time you noticed anything the matter with her?'

She babbled: 'About two thirty, three o'clock. They were all in here – the place was still crowded – and someone knocked on the door. He was standing out there with her in his arms and he passed her to me and whispered, "Look after her, will you?" That's when he begged me not to tell anyone. He said he'd—' She stopped.

'Go on!' snapped Smitty.

'He said he'd cut me in on the thousand if they won it. Then when the whistle blew and they all went out again, he was standing there waiting to take her back in his arms – and off he goes with her. They all had to be helped out by that time, anyway, so nobody noticed anything wrong. After that, the same thing happened each time – until you came. But I didn't dream she was dead.' She crossed herself. 'If I'da thought that, you couldn't have got me to touch her for love nor money—'

'I've got my doubts,' Smitty told her, 'about the money part of that, anyway. Outside – and consider yourself a material witness.'

If the old crone was to be believed, it had happened outside on the

314

dance floor under the bright arc lights, and not in here. He was pretty sure it had, at that. Monahan wouldn't have dared try to force his way in here. The screaming of the other occupants would have blown the roof off. Secondly, the very fact that the floor had been more crowded at that time than later, had helped cover it up. They'd probably quarrelled when she tried to quit. He'd whipped out the pencil and struck her while she clung to him. She'd either fallen and killed herself on it, and he'd picked her up again immediately before anyone noticed, or else the Falvey woman had handled her carelessly in the washroom and the impaled pencil had reached her heart.

Smitty decided he wanted to know if any of the feminine entries had been seen to fall to the floor at any time during the evening. Pasternack had been in his office from ten on, first giving out publicity items and then taking a nap, so Smitty put him back on the shelf. Moe, however, came across beautifully.

'Did I see anyone fall?' he echoed shrilly. 'Who didn't! Such a commotion you never saw in your life. About half-past two. Right when we were on the air, too.'

'Go on, this is getting good. What'd he do, pick her right up again?'

'Pick her up! She wouldn't get up. You couldn't go near her! She just sat there swearing and screaming and throwing things. I thought we'd have to send for the police. Finally they sneaked up behind her and hauled her off on her fanny to the bleachers and disqualified her—'

'Wa-a-ait a minute,' gasped Smitty. 'Who you talking about?'

Moe looked surprised. 'That Standish dame, who else? You saw her, the one with the bum pin. That was when she sprained it and couldn't dance any more. She wouldn't go home. She hung around saying she was framed and gypped and we couldn't get rid of her—'

'Wrong number,' said Smitty disgustedly. 'Back where you came from.' And to the cop: 'Now we'll get down to brass tacks. Let's have a crack at Monahan—'

He was thumbing his notebook with studied absorption when the fellow was shoved in the door. 'Be right with you,' he said offhandedly, tapping his pockets, 'soon as I jot down – Lend me your pencil a minute, will you?'

'I – I had one, but I lost it,' said Monahan dully.

'How come?' asked Smitty quietly.

'Fell out of my pocket, I guess. The clip was broken.'

'This it?'

The fellow's eyes grew big, while it almost touched their lashes, twirling from left to right and right to left. 'Yeah, but what's the matter with it, what's it got on it?'

'You asking me that?' leered Smitty. 'Come on, show me how you did it!'

315

Monahan cowered back against the wall, looked from the body on the floor to the pencil, and back again. 'Oh no,' he moaned, 'no. Is that what happened to her? I didn't even know—'

'Guys as innocent as you rub me the wrong way,' said Smitty. He reached for him, hauled him out into the centre of the room, and then sent him flying back again. His head bonged the door and the cop looked in inquiringly. 'No, I didn't knock,' said Smitty, 'that was just his dome.' He sprayed a little of the alcohol into Monahan's stunned face and hauled him forward again. 'The first peep out of you was, "I killed her." Then you keeled over. Later on you kept saying "I'm to blame, I'm to blame." Why try to back out now?'

'But I didn't mean I did anything to her,' wailed Monahan, 'I thought I killed her by dancing too much. She was all right when I helped her in here about two. Then when I came back for her, the old dame whispered she couldn't wake her up. She said maybe the motion of dancing would bring her to. She said, "You want that thousand dollars, don't you? Here, hold her up, no one'll be any the wiser." And I listened to her like a fool and faked it from then on.'

Smitty sent him hurling again. 'Oh, so now it's supposed to have happened in here – with your pencil, no less! Quit trying to pass the buck!'

The cop, who didn't seem to be very bright, again opened the door, and Monahan came sprawling out at his feet. 'Geez, what a hard head he must have,' he remarked.

'Go over and start up that phonograph over there,' ordered Smitty. 'We're going to have a little demonstration – of how he did it. If banging his conk against the door won't bring back his memory, maybe dancing with her will do it.' He hoisted Monahan upright by the scruff of the neck. 'Which pocket was the pencil in?'

The man motioned towards his breast. Smitty dropped it in point-first. The cop fitted the needle into the groove and threw the switch. A blare came from the amplifier. 'Pick her up and hold her,' grated Smitty.

An animal-like moan was the only answer he got. The man tried to back away. The cop threw him forward again. 'So you won't dance, eh?'

'I won't dance,' gasped Monahan.

When they helped him up from the floor, he would dance.

'You held her like that dead, for two solid hours,' Smitty reminded him. 'Why mind an extra five minutes or so?'

The moving scarecrow crouched down beside the other inert scarecrow on the floor. Slowly his arms went around her. The two scarecrows rose to their feet, tottered drunkenly together, then moved out of the doorway into the open in time to the music. The cop began to perspire.

Smitty said: 'Any time you're willing to admit you done it, you can quit.'

'God forgive you for this!' said a tomb-like voice.

'Take out the pencil,' said Smitty, 'without letting go of her – like you did the first time .'

'This is the first time,' said that hollow voice. 'The time before – it dropped out.' His right hand slipped slowly away from the corpse's back, dipped into his pocket.

The others had come out of Pasternack's office, drawn by the sound of the macabre music, and stood huddled together, horror and unbelief written all over their weary faces. A corner of the bleachers hid both Smitty and the cop from them; all they could see was that grisly couple moving slowly out into the centre of the big floor, alone under the funeral heliotrope arc light. Monahan's hand suddenly went up, with something gleaming in it; stabbed down again and was hidden against his partner's back. There was an unearthly howl and the girl with the turned ankle fell flat on her face amidst the onlookers.

Smitty signalled the cop; the music suddenly broke off. Monahan and his partner had come to a halt again and stood there like they had when the contest first ended, upright, tent-shaped, feet far apart, heads locked together. One pair of eyes was as glazed as the other now.

'All right break, break!' said Smitty.

Monahan was clinging to her with a silent, terrible intensity as though he could no longer let go.

The Standish girl had sat up, but promptly covered her eyes with both hands and was shaking all over as if she had a chill.

'I want that girl in here,' said Smitty. 'And you, Moe. And the old lady.'

He closed the door on the three of them. 'Let's see that book of entries again.'

Moe handed it over jumpily.

'Sylvia Standish, eh?' The girl nodded, still sucking in her breath from the fright she'd had.

'Toodles McGuire was Rose Lamont – now what's your real name?' He thumbed at the old woman. 'What are you two to each other?'

The girl looked away. 'She's my mother, if you gotta know,' she said.

'Might as well admit it, it's easy enough to check up on,' he agreed. 'I had a hunch there was a tie-up like that in it somewhere. You were too ready to help her carry the body in here the first time.' He turned to the cringing Moe. 'I understood you to say she carried on like nobody's never-mind when she was ruled out, had to be hauled off the floor by main force and wouldn't go home. Was she just a bum loser, or what was her grievance?'

'She claimed it was done purposely,' said Moe. 'Me, I got my doubts. It was like this. That girl the feller killed, she had on a string of glass beads, see? So the string broke and they rolled all over the floor under everybody's feet. So this one, she slipped on 'em, fell and turned her ankle and couldn't dance no more. Then she starts hollering blue murder.' He shrugged. 'What should we do, call off the contest because she couldn't dance no more?'

'She did it purposely,' broke in the girl hotly, 'so she could hook the award herself! She knew I had a better chance than anyone else—'

'I suppose it was while you were sitting there on the floor you picked up the pencil Monahan had dropped,' Smitty said casually.

'I did like hell! It fell out in the bleachers when he came over to apolo—' She stopped abruptly. 'I don't know what pencil you're talking about.'

'Don't worry about a little slip-up like that,' Smitty told her. 'You're down for it anyway – and have been ever since you folded up out there just now. You're not telling me anything I don't know already.'

'Anyone woulda keeled over; I thought I was seeing her ghost—'

'That ain't what told me. It was seeing him pretend to do it that told me he never did it. It wasn't done outside at all, in spite of what your old lady tried to hand me. Know why? The pencil didn't go through her dress. There's no hole in the back of her dress. Therefore she had her dress off and was cooling off when it happened. Therefore it was done here in the restroom. For Monahan to do it outside he would have had to hitch her whole dress up almost over her head in front of everybody – and maybe that wouldn't have been noticed!

'He never came in here after her; your own mother would have been the first one to squawk for help. You did, though. She stayed a moment after the others. You came in the minute they cleared out and stuck her with it. She fell on it and killed herself. Then your old lady tried to cover you by putting a pad on the wound and giving Monahan the idea she was stupefied from fatigue. When he began to notice the coldness, if he did, he thought it was from the alcohol-rubs she was getting every rest-period. I guess he isn't very bright anyway – a guy like that, that dances for his coffee-and. He didn't have any motive. He wouldn't have done it even if she wanted to quit, he'd have let her. He was too penitent later on when he thought he'd tired her to death. But you had all the motive I need – those broken beads. Getting even for what you thought she did. Have I left anything out?'

'Yeah,' she said curtly, 'look up my sleeve and tell me if my hat's on straight!'

DEAD ON HER FEET

On the way out to the Black Maria that had backed up to the entrance, with the two Falvey women, Pasternack, Moe, and the other four dancers marching single file ahead of him, Smitty called to the cop: 'Where's Monahan? Bring him along!'

The cop came up mopping his brow. 'I finally pried him loose,' he said, 'when they came to take her away, but I can't get him to stop laughing. He's been laughing ever since. I think he's lost his mind. Makes your blood run cold. Look at that!'

Monahan was standing there, propped against the wall, a lone figure under the arclight, his arms still extended in the half-embrace in which he had held his partner for nine days and nights, while peal after peal of macabre mirth came from him, shaking him from head to foot.

Geoffrey Household

Taboo

I had this story from Lewis Banning, the American; but as I also know Shiravieff pretty well and have heard some parts of it from him since, I think I can honestly reconstruct his own words.

Shiravieff had asked Banning to meet Colonel Romero, and after lunch took them, as his habit is, into his consulting-room; his study, I should call it, for there are no instruments or white enamel to make a man unpleasantly conscious of the workings of his own body, nor has Shiravieff, among the obscure groups of letters that he is entitled to write after his name, any one which implies a medical degree. It is a long, restful room, its harmony only broken by sporting trophies. The muzzle of an enormous wolf grins over the mantelpiece, and there are fine heads of ibex and aurochs on the opposite wall. No doubt Shiravieff put them there deliberately. His patients from the counties came in expecting a quack doctor but at once gained confidence when they saw he had killed wild animals in a gentlemanly manner.

The trophies suit him. With his peaked beard and broad smile, he looks more the explorer than the psychologist. His unvarying calm is not the priestlike quality of the doctor; it is the disillusionment of the traveller and exile, of one who has studied the best and the worst in human nature and discovered that there is no definable difference between them.

Romero took a dislike to the room. He was very sensitive to atmosphere, though he would have denied it indignantly.

'A lot of silly women,' he grumbled obscurely, 'pouring out emotions.'

They had, of course, poured out plenty of emotions from the same chair that he was occupying; but, since Shiravieff made his reputation on cases of shell-shock, there must have been a lot of silly men too.

Romero naturally would not mention that. He preferred to think that hysteria was confined to the opposite sex. Being a Latin in love with England, he worshipped and cultivated our detachment.

'I assure you that emotions are quite harmless once they are out of the system,' answered Shiravieff, smiling. 'It's when they stay inside that they give trouble.'

'*Cá!* I like people who keep their emotions inside,' said Romero. 'It is why I live in London. The English are not cold – it is nonsense to say they are cold – but they are well bred. They never show a sign of what hurts them most. I like that.'

Shiravieff tapped his long forefinger on the table in a fast, nervous rhythm.

'And what if they *must* display emotion?' he asked irritably. 'Shock them – shock them, you understand, so that they must! They can't do it, and they are hurt for life.'

They had never before seen him impatient. Nobody had. It was an unimaginable activity, as if your family doctor were to come and visit you without his trousers. Romero had evidently stirred up the depths.

'I've shocked them, and they displayed plenty of emotion,' remarked Banning.

'Oh, I do not mean their little conventions,' said Shiravieff slowly and severely. 'Shock them with some horrid fact that they can't blink away, something that would outrage the souls of any of us. Do you remember de Maupassant's story of the man whose daughter was buried alive – how she returned from the grave and how all his life he kept the twitching gesture with which he tried to push her away? Well, if that man had shrieked or thrown a fit or wept all night he mightn't have suffered from the twitch.'

'Courage would have saved him,' announced the colonel superbly.

'No!' shouted Shiravieff. 'We're all cowards, and the healthiest thing we can do is to express fear when we feel it.'

'The fear of death—' began Romero.

'I am not talking about the fear of death. It is not that. It is our horror of breaking a taboo that causes shock. Listen to me. Do either of you remember the Zweibergen case in 1926?'

'The name's familiar,' said Banning. 'But I can't just recall . . . was it a haunted village?'

'I congratulate you on your healthy mind,' said Shiravieff ironically. 'You can forget what you don't want to remember.'

He offered them cigars and lit one himself. Since he hardly ever smoked it calmed him immediately. His grey eyes twinkled as if to assure them that he shared their surprise at his irritation. Banning had never before realized, so he said, that the anti-smoke societies were right, that tobacco was a drug.

'I was at Zweibergen that summer. I chose it because I wanted to be alone. I can only rest when I am alone,' began Shiravieff abruptly. 'The eastern Carpathians were remote ten years ago – cut off from the tourists by too many frontiers. The Hungarian magnates who used to shoot the forests before the war had vanished, and their estates were sparsely settled. I didn't expect any civilized company.

'I was disappointed to find that a married couple had rented the old shooting-box. They were obviously interesting, but I made no advances to them beyond passing the time of day whenever we met on the village street. He was English and she American – one of those delightful women who are wholly and typically American. No other country can fuse enough races to produce them. Her blood, I should guess, was mostly Slav. They thought me a surly fellow, but respected my evident desire for privacy – until the time when all of us in Zweibergen wanted listeners. Then the Vaughans asked me to dinner.

'We talked nothing but commonplaces during the meal, which was, by the way, excellent. There were a joint of venison and some wild strawberries, I remember. We took our coffee on the lawn in front of the house, and sat for a moment in silence – the mountain silence – staring out across the valley. The pine forest, rising tier upon tier, was very black in the late twilight. White, isolated rocks were scattered through it. They looked as if they might move on at any minute – like the ghosts of great beasts pasturing upon the tree-tops. Then a dog howled on the alp above us. We all began talking at once. About the mystery, of course.

'Two men had been missing in that forest for nearly a week. The first of them belonged to a little town about ten miles down the valley; he was returning after nightfall from a short climb in the mountains. He might have vanished into a snowdrift or ravine, for the paths were none too safe. There were no climbing clubs in that district to keep them up. But it seemed to be some less common accident that had overtaken him. He was out of the high peaks. A shepherd camping on one of the lower alps had exchanged a goodnight with him, and watched him disappear among the trees on his way downwards. That was the last that had been seen or heard of him.

'The other was one of the search party that had gone out on the following day. The man had been posted as a stop, while the rest beat the woods towards him. It was the last drive, and already dark. When the line came up to his stand he was not there.

'Everybody suspected wolves. Since 1914 there had been no shooting over the game preserves, and animal life of all sorts was plentiful. But the wolves were not in pack, and the search parties did not find a trace of blood. There were no tracks to help. There was no sign of a struggle.

Vaughan suggested that we were making a mystery out of nothing –
probably the two men had become tired of domestic routine, and taken
the opportunity to disappear. By now, he expected, they were on their
way to the Argentine.

'His cool dismissal of tragedy was inhuman. He sat there, tall, distant,
and casually strong. His face was stamped ready-made out of that
pleasant upper-class mould. Only his firm mouth and thin sensitive
nostrils showed that he had any personality of his own. Kyra Vaughan
looked at him scornfully.

' "Is that what you really think?" she asked.

' "Why not?" he answered. "If those men had been killed it must have
been by something prowling about and waiting for its chance. And there
isn't such a thing."

' "If you want to believe the men aren't dead, believe it!" Kyra said.

'Vaughan's theory that the men had disappeared of their own free will
was, of course, absurd; but his wife's sudden coldness to him seemed to
me to be needlessly impatient. I understood when I knew them better.
Vaughan – your reserved Englishman, Romero! – was covering up his
thoughts and fears, and chose, quite unconsciously, to appear stupid
rather than to show his anxiety. She recognized the insincerity without
understanding its cause, and it made her angry.

'They were a queer pair, those two; intelligent, cultured, and so interested in themselves and each other that they needed more than one life
to satisfy their curiosity. She was a highly strung creature, with swift
brown eyes and a slender, eager body that seemed to grow like a flower
from the ground under her feet. And natural! I don't mean she couldn't
act. She could – but when she did, it was deliberate. She was defenceless
before others' suffering and joy, and she didn't try to hide it.

'Lord! She used to live through enough emotions in one day to last her
husband for a year!

'Not that he was unemotional. Those two were very much alike,
though you'd never have guessed it. But he was shy of tears and laughter,
and he had armed his whole soul against them. To a casual observer he
seemed the calmer of the two, but at bottom he was an extremist. He
might have been a poet, a Saint Francis, a revolutionary. But was he?
No! He was an Englishman. He knew he was in danger of being swayed
by emotional ideas, of giving his life to them. And so? And so he balanced
every idea with another, and secured peace for himself between the
scales. She, of course, would always jump into one scale or the other.
And he loved her for it. But his non-committal attitudes got on her
nerves.'

'She could do no wrong in your eyes,' said Romero indignantly. His
sympathies had been aroused on behalf of the unknown Englishman. He

admired him.

'I adored her,' said Shiravieff frankly. 'Everybody did. She made one live more intensely. Don't think I undervalued him, however. I couldn't help seeing how his wheels went round, but I liked him thoroughly. He was a man you could trust, and good company as well. A man of action. What he did had little relation to the opinions he expressed.

'Well, after that dinner with the Vaughans I had no more desire for a lonely holiday; so I did the next best thing, and took an active interest in everything that was going on. I heard all the gossip, for I was staying in the general clearing-house, the village inn. In the evenings I often joined the district magistrate as he sat in the garden with a stein of beer in front of him and looked over the notes of the depositions which he had taken that day.

'He was a very solid functionary – a good type of man for a case like that. A more imaginative person would have formed theories, found evidence to fit them, and only added to the mystery. He did not want to discuss the case. No, he had no fear of an indiscretion. It was simply that he had nothing to say, and was clear-headed enough to realize it. He admitted that he knew no more than the villagers whose depositions filled his portfolio. But he was ready to talk on any other subject – especially politics – and our long conversations gave me a reputation for profound wisdom among the villagers. Almost I had the standing of a public official.

'So, when a third man disappeared, this time from Zweibergen itself, the mayor and the village constable came to me for instructions. It was the local grocer who was missing. He had climbed up through the forest in the hope of bagging a blackcock at dusk. In the morning the shop did not open. Only then was it known that he had never returned. A solitary shot had been heard about 10.30 p.m., when the grocer was presumably trudging homewards.

'All I could do, pending the arrival of the magistrate, was to send out search parties. We quartered the forest, and examined every path. Vaughan and I, with one of the peasants, went up to my favourite place for blackcock. It was there, I thought, that the grocer would have gone. Then we inspected every foot of the route which he must have taken back to the village. Vaughan knew something about tracking. He was one of those surprising Englishmen whom you may know for years without realizing that once there were coloured men in Africa or Burma or Borneo who knew him still better, and drove game for him, and acknowledged him as someone juster than their gods, but no more comprehensible.

'We had covered some four miles when he surprised me by suddenly showing interest in the undergrowth. Up to then I had been fool enough to think that he was doing precisely nothing.

' "Someone has turned aside from the path here," he said. "He was in a hurry. I wonder why."

'A few yards from the path there was a white rock about thirty feet high. It was steep, but projecting ledges gave an easy way up. A hot spring at the foot of it bubbled out of a cavity hardly bigger than a fox's earth. When Vaughan showed me the signs, I could see that the scrub which grew between the rocks and the path had been roughly pushed aside. But I pointed out that no one was likely to dash off the path through that thicket.

' "When you know you're being followed, you like to have a clear space around you," Vaughan answered. "It would be comforting to be on top of that rock with a gun in your hands – if you got there in time. Let's go up."

'The top was bare stone, with clumps of creeper and ivy growing from the crannies. Set back some three yards from the edge was a little tree, growing in a pocket of soil. One side of its base was shattered into slivers. It had received a full charge of shot at close quarters. The peasant crossed himself. He murmured:

' "They say there's always a tree between you and it."

'I asked him what "it" was. He didn't answer immediately, but played with his stick casually, and as if ashamed, until the naked steel point was in his hand. Then he muttered:

' "The werewolf."

'Vaughan laughed and pointed to the shot marks six inches from the ground.

' "The werewolf must be a baby one, if it's only as tall as that," he said. "No, the man's gun went off as he fell. Perhaps he was followed too close as he scrambled up. About there is where his body would have fallen."

'He knelt down to examine the ground.

' "What's that?" he asked me. "If it's blood, it has something else with it."

'There was only a tiny spot on the bare rock. I looked at it. It was undoubtedly brain tissue. I was surprised that there was no more of it. It must, I suppose, have come from a deep wound in the skull. Might have been made by an arrow, or a bird's beak, or perhaps a too·h.

'Vaughan slid down the rock, and prodded his stick into the sulphurous mud of the stream bed. Then he hunted about in the bushes like a dog.

' "There was no body dragged away in that direction," he said.

'We examined the farther side of the rock. It fell sheer, and seemed an impossible climb for man or beast. The edge was matted with growing things. I was ready to believe that Vaughan's eyes could tell if anything had passed that way.

' "Not a sign!" he said. "Where the devil has his body gone to?"

'The three of us sat on the edge of the rock in silence. The spring bubbled and wept beneath, and the pines murmured above us. There was no need of a little particle of human substance, recognizable only to a physiologist's eye, to tell us that we were on the scene of a kill. Imagination? Imagination is so often only a forgotten instinct. The man who ran up that rock wondered in his panic why he gave way to his imagination.

'We found the magistrate in the village when we returned and reported our find to him.

' "Interesting! But what does it tell us?" he said.

'I pointed out that at least we knew the man was dead or dying.

' "There's no certain proof. Show me his body. Show me any motive for killing him."

'Vaughan insisted that it was the work of an animal. The magistrate disagreed. If it were wolf, he said, we might have some difficulty in collecting the body, but none in finding it. And as for bear – well, they were so harmless that the idea was ridiculous.

'Nobody believed in any material beast, for the whole countryside had been beaten. But tales were told in the village – the old tales. I should never have dreamed that those peasants accepted so many horrors as fact if I hadn't heard those tales in the village inn. The odd thing is that I couldn't say then, and I can't say now, that they were altogether wrong. You should have seen the look in those men's eyes as old Weiss, the game warden, told how time after time his grandfather had fired point-blank at a grey wolf whom he met in the woods at twilight. He had never killed it until he loaded his gun with silver. Then the wolf vanished after the shot, but Heinrich the cobbler was found dying in his house with a beaten silver dollar in his belly.

'Josef Weiss, his son, who did most of the work on the preserves and was seldom seen in the village unless he came down to sell a joint or two of venison, was indignant with his father. He was a heavily built, sullen fellow, who had read a little. There's nobody so intolerant of superstition as your half-educated man. Vaughan, of course, agreed with him – but then capped the villagers' stories with such ghastly tales from native folklore and mediæval literature that I couldn't help seeing he had been brooding on the subject. The peasants took him seriously. They came and went in pairs. No one would step out into the night without a companion. Only the shepherd was unaffected. He didn't disbelieve, but he was a mystic. He was used to passing to and fro under the trees at night.

' "You've got to be a part of those things, sir," he said to me, "then you'll not be afraid of them. I don't say a man can turn himself into a wolf – the Blessed Virgin protect us! – but I know why he'd want to."

'That was most interesting.

' "I think I know too," I answered. "But what does it feel like?"

' "It feels as if the woods had got under your skin, and you want to walk wild and crouch at the knees."

' "He's perfectly right," said Vaughan convincingly.

'That was the last straw for those peasants. They drew away from Vaughan, and two of them spat into the fire to avert his evil eye. He seemed to them much too familiar with the black arts.

' "How do you explain it?" asked Vaughan, turning to me.

'I told him it might have a dozen different causes, just as fear of the dark has. And physical hunger might also have something to do with it.

'I think our modern psychology is inclined to give too much importance to sex. We forget that man is, or was, a fleet-footed hunting animal equipped with all the necessary instincts.

'As soon as I mentioned hunger, there was a chorus of assent – though they really didn't know what I or the shepherd or Vaughan was talking about. Most of those men had experienced extreme hunger. The innkeeper was reminded of a temporary famine during the war. The shepherd told us how he had once spent a week stuck on the face of a cliff before he was found. Josef Weiss, eager to get away from the supernatural, told his experiences as a prisoner of war in Russia. With his companions he had been forgotten behind the blank walls of a fortress while their guards engaged in revolution. Those poor devils had been reduced to very desperate straits indeed.

'For a whole week Vaughan and I were out with the search parties day and night. Meanwhile Kyra wore herself out trying to comfort the womenfolk. They couldn't help loving her – yet half suspected that she herself was at the bottom of the mystery. I don't blame them. They couldn't be expected to understand her intense spirituality. To them she was like a creature from another planet, fascinating and terrifying. Without claiming any supernatural powers for her, I've no doubt that Kyra could have told the past, present, and future of any of those villagers much more accurately than the travelling gipsies.

'On our first day of rest I spent the afternoon with the Vaughans. He and I were refreshed by twelve hours' sleep, and certain that we could hit on some new solution to the mystery that might be the right one. Kyra joined in the discussion. We went over the old theories again and again, but could make no progress.

' "We shall be forced to believe the tales they tell in the village," I said at last.

' "Why don't you?" asked Kyra Vaughan.

'We both protested. Did she believe them, we asked.

' "I'm not sure," she answered. "What does it matter? But I know that evil has come to those men. Evil . . ." she repeated

'We were startled You smile, Romero, but you don't realize how that atmosphere of the uncanny affected us.

'Looking back on it, I see how right she was. Women – good Lord, they get hold of the spiritual significance of something, and we take them literally!

'When she left us I asked Vaughan whether she really believed in the werewolf.

' "Not exactly," he explained. "What she means is that our logic isn't getting us anywhere – that we ought to begin looking for something which, if it isn't a werewolf, has the spirit of the werewolf. You see, even if she saw one, she would be no more worried than she is. The outward form of things impresses her so little."

'Vaughan appreciated his wife. He didn't know what in the world she meant, but he knew that there was always sense in her parables, even if it took one a long time to make the connection between what she actually said and the way in which one would have expressed the same thing oneself. That, after all, is what understanding means.

'I asked what he supposed she meant by evil.

' "Evil?" he replied. "Evil forces – something that behaves as it has no right to behave. She means almost – possession. Look here! Let's find out in our own way what she means. Assuming it's visible, let's see this thing."

'It was, he still thought, an animal. Its hunting had been successful, and now that the woods were quiet it would start again. He didn't think it had been driven away for good.

' "It wasn't driven away by the first search parties," he pointed out. "They frightened all the game for miles around, but this thing simply took one of them. It will come back, just as surely as a man-eating lion comes back. And there's only one way to catch it – bait!"

' "Who's going to be the bait?" I asked.

' "You and I."

'I suppose I looked startled. Vaughan laughed. He said that I was getting fat, that I would make most tempting bait. Whenever he made jokes in poor taste, I knew that he was perfectly serious.

' "What are you going to do?" I asked. "Tie me to a tree and watch out with a gun?"

' "That's about right, except that you needn't be tied up – and as the idea is mine you can have first turn with the gun. Are you a good shot?"

'I am and so was he. To prove it, we practised on a target after dinner, and found that we could trust each other up to fifty yards in clear moonlight. Kyra disliked shooting. She had a horror of death. Vaughan's excuse didn't improve matters. He said that we were going deer-stalking the next night and needed some practice.

' "Are you going to shoot them while they are asleep?" she asked disgustedly.

' "While they are having their supper, dear."

' "Before, if possible," I added.

'I disliked hurting her by jokes that to her were pointless, but we chose that method deliberately. She couldn't be told the truth, and now she would be too proud to ask questions.

'Vaughan came down to the inn the following afternoon, and we worked out a plan of campaign. The rock was the starting-point of all our theories, and on it we decided to place the watcher. From the top there was a clear view of the path for fifty yards on either side. The watcher was to take up his stand, while covered by the ivy, before sunset, and at a little before ten the bait was to be on the path and within shot. He should walk up and down, taking care never to step out of sight of the rock, until midnight, when the party would break up. We reckoned that our quarry, if it reasoned, would take the bait to be a picket posted in that part of the forest.

'The difficulty was getting home. We had to go separately in case we were observed, and hope for the best. Eventually we decided that the man on the path, who might be followed, should go straight down to the road as fast as he could. There was a timber slide quite close, by which he could cut down in ten minutes. The man on the rock should wait awhile and then go home by the path.

' "Well, I shall not see you again until to-morrow morning," said Vaughan as he got up to go. "You'll see me but I shan't see you. Just whistle once, very softly, as I come up the path, so that I know you're there."

'He remarked that he had left a letter for Kyra with the notary in case of accidents, and added, with an embarrassed laugh, that he supposed it was silly.

'I thought it was anything but silly, and said so.

'I was on the rock by sunset. I wormed my legs and body back into the ivy, leaving head and shoulders free to pivot with the rifle. It was a little .300 with a longish barrel. I felt certain that Vaughan was as safe as human science and a steady hand could make him.

'The moon came up, and the path was a ribbon of silver in front of me. There's something silent about moonlight. It's not light. It's a state of things. When there was sound it was unexpected, like the sudden shiver on the flank o. a sleeping beast. A twig cracked now and then. An owl hooted. A fox slunk across the pathway, looking back over his shoulder. I wished that Vaughan would come. Then the ivy rustled behind me. I couldn't turn round. My spine became very sensitive, and a point at the back of my skull tingled as if expecting a blow. It was no good my telling myself that nothing but a bird could possibly be behind me – but of course it was a bird. A nightjar whooshed out of the ivy, and my body became suddenly cold with sweat. That infernal fright cleared all vague fears right out of me. I continued to be uneasy, but I was calm.

'After a while I heard Vaughan striding up the path. Then he stepped within range, a bold, clear figure in the moonlight. I whistled softly, and he waved his hand from the wrist in acknowledgment. He walked up and down, smoking a cigar. The point of light marked his head in the shadows. Wherever he went, my sights were lined a yard or two behind him. At midnight he nodded his head towards my hiding-place and trotted rapidly away to the timber slide. A little later I took the path home.

'The next night our rôles were reversed. It was my turn to walk the path. I found that I preferred to be the bait. On the rock I had longed for another pair of eyes, but after an hour on the ground I did not even want to turn my head. I was quite content to trust Vaughan to take care of anything going on behind me. Only once was I uneasy. I heard, as I thought, a bird calling far down in the woods. It was a strange call, almost a whimper. It was like the little frightened exclamation of a woman. Birds weren't popular with me just then. I had a crazy memory of some Brazilian bird which drives a hole in the back of your head and lives on brains. I peered down through the trees, and caught a flicker of white in a moonlight clearing below. It showed only for a split second, and I came to the conclusion that it must have been a ripple of wind in the silver grass. When the time was up I went down the timber slide and took the road home to the inn. I fell asleep wondering whether we hadn't let our nerves run away with us.

'I went up to see the Vaughans in the morning. Kyra looked pale and worried. I told her at once that she must take more rest.

' "She won't," said Vaughan. "She can't resist other people's troubles."

' "You see, I can't put them out of my mind as easily as you," she answered provocatively.

' "Oh Lord!" Vaughan exclaimed. "I'm not going to start an argument."

' "No – because you know you're in the wrong. Have you quite forgotten this horrible affair?"

'I gathered up the reins of the conversation, and gentled it into easier topics. As I did so, I was conscious of resistance from Kyra; she evidently wanted to go on scrapping. I wondered why. Her nerves, no doubt, were overstrained, but she was too tired to wish to relieve them by a quarrel.

I decided that she was deliberately worrying her husband to make him admit how he was spending his evenings.

'That was it. Before I left, she took me apart on the pretext of showing me the garden and pinned the conversation to our shooting expeditions. Please God I'm never in the dock if the prosecuting counsel is a woman! As it was, I had the right to ask questions in my turn, and managed to slip from under her cross-examination without allowing her to feel it. It hurt. I couldn't let her know the truth, but I hated to leave her in that torment of uncertainty. She hesitated an instant before she said good-bye to me. Then she caught my arm, and cried:

' "Take care of him!"

'I smiled and told her that she was overwrought, that we were doing nothing dangerous. What else could I say?

'That night, the third of the watching, the woods were alive. The world which lives just below the fallen leaves – mice and moles and big beetles – was making its surprising stir. The night birds were crying. A deer coughed far up in the forest. There was a slight breeze blowing, and from my lair on top of the rock I watched Vaughan trying to catch the scents it bore. He crouched down in the shadows. A bear ambled across the path up wind, and began to grub for some succulent morsel at the roots of a tree. It looked as woolly and harmless as a big dog. Clearly neither it nor its kind were the cause of our vigil. I saw Vaughan smile, and knew that he was thinking the same thought.

'A little after eleven the bear looked up, sniffed the air, and disappeared into the black bulk of the undergrowth as effortlessly and completely as if a spotlight had been switched off him. One by one the sounds of the night ceased. Vaughan eased the revolver in his pocket. The silence told its own tale. The forest had laid aside its business, and was watching like ourselves.

'Vaughan walked up the path to the far end of his beat. I looked away from him an instant, and down the path through the trees my eyes caught that same flicker of white. He turned to come back, and by the time that he was abreast of the rock I had seen it again. A bulky object it seemed to be, soft white, moving fast. He passed me, going towards it, and I lined my sights on the path ahead of him. Bounding up through the woods it came, then into the moonlight, and on to him. I was saved only by the extreme difficulty of the shot. I took just a fraction of a second longer than I needed, to make very sure of not hitting Vaughan. In that fraction of a second, thank God, she called to him! It was Kyra. A white ermine coat and her terrified running up the path had made of her a strange figure.

'She clung to him while she got her breath back. I heard her say:

' "I was frightened. There was something after me. I know it."

'Vaughan did not answer, but held her very close and stroked her hair. His upper lip curled back a little from his teeth. For once his whole being was surrendered to a single emotion: the desire to kill whatever had frightened her.

' "How did you know I was here?" he asked.

' "I didn't. I was looking for you. I looked for you last night, too."

' "You mad, brave girl!" he said.

' "But you mustn't, mustn't be alone. Where's Shiravieff?"

' "Right there." He pointed to the rock.

' "Why don't you hide yourself, too?"

' "One of us must show himself," he answered.

'She understood instantly the full meaning of his reply.

' "Come back with me!" she cried. "Promise me to stop it!"

' "I'm very safe, dear," he answered. "Look!"

'I can hear his tense voice right now, and remember their exact words. Those things eat into the memory. He led her just below the rock. His left arm was round her. At the full stretch of his right arm he held out his handkerchief by two corners. He did not look at me, nor alter his tone.

' "Shiravieff," he said, "make a hole in that!"

'It was just a theatrical bit of nonsense, for the handkerchief was the easiest of easy marks. At any other time I would have been as sure as he of the result of the shot. But what he didn't know was that I had so nearly fired at another white and much larger mark – I was trembling so that I could hardly hold the rifle. I pressed the trigger. The hole in the handkerchief was dangerously near his hand. He put it down to bravado rather than bad shooting.

'Vaughan's trick had its effect. Kyra was surprised. She did not realize how easy it was, any more than she knew how much harder to hit is a moving mark seen in a moment of excitement.

' "But let me stay with you," she appealed.

' "Sweetheart, we're going back right now. Do you think I'm going to allow my most precious possession to run wild in the woods?"

' "What about mine?" she said, and kissed him.

'They went away down the short cut. He made her walk a yard in front of him, and I caught the glint of moonlight on the barrel of his revolver. He was taking no risks.

'I myself went back by the path – carelessly, for I was sure that every living thing had been scared away by the voices and the shot. I was nearly down when I knew I was being followed. You've both lived in strange places – do you want me to explain the sensation? No? Well then, I knew I was being followed. I stopped and faced back up the path. Instantly something moved past me in the bushes, as if to cut off my retreat. I'm not superstitious. Once I heard it, I felt safe, for I knew where it was. I was sure I could move faster down that path than anything in the undergrowth – and if it came out into the open, it would have to absorb five steel explosive bullets. I ran. So far as I could hear, it didn't follow.

'I told Vaughan the next morning what had happened.

' "I'm sorry," he said, "I had to take her back. You understand, don't you?"

' "Of course," I answered in surprise. "What else could you do?"

' "Well, I didn't like leaving you alone. We had advertised our presence pretty widely. True, we should have frightened away any animal – but all we know about this animal is that it doesn't behave like one. There was a chance of our attracting instead of frightening it. We're going to get it to-night," he added savagely.

'I asked if Kyra would promise to stay at home.

' "Yes. She says we're doing our duty, and that she won't interfere. Do you think this is our duty?"

' "No!" I said.

' "Nor do I. I never feel that anything which I enjoy can possibly be my duty. And, by God, I enjoy this now!"

'I think he did enjoy it as he waited on the rock that night. He wanted revenge. There was no reason to believe that Kyra had been frightened by anything more than night and loneliness, but he was out against the whole set of circumstances that had dared to affect her. He wanted to be the bait instead of the watcher – I believe, with some mad hope of getting his hands on his enemy. But I wouldn't let him. After all, it was my turn.

'Bait! As I walked up and down the path, the word kept running through my mind. There wasn't a sound. The only moving thing was the moon which passed from tree-top to tree-top as the night wore on. I pictured Vaughan on the rock, the foresight of his rifle creeping backwards and forwards in a quarter-circle as it followed my movements. I visualized the line of his aim as a thread of light passing down and across in front of my eyes. Once I heard Vaughan cough. I knew that he had seen my nervousness and was reassuring me. I stood by a clump of bushes some twenty yards away, watching a silver leaf that shook as some tiny beast crawled up it.

'Hot breath on the back of my neck – crushing weight on my shoulders – hardness against the back of my skull – the crack of Vaughan's rifle – they were instantaneous, but not too swift for me to know all the terror of death. Something leapt away from me, and squirmed into the spring-head beneath the rock.

' "Are you all right?" shouted Vaughan, crashing down through the ivy.

' "What was it?"

' "A man. I've winged him. Come on! I'm going in after him!"

'Vaughan was berserk mad. I've never seen such flaming disregard of danger. He drew a deep breath, and tackled the hole as if it were a man's ankles. Head and shoulders, he sloshed into the mud of the cavity, emptying his Winchester in front of him. If he couldn't wriggle forward swiftly without drawing breath he would be choked by the sulphur fumes or drowned. If his enemy were waiting for him, he was a dead man. He disappeared and I followed. No, I didn't need any courage. I was covered by the whole length of Vaughan's body. But it was a vile moment. We'd never dreamed that anything could get in and out through that spring. Imagine holding your breath, and trying to squirm through hot water, using your hips and shoulders like a snake, not knowing how you would return if the way forward was barred. At last I was able to raise myself on my hands and draw a breath. Vaughan had dragged himself clear and was on his feet, holding a flashlight in front of him.

' "Got him!" he said.

'We were in a low cave under the rock. There was air from the cracks above us. The floor was of dry sand, for the hot stream flowed into the cave close to the hole by which it left. A man lay crumpled up at the far end of the hollow. We crossed over to him. He held a sort of long pistol in his hand. It was a spring humane-killer. The touch of that wide muzzle against my skull is not a pleasant memory. The muzzle is jagged, you see, so that it grips the scalp while the spike is released.

'We turned the body over – it was Josef Weiss. Werewolf? Possession? I don't know. I would call it an atavistic neurosis. But that's a name, not an explanation.

'Beyond the body there was a hole some six feet in diameter, as round as if it had been bored by a rotary drill. The springs which had forced that passage had dried up, but the mottled-yellow walls were smooth as marble with the deposit left by the water. Evidently Weiss had been trying to reach that opening when Vaughan dropped him. We climbed that natural sewer pipe. For half an hour the flashlight revealed nothing but the sweating walls of the hole. Then we were stopped by a roughly hewn ladder which sprawled across the passage. The rungs were covered with mud, and here and there were dark stains on the wood. We went up. It led to a hollow evidently dug out with spade and chisel. The roof was of planks, with a trap-door at one end. We lifted it with our shoulders, and stood up within the four walls of a cottage. A fire was smouldering on the open hearth, and as we let in the draught of air, a log burst into flame. A gun stood in the ingle. On a rack were some iron traps and a belt of cartridges. There was a table in the centre of the room with a long knife on it. That was all we saw with our first glance. With our second we saw a lot more. Weiss had certainly carried his homicidal mania to extremes. I imagine his beastly experiences as a prisoner of war had left a kink in the poor devil's mind. Then, digging out a cellar or repairing the floor, he had accidentally discovered the dry channel beneath the cottage, and followed it to its hidden outlet. That turned his secret desires into action. He could kill and remove his victim without any trace. And so he let himself go.

'At dawn we were back at the cottage with the magistrate. When he came out, he was violently, terribly sick. I have never seen a man be so sick. It cleared him. No, I'm not being humorous. It cleared him mentally. He needed none of those emotional upheavals which we have to employ to drive shock out of our system. Didn't I tell you he was unimaginative? He handled the subsequent inquiry in a masterly fashion. He accepted as an unavoidable fact the horror of the thing, but he wouldn't listen to tales which could not be proved. There was never any definite proof of the extra horror in which the villagers believed.'

There was an exclamation from Lewis Banning.

'Ah – you remember now. I thought you would. The press reported that rumour as a fact, but there was no definite proof, I tell you.

'Vaughan begged me to keep it from his wife. I was to persuade her to go away at once before a breath of it could reach her. I was to tell her that he might have received internal injuries, and should be examined without delay. He himself believed the tale that was going round, but he was very conscious of his poise. I suspect that he was feeling a little proud of himself – proud that he was unaffected. But he dreaded the effect of the shock on his wife.

'We were too late. The cook had caught the prevailing fever, and told that unpleasant rumour to Kyra. She ran to her husband, deadly pale, desperate, instinctively seeking protection against the blow. He could protect himself, and would have given his life to be able to protect her. He tried, but only gave her words and more words. He explained that, looking at the affair calmly, it didn't matter; that no one could have known; that the best thing was to forget it; and so on. It was absurd. As if anyone who believed what was being said could look at the affair calmly!

'Sentiments of that kind were no comfort to his wife. She expected him to show his horror, not to isolate himself as if he had shut down a lid, not to leave her spiritually alone. She cried out at him that he had no feeling and rushed to her room. Perhaps I should have given her a sedative, but I didn't. I knew that the sooner she had it out with herself, the better, and that her mind was healthy enough to stand it.

'I said so to Vaughan, but he did not understand. Emotion, he thought, was dangerous. It mustn't be let loose. He wanted to tell her again not to "worry". He didn't see that he was the only person within ten miles who wasn't "worried".

'She came down later. She spoke to Vaughan scornfully, coldly, as if she had found him unfaithful to her. She said to him:

' "I can't see the woman again. Tell her to go, will you?"

'She meant the cook. Vaughan challenged her. He was just obstinately logical and fair.

' "It's not her fault," he said. "She's an ignorant woman, not an anatomist. We'll call her in, and you'll see how unjust you are."

' "Oh no!" she cried – and then checked herself.

' "Send for her then!" she said.

'The cook came in. How could she know, she sobbed – she had noticed nothing – she was sure that what she had bought from Josef Weiss was really venison – she didn't think for a moment. . . . Well, blessed are the simple!

' "My God! Be quiet!" Kyra burst out. "You all of you think what you want to think. You all lie to yourselves and pretend and have no feelings!"

'I couldn't stand any more. I begged her not to torture herself and not to torture me. It was the right note. She took my hands and asked me to forgive her. Then the tears came. She cried, I think, till morning. At breakfast she had a wan smile for both of us, and I knew that she was out of danger – clear of the shock for good. They left for England the same day.

'I met them in Vienna two years ago, and they dined with me. We never mentioned Zweibergen. They still adored one another, and still quarrelled. It was good to hear them talk and watch them feeling for each other's sympathy.

'Vaughan refused his meat at dinner, and said that he had become a vegetarian.

' "Why?" I asked deliberately.

'He answered that he had recently had a nervous breakdown – could eat nothing, and had nearly died. He was all right now, he said; no trace of the illness remained but his distaste for meat . . . it had come over him quite suddenly . . . he could not think why.

'I tell you the man was absolutely serious. He could *not* think why. Shock had lain hidden in him for ten years, and then had claimed its penalty.'

'And you?' asked Banning. 'How did you get clear of shock? You had to control your emotions at the time.'

'A fair question,' said Shiravieff. 'I've been living under a suspended sentence. There have been days when I thought I should visit one of my colleagues and ask him to clean up the mess. If I could only have got the story out of my system, it would have helped a lot – but I couldn't bring myself to tell it.'

'You have just told it,' said Colonel Romero solemnly.

Graham Greene

A Little Place off the
Edgware Road

Craven came up past the Achilles statue in the thin summer rain. It was only just after lighting-up time, but already the cars were lined up all the way to the Marble Arch, and the sharp acquisitive faces peered out ready for a good time with anything possible which came along. Craven went bitterly by with the collar of his mackintosh tight round his throat: it was one of his bad days.

All the way up the Park he was reminded of passion, but you needed money for love. All that a poor man could get was lust. Love needed a good suit, a car, a flat somewhere, or a good hotel. It needed to be wrapped in cellophane. He was aware all the time of the stringy tie beneath the mackintosh, and the frayed sleeves: he carried his body about with him like something he hated. (There were moments of happiness in the British Museum reading-room, but the body called him back.) He bore, as his only sentiment, the memory of ugly deeds committed on park chairs. People talked as if the body died too soon – that wasn't the trouble, to Craven, at all. The body kept alive – and through the glittering tinselly rain, on his way to a rostrum, he passed a little man in a black suit carrying a banner, 'The Body shall rise again'. He remembered a dream from which three times he had woken trembling: he had been alone in the huge dark cavernous burying ground of all the world. Every grave was connected to another under the ground: the globe was honeycombed for the sake of the dead, and on each occasion of dreaming he had discovered anew the horrifying fact that the body doesn't decay. There are no worms and dissolution. Under the ground the world was littered with masses of dead flesh ready to rise again with their warts and boils and eruptions. He had lain in bed and remembered – as 'tidings of great joy' – that the body after all was corrupt.

He came up into the Edgware Road walking fast – the Guardsmen were out in couples, great languid elongated beasts – the bodies like worms in their tight trousers. He hated them, and hated his hatred because he knew what it was, envy. He was aware that every one of them had a better body than himself: indigestion creased his stomach: he felt sure that his breath was foul – but who could he ask? Sometimes he secretly touched himself here and there with scent: it was one of his ugliest secrets. Why should he be asked to believe in the resurrection of this body he wanted to forget? Sometimes he prayed at night (a hint of religious belief was lodged in his breast like a worm in a nut) that *his* body at any rate should never rise again.

He knew all the side streets round the Edgware Road only too well: when a mood was on, he simply walked until he tired, squinting at his own image in the windows of Salmon & Gluckstein and the A.B.C.s. So he noticed at once the posters outside the disused theatre in Culpar Road. They were not unusual, for sometimes Barclays Bank Dramatic Society would hire the place for an evening – or an obscure film would be trade-shown there. The theatre had been built in 1920 by an optimist who thought the cheapness of the site would more than counter-balance its disadvantage of lying a mile outside the conventional theatre zone. But no play had ever succeeded, and it was soon left to gather rat-holes and spider-webs. The covering of the seats was never renewed, and all that ever happened to the place was the temporary false life of an amateur play or a trade show.

Craven stopped and read – there were still optimists it appeared, even in 1939, for nobody but the blindest optimist could hope to make money out of the place as 'The Home of the Silent Film'. The first season of 'primitives' was announced (a high-brow phrase): there would never be a second. Well, the seats were cheap, and it was perhaps worth a shilling to him, now that he was tired, to get in somewhere out of the rain. Craven bought a ticket and went in to the darkness of the stalls.

In the dead darkness a piano tinkled something monotonous recalling Mendelssohn: he sat down in a gangway seat, and could immediately feel the emptiness all round him. No, there would never be another season. On the screen a large woman in a kind of toga wrung her hands, then wobbled with curious jerky movements towards a couch. There she sat and stared out like a sheep-dog distractedly through her loose and black and stringy hair. Sometimes she seemed to dissolve altogether into dots and flashes and wiggly lines. A sub-title said, 'Pompilia betrayed by her beloved Augustus seeks an end to her troubles.'

Craven began at last to see – a dim waste of stalls. There were not twenty people in the place – a few couples whispering with their heads touching, and a number of lonely men like himself, wearing the same uniform of the cheap mackintosh. They lay about at intervals like corpses – and again Craven's obsession returned: the tooth-ache of horror. He thought miserably – I am going mad: other people don't feel like this. Even a disused theatre reminded him of those interminable caverns where the bodies were waiting for resurrection.

'A slave to his passion Augustus calls for yet more wine.'

A gross middle-aged Teutonic actor lay on an elbow with his arm round a large woman in a shift. The Spring Song tinkled ineptly on, and the screen flickered like indigestion. Somebody felt his way through the darkness, scrabbling past Craven's knees – a small man: Craven experienced the unpleasant feeling of a large beard brushing his mouth. Then there was a long sigh as the newcomer found the next chair, and on the screen events had moved with such rapidity that Pompilia had already stabbed herself – or so Craven supposed – and lay still and buxom among her weeping slaves.

A low breathless voice sighed out close to Craven's ear, 'What's happened? Is she asleep?'

'No. Dead.'

'Murdered?' the voice asked with a keen interest.

'I don't think so. Stabbed herself.'

Nobody said 'Hush': nobody was enough interested to object to a voice. They drooped among the empty chairs in attitudes of weary inattention.

The film wasn't nearly over yet: there were children somehow to be considered: was it all going on to a second generation? But the small bearded man in the next seat seemed to be interested only in Pompilia's death. The fact that he had come in at that moment apparently fascinated him. Craven heard the word 'coincidence' twice, and he went on talking to himself about it in low out-of-breath tones. 'Absurd when you come to think of it,' and then 'no blood at all'. Craven didn't listen: he sat with his hands clasped between his knees, facing the fact as he had faced it so often before, that he was in danger of going mad. He had to pull himself up, take a holiday, see a doctor (God knew what infection moved in his veins). He became aware that his bearded neighbour had addressed him directly. 'What?' he asked impatiently, 'what did you say?'

'There would be more blood than you can imagine.'

'What are you talking about?'

When the man spoke to him, he sprayed him with damp breath. There was a little bubble in his speech like an impediment. He said, 'When you murder a man . . .'

340

'This was a woman,' Craven said impatiently.

'That wouldn't make any difference.'

'And it's got nothing to do with murder anyway.'

'That doesn't signify.' They seemed to have got into an absurd and meaningless wrangle in the dark.

'I know, you see,' the little bearded man said in a tone of enormous conceit.

'Know what?'

'About such things,' he said with guarded ambiguity.

Craven turned and tried to see him clearly. Was he mad? Was this a warning of what he might become – babbling incomprehensibly to strangers in cinemas? He thought, By God, no, trying to see: I'll be sane yet. I *will* be sane. He could make out nothing but a small black hump of body. The man was talking to himself again. He said, 'Talk. Such talk. They'll say it was all for fifty pounds. But that's a lie. Reasons and reasons. They always take the first reason. Never look behind. Thirty years of reasons. Such simpletons,' he added again in that tone of breathless and unbounded conceit. So this was madness. So long as he could realize that, he must be sane himself – relatively speaking. Not so sane perhaps as the seekers in the park or the Guardsmen in the Edgware Road, but saner than this. It was like a message of encouragement as the piano tinkled on.

Then again the little man turned and sprayed him. 'Killed herself, you say? But who's to know that? It's not a mere question of what hand holds the knife.' He laid a hand suddenly and confidingly on Craven's: it was damp and sticky: Craven said with horror as a possible meaning came to him, 'What are you talking about?'

'I know,' the little man said. 'A man in my position gets to know almost everything.'

'What is your position?' Craven asked, feeling the sticky hand on his, trying to make up his mind whether he was being hysterical or not – after all, there were a dozen explanations – it might be treacle.

'A pretty desperate one *you'd* say.' Sometimes the voice almost died in the throat altogether. Something incomprehensible had happened on the screen – take your eyes from these early pictures for a moment and the plot had proceeded on at such a pace. . . . Only the actors moved slowly and jerkily. A young woman in a nightdress seemed to be weeping in the arms of a Roman centurion: Craven hadn't seen either of them before. '*I am not afraid of death, Lucius – in your arms.*'

The little man began to titter – knowingly. He was talking to himself again. It would have been easy to ignore him altogether if it had not been for those sticky hands which he now removed: he seemed to be fumbling at the seat in front of him. His head had a habit of lolling sideways – like an idiot child's. He said distinctly and irrelevantly: 'Bayswater Tragedy.'

'What was that?' Craven said. He had seen those words on a poster before he entered the park.

'What?'

'About the tragedy.'

'To think they call Cullen Mews Bayswater.' Suddenly the little man began to cough – turning his face towards Craven and coughing right at him: it was like vindictiveness. The voice said, 'Let me see. My umbrella.' He was getting up.

'You didn't have an umbrella.'

'My umbrella,' he repeated. 'My —' and seemed to lose the word altogether. He went scrabbling out past Craven's knees.

Craven let him go, but before he had reached the billowy dusty curtains of the Exit the screen went blank and bright – the film had broken, and somebody immediately turned up one dirt-choked chandelier above the circle. It shone down just enough for Craven to see the smear on his hands. This wasn't hysteria: this was a fact. He wasn't mad: he had sat next a madman who in some mews – what was the name, Colon, Collin. . . . Craven jumped up and made his own way out: the black curtain flapped in his mouth. But he was too late: the man had gone and there were three turnings to choose from. He chose instead a telephone-box and dialled with a sense odd for him of sanity and decision 999.

It didn't take two minutes to get the right department. They were interested and very kind. Yes, there had been a murder in a mews – Cullen Mews. A man's neck had been cut from ear to ear with a bread knife – a horrid crime. He began to tell them how he had sat next the murderer in a cinema: it couldn't be anyone else: there was blood on his hands – and he remembered with repulsion as he spoke the damp beard. There must have been a terrible lot of blood. But the voice from the Yard interrupted him. 'Oh no,' it was saying, 'we have the murderer – no doubt of it at all. It's the body that's disappeared.'

Craven put down the receiver. He said to himself aloud, 'Why should this happen to *me*? Why to *me*?' He was back in the horror of his dream – the squalid darkening street outside was only one of the innumerable tunnels connecting grave to grave where the imperishable bodies lay. He said, 'It was a dream, a dream,' and leaning forward he saw in the mirror above the telephone his own face sprinkled by tiny drops of blood like dew from a scent-spray. He began to scream, 'I won't go mad. I won't go mad. I'm sane. I won't go mad.' Presently a little crowd began to collect, and soon a policeman came.

C. M. Kornbluth

The Words of Guru

Yesterday, when I was going to meet Guru in the woods a man stopped me and said: 'Child, what are you doing out at one in the morning? Does your mother know where you are? How old are you, walking around this late?'

I looked at him, and saw that he was white-haired, so I laughed. Old men never see; in fact men hardly see at all. Sometimes young women see part, but men rarely ever see at all. 'I'm twelve on my next birth-day,' I said. And then, because I would not let him live to tell people, I said, 'And I'm out this late to see Guru.'

'Guru?' he asked. 'Who is Guru? Some foreigner, I suppose? Bad business mixing with foreigners, young fellow. Who is Guru?'

So I told him who Guru was, and just as he began talking about cheap magazines and fairy tales I said one of the words that Guru taught me and he stopped talking. Because he was an old man and his joints were stiff he didn't crumple up but fell in one piece, hitting his head on the stone. Then I went on.

Even though I'm going to be only twelve on my next birthday I know many things that old people don't. And I remember things that other boys can't. I remember being born out of darkness, and I remember the noises that people made about me. Then when I was two months old I began to understand that the noises meant things like the things that were going on inside my head. I found out that I could make the noises too, and everybody was very much surprised. 'Talking!' they said, again and again. 'And so very young! Clara, what do you make of it?' Clara was my mother.

And Clara would say: 'I'm sure I don't know. There never was any genius in my family, and I'm sure there was none in Joe's.' Joe was my father.

C. M. KORNBLUTH

Once Clara showed me a man I had never seen before, and told me that he was a reporter – that he wrote things in newspapers. The reporter tried to talk to me as if I were an ordinary baby. I didn't even answer him, but just kept looking at him until his eyes fell and he went away. Later Clara scolded me and read me a little piece in the reporter's newspaper that was supposed to be funny – about the reporter asking me very complicated questions and me answering with baby noises. It was not true, of course. I didn't say a word to the reporter, and he didn't ask me even one of the questions.

I heard her read the little piece, but while I listened I was watching the slug crawling on the wall. When Clara was finished I asked her: 'What is that grey thing?'

She looked where I pointed, but couldn't see it. 'What grey thing, Peter?' she asked. I had her call me by my whole name, Peter, instead of anything silly like Petey. 'What grey thing?'

'It's as big as your hand, Clara, but soft. I don't think it has any bones at all. It's crawling up, but I don't see any face on the topward side. And there aren't any legs.'

I think she was worried, but she tried to baby me by putting her hand on the wall and trying to find out where it was. I called out whether she was right or left of the thing. Finally she put her hand right through the slug. And then I realized that she really couldn't see it, and didn't believe it was there. I stopped talking about it then and only asked her a few days later: 'Clara, what do you call a thing which one person can see and another person can't?'

'An illusion, Peter,' she said. 'If that's what you mean.' I said nothing, but let her put me to bed as usual, but when she turned out the light and went away I waited a little while and then called out softly, 'Illusion! Illusion!'

At once Guru came for the first time. He bowed, the way he always has since, and said: 'I have been waiting.'

'I didn't know that was the way to call you,' I said.

'Whenever you want me I will be ready. I will teach you, Peter – if you want to learn. Do you know what I will teach you?'

'If you will teach me about the grey thing on the wall,' I said, 'I will listen. And if you will teach me about real things and unreal things I will listen.'

'These things,' he said thoughtfully, 'very few wish to learn. And there are some things that nobody ever wished to learn. And there are some things that I will not teach.'

Then I said: 'The things nobody has ever wished to learn I will learn. And I will even learn the things you do not wish to teach.'

He smiled mockingly. 'A master has come,' he said, half-laughing. 'A

344

master of Guru.'

That was how I learned his name. And that night he taught me a word which would do little things, like spoiling food.

From that day, to the time I saw him last night he has not changed at all, though now I am as tall as he is. His skin is still as dry and shiny as ever it was, and his face is still bony, crowned by a head of very coarse, black hair.

When I was ten years old I went to bed one night only long enough to make Joe and Clara suppose I was fast asleep. I left in my place something which appears when you say one of the words of Guru and went down the drainpipe outside my window. It always was easy to climb down and up, ever since I was eight years old.

I met Guru in Inwood Hill Park. 'You're late,' he said.

'Not too late,' I answered. 'I know it's never too late for one of these things.'

'How do you know?' he asked sharply. 'This is your first.'

'And maybe my last,' I replied. 'I don't like the idea of it. If I have nothing more to learn from my second than my first I shan't go to another.'

'You don't know,' he said. 'You don't know what it's like – the voices, and the bodies slick with unguent, leaping flames, mind-filling ritual! You can have no idea at all until you've taken part.'

'We'll see,' I said. 'Can we leave from here?'

'Yes,' he said. Then he taught me the word I would need to know, and we both said it together.

The place we were in next was lit with red lights, and I think that the walls were of rock. Though of course there was no real seeing there, and so the lights only seemed to be red, and it was not real rock.

As we were going to the fire one of them stopped us. 'Who's with you?' she asked, calling Guru by another name. I did not know that he was also the person bearing that name, for it was a very powerful one.

He cast a hasty, sidewise glance at me and then said: 'This is Peter of whom I have often told you.'

She looked at me then and smiled, stretching out her oily arms. 'Ah,' she said, softly, like the cats when they talk at night to me. 'Ah, this is Peter. Will you come to me when I call you, Peter? And sometimes call for me – in the dark – when you are alone?'

'Don't do that!' said Guru, angrily pushing past her. 'He's very young – you might spoil him for his work.'

She screeched at our backs: 'Guru and his pupil – fine pair! Boy, he's no more real than I am – you're the only real thing here!'

'Don't listen to her,' said Guru. 'She's wild and raving. They're always tight-strung when this time comes around.'

We came near the fires then, and sat down on rocks. They were killing animals and birds and doing things with their bodies. The blood was being collected in a basin of stone, which passed through the crowd. The one to my left handed it to me. 'Drink,' she said, grinning to show me her fine, white teeth. I swallowed twice from it and passed it to Guru.

When the bowl had passed all around we took off our clothes. Some, like Guru, did not wear them, but many did. The one to my left sat closer to me, breathing heavily at my face. I moved away. 'Tell her to stop, Guru,' I said. 'This isn't part of it, I know.'

Guru spoke to her sharply in their own language, and she changed her seat, snarling.

Then we all began to chant, clapping our hands and beating our thighs. One of them rose slowly and circled about the fires in a slow pace, her eyes rolling wildly. She worked her jaws and flung her arms about so sharply that I could hear the elbows crack. Still shuffling her feet against the rock floor she bent her body backwards down to her feet. Her belly muscles were bands standing out from her skin, nearly, and the oil rolled down her body and legs. As the palms of her hands touched the ground she collapsed in a twitching heap and began to set up a thin wailing noise against the steady chant and hand-beat that the rest of us were keeping up.

Another of them did the same as the first, and we chanted louder for her and still louder for the third. Then, while we still beat our hands and thighs, one of them took up the third, laid her across the altar and made her ready with a stone knife. The fire's light gleamed off the chipped edge of obsidian. As her blood drained down the groove cut as a gutter into the rock of the altar, we stopped our chant and the fires were snuffed out.

But still we could see what was going on, for these things were, of course, not happening at all – only seeming to happen, really, just as all the people and things there only seemed to be what they were. Only I was real. That must be why they desired me so.

As the last of the fires died Guru excitedly whispered: 'The Presence!' He was very deeply moved.

From the pool of blood from the third dancer's body there issued the Presence. It was the tallest one there, and when it spoke its voice was deeper, and when it commanded its commands were obeyed.

'Let blood!' it commanded, and we gashed ourselves with flints. It smiled and showed teeth bigger and sharper and whiter than any of the others.

'Make water!' it commanded, and we all spat on each other. It flapped its wings and rolled its eyes, that were bigger and redder than any of the others.

'Pass flame!' it commanded, and we breathed smoke and fire on our limbs. It stamped its feet, let blue flames roar from its mouth, and they were bigger and wilder than any of the others.

Then it returned to the pool of blood and we lit the fires again. Guru was staring straight before him; I tugged his arm. He bowed as though we were meeting for the first time that night.

'What are you thinking of?' I asked. 'We shall go now.'

'Yes,' he said heavily. 'Now we shall go.' Then we said the word that had brought us there.

The first man I killed was Brother Paul, at the school where I went to learn the things that Guru did not teach me.

It was less than a year ago, but it seems like a very long time. I have killed so many times since then.

'You're a very bright boy, Peter,' said the brother.

'Thank you, brother.'

'But there are things about you that I don't understand. Normally I'd ask your parents but – I feel that they don't understand either. You were an infant prodigy, weren't you?'

'Yes, brother.'

'There's nothing very unusual about that – glands, I'm told. You know what glands are?'

Then I was alarmed. I had heard of them, but I was not certain whether they were the short, thick green men who wear only metal or the things with many legs with whom I talked in the woods.

'How did you find out?' I asked him.

'But Peter! You look positively frightened, lad! I don't know a thing about them myself, but Father Frederick does. He has whole books about them, though I sometimes doubt whether he believes them himself.'

'They aren't good books, brother,' I said. 'They ought to be burned.'

'That's a savage thought, my son. But to return to your own problem—'

I could not let him go any further knowing what he did about me. I said one of the words Guru taught me and he looked at first very surprised and then seemed to be in great pain. He dropped across his desk and I felt his wrist to make sure, for I had not used that word before. But he was dead.

There was a heavy step outside and I made myself invisible. Stout Father Frederick entered, and I nearly killed him too with the word, but I knew that that would be very curious. I decided to wait, and went through the door as Father Frederick bent over the dead monk. He thought he was asleep.

I went down the corridor to the book-lined office of the stout priest and, working quickly, piled all his books in the centre of the room and lit them with my breath. Then I went down to the schoolyard and made myself visible again when there was nobody looking. It was very easy. I killed a man I passed on the street the next day.

There was a girl named Mary who lived near us. She was fourteen then, and I desired her as those in the Cavern out of Time and Space had desired me.

So when I saw Guru and he had bowed, I told him of it, and he looked at me in great surprise. 'You are growing older, Peter,' he said.

'I am, Guru. And there will come a time when your words will not be strong enough for me.'

He laughed. 'Come, Peter,' he said. 'Follow me if you wish. There is something that is going to be done—' He licked his thin, purple lips and said: 'I have told you what it will be like.'

'I shall come,' I said. 'Teach me the word.' So he taught me the word and we said it together.

The place we were in next was not like any of the other places I had been to before with Guru. It was No-place. Always before there had been the seeming passage of time and matter, but here there was not even that. Here Guru and the others cast off their forms and were what they were, and No-place was the only place where they could do this.

It was not like the Cavern, for the Cavern had been out of time and space, and this place was not enough of a place even for that. It was No-place.

What happened there does not bear telling, but I was made known to certain ones who never departed from there. All came to them as they existed. They had not colour or the seeming of colour, or any seeming of shape.

There I learned that eventually I would join with them; that I had been selected as the one of my planet who was to dwell without being forever in that No-place.

Guru and I left, having said the word.

'Well?' demanded Guru, staring me in the eye.

'I am willing,' I said. 'But teach me one word now—'

'Ah,' he said grinning. 'The girl?'

'Yes,' I said. 'The word that will mean much to her.'

Still grinning, he taught me the word.

Mary, who had been fourteen, is now fifteen and what they call incurably mad.

Last night I saw Guru again and for the last time. He bowed as I approached him. 'Peter,' he said warmly.

'Teach me the word,' said I.

'It is not too late.'

'Teach me the word.'

'You can withdraw – with what you master you can master also this world. Gold without reckoning; sardonyx and gems, Peter! Rich crushed velvet – stiff, scraping, embroidered tapestries!'

'Teach me the word.'

'Think, Peter, of the house you could build. It could be of white marble, and every slab centred by a winking ruby. Its gate could be of beaten gold within and without and it could be built about one slender tower of carven ivory, rising mile after mile into the turquoise sky. You could see the clouds float underneath your eyes.'

'Teach me the word.'

'Your tongue could crush the grapes that taste like melted silver. You could hear always the song of the bulbul and the lark that sounds like the dawnstar made musical. Spikenard that will bloom a thousand thousand years could be ever in your nostrils. Your hands could feel the down of purple Himalayan swans that is softer than a sunset cloud.'

'Teach me the word.'

'You could have women whose skin would be from the black of ebony to the white of snow. You could have women who would be as hard as flints or as soft as a sunset cloud.'

'Teach me the word.'

Guru grinned and said the word.

Now, I do not know whether I will say that word, which was the last that Guru taught me, today or tomorrow or until a year has passed.

It is a word that will explode this planet like a stick of dynamite in a rotten apple.

Robert Bloch

Yours truly, Jack the Ripper

I looked at the stage Englishman. He looked at me.

'Sir Guy Hollis?' I asked.

'Indeed. Have I the pleasure of addressing John Carmody, the psychiatrist?'

I nodded. My eyes swept over the figure of my distinguished visitor. Tall, lean, sandy-haired – with the traditional tufted moustache. And the tweeds. I suspected a monocle concealed in a vest pocket, and wondered if he'd left his umbrella in the outer office.

But more than that, I wondered what the devil had impelled Sir Guy Hollis of the British Embassy to seek out a total stranger here in Chicago.

Sir Guy didn't help matters any as he sat down. He cleared his throat, glanced around nervously, tapped his pipe against the side of the desk. Then he opened his mouth.

'What do you think of London?' he said.

'Why—'

'I'd like to discuss London with you, Mr Carmody.'

I meet all kinds. So I merely smiled, sat back, and gave him his head.

'Have you ever noticed anything strange about that city?' he asked.

'Well, the fog is famous.'

'Yes, the fog. That's important. It usually provides the perfect setting.'

'Setting for what?'

Sir Guy Hollis gave me an enigmatic grin.

'Murder,' he murmured.

'Murder?'

'Yes. Hasn't it struck you that London, of all cities, has a peculiar affinity for those who contemplate homicide?'

They don't talk that way, except in books. Still, it was an interesting

350

thought. London as an ideal spot for a murder!

'As you mentioned,' said Sir Guy, 'there is a natural reason for this. The fog is an ideal background. And then too the British have a peculiar attitude in such matters. You might call it their sporting instinct. They regard murder as sort of a game.'

I sat up straight. Here was a theory.

'Yes, I needn't bore you with homicide statistics. The record is there. Aesthetically, temperamentally, the Englishman is interested in crimes of violence.

'A man commits murder. Then the excitement begins. The game starts. Will the criminal outwit the police? You can read between the lines in their newspaper stories. Everybody is waiting to see who will score.

'British law regards a prisoner as guilty until proven innocent. That's *their* advantage. But first they must catch their prisoner. And London bobbies are not allowed to carry fire-arms. That's a point for the fugitive. You see? All part of the rules of the game.'

I wondered what Sir Guy was driving at. Either a point or a strait jacket. But I kept my mouth shut and let him continue.

'The logical result of this British attitude towards murder is – Sherlock Holmes,' he said.

'Have you ever noticed how popular the theme of murder is in British fiction and drama?'

I smiled. I was back on familiar ground.

'*Angel Street*,' I suggested.

'*Ladies in Retirement*,' he continued. '*Night Must Fall*.'

'*Payment Deferred*,' I added. '*Laburnum Grove. Kind Lady. Love from a Stranger. Portrait of a Man with Red Hair. Black Limelight*.'

He nodded. 'Think of the motion pictures of Alfred Hitchcock and Emlyn Williams. The actors – Wilfred Lawson and Leslie Banks.'

'Charles Laughton,' I continued for him. 'Edmund Gwenn. Basil Rathbone. Raymond Massey. Sir Cedric Hardwicke.'

'You're quite an expert on this sort of thing yourself,' he told me.

'Not at all.' I smiled. 'I'm a psychiatrist.'

Then I leaned forward. I didn't change my tone of voice. 'All I want to know,' I said sweetly, 'is why you come up to my office and discuss murder melodramas with me.'

It stung him. He sat back and blinked a little.

'That isn't my intention,' he murmured. 'No. Not at all. I was just advancing a theory—'

'Stalling,' I said. 'Stalling. Come on, Sir Guy – spit it out.'

Talking like a gangster is all part of the applied psychiatric technique.

At least, it worked for me.

It worked this time.

Sir Guy stopped bleating. His eyes narrowed. When he leaned forward again he meant business.

'Mr Carmody,' he said, 'have you ever heard of – Jack the Ripper?'

'The murderer?' I asked.

'Exactly. The greatest monster of them all. Worse than Spring-heel Jack or Crippen. Jack the Ripper. Red Jack.'

'I've heard of him,' I said.

'Do you know his history?'

I got tough again. 'Listen, Sir Guy,' I muttered. 'I don't think we'll get any place swapping old wives' tales about famous crimes of history.'

Another bull's-eye. He took a deep breath.

'This is no old wives' tale. It's a matter of life or death.'

He was so wrapped up in his obsession he even talked that way. Well – I was willing to listen. We psychiatrists get paid for listening.

'Go ahead,' I told him. 'Let's have the story.'

Sir Guy lit a cigarette and began to talk.

'London, 1888,' he began. 'Late summer and early fall. That was the time. Out of nowhere came the shadowy figure of Jack the Ripper – a stalking shadow with a knife, prowling through London's East End. Haunting the squalid dives of Whitechapel, Spitalfields. Where he came from no one knew. But he brought death. Death in a knife.

'Six times that knife descended to slash the throats and bodies of London's women. Drabs and alley sluts. August 7th was the date of the first butchery. They found her body lying there with thirty-nine stab wounds. A ghastly murder. On August 31st, another victim. The press became interested. The slum inhabitants were more deeply interested still.

'Who was this unknown killer who prowled in their midst and struck at will in the deserted alleyways of night-town? And what was more important – when would he strike again?

'September 8th was the date. Scotland Yard assigned special deputies. Rumours ran rampant. The atrocious nature of the slayings was the subject for shocking speculation.

'The killer used a knife – expertly. He cut throats. He chose victims and settings with a fiendish deliberation. No one saw him or heard him. But watchmen making their grey rounds in the dawn would stumble across the hacked and horrid thing that was the Ripper's handiwork.

'Who was he? What was he? A mad surgeon? A butcher? An insane scientist? A pathological degenerate escaped from an asylum? A deranged nobleman? A member of the London police?

'Then the poem appeared in the newspapers. The anonymous poem, designed to put a stop to speculations – but which only aroused public interest to a further frenzy. A mocking little stanza:

> *I'm not a butcher, I'm not a kid*
> *Nor yet a foreign skipper,*
> *But I'm your own true loving friend,*
> *Yours truly – Jack the Ripper.*

'And on September 30th, two more throats were slashed open.'

I interrupted Sir Guy for a moment.

'Very interesting,' I commented. I'm afraid a faint hint of sarcasm crept into my voice.

He winced, but didn't falter in his narrative.

'There was silence, then, in London for a time. Silence, and a nameless fear. When would Red Jack strike again? They waited through October. Every figment of fog concealed his phantom presence. Concealed it well – for nothing was learned of the Ripper's identity, or his purpose. The drabs of London shivered in the raw wind of early November. Shivered, and were thankful for the coming of each morning's sun.

'November 9th. They found her in her room. She lay there very quietly, limbs neatly arranged. And beside her, with equal neatness, were laid her head and heart. The Ripper had outdone himself in execution.

'Then, panic. But needless panic. For though press, police and populace alike awaited in sick dread, Jack the Ripper did not strike again.

'Months passed. A year. The immediate interest died, but not the memory. They said Jack had skipped to America. That he had committed suicide. They said – and they wrote. They've written ever since. Theories, hypotheses, arguments, treatises. But to this day no one knows who Jack the Ripper was. Or why he killed. Or why he stopped killing.'

Sir Guy was silent. Obviously he expected some comment from me.

'You tell the story well,' I remarked. 'Though with a slight emotional bias.'

'I've got all the documents,' said Sir Guy Hollis. 'I've made a collection of existing data and studied it.'

I stood up. 'Well,' I yawned, in mock fatigue, 'I've enjoyed your little bedtime story a great deal, Sir Guy. It was kind of you to abandon your duties at the British Embassy to drop in on a poor psychiatrist and regale him with your anecdotes.'

Goading him always did the trick.

'I suppose you want to know why I'm interested?' he snapped.

'Yes. That's exactly what I'd like to know. Why are you interested?'

'Because,' said Sir Guy Hollis, 'I am on the trail of Jack the Ripper now. I think he's here – in Chicago!'

I sat down again. This time I did the blinking act.

'Say that again,' I stuttered.

'Jack the Ripper is alive, in Chicago, and I'm out to find him.'

'Wait a minute,' I said. 'Wait – a – minute!'

He wasn't smiling. It wasn't a joke.

'See here,' I said. 'What was the date of these murders?'

'August to November 1888.'

'1888? But if Jack the Ripper was an able-bodied man in 1888, he'd surely be dead today! Why look, man – if he were merely *born* in that year, he'd be fifty-five years old today!'

'Would he?' smiled Sir Guy Hollis. 'Or should I say, "Would she?" Because Jack the Ripper may have been a woman. Or any number of things.'

'Sir Guy,' I said. 'You came to the right person when you looked me up. You definitely need the services of a psychiatrist.'

'Perhaps. Tell me, Mr Carmody, do you think I'm crazy?'

I looked at him and shrugged. But I had to give him a truthful answer.

'Frankly – no.'

'Then you might listen to the reasons I believe Jack the Ripper is alive today.'

'I might.'

'I've studied these cases for thirty years. Been over the actual ground. Talked to officials. Talked to friends and acquaintances of the poor drabs who were killed. Visited with men and women in the neighbourhood. Collected an entire library of material touching on Jack the Ripper. Studied all the wild theories or crazy notions.

'I learned a little. Not much, but a little. I won't bore you with my conclusions. But there was another branch of inquiry that yielded more fruitful returns. I have studied unsolved crimes. Murders.

'I could show you clippings from the papers of half the world's great cities. San Francisco. Shanghai. Calcutta. Omsk. Paris. Berlin. Pretoria. Cairo. Milan. Adelaide.

'The trail is there, the pattern. Unsolved crimes. Slashed throats of women. With the peculiar disfigurations and removals. Yes, I've followed a trail of blood. From New York westward across the continent. Then to the Pacific. From there to Africa. During the World War of 1914–18 it was Europe. After that, South America. And since 1930, the United States again. Eighty-seven such murders – and to the trained criminologist, all bear the stigma of the Ripper's handiwork.

'Recently there were the so-called Cleveland torso slayings. Remember? A shocking series. And finally, two recent deaths in Chicago. Within the past six months. One out on South Dearborn. The other somewhere up on Halsted. Same type of crime, same technique. I tell you, there are unmistakable indications in all these affairs – indications of the work of Jack the Ripper!'

I smiled.

'A very tight theory,' I said. 'I'll not question your evidence at all, or the deductions you draw. You're the criminologist, and I'll take your word for it. Just one thing remains to be explained. A minor point, perhaps, but worth mentioning.'

'And what is that?' asked Sir Guy.

'Just how could a man of, let us say, eighty-five years commit these crimes? For if Jack the Ripper was around thirty in 1888 and lived, he'd be eighty-five today.'

Sir Guy Hollis was silent. I had him there. But—

'*Suppose he didn't get any older?*' whispered Sir Guy.

'What's that?'

'Suppose Jack the Ripper didn't grow old? Suppose he is still a young man today?'

'All right,' I said. 'I'll suppose for a moment. Then I'll stop supposing and call for my nurse to restrain you.'

'I'm serious,' said Sir Guy.

'They all are,' I told him. 'That's the pity of it all, isn't it? They *know* they hear voices and see demons. But we lock them up just the same.'

It was cruel, but it got results. He rose and faced me.

'It's a crazy theory, I grant you,' he said. 'All the theories about the Ripper are crazy. The idea that he was a doctor. Or a maniac. Or a woman. The reasons advanced for such beliefs are flimsy enough. There's nothing to go by. So why should my notion be any worse?'

'Because people grow older,' I reasoned with him. 'Doctors, maniacs and women alike.'

'What about – *sorcerers*?'

'Sorcerers?'

'Necromancers. Wizards. Practisers of Black Magic?'

'What's the point?'

'I studied,' said Sir Guy. 'I studied everything. After a while I began to study the dates of the murders. The pattern those dates formed. The rhythm. The solar, lunar, stellar rhythm. The sidereal aspect. The astrological significance.'

He *was* crazy. But I still listened.

'Suppose Jack the Ripper didn't murder for murder's sake alone? Suppose he wanted to make – a sacrifice?'

'What kind of a sacrifice?'

Sir Guy shrugged. 'It is said that if you offer blood to the dark gods they grant boons. Yes, if a blood offering is made at the proper time – when the moon and the stars are right – and with the proper ceremonies – they grant boons. Boons of youth. Eternal youth.'

'But that's nonsense!'

'No. That's – Jack the Ripper.'

I stood up. 'A most interesting theory,' I told him. 'But Sir Guy – there's just one thing I'm interested in. Why do you come here and tell it to me? I'm not an authority on witchcraft. I'm not a police official or criminologist. I'm a practising psychiatrist. What's the connection?'

Sir Guy smiled.

'You are interested, then?'

'Well, yes. There must be some point.'

'There is. But I wished to be assured of your interest first. Now I can tell you my plan.'

'And just what is that plan?'

Sir Guy gave me a long look. Then he spoke.

'John Carmody,' he said, 'you and I are going to capture Jack the Ripper.'

That's the way it happened. I've given the gist of that first interview in all its intricate and somewhat boring detail, because I think it's important. It helps to throw some light on Sir Guy's character and attitude. And in view of what happened after that—

But I'm coming to those matters.

Sir Guy's thought was simple. It wasn't even a thought. Just a hunch.

'You know the people here,' he told me. 'I've inquired. That's why I came to you as the ideal man for my purpose. You number among your acquaintances many writers, painters, poets. The so-called intelligentsia. The Bohemians. The lunatic fringe from the near north side.

'For certain reasons – never mind what they are – my clues lead me to infer that Jack the Ripper is a member of that element. He chooses to pose as an eccentric. I've a feeling that with you to take me around and introduce me to your set, I might hit upon the right person.'

'It's all right with me,' I said. 'But just how are you going to look for him? As you say, he might be anybody, anywhere. And you have no idea what he looks like. He might be young or old. Jack the Ripper – a Jack of all trades? Rich man, poor man, beggar man, thief, doctor, lawyer – how will you know?'

'We shall see.' Sir Guy sighed heavily. 'But I must find him. At once.'

'Why the hurry?'

Sir Guy sighed again. 'Because in two days he will kill again.'

'Are you sure?'

'Sure as the stars. I've plotted his chart, you see. All eighty-seven of the murders correspond to certain astrological rhythm patterns. If, as I suspect, he makes a blood sacrifice to renew his youth, he must murder within two days. Notice the pattern of his first crimes in London. August 7th. Then August 31st. September 8th. September 30th. November 9th. Intervals of 24 days, 9 days, 22 days – he killed two this time – and then 40 days. Of course there were crimes in between. There had to be. But they weren't discovered and pinned on him.

'At any rate, I've worked out a pattern for him, based on all my data. And I say that within the next two days he kills. So I must seek him out, somehow, before then.'

'And I'm still asking you what you want me to do.'

'Take me out,' said Sir Guy. 'Introduce me to your friends. Take me to parties.'

'But where do I begin? As far as I know, my artistic friends, despite their eccentricities, are all normal people.'

'So is the Ripper. Perfectly normal. Except on certain nights.' Again that faraway look in Sir Guy's eyes. 'Then he becomes an ageless pathological monster, crouching to kill, on evenings when the stars blaze down in the blazing patterns of death.'

'All right,' I said. 'All right. I'll take you to parties, Sir Guy. I want to go myself, anyway. I need the drinks they'll serve there, after listening to your kind of talk.'

We made our plans. And that evening I took him over to Lester Baston's studio.

As we ascended to the penthouse roof in the elevator I took the opportunity to warn Sir Guy.

'Baston's a real screwball,' I cautioned him. 'So are his guests. Be prepared for anything and everything.'

'I am.' Sir Guy Hollis was perfectly serious. He put his hand in his trousers pocket and pulled out a gun.

'What the—' I began.

'If I see him I'll be ready,' Sir Guy said. He didn't smile, either.

'But you can't go running around at a party with a loaded revolver in your pocket, man!'

'Don't worry, I won't behave foolishly.'

I wondered. Sir Guy Hollis was not, to my way of thinking, a normal man.

We stepped out of the elevator, went towards Baston's apartment door.

'By the way,' I murmured, 'just how do you wish to be introduced? Shall I tell them who you are and what you are looking for?'

357

'I don't care. Perhaps it would be best to be frank.'

'But don't you think that the Ripper – if by some miracle he or she is present – will immediately get the wind up and take cover?'

'I think the shock of the announcement that I am hunting the Ripper would provoke some kind of betraying gesture on his part,' said Sir Guy.

'You'd make a pretty good psychiatrist yourself,' I conceded. 'It's a fine theory. But I warn you, you're going to be in for a lot of ribbing. This is a wild bunch.'

Sir Guy smiled.

'I'm ready,' he announced. 'I have a little plan of my own. Don't be shocked by anything I do,' he warned me.

I nodded and knocked on the door.

Baston opened it and poured out into the hall. He teetered back and forth regarding us very gravely. He squinted at my square-cut homburg hat and Sir Guy's moustache.

'Aha,' he intoned. 'The Walrus and the Carpenter.'

I introduced Sir Guy.

'Welcome,' said Baston, gesturing us inside with over-elaborate courtesy. He stumbled after us into the garish parlour.

I stared at the crowd that moved restlessly through the fog of cigarette smoke.

It was the shank of the evening for this mob. Every hand held a drink. Every face held a slightly hectic flush. Over in one corner the piano was going full blast.

Sir Guy got a monocle-full right away. He saw LaVerne Gonnister, the poetess, hit Hymie Kralik in the eye. He saw Hymie sit down on the floor and cry until Dick Pool accidentally stepped on his stomach as he walked through to the dining-room for a drink.

He heard Nadia Vilinoff the commercial artist tell Johnny Odcutt that she thought his tattooing was in dreadful taste.

His zoological observations might have continued indefinitely if Lester Baston hadn't stepped to the centre of the room and called for silence by dropping a vase on the floor.

'We have distinguished visitors in our midst,' bawled Lester, waving his empty glass in our direction. 'None other than the Walrus and the Carpenter. The Walrus is Sir Guy Hollis, a something-or-other from the British Embassy. The Carpenter, as you all know, is our own John Carmody, the prominent dispenser of libido-liniment.'

He turned and grabbed Sir Guy by the arm, dragging him to the middle of the carpet. For a moment I thought Hollis might object, but a quick wink reassured me. He was prepared for this.

'It is our custom, Sir Guy,' said Baston, loudly, 'to subject our new friends to a little cross-examination. Just a little formality at these very formal gatherings, you understand. Are you prepared to answer questions?'

Sir Guy nodded and grinned.

'Very well,' Baston muttered. 'Friends – I give you this bundle from Britain. Your witness.'

Then the ribbing started. I meant to listen, but at that moment Lydia Dare saw me and dragged me off into the vestibule for one of those Darling-I-waited-for-your-call-all-day routines.

By the time I got rid of her and went back, the impromptu quiz session was in full swing. From the attitude of the crowd, I gathered that Sir Guy was doing all right for himself.

Then Baston himself interjected a question that upset the applecart.

'And what, may I ask, brings you to our midst tonight? What is your mission, oh Walrus?'

'I'm looking for Jack the Ripper.'

Nobody laughed.

Perhaps it struck them all the way it did me. I glanced at my neighbours and began to *wonder*.

LaVerne Gonnister. Hymie Kralik. Harmless. Dick Pool. Nadia Vilinoff. Johnny Odcutt and his wife. Barclay Melton. Lydia Dare. All harmless.

But what a forced smile on Dick Pool's face! And that sly, self-conscious smirk that Barclay Melton wore!

Oh, it was absurd, I grant you. But for the first time I saw these people in a new light. I wondered about their lives – their secret lives beyond the scenes of parties.

How many of them were playing a part, concealing something?

Who here would worship Hecate and grant that horrid goddess the dark boon of blood?

Even Lester Baston might be masquerading.

The mood was upon us all, for a moment. I saw questions flicker in the circle of eyes around the room.

Sir Guy stood there, and I could swear he was fully conscious of the situation he'd created, and enjoyed it.

I wondered idly just what was *really* wrong with him. Why he had this odd fixation concerning Jack the Ripper. Maybe he was hiding secrets, too . . .

Baston, as usual, broke the mood. He burlesqued it.

'The Walrus isn't kidding, friends,' he said. He slapped Sir Guy on the back and put his arm around him as he orated. 'Our English cousin is really on the trail of the fabulous Jack the Ripper. You all remember Jack the Ripper, I presume? Quite a cutup in the old days, as I recall.

Really had some ripping good times when he went out on a tear.

'The Walrus has some idea that the Ripper is still alive, probably prowling around Chicago with a Boy Scout knife. In fact' – Baston paused impressively and shot it out in a rasping stage-whisper – 'in fact, he has reason to believe that Jack the Ripper might even be right here in our midst tonight.'

There was the expected reaction of giggles and grins. Baston eyed Lydia Dare reprovingly. 'You girls needn't laugh,' he smirked. 'Jack the Ripper might be a woman, too, you know. Sort of a Jill the Ripper.'

'You mean you actually suspect one of us?' shrieked LaVerne Gonnister, simpering up to Sir Guy. 'But that Jack the Ripper person disappeared ages ago, didn't he? In 1888?'

'Aha!' interrupted Baston. 'How do you know so much about it, young lady? Sounds suspicious! Watch her, Sir Guy – she may not be as young as she appears. These lady poets have dark pasts.'

The tension was gone, the mood was shattered, and the whole thing was beginning to degenerate into a trivial party joke.

Then Baston caught it.

'Guess what?' he yelled. 'The Walrus has a gun.'

His embracing arm had slipped and encountered the hard outline of the gun in Sir Guy's pocket. He snatched it out before Hollis had the opportunity to protest.

I stared hard at Sir Guy, wondering if this thing had carried far enough. But he flicked a wink my way and I remembered he had told me not to be alarmed.

So I waited as Baston broached a drunken inspiration.

'Let's play fair with our friend the Walrus,' he cried. 'He came all the way from England to our party on this mission. If none of you is willing to confess, I suggest we give him a chance to find out – the hard way.'

'What's up?' asked Johnny Odcutt.

'I'll turn out the lights for one minute. Sir Guy can stand here with his gun. If anyone in this room is the Ripper he can either run for it or take the opportunity to – well, eradicate his pursuer. Fair enough?'

It was even sillier than it sounds, but it caught the popular fancy. Sir Guy's protests went unheard in the ensuing babble. And before I could stride over and put in my two cents' worth, Lester Baston had reached the light switch.

'Don't anybody move,' he announced, with fake solemnity. 'For one minute we will remain in darkness – perhaps at the mercy of a killer. At the end of that time, I'll turn up the lights again and look for bodies. Choose your partners, ladies and gentlemen.'

The lights went out.

Somebody giggled.

I heard footsteps in the darkness. Mutterings.

A hand brushed my face.

The watch on my wrist ticked violently. But even louder, rising above it, I heard another thumping. The beating of my heart.

Absurd. Standing in the dark with a group of tipsy fools. And yet there was real terror lurking here, rustling through the velvet blackness.

Jack the Ripper prowled in darkness like this. And Jack the Ripper had a knife. Jack the Ripper had a madman's brain and a madman's purpose.

But Jack the Ripper was dead, dead and dust these many years – by every human law.

Only there are no human laws when you feel yourself in the darkness, when the darkness hides and protects and the outer mask slips off your face and you feel something welling up within you, a brooding shapeless purpose that is brother to the blackness.

Sir Guy Hollis shrieked.

There was a grisly thud.

Baston had the lights on.

Everybody screamed.

Sir Guy Hollis lay sprawled on the floor in the centre of the room. The gun was still clutched in his hand.

I glanced at the faces, marvelling at the variety of expressions human beings can assume when confronting horror.

All the faces were present in the circle. Nobody had fled. And yet Sir Guy Hollis lay there . . .

LaVerne Gonnister was wailing and hiding her face.

'All right.'

Sir Guy rolled over and jumped to his feet. He was smiling.

'Just an experiment, eh? If Jack the Ripper *were* among those present, and thought I had been murdered, he would have betrayed himself in some way when the lights went on and he saw me lying there.

'I am convinced of your individual and collective innocence. Just a gentle spoof, my friends.'

Hollis stared at the goggling Baston and the rest of them crowding in behind him.

'Shall we leave, John?' he called to me. 'It's getting late, I think.'

Turning, he headed for the closet. I followed him. Nobody said a word.

It was a pretty dull party after that.

I met Sir Guy the following evening as we agreed, on the corner of 29th and South Halsted.

After what had happened the night before, I was prepared for almost anything. But Sir Guy seemed matter-of-fact enough as he stood huddled against a grimy doorway and waited for me to appear.

'Boo!' I said, jumping out suddenly. He smiled. Only the betraying gesture of his left hand indicated that he'd instinctively reached for his gun when I startled him.

'All ready for our wild goose chase?' I asked.

'Yes.' He nodded. 'I'm glad that you agreed to meet me without asking questions,' he told me. 'It shows you trust my judgment.' He took my arm and edged me along the street slowly.

'It's foggy tonight, John,' said Sir Guy Hollis. 'Like London.'

I nodded.

'Cold, too, for November.'

I nodded again and half-shivered my agreement.

'Curious,' mused Sir Guy. 'London fog and November. The place and the time of the Ripper murders.'

I grinned through darkness. 'Let me remind you, Sir Guy, that this isn't London, but Chicago. And it isn't November 1888. It's over fifty years later.'

Sir Guy returned my grin, but without mirth. 'I'm not so sure, at that,' he murmured. 'Look about you. These tangled alleys and twisted streets. They're like the East End. Mitre Square. And surely they are as ancient as fifty years, at least.'

'You're in the poor neighbourhood off South Clark Street,' I said, shortly. 'And why you dragged me down here I still don't know.'

'It's a hunch,' Sir Guy admitted. 'Just a hunch on my part, John. I want to wander around down here. There's the same geographical conformation in these streets as in those courts where the Ripper roamed and slew. That's where we'll find him, John. Not in the bright lights of the Bohemian neighbourhood, but down here in the darkness. The darkness where he waits and crouches.'

'Is that why you brought a gun?' I asked. I was unable to keep a trace of sarcastic nervousness from my voice. All of this talk, this incessant obsession with Jack the Ripper, got on my nerves more than I cared to admit.

'We may need the gun,' said Sir Guy, gravely. 'After all, tonight is the appointed night.'

I sighed. We wandered on through the foggy, deserted streets. Here and there a dim light burned above a doorway. Otherwise, all was darkness and shadow. Deep, gaping alley-ways loomed as we proceeded down a slanting side street.

We crawled through that fog, alone and silent, like two tiny maggots floundering within a shroud.

When that thought hit me, I winced. The atmosphere was beginning to get *me*, too. If I didn't watch my step I'd go as loony as Sir Guy.

'Can't you see there's not a soul around these streets?' I said, tugging at his coat impatiently.

'He's bound to come,' said Sir Guy. 'He'll be drawn here. This is what I've been looking for. A *genius loci*. An evil spot that attracts evil. Always, when he slays, it's in the slums.

'You see, that must be one of his weaknesses. He has a fascination for squalor. Besides, the women he needs for sacrifice are more easily found in the dives and stewpots of a great city.'

I smiled. 'Well, let's go into one of the dives or stewpots,' I suggested. 'I'm cold. Need a drink. This fog gets into your bones. You Britishers can stand it, but I like warmth and dry heat.'

We emerged from our side street and stood upon the threshold of an alley.

Through the white clouds of mist ahead, I discerned a dim blue light, a naked bulb dangling from a beer sign above an alley tavern.

'Let's take a chance,' I said. 'I'm beginning to shiver.'

'Lead the way,' said Sir Guy. I led him down the alley passage. We halted before the door of the dive.

'What are you waiting for?' he asked.

'Just looking in,' I told him. 'This is a tough neighbourhood, Sir Guy. Never know what you're liable to run into. And I'd prefer we didn't get into the wrong company.'

'Good idea, John.'

I finished my inspection through the doorway. 'Looks deserted,' I murmured. 'Let's try it.'

We entered a dingy bar. A feeble light flickered above the counter and railing, but failed to penetrate the farther gloom of the back booths.

A gigantic Negro lolled across the bar. He scarcely stirred as we came in, but his eyes flickered open quite suddenly and I knew he noted our presence and was judging us.

'Evening,' I said.

He took his time before replying. Still sizing us up. Then he grinned. 'Evening, gents. What's your pleasure?'

'Gin,' I said. 'Two gins. It's a cold night.'

'That's right, gents.'

He poured, I paid, and took the glasses over to one of the booths. We wasted no time in emptying them. The fiery liquor warmed.

I went over to the bar and got the bottle. Sir Guy and I poured ourselves another drink. The big Negro went back into his doze, with one wary eye half-open against any sudden activity.

The clock over the bar ticked on. The wind was rising outside, tearing the shroud of fog to ragged shreds. Sir Guy and I sat in the warm booth and drank our gin.

He began to talk, and the shadows crept up about us to listen.

He rambled a great deal. He went over everything he'd said in the office when I met him, just as though I hadn't heard it before. The poor devils with obsessions are like that.

I listened very patiently. I poured Sir Guy another drink. And another.

But the liquor only made him more talkative. How he did run on! About ritual killings and prolonging life unnaturally – the whole fantastic tale came out again. And, of course, he maintained his unyielding conviction that the Ripper was abroad tonight.

I suppose I was guilty of goading him.

'Very well,' I said, unable to keep the impatience from my voice. 'Let us say that your theory is correct – even though we must overlook every natural law and swallow a lot of superstition to give it any credence.

'But let us say, for the sake of argument, that you are right. Jack the Ripper was a man who discovered how to prolong his own life through making human sacrifices. He did travel around the world as you believe. He is in Chicago now and he is planning to kill. In other words, let us suppose that everything you claim is gospel truth. So what?'

'What do you mean, "so what"?' said Sir Guy.

'I mean – so what?' I answered. 'If all this is true, it still doesn't prove that by sitting down in a dingy gin-mill on the South Side, Jack the Ripper is going to walk in here and let you kill him, or turn him over to the police. And come to think of it, I don't even know now just what you intend to *do* with him if you ever did find him.'

Sir Guy gulped his gin. 'I'd capture the bloody swine,' he said. 'Capture him and turn him over to the government, together with all the papers and documentary evidence I've collected against him over a period of many years. I've spent a fortune investigating this affair, I tell you, a fortune! His capture will mean the solution of hundreds of unsolved crimes, of that I am convinced.

'I tell you, a mad beast is loose on this world! An ageless, eternal beast, sacrificing to Hecate and the dark gods!'

In vino veritas. Or was all this babbling the result of too much gin? It didn't matter. Sir Guy Hollis had another. I sat there and wondered what to do with him. The man was rapidly working up to a climax of hysterical drunkenness.

'One other point,' I said, more for the sake of conversation than in any hopes of obtaining information. 'You still don't explain how it is that you hope to just blunder into the Ripper.'

'He'll be around,' said Sir Guy. 'I'm psychic. I know.'

Sir Guy wasn't psychic. He was maudlin.

The whole business was beginning to infuriate me. We'd been sitting here an hour, and during all this time I'd been forced to play nursemaid and audience to a babbling idiot. After all, he wasn't a regular patient of mine.

'That's enough,' I said, putting out my hand as Sir Guy reached for the half-emptied bottle again. 'You've had plenty. Now I've got a suggestion to make. Let's call a cab and get out of here. It's getting late and it doesn't look as though your elusive friend is going to put in his appearance. Tomorrow, if I were you, I'd plan to turn all those papers and documents over to the F.B.I. If you're so convinced of the truth of your wild theory, they are competent to make a very thorough investigation and find your man.'

'No.' Sir Guy was drunkenly obstinate. 'No cab.'

'But let's get out of here anyway,' I said, glancing at my watch. 'It's past midnight.'

He sighed, shrugged, and rose unsteadily. As he started for the door, he tugged the gun free from his pocket.

'Here, give me that!' I whispered. 'You can't walk around the street brandishing that thing.'

I took the gun and slipped it inside my coat. Then I got hold of his right arm and steered him out of the door. The Negro didn't look up as we departed.

We stood shivering in the alleyway. The fog had increased. I couldn't see either end of the alley from where we stood. It was cold. Damp. Dark. Fog or no fog, a little wind was whispering secrets to the shadows at our backs.

The fresh air hit Sir Guy just as I had expected it would. Fog and gin fumes don't mingle very well. He lurched as I guided him slowly through the mist.

Sir Guy, despite his incapacity, still stared apprehensively at the alley, as though he expected to see a figure approaching.

Disgust got the better of me.

'Childish foolishness,' I snorted. 'Jack the Ripper, indeed! I call this carrying a hobby too far.'

'Hobby?' He faced me. Through the fog I could see his distorted face. 'You call this a hobby?'

'Well, what is it?' I grumbled. 'Just why else are you so interested in tracking down this mythical killer?'

My arm held him. But his stare held me.

'In London,' he whispered. 'In 1888 . . . one of those women the

Ripper slew . . . was my mother.'

'What?'

'My father and I swore to give our lives to find the Ripper. My father was the first to search. He died in Hollywood in 1926 – on the trail of the Ripper. They said he was stabbed by an unknown assailant in a brawl. But I know who that assailant was.

'So I've taken up his work, do you see, John? I've carried on. And I will carry on until I do find him and kill him with my own hands.

'He took my mother's life and the lives of hundreds to keep his own hellish being alive. Like a vampire, he battens on blood. Like a ghoul, he is nourished by death. Like a fiend, he stalks the world to kill. He is cunning, devilishly cunning. But I'll never rest until I find him, never!'

I believed him then. He wouldn't give up. He wasn't just a drunken babbler any more. He was as fanatical, as determined, as relentless as the Ripper himself.

Tomorrow he'd be sober. He'd continue the search. Perhaps he'd turn those papers over to the F.B.I. Sooner or later, with such persistence – and with his motive – he'd be successful. I'd always known he had a motive.

'Let's go,' I said, steering him down the alley.

'Wait a minute,' said Sir Guy. 'Give me back my gun.' He lurched a little. 'I'd feel better with the gun on me.'

He pressed me into the dark shadows of a little recess.

I tried to shrug him off, but he was insistent.

'Let me carry the gun now, John,' he mumbled.

'All right,' I said.

I reached into my coat, brought my hand out.

'But that's not a gun,' he protested. 'That's a knife.'

'I know.'

I bore down on him swiftly.

'John!' he screamed.

'Never mind the "John",' I whispered, raising the knife. 'Just call me . . . Jack.'

John Keir Cross

The Glass Eye

There are things that are funny so that you laugh at them, and there are things that are funny but you don't laugh at them at all – at least, if you do, you aren't laughing because they amuse you: you are doing what Bergson says you do when you laugh – you are snarling. You are up against something you don't understand – or something you understand too well, but don't want to give in to. It's the other side of the familiar thing – the shadow turned inside out – the dog beneath the skin of the dog beneath the skin.

You can take, for example, the case of Julia. Is it possible to laugh at people like Julia? I have never been able to. Yet Julia is funny – there is something monumentally funny in that terrible gaunt shape, in those wide and earnest eyes, in the red, moist tip of that nose of hers that seems longer than any nose in the world. There is something funny in her uncanny genius for saying the wrong thing – but when she does say the wrong thing a whole world of tragic miscomprehension comes to the surface. The blue eyes smile seriously – the whole pose and attitude register the fact that a remark has been made. Behold! Julia seems to say – a remark, my friends, a remark! . . . And everyone shuffles a little and looks the other way, or hastily talks about something else.

For example: Some people with a young baby came to see my wife and me just after we were married. The mother went out for a walk, leaving my wife to look after the child. She suddenly said, glancing at the clock:

'Heavens, it's time I went upstairs to feed Celia's infant!'

And Julia (the blue eyes smiling) looked up from the magazine she was reading.

'Is it bottle-fed?' she asked . . .

367

Julia is over forty – forty-two, to be exact.

A friend of mine, a man who makes up verse for the magazines, wrote a poem about Julia. He called it:

To Julia: *A Song for a lost, mad girl.*

> *O, she thought she was in China*
> *And a million miles away,*
> *All among the tall pagodas*
> *Where the shining geishas play;*
>
> *And the mocking-birds were singing,*
> *And the lanterns burning red,*
> *And the temple bells were ringing –*
> *Softly, softly in her head.*
>
> *And those high and frozen mountains*
> *Brought her comfort in the night –*
> *Golden fish in silver fountains*
> *Wove her garments of delight;*
>
> *And the rich mimosa blossoms*
> *Scented all the shining air,*
> *And the mocking-birds were nesting –*
> *Quietly, quietly in her hair . . .*

Now, I want to tell you a story about Julia. Is it a funny story? I don't know – I just don't know. There are two people concerned in it, and in a sense they were both funny – Julia and this man, Max Collodi, I mean. But I don't think the story is funny. It is grotesque. There is one small twist in it, one odd and unaccountable thing . . .

I must tell you something first. If you call on Julia in her little flat in West Kensington where everything is just so – where the Burne-Jones panels by the mantelshelf harmonise so beautifully with the William Morris design on the wallpaper, where the volumes of the Tauchnitz edition of the Best English Authors smile on you from the bookshelves like rows of well-kept false teeth – if you call on her for tea, say, from the Japanese handpainted cups – you will see, on the mantelpiece, something that will haunt you more than any other thing in that room of ghosts. You will go away with your brows drawn together in a frown and your lips pursed up in an effort to understand, to piece things together. But you will see no more than it can see.

It is the story of that thing that I want to tell you – the story of that unaccountable Glass Eye, nestling on its little bed of black velvet on Julia's marble mantelshelf.

Somewhere in one of the philosophic books of the East there is another story about a Glass Eye. It concerns, if I remember rightly, a beggar who one day asked a philosopher for alms. The philosopher refused and went on his way. But the beggar was a trier and pursued him, shrilly demanding money. He pursued him right out of the city, till at last the philosopher stopped in exasperation and said:

'All right, I'll give you money. But on one condition. One of my eyes is a glass eye. Tell me which eye it is and you shall have all I possess.'

The beggar looked at him intently, and at length said solemnly:

'Your right eye, Master, is the glass eye.'

The philosopher was astonished.

'Tell me how you knew,' he cried. 'That eye was made by the greatest craftsman in the world – it should be impossible to tell it from a real eye. How did you know that my right eye was the glass eye?'

'Because Master,' said the beggar slowly, 'because your right eye was the one that had a compassionate look in it.'

Five years ago, when Julia was thirty-seven, she lived in a bed-sitting-room in a narrow-shouldered house between West Kensington and Fulham. It was a small room, with yellow wallpaper stained with damp at the corners. There was a marble-topped washstand with a flowered basin and ewer on it. The pictures on the walls were coloured engravings of old sailing ships – the landlady's father had been captain once of one of those long, slender vessels that had paddles as well as sails. On the mantelshelf was an eight-day clock, and in the tiled hearth stood a rusty gas-ring on which Julia did her cooking.

At this time Julia did not have the reasonably good job she has now. She was clerk to an old-fashioned solicitor, a man named Maufry, who still wore a square black top hat and wrote to his clients by hand, taking copies by the old moist-paper method.

The loneliness and desolation of Julia's life were appalling. She did not know any of us in those days, so she did not have even the slight companionship and relief we afford her. She got up in the mornings, made herself tea on the gas-ring and cooked a slice of toast before the gas-fire. She lunched cheaply at an A.B.C. tea shop, with a book propped up before her. In the evenings she cooked a simple meal – fried some gammon, perhaps, or a chop, and boiled some vegetables (all on the same gas-ring, of course – a complicated conjuring trick this, involving much juggling with pots and pans). Then, having washed up, she read, or wrote letters to her sister in Leicester. And went to bed, generally at ten or half-past.

What went on in her mind? Did she ever gaze at the engravings on the walls and wish she might sail in those vanished ships to unimaginable places? Did she, as she read her books – dull novels by dead authors about people who had never lived – did she ever permit herself to be wafted away in fancy to some other and more picturesque life, in Spain, Italy, Morocco? Did she long for a knock at the door? Did she hope that the young man in the flat above might come home drunk one night and enter the wrong room? Did she look back on the past and speculate on why it was that things had slipped so unnoticeably away from her?

That past of hers . . . Did she realise, do you think, that such lost souls as hers are doomed to fail in everything they touch? She was not a virgin: she had been seduced at the age of eighteen by an elderly Midlands business man she never saw again. She had been in love – at one time she had even been engaged (to a young man she had met on a holiday at a sea-side resort). But she never met the object of her love – a lecturer at a church discussion group she had once attended: and her fiancé, after six months' tergiversation, finally sent back her letters and the gifts she had showered on him, and disappeared. The last she heard of him he was living at Liverpool, having married a show-girl from Manchester. So, through the long years, old Maufry got all her devotion, and the small crippled son of her sister got all her love – her chilly and half-frightened love.

Once a year this child was sent to London to stay with Julia while his mother went to visit her husband's people in Wales. The spinster curtained off a corner of her room and borrowed a cot from her landlady for the boy to sleep in. She fed him magnificently, took him to cinemas and theatres, bought him toys and books galore. And he, a pale, large-headed child, with eyes like balls of putty, accepted everything unquestioningly. The only reward he ever gave her was a wan, abstracted smile.

It was late one summer, during one of Bernard's visits, that the tragic episode of the Glass Eye began. Julia had bought tickets for the Old Palace Music Hall in Fulham. She and Bernard sat in the red plush stalls indifferently watching the show. It began with an act by two acrobats, a man and a woman in white tights and spangled pantees. The only thrilling moment was when, at the end, the woman climbed a chromium-plated pole that was balanced on the man's chin. She slipped and almost fell. Julia, visualising the white-clad figure falling into the stalls – as seemed inevitable, on top of Bernard's crippled legs – clasped the boy convulsively to her. He looked up at her in surprise, repelled by the smell of camphor from her clothes. She, as the woman on the stage righted herself, felt sweeping over her an immense wave of relief and tenderness. For the rest of the first part of the programme she trembled violently from time to time, looking down at the pale, abstracted boy. If anything should happen to him, while he was in her charge! . . . She had an almost uncontrollable longing to touch the boy's bare, warped knees – only to touch him. She had never touched anyone.

After the interval there were some ballads by two stout operatic singers, then an eccentric cyclist took the stage, and then came the high spot of the show. It was announced on the programme thus:

MAX COLLODI
The Gentleman Ventriloquist
with his amazing
Dummy
'GEORGE.'

The curtain rose, and in a moment Julia forgot everything. She forgot Bernard, she forgot the little room with yellow wallpaper, she forgot Mr Maufry and the high stool on which she sat in his office. Only one thing in the world existed for her – the figure of Max Collodi.

As he sat there on the stage with the spotlight on him it was impossible to conceive anything more handsome. His dark hair gleamed, his jaw showed a slight blue shadow. His moustache was exquisitely clipped, his high square shoulders spoke of great strength. His temples were narrow, his eyes deep set, his chin was cleft, his teeth, when he spoke, shone like jewels.

George, the dummy on his knee, was a grotesque doll about three feet high, with a huge tow head and staring eyes. Its head moved quickly from left to right, its voice was high-pitched and nasal as it answered Max's questions with clumsy wit. Julia did not notice the act – she did not hear the cross-talk, paid no attention to the pathetic little song that George sang. She was staring at the incredibly handsome young man, watching every suave, slightly stiff movement. When the tab curtains swung together at the end of the act she was still staring, motionless, her blue eyes shining, the end of her long nose slightly and pathetically damp. In that one moment she realised that there could be no other man in all the world for her but Max Collodi. All the empty years, the acres of desolation, had been leading up to this glorious climax.

As if she were in a dream she took Bernard home. She gave him some hot Ovaltine and put him to bed in the cot behind the curtain. Then she went to bed herself and lay for a long time staring up at the dim ceiling and listening to the night noises. Footsteps, echoed through the open window from the street – the slow, measured footsteps of a policeman, the quick patter of a young man going home, from a dance perhaps, the strolling, mingled footsteps of lovers. Now and again, from somewhere inside the house, a board creaked. A mouse scuttled across the floor – shivering slightly she heard it scraping round the gas-ring, at the spot she had spilt some grease earlier in the day. From somewhere beneath her came the resonant snoring of the landlady.

And all the time, as she lay there, she was thinking of Max Collodi. She could not get his image out of her mind – but she did not want to get his image out of her mind. He was, she reckoned, thirty – thirty-two: only five years younger than she was. What had been his life? Was he (hideous thought – push it under) – was he married? Max Collodi, the Gentleman Ventriloquist . . . A ventriloquist. A man who could throw his voice. A superb accomplishment, it seemed. Thirty-two . . . She, if she took proper care, if she learned to make-up properly, might pass for thirty-five. Was he tall? All the time, on the stage, he had been sitting down – he had not risen even to take his curtain call. But he seemed tall – the broad shoulders vouched for his tallness. Max Collodi . . . A wonderful name – a name full of poetry. Max Collodi. Mrs Max Collodi. Madame Collodi. Or was it Señora Collodi?

She heard footsteps mounting the stairs outside. The young man in the flat above had come home. Suppose – suppose she *was* Señora Collodi? She was lying in the upper room of their villa in Italy – on the outskirts of Rome. Max had been appearing at the theatre. He was coming home, dead tired. It was his footsteps she could hear dragging up the stairs. In another moment the door would open. He would come in. He would get into bed beside her. She would hold him, she would comfort him, she would send him to sleep.

The footsteps passed, and a few moments later she heard the door of the flat above open and shut. She sighed and turned over in bed. Señora Collodi . . .

Next day, Bernard was due to leave for home. Julia got permission from Mr Maufry to have the morning off and took him to the station. She hardly noticed him. She kissed him goodbye mechanically, then sent a telegram to her sister to say that he was safely on the train. Then she had lunch – and for the first time in years she did not have it at the A.B.C. She went to a small café opposite the Old Palace Music Hall. There was just the chance, as she sat there, that she might see Max going in or coming out.

The afternoon passed somehow. Even old Mr Maufry noticed Julia's abstraction, but he attributed it to the fact that she had been seeing her nephew off. He himself was not feeling very well these days, so he gave Julia orders to close the office early, set his square hat firmly on his head and went woodenly off to his old-fashioned house out Chiswick way.

Julia, for her part, locked up the office, hurried home, boiled herself an egg by way of supper and then went out – to the Old Palace Music Hall. There, in a ferment of impatience, she sat through the acrobat act, the eccentric cyclist act, the ballad-singing act. By the time the indicator showed her that Max Collodi was next on the bill her heart was beating painfully, her hands had grown warm and clammy, her eyes were staring wide.

'Oh, I'm only a ventriloquist's doll,'

sang the ridiculous George –

'Only a ventriloquist's doll, that's all . . .'

But Julia did not care what George was. It was Max, his master, she was interested in. She stared at the well-groomed, suave, poised figure, smiling so gently and pityingly at George's *bêtises*. She noted the small bow that he gave to acknowledge applause, the gentlemanly restraint of him – so wonderfully unlike the exuberance of most Music Hall artistes. Max Collodi . . . Of course – he was made up. It was possible that off stage he didn't look *quite* so young. Thirty-five, perhaps. Yes – thirty-five . . .

The curtains swung together. The audience applauded. Julia sat still, entranced. They were applauding him – her Max. The curtains parted again. He was still sitting there, bowing a little and smiling, with the fatuous George grinning oafishly on his knee. Max looked straight ahead. By sheer will-power Julia tried to make him look in her direction – she had read of such things being possible. But perhaps her will was not strong enough. Max continued to look straight ahead, at the audience in general. It was impossible to believe that anyone could be so handsome. A woman in front said so in a loud whisper to her neighbour, and the neighbour replied with a sneer: 'Yes – *too* handsome, if you ask me.' Julia glared at her fiercely. She could have murdered her.

She walked home slowly. On a bill on the hoarding near her house she saw his name in large lettering – 'Max Collodi, the Gentleman Ventriloquist, with "George" . . .' She looked hastily about her to see no one was near, then quickly tore away that corner of the bill. In her room she straightened out the crumpled piece of paper and stared at it for a long time before tucking it away between the leaves of one of her favourite books.

Now I must ask you to believe what may seem to you, a normal human being, the impossible. But remember the thirty-seven desolate years, the long empty hours in that terrible room with its peeling yellow wallpaper and its engravings of long-lost ships. Remember the far-off seduction almost twenty years before, the broken engagement, the square, soulless hat of Mr Maufry. Remember the solitary meals conjured from that single gas-ring, the cold, unlovely love that had concentrated itself on the distant and unresponsive Bernard. And remember the story of the Eastern philosopher's Glass Eye. That other Glass Eye – the one that now rests on black velvet on Julia's mantelshelf – that is all that remains these days of Julia's affair with Max Collodi. A Glass Eye – a curious, even a terrible relic . . .

Every night, for the rest of that first week of her passion for Max Collodi, Julia paid her three shillings and sixpence to sit in the fauteuils (as they were called) at the Old Palace Music Hall. She sat with her gaunt fingers picking convulsively at the plush-covered arms of her seat: she sat with her earnest eyes fixed in fascination on the suave spotlighted figure of the ventriloquist: she sat with her long nose twitching, a minute drop of moisture forming always on the red tip of it.

She found, on the counter of a nearby newsagent's shop, a little pile of what professional theatricals call hand-outs – postcard size photographs of celebrities, with quotations from their press notices on them. Some of these featured Collodi, and without hesitation (but with a furtive look round to see that no one was watching) Julia swept half-a-dozen of them into her handbag. They showed the ventriloquist sitting with his dummy, George, on his knee. His signature – a large, bold scrawl – was written across the bottom right-hand corner of the photograph. The extracts from the notices were printed in a column on the reverse side of the card:

'. . . An extremely skilful exponent of the polyphonic art . . .'
'. . . Mr Collodi succeeds in convincing us in the course of his exhibition that the term "artist", so often misapplied these days, can still be used with accuracy to refer to a Music Hall performer . . .'
'. . . A great, a memorable display . . .'

Julia took the cards home, and placed them with the torn fragment of the playbill, in her copy of the *Journal of Marie Bashkirtseff*. She looked at them every night before going to bed. She looked at them every morning before setting off to work.

At the same newsagent's she bought, at the end of the week, a copy of *The Stage*. She knew (from her fiancé in the old days, who had always been interested in theatricals) that show people usually inserted notices in this journal to say what theatres they were appearing in. To her joy, Max Collodi had done this: after his engagement at the Old Palace he was due for a week's appearance at the Pavilion, Finsbury.

Every night she travelled across London and paid her three and six-pence to sit in the fauteuils of the Pavilion, Finsbury.

And the following week, acting as before on the information in *The Stage*, she paid her three and sixpence at the Hippodrome, Streatham.

I said I expected you to believe impossible things. This is one of them: the foolish infatuation of an ageing woman of great ugliness for a Music Hall performer. Julia was blind. Yet she did not have Glass Eyes. You, perhaps, are the one in the position of the Philosopher in the Eastern tale. She was the beggar – without his wit and acuteness.

The end of it was that when Max Collodi was going on tour (as she was informed by *The Stage*), Julia gave her employer, Maufry, a week's notice. She had a small capital, simply invested, accumulated through many years of saving: it was this that, with no thought for the future, she proposed living on while she followed Collodi about the country.

And she did one other thing. She wrote Collodi a letter.

I am not able to quote the letter – I don't know what it said. I know that somewhere in the course of it she asked if she might meet the ventriloquist. And I know that she got a reply, written in the large hand of the signature on the postcard (the hand of an egotist – or a man in need of asserting himself), to say that Mr Max Collodi was grateful for her praises, but that he never gave interviews.

I know also that Julia went on writing to Collodi. And that he went on replying. And that, as time passed, he seemed to grow warmer to-wards her – even friendly. Once – in Bradford – he asked her to send him a photograph: and Julia, with great trepidation, sent him a blurred snapshot taken long ago by her fiancé. She appeared in it sitting on a lawn against a background of fuchsia and veronica bushes – very shy, with her head to one side. A very old snapshot it was – a daylight-exposure print on matt paper. They had said, in those days, that it was the dead-spit of her: the bobbed hair caught up in a bandeau of Japanese silk, the frock with no waist that ended above the knee, the ear-rings of emerald cut glass – they were all very much a part of Julia at twenty-three. And she sent this snapshot to Max Collodi as a portrait – a dead-spit portrait – of Julia at thirty-seven. Close your left eyes, my friends – look at Julia with the Glass Ones.

* * *

It was at Blackpool that Julia eventually met Max Collodi, in a small hotel in a street off the Promenade – the Seabank Temperance Hotel, Bed and Breakfast 16/6. The meeting was the end of the episode – or the beginning of it.

It happened in this way.

Julia, in her letters to Collodi, kept suggesting that they might meet.

In the beginning he reiterated his statement that he never gave interviews. But later, as she grew more persistent and he more benevolent, he began to hint that a meeting might be possible. Perhaps it was the dead-spit portrait. Perhaps he wanted to savour the adulation at closer quarters. It was, I think he felt, worth risking. I said at the beginning of this tale that Max Collodi too, in his way, was funny.

In the letter he finally wrote consenting to a meeting and fixing a time and place, he made, like the true theatrical he was, certain conditions. She was to stay only for five minutes this first time. Later on, perhaps, if she still wanted to go on seeing him, they might arrange longer appointments. And he had (he said) an aversion in real life to strong light, being so much in his professional life under the glare of the limes and the footlights. So the hotel room would be dimly lit. If she did not mind (an arch touch this) being received in a half-lit hotel bedroom by a strange man, with no other chaperone besides his dummy, George, then would she go to the Seabank Temperance Hotel, Mortimer Street, Blackpool, at 10 p.m. on Saturday evening, after his show at the Winter Garden Theatre. And he would be happy to tell her something about himself and to hear, in his turn, something about her.

You will not want me to go into details about the hour and a half that Julia spent that evening before the mirror in the boarding-house at which she was staying. It was a large mirror with a chipped gilt frame. The quicksilver had come off from the back of it in sporadic, smallpox-like patches, and in one corner the glass was warped, so that you appeared curiously elongated in it, as if El Greco had painted you. Nor will I say anything about the agonies that Julia underwent before she could make up her mind what to wear. Did she, in the end, decide that there was no hope of appearing exactly like the dead-spit snapshot? Did she, with an unadmitted joy, bless Max for arranging the dimly-lighted room and an interview of only five minutes? Did she have qualms that when he had said 'if she still wanted to go on seeing him,' he might have meant: 'if I still want to go on seeing you'? It is impossible to answer these questions. I only speculate and tell the story.

At ten minutes to ten Julia was walking to and fro near the Seabank Hotel, waiting for the hour to strike. She was shivering – and not alone from the slight chill of the night. On all sides of her people were enjoying themselves. The town was ablaze with coloured lights, there were a thousand conflicting jazz tunes in the air, from the dance halls, from the piano-accordions and ukeleles of the young men and women who strolled about the Promenade in groups with little white paper hats on their heads that had 'Kiss me quick, Charlie' written round the brim. Beyond all these things was the sea, glittering under the lights but cold and detached, no part of the scene at all – the 'broad Atlantic' as Julia automatically referred to it, remembering all the books she had read.

She glanced at her watch. It was two minutes to ten. She pushed open the swing door of the hotel and walked up to the reception desk.

An old man, bald, with a hare lip, peered at her. She stumblingly asked for the number of Mr Max Collodi's room. Number Seven, he told her – on the first floor, stairway to her left.

She blushed a bit as she walked across the hall feeling his eyes on her back. As she mounted the stairs, taking care not to trip over the worn carpet where it had escaped from the brass stair-rods, she dabbed at the damp tip of her nose with a small scented handkerchief – Attar of Roses from Boots, at 4/6 the bottle. She prayed to God – and she believed in God – that no one would see her. And no one did – if you except the stucco cherubs that decorated the pillar tops of the Seabank Temperance Hotel.

She reached Number Seven.

'O God,' she prayed, 'help me, oh help me!'

She tapped on the door. His voice came through it to her – unmistakably his voice, the voice she had heard from her seat in the fauteuils of a hundred different Music Halls.

She repeated her prayer and walked in.

He was sitting facing her behind a large mahogany table. Even in the dim light she could not mistake him: every line of those handsome features was printed deep on her memory.

He inclined his head in the brusque, slightly stiff way she knew so well – it was the bow with which he acknowledged applause in the theatre.

'Dear lady,' he said. 'Pray sit down.'

And she timidly sat down – at the table, facing him. She did not know what to say – what was there to say? To gain time she quickly and nervously glanced round the room. An ordinary room, with flowered wallpaper. There was a high box-spring bed, the striped ticking of it showing beneath the bedcover of lilac damask. There was a wardrobe and a small chest-of-drawers – and (she noticed, God help her!) a white china chamber pot peeping out from the half-open door of a commode. Lolling grotesquely on a chair to Collodi's left was the dummy, George: a fantastic figure in that half light with its huge tow head and painted smile.

She looked quickly back at the ventriloquist. He had not moved – still held his head slightly forward. He was smiling in his chilly professional way. She remembered the woman in front of her at the Old Palace in Fulham – 'too handsome, for my liking . . .'

'Mr Collodi?' she said, hesitantly. Her voice sounded thin and false – not herself speaking at all, but someone else; someone else in her body, trembling, aching, sick in the stomach.

'Max Collodi, at your service,' he replied, still smiling.

And suddenly there swept into her, as she sat there, a terrible, an overwhelming desire. It was a desire she had experienced before, in the Old Palace, when it had seemed that the acrobat was going to fall on top of Bernard – the desire to touch. She wanted to touch Collodi – to touch his hand, his forehead, his blue-tinted jaw. And after those thirty-seven years this craving, gathered and condensed in this one moment, was not possibly to be denied.

She got up. She stood for a moment staring wildly, breathing in hasty, dry gasps. She walked quickly round the table and touched Collodi on the cheek with her gaunt quivering fingers. Then she screamed – or she made the movements of screaming, though no sound came from her but a terrible dry croak. For Collodi, with the fixed professional smile still on his face, toppled sideways and fell from his chair with a crash to the floor.

There was one moment of beastly silence and then there was a scream: but not from Julia or the someone else who seemed to have taken possession of her body. No. It came from the chair where George had been lolling grotesquely. Now, as she stared, it was to see George standing up on the chair, his hideous painted face twisted with rage and fear and sorrow. And, as she stared, she realised that at last she had met Max Collodi, the ventriloquist.

She started to laugh. Sobs of laughter shook her whole angular frame. She stared at the dummy on the floor – the beautiful staring face she had loved so much. And, not fully knowing what she was doing, she gave in to the storm that was racking her. Screaming terribly, she drove the high heels of her shoes into the padded body and waxen mask of the thing. It still smiled. One of its eyes shot out and rolled across the floor, but it still smiled. And all the time the misshapen being on the chair who was the real Max Collodi, the writer of that bold, assertive hand, the big-headed painted dwarf who had sat on the knee of the thing on the floor, who had spoken in two voices, a fair one and a foul one, working the movements of that handsome mouth and head by means of small pneumatic bulb controls – that misshapen, unlovable creature was weeping. How could he have hoped to get away with it? – he who was, in his own way, as hungry as Julia?

Gasping, blinded by her tears, Julia turned to run from the room. Her foot trod on something round and hard. She stooped half-wittedly to pick it up, then ran down the corridor, past the stucco cherubs, clutching it in her hand so tightly that it socketed itself in her palm. It was the

Glass Eye of the thing on the floor – the Glass Eye that now rests, as a terrible relic, on its black velvet bed on Julia's mantelpiece.

* * *

Well, that is the story of Julia and Max Collodi. I think of it every time I go to see her in that little flat where everything is just so. And I think of that other story about the Eastern Philosopher. And I wonder, every time I look at the thing on the mantelshelf: Which of my eyes is a Glass One?

I think of the thirty-seven years – forty-two years now. I think of the yellow wallpaper and the vanished ships and the white paper hats on the Promenade at Blackpool. I think of the A.B.C. lunches, the volumes of the Tauchnitz Edition, the broad, cold sea with the lights on it. And I think of my friend's verses:

> *O, she thought she was in China*
> *And a million miles away,*
> *All among the tall pagodas*
> *Where the shining geishas play;*
>
> *And the mocking-birds were singing,*
> *And the lanterns burning red,*
> *And the temple bells were ringing –*
> *Softly, softly in her head . . .*

There is one more word.

Max Collodi, the Gentleman Ventriloquist, made no more appearances. There are no notices about him in *The Stage*.

But about a year ago I had a letter from a friend of mine who was holidaying in Scotland.

'Things have been brighter here these past few days,' he wrote. 'A small travelling circus has been visiting the district. One of the clowns is a sad-faced, large-headed dwarf, about three feet high. He calls himself Maximilian. I've seen him several times walking in the village – a fantastic little figure. He has a beautiful voice, which comes (I don't know why it should) as a surprise. He has an odd affectation too (it must be an affectation, for he doesn't do it during his circus act): he wears a black patch over one of his eyes.'

My friend did not say which eye. Remembering the Eastern tale I have often wondered. Left? – or Right?

D'Arcy Niland

The Web

The old man was sitting in the drawing room, still and calm like a sculptor's model, the sun splashing weakly on his legs; and the boy came in from school, the red of the romp in his cheeks and his eyes bright.

'That you, Joe?'

'Hi, Gramp.'

They had known each other a week. The old man was still strange in the house, but he had encompassed the family, his daughter, her husband, both except the boy. The boy seemed to be walking around the outskirts of his friendliness, now and then edging over the line, but scuttling back again. He sensed about him a manner he could not fathom.

Now the boy threw his schoolbag down, went to the sideboard and picked up an apple. Slowly, he tiptoed towards his grandfather, cautiously moved all around him, taking in the big-boned frame, and warily moving to the front and staring at the serene blue eyes; staring.

He felt the impact of incomprehension; the incredulity of eyes that were eyes in every way, that looked at him and yet could not see him; and he knew in his own way the inertness of that mass that was yet alive; the helplessness. It horrified him.

'Have a good day at school, son?'

'Okay. Got the cuts for fightin', but.'

He saw the old man's mouth break open, while the expression of the eyes remained unaltered; and he saw on that part of the face under the eyes a curious vivacity of amusement.

Suddenly the boy's eyes shifted, his neck craned forward, and he said: 'Don't move, Gramp. There's a spider on your arm.'

He might have told the old man there was a stick of dynamite at his feet, for he was electrified into movement, while horror jumped on to his face, and he struggled forward in his chair, brushing his clothes wildly and blindly, and crying: 'Get it off me! Get it off me!'

The boy fell back in amazement at the alarm and panic in his grandfather. Then he bustled up to him and said: 'Keep still, and I'll get him. He's on your leg now. He's only a little one.' He slapped at the man's thigh and brushed the spider to the carpet, grinding it with his boot and making sounds of emphasis with his mouth.

'There, he's dead now. I got him.'

He saw the old man collapse in his chair, panting, his face chalky, and his hands shaking; trying to speak.

'I hate them things,' he muttered huskily.

'Well, he's dead now. I squashed him.'

'Good boy, Joe.' There was relief and pleasure in the old man's voice. He fumbled in his pocket, and the boy's face lit greedily at the jingle of coins. 'Here. Here's thrippence. You go and buy some lollies. That's the boy.'

The boy took the money and backed away, delighted, but still astonished at the change that had come over his grandfather.

A week later the boy with two of his schoolmates came up to the old man sitting in the back yard, and said: 'Gramp, did you ever eat aniseed balls?'

'Years ago.'

'Did you like them?' asked the boy eagerly.

'I certainly did.'

'Well, I know where I can get some, Gramp. Down at the corner shop. They're all in the window. Would you like me to get you some?'

The old man put his hand in his pocket, and with a chuckle handed the boy sixpence. 'You get some for you and your pals, Joe; I'll have some another day.'

'Gee, thanks, Gramp.'

That evening the old man's daughter said to him: 'You mustn't be giving money to Joe.'

'Only sixpence,' he said.

'I don't want you to do it, Father. He gets enough pocket-money without bothering you. And besides, I don't want him to be filling himself up with gut-rot all the time. Please don't give him any more.'

'All right,' he said. He knew the tone of her voice, and he was a prisoner of their stewardship. But he didn't mind giving the boy money. It was helping to bridge the gulf between them, coaxing the boy into fearless friendship, subtly easing away whatever strangeness it was that kept him vaguely remote.

When the boy asked again the old man refused him. The boy tried all sorts of subterfuges, but his grandfather would not relent. He told him he was short of change, or gave some other excuse. The boy was broodingly bitter. He had wanted the money especially. He was desperate in his rage, furious because he had suffered a knockback at what he had come to take for granted, and because there was no other source of extra income open to him.

'Mingy old cow,' he said with hate.

He affected not to hold any animosity. He had his scheme worked out. He tried it one day when his mother and father were out, and he was alone with the old man in the house.

He suddenly chirruped excitedly: 'Oh look, Gramp, there's another spider.'

'Where? Where?' cried the old man, disturbance shaking him again.

'It's not near you. It's on the table.'

'Kill it, then. Kill it. Don't let it come near me.'

'But it won't touch you, Gramp. It's on the table, I said.'

The old man was stumbling out of his chair, the sweat on his face. He sat still for a second, panting.

'Oh, it's moving across the table now. It's moving. Can spiders smell you, Gramp?'

'Kill it!' screamed the old man. 'Kill it before it drops to the floor.'

The boy watched with hypnotic delight, sensing the power that he wielded: this huge old man subject to him.

'What'll you give me if I kill it?' he breathed.

'Anything, anything. Where is it now?'

'Sixpence?'

'Yes, yes.'

The boy made a slapping sound. Then he breathed with triumph. 'Now it'll never get you, Gramp. Gimme the sixpence that you said you would. Oh, it's not quite dead. Gimme the sixpence, Gramp, and I'll squash it with the sixpence.'

The old man's money jingled and spilt in a jingle out of his hand. The boy gathered up the coins. He put sixpence in his pocket. Then he held out the money, and tipped it into the man's hand. The man searched with his fingers, and gave the boy sixpence.

'Thanks, Gramp. Gee, he was a big spider, too. Brown. Hairy legs.'

'Don't tell me about it!' yelled the old man. 'I don't want to hear about it. Get out of here. Are you sure you killed it?'

'Oh yes, Gramp. It's all squashed up. You can feel it here.'

'No, no. Get it away from me.'

The boy's lips eased apart over his sharp little teeth, and his hand was on the two sixpences in his pocket.

'Crikey, Gramp, I don't know what makes you so scared of spiders.'

'I hate 'em. I hated 'em all my life. I killed every one I saw. There's a lot of spiders in this house.'

'But you needn't worry, Gramp. I'll kill every spider I see, and I'll kill 'em just for you, and you needn't gimme any more than a penny if you don't want to.'

The old man's breathing came stiffly. He waved a hand: 'All right. All right. Leave me alone now. And don't tell your mother I gave you that sixpence.'

'No fear, Gramp. It's just a secret between you and me.'

He raced out joyfully.

The boy was very cunning. He didn't try again for a fortnight. And in the meantime, when he was sitting outside one day with the old man, the old man said: 'You don't dislike spiders, do you, Joey?'

'No, Gramp,' the boy said ingenuously.

'I hate 'em,' the old man said emphatically.

The boy got away with it once more. He waited until the old man was well on in his pitiable terror. Then he played for the stakes.

'Will you gimme a shilling if I kill it?'

As soon as he had said it, he noticed a sudden change in the old man; it was only momentarily, but he noticed it. The old man, still gripped in terror, only nodded.

'Gimme the shilling first, then,' the boy said warily.

When he had it he made a great business of killing the imaginary red-back; and he talked a lot, but the old man said nothing. He tried to get some assurance from the old man that he was a good boy, and had made the old man happy by killing the spider. But all he got was silence. He went away worried, yet defiant and joyous.

When he tried again, the old man's lips came together, and a great anger shook him: 'You dirty little blackmailer. Get out of my sight. Get out, or I'll tell your mother what sort of a son she's got. Get out!' he yelled. And the boy ran frightened at the wrath in him, but his blood on fire with hate.

The old man shook not with fear, but with a nervous emotion of un-pleasantness. Now he had driven the boy like a wild cat beyond the confines of his friendship. He had alienated him. Soon he began to sense the boy's loss about him, and that loss gave the silence chimeras which had never been there before. He began to see spiders as if the boy were pointing them out to him.

In his sleep at night it was not with the terror of an explosion that he awoke. The nightmare descent of dusty darkness and wheels of light spinning in his brain; and noises that were rescuers; and the fresh air meeting his face after the foul stink of the mine; and the great palling abyss of non-independence that had enclosed him until the words of his daughter in his ear gave him knowledge of security and care – four walls and a roof and a watcher.

That was terrible enough, but it was horror that woke him raving; drenched in sweat, crazily slapping at the bed-clothes, at the thousand crawling things on his flesh; and spitting out the spiders that crawled down his throat, their bulbous eyes seeking, and their hairy legs spiking his tongue. It was spiders, hundreds of thousands of them, creeping out of the darkness – the real ghosts of his sleep.

And there was one that came, standing on the floor; its body above the bed, black as tar and yellow-streaked, the hair bristling on it, its leg joints like fractured sticks, its eyes as big as oranges and its mouth scarlet. And swiftly it worked, netting the bed in silken cables, enmeshing him. He sobbed and ranted against it; and only a woman's voice full of agitation could assure him that it was driven away, and was no part, had never been a part, of that other darkness.

The old man tried to get on with the boy, speaking kindly to him, coaxing and cajoling, but he couldn't. Yet the boy did not worry him for weeks. He was thus not prepared for the incident when it did happen. He was sitting in the drawing room again, the sun through the window warming his legs. He was dozing. The boy, with a companion, sneaked into the porch, tiptoed to the door and looked in.

He put a finger to his lips and said in a whisper: 'You watch.'

Then he said in alarm: 'Oh, Grandpa, Grandpa, look! There's a spider!'

The old man started up, jabbering. Then his face darkened, and he cried out to the boy to get away.

'But Gramp, it's true. It's true,' piped the boy shrilly.

'You little devil, get when I tell you!'

'All right, don't believe me. He's on your knee! He's on your knee!'

The old man's mouth opened. Perhaps the boy was right. He slapped at his knee, the panic working up in him, the shock and terror paralysing and activating him.

Then he cried: 'You lying hound! God, if I only had my eyes.'

The boy grinned at his companion, who grinned back. Then he took a matchbox from his pocket, and edging closer to the agitated old man, opened the box and dropped the half-stunned spider on his hand, at the same time stepping back quickly and yelling: 'He's on your hand! Look out!'

The old man pulled his hand away with a ghastly expression on his face, and terror gurgling in his voice, and he smashed with his hands, squashing the spider against his knee, and then in a frenzy slapping it off, and rising to his feet, choking and sobbing, groping and blundering.

Then he heard the snickering titter of the boy, and the echo of it from the other, and he knew he was the dupe of a cruel joke; it went like a storm through him, and his hand closed on his walking stick; he went berserk, a scream of fury bursting from his iron lungs, as he swished blindly, the cane singing through space.

The boy fell back in fright as though caught in the vestiges of a tornado. His companion at the door bolted. The old man slashed and the sound of a globe shattered about his ears; glass and wood crashed and tinkled; and the boy's affrighted cries blabbed his whereabouts, pinpointed the target. He was screaming, darting behind chairs, under the table; the cane met his shoulder and cracked against his head, and cracked, and he fell with a sob, fell and crawled towards the door, bloody and stunned to a silence; and sat huddled on the threshold.

And then the old man, aware of the silence, stopped his swishing. He stood upright, gaping in horror. He dropped the cane from his nerveless fingers and cried out in a distracted voice: 'Joe! Joe!'

The silence shouted back, and it put him on the floor in a craze of fear, down on his hands and knees, groping and crawling, shrieking: 'Joe! Joe! Where are you, Joe?'

And the boy, numb with shock, watching him from the door, began to cry deeply with the outrageous self-pity of his experience.

C. M. Kornbluth

The Little Black Bag

Old Dr Full felt the winter in his bones as he limped down the alley. It was the alley and the back door he had chosen rather than the sidewalk and the front door because of the brown paper bag under his arm. He knew perfectly well that the flat-faced stringy-haired women of his street and their gap-toothed, sour-smelling husbands did not notice if he brought a bottle of cheap wine to his room. They all but lived on the stuff themselves, varied by whisky when pay cheques were boosted by overtime. But Dr Full, unlike them, was ashamed.

A complicated disaster occurred as he limped down the littered alley. One of the neighbourhood dogs – a mean little black one he knew and hated with its teeth always bared and always snarling with menace – hurled at his legs through a hole in the board fence that lined his path. Dr Full flinched, then swung his leg in what was to have been a satisfying kick to the animal's gaunt ribs. But the winter in his bones weighed down the leg. His foot failed to clear a half-buried brick, and he sat down abruptly, cursing. When he smelled unbottled wine and realised his brown paper package had slipped from under his arm and smashed, his curses died on his lips. The snarling dog was circling him at a yard's distance, tensely stalking, but he ignored it in the greater disaster.

With stiff fingers as he sat in the filth of the alley, Dr Full unfolded the brown paper bag's top, which had been crimped over, grocer-wise. The early autumnal dusk had come; he could not see plainly what was left. He lifted out the jug-handled top of his half-gallon, and some fragments, and then the bottom of the bottle. Dr Full was far too occupied to exult as he noted that there was a good pint left. He had a problem, and emotions could be deferred until the fitting time.

The dog closed in, its snarl rising in pitch. He set down the bottom of the bottle and pelted the dog with the curved triangular glass fragments of its top. One of them connected, and the dog ducked back through the fence, howling. Dr Full then placed a razorlike edge of the half-gallon bottle's foundation to his lips and drank from it as though it were a giant's cup. Twice he had to put it down to rest his arms, but in one minute he had swallowed the pint of wine.

He thought of rising to his feet and walking through the alley to his room, but a flood of well-being drowned the notion. It was, after all, inexpressibly pleasant to sit there and feel the frost-hardened mud of the alley turn soft, or seem to, and to feel the winter evaporating from his bones under a warmth which spread from his stomach through his limbs.

A three-year-old girl in a cut-down winter coat squeezed through the same hole in the board fence from which the black dog had sprung its ambush. Gravely she toddled up to Dr Full and inspected him, with her dirty forefinger in her mouth. Dr Full's happiness had been providentially made complete; he had been supplied with an audience.

'Ah, my dear,' he said hoarsely. And then: 'Preposserous accusation. "If that's what you call evidence," I should have told them, "you better stick to your doctoring." I should have told them: "I was here before your County Medical Society. And the Licence Commissioner never proved a thing on me. So, gennulmen, doesn't it stand to reason? I appeal to you as fellow memmers of a great profession—" '

The little girl, bored, moved away, picking up one of the triangular pieces of glass to play with as she left. Dr Full forgot her immediately, and continued to himself earnestly: 'But so help me, they *couldn't* prove a thing. Hasn't a man got any *rights*?' He brooded over the question, of whose answer he was so sure, but on which the Committee on Ethics of the County Medical Society had been equally certain. The winter was creeping into his bones again, and he had no money and no more wine.

Dr Full pretended to himself that there was a bottle of whisky somewhere in the fearful litter of his room. It was an old and cruel trick he played on himself when he simply had to be galvanised into getting up and going home. He might freeze there in the alley. In his room he would be bitten by bugs and would cough at the mouldy reek from his sink, but he would not freeze and be cheated of the hundreds of bottles of wine that he still might drink, the thousands of hours of glowing content he still might feel. He thought about that bottle of whisky – was it back of a mounded heap of medical journals? No; he had looked there last time. Was it under the sink, shoved well to the rear, behind the rusty drain? The cruel trick began to play itself out again. Yes, he told himself with mounting excitement, yes, it might be! Your memory isn't so good nowadays, he told himself with rueful good-fellowship. You know perfectly well you might have bought a bottle of whisky and shoved it behind the sink drain for a moment just like this.

The amber bottle, the crisp snap of the sealing as he cut it, the pleasureable exertion of starting the screw cap on its threads, and then the refreshing tangs in his throat, the warmth in his stomach, the dark, dull happy oblivion of drunkenness – they became real to him. You *could* have, you know! You *could* have! he told himself. With the blessed conviction growing in his mind – it *could* have happened, you know! It *could* have! – he struggled to his right knee. As he did, he heard a yelp behind him, and curiously craned his neck around while resting. It was the little girl, who had cut her hand quite badly on her toy, the piece of glass. Dr Full could see the rilling bright blood down her coat, pooling at her feet.

He almost felt inclined to defer the image of the amber bottle for her, but not seriously. He knew that it was there, shoved well to the rear under the sink, behind the rusty drain where he had hidden it. He would have a drink and then magnanimously return to help the child. Dr Full got to his other knee and then his feet, and proceeded at a rapid totter down the littered alley towards his room, where he would hunt with calm optimism at first for the bottle that was not there, then with anxiety, and then with frantic violence. He would hurl books and dishes about before he was done looking for the amber bottle of whisky, and finally would beat his swollen knuckles against the brick wall until old scars on them opened and his thick old blood oozed over his hands. Last of all, he would sit down somewhere on the floor, whimpering, and would plunge into the abyss of purgulent nightmare that was his sleep.

After twenty generations of shilly-shallying and 'we'll cross that bridge when we come to it', *genus homo* had bred himself into an impasse. Dogged biometricians had pointed out with irrefutable logic that mental subnormals were outbreeding mental normals and supernormals, and that the process was occurring on an exponential curve. Every fact that could be mustered in the argument proved the biometricians' case, and led inevitably to the conclusion that *genus homo* was going to wind up in a preposterous jam quite soon. If you think that had any effect on breeding practices, you do not know *genus homo*.

There was, of course, a sort of masking effect produced by that other exponential function, the accumulation of technological devices. A moron trained to punch an adding machine seems to be a more skilful computer than a medieval mathematician trained to count on his fingers. A moron trained to operate the twenty-first century equivalent of a linotype seems to be a better typographer than a Renaissance printer limited to a few founts of movable type. This is also true of medical practice.

It was a complicated affair of many factors. The supernormals 'improved the product' at greater speed than the subnormals degraded it, but in smaller quantity because elaborate training of their children was practised on a custom-made basis. The fetish of higher education had some weird avatars by the twentieth generation: 'colleges' where not a member of the student body could read words of three syllables; 'universities' where such degrees as 'Bachelor of Typewriting', 'Master of Shorthand' and 'Doctor of Philosophy (Card Filing)' were conferred, with the traditional pomp. The handful of supernormals used such devices in order that the vast majority might keep some semblance of a social order going.

Some day the supernormals would mercilessly cross the bridge; at the twentieth generation they were standing irresolutely at its approaches wondering what had hit them. And the ghosts of twenty generations of biometricians chuckled malignantly.

It is a certain Doctor of Medicine of this twentieth generation that we are concerned with. His name was Hemingway – John Hemingway, B.Sc., M.D. He was a general practitioner, and did not hold with running to specialists with every trifling ailment. He often said as much, in approximately these words: 'Now, uh, what I mean is you got a good old G.P. See what I mean? Well, uh, now a good old G.P. don't claim he knows all about lungs and glands and them things, get me? But you got a G.P., you got, uh, you got a, well, you got a . . . *all-round man*! That's what you got when you got a G.P. – you got a all-round man.'

But from this, do not imagine that Dr Hemingway was a poor doctor. He could remove tonsils or appendixes, assist at practically any confinement and deliver a living, uninjured infant, correctly diagnose hundreds of ailments and prescribe and administer the correct medication or treatment for each. There was, in fact, only one thing he could not do in the medical line, and that was violate the ancient canons of medical ethics. And Dr Hemingway knew better than to try.

Dr Hemingway and a few friends were chatting one evening when the event occurred that precipitates him into our story. He had been through a hard day at the clinic, and he wished his physicist friend Walter Gillis, B.Sc., M.Sc., Ph.D., would shut up so he could tell everybody about it. But Gillis kept rambling on, in his stilted fashion: 'You got to hand it to old Mike; he don't have what we call the scientific method, but you got to hand it to him. There this poor little dope is, puttering around with some glassware and I come up and I ask him, kidding of course, "How's about a time-travel machine, Mike?" '

Dr Gillis was not aware of it, but 'Mike' had an I.Q. six times his own, and was – to be blunt – his keeper. 'Mike' rode herd on the pseudo-physicists in the pseudo-laboratory, in the guise of a bottle washer. It was a social waste – but as has been mentioned before, the supernormals were still standing at the approaches to a bridge. Their irresolution led to many such preposterous situations. And it happens that 'Mike', having grown frantically bored with his task, was malevolent enough to . . . but let Dr Gillis tell it:

'So he gives me those here tube numbers and says, "Series circuit. Now stop bothering me. Build your time machine, sit down at it and turn on the switch. That's all I ask, Dr Gillis – that's all I ask." '

'Say,' marvelled a brittle and lovely blonde guest, 'you remember real good, don't you, doc?' She gave him a melting smile.

'Heck,' said Gillis modestly, 'I always remember good. It's what you call an inherent facility. And besides I told it quick to my secretary, so she wrote it down. I don't read so good, but I sure remember good, all right. Now, where was I?'

Everybody thought hard, and there were various suggestions:

'Something about bottles, doc?'

'You was starting a fight. You said, "Time somebody was travelling." '

'Yeah – you called somebody a swish. Who did you call a swish?'

'Not swish – *switch*.'

Dr Gillis' noble brow grooved with thought, and he declared: 'Switch is right. It was about time travel. What we call travel through time. So I took the tube numbers he gave me and I put them into the circuit builder, I set it for "series" and there it is – my time-travelling machine. It travels things through time real good.' He displayed a box.

'What's in the box?' asked the lovely blonde.

Dr Hemingway told her: 'Time travel. It travels things through time.'

'Look,' said Gillis, the physicist. He took Dr Hemingway's little black bag and put it on the box. He turned on the switch and the little black bag vanished.

'Say,' said Dr Hemingway, 'that was, uh, swell. Now bring it back.'

'Huh?'

'Bring back my little black bag.'

'Well,' said Dr Gillis, 'they don't come back. I tried it backwards and they don't come back. I guess maybe that dummy Mike give me a bum steer.'

There was wholesale condemnation of 'Mike' but Dr Hemingway took no part in it. He was nagged by a vague feeling that there was something he would have to do. He reasoned: 'I am a doctor, and a doctor has got to have a little black bag. I ain't got a little black bag – so ain't I a doctor no more?' He decided that this was absurd. He *knew* he was a doctor. So it must be the bag's fault for not being there. It was no good, and he would get another one tomorrow from that dummy Al, at the clinic. Al could find things good, but he was a dummy – never liked to talk sociable to you.

So the next day Dr Hemingway remembered to get another little black bag from his keeper – another little black bag with which he could perform tonsilectomies, appendectomies and the most difficult confinements, and with which he could diagnose and cure his kind until the day when the supernormals could bring themselves to cross that bridge. Al was kinda nasty about the missing little black bag, but Dr Hemingway didn't exactly remember what had happened, so no tracer was sent out, so. . . .

Old Dr Full awoke from the horrors of the night to the horrors of the day. His gummy eyelashes pulled apart convulsively. He was propped against a corner of his room, and something was making a little drumming noise. He felt very cold and cramped. As his eyes focused on his lower body, he croaked out a laugh. The drumming noise was being made by his left heel, agitated by fine tremors against the bare floor. It was going to be the D.T.s again, he decided dispassionately. He wiped his mouth with his bloody knuckles, and the fine tremor coarsened; the snare-drum beat became louder and slower. He was getting a break this fine morning, he decided sardonically. You didn't get the horrors until you had been tightened like a violin string, just to the breaking point. He had a reprieve, if a reprieve into his old body with the blazing, endless headache just back of his eyes and the screaming stiffness in the joints were anything to be thankful for.

There was something or other about a kid, he thought vaguely. He was going to doctor some kid. His eyes rested on a little black bag in the centre of the room, and he forgot about the kid. 'I could have sworn,' said Dr Full, 'I hocked that two years ago!' He hitched over and reached the bag, and then realised it was some stranger's kit, arriving here he did not know how. He tentatively touched the lock and it snapped open and lay flat, rows and rows of instruments and medications tucked into loops in its four walls. It seemed vastly larger open than closed. He didn't see how it could possibly fold up into that compact size again, but decided it was some stunt of the instrument makers. Since his time – that made it worth more at the hock shop, he thought with satisfaction.

Just for old times' sake, he let his eyes and fingers rove over the instruments before he snapped the bag shut and headed for Uncle's. More than a few were a little hard to recognise – exactly that. You could see the things with blades for cutting, the forceps for holding and pulling, the retractors for holding fast, the needles and gut for suturing, the hypos – a fleeting thought crossed his mind that he could peddle the hypos separately to drug addicts.

Let's go, he decided, and tried to fold up the case. It didn't fold until he happened to touch the lock, and then it folded all at once into a little black bag. Sure have forged ahead, he thought, almost able to forget that what he was primarily interested in was its pawn value.

With a definite objective, it was not too hard for him to get to his feet. He decided to go down the front steps, out the front door and down the sidewalk. But first. . . .

He snapped the bag open again on his kitchen table, and pored through the medication tubes. 'Anything to sock the autonomic nervous system good and hard,' he mumbled. The tubes were numbered, and there was a plastic card which seemed to list them. The left margin of the card was a rundown of the systems – vascular, muscular, nervous. He followed the last entry across to the right. There were columns for 'stimulant', 'depressant', and so on. Under 'nervous system' and 'depressant' he found the number 17, and shakily located the little glass tube which bore it. It was full of pretty blue pills and he took one.

It was like being struck by a thunderbolt.

Dr Full had so long lacked any sense of well-being except the brie glow of alcohol that he had forgotten its very nature. He was panic-stricken for a long moment at the sensation that spread through him slowly, finally tingling in his fingertips. He straightened up, his pains gone and his leg tremor stilled.

That was great, he thought. He'd be able to *run* to the hock shop, pawn the little black bag and get some booze. He started down the stairs. Not even the street, bright with midmorning sun, into which he emerged made him quail. The little black bag in his left hand had a satisfying, authoritative weight. He was walking erect, he noted, and not in the somewhat furtive crouch that had grown on him in recent years. A little self-respect, he told himself, that's what I need. Just because a man's down doesn't mean—

'Docta, please-a come wit'!' somebody yelled at him, tugging his arm. 'Da litt-la girl, she's-a burn' up!' It was one of the slum's innumerable flat-faced, stringy-haired women, in a slovenly wrapper.

'Ah, I happen to be retired from practice –' he began hoarsely, but she would not be put off.

'In by here, docta!' she urged, tugging him to a doorway. 'You come look-a da litt-la girl. I got two dolla, you come look!' That put a different complexion on the matter. He allowed himself to be towed through the doorway into a mussy, cabbage-smelling flat. He knew the woman now, or rather knew who she must be – a new arrival who had moved in the other night. These people moved at night, in motorcades of battered cars supplied by friends and relations, with furniture lashed to the tops, swearing and drinking until the small hours. It explained why she had stopped him: she did not yet know he was old Dr Full, a drunken reprobate whom nobody would trust. The little black bag had been his guarantee, outweighing his whiskery face and stained black suit.

He was looking down on a three-year-old girl who had, he rather suspected, just been placed in the mathematical centre of a freshly changed double bed. God knew what sour and dirty mattress she usually slept on. He seemed to recognise her as he noted a crusted bandage on her right hand. Two dollars, he thought. . . . An ugly flush had spread up her pipestem arm. He poked a finger into the socket of her elbow, and felt little spheres like marbles under the skin and ligaments roll apart. The child began to squall thinly; beside him, the woman gasped and began to weep herself.

'Out,' he gestured briskly at her, and she thudded away, still sobbing.

Two dollars, he thought – give her some mumbo jumbo, take the money and tell her to go to a clinic. Strep, I guess, from that stinking alley. It's a wonder any of them grow up. He put down the little black bag and forgetfully fumbled for his key, then remembered and touched the lock. It flew open, and he selected a bandage shears, with a blunt wafer for the lower jaw. He fitted the lower jaw under the bandage, trying not to hurt the kid by its pressure on the infection, and began to cut. It was amazing how easily and swiftly the shining shears snipped through the crusty rag around the wound. He hardly seemed to be driving the shears with fingers at all. It almost seemed as though the shears were driving his fingers instead as they scissored a clean, light line through the bandage.

Certainly have forged ahead since my time, he thought – sharper than a microtome knife. He replaced the shears in their loop on the extraordinarily big board that the little black bag turned into when it unfolded, and leaned over the wound. He whistled at the ugly gash, and the violent infection which had taken immediate root in the sickly child's thin body. Now what can you do with a thing like that? He pawed over the contents of the little black bag, nervously. If he lanced it and let some of the pus out, the old woman would think he'd done something for her and he'd get the two dollars. But at the clinic they'd want to know who did it and if they got sore enough they might send a cop around. Maybe there was something in the kit. . . .

He ran down the left edge of the card to 'lymphatic' and read across to the column under 'infection'. It didn't sound right at all to him; he checked again, but it still said that. In the square to which the line and column led were the symbols: 'IV-g-3cc.' He couldn't find any bottles marked with Roman numerals, and then noticed that that was how the hypodermic needles were designated. He lifted number IV from its loop, noting that it was fitted with a needle already and even seemed to be charged. What a way to carry those things around! So – three c.c.s o whatever was in hypo number IV ought to do something or other about infections settled in the lymphatic system – which, God knows, this one was. What did the lower case 'g' mean, though? He studied the glass hypo and saw letters engraved on what looked like a rotating disc at the top of the barrel. They ran from 'a' to 'i', and there was an index line engraved on the barrel on the opposite side from the calibrations.

Shrugging, old Dr Full turned the disc until 'g' coincided with the index line, and lifted the hypo to eye level. As he pressed in the plunger h˙ did not see the tiny thread of fluid squirt from the tip of the needle. There was a sort of dark mist for a moment about the tip. A closer inspection showed that the needle was not even pierced at the tip. It had the usual slanting cut across the bias of the ɔhaft, but the cut did not expose an oval hole. Baffled, he tried pressing the plunger again. Again *something* appeared around the tip and vanished. 'We'll settle this,' said the doctor. He slipped the needle into the skin of his forearm. He thought at first that he had missed – that the point had glided over the top of his skin instead of catching and slipping under it. But he saw a tiny blood spot and realised that somehow he just hadn't felt the puncture. Whatever was in the barrel, he decided, couldn't do him any harm if it lived up to its billing – and if it could come out through a needle that had no hole. He gave himself three c.c. and twitched the needle out. There was the swelling – painless, but otherwise typical.

Dr Full decided it was his eyes or something, and gave three c.c. of 'g' from hypodermic IV to the feverish child. There was no interruption to her wailing as the needle went in and the swelling rose. But a long instant later, she gave a final gasp and was silent.

Well, he told himself, cold with horror, you did it that time. You killed her with that stuff.

Then the child sat up and said: 'Where's my mommy?'

Incredulously, the doctor seized her arm and palpated the elbow. The gland infection was zero, and the temperature seemed normal. The blood-congested tissues surrounding the wound were subsiding as he watched. The child's pulse was stronger and no faster than a child's should be. In the sudden silence of the room he could hear the little girl's mother sobbing in her kitchen, outside. And he also heard a girl's insinuating voice:

'She gonna be O.K., doc?'

He turned and saw a gaunt-faced, dirty-blonde sloven of perhaps eighteen leaning in the doorway and eyeing him with amused contempt. She continued: 'I heard about you, *Doc-tor* Full. So don't go try and put the bite on the old lady. You couldn't doctor up a sick cat.'

'Indeed?' he rumbled. This young person was going to get a lesson she richly deserved. 'Perhaps you would care to look at my patient?'

'Where's my mommy?' insisted the little girl, and the blonde's jaw fell. She went to the bed and cautiously asked: 'You O.K. now, Teresa? You all fixed up?'

'Where's my mommy?' demanded Teresa. Then, accusingly, she gestured with her wounded hand at the doctor. 'You *poke* me!' she complained, and giggled pointlessly.

'Well –' said the blonde girl, 'I guess I got to hand it to you, doc. These loudmouth women around here said you didn't know your . . . I mean, didn't know how to cure people. They said you ain't a real doctor.'

'I *have* retired from practice,' he said. 'But I happened to be taking this case to a colleague as a favour, your good mother noticed me, and –' a deprecating smile. He touched the lock of the case and it folded up into the little black bag again.

'You stole it,' the girl said flatly.

He sputtered.

'Nobody'd trust you with a thing like that. It must be worth plenty. You stole that case. I was going to stop you when I come in and saw you working over Teresa, but it looked like you wasn't doing her any harm. But when you give me that line about taking that case to a colleague I know you stole it. You gimme a cut or I go to the cops. A thing like that must be worth twenty-thirty dollars.'

The mother came timidly in, her eyes red. But she let out a whoop of joy when she saw the little girl sitting up and babbling to herself, embraced her madly, fell on her knees for a quick prayer, hopped up to kiss the doctor's hand, and then dragged him into the kitchen, all the while rattling in her native language while the blonde girl let her eyes go cold with disgust. Dr Full allowed himself to be towed into the kitchen, but flatly declined a cup of coffee and a plate of anise cakes and St John's Bread.

'Try him on some wine, ma,' said the girl sardonically.

'Hyass! Hyass!' breathed the woman delightedly. 'You like-a wine, docta?' She had a carafe of purplish liquid before him in an instant, and the blonde girl snickered as the doctor's hand twitched out at it. He drew his hand back, while there grew in his head the old image of how it would smell and then taste and then warm his stomach and limbs. He made the kind of calculation at which he was practised; the delighted woman would not notice as he downed two tumblers, and he could overawe her through two tumblers more with his tale of Teresa's narrow brush with the Destroying Angel, and then – why, then it would not matter. He would be drunk.

But for the first time in years, there was a sort of counter-image: a blend of the rage he felt at the blonde girl to whom he was so transparent, and of pride at the cure he had just effected. Much to his own surprise, he drew back his hand from the carafe and said, luxuriating in the words: 'No, thank you. I don't believe I'd care for any so early in the day.' He covertly watched the blonde girl's face, and was gratified at her surprise. Then the mother was shyly handing him two bills and saying 'Is no much-a money, docta – but you come again, see Teresa?'

'I shall be glad to follow the case through,' he said. 'But now excuse me – I really must be running along.' He grasped the little black bag firmly and got up; he wanted very much to get away from the wine and the older girl.

'Wait up, doc,' she said, 'I'm going your way.' She followed him out and down the street. He ignored her until he felt her hand on the black bag. Then old Dr Full stopped and tried to reason with her:

'Look, my dear. Perhaps you're right. I might have stolen it. To be perfectly frank, I don't remember how I got it. But you're young and you can earn your own money –'

'Fifty-fifty,' she said, 'or I go to the cops. And if I get another word outta you, it's sixty-forty. And you know who gets the short end, don't you, doc?'

Defeated, he marched to the pawnshop, her impudent hand still on the handle with his, and her heels beating out a tattoo against his stately tread.

In the pawnshop, they both got a shock.

'It ain't stendard,' said Uncle, unimpressed by the ingenious lock. 'I ain't nevva seen one like it. Some cheap Jap stuff, maybe? Try down the street. This I nevva could sell.'

Down the street they got an offer of one dollar. The same complaint was made: 'I ain't a collecta, mista – I buy stuff that got resale value. Who could I sell this to, a Chinaman who don't know medical instruments? Every one of them looks funny. You sure you didn't make these yourself?' They didn't take the one-dollar offer.

The girl was baffled and angry; the doctor was baffled too, but triumphant. He had two dollars, and the girl had a half-interest in something nobody wanted. But he suddenly marvelled, the thing had been all right to cure the kid, hadn't it?

'Well,' he asked her, 'do you give up? As you see, the kit is practically valueless.'

She was thinking hard. 'Don't fly off the handle, doc. I don't get this but something's going on all right ... would those guys know good stuff if they saw it?'

'They would. They make a living from it. Wherever this kit came from –'

She seized on that, with a devilish faculty she seemed to have of eliciting answers without asking questions. 'I thought so. You don't know either, huh? Well, maybe I can find out for you. C'mon in here. I ain't letting go of that thing. There's money in it – some way, I don't know how, there's money in it.' He followed her into a cafeteria and to an almost empty corner. She was oblivious to stares and snickers from the other customers as she opened the little black bag – it a most covered a cafeteria table – and ferreted through it. She picked out a retractor from a loop, scrutinised it, contemptuously threw it down, picked out a speculum, threw it down, picked out the lower half of an O.B. forceps, turned it over, close to her sharp young eyes – and saw what the doctor's dim old ones could not have seen.

All old Dr Full knew was that she was peering at the neck of the forceps and then turned white. Very carefully, she placed the half of the forceps back in its loop of cloth and then replaced the retractor and the speculum. 'Well?' he asked. 'What did you see?'

' "Made in U.S.A.," ' she quoted hoarsely. ' "Patent Applied for July 2450." '

He wanted to tell her she must have misread the inscription, that it much be a practical joke, that. . . .

But he knew she had read correctly. Those bandage shears: they *had* driven his fingers, rather than his fingers driving them. The hypo needle that had no hole. The pretty blue pill that had struck him like a thunderbolt.

'You know what I'm going to do?' asked the girl, with sudden animation. 'I'm going to go to charm school. You'll like that, won't ya, doc? Because we're sure going to be seeing a lot of each other.'

Old Dr Full didn't answer. His hands had been playing idly with that plastic card from the kit on which had been printed the rows and columns that had guided him twice before. The card had a slight convexity; you could snap the convexity back and forth from one side to the other. He noted, in a daze, that with each snap a different text appeared on the cards. *Snap.* 'The knife with the blue dot in the handle is for tumours only. Diagnose tumours with your Instrument Seven, the Swelling Tester. Place the Swelling Tester –' *Snap.* 'An overdose of the pink pills in Bottle 3 can be fixed with one white pill from Bottle –' *Snap.* 'Hold the suture needle by the end without the hole in it. Touch it to one end of the wound you want to close and let go. After it has made the knot, touch it –' *Snap.* 'Place the top half of the O.B. Forceps near the opening. Let go. After it has entered and conformed to the shape of –' *Snap.*

The slot man saw 'FLANNERY 1 – MEDICAL' in the upper left corner of the hunk of copy. He automatically scribbled 'trim to .75' on it and skimmed it across the horseshoe-shaped copy desk to Piper, who had been handling Edna Flannery's quack exposé series. She was a nice youngster, he thought, but like all youngsters she overwrote. Hence, the '*trim*'.

Piper dealt back a city hall story to the slot, pinned down Flannery's feature with one hand and began to tap his pencil across it, one tap to a word, at the same steady beat as a teletype carriage travelling across the roller. He wasn't exactly reading it this first time. He was just looking at the letters and words to find out whether, as letters and words, they conformed to *Herald* style. The steady tap of his pencil ceased at intervals as it drew a black line ending with a stylised letter 'd' through the word 'breast' and scribbled in 'chest' instead, or knocked down the capital 'E' in 'East' to lower case with a diagonal, or closed up a split word – in whose middle Flannery had bumped the space bar of her typewriter – with two curved lines like parentheses rotated through ninety degrees. The thick black pencil zipped a ring around the '30' which, like all youngsters, she put at the end of her stories. He turned back to the first page for the second reading. This time, the pencil drew lines with the stylised 'd's' at the end of them through adjectives and whole phrases, printed big 'L's' to mark paragraphs, hooked some of Flannery's own paragraphs together with swooping recurved lines.

At the bottom of 'FLANNERY ADD 2 – MEDICAL' the pencil slowed down and stopped. The slot man, sensitive to the rhythm of his beloved copy desk, looked up almost at once. He saw Piper squinting at the story, at a loss. Without wasting words, the copy reader skimmed it back across the masonite horseshoe to the chief, caught a police story in return and buckled down, his pencil tapping. The slot man read as far as the fourth add, barked at Howard, on the rim: 'Sit in for me,' and stumped through the clattering city room towards the alcove where the managing editor presided over his own bedlam.

The copy chief waited his turn while the make-up editor, the press-room foreman and the chief photographer had words with the M.E. When his turn came, he dropped Flannery's copy on his desk and said: 'She says this one isn't a quack.'

The M.E. read:

'FLANNERY 1 – MEDICAL, by Edna Flannery, *Herald* Staff Writer.

'The sordid tale of medical quackery which the *Herald* has exposed in this series of articles undergoes a change of pace today which the reporter found a welcome surprise. Her quest for the facts in the case of today's subject started just the same way that her exposure of one dozen shyster M.D.'s and faith-healing phonies did. But she can report for a change that Dr Bayard Kendrick Full is, despite unorthodox practices which have drawn the suspicion of the rightly hypersensitive medical associations, a true healer living up to the highest ideals of his profession.

'Dr Full's name was given to the *Herald*'s reporter by the ethical committee of a county medical association, which reported that he had been expelled from the association on July 18, 1941 for allegedly "milking" several patients suffering from trivial complaints. According to sworn statements in the committee's files, Dr Full had told them they suffered from cancer, and that he had a treatment which would prolong their lives. After his expulsion from the association, Dr Full dropped out of their sight – until he opened a midtown "sanatorium" in a brownstone front which had for years served as a rooming house.

'The *Herald*'s reporter went to that sanatorium, on East 89th Street, with the full expectation of having numerous imaginary ailments diagnosed and of being promised a sure cure for a flat sum of money. She expected to find unkempt quarters, dirty instruments and the mumbo-jumbo paraphernalia of the shyster M.D. which she had seen a dozen times before.

'She was wrong.

'Dr Full's sanatorium is spotlessly clean, from its tastefully furnished entrance hall to its shining, white treatment rooms. The attractive blonde receptionist who greeted the reporter was soft-spoken and correct, asking only the reporter's name, address and the general nature of her complaint. This was given, as usual, as "nagging backache". The receptionist asked the *Herald*'s reporter to be seated, and a short while later conducted her to a second-floor treatment room and introduced her to Dr Full.

'Dr Full's alleged past, as described by the medical society spokesman, is hard to reconcile with his present appearance. He is a clear-eyed, white-haired man in his sixties, to judge by his appearance – a little above middle height and apparently in good physical condition. His voice was firm and friendly, untainted by the ingratiating whine of the shyster M.D. which the reporter has come to know too well.

'The receptionist did not leave the room as he began his examination after a few questions as to the nature and location of the pain. As the reporter lay face down on a treatment table the doctor pressed some instrument to the small of her back. In about one minute he made this astounding statement: "Young woman, there is no reason for you to have any pain where you say you do. I understand they're saying nowadays that emotional upsets cause pains like that. You'd better go to a psychologist or psychiatrist if the pain keeps up. There is no physical cause for it, so I can do nothing for you."

'His frankness took the reporter's breath away. Had he guessed she was, so to speak, a spy in his camp? She tried again: "Well, doctor, perhaps you'd give me a physical checkup. I feel rundown all the time, besides the pains. Maybe I need a tonic." This is never-failing bait to shyster M.D.'s – an invitation for them to find all sorts of mysterious conditions wrong with a patient, each of which "requires" an expensive treatment. As explained in the first article of this series, of course, the reporter underwent a thorough physical checkup before she embarked on her quack hunt, and was found to be in one hundred per cent perfect condition, with the exception of a "scarred" area at the bottom tip of her left lung resulting from a childhood attack of tuberculosis and a tendency towards "hyperthyroidism" – overactivity of the thyroid gland which makes it difficult to put on weight and sometimes causes a slight shortness of breath.

'Dr Full consented to perform the examination, and took a number of shining, spotlessly clean instruments from loops in a large board literally covered with instruments – most of them unfamiliar to the reporter. The instrument with which he approached first was a tube with a curved dial in its surface and two wires that ended on flat discs growing from its ends. He placed one of the discs on the back of the reporter's right hand and the other on the back of her left. "Reading the meter", he called out some number which the attentive receptionist took down on a ruled form. The same procedure was repeated several times, thoroughly covering the reporter's anatomy and thoroughly convincing her that the doctor was a complete quack. The reporter had never seen any such diagnostic procedure practised during the weeks she put in preparing for this series.

'The doctor then took the ruled sheet from the receptionist, conferred with her in low tones and said: "You have a slightly overactive thyroid, young woman. And there's something wrong with your left lung – not seriously, but I'd like to take a closer look."

'He selected an instrument from the board which, the reporter knew, is called a "speculum" – a scissorlike device which spreads apart body openings such as the orifice of the ear, the nostril and so on, so that a doctor can look in during an examination. The instrument was, however, too large to be an aural or nasal speculum but too small to be anything else. As the *Herald*'s reporter was about to ask further questions, the attending receptionist told her: "It's customary for us to blindfold our patients during lung examinations – do you mind?" The reporter, bewildered, allowed her to tie a spotlessly clean bandage over her eyes, and waited nervously for what would come next.

'She still cannot say exactly what happened while she was blind-folded – but X-rays confirm her suspicions. She felt a cold sensation at her ribs on the left side – a cold that seemed to enter inside her body. Then there was a snapping feeling, and the cold sensation was gone. She heard Dr Full say in a matter-of-fact voice: "You have an old tubercular scar down there. It isn't doing any particular harm, but an active person like you needs all the oxygen she can get. Lie still and I'll fix it for you."

'Then there was a repetition of the cold sensation, lasting for a longer time. "Another batch of alveoli and some more vascular glue," the *Herald*'s reporter heard Dr Full say, and the receptionist's crisp response to the order. Then the strange sensation departed and the eye bandage was removed. The reporter saw no scar on her ribs, and yet the doctor assured her: "That did it. We took out the fibrosis – and a good fibrosis it was, too; it walled off the infection so you're still alive to tell the tale. Then we planted a few clumps of alveoli – they're the little gadgets that get the oxygen from the air you breathe into your blood. I won't monkey with your thyroxin supply. You've got used to being the kind of person you are, and if you suddenly found yourself easy-going and all the rest of it, chances are you'd only be upset. About the backache: just check with the county medical society for the name of a good psychologist or psychiatrist. And look out for quacks; the woods are full of them."

'The doctor's self-assurance took the reporter's breath away. She asked what the charge would be, and was told to pay the receptionist fifty dollars. As usual, the reporter delayed paying until she got a receipt signed by the doctor himself, detailing the services for which it paid. Unlike most, the doctor cheerfully wrote: "For removal of fibrosis from left lung and restoration of alveoli," and signed it.

'The reporter's first move when she left the sanatorium was to head for the chest specialist who had examined her in preparation for this series. A comparison of X-rays taken on the day of the "operation" and those taken previously would, the *Herald*'s reporter then thought, expose Dr Full as a prince of shyster M.D.'s and quacks.

'The chest specialist made time on his crowded schedule for the reporter, in whose series he has shown a lively interest from the planning stage on. He laughed uproariously in his staid Park Avenue examining room as she described the weird procedure to which she had been subjected. But he did not laugh when he took a chest X-ray of the reporter, developed it, dried it and compared it with the ones he had taken earlier. The chest specialist took six more X-rays that afternoon, but finally admitted that they all told the same story. The *Herald*'s reporter has it on his authority that the scar she had eighteen days ago from her tuberculosis is now gone and has been replaced by healthy lung tissue. He declared that this is a happening unparalleled in medical history. He does not go along with the reporter in her firm conviction that Dr Full is responsible for the change.

'The *Herald*'s reporter, however, sees no two ways about it. She concludes that Dr Bayard Kendrick Full – whatever his alleged past may have been – is now an unorthodox but highly successful practitioner of medicine, to whose hands the reporter would trust herself in any emergency.

'Not so is the case of "Rev." Annie Dimsworth – a female harpy who, under the guise of "faith" preys on the ignorant and suffering who come to her sordid "healing parlour" for help and remain to feed "Rev." Annie's bank account, which now totals up to $53,283.64. Tomorrow's article will show, with photostats of bank statements and sworn testimoney, that –'

The managing editor turned down 'FLANNERY LAST ADD – MEDICAL' and tapped his front teeth with a pencil, trying to think straight. He finally told the copy chief: 'Kill the story. Run the teaser as a box.' He tore off the last paragraph – the 'teaser' about 'Rev.' Annie and handed it to the desk man, who stumped back to his masonite horseshoe.

The make-up editor was back, dancing with impatience as he tried to catch the M.E.'s eye. The interphone buzzed with the red light which indicated that the editor and publisher wanted to talk to him. The M.E. thought briefly of a special series on this Dr Full, decided nobody would believe it and that he probably was a phony anyway. He spiked the story on the 'dead' hook and answered his interphone.

Dr Full had become almost fond of Angie. As his practice had grown to engross the neighbourhood illnesses, and then to a corner suite in an uptown taxpayer building, and finally to the sanatorium, she seemed to have grown with it. Oh, he thought, we have our little disputes. . . .

The girl, for instance, was too much interested in money. She had wanted to specialise in cosmetic surgery – removing wrinkles from wealthy old women and whatnot. She didn't realise, at first, that a thing like this was in their trust, that they were the stewards and not the owners of the little black bag and its fabulous contents.

He had tried, ever so cautiously, to analyse them, but without success. All the instruments were slightly radioactive, for instance, but not quite so. They would make a Geiger-Mueller counter indicate, but they would not collapse the leaves of an electroscope. He didn't pretend to be up on the latest developments, but as he understood it, that was just plain *wrong*. Under the highest magnification, there were lines on the instruments' superfinished surfaces: incredibly fine lines, engraved in random hatchments which made no particular sense. Their magnetic properties were preposterous. Sometimes the instruments were strongly attracted to magnets, sometimes less so, and sometimes not at all.

Dr Full had taken X-rays in fear and trembling lest he disrupt whatever delicate machinery worked in them. He was *sure* they were not solid, that the handles and perhaps the blades must be mere shells filled with busy little watchworks – but the X-rays showed nothing of the sort. Oh, yes – and they were always sterile, and they wouldn't rust. Dust *fell* off them if you shook them: now, that was something he understood. They ionised the dust, or were ionised themselves, or something of the sort. At any rate, he had read of something similar that had to do with phonograph records.

She wouldn't know about that, he proudly thought. She kept the books well enough, and perhaps she gave him a useful prod now and then when he was inclined to settle down. The move from the neighbourhood slum to the uptown quarters had been her idea, and so had the sanatorium. Good; good; it enlarged his sphere of usefulness. Let the child have her mink coats and her convertible, as they seemed to be calling roadsters nowadays. He himself was too busy and too old. He had so much to make up for.

Dr Full thought happily of his master plan. She would not like it much, but she would have to see the logic of it. This marvellous thing that had happened to them must be handed on. She was herself no doctor even though the instruments practically ran themselves, there was more to doctoring than skill. There were the ancient canons of the healing art. And so, having seen the logic of it, Angie would yield; she would assent to his turning over the little black bag to all humanity.

He would probably present it to the College of Surgeons, with as little fuss as possible – well, perhaps a *small* ceremony, and he would like a souvenir of the occasion, a cup or a framed testimonial. It would be a relief to have the thing out of his hands, in a way; let the giants of the healing art decide who was to have its benefits. No; Angie would understand. She was a good-hearted girl.

It was nice that she had been showing so much interest in the surgical side lately – asking about the instruments, reading the instruction card for hours, even practising on guinea pigs. If something of his love for humanity had been communicated to her, old Dr Full sentimentally thought, his life would not have been in vain. Surely she would realise that a greater good would be served by surrendering the instruments to wiser hands than theirs, and by throwing aside the cloak of secrecy necessary to work on their small scale.

Dr Full was in the treatment room that had been the brownstone's front parlour; through the window he saw Angie's yellow convertible roll to a stop before the stoop. He liked the way she looked as she climbed the stairs; neat, not flashy, he thought. A sensible girl like her, she'd understand. There was somebody with her – a fat woman, puffing up the steps, overdressed and petulant. Now, what could she want?

Angie let herself in and went into the treatment room, followed by the

C. M. KORNBLUTH

fat woman. 'Doctor,' said the blonde girl gravely, 'may I present Mrs Coleman?' Charm school had not taught her everything, but Mrs Coleman, evidently *nouveau riche* thought the doctor, did not notice the blunder.

'Miss Aquella told me *so* much about you, doctor, and your remarkable system!' she gushed.

Before he could answer, Angie smoothly interposed: 'Would you excuse us for just a moment, Mrs Coleman?'

She took the doctor's arm and led him into the reception hall. 'Listen,' she said swiftly, 'I know this goes against your grain, but I couldn't pass it up. I met this old thing in the exercise class at Elizabeth Barton's. Nobody else'll talk to her there. She's a widow, I guess her husband was a black marketeer or something, and she has a pile of dough. I gave her a line about how you had a system of massaging wrinkles out. My idea is, you blindfold her, cut her neck open with the Cutaneous Series knife, shoot some Firmol into the muscles, spoon out some of that blubber with an Adipose Series curette and spray it all with Skintite. When you take the blindfold off she's got rid of a wrinkle and doesn't know what happened. She'll pay five hundred dollars. Now, don't say "no", doc. Just this once, let's do it my way, can't you? I've been working on this deal all along too, haven't I?'

'Oh,' said the doctor, 'very well.' He was going to have to tell her about the master plan before long anyway. He would let her have it her way this time.

Back in the treatment room, Mrs Coleman had been thinking things over. She told the doctor sternly as he entered: 'Of course, your system is permanent, isn't it?'

'It is, madam,' he said shortly. 'Would you please lie down there? Miss Aquella, get a sterile three-inch bandage for Mrs Coleman's eyes.' He turned his back on the fat woman to avoid conversation, and pretended to be adjusting the lights. Angie blindfolded the woman, and the doctor selected the instruments he would need. He handed the blonde girl a pair of retractors, and told her: 'Just slip the corners of the blades in as I cut –' She gave him an alarmed look, and gestured at the reclining woman. He lowered his voice: 'Very well. Slip in the corners and rock them along the incision. I'll tell you when to pull them out.'

Dr Full held the Cutaneous Series knife to his eyes as he adjusted the little slide for 3 cm. depth. He sighed a little as he recalled that its last use had been in the extirpation of an 'inoperable' tumour of the throat.

'Very well,' he said, bending over the woman. He tried a tentative pass through her tissues. The blade dipped in and flowed through them, like a finger through quicksilver, with no wound left in the wake. Only the retractors could hold the edges of the incision apart.

404

Mrs Coleman stirred and jabbered: 'Doctor, that felt so peculiar! Are you sure you're rubbing the right way?'

'Quite sure, madam,' said the doctor wearily. 'Would you please try not to talk during the massage?'

He nodded at Angie, who stood ready with the retractors. The blade sank in to its three centimetres, miraculously cutting only the dead horny tissues of the epidermis and the live tissue of the dermis, pushing aside mysteriously all major and minor blood vessels and muscular tissue, declining to affect any system or organ except the one it was – tuned to, could you say? The doctor didn't know the answer, but he felt tired and bitter at this prostitution. Angie slipped in the retractor blades and rocked them as he withdrew the knife, then pulled to separate the lips of the incision. It bloodlessly exposed an unhealthy string of muscle, sagging in a dead-looking loop from blue-grey ligaments. The doctor took a hypo, Number IX, preset to 'g' and raised it to his eye level. The mist came and went; there probably was no possibility of an embolus with one of these gadgets, but why take chances? He shot one c.c. of 'g' – identified as 'Firmol' by the card – into the muscle. He and Angie watched as it tightened up against the pharynx.

He took the Adipose Series curette, a small one, and spooned out yellowish tissue, dropping it into the incinerator box, and then nodded to Angie. She eased out the retractors and the gaping incision slipped together into unbroken skin, sagging now. The doctor had the atomiser – dialled to 'Skintite' – ready. He sprayed, and the skin shrank up into the now firm throat line.

As he replaced the instruments, Angie removed Mrs Coleman's bandage and gaily announced: 'We're finished! And there's a mirror in the reception hall –'

Mrs Coleman didn't need to be invited twice. With incredulous fingers she felt her chin, and then dashed for the hall. The doctor grimaced as he heard her yelp of delight, and Angie turned to him with a tight smile. 'I'll get the money and get her out,' she said. 'You won't have to be bothered with her any more.'

He was grateful for that much.

She followed Mrs Coleman into the reception hall, and the doctor dreamed over the case of instruments. A ceremony, certainly – he was *entitled* to one. Not everybody, he thought, would turn such a sure source of money over to the good of humanity. But you reached an age when money mattered less, and when you thought of these things you had done that *might* be open to misunderstanding if, just if, there chanced to be any of that, well, that judgment business. The doctor wasn't a religious man, but you certainly found yourself thinking hard about some things when your time drew near. . . .

Angie was back, with a bit of paper in her hands. 'Five hundred dollars,' she said matter-of-factly. 'And you realise, don't you, that we could go over her an inch at a time – at five hundred dollars an inch?'

'I've been meaning to talk to you about that,' he said.

There was bright fear in her eyes, he thought – but why?

'Angie, you've been a good girl and an understanding girl, but we can't keep this up forever, you know.'

'Let's talk about it some other time,' she said flatly. 'I'm tired now.'

'No – I really feel we've gone far enough on our own. The instruments –'

'Don't say it, doc!' she hissed. 'Don't say it, or you'll be sorry!' In her face there was a look that reminded him of the hollow-eyed, gaunt-faced, dirty-blonde creature she had been. From under the charm-school finish there burned the gutter-snipe whose infancy had been spent on a sour and filthy mattress, whose childhood had been play in the littered alley and whose adolescence had been the sweatshops and the aimless gatherings at night under the glaring streetlamps.

He shook his head to dispel the puzzling notion. 'It's this way,' he patiently began. 'I told you about the family that invented the O.B. forceps and kept them a secret for so many generations, how they could have given them to the world but didn't?'

'They knew what they were doing,' said the guttersnipe flatly.

'Well, that's neither here nor there,' said the doctor, irritated. 'My mind is made up about it. I'm going to turn the instruments over to the College of Surgeons. We have enough money to be comfortable. You can even have the house. I've been thinking of going to a warmer climate, myself.' He felt peeved with her for making the unpleasant scene. He was unprepared for what happened next.

Angie snatched the little black bag and dashed for the door, with panic in her eyes. He scrambled after her, catching her arm, twisting it in a sudden rage. She clawed at his face with her free hand, babbling curses. Somehow, somebody's finger touched the little black bag, and it opened grotesquely into that enormous board, covered with shining instruments, large and small. Half a dozen of them joggled loose and fell to the floor.

'*Now* see what you've done!' roared the doctor, unreasonably. Her hand was still vicelike on the handle, but she was standing still, trembling with choked-up rage. The doctor bent stiffly to pick up the fallen instruments. Unreasonable girl! he thought bitterly. Making a scene. . . .

Pain drove in between his shoulder-blades and he fell face down. The light ebbed. 'Unreasonable girl!' he tried to croak. And then: 'They'll know I tried, anyway –'

Angie looked down on his prone body, with the handle of the Number

Six Cautery Series knife protruding from it. '. . . will cut through all tissues. Use for amputations before you spread on the Re-Gro. Extreme caution should be used in the vicinity of vital organs and major blood vessels or nerve trunks –'

'I didn't mean to do that,' said Angie, dully, cold with horror. Now the detective would come, the implacable detective who would reconstruct the crime from the dust in the room. She would run and turn and twist, but the detective would find her out and she would be tried in a courtroom before a judge and jury; the lawyer would make speeches, but the jury would convict her anyway, and the headlines would scream: 'BLONDE KILLER GUILTY!' and she'd maybe get the chair, walking down a plain corridor where a beam of sunlight struck through the dusty air, with an iron door at the end of it. Her mink, her convertible, her dresses, the handsome man she was going to meet and marry. . . .

The mist of cinematic clichés cleared, and she knew what she would do next. Quite steadily, she picked the incinerator box from its loop in the board – a metal cube with a different-textured spot on one side. '. . . to dispose of fibroses or other unwanted matter, simply touch the disc –' You dropped something in and touched the disc. There was a sort of soundless whistle, very powerful and unpleasant if you were too close, and a sort of lightless flash. When you opened the box again, the contents were gone. Angie took another of the Cautery Series knives and went grimly to work. Good thing there wasn't any blood to speak of. . . . She finished the awful task in three hours.

She slept heavily that night, totally exhausted by the wringing emotional demands of the slaying and the subsequent horror. But in the morning, it was as though the doctor had never been there. She ate breakfast, dressed with unusual care – and then undid the unusual care. Nothing out of the ordinary, she told herself. Don't do one thing different from the way you would have done it before. After a day or two, you can phone the cops. Say he walked out spoiling for a drink, and you're worried. But don't rush it, baby – *don't rush it.*

Mrs Coleman was due at 10:00 A.M. Angie had counted on being able to talk the doctor into at least one more five-hundred-dollar session. She'd have to do it herself now – but she'd have to start sooner or later.

The woman arrived early. Angie explained smoothly: 'The doctor asked me to take care of the massage today. Now that he has the tissue-firming process beginning, it only requires somebody trained in his methods –' As she spoke, her eyes swivelled to the instrument case – open! She cursed herself for the single flaw as the woman followed her gaze and recoiled.

'What are those things?' she demanded. 'Are you going to cut me with them? I *thought* there was something fishy –'

'Please, Mrs Coleman,' said Angie, 'please, *dear* Mrs Coleman – you don't understand about the . . . the massage instruments!'

'Massage instruments, my foot!' squabbled the woman shrilly. 'That doctor *operated* on me. Why, he might have killed me!'

Angie wordlessly took one of the smaller Cutaneous Series knives and passed it through her forearm. The blade flowed like a finger through quicksilver, leaving no wound in its wake. *That* should convince the old cow!

It didn't convince her, but it did startle her. 'What did you do with it? The blade folds up into the handle – that's it!'

'Now look closely, Mrs Coleman,' said Angie, thinking desperately of the five hundred dollars. 'Look very closely and you'll see that the, uh, the subskin massager simply slips beneath the tissues without doing any harm, tightening and firming the muscles themselves instead of having to work through the layers of skin and adipose tissue. It's the secret of the doctor's method. Now, how can outside massage have the effect that we got last night?'

Mrs Coleman was beginning to calm down. 'It *did* work, all right,' she admitted, stroking the new line of her neck. 'But your arm's one thing and my neck's another! Let me see you do that with your neck!'

Angie smiled. . . .

Al returned to the clinic after an excellent lunch that had almost reconciled him to three more months he would have to spend on duty. And then, he thought, and then a blessed year at the blessedly supernormal South Pole working on his specialty – which happened to be telekinesis exercises for ages three to six. Meanwhile, of course, the world had to go on and of course he had to shoulder his share in the running of it.

Before settling down to deskwork he gave a routine glance at the bag board. What he saw made him stiffen with shocked surprise. A red light was on next to one of the numbers – the first since he couldn't think when. He read off the number and murmured: 'O.K., 674,101. That fixes *you*.' He put the number on a card sorter and in a moment the record was in his hand. Oh, yes – Hemingway's bag. The big dummy didn't remember how or where he had lost it; none of them ever did. There were hundreds of them floating around.

Al's policy in such cases was to leave the bag turned on. The things practically ran themselves – it was practically impossible to do harm with them – so whoever found a lost one might as well be allowed to use it. You turn it off, you have a social loss – you leave it on, it may do some good. As he understood it, and not very well at that, the stuff wasn't 'used up'. A temporalist had tried to explain it to him with little success that the prototypes in the transmitter *had been transducted* through a series of point events of transfinite cardinality. Al had innocently asked whether that meant prototypes had been stretched, so to speak, through all time, and the temporalist had thought he was joking and left in a huff.

'Like to see him do this,' thought Al darkly, as he telekinised himsel to the combox, after a cautious look to see that there were no medics around. To the box he said: 'Police chief,' and then to the police chief: 'There's been a homicide committed with Medical Instrument Kit 674,101. It was lost some months ago by one of my people, Dr John Hemingway. He didn't have a clear account of the circumstances.'

The police chief groaned and said: 'I'll call him in and question him.' He was to be astonished by the answers, and was to learn that the homicide was well out of his jurisdiction.

Al stood for a moment at the bag board by the glowing red light that had been sparked into life by a departing vital force giving, as its last act, the warning that Kit 674,101 was in homicidal hands. With a sigh, Al pulled the plug and the light went out.

'Yah,' jeered the woman. 'You'd fool around with my neck, but you wouldn't risk your own with that thing!'

Angie smiled with serene confidence, a smile that was to shock hardened morgue attendants. She set the Cutaneous Series knife to 3 centimetres before drawing it across her neck. Smiling, knowing the blade would cut only the dead horny tissue of the epidermis and the live tissue of the dermis, mysteriously push aside all major and minor blood vessels and muscular tissue. . . .

Smiling, the knife plunging in and its microtome-sharp metal shearing through major and minor blood vessels and muscular tissue and pharynx, Angie cut her throat.

In the few minutes it took the police, summoned by the shrieking Mrs Coleman, to arrive, the instruments had become crusted with rust, and the flasks which had held vascular glue and clumps of pink, rubbery alveoli and spare grey cells and coils of receptor nerves held only black slime, and from them when opened gushed the foul gases of decomposition.

C. S. Forester

The Physiology of Fear

Dr Georg Schmidt was not a young man, and perhaps because of that he sometimes found it hard to believe that this was a real, permanent world in which he was moving and living. He had qualified as a doctor in the days of the Kaiser, before 1914. A man who had vivid recollections of the Hohenzollern empire, with all its tradition and appearance of permanence, and who had then seen the Weimar Republic come and go, and who had lived through the inflation and through several revolutions, abortive and otherwise, found it a little difficult to believe in the prospective existence of the Third Reich for a thousand years, which its supporters predicted for it. This was especially the case because Schmidt was of a cynical turn of mind, with his cynicism accentuated by a scientific education. But his cynicism was not of the right type to be of use to him under Hitler and the Nazis, considering the sort of work he was called upon by them to do. For he was appointed a surgeon in the SS, and posted as medical officer to the Rosenberg Concentration Camp. There he could inspect water supply and sanitary arrangements, he could combat epidemics, and do all the things he had learned to do thoroughly well between 1914 and 1918, but a medical officer in a concentration camp had other duties as well, which were hard to perform; there is no need to enlarge upon them, except to comment that perhaps the easiest duty was to advise upon the issue of rations so that the prisoners had the minimum diet on which life could be sustained.

All the hideous things that Schmidt had to do, he had to do. That was simple. The Party cast a cold eye upon any man who flinched from obeying orders; those orders came down from the Fuehrer himself, and they were not rendered any less sacred by the fact that they were transmitted, interpreted, and expanded by a number of officials before they reached Schmidt. Those officials held their authority from the Fuehrer, and a man who cavilled at doing what he was told by them to do was guilty of treason against the Fuehrer, against the Reich, and no fate could be too bad for him – even though anyone who knew the sort of fate that was meted out (and Schmidt saw it meted out) might have thought it was too bad for anyone. Schmidt knew all about the gallows and the block, the torture cells and the gas chambers, so he did what he was told, moving in a world that was like a bad dream, hoping that what he saw and did was not really happening, hoping that some time soon he would wake up and find it was only a dream after all.

So, when his leave came round in the summer of 1940, he welcomed it with as much gladness as he had done in the old days of 1917. He handed over to the doctor who came to relieve him; he packed his fibre suitcase, saw that his papers were in order, and started off for the railway station and for the city that he called 'home'. He had few relations – his wife was dead – but his brilliant nephew Heinrich had invited him to spend his leave at his house there, and Schmidt was looking forward to that. Young Heinz was a product of the new generation, he knew – because of the exigencies of the service he had seen little of him lately – but Schmidt was quite certain that he was a nephew to be proud of. He had not only qualified in medicine, but he had attained a Doctorate of Science, and even now, with Germany mobilised, he was still a civilian, holding a research fellowship at the university – a sure proof of the esteem in which he was held. Schmidt had read the early papers he had contributed to the university 'Transactions' and had glowed with pride. His nephew was clearly destined to be one of the great physiologists of the world, a man whose name would always be remembered. Schmidt would have liked to have been a famous research worker himself, and he found a vicarious, almost a parental, pleasure in his nephew's achievements.

Heinz himself opened the door to him when he rang the door-bell after a tedious night journey across wartime Germany.

'Welcome, uncle,' he said, relieving him of his suitcase.

Heinz was everything an uncle might wish for, tall and blond and handsome, smartly dressed, vigorous – he had all those advantages as well as being a man of brilliant mind. And his wife, Caecilie, was a desirable niece, too, a very pretty girl in a uniform not too obtrusive. She made Schmidt welcome with the utmost kindness and hospitality.

'You look tired, uncle,' said Caecilie, 'we must try and remedy that while you are with us.'

Schmidt glowed with something like happiness as they showed him his room and saw to his comfort. More than ever at that moment did his duties at the Rosenberg Concentration Camp appear like a bad dream.

'You and I have an appointment for luncheon, uncle,' said Heinz.
'Indeed?'

'With Standartenfuehrer Kroide. The president himself.'

There was a humorous twinkle in Heinz' eye as he spoke. He could see the incongruity of having a Nazi official as president of a university which dated back to the Middle Ages.

'How is it that I am invited?' asked Schmidt.

'I mentioned to him that I was expecting you,' explained Heinz, 'and that you were my uncle.'

'And he wanted to meet the uncle of the great physiologist?' said Schmidt. 'I have attained fame at last.'

'Turn round, uncle,' said Caecilie, clothes-brush in hand. 'I want to brush your shoulders.'

On the way to the university, walking through the streets multi-coloured with uniforms, Schmidt asked his nephew about his work.

'Is it still inter-cellular osmosis?' he asked.

'No,' said Heinz. 'It's a larger project altogether. Immensely larger, and it may prove to be of great importance to the Reich.'

'Is it a war secret?'

'The results may be, when we see what they are. But there is no need for secrecy at present. I'm working on the physiology of fear.'

'Very interesting.'

'Very interesting indeed. The government is of course assisting the university. I understand that the Fuehrer himself knows about my research. At any rate, it is the government, of course, that is providing me with suitable subjects.'

'That must be a great help,' said Schmidt.

'Oh, yes, of course. It would be hard to conduct such a research without a plentiful supply. And the university has been most co-operative. I have a thousand cubic metres of laboratory space for my use. Actually I am using the laboratories once used by Liebig and Hertz – remodelled, of course.'

'That's a compliment in itself,' said Schmidt.

The university had a long and honourable record for scientific research. The world was at least a healthier place, if not a happier, as a result of the labours of the university's scientists.

'I'll take you round and show you after lunch,' said Heinz.

'Thank you. That will be very interesting.'

Schmidt was not quite sure that he wanted to be shown. The physiology of fear could hardly be investigated without causing fear, and he did not specially want to be shown terrified animals; many animals, obviously, with the government undertaking to supply them.

'I suppose rats and guinea pigs are unsuitable for your investigation?'

asked Schmidt.

'Of course,' said Heinz, and then the glow of enthusiasm in his face died away as he changed the subject and pointed across the road. 'Here's the president's house.'

Standartenfuehrer Kroide was no scientist, not even a scientist in uniform. As head of the university he represented the Ministry of Enlightenment and Propaganda, naturally. It was his business to see that German youth not only was educated along the lines most useful to the Reich, but also that it was not educated along the lines that were improper.

'We are proud of our young man, here,' said Kroide, indicating Heinz. 'A splendid example of the new growth of scientists of the Third Reich. One of our earliest, but with the example he has set he will not be our last.'

Kroide was a man with the same personal charm as the head of his ministry. He could talk charmingly and interestingly, and at luncheon he entertained Schmidt, who sat at his right, with a vivid account of the success of the new system of education, a success demonstrated by the correct thinking of all the new generation, and resulting from consistent methods employed from earliest childhood.

'Your nephew himself was distinguished as a boy in the Hitler Youth,' said Kroide.

'I remember,' answered Schmidt, and that was only true as he said it. He had forgotten about Heinz' early activities, and he thought Heinz probably had forgotten them too. The notion crept into his mind that it might be difficult to retain the ideas of Nazism when one was a true scientist, but he put it hastily aside. Some people would have thought it blasphemous; Schmidt knew it was dangerous.

When lunch was over Kroide shook Schmidt's hand.

'I have no doubt your nephew is impatient to carry you off,' he said. 'He wants to get back to his experiments as well as to show you his work. I hope when your leave comes round again you will let me know so that I can again have the pleasure of entertaining you.'

'Thank you, Standartenfuehrer,' said Schmidt.

Walking from the president's house over to the laboratory Heinz began to go into further detail regarding his work.

'Thanks to the Reich and the Fuehrer,' he said, 'I am able to investigate the subject in a way that has not been possible before. There could never be exact measurements of any sort, and I expect that is why fear has never been analysed physiologically until now. All that is known is contained in two paragraphs in any standard text-book of physiology, as I expect you remember, uncle.'

'A line or two about the suprarenals,' agreed Schmidt. 'A little about

413

blood-pressure.'

'Exactly. All vague and unscientific. But now we can tackle the subject quantitatively and scientifically. Some of the results I have already obtained are most significant and illuminating.'

Schmidt wondered vaguely how fear could be measured with any exactness, even if intelligent animals, even if monkeys were employed. But now conversation was interrupted, as they were passing through doors guarded by SS sentries, and crossing courtyards similarly patrolled. There were salutes in plenty for the Herr Professor, and it occurred to Schmidt that the government must be anxious to keep the research a secret to provide these guards.

'And here we are,' said Heinz, holding open a door for Schmidt to pass through.

There were guards here as well, in the long well-lit laboratory, guards in black uniforms with death's-head insignia; guards carrying whips – it was they whom Schmidt saw first, and the sight puzzled him. There were seated workers and standing workers; the seated workers, each at a separate bench, were covered with scientific instruments of all sorts applied to their naked bodies. Schmidt could guess at the use of most of them; there were instruments for measuring blood-pressure, and instruments for measuring the amount of air inspired, for recording respiration and heart beat. Beside each seated worker another, standing, was diligently employed in noting the recordings. The nakedness of the seated workers was surprising. Most surprising still was the sight of the apparatus before each one, when Schmidt came to notice it. Each one had a roulette wheel in front of him, and was spinning it, and was dropping the little ivory ball into the basin as he spun it. Schmidt could understand nothing of what he saw, and looked at his nephew in complete bewilderment.

'What is happening here?' he asked. 'Where are the animals?'

'Animals?' said Heinz, 'I thought I made it plain to you that I do not use animals. These are my subjects. These.'

He indicated with a sweep of his hand the twelve naked men sitting at the roulette wheels.

'Oh,' said Schmidt, weakly.

'With animals,' said Heinz, and something faintly professorial crept into his manner as he spoke, 'it would be quite impossible, as I told you, to obtain quantitative results of any value. For those, intelligence on the part of the subject is necessary. Besides, I have already proved that there is almost no analogy between the physiological effects of fear in animals and in man.'

'But what are they doing?' asked Schmidt.

'It is simple,' explained Heinz, 'as practical ideas usually are. They spin their roulette wheels, as you see. The numbers that turn up are immaterial. It is the red and black that count.'

'Yes?'

'It is explained to each subject when he is brought here that when he spins eight consecutive reds it is the end for him.'

'The end?'

'These subjects are all people who are destined for liquidation, of course. They might as well be usefully employed first. And some of my most valuable data are acquired at the autopsies, as you can understand.'

'Yes.'

'And so these subjects are spinning their roulette wheels, and that is how I get my quantitative results. It is remarkable how exact they can be. A man spins a single red, and he hardly cares. Two, he is not much more concerned either. With the third and the fourth the physiological effects become more marked, and when it reaches seven the graphs show a very steep incline.'

'I suppose so,' said Schmidt.

He told himself that he was in a real world, with these things actually happening in it, and yet he found himself still wishing wildly that he would awake from the nightmare. There was a sharp crack and a cry of pain from the far end of the room, and Schmidt looked in that direction in time to see a guard turn away from one of the subjects after dealing a blow with his whip.

'As the number of consecutive reds increases the subject grows reluctant to go on spinning the wheel,' explained Heinz. 'Compulsion has to be employed with most of them.'

'Naturally,' said Schmidt. He knew perfectly well that if he blazed out in protest he would be proved not to be wholeheartedly for the régime – he might even find himself sitting spinning a roulette wheel.

'And yet the psychology is as interesting as the physiology,' went on Heinz. 'There are some who spin feverishly as if anxious to reach the end. We have even had a few who anticipated it, killing themselves in their cells at night – a nuisance, because it means a premature termination of the results in their case.'

'That must be a nuisance,' said Schmidt.

'The psychological findings are of course being analysed by another department,' said Heinz. 'Old Engel has a team of assistants at work on them. But psychology is by no means as exact a science as physiology – it can hardly be called a science at all, can it?'

'I suppose not.'

'With half these subjects,' explained Heinz, 'it is made clear to them that when they spin their eight reds they will meet their end by the quick SS neck shot, all over in a second. The other half are told that it will be a more painful process, prolonged as far as the SS can manage it. But it is quite surprising how little difference that prospect makes to the physiological results – the subjects really do not look beyond the act that they will die when they spin their eight consecutive reds. In fact, I am thinking of discontinuing that part of the investigation, for the treatment administered by the SS brings about a serious confusion in the eventual findings at the autopsy. My work is more important than that of the psychologists.'

'Of course,' said Schmidt. He wanted to sit down, but Heinz went on talking, enthusiastic about his subject.

'Most of this apparatus I designed myself,' he said. 'This one here provides a continuous record of the rate of sweat secretion. The curves I am obtaining with it sometimes offer interesting contrasts with the graphs of blood-pressure and respiration.'

He bent over to show the apparatus to Schmidt, standing close to the subject, a heavily built and swarthy man, who at that moment uttered a groan of despair.

'Seven, I see,' said Heinz. 'You notice how the blood-pressure rises?'

The subject struggled on his stool – it was only then that Schmidt noticed that the subjects were leg-ironed and chained in their places. A guard came sidling up, his whip whistling shrilly as he swung it in the air, and at the sound of it the subject subsided.

'Spin,' said the assistant who was taking the recordings, and the subject spun the wheel and dropped in the ivory ball, which bounced clicking against the metal studs.

'Ah, black,' said Heinz. 'Most of his curves will show an abrupt decline at this point.'

Schmidt felt relief that it had been black this time.

'Some of these subjects last literally for weeks,' commented Heinz. 'It takes that long sometimes for them to spin their eight consecutive reds. And yet there is very little flattening of the curves – you would be surprised at the consistency of the results. I'll show you some of my graphs in a moment.'

'That would be very interesting,' said Schmidt.

'One at least of my preconceived notions has been disposed of already,' said Heinz. 'I had formed a theory regarding possible fatigue of the suprarenals, but I've proved myself wrong. It was one more example of the necessity to correlate relevant facts before forming an hypothesis.'

Heinz twinkled at the memory; he did not mind admitting the human weakness.

'Yes, it is very necessary,' agreed Schmidt.

It was in the adjoining smaller laboratory that the graphs were kept.

Heinz dilated on them with enthusiasm as he displayed them to his uncle, the saw-backed curves, continuous lines and broken lines, dotted lines and starred lines, lines of different colours, a dozen curves on each sheet for the various physiological measurements of an individual subject, mounting irregularly upwards towards an abrupt end; each sheet told the physiological history of the last days of a man.

'Extremely interesting,' said Schmidt, trying not to think about that part of it.

Back at the house Caecilie was quite indignant with her husband.

'Uncle looks more tired than ever, Heinz,' she said. 'You've worn him out to-day. I'm sorry, uncle. These scientists never know when to stop when they get started on their hobby. Why don't you have a little rest before the evening meal?'

Schmidt certainly needed a rest, and at dinner fortunately the conversation was not directed towards the physiology of fear. The Luftwaffe was at that time engaged upon the subjugation of England, so there were plenty of other subjects to discuss – the results of the day's air fighting, and the possibility that England might accept the Fuehrer's magnanimous offer of peace without the necessity of submitting to invasion, and the future of a world enlightened by the ideas of Nazidom. It was only at intervals during the rest of Schmidt's stay that Heinz discussed his research work. Once was when Caecilie had displayed some feminine weakness or other.

'Odd,' said Heinz when he was alone with his uncle, 'how inconsistent women can be. Some of the curves I've obtained with women subjects at the laboratory show the most remarkable variations from normal. The psychologists have seized upon them to help prove some of their theories. And I have to admit there's something to be said for them, too.'

And other time, after they had listened to a broadcast speech by Baldur von Schirach, Heinz talked about race in connection with his research.

'Of course,' he said, 'most of my subjects are Poles and Czechs. I expect you noticed that they were all of the Alpine or Mediterranean types. Even the non-Slavs were of those types. Naturally there are Semitics as well in plenty, but to make my research more complete I need Nordic types.'

'Naturally,' said Schmidt.

'And Nordic types are not so readily available. But I have asked the president to make the strongest representations on the point, and he is doing so. A Nordic type may commit a murder, perhaps. Or there is always the chance of a few Norwegians.'

'Of course that's possible.'

'And then I shall get a new set of curves. And the postmortem appearances should be most interesting.'

'Yes.'

It was a great surprise to Schmidt to hear his nephew talking the Nazi nonsense about race, about Nordics and Alpines. It was hard to believe that a scientist, a scientist with a good mind – even though completely heartless in his work – could possibly give any weight at all to those old theories. Schmidt had to remind himself that Heinz had been exposed to that sort of talk since his boyhood, had hardly known a world where Nordic superiority was not assumed as an article of faith – at least publicly – by everyone. That upbringing of his would largely account for the utter heartlessness, too. So that to Schmidt it was hard to decide which was the greater strain, to stay and listen to his nephew talking about his physiological research or to go back to his nightmare duties at the concentration camp. But he had no choice; when his leave was up he had to go back to Rosenberg camp, into the dreadful conditions there, and he had to do the dreadful things he was called upon to do. It was in the winter that he received a letter from Caecilie. He recognised the writing on the envelope, but the postmark was strange.

They have taken Heinz away [wrote Caecilie]. *Two SS men came and arrested him at night and of course they did not say why. Uncle, I am very worried and I am writing to you to ask you to help because you are in the SS. I am going to post this letter in another town in case they see me posting it and open it. Uncle, please help me. Please find out where he is and try and help him. He was always a good Nazi, as you know. He has never said anything or thought anything that the SS could say was treason. I pray you to help me, uncle. He would have been an army doctor gladly except that the Ministry decided he would be more useful in research. Please help me.*

The first thing that Schmidt did after reading that letter was to burn it. It was dangerous enough to be related to a man who had been arrested by the SS; to be asked by that man's wife to help was very dangerous indeed. And there was nothing he could do, either. The SS kept its secrets, and no insignificant surgeon could hope to be admitted to them, and if that surgeon began to ask questions it might be – it would certainly be – too bad for him. Schmidt did not even answer Caecilie's letter; her mail would undoubtedly be opened and read, and he could not risk even expressing sympathy for a man whose guilt was obvious because of his arrest. He worried about it, though.

The following summer, after the invasion of Russia had begun, Schmidt attended a selection parade in his official capacity.

'A hundred and twenty,' said the camp commandant to him; from the little office they could hear the shouts of the guards and the kapos as they formed up their party for the parade. 'There will be five hundred present, so you can take one in four. A few more than a hundred and twenty will not matter.'

This was the worst of Schmidt's duties, to select the men and women who were to die in the Rosenberg gas chamber. Those were the times when he almost thought he would rather have the gas chamber for himself – almost. That 'almost' might explain how he had come to be selected as surgeon in the SS, and posted to a concentration camp; the SS picked their instruments carefully, and they had noted how fear had forced Schmidt into accepting duties progressively more revolting.

Schmidt drank a glass of schnapps, saw to it that his uniform was correct, and stepped out into the blinding sunshine on the parade ground. Perhaps it was not as bad to select men victims as women. Usually the men made less commotion about it; many of them tried to appear brave, and were ashamed to show emotion before their fellows – some of them, not very many, would try desperately to make a joke when they were selected. And on the other hand they were often so worn down with harsh treatment that they were apathetic. Schmidt hoped that would be the case now.

He walked along the line. Behind him followed the guards to herd away the victims he selected. He had to choose one in four. He might merely have indicated every fourth man, by pure chance, but he dared not do so, lest the anomalies should be too glaring. If he picked those who were still fit and able and left the old, the sick, and the wornout it would be noticed. He had to exercise some care in the selection.

He did not look at the faces; he could not. He looked at the bodies. The diseased, the old, the starved; he had to keep his head clear and his mind active so as to keep count and maintain the proportion of roughly one in four. He pointed to those he selected and passed on. Behind him there were groans of despair; sometimes hysterical screams, the sharp sound of blows, sometimes even a shot as some desperate man resisted and was given his end on the spot. Half-way down the line Schmidt heard a sudden whisper from the line; a single word.

'Uncle!'

He looked up from the body to the face. It was Heinz; but if the word had not been spoken he would not have recognised him. The growth of dirty beard alone was a disguise. And Heinz had lost some of his teeth, and his nose was not quite straight now, and his cheeks were hollow, with the cheekbones standing out. Schmidt looked down again at the scars and sores on the body. If he had not looked at the face he might well have selected Heinz for the gas chamber, young and vigorous though he had recently been.

Neither men dared show further sign of recognition. Luckily the SS men were some yards behind and had not heard the whispered word. Luckily the men on either side of Heinz were old and could be picked as victims – luckily Schmidt's mind was clear enough for him to think of that, lest they should talk and should involve him in Heinz's catastrophe. Schmidt passed on and left Heinz standing in the line, unchosen. Schmidt was shaking with the shock, after his moment of clear thinking, and it was all he could do to complete the parade.

As medical officer Schmidt had access to the files in the central office, and after a decent interval he went to examine them. He went through the card index elaborately, looking at many names, so that the corporal on duty there would not guess what was the real object of his search. Heinz' card was there, but – as Schmidt fully expected – it told him nothing of importance. There were only dates and the names of camps. Heinz had been in two bad ones before coming to Rosenberg, which accounted for the scars and the sores. But there was no indication of what his offence had been – that was only given on the cards of prisoners who were guilty of crimes in the old sense. The SS kept its secrets; Schmidt came away from his examination of the files knowing no more than he had done before. Nor was he going to make further inquiries. No one ever inquired about an SS prisoner; nobody wanted to be thought interested in an SS prisoner's fate.

He was due to have leave soon again, and it called for an effort to decide what he was to do then. He had heard from Caecilie that she had been conscripted into factory work, but her house was still open to him, of course. There was almost nowhere else that he could go, and he went, eventually, and Caecilie made him welcome as always. The house was by no means entirely hers now, as a number of technical workers had been billeted in it – to Schmidt that was something of a relief, because it restricted conversation about Heinz. Caecilie could only speak about him when they were quite alone, and then no louder than a whisper. Schmidt was sympathetic but non-committal; he had decided after prolonged thought not to tell her about his encounter with Heinz. It would do her no good, and it might do her a great deal of harm. She would want to know all about him, how his health was and how he looked, and Schmidt neither wanted to tell her nor could he trust himself to lie convincingly. And moreover Caecilie would expect him to do something to alleviate Heinz' fate, and Schmidt knew that to be downright impossible. He could not bear having to tell her that.

And there was the question of his oaths; at the time of his induction into the SS he had sworn to keep the secrets of the organisation, and he had sworn a further oath never to reveal to the outside world anything about what went on in concentration camps; secrecy made the SS more dreaded than ever, and it was even possible that the SS did not feel happy at the thought that the outside world should know about the nature of the punishments it inflicted. Schmidt had no scruples about the oaths he had taken, but he did not want to violate them by telling Caecilie what he knew. Caecilie might at any time be arrested and under questioning by the SS she would certainly reveal (Schmidt knew about that questioning) anything Schmidt had told her. It was best not to tell her anything.

But because of the prickings of his conscience in the matter he decided in the end to do what he had had in the back of his mind for some time. There was a risk about it, but it was the best he could do. He sent a polite note to Standartenfuehrer Kroide at the university. telling him of his presence in the city on leave, and – he had not really expected it, but only hoped for it – received in return an invitation to luncheon.

It was the usual large party, and Kroide was his usual charming self, the perfect host. It occurred to Schmidt as he listened to the conversation that these parties were one tiny strand in a vast spider's web spread all over the country, in the centre of which was the spider, Dr Goebbels himself, attentive to all the vibrations that passed along the strands. There was wine, there was the freest of conversation, and after such a party Kroide would be able to pass along a good deal of information regarding the attitude of the local intellectuals.

To-day there was no lack of a subject to talk about. The army was pressing far and fast into Russia, and the communiques were blaring victory. There could be no doubt that the Russian colossus wou'd soon be beaten to the ground. No army could long endure the defeats the Fuehrer was inflicting on the Russians. They would collapse, and that would be the end of Germany's last rival save for England. impotent across the sea and fast being strangled by the U-boat campaign. There were some quite amusing jokes about what the Fuehrer would do with Stalin when he fell into his hands. Standartenfuehrer Kroide sat beaming as he listened to the talk, and he let it be understood, by his significant reticences, that he could, if security did not forbid, add much to the conversation, and that, as a high official of the Ministry of Propaganda, he was cognisant of many secrets regarding the further surprises the Fuehrer had up his sleeve for the enemies of the Reich. He beamed and he drank wine, mellowed by alcohol and victory. It was after lunch was over, as the guests still stood chatting, that he addressed himself to Schmidt.

'Too bad about that young nephew of yours,' he said.

'My nephew Heinrich?' asked Schmidt, without committing himself.

'Yes. I once had great hopes of him. I thought he was a talented scientist and a fervent friend of the Reich, but to my disappointment I found he was neither.'

'I am sorry about that, Standartenfuehrer,' said Schmidt. It was safe to be sorry about Kroide's hurt feelings, even if it was not safe to be sorry about Heinz' fate.

'The silly young fool,' said Kroide. 'Not only was he completely wrong-headed, but he wanted to proclaim the fact publicly.'

'How very extraordinary!' said Schmidt.

'Yes, indeed. He told me he had completed the piece of physiological research on which he was engaged – you remember – and I was quite delighted. I encouraged him all the time he was writing his paper regarding his results, and I looked forward to the time when it should be completed.'

'And did he complete it, Standartenfuehrer?'

'Yes. Of course I did not read it; it was far too technical for me. I forwarded it, just as it was, graphs, statistics and all, to Dr Goebbels' office, as was my duty, of course.'

'Yes?' Schmidt hoped he was not displaying too much interest. Despite the wine which made his head swim he tried to put exactly the right intonation into what he said.

'I was really only concerned with security – I thought it was possible, or even likely, that the paper might contain material that our enemies could find useful as well as us. It was a routine step, to decide whether it would be desirable to publish the paper in the university "Transactions."'

Kroide took off his spectacles and polished them, and blinked short-sightedly at Schmidt.

'It was a great shock to me,' went on Kroide, 'when the teletype message came in ordering me to suppress everything to do with your nephew's paper. The SS, of course, had already arrested him by the time the message reached me.'

'How shocking!' said Schmidt. He still did not dare to ask the obvious question, but he waited hopefully and his hope was not disappointed.

'Yes,' said Kroide, almost with regret. 'The SS had no choice but to arrest him and put him where his ridiculous theories could do no harm. Do you know what the madman had written?'

'I simply cannot guess,' said Schmidt.

Kroide leaned forward confidentially and tapped Schmidt on the chest with his spectacles.

'He had it all wrong. I even think he might have had insane delusions. He thought he had proved that fear had exactly the same physiological results with Nordics as with the lesser races! Can you imagine anything more insane or more treasonable?'

'No,' said Schmidt.

C. S. Forester

The Head and the Feet

Georg Schmidt was not happy in his job as medical officer of the Rosenberg Concentration Camp. There were many days when he regretted, when he sorrowed deeply over, his initial weaknesses which had given the SS the hint that he was a suitable and pliable instrument for them. Now he was in their clutches and there was no way out for him – the only possible way, that of volunteering for active service with the Waffen SS in the field, was barred by reason of his advanced age. Schmidt often remembered the brutal speech of an SS officer to a newly-arrived batch of prisoners.

'You are here to work, and work you shall. For the man who cannot work, and for the man who will not work, there is the gas chamber. Work or death – there is no other future for you.'

There was no other future for Schmidt, either, and he knew it well. Nor could he ever allow the world a glimpse if his feelings; they must always be concealed. The SS was proud of the intensity of its patriotism and of the fervour of its faith in national socialism and it would never tolerate the existence of a half-hearted member. The knowledge made Schmidt's situation all the worse, for it deprived him of any pleasure in getting drunk; in alcoholic stupor he could be oblivious of his troubles, but while he was achieving that condition he was always gnawed at by the thought of what might blurt out before he was quite drunk, and the fears that thought aroused poisoned his liquor and delayed its action, so that he would sometimes spend the evening in his quarters, unable to get drunk, yammering to himself in a nightmare of misery. The world thinks of the men who staffed the concentration camps as fiends of Hell; fiends they were, but they were in Hell too, some of them.

That was not true of Sturmbannfuehrer Schiller, the camp commandant, who was a man without humour or moods, whose conscience was in the keeping of the SS, and who was actuated by no motives beyond a mild personal ambition and a desire to carry out to the letter the orders of higher authority. As long as headquarters at Oranienburg couched the order in the proper form, and it bore the correct signature, Sturm-bannfuehrer Schiller would have pushed his own mother into the gas chamber without a moment's hesitation or regret, Schmidt thought. The two men were together in the commandant's office; Schmidt had just made his report after his morning rounds, and had laid stress on the necessity for temporary isolation and thorough delousing of a new batch of Ruthenians who had just arrived; he suspected they had brought typhus with them.

'I have made a note of it,' said Schiller. 'Meanwhile there is a question of some other arrivals beside the Ruthenians.'

'Yes, commandant,' said Schmidt.

He knew perfectly well there had been some other arrivals, and so did all the rest of the staff, and probably the prisoners as well, but as there had been ostentatious secrecy about the matter he judged it best to make a show of ignorance. But during the night a small amount of motor transport had arrived, conveying a number of new SS troopers and presumably some other people, for one of the detached huts on the perimeter of the camp was now guarded by sentries with new faces, and foot traffic along the path leading past it was now prohibited.

'There are four new prisoners in Block Eleven,' explained Schiller. 'They have been sent here with their papers marked "for special treatment!" '

'I understand, commandant,' said Schmidt.

He knew those fatal words well. The prisoner whose papers bore them – besondere Behandlung – was marked by Oranienburg for execution. Death stalked about Rosenberg camp in many forms. Death in the gas chamber – that was of everyday occurrence; death under the whips and rifle butts of the guards; death from disease and privation; death from suicide. But 'special treatment' meant something far more formal and far less casual than all those; it meant capital punishment carried out with the ritual and elaboration of the old days when execution only followed murder. It meant a fixed time and place, the presence of witnesses, the signing of certificates, even if the methods of execution were sometimes strange and even if the whole affair was shrouded in secrecy. Now and then there would be public and formal hangings, carried out on the central parade ground in sight of all the mustered prisoners – that would be when some prisoner had been guilty of sabotage or insubordination or attempted escape. Sometimes there would be private hangings, in a little hut at the back of the crematorium to which the bodies would be speedily and secretly transferred; there was a row of hooks in a beam in that hut, and lengths of supple rope kept ready, and a heavy bench from which the victims could be pushed. Who those victims were, and why they were accorded this particular 'special treatment,' their crimes and the reasons for secrecy, were matters with which only headquarters were concerned, and it would be better if no one else were to inquire into them.

There had been two victims – both women – who had had very special treatment indeed; at Schiller's orders Schmidt had told them that they were to be inoculated against typhus, and Schmid thad injected subcutaneously so large a dose of morphine that they had slipped away into final unconsciousness without any of the bitterness of death, but on the other hand there had been some men who had been slowly strangled – slowly, and with many intermissions – while an official photographer had recorded the process for the subsequent delectation of some unknown but certainly lofty official, perhaps the same one whose soft-heartedness had selected the fate of the women.

So with all these possibilities Schmidt had to await further instructions from Schiller.

'The special treatment indicated by the orders I have received,' said the latter, 'is decapitation.'

Schmidt knew he should answer 'Yes commandant' as always, but this time the words would not come, for he was surprised, even though seven years of service in a concentration camp should have rendered him immune to surprise. But Schiller waited patiently for his reply, and he made it at last. He should not have been surprised, for a very early decree by the Fuehrer years ago, had re-established decapitation as a method of punishment in the Reich.

'The headsman,' went on Schiller, 'is here. He was brought by the same convoy as brought the prisoners. He is under confinement too, to make sure he will be sober when the time comes.'

'And when is the time?' asked Schmidt, knowing the question was expected of him. Schiller tapped thoughtfully on his desk with the butt end of his pen. The length of four human lives was being determined by his decision, but Schiller really did not give a thought to that. If he named an early hour in the morning his wife would be distressed at having to rise unusually early to sit with him at breakfast, but if he left it until later his necessary attendance at the function would break into his comfortable morning routine of correspondence and reports. But it would be best to get it over before the camp was roused at dawn, because otherwise the prisoners with their lively powers of observation would perhaps guess what was going on. He made a compromise decision.

'Five-thirty,' he said, at length. 'You will be present from five-fifteen.'

'Very well, commandant,' said Schmidt.

'The certificates must be prepared immediately after the execution,' added Schiller. 'The escort will leave as soon as cremation is complete and the officer in command is to take them with him.'

'Very well,' said Schmidt.

Even he, even in his present mood, quite failed to see anything odd about the regulations that made it necessary to have a qualified medical man in attendance to certify the cause of death when men were going to have their heads severed from their bodies; routine, regulations, precedents all demanded his presence, and it did not occur to him to revolt against them – not that he would have done so, in any case, naturally.

'I will see you there,' said Schiller. 'Heil Hitler!'

'Heil Hitler!' said Schmidt.

At five o'clock in the morning, when Schmidt was called, it was still perfectly dark and shuddering cold. He huddled himself into his uniform and drank a hurried cup of coffee – even at this stage of the war coffee was the only unsatisfactory ration allotted to the SS – and walked across the parade ground from his quarters. A few shaded lamps threw beams of light along the fences of barbed wire so that the guards in the towers had the whole perimeter under observation. The whole camp was deadly quiet, even though five thousand men and women lay there in confinement. He saw a sudden gleam of flame from the chimney of the crematorium; a Kapo – one of the internees who did duties in return for a little more food and a little less ill-treatment – was firing it up in readiness. But there was no one near the little shed with the beam and the hooks. Schmidt realised that of course there would not be room enough there for the swing of an axe, and in a sudden fear lest he should be late he hurried on to where light from an opening door revealed dark figures moving about. He arrived a little short of breath and only just in time at the vacant shed near the guard-house. Schiller was just entering, his adjutant with him.

'Heil Hitler!' said Schmidt, saluting.

'Heil Hitler!' grunted Schiller, who was never at his best early in the morning.

Preparations had already been made in the shed. The floorboards – if there ever had been any – had been removed to reveal the naked earth, and in the middle of the shed stood a large cube of wood; dangling over the cube, illuminating it starkly against the sawdust, hung a bright electric lamp. Schiller and Schmidt and the adjutant took their position beside the block, and as they did so three more men came in through the door. They all wore leather aprons, but one of them was bare to the waist despite the cold. He was a man of immense physique, something under thirty, bulging with muscle, and he carried the largest axe that

Schmidt had ever seen; along the edge it certainly measured forty centimetres, and it was clear, from the way the big man handled it, that the huge head weighed several kilograms. Schmidt found himself thinking that the axe-head would do the job of its own weight, but he next decided that it would be all the more necessary to have a powerful man to wield it, to swing it up and bring it down. The executioner took his place by the block; he measured his distance from it with his eye, lifted the axe to it, bending his knees and shifting his feet until he was satisfied with his position, like a golfer addressing his ball. At length he stood erect, the axe-head resting by his feet, and the helve in his hands, and then in came an SS officer and two SS men with the first victim. He was frightened. He dragged his feet and he moaned pitifully, but not for long.

'Next!' called the officer – hardly necessary after that loud thump. And then again, after the axe had once more swung slowly up and come hurtling down, 'Next!'

Schmidt found he had to look away. He shifted his position a little, and, holding himself at attention with his eyes looking straight before him he could direct his rigid stare away from what was going on, even though he could not close his ears to it. Nor could he numb his sensation of touch. Immediately after the next thump he heard something bounce in front of him, and he felt something bump against his feet, and he looked down with something of horror at what had struck him, until one of the men in the leather aprons stooped and lifted it away.

'Next!' said the SS officer.

The horror grew inside Schmidt as he thought again of what had bumped against his feet. He was shuddering and felt sick so that this time he paid no attention to what was going on and was only recalled to reality by the clear expressionless voice of the SS officer.

'So perish all enemies of the Reich! Heil Hitler!'

'Heil Hitler!' chorused most the those present – most of those present who were still alive – and then Schiller turned to Schmidt.

'The certificates are in my office. Please come and sign them.'

When Schmidt straightened himself up from the desk, recapping his fountain-pen, Schiller had an invitation for him.

'Next Wednesday is my birthday,' he said, with a smile. 'I hope you will come to a party at my house. A little wine – a little coffee – at four o'clock? Next Wednesday?'

'Of course I shall be delighted,' said Schmidt.

It was an effort to smile and bow; Schmidt was sure he must be looking white and sick – he could still feel that thing bumping against his feet, so that it was all he could do not to look down at his boots.

'Excellent! My wife will be pleased,' said Schiller, and then in

427

dismissal, 'Heil Hitler!'

Outside it was still quite dark, only the barest hint of dawn in the east, but a gush of flames flared up again from the chimney of the crematorium. By the guard-house stood the trucks which were to take the SS men away to their next duty. Two dark figures were lifting a heavy cube up into one of the trucks. And in the darkness as he walked along Schmidt could still feel the sensation of that bump against his feet.

It was strange how it still lingered with him. He went back to his quarters, stripped, and stood under the shower and scrubbed his feet, telling himself at the same time that it was quite absurd that he should do so, for he had been wearing his uniform boots when it had happened and it was impossible that he should be polluted, that anything could have infected him. But when, dressed again, he went over to the mess and sat down to breakfast he bumped his foot against the table-leg, not hard, almost gently, the way – the way his foot had been bumped before. The result was that he snarled at the morning greetings of his brother officers in a way that made the adjutant cock an eye at him; part of the oath of the SS was to swear true comradeship with all one's fellow members and Schmidt's behaviour was therefore suspicious.

Schmidt's upset temper continued. At the sick parade he was testy and curt. To-day he did not draw even his usual consolation from the fact that he never had to combat malingering; the prison sick always did their pathetic best to appear as well as possible, for they knew that the gas chamber awaited the seriously ill. The man to-day whom he ordered to hospital actually begged not to be sent; he dropped on his knees – he was an oldish man of no spirit – and tried to grasp the skirt of Schmidt's tunic in supplication, and when Schmidt drew back he overbalanced forward and grasped at Schmidt's feet, provoking a burst of wrath which took Schmidt's assistants by surprise, as he was usually even-tempered; they sought to please him (they were all Kapos – hated by their fellow prisoners and despised by their masters) by beating the old man with their sticks as they dragged him away. But after Schmidt had completed his morning duties he went under the shower again, as he usually did, and he found himself scrubbing his feet again. He remembered that bump against them so well; the memory kept on returning to him.

He could not lose that memory however much he tried; there were little incidents all through the day that brought it back to him, a touch here, a bump there. He found himself, when he wanted to put on his slippers, actually shrinking from putting his hands to his boots, and when he drank his fourth glass of schnapps he suddenly leaped up from his chair, shaking, for he was sure he had felt something strike against his feet again. It was the same when he went to bed; he composed himself for sleep, and he drifted off, stupefied, and then woke instantly with a start, sweating, his heart thumping, for he had dreamed in those few seconds of sleep that something had struck against his feet. He hated his feet, down there at the far end of the bed. Muzzy with drink and yet at the same time tense and nervous he had to get up and stagger over to the dispensary for a drug to induce sleep, and then that was worse, for the drug seemed to bind and shackle him in his dreams, holding him helpless while things – not well-defined things but things with eyes and mouths – bounced and touched his feet.

Next morning, standing by his bed with his hand on his dressing-table to steady himself, he addressed himself seriously, as seriously as his aching head would permit. This was all nonsense. He would be going insane if he allowed this to go on. After all he had seen and endured it was absurd to allow one single petty incident to upset him in this fashion. He must put it out of his mind altogether. He must not shudder like that at the recollection of his dreams. Nor must he step aside hastily as he had just done at the thought of things touching his feet. No, he must not. He had a professional familiarity with insanity, naturally, and he knew about the growth of delusions; he had seen delusions of touch before. But in the shower it was hard not to stoop down with the scrubbing-brush and scrub and scrub at his feet in the hope of abolishing the feeling of a cold poison upon their skin. Did a snake have saliva? The cold saliva of a snake was the idea in his mind at the moment. Absurd, of course – that had no relation at all to – to what had actually happened. He swore violently.

In the mess the adjutant cocked an eye at him again, noting the imperfect shave and the dirty handkerchief. They were affronts to the tradition of the SS, which demanded the most careful, ritual bodily cleanliness. The adjutant had to think about his duty, for he was a member of a very special body, of the police within the police. Juvenal had asked, eighteen hundred years earlier, 'Who shall guard the guards?' and Himmler had found the answer to that question; the adjutant was one of those people who reported to Himmler on the people who reported to Himmler. Schmidt was aware of the glance the adjutant shot at him, and his condition was not bettered on that account. It made him concerned about his feet again. He dragged the polluted things about with him all day as he did his day's duty, most painfully conscious of them, and the night was even worse. The delusions were out of control altogether now; they had fastened upon him and could not let him go. Rosenberg Concentration Camp was a hell-pit of despair and misery, and the camp doctor now had his share too. His word could deal out death – and it did, hundreds of times – and the prisoners in their profound misery did their best to flatter him, to please him, to gain his favour. They cringed to him like beaten dogs, while he walked among them on a pair of feet that he believed to be spongy and rotten with poison; feet that, whenever his attention was diverted, might be bumped against by things. There were days of this life, days and days – and nights and nights.

Then came the commandant's birthday, to be celebrated with all the sentiment of the German tradition, and Schmidt made a serious effort to pull himself together for the occasion. He shaved a second time, even though it was only early afternoon, trying to smile with sympathy at the haggard old face that looked back at him from the mirror. He had his clothes most carefully brushed, and he was proud of himself for being able to order without a quaver a special polishing of his boots without a thought of – of what he must not think about. He must not think about his feet as they went one-two one-two when he marched out through the prison gate; the SS were always smart and military in appearance and movement, and though he was middle-aged he could be as smart and military as the spotless sentry at the gate who saluted him. Smart and upright even with feet that – that— No, he must not think about his feet.

The commandant lived a domestic life in the bosom of his family during the hours when he was not engaged on the business of the state in Rosenberg Concentration Camp. He had taken a little house in the village a mile from the gate, where he dwelt with his wife and children, happily uxorious, indulgent to his children, and polite to his neighbours despite his rank, although they could not forget the dreaded uniform he wore, while they tried to be ignorant of what happened behind the barbed-wire fences of the camp a mile up the road which they never walked along. The commandant was a good host now; he made Schmidt welcome, and received his felicitations on his birthday with delighted modesty. Schmidt bowed over Frau Sturmbannfuehrer Schiller's hand and told her that every day she looked younger and more charming. He bowed to his brother officers – the adjutant was there, of course – and he made himself agreeable to their wives. Five of the officers had been fortunate enough to be able to establish their wives in the village, and they and their wives and a couple of other officers from the camp constituted the party, no one else. The black uniforms lived in isolation; they saw each other every day, but for this occasion they made polite conversation as if they had not met for weeks, and they talked to the wives, and the wives talked to them, as if they were people of normal life, as if the hideous cruelty in which they dealt daily had never been thought of.

What went on in the concentration camp was supposed to be kept secret and never described in the outside world, but perhaps husbands talked to wives; perhaps those wives knew, as they talked to their husbands' colleagues, what frightful deeds of blood those colleagues had perpetrated, but they showed no sign of it. They smiled and they discussed airy nothings; perhaps as a butcher's wife will talk with another butcher. And the children, when they were brought into the party, in their best clothes and with their hair tidy, were cooed over and complimented. The five-year-old and the three-year-old bobbed and curtsied as they were told, but little Hildegard was only one-and-a-half, and when she was put down on the floor she escaped from her mother with a gurgle of glee and ran with unsteady steps and outspread arms into the crowded room. Schmidt drew hastily back to avoid her clutch round his legs – he did not want his feet touched as the hospital patient had touched them – and she fell with a bump on her nose at his feet and wailed in consequence. The woman looked their disapprobation at Schmidt for allowing it to happen, but he was only an old widower, after all, and had had nothing to do with children, so they decided he was to be pitied rather than to be condemned. But the adjutant saw and was not so lenient in his judgment, for kindness to children and animals should be, as the SS doctrine laid down, characteristic of a member of the SS.

It was even worse ten minutes later, just when Schmidt was talking again to Frau Neumann and priding himself on behaving naturally. Something bumped against his feet, something solid. Frau Neumann saw the expression on his face change, saw the horror in it. The wine in the glass that Schmidt held was jerked out in a golden arc as he kicked out wildly. There was a sharp yelp, and everyone looked down and round to see Sturmbannfuehrer Schiller's little dachshund, which had managed to make its way into the room when the children were taken out, proclaiming the sorrow of an affectionate advance being received by a kick in the ribs. There was more reproach in the eyes of the women as they looked at Schmidt, but he was hardly aware of it, with the sweat standing out on his forehead and his hands shaking.

Schmidt was the first guest to leave that party, even though the sane part of his mind told him that perhaps it was a little unwise to do so. The others would be given an opportunity to discuss him and his peculiarities. He was not in any case a man who enjoyed the company of other people; moreover although the same part of his mind told him, too, that he should stay here amid the lights and the distractions, the insane part wanted to take him away like a wounded animal, into darkness and solitude. The sane part of his mind made him shake Sturmbannfuehrer's hand politely and renew his congratulations on the anniversary, and made him thank Frau Sturmbannfuehrer Schiller for a magnificent party, but the insane part asserted itself again as he walked in the darkness back to the camp.

A strange suggestion was making itself felt in his mind. These feet, these horrible feet of his, might be got rid of. He pictured himself lying on his back in his bed, revolver in hand, taking aim at those feet and shooting them off, bit by bit. There was something strangely tempting in the idea; it would mean the end of his troubles. But what was left of his sanity asserted itself again and argued with his insanity. It would be painful (but was that not really an argument in its favour?) and it would be impractical (but perhaps not to a man as filled with an inward spirit as he was) and it was the insane who practised horrible mutilations upon themselves (but the insane did not have the justification he had – they had not had his experience) and he would feel better in the morning (but before morning he had still to go through the night).

As he plodded on up the road to the camp the arguments presented by his sanity fought a losing battle with those presented by his insanity. By the time he had reached the gate he was thinking about his project with something of warm anticipation. He would free himself from his disgusting feet; he had practically decided upon it as he stood by the gate for the sergeant of the guard to identify him – he was even a little afraid lest the sergeant should read his intention in his expression and prevent him for some reason.

That started another train of thought as he walked into the dark camp. The SS would look upon his act as self-mutilation to avoid duty. Then he would be misunderstood – that was the trouble, not the fear of what would be done to the remainder of him in that event. He did not like that thought, and he felt bitter disappointment at having to give up the project. He stamped with his disgusting feet in rage as he walked along through the camp.

There, hardly visible in the darkness, was the shed where – where it had happened. There was the gas chamber which had so often held the heaped-up dead. There was the private execution shed with its beam and its hooks and its supple ropes with running nooses. A new idea struck him, one which was not disapproved by any part of his mind. He walked in the darkness to the shed; even in the deeper darkness within it he could find his way about, feel for a hook and a rope, climb up on to the bench. This was gratifying; this was an ingenious way round the difficulties which no one less clever than he could have thought of. There was something wayward and pixie-like in his mood now in his moment of triumph. It was that which made him say 'Heil Hitler!' before he stepped off the bench.

Ray Bradbury

The Veld

'George, I wish you'd look at the nursery.'

'What's wrong with it?'

'I don't know.'

'Well, then.'

'I just want you to look at it, is all, or call a psychologist in to look at it.'

'What would a psychologist want with a nursery?'

'You know very well what he'd want.' His wife paused in the middle of the kitchen and watched the stove busy humming to itself, making supper for four.

'It's just that the nursery is different now than it was.'

'All right, let's have a look.'

They walked down the hall of their sound-proofed, Happy-life Home, which had cost them thirty thousand dollars installed, this house which clothed and fed and rocked them to sleep and played and sang and was good to them. Their approach sensitised a switch somewhere and the nursery light flicked on when they came within ten feet of it. Similarly, behind them, in the halls, lights went on and off as they left them behind, with a soft automaticity.

'Well,' said George Hadley.

They stood on the thatched floor of the nursery. It was forty feet across by forty feet long and thirty feet high, it had cost half again as much as the rest of the house. 'But nothing's too good for our children,' George had said.

The nursery was silent. It was empty as a jungle glade at hot high noon. The walls were blank and two-dimensional. Now, as George and Lydia Hadley stood in the centre of the room, the walls began to purr and recede into crystalline distance, it seemed, and presently an African veld appeared, in three dimensions, on all sides, in colour, reproduced to the final pebble and bit of straw. The ceiling above them became a deep sky with a hot yellow sun.

George Hadley felt the perspiration start on his brow.

'Let's get out of this sun,' he said. 'This is a little too real. But I don't see anything wrong.'

'Wait a moment, you'll see,' said his wife.

Now the hidden odorophonics were beginning to blow a wind o odour at the two people in the middle of the baked veldland. The hot straw smell of lion grass, the cool green smell of the hidden water hole, the great rusty smell of animals, the smell of dust like a red paprika in the hot air. And now the sounds: the thump of distant antelope feet on grassy sod, the papery rustling of vultures. A shadow passed through the sky. The shadow flickered on George Hadley's upturned, sweating face.

'Filthy creatures,' he heard his wife say.

'The vultures.'

'You see, there are the lions, far over, that way. Now they're on their way to the water hole. They've just been eating,' said Lydia. 'I don't know what.'

'Some animal.' George Hadley put his hand up to shield off the burning light from his squinted eyes. 'A zebra or a baby giraffe, maybe.'

'Are you *sure*?' His wife sounded peculiarly tense.

'No, it's a little late to be *sure*,' he said, amused. 'Nothing over there I can see but cleaned bone, and the vultures dropping for what's left.'

'Did you hear that scream?' she asked.

'No.'

'About a minute ago?'

'Sorry, no.'

The lions were coming. And again George Hadley was filled with admiration for the mechanical genius who had conceived this room. A miracle of efficiency selling for an absurdly low price. Every home should have one. Oh, occasionally they frightened you with their clinical accuracy, they startled you, gave you a twinge, but most of the time what fun for everyone, not only your own son and daughter, but for yourself when you felt like a quick jaunt to a foreign land, a quick change of scenery. Well, here it was!

And here were the lions now, fifteen feet away, so real, so feverishly and startlingly real that you could feel the prickling fur on your hand, and your mouth was stuffed with the dusty upholstery smell of their heated pelts, and the yellow of them was in your eyes like the yellow of an exquisite French tapestry, the yellows of lions and summer grass, and the sound of the matted lion lungs exhaling on the silent noontide,

434

and the smell of meat from the panting, dripping mouths.

The lions stood looking at George and Lydia Hadley with terrible green-yellow eyes.

'Watch out!' screamed Lydia.

The lions came running at them.

Lydia bolted and ran. Instinctively, George sprang after her. Outside, in the hall, with the door slammed, he was laughing and she was crying, and they both stood appalled at the other's reaction.

'George!'

'Lydia! Oh, my dear poor sweet Lydia!'

'They almost got us!'

'Walls, Lydia, remember; crystal walls, that's all they are. Oh, they look real, I must admit – Africa in your parlour – but it's all dimensional super-reactionary, super-sensitive colour film and mental tape film behind glass screens. It's all odorophonics and sonics, Lydia. Here's my handkerchief.'

'I'm afraid.' She came to him and put her body against him and cried steadily. 'Did you see? Did you feel? It's too real.'

'Now, Lydia . . .'

'You've got to tell Wendy and Peter not to read any more on Africa.'

'Of course – of course.' He patted her.

'Promise?'

'Sure.'

'And lock the nursery for a few days until I get my nerves settled.'

'You know how difficult Peter is about that. When I punished him a month ago by locking the nursery for even a few hours – the tantrum he threw! And Wendy too. They live for the nursery.'

'It's got to be locked, that's all there is to it.'

'All right.' Reluctantly he locked the huge door. 'You've been working too hard. You need a rest.'

'I don't know – I don't know,' she said, blowing her nose, sitting down in a chair that immediately began to rock and comfort her. 'Maybe I don't have enough to do. Maybe I have time to think too much. Why don't we shut the whole house off for a few days and take a vacation?'

'You mean you want to ry my eggs for me?'

'Yes.' She nodded.

'And darn my socks?'

'Yes.' A frantic, watery-eyed nodding.

'And sweep the house?'

'Yes, yes – oh, yes!'

'But I thought that's why we bought this house, so we wouldn't have to do anything?'

'That's just it. I feel like I don't belong here. The house is wife and mother now and nursemaid. Can I compete with an African veld? Can I have a bath and scrub the children as efficiently or quickly as the automatic scrub bath can? I cannot. And it isn't just me. It's you. You've been awfully nervous lately.'

'I suppose I have been smoking too much.'

'You look as if you didn't know what to do with yourself in this house, either. You smoke a little more every morning and drink a little more every afternoon and need a little more sedative every night. You're beginning to feel unnecessary too.'

'Am I?' He paused and tried to feel into himself to see what was really there.

'Oh, George!' She looked beyond him, at the nursery door. 'Those lions can't get out of there, can they?'

He looked at the door and saw it tremble as if something had jumped against it from the other side.

'Of course not,' he said.

At dinner they ate alone, for Wendy and Peter were at a special plastic carnival across town and had televised home to say they'd be late, to go ahead eating. So George Hadley, bemused, sat watching the dining-room table produce warm dishes of food from its mechanical interior.

'We forgot the ketchup,' he said.

'Sorry,' said a small voice within the table, and ketchup appeared.

As for the nursery, thought George Hadley, it won't hurt for the children to be locked out of it awhile. Too much of anything isn't good for anyone. And it was clearly indicated that the children had been spending a little too much time on Africa. That *sun*. He could feel it on his neck, still, like a hot paw. And the *lions*. And the smell of blood. Remarkable how the nursery caught the telepathic emanations of the children's minds and created life to fill their every desire. The children thought lions, and there were lions. The children thought zebras, and there were zebras. Sun – sun. Giraffes – giraffes. Death and death.

That *last*. He chewed tastelessly on the meat that the table had cut for him. Death thoughts. They were awfully young, Wendy and Peter, for death thoughts. Or, no, you were never too young, really. Long before you knew what death was you were wishing it on someone else. When you were two years old you were shooting people with cap pistols.

But this – the long, hot African veld – the awful death in the jaws of a lion. And repeated again and again.

'Where are you going?'

He didn't answer Lydia. Preoccupied, he let the lights glow softly on ahead of him, extinguish behind him as he padded to the nursery door. He listened against it. Far away, a lion roared.

He unlocked the door and opened it. Just before he stepped inside, he heard a far-away scream. And then another roar from the lions, which subsided quickly.

He stepped into Africa. How many times in the last year had he opened this door and found Wonderland, Alice, the Mock Turtle, or Aladdin and his Magical Lamp, or Jack Pumpkinhead of Oz, or Dr Doolittle, or the cow jumping over a very real-appearing moon – all the delightful contraptions of a make-believe world. How often had he seen Pegasus flying in the sky ceiling, or seen fountains of red fireworks, or heard angel voices singing. But now, this yellow hot Africa, this bake oven with murder in the heat. Perhaps Lydia was right. Perhaps they needed a little vacation from the fantasy which was growing a bit too real for ten-year-old children. It was all right to exercise one's mind with gymnastic fantasies, but when the lively child mind settled on one pattern . . ? It seemed that, at a distance, for the past month, he had heard lions roaring, and smelled their strong odour seeping as far away as his study door. But, being busy, he had paid it no attention.

George Hadley stood on the African grassland alone. The lions looked up from their feeding, watching him. The only flaw to the illusion was the open door through which he could see his wife, far down the dark hall, like a framed picture, eating her dinner abstractedly.

'Go away,' he said to the lions.

They did not go.

He knew the principle of the room exactly. You sent out your thoughts. Whatever you thought would appear.

'Let's have Aladdin and his lamp,' he snapped.

The veldland remained, the lions remained.

'Come on, room! I demand Aladdin!' he said.

Nothing happened. The lions mumbled in their baked pelts.

'Aladdin!'

He went back to dinner. 'The fool room's out of order,' he said. 'It won't respond.'

'Or—'

'Or what?'

'Or it *can't* respond,' said Lydia, 'because the children have thought about Africa and lions and killing so many days that the room's in a rut.'

'Could be.'

'Or Peter's set it to remain that way.'

'*Set* it?'

'He may have got into the machinery and fixed something.'

'Peter doesn't know machinery.'

'He's a wise one for ten. That I.Q. of his—'

'Nevertheless—'

'Hello, Mom. Hello, Dad.'

The Hadleys turned. Wendy and Peter were coming in the front door, cheeks like peppermint candy, eyes like bright blue agate marbles, a smell of ozone on their jumpers from their trip in the helicopter.

'You're just in time for supper,' said both parents.

'We're full of strawberry ice cream and hot dogs,' said the children, holding hands. 'But we'll sit and watch.'

'Yes, come tell us about the nursery,' said George Hadley.

The brother and sister blinked at him and then at each other. 'Nursery?'

'All about Africa and everything,' said the father with false joviality.

'I don't understand,' said Peter.

'Your mother and I were just travelling through Africa with rod and reel; Tom Swift and his Electric Lion,' said George Hadley.

'There's no Africa in the nursery,' said Peter simply.

'Oh, come now, Peter. We know better.'

'I don't remember any Africa,' said Peter to Wendy. 'Do you?'

'No.'

'Run see and come tell.'

She obeyed.

'Wendy, come back here!' said George Hadley, but she was gone. The house lights followed her like a flock of fireflies. Too late, he realised he had forgotten to lock the nursery door after his last inspection.

'Wendy'll look and come tell us,' said Peter.

'She doesn't have to tell *me*. I've seen it.'

'I'm sure you're mistaken, Father.'

'I'm not, Peter. Come along now.'

But Wendy was back. 'It's not Africa,' she said breathlessly.

'We'll see about this,' said George Hadley, and they all walked down the hall together and opened the nursery door.

There was a green, lovely forest, a lovely river, a purple mountain, high voices singing, and Rima, lovely and mysterious, lurking in the trees with colourful flights of butterflies, like animated bouquets, lingering in her long hair. The African veldland was gone. The lions were gone. Only Rima was here now, singing a song so beautiful that it brought tears to your eyes.

George Hadley looked in at the changed scene. 'Go to bed,' he said to the children.

They opened their mouths.

'You heard me,' he said.

They went off to the air closet, where a wind sucked them like brown leaves up the flue to their slumber rooms.

438

George Hadley walked through the singing glade and picked up something that lay in the corner near where the lions had been. He walked slowly back to his wife.

'What is that?' she asked.

'An old wallet of mine,' he said.

He showed it to her. The smell of hot grass was on it and the smell of a lion. There were drops of saliva on it, it had been chewed, and there blood smears on both sides.

He closed the nursery door and locked it, tight.

In the middle of the night he was still awake and he knew his wife was awake. 'Do you think Wendy changed it?' she said at last, in the dark room.

'Of course.'

'Made it from a veld into a forest and put Rima there instead of lions?'

'Yes.'

'Why?'

'I don't know. But it's staying locked until I find out.'

'How did your wallet get there?'

'I don't know anything,' he said, 'except that I'm beginning to be sorry we bought that room for the children. If children are neurotic at all, a room like that—'

'It's supposed to help them work off their neuroses in a healthful way.'

'I'm starting to wonder.' He stared at the ceiling.

'We've given the children everything they ever wanted. Is this our reward – secrecy, disobedience?'

'Who was it said, "Children are carpets, they should be stepped on occasionally"? We've never lifted a hand. They're insufferable – let's admit it. They come and go when they like; they treat us as if *we* were offspring. They're spoiled and we're spoiled.'

'They've been acting funny ever since you forbade them to take the rocket to New York a few months ago.'

'They're not old enough to do that alone, I explained.'

'Nevertheless, I've noticed they've been decidedly cool toward us since.'

'I think I'll have David McClean come tomorrow morning to have a look at Africa.'

'But it's not Africa now, it's Green Mansions country and Rima.'

'I have a feeling it'll be Africa again before then.'

A moment later they heard the screams.

Two screams. Two people screaming from downstairs. And then a roar of lions.

'Wendy and Peter aren't in their rooms,' said his wife.

He lay in his bed with his beating heart. 'No,' he said. 'They've broken into the nursery.'

'Those screams – they sound familiar.'

'Do they?'

'Yes, awfully.'

And although their beds tried very hard, the two adults couldn't be rocked to sleep for another hour. A smell of cats was in the night air.

'Father?' said Peter.

'Yes.'

Peter looked at his shoes. He never looked at his father any more, nor at his mother. 'You aren't going to lock up the nursery for good, are you?'

'That all depends.'

'On what?' snapped Peter.

'On you and your sister. If you intersperse this Africa with a little variety – oh, Sweden perhaps, or Denmark or China—'

'I thought we were free to play as we wished.'

'You are, within reasonable bounds.'

'What's wrong with Africa, Father?'

'Oh, so now you admit you have been conjuring up Africa, do you?'

'I wouldn't want the nursery locked up,' said Peter coldly. 'Ever.'

'Matter of fact, we're thinking of turning the whole house off for about a month. Live sort of a carefree one-for-all existence.'

'That sounds dreadful! Would I have to tie my own shoes instead of letting the shoe tier do it? And brush my own teeth and comb my hair and give myself a bath?'

'It would be fun for a change, don't you think?'

'No, it would be horrid. I didn't like it when you took out the picture painter last month.'

'That's because I wanted you to learn to paint all by yourself, son.'

'I don't want to do anything but look and listen and smell; what else is there to do?'

'All right, go play in Africa.'

'Will you shut off the house sometime soon?'

'We're considering it.'

'I don't think you'd better consider it any more, Father.'

'I won't have any threats from my son!'

'Very well.' And Peter strolled off to the nursery.

'Am I on time?' said David McClean.

'Breakfast?' asked George Hadley.

'Thanks, had some. What's the trouble?'

'David, you're a psychologist.'

'I should hope so.'

'Well, then, have a look at our nursery. You saw it a year ago when you dropped by; did you notice anything peculiar about it then?'

'Can't say I did; the usual violences, a tendency toward a slight paranoia here or there, usual in children because they feel persecuted by parents constantly, but, oh, really nothing.'

They walked down the hall. 'I locked the nursery up,' explained the father, 'and the children broke back into it during the night. I let them stay so they could form the patterns for you to see.'

There was a terrible screaming from the nursery.

'There it is,' said George Hadley. 'See what you make of it.'

They walked in on the children without rapping.

The screams had faded. The lions were feeding.

'Run outside a moment, children,' said George Hadley. 'No, don't change the mental combination. Leave the walls as they are. Get!'

With the children gone, the two men stood studying the lions clustered at a distance, eating with great relish whatever it was they had caught.

'I wish I knew what it was,' said George Hadley. 'Sometimes I can almost see. Do you think if I brought highpowered binoculars here and—'

David McClean laughed dryly. 'Hardly.' He turned to study all four walls. 'How long has this been going on?'

'A little over a month.'

'It certainly doesn't feel good.'

'I want facts, not feelings.'

'My dear George, a psychologist never saw a fact in his life. He only hears about feelings; vague things. This doesn't feel good, I tell you. Trust my hunches and my instincts, I have a nose for something bad. This is very bad. My advice to you is to have the whole damn room torn down and your children brought to me every day during the next year for treatment.'

'Is it that bad?'

'I'm afraid so. One of the original uses of these nurseries was so that we could study the patterns left on the walls by the child's mind, study at our leisure, and help the child. In this case, however, the room has become a channel toward – destructive thoughts, instead of a release away from them.'

'Didn't you sense this before?'

'I sensed only that you had spoiled your children more than most. And now you're letting them down in some way. What way?'

'I wouldn't let them go to New York.'

'What else?'

'I've taken a few machines from the house and threatened them, a month ago, with closing up the nursery unless they did their homework. I did close it for a few days to show I meant business.'

'Ah, ha!'

'Does that mean anything?'

'Everything. Where before they had a Santa Claus now they have a Scrooge. Children prefer Santas. You've let this room and this house replace you and your wife in your children's affections. This room is their mother and father, far more important in their lives than their real parents. And now you come along and want to shut it off. No wonder there's hatred here. You can feel it coming out of the sky. Feel that sun. George, you'll have to change your life. Like too many others, you've built it around creature comforts. Why, you'd starve tomorrow if something went wrong in your kitchen. You wouldn't know how to tap an egg. Nevertheless, turn everything off. Start new. It'll take time. But we'll make good children out of bad in a year, wait and see.'

'But won't the shock be too much for the children, shutting the room up abruptly, for good?'

'I don't want them going any deeper into this, that's all.'

The lions were finished with their red feast.

The lions were standing on the edge of the clearing watching the two men.

'Now *I'm* feeling persecuted,' said McClean. 'Let's get out of here. I never have cared for these damned rooms. Make me nervous.'

'The lions look real, don't they?' said George Hadley. 'I don't suppose there's any way—'

'What?'

'– that they could *become* real?'

'Not that I know.'

'Some flaw in the machinery, a tampering or something?'

'No.'

They went to the door.

'I don't imagine the room will like being turned off,' said the father.

'Nothing ever likes to die – even a room.'

'I wonder if it hates me for wanting to switch it off?'

'Paranoia is thick around here today,' said David McClean. 'You can follow it like a spoor. Hello.' He bent and picked up a bloody scarf. 'This yours?'

'No.' George Hadley's face was rigid. 'It belongs to Lydia.'

They went to the fuse box together and threw the switch that killed the nursery.

The two children were in hysterics. They screamed and pranced and threw things. They yelled and sobbed and swore and jumped at the furniture.

'You can't do that to the nursery, you can't?'

'Now, children.'

The children flung themselves on to a couch, weeping.

'George,' said Lydia Hadley, 'turn on the nursery, just for a few moments. You can't be so abrupt.'

'No.'

'You can't be so cruel.'

'Lydia, it's off, and it stays off. And the whole damn house dies as of here and now. The more I see of the mess we've put ourselves in, the more it sickens me. We've been contemplating our mechanical, electronic navels for too long. My God, how we need a breath of honest air!'

And he marched about the house turning off the voice clocks, the stoves, the heaters, the shoe shiners, the shoe lacers, the body scrubbers and swabbers and massagers, and every other machine he could put his hand to.

The house was full of dead bodies, it seemed. It felt like a mechanical cemetery. So silent. None of the humming hidden energy of machines waiting to funtion at the tap of a button.

'Don't let them do it!' wailed Peter at the ceiling, as if he was talking to the house, the nursery. 'Don't let Father kill everything.' He turned to his father. 'Oh, I hate you!'

'Insults won't get you anywhere.'

'I wish you were dead!'

'We were, for a long while. Now we're going to really start living. Instead of being handled and massaged, we're going to live.'

Wendy was still crying and Peter joined her again. 'Just a moment, just one moment, just another moment of nursery,' they wailed.

'Oh George,' said the wife, 'it can't hurt.'

'All right – all right, if they'll only just shut up. One minute, mind you, and then off forever.'

'Daddy, Daddy, Daddy!' sang the children, smiling with wet faces.

'And then we're going on a vacation. David McClean is coming back in half an hour to help us move out and get to the airport. I'm going to dress. You turn the nursery on for a minute, Lydia, just a minute, mind you.'

And the three of them went babbling off while he let himself be vacuumed upstairs through the air flue and set about dressing himself. A minutes later Lydia appeared.

'I'll be glad when we get away,' she sighed.

'Did you leave them in the nursery?'

'I wanted to dress too. Oh, that horrid Africa. What can they see in it?'

'Well, in five minutes we'll be on our way to Iowa. Lord, how did we ever get in this house? What prompted us to buy a nightmare?'

'Pride, money, foolishness.'

'I think we'd better get downstairs before those kids get engrossed with those damned beasts again.'

Just then they heard the children calling, 'Daddy, Mommy, come quick – quick!'

They went downstairs in the air flue and ran down the hall. The children were nowhere in sight. 'Wendy? Peter!'

They ran into the nursery. The veldland was empty save for the lions waiting, looking at them. 'Peter, Wendy?'

The door slammed.

'Wendy, Peter!'

George Hadley and his wife whirled and ran back to the door.

'Open the door!' cried George Hadley, trying the knob. 'Why, they've locked it from the outside! Peter!' He beat at the door. 'Open up!'

He heard Peter's voice outside, against the door.

'Don't let them switch off the nursery and the house,' he was saying.

Mr and Mrs George Hadley beat at the door. 'Now, don't be ridiculous, children. It's time to go. Mr McClean'll be here in a minute and ...'

And then they heard the sounds.

The lions on three sides of them, in the yellow veld grass, padding through the dry straw, rumbling and roaring in their throats.

The lions.

Mr Hadley looked at his wife and they turned and looked back at the beasts edging slowly forward, crouching, tails stiff.

Mr and Mrs Hadley screamed.

And suddenly they realised why those other screams had sounded familiar.

'Well, here I am,' said David McClean in the nursery doorway. 'Oh, hello,' He stared at the two children seated in the centre of the open glade eating a little picnic lunch. Beyond them was the water hole and the yellow veldland; above was the hot sun. He began to perspire. 'Where are your father and mother?'

The children looked up and smiled. 'Oh, they'll be here directly.'

'Good, we must get going.' At a distance Mr McClean saw the lions fighting and clawing and then quieting down to feed in silence under the shady trees.

He squinted at the lions with his hand up to his eyes.

Now the lions were done feeding. They moved to the water hole to drink.

A shadow flickered over Mr McClean's hot face. Many shadows flickered. The vultures were dropping down the blazing sky.

'A cup of tea?' asked Wendy in the silence.

Ray Bradbury

Skeleton

It was past time for him to see the doctor again. Mr Harris turned palely in at the stair well, and on his way up the flight saw Dr Burleigh's name gilded over a pointing arrow. Would Dr Burleigh sigh when he walked in? After all, this would make the tenth trip so far this year. But Burleigh shouldn't complain; he was paid for the examinations!

The nurse looked Mr Harris over and smiled, a bit amusedly, as she tiptoed to the glazed glass door, opened it, and put her head in. Harris thought he heard her say, 'Guess who's here, Doctor.' And didn't the doctor's voice reply, faintly, 'Oh, my God, *again*?' Harris swallowed uneasily.

When Harris walked in, Dr Burleigh snorted. 'Aches in your bones again! Ah!!' He scowled and adjusted his glasses. 'My dear Harris, you've been curried with the finest-tooth combs and bacteria-brushes known to science. You're just nervous. Let's see your fingers. Too many cigarettes. Let's smell your breath. Too much protein. Let's see your eyes. Not enough sleep. My response? Go to bed, stop the protein, no smoking. Ten dollars, please.'

Harris stood sulking.

The doctor glanced up from his papers. '*You* still here? You're a hypochondriac! That's *eleven* dollars, now.'

'But why should my bones ache?' asked Harris.

Dr Burleigh spoke as to a child. 'You ever had a sore muscle, and kept irritating it, fussing with it, rubbing it? It gets worse the more you bother it. Then you leave it alone and the pain vanishes. You realize you caused most of the soreness yourself. Well, son, that's what's with you. Leave yourself alone. Take a dose of salts. Get out of here and take that trip to Phoenix you've stewed about for months. Do you good to travel!'

Five minutes later, Mr Harris riffled through a classified phone directory at the corner druggist's. A fine lot of sympathy one got from blind fools like Burleigh! He passed his finger down a list of BONE SPECIALISTS, found one named M. Munigant. Munigant lacked an M.D., or any other academic lettering behind his name, but his office was conveniently near. Three blocks down, one block over. . . .

M. Munigant, like his office, was small and dark. Like his office he smelled of iodoform, iodine, and other odd things. He was a good listener, though, and listened with eager shiny moves of his eyes, and when he talked to Harris, his accent was such that he softly whistled each word; undoubtedly because of imperfect dentures.

Harris told all.

M. Munigant nodded. He had seen cases like this before. The bones of the body. Man was not aware of his bones. Ah, yes, the bones. The skeleton. Most difficult. Something concerning an imbalance, an unsympathetic coordination between soul, flesh and skeleton. Very complicated, softly whistled M. Munigant. Harris listened, fascinated. Now, *here* was a doctor who understood his illness! Psychological, said M. Munigant. He moved swiftly, delicately to a dingy wall and slashed down half a dozen X-rays to haunt the room with their look of things found floating in an ancient tide. Here, here! The skeleton surprised! Here luminous portraits of the long, the short, the large, the small bones. Mr Harris must be aware of his position, his problem! M. Munigant's hand tapped, rattled, whispered, scratched at faint nebulae of flesh in which hung ghosts of cranium, spinal-cord, pelvis, lime, calcium, marrow, here, there, this, that, these, those, and others! Look!

Harris shuddered. The X-rays and the paintings blew in a green and phosphorescent wind from a land peopled by the monsters of Dali and Fuseli.

M. Munigant whistled quietly. Did Mr Harris wish his bones – treated?

'That depends,' said Harris.

Well, M. Munigant could not help Harris unless Harris was in the proper mood. Psychologically, one had to *need* help, or the doctor was useless. But (shrugging) M. Munigant would 'try'.

Harris lay on a table with his mouth open. The lights were switched off, the shades drawn. M. Munigant approached his patient.

Something touched Harris's tongue.

He felt his jawbones forced out. They creaked and made faint cracking noises. One of those skeleton charts on the dim wall seemed to quiver and jump. A violent shudder seized Harris. Involuntarily, his mouth snapped shut.

M. Munigant shouted. His nose had almost been bitten off! No use, no use! Now was not the time! M. Munigant whispered the shades up,

446

dreadfully disappointed. When Mr Harris felt he could cooperate psychologically, when Mr Harris really *needed* help and trusted M. Munigant to help him, then maybe something could be done. M. Munigant held out his little hand. In the meantime, the fee was only two dollars. Mr Harris must begin to think. Here was a sketch for Mr Harris to take home and study. It would acquaint him with his body. He must be tremblingly aware of himself. He must be on guard. Skeletons were strange, unwieldy things. M. Munigant's eyes glittered. Good day to Mr Harris. Oh, and would he care for a breadstick? M. Munigant proffered a jar of long hard salty breadsticks to Harris, taking one himself, saying that chewing breadsticks kept him in – ah – practice. Good day, good day, to Mr Harris! Mr Harris went home.

The next day, Sunday, Mr Harris discovered innumerable fresh aches and pains in his body. He spent the morning, his eyes fixed staring with new interest at the small, anatomically perfect painting of a skeleton M. Munigant had given him.

His wife, Clarisse, startled him at dinner when she cracked her exquisitely thin knuckles, one by one, until he clapped his hands to his ears and cried, 'Stop!'

The rest of the afternoon he quarantined himself in his room. Clarisse played bridge in the parlour laughing and chatting with three other ladies while Harris, hidden away, fingered and weighed the limbs of his body with growing curiosity. After an hour he suddenly rose and called:

'Clarisse!'

She had a way of dancing into any room, her body doing all sorts of soft, agreeable things to keep her feet from ever quite touching the nap of a rug. She excused herself from her friends and came to see him now, brightly. She found him re-seated in a far corner and she saw that he was staring at the anatomical sketch. 'Are you still brooding, sweet?' she asked. 'Please don't.' She sat upon his knees.

Her beauty could not distract him now in his absorption. He juggled her lightness, he touched her kneecap, suspiciously. It seemed to move under her pale, glowing skin. 'Is it supposed to do that?' he asked, sucking in his breath.

'Is what supposed to do what?' she laughed. 'You mean my kneecap?'

'Is it supposed to run around on top your knee that way?'

She experimented. 'So it *does*,' she marvelled.

'I'm glad yours slithers, too,' he sighed. 'I was beginning to worry.'

'About what?'

He patted his ribs. 'My ribs don't go all the way down, they stop *here*. And I found some confounded ones that dangle in mid-air!'

Beneath the curve of her small breasts, Clarisse clasped her hands.

447

'Of course, silly, everybody's ribs stop at a given point. And those funny short ones are floating ribs.'

'I hope they don't float around too much.' The joke was most uneasy. Now, above all, he wished to be alone. Further discoveries, newer and stranger archaeological diggings, lay within reach of his trembling hands, and he did not wish to be laughed at.

'Thanks for coming in, dear,' he said.

'Any time.' She rubbed her small nose softly against his.

'Wait! Here, now . . .' He put his finger to touch his nose and hers. 'Did you realize? The nose-bone grows down only *this* far. From there on a lot of gristly tissue fills out the rest!'

She wrinkled hers. 'Of course, darling!' And she danced from the room.

Now, sitting alone, he felt the perspiration rise from the pools and hollows of his face, to flow in a thin tide down his cheeks. He licked his lips and shut his eyes. Now . . . now . . . next on the agenda, what . . . ? The spinal cord, yes. Here. Slowly, he examined it, in the same way he operated the many push-buttons in his office, thrusting them to summon secretaries, messengers. But now, in these pushings of his spinal column, fears and terrors answered, rushed from a million doors in his mind to confront and shake him! His spine felt horribly – unfamiliar. Like the brittle shards of a fish, freshly eaten, its bones left strewn on a cold china platter. He seized the little rounded knobbins. 'Lord! Lord!'

His teeth began to chatter. God All-Mighty! he thought, why haven't I realized it all these years? All these years I've gone around with a – SKELETON – inside me! How is it we take ourselves for granted? How is it we never question our bodies and our being?

A skeleton. One of those jointed, snowy, hard things, one of those foul, dry brittle, gouge-eyed, skull-faced, shake-fingered, rattling things that sway from neck-chains in abandoned webbed closets, one of those things found on the desert all along and scattered like dice!

He stood upright, because he could not bear to remain seated. Inside me now, he grasped his stomach, his head, inside my head is a – skull. One of those curved carapaces which holds my brain like an electrical jelly, one of those cracked shells with the holes in front like two holes shot through it by a double-barrelled shotgun! With its grottoes and caverns of bone, its revetments and placements for my flesh, my smelling, my seeing, my hearing, my thinking! A skull, encompassing my brain, allowing it exit through its brittle windows to see the outside world!

He wanted to dash into the bridge party, upset it, a fox in a chicken-yard, the cards fluttering all around like chicken feathers burst upward in clouds! He stopped himself only with a violent, trembling effort. Now, now, man, control yourself. This is a revelation, take it for what it's worth, understand it, savour it. BUT A SKELETON! screamed his subconscious. I won't stand for it. It's vulgar, it's terrible, it's frightening. Skeletons are horrors; they clink and tinkle and rattle in old castles, hung from oaken beams, making long, indolently rustling pendulums on the wind. . . .

'Darling, will you come meet the ladies?' His wife's clear, sweet voice called from far away.

Mr Harris stood. His SKELETON held him up! This thing inside, this invader, this horror, was supporting his arms, legs, and head! It was like feeling someone just behind you who shouldn't be there. With every step, he realized how dependent he was on this other Thing.

'Darling, I'll be with you in a moment,' he called weakly. To himself he said, come on, brace up! You've got to go back to work tomorrow. Friday you must make that trip to Phoenix. It's a long drive. Hundreds of miles. Must be in shape for that trip or you won't get Mr Creldon to invest in your ceramics business. Chin up, now!

A moment later he stood among the ladies, being introduced to Mrs Withers, Mrs Abblematt, and Miss Kirthy, all of whom had skeletons inside them, but took it very calmly, because nature had carefully clothed the bare nudity of clavicle, tibia, and femur with breasts, thighs, calves, with coiffure and eyebrow satanic, with bee-stung lips and – LORD! shouted Mr Harris inwardly – when they talk or eat, part of their skeleton shows – their *teeth*! I never thought of that. 'Excuse me,' he gasped, and ran from the room only in time to drop his lunch among the petunias over the garden balustrade.

That night, seated on the bed as his wife undressed, he pared his toenails and fingernails scrupulously. These parts, too, were where his skeleton was shoving, indignantly growing out. He must have muttered part of this theory, because next thing he knew his wife, in negligee, was on the bed, her arms about his neck, yawning, 'Oh, my darling, finger-nails are *not* bone, they're only hardened epidermis!'

He threw the scissors down. 'Are you certain? I hope so. I'd feel better.' He looked at the curve of her body, marvelling. 'I hope all people are made the same way.'

'If you aren't the darndest hypochondriac!' She held him at arm's length. 'Come on. What's wrong? Tell ma-ma.'

'Something inside me,' he said 'Something – I ate.'

The next morning and all afternoon at his downtown office, Mr Harris sorted out the sizes, shapes, and construction of various bones in his body with displeasure. At ten A.M. he asked to feel Mr Smith's elbow one moment. Mr Smith obliged, but scowled suspiciously. And after lunch Mr Harris asked to touch Miss Laurel's shoulder blade and she immediately pushed herself back against him, purring like a kitten and shutting her eyes.

'Miss Laurel!' he snapped. 'Stop that!'

Alone, he pondered his neuroses. The war was just over, the pressure of his work, the uncertainty of the future, probably had much to do with his mental outlook. He wanted to leave the office, get into business for himself. He had more than a little talent for ceramics and sculpture. As soon as possible he'd head for Arizona, borrow that money from Mr Creldon, build a kiln and set up shop. It was a worry. What a case he was. But luckily he had contacted M. Munigant, who seemed eager to understand and help him. He would fight it out with himself, not go back to either Munigant or Dr Burleigh unless he was forced to. The alien feeling would pass. He sat staring into space.

The alien feeling did not pass. It grew.

On Tuesday and Wednesday it bothered him terrifically that his epidermis, hair and other appendages were of a high disorder, while his integumented skeleton of himself was a slick clean structure of efficient organization. Sometimes, in certain lights with his lips drawn morosely down, weighted with melancholy, he imagined he saw his skull grinning at him behind the flesh.

Let go! he cried. Let go of me! My lungs! Stop!

He gasped convulsively, as if his ribs were crushing the breath from him.

My brain – stop squeezing it!

And terrifying headaches burnt his brain to a blind cinder.

My insides, let them be, for God's sake! Stay away from my heart!

His heart cringed from the fanning motion of ribs like pale spiders crouched and fiddling with their prey.

Drenched with sweat, he lay upon the bed one night while Clarisse was out attending a Red Cross meeting. He tried to gather his wits but only grew more aware of the conflict between his dirty exterior and this beautiful cool clean calciumed thing inside.

His complexion: wasn't it oily and lined with worry?

Observe the flawless, snow-white perfection of the skull.

His nose: wasn't it too large?

Then observe the tiny bones of the skull's nose before that monstrous nasal cartilage begins forming the lopsided proboscis.

His body: wasn't it plump?

Well, consider the skeleton; slender, svelte, economical of line and contour. Exquisitely carved oriental ivory! Perfect, thin as a white praying mantis!

His eyes: weren't they protuberant, ordinary, numb-looking?

Be so kind as to note the eye-sockets of the skull; so deep and rounded, sombre, quiet pools, all-knowing, eternal. Gaze deep and you never touch the bottom of their dark understanding. All irony, all life, all everything is there in the cupped darkness.

Compare. Compare. Compare.

He raged for hours. And the skeleton, ever the frail and solemn philosopher, hung quietly inside, saying not a word, suspended like a delicate insect within a chrysalis, waiting and waiting.

Harris sat slowly up.

'Wait a minute. Hold on!' he exclaimed. 'You're helpless, too. I've got you, too. I can make you do anything I want! You can't prevent it! I say move your carpals, metacarpals, and phalanges and – sswtt – up they go, as I wave to someone!' He laughed. 'I order the fibula and femur to locomote and *Hunn* two three four, *Hunn* two three four – we walk around the block. There!'

Harris grinned.

'It's a fifty-fifty fight. Even-Stephen. And we'll fight it out, we two! After all, I'm the part that *thinks*! Yes, by God! yes. Even if I didn't have you, I could still think!'

Instantly, a tiger's jaw snapped shut, chewing his brain in half. Harris screamed. The bones of his skull grabbed hold and gave him nightmares. Then slowly, while he shrieked, nuzzled and ate the nightmares one by one, until the last one was gone and the light went out. . .

At the end of the week he postponed the Phoenix trip because of his health. Weighing himself on a penny scale he saw the slow gliding red arrow point to: 165.

He groaned. Why, I've weighed 175 for years. I can't have lost ten pounds! He examined his cheeks in the fly-dotted mirror. Cold, primitive fear rushed over him in odd little shivers. You, you! I know what you're about, *you*!

He shook his fist at his bony face, particularly addressing his remarks to his superior maxillary, his inferior maxillary, to his cranium and to his cervical vertebrae.

'You damn thing, you! Think you can starve me, make me lose weight, eh? Peel the flesh off, leave nothing, but skin on bone. Trying to ditch me, so you can be supreme, ah? No, no!'

He fled into a cafeteria.

Turkey, dressing, creamed potatoes, four vegetables, three desserts, he could eat none of it, he was sick to his stomach. He forced himself. His teeth began to ache. Bad teeth, is it? he thought angrily. I'll eat in spite of every tooth clanging and banging and rattling so they fall in my gravy.

His head blazed, his breath jerked in and out of a constricted chest, his teeth raged with pain, but he knew one small victory. He was about to drink milk when he stopped and poured it into a vase of nasturtiums. No calcium for you, my boy, no calcium for you. Never again shall I eat foods with calcium or other bone-fortifying minerals. I'll eat for one of us, not both, my lad.

'One hundred and fifty pounds,' he said, the following week to his wife. 'Do you *see* how I've changed?'

'For the better,' said Clarisse. 'You were always a little plump for your height, darling.' She stroked his chin. 'I like your face. It's so much nicer; the lines of it are so firm and strong now.'

'They're not *my* lines, they're his, damn him! You mean to say you like him better than you like me?'

'Him? Who's "*him*?"'

In the parlour mirror, beyond Clarisse, his skull smiled back at him behind his fleshy grimace of hatred and despair.

Fuming, he popped malt tablets into his mouth. This was one way of gaining weight when you couldn't keep other foods down. Clarisse noticed the malt pellets.

'But, darling, really, you don't have to regain the weight for me,' she said.

Oh, shut up! he felt like saying.

She made him lie with his head in her lap. 'Darling,' she said, 'I've watched you lately. You're so – badly off. You don't say anything, but you look – hunted. You toss in bed at night. Maybe you should go to a psychiatrist. But I think I can tell you everything he would say. I've put it all together from hints you've let escape you. I can tell you that you and your skeleton are one and the same, 'one nation, indivisible, with liberty and justice for all.' United you stand, divided you fall. If you two fellows can't get along like an old married couple in the future, go back and see Dr Burleigh. But, first, relax. You're in a vicious circle; the more you worry, the more your bones stick out, the more you worry. After all, who picked this fight – you or that anonymous entity you claim is lurking around behind your alimentary canal?'

He closed his eyes. 'I did. I guess I did. Go on Clarisse, keep talking.'

'You rest now,' she said softly, 'Rest and forget.'

Mr Harris felt buoyed up for half a day, then he began to sag. It was all very well to blame his imagination, but this particular skeleton, by God, was fighting back.

Harris set out for M. Munigant's office late in the day. Walking for half an hour until he found the address, he caught sight of the name 'M. Munigant' initialled in ancient, flaking gold on a glass plate outside the building. Then, his bones seemed to explode from their moorings, blasted and erupted with pain. Blinded, he staggered away. When he opened his eyes again he had rounded a corner. M. Munigant's office was out of sight.

The pains ceased.

M. Munigant was the man to help him. If the sight of his name could cause so titanic a reaction of course M. Munigant *must* be just the man.

But, not today. Each time he tried to return to that office, the terrible pains took hold. Perspiring, he had to give up and swayed into a cocktail bar.

Moving across the dim lounge, he wondered briefly if a lot of blame couldn't be put on M. Munigant's shoulders. After all, it was Munigant who'd first drawn specific attention to his skeleton, and letthe psychological impact of it slam home! Could M. Munigant be using him for some nefarious purpose? But what purpose? Silly to suspect him. Just a little doctor. Trying to be helpful. Munigant and his jar of breadsticks. Ridiculous. M. Munigant was okay, okay . . .

There was a sight within the cocktail lounge to give him hope. A large, fat man, round as a butterball, stood drinking consecutive beers at the bar. Now *there* was a successful man. Harris repressed a desire to go up, clap the fat man's shoulder, and inquire as to how he'd gone about impounding his bones. Yes, the fat man's skeleton was luxuriously closeted. There were pillows of fat here, resilient bulges of it there, with several round chandeliers of fat under his chin. The poor skeleton was lost; it could never fight clear of that blubber. It might have tried once – but not now, overwhelmed, not a bony echo of the fat man's supporter remained.

Not without envy, Harris approached the fat man as one might cut across the bow of an ocean liner. Harris ordered a drink, drank it, and then dared to address the fat man:

'Glands?'

'You talking to me?' asked the fat man.

'Or is there a special diet?' wondered Harris. 'I beg your pardon, but as you see, I'm down. Can't seem to put on any weight. I'd like a stomach like that one of yours. Did you grow it because you were afraid of something?'

'You,' announced the fat man, 'are drunk. But – I like drunkards.' He ordered more drinks. 'Listen close, I'll tell you. Layer by layer,' said the fat man, 'twenty years, man and boy, I built this.' He held his vast stomach like a globe of the world, teaching his audience its gastronomical geography. 'It was no overnight circus. The tent was not raised before dawn on the wonders installed within. I have cultivated my inner organs as if they were thoroughbred dogs, cats, and other animals. My stomach is a fat pink Persian tom slumbering, rousing at intervals to purr, mew, growl, and cry for chocolate titbits. I feed it well, it will 'most sit up for me. And, my dear fellow, my intestines are the rarest pure-bred Indian anacondas you ever viewed in the sleekest, coiled, fine and ruddy health. Keep 'em in prime, I do, all my pets. For fear of something? Perhaps.'

This called for another drink for everyone.

'Gain weight?' The fat man savored the words on his tongue. 'Here's what you do: get yourself a quarrelling bird of a wife, a baker's dozen of relatives who can flush a covey of troubles out from behind the veriest molehill. Add to these a sprinkling of business associates whose prime motivation is snatching your last lonely quid, and you are well on your way to getting fat. How so? In no time you'll begin subconsciously building fat betwixt yourself and them. A buffer epidermal state, a cellular wall. You'll soon find that eating is the only fun on earth. But one needs to be bothered by outside sources. Too many people in this world haven't enough to worry about, then they begin picking on themselves, and they lose weight. Meet all of the vile, terrible people you can possibly meet, and pretty soon you'll be adding the good old fat!'

And with that advice, the fat man launched himself out into the dark tide of night, swaying mightily and wheezing.

'That's exactly what Dr Burleigh told me, slightly changed,' said Harris thoughtfully. 'Perhaps that trip to Phoenix, now, at this time—'

The trip from Los Angeles to Phoenix was a sweltering one, crossing, as it did, the Mojave desert on a broiling yellow day. Traffic was thin and inconstant, and for long stretches there would not be a car on the road for miles ahead or behind. Harris twitched his fingers on the steering wheel. Whether or not Creldon, in Phoenix, lent him the money he needed to start his business, it was still a good thing to get away, to put distance behind.

The car moved in the hot sluice of desert wind. The one Mr H. sat inside the other Mr H. Perhaps both perspired. Perhaps both were miserable.

On a curve, the inside Mr H. suddenly constricted the outer flesh, causing him to jerk forward on the hot steering wheel.

The car plunged off the road into boiling sand and turned half over.

Night came, a wind rose, the road was lonely and silent. The few cars that passed went swiftly on their way, their view obstructed. Mr Harris lay unconscious, until very late he heard a wind rising out of the desert, felt the sting of little sand needles on his cheeks, and opened his eyes.

Morning found him gritty-eyed and wandering in thoughtless senseless circles, having, in his delirium, got away from the road. At noon he sprawled in the poor shade of a bush. The sun struck him with a keen sword edge, cutting through to his – bones. A vulture circled.

Harris' parched lips cracked open. 'So that's it?' he whispered, red-eyed, bristle-cheeked. 'One way or another you'll walk me, starve me, thirst me, kill me.' He swallowed dry burrs of dust. 'Sun cook off my flesh so you can peek out. Vultures lunch off me, and there you'll lie, grinning. Grinning with victory. Like a bleached xylophone strewn and

454

played by vultures with an ear for odd music. You'd like that. Freedom.

He walked on through a landscape that shivered and bubbled in the direct pour of sunlight; stumbling, falling flat, lying to feed himself little mouths of fire. The air was blue alcohol flame, and vultures roasted and steamed and glittered as they flew in glides and circles. Phoenix. The road. Car. Water. Safety.

'Hey!'

Someone called from way off in the blue alcohol flame.

Mr Harris propped himself up.

The call was repeated. A crunching of footsteps, quick.

With a cry of unbelievable relief, Harris rose, only to collapse again into the arms of someone in a uniform with a badge.

The car tediously hauled, repaired, Phoenix reached, Harris found himself in such an unholy state of mind that the business transaction was a numb pantomime. Even when he got the loan and held the money in his hand, it meant nothing. This Thing within him like a hard white sword in a scabbard tainted his business, his eating, coloured his love for Clarisse, made it unsafe to trust an automobile; all in all this Thing had to be put in its place. The desert incident had brushed too close. Too near the bone, one might say with an ironic twist of one's mouth. Harris heard himself thanking Mr Creldon, dimly, for the money. Then he turned his car and motored back across the long miles, this time cutting across to San Diego, so he would miss that desert stretch between El Centro and Beaumont. He drove north along the coast. He didn't trust that desert. But – careful! Salt waves boomed, hissing on the beach outside Laguna. Sand, fish and crustacea would cleanse his bones as swiftly as vultures. Slow down on the curves over the surf.

Damn, he was sick!

Where to turn? Clarisse? Burleigh? Munigant? Bone specialist. Munigant. Well?

'Darling!' Clarisse kissed him. He winced at the solidness of the teeth and jaw behind the passionate exchange.

'Darling,' he said, slowly, wiping his lips with his wrist, trembling.

'You look thinner; oh, darling, the business deal—?'

'It went through. I guess. Yes, it did.'

She kissed him again. They ate a slow, falsely cheerful dinner, with Clarisse laughing and encouraging him. He studied the phone; several times he picked it up indecisively, then laid it down.

His wife walked in, putting on her coat and hat. 'Well, sorry, but I have to leave.' She pinched him on the cheek. 'Come on now, cheer up! I'll be back from Red Cross in three hours. You lie around and snooze. I simply *have* to go.'

When Clarisse was gone, Harris dialled the phone, nervously.

'M. Munigant?'

The explosions and the sickness in his body after he set the phone down were unbelievable. His bones were racked with every kind of pain, cold and hot, he had ever thought of or experienced in wildest nightmare. He swallowed all the aspirin he could find, in an effort to stave off the assault; but when the doorbell finally rang an hour later, he could not move; he lay weak and exhausted, panting, tears streaming down his cheeks.

'Come in! Come in, for God's sake!'

M. Munigant came in. Thank God the door was unlocked.

Oh, but Mr Harris looked terrible. M. Munigant stood in the centre of the living room, small and dark. Harris nodded. The pains rushed through him, hitting him with large iron hammers and hooks. M. Munigant's eye glittered as he saw Harris' protuberant bones. Ah, he saw that Mr Harris was now psychologically prepared for aid. Was it not so? Harris nodded again, feebly, sobbing. M. Munigant still whistled when he talked; something about his tongue and the whistling. No matter. Through his shimmering eyes Harris seemed to see M. Munigant shrink, get smaller. Imagination, of course. Harris sobbed out his story of the Phoenix trip. M. Munigant sympathized. This skeleton was a – a traitor! They would fix him for once and for all!

'Mr Munigant,' sighed Harris, faintly, 'I – I never noticed before. Your tongue. Round, tube-like. Hollow? My eyes. Delirious. What do I do?'

M. Munigant whistled softly, appreciatively, coming closer. If Mr Harris would relax in his chair, and open his mouth? The lights were switched off. M. Munigant peered into Harris' dropped jaw. Wider, please? It had been so hard, that first visit, to help Harris, with both body and bone in revolt. Now, he had cooperation from the flesh of the man, anyway, even if the skeleton protested. In the darkness, M. Munigant's voice got small, small, tiny, tiny. The whistling became high and shrill. Now. Relax, Mr Harris. NOW!

Harris felt his jaw pressed violently in all directions, his tongue depressed as with a spoon, his throat clogged. He gasped for breath. Whistle. He couldn't breathe! Something squirmed, corkscrewed his cheeks out, bursting his jaws. Like a hot-water douche, something squirted into his sinuses, his ears clanged! 'Ahhhh!' shrieked Harris, gagging. His head, its carapaces riven, shattered, hung loose. Agony shot fire through his lungs.

Harris could breathe again, momentarily. His watery eyes sprang wide. He shouted. His ribs, like sticks picked up and bundled, were loosened in him. Pain! He fell to the floor, wheezing out his hot breath.

Lights flickered in his senseless eyeballs, he felt his limbs swiftly cast loose and free. Through streaming eyes he saw the parlour.

The room was empty.

'M. Munigant? In God's name, where are you, M. Munigant? Come help me!'

M. Munigant was gone.

'Help!'

Then he heard it.

Deep down in the subterranean fissures of his body, the minute, unbelievable noises; little smackings and twistings and little dry chippings and grindings and nuzzling sounds – like a tiny hungry mouse down in the red-blooded dimness, gnawing ever so earnestly and expertly at what might have been, but was not, a submerged timber . . . !

Clarisse, walking along the sidewalk, held her head high and marched straight toward her house on Saint James Place. She was thinking of the Red Cross as she turned the corner and almost ran into this little dark man who smelled of iodine.

Clarisse would have ignored him if it were not for the fact that as she passed, he took something long, white and oddly familiar from his coat and proceeded to chew on it, as on a peppermint stick. Its end devoured, his extraordinary tongue darted within the white confection, sucking out the filling, making contented noises. He was still crunching his goody as she proceeded up the sidewalk to her house, turned the doorknob and walked in.

'Darling?' she called, smiling around. 'Darling, where are you?' She shut the door, walked down the hall and into the living room. 'Darling . .'

She stared at the floor for twenty seconds, trying to understand.

She screamed.

Outside in the sycamore darkness, the little man pierced a long white stick with intermittent holes; then, softly, sighing, his lips puckered, played a little sad tune upon the improvised instrument to accompany the shrill and awful singing of Clarisse's voice as she stood in the living room.

Many times as a little girl Clarisse had run on the beach sands, stepped on a jellyfish and screamed. It was not so bad, finding an intact, gelatin-skinned jellyfish in one's living room. One could step back from it.

It was when the jellyfish *called you by name* . . .

John Collier

Evening Primrose

March 21
In a pad of Highlife Bond, bought by Miss Sadie Broadribb at Bracey's for 25c

Today I made my decision. I would turn my back for good and all upon the *bourgeois* world that hates a poet. I would leave, get out, break away—

And I have done it. I am free! Free as the mote that dances in the sunbeam! Free as a house-fly crossing first-class in the largest of luxury liners! Free as my verse! Free as the food I shall eat, the paper I shall write upon, the lamb's-wool-lined, softly slithering slippers I shall wear.

This morning I had not so much as a car-fare. Now I am here, on velvet. You are itching to learn of this haven; you would like to organise trips here, spoil it, send your relations-in-law, perhaps even come yourself. After all, this journal will hardly fall into your hands till I am dead. I'll tell you.

I am at Bracey's Giant Emporium, as happy as a mouse in the middle of an immense cheese, and the world shall know me no more.

Merrily, merrily shall I live now, secure behind a towering pile of carpets, in a corner-nook which I propose to line with eiderdowns, angora vestments, and the Cleopatraean tops in pillows. I shall be cosy.

I nipped into this sanctuary late this afternoon, and soon heard the dying footfalls of closing time. From now on, my only effort will be to dodge the night-watchman. Poets can dodge.

I have already made my first mouse-like exploration. I tiptoed as far as the stationery department, and, timid, darted back with only these writing materials, the poet's first need. Now I shall lay them aside and seek other necessities: food, wine, the soft furniture of my couch, and a

458

natty smoking-jacket. This place stimulates me. I shall write here.

Dawn, Next Day

I suppose no one in the world was ever more astonished and over-whelmed than I have been tonight. It is unbelievable. Yet I believe it. How interesting life is when things get like that!

I crept out, as I said I would, and found the great shop in mingled light and gloom. The central well was half illuminated; the circling galleries towered in a pansy Piranesi of toppling light and shade. The spidery stairways and flying bridges had passed from purpose into fantasy. Silks and velvets glimmered like ghosts, a hundred pantie-clad models offered simpers and embraces to the desert air. Ring, clips, and bracelets glittered frostily in a desolate absence of Honey and Daddy.

Creeping along the transverse aisles, which were in deeper darkness, I felt like a wandering thought in the dreaming brain of a chorus girl down on her luck. Only, of course, their brains are not so big as Bracey's Giant Emporium. And there was no man there.

None, that is, except the night-watchman. I had forgotten him. As I crossed an open space on the mezzanine floor, hugging the lee of a display of sultry shawls, I became aware of a regular thudding, which might almost have been that of my own heart. Suddenly it burst upon me that it came from outside. It was the sound of footsteps, and they were only a few paces away. Quick as a flash I seized a flamboyant mantilla, whirled it about me and stood with one arm outflung, like a Carmen petrified in a gesture of disdain.

I was successful. He passed me, jingling his little machine on its chain; humming his little tine; he eyes scaled with refractions of the blaring day. 'Go, worldling!' I whispered, and permitted myself a soundless laugh.

It froze on my lips. My heart faltered. A new fear seized me.

I was afraid to move. I was afraid to look round. I felt I was being watched, by something that could see right through me. This was a very different feeling from the ordinary emergency caused by the very ordinary night-watchman. My conscious impulse was the obvious one; to glance behind me. But my eyes knew better. I remained absolutely petrified, staring straight ahead.

My eyes were trying to tell me something that my brain refused to believe. They made their point. I was looking straight into another pair of eyes, human eyes, but large, flat, luminous. I have seen such eyes among the nocturnal creatures, which creep out under the artificial blue moonlight in the zoo.

The owner was only a dozen feet away from me. The watchman had passed between us, nearer him than me. Yet he had not seen him. I must have been looking straight at him for several minutes at a stretch. I had not seen him either.

He was half reclining against a low dais where, on a floor of russet leaves, and flanked by billows of glowing home-spun, the fresh-faced waxen girls modelled spectator sports suits in herringbones, checks, and plaids. He leaned against the skirt of one of these Dianas; its folds concealed perhaps his ear, his shoulder, and a little of his right-hand side. He, himself, was clad in dim but large-patterned Shetland tweeds of the latest cut, suede shoes, a shirt in a rather broad *motif* in olive, pink, and grey. He was as pale as a creature found under a stone. His long, thin arms ended in hands that hung floatingly, more like trailing, transparent fins, or wisps of chiffon, than ordinary hands.

He spoke. His voice was not a voice; it was a mere whistling under the tongue. 'Not bad, for a beginner!'

I grasped that he was complimenting me, rather satirically, on my own, more amateurish, feat of camouflage. I stuttered. I said, 'I'm sorry. I didn't know anyone else lived here.' I noticed, even as I spoke, that I was imitating his own whistling sibilant utterance.

'Oh, yes,' he said. '*We* live here. It's delightful.'

'We?'

'Yes, all of us. Look!'

We were near the edge of the first gallery. He swept his long hand round, indicating the whole well of the shop. I looked. I saw nothing. I could hear nothing, except the watchman's thudding step receding infinitely far along some basement aisle.

'Don't you see?'

You know the sensation one has, peering into the half-light of a vivarium? One sees bark, pebbles, a few leaves, nothing more. And then suddenly, a stone breathes – it is a toad; there is a chameleon, another, a coiled adder, a mantis among the leaves. The whole case seems crepitant with life. Perhaps the whole world is. One glances at one's sleeve, one's feet.

So it was with thet ad,n. I loo iked shopwas empty. I looked, and there was an old lady, clambering out from behind the monstrous clock. There were three girls, elderly *ingénues*, incredibly emaciated, simpering at the entrance of the perfumery. Their hair was a fine floss, pale as gossamer. Equally brittle and colourless was a man with the appearance of a colonel of southern extraction, who stood regarding me while he caressed moustachios that would have done credit to a crystal shrimp. A chintzy woman, possibly of literary tastes, swam forward from the curtains and drapes.

They came thick about me, fluttering, whistling, like a waving of gauze in the wind. Their eyes were wide and flatly bright. I saw there was no colour to the iris.

'How raw he looks!'

'A detective! Send for the Dark Men!'

'I'm not a detective. I am a poet. I have renounced the world.'

'He is a poet. He has come over to us. Mr Roscoe found him.'

'He admires us.'

'He must meet Mrs Vanderpant.'

I was taken to meet Mrs Vanderpant. She proved to be the Grand Old Lady of the store, almost entirely transparent.

'So you are a poet, Mr Snell? You will find inspiration here. I am quite the oldest inhabitant. Three mergers and a complete rebuilding, but they didn't get rid of me!'

'Tell how you went out by daylight, dear Mrs Vanderpant, and nearly got bought for Whistler's *Mother*.'

'That was in pre-war days. I was more robust then. But at the cash desk they suddenly remembered there was no frame. And when they came back to look at me—'

'—She was gone.'

Their laughter was like the stridulation of the ghosts of grasshoppers.

'Where is Ella? Where is my broth?'

'She is bringing it, Mrs Vanderpant. It will come.'

'Tiresome little creature! She is our foundling, Mr Snell. She is not quite our sort.'

'Is that so, Mrs Vanderpant? Dear, dear!'

'I lived alone here, Mr Snell, for many years. I took refuge here in the terrible times in the 'eighties. I was a young girl then, a beauty, people were kind enough to say, but poor Papa lost his money. Bracey's meant a lot to a young girl, in the New York of those days, Mr Snell. It seemed to me terrible that I should not be able to come here in the ordinary way. So I came here for good. I was quite alarmed when others began to come in, after the crash of 1907. But it was the dear Judge, the Colonel, Mrs Bilbee—'

I bowed. I was being introduced.

'Mrs Bilbee writes plays. *And* of a very old Philadelphia family. You will find us quite *nice* here, Mr Snell.'

'I feel it a great privilege, Mrs Vanderpant.'

'And of course, all our dear *young* people came in '29. *Their* poor papas jumped from skyscrapers.'

I did a great deal of bowing and whistling. The introductions took a long time. Who would have thought so many people lived in Bracey's?

'And here at last is Ella with my broth.'

It was then that I noticed the young people were not so young after all, in spite of their smiles, their little ways, the *ingénue* dress. Ella was in her teens. Clad only in something from the shop-soiled counter, she nevertheless had the appearance of a living flower in a French cemetery, or a mermaid among polyps.

'Come, you stupid thing!'

'Mrs Vanderpant is waiting.'

Her pallor was not like theirs; not like the pallor of something that glistens or scuttles when you turn over a stone. Hers was that of a pearl.

Ella! Pearl of this remotest, most fantastic cave! Little mermaid, brushed over, pressed down by objects of a deadlier white – tentacles – ! I can write no more.

March 28

Well, I am rapidly becoming used to my new and half-lit world, to my strange company. I am learning the intricate laws of silence and camouflage which dominate the apparently casual strollings and gatherings of the mid-night clan. How they detest the night-watchman, whose existence imposes these laws on their idle festivals!

'Odious, vulgar creature! He reeks of the coarse sun!'

Actually, he is quite a personable young man, very young for a night-watchman, so young that I think he must have been wounded in the war. But they would like to tear him to pieces.

They are very pleasant to me, though. They are pleased that a poet should have come among them. Yet I cannot like them entirely. My blood is a little chilled by the uncanny ease with which even the old ladies can clamber spider-like from balcony to balcony. Or is it because they are so unkind to Ella?

Yesterday we had a bridge party. Tonight, Mrs Bilbee's little play, *Love in Shadowland*, is going to be presented. Would you believe it? – another colony, from Wanamaker's, is coming over *en masse* to attend. Apparently people live in all the great stores. This visit is considered a great honour, for there is an intense snobbery in these creatures. They speak with horror of a social outcast who left a high-class Madison Avenue establishment, and now leads a wallowing, beachcomberish life in a delicatessen. And they relate with tragic emotions the story of the man in Altman's, who conceived such a passion for a model plaid dressing jacket that he emerged and wrested it from the hands of a purchaser. It seems that all the Altman colony, dreading an investigation, were forced to remove beyond the social pale, into a five-and-dime. Well, I must get ready to attend the play.

April 14

I have found an opportunity to speak to Ella. I dared not before;

here one has a sense always of pale eyes secretly watching. But last night, at the play, I developed a fit of hiccups. I was somewhat sternly told to go and secrete myself in the basement, among the garbage cans, where the watchman never comes.

There, in the rat-haunted darkness. I heard a stifled sob. 'What's that? Is it you? Is it Ella? What ails you, child? Why do you cry?'

'They wouldn't even let me see the play.'

'Is that all? Let me console you.'

'I am so unhappy.'

She told me her tragic little story. What do you think? When she was a child, a little tiny child of only six, she strayed away and fell asleep behind a counter, while her mother tried on a new hat. When she woke, the store was in darkness.

'And I cried, and they all came around, and took hold of me. "She will tell, if we let her go," they said. Some said, "Call in the Dark Men." "Let her stay here," said Mrs Vanderpant. "She will make me a nice little maid." '

'Who are these Dark Men, Ella? They spoke of them when I came here.'

'Don't you know? Oh, it's horrible! It's horrible!'

'Tell me, Ella. Let us share it.'

She trembled. 'You know the morticians, "Journey's End", who go to houses when people die?'

'Yes, Ella.'

'Well, in that shop, just like here, and at Gimbel's, and at Bloomingdale's, there are people living, people like these.'

'How disgusting! But what can they live upon, Ella, in a funeral home?'

'Don't ask me! Dead people are sent there, to be embalmed. Oh, they are terrible creatures! Even the people here are terrified of them. But if anyone dies, or if some poor burglar breaks in, and sees these people, and might tell—'

'Yes? Go on.'

'Then they send for the others, the Dark Men.'

'Good heavens!'

'Yes, and they put the body in Surgical Supplies – or the burglar, all tied up, if it's a burglar – and they send for these others, and then they all hide, and in they come, the others – Oh! They're like pieces of blackness. I saw them once. It was terrible.'

'And then?'

'They go in, to where the dead person is, or the poor burglar. And they have wax there – and all sorts of things. And when they're gone there's just one of these wax models left on the table. And then our people put a dress on it, or a bathing suit, and they mix it up with all the others, and nobody ever knows.'

'But aren't they heavier than the others, these wax models? You would think they'd be heavier.'

'No, they're not heavier. I think there's a lot of them – gone.'

'Oh, dear! So they were going to do that to you, when you were a little child?'

'Yes, only Mrs Vanderpant said I was to be her maid.'

'I don't like these people, Ella.'

'Nor do I. I wish I could see a bird.'

'Why don't you go into the pet shop?'

'It wouldn't be the same. I want to see it on a twig, with leaves.'

'Ella, let us meet often. Let us creep away down here and meet. I will tell you about birds, and twigs and leaves.'

May 1

For the last few nights the store has been feverish with the shivering whisper of a huge crush at Bloomingdale's. Tonight was the night.

'Not changed yet? We leave on the stroke of two.' Roscoe has appointed himself, or been appointed, my guide or my guard.

'Roscoe, I am still a greenhorn. I dread the streets.'

'Nonsense! There's nothing to it. We slip out by twos and threes, stand on the sidewalk, pick up a taxi. Were you never out late in the old days? If so, you must have seen us, many a time.'

'Good heavens, I believe I have! And often wondered where you came from. And it was from here! But, Roscoe, my brow is burning. I find it hard to breathe. I fear a cold.'

'In that case you must certainly remain behind. Our whole party would be disgraced in the unfortunate event of a sneeze.'

I had relied on their rigid etiquette, so largely based on fear of discovery, and I was right. Soon they were gone, drifting out like leaves aslant on the wind. At once I dressed in flannel slacks, canvas shoes and a tasteful sport shirt, all new in stock today. I found a quiet spot, safely off the track beaten by the night-watchman. There, in a model's lifted hand, I set a wide fern frond culled from the florist's shop, and at once had a young spring tree. The carpet was sandy, sandy as a lake-side beach. A snowy napkin; two cakes, each with a cherry on it; I had only to imagine the lake and to find Ella.

'Why, Charles, what's this?'

'I'm a poet, Ella, and when a poet meets a girl like you he thinks of a day in the country. Do you see this tree? Let's call it *our* tree. There's the lake – the prettiest lake imaginable. Here is grass, and there are flowers. There are birds too, Ella. You told me you like birds.'

'Oh, Charles, you're so sweet. I feel I hear them singing.'

'And here's our lunch. But before we eat, go behind the rock there, and see what you find.'

I heard her cry out in delight when she saw the summer dress I had put there for her. When she came back the spring day smiled to see her, and the lake shone brighter than before. 'Ella, let us have lunch. Let us have fun. Let us have a swim. I can just imagine you in one of those new bathing suits.'

'Let's just sit here, Charles, and talk.'

So we sat and talked, and the time was gone like a dream. We might have stayed there, forgetful of everything, had it not been for the spider.

'Charles, what are you doing?'

'Nothing, my dear. Just a naughty little spider, crawling over your knee. Purely imaginary, of course, but that sort are sometimes the worst. I had to try to catch him.'

'Don't Charles! It's late. It's terribly late. They'll be back any minute. I'd better go home.'

I took her home to the kitchenware on the sub-ground floor, and kissed here good-day. She offered me her cheek. This troubles me.

May 10

'Ella, I love you.'

I said it to her just like that. We have met many times. I have dreamt of her by day. I have not even kept up my journal. Verse has been out of the question.

'Ella, I love you. Let us move into the trousseau department. Don't look so dismayed, darling. If you like, we will go right away from here. We will live in that little restaurant in Central Park. There are thousands of birds there.'

'Please – please don't talk like that!'

'But I love you with all my heart.'

'You mustn't.'

'But I find I must. I can't help it. Ella, you don't love another?'

She wept a little. 'Oh, Charles, I do.'

'Love another, Ella? One of these? I thought you dreaded them all. It must be Roscoe. He is the only one that's any way human. We talk of art, life, and such things. And he has stolen your heart!'

'No, Charles, no. He's just like the rest, really. I hate them all. They make me shudder.'

'Who is it, then?'

'It's him.'

'Who?'

'The night-watchman.'

465

'Impossible!'

'No. He smells of the sun.'

'Oh, Ella, you have broken my heart.'

'Be my friend, though.'

'I will. I'll be your brother. How did you fall in love with him?'

'Oh, Charles, it was wonderful. I was thinking of birds, and I was careless. Don't tell on me, Charles. They'll punish me.'

'No. No. Go on.'

'I was careless, and there he was, coming round the corner. And there was no place for me; I had this blue dress on. There were some wax models in their underthings.'

'Please go on.'

'I couldn't help it. I slipped off my dress, and stood still.'

'I see.'

'And he stopped just by me, Charles. And he looked at me. And he touched my cheek.'

'Did he notice nothing?'

'No. It was cold. But Charles, he said – he said – "Say, honey, I wish they made 'em like you on Eighth Avenue." Charles, wasn't that a lovely thing to say?'

'Personally, I should have said Park Avenue.'

'Oh, Charles, don't get like these people here. Sometimes I think you're getting like them. It doesn't matter what street, Charles; it was a lovely thing to say.'

'Yes, but my heart's broken. And what can you do about him? Ella, he belongs to another world.'

'Yes, Charles, Eighth Avenue. I want to go there. Charles, are you truly my friend?'

'I'm your brother, only my heart's broken.'

'I'll tell you. I will. I'm going to stand there again. So he'll see me.'

'And then?'

'Perhaps he'll speak to me again.'

'My dearest Ella, you are torturing yourself. You are making it worse.'

'No, Charles. Because I shall answer him. He will take me away.'

'Ella, I can't bear it.'

'Ssh! There is someone coming. I shall see birds – real birds, Charles – and flowers growing. They're coming. You must go.'

May 13

The last three days have been torture. This evening I broke. Roscoe had joined me. He sat eyeing me for a long time. He put his hand on my shoulder.

466

He said, 'You're looking seedy, old fellow. Why don't you go over to Wanamaker's for some ski-ing?'

His kindness compelled a frank response. 'It's deeper than that, Roscoe. I'm done for. I can't eat, I can't sleep. I can't write, man. I can't even write.'

'What is it? Day starvation?'

'Roscoe – it's love.'

'Not one of the staff, Charles, or the customers? That's absolutely forbidden.'

'No, it's not that, Roscoe. But just as hopeless.'

'My dear fellow, I can't bear to see you like this. Let me help you. Let me share your trouble.'

Then it all came out. It burst out. I trusted him. I think I trusted him. I really think I had no intention of betraying Ella, of spoiling her escape, of keeping her here till her heart turned towards me. If I had, it was subconscious, I swear it.

But I told him all. He was sympathetic, but I detected a sly reserve in his sympathy. 'You will respect my confidence, Roscoe? This is to be a secret between us.'

'As secret as the grave, old chap.'

And he must have gone straight to Mrs Vanderpant. This evening the atmosphere has changed. People flicker to and fro, smiling nervously, horribly, with a sort of frightened sadistic exaltation. When I speak to them they answer evasively, fidget, and disappear. An informal dance has been called off. I cannot find Ella. I will creep out. I will look for her again.

Later

Heaven! It has happened. I went in desperation to the manager's office, whose glass front overlooks the whole shop. I watched till midnight. Then I saw a little group of them, like ants bearing a victim. They were carrying Ella. They took her to the surgical department. They took other things.

And, coming back here, I was passed by a flittering, whispering horde of them, glancing over their shoulders in a thrilled ecstasy of panic, making for their hiding places. I, too, hid myself. How can I describe the dark inhuman creatures that passed me, silent as shadows? They went there – where Ella is.

What can I do? There is only one thing. I will find the watchman. I will tell him. He and I will save her. And if we are overpowered— Well, I will leave this on a counter. Tomorrow, if we live, I can recover it.

If not, look in the windows. Look for three new figures; two men, one rather sensitive-looking, and a girl. She has blue eyes, like periwinkle flowers, and her upper lip is lifted a little.

Look for us.

Smoke them out! Obliterate them! Avenge us!

Robert Silverberg

Back from the Grave

Massey woke slowly, as if the return to awareness were almost painful to him. He had the ghastly sensation of being closed in. The air around him was warm and moist and faintly foul-tasting as it passed into his lungs, and everything was dark.

He yawned, tried to stretch. Probably the windows were closed in the bedroom, that was all. That was why everything seemed so muggy in here. All he had to do was call his wife, have her get the maid or someone else to draw back the curtains and let some fresh air into the room. . . .

'Louise! Louise!'

His voice sounded oddly muffled, flat, and indistinct in his own ears. It seemed to bounce back at him from the walls and ceiling of his bedroom.

'Louise? I'm calling you!'

There was no answer.

Massey suddenly became conscious of the noxious humidity all about him. *Very well*, he thought, *if there's no one else here I'll have to open the windows myself!* He levered himself up on his elbows, tried to swing himself out of bed.

He realised that he was not in a bed at all.

A pallid quiver of fear lanced through him as he discovered he did not have room to rise to a sitting position. Above him, only inches above his head, he felt the smooth sheen of satin. There was satin all about. He reached to his left in the darkness and felt satin again, barely an inch from his shoulder. It was the same to his right.

Moment after moment, the air was growing murkier and harder to breathe. And he did not have room to move. He seemed to be in a container just about the length and width of his own body.

There is only one purpose for a container of such dimensions.

Massey felt the clammy hand of panic brush his cheeks. My *God*, he thought. *They've made a mistake! They thought I was dead and they buried me! I'm not dead! I'm – I'm – buried alive!*

Massey lay quite still for several moments after the terrible truth had become apparent. He did not want to panic. He was a reasonable man; he knew that to panic now would mean certain death. He had to be calm. Think this thing out. Don't panic.

The first fact to consider was that he was in a coffin. Coffins are not built with much air-space. Massey was a heavy-set man, and that meant not only that he needed a lot of air but that there could be little air in the coffin to begin with. And that air was rapidly being exhausted. He began taking shallower, and less frequent breaths.

Perhaps they had not buried him yet. Maybe he was still lying in state in a funeral parlour somewhere. They had lowered the coffin lid already, but there was still the chance they had not yet placed him in the grave. In that case –

He summoned up his energy and released it in one mighty cry for help. He waited.

Nothing happened.

Massey realised that such shouting was wasteful of oxygen. Probably they could not hear him through the heavy lid of the coffin. Or – he quivered at the possibility – perhaps they had lowered him into the ground already, said the proper words over him, shovelled the soil back into the cavity.

That would mean that five feet of packed-down earth lay above his head. Not even superman could raise a coffin lid with that kind of weight pressing down. Lying there in the darkness, Massey tried to force himself not to think of that possibility. Despite himself, the vision came – of himself, two yards beneath the ground, wasting his last strength in a desperate and ultimately futile attempt to raise a coffin lid held down by hundreds of pounds of soil Pushing and pushing, while the moist air around him gradually gave up its life-saving oxygen and became unfit to breathe, until finally he clutched at his purpling throat in agony, unable even to double up because of the dimensions of the coffin.

No, he thought. *I won't think of it!*

The only situation he would allow his numbed mind to consider was a hopeful one, that he was still above the surface of the ground. Otherwise there would be no hope, and he might as well lie back and die.

But. . . .

How could such a thing happen to me?

He had heard of cases of premature burial before. Most of them were apocryphal, of course – tales out of Poe, placed in real life by glib-tongued liars. But this was no lie, nor was it a story by Poe. Here he was: James Ronald Massey, forty-four years old, assets better than five hundred thousand dollars, holding responsible positions in no less than seven important corporations – here he was, lying in a coffin hardly bigger than his own body, while his life flickered like a dying candle.

It was like a dream – a nightmare. But it was real.

Massey allowed himself the luxury of a deep breath and raised his arms until his hands pressed against the satin-lined lid of the coffin. Tensing his body, he pushed upward until his wrists ached. Nothing happened; not even the smallest upward motion of the coffin lid was apparent.

He let his hands drop.

Droplets of sweat broke out all over his body. His clothes itched; he was wearing, not one of his own costly suits, but some cheap outfit supplied by the undertaker, and the coarse fabric felt rough and un-familiar against his skin.

He wondered how much more time he had, before the air would be totally vitiated. Ten minutes? An hour? A day, perhaps?

He wondered how he could possibly have been buried alive at all.

As he lay there, gathering his strength for another attempt to raise the lid, his thoughts drifted back – back over an entire lifetime, really, but centring on only the last three years, the years of his marriage to Louise. Massey had been past forty when he married her: she had been only twenty-three.

He had never had time to marry when he was young. He was always too busy, involved in complex corporate schemes, pyramiding his investments, building up his money to provide himself with a luxurious middle age. Despite himself he smiled ironically, lying in the coffin, as he recalled his frantic planning, the long hours of pacing the floor at night to devise yet another investment plan.

For what? Here at the age of forty-four he lay trapped alive in his coffin – with his life ticking away with every beat of his heart. Unless he freed himself through a miracle, there would be no old age for him.

And he would not have Louise any more.

The thoughts of Louise made the fear return. He had met her at a summer resort, one of his rare vacations; she was with her parents, and they had danced a few times, and before the two weeks were over Massey had astonished himself by proposing marriage to her. She had astonished him even more by accepting.

They had been married a month later. It was a small ceremony, though he did send announcements to all of his business associates, and they honeymooned for a month in South America. Massey could not spare more than a month away from his desk. Louise didn't seem to object to his devotion to his work, especially when he explained his financial status to her and their children after he was gone.

Those early married months had been the happiest of his life. Massey thought. To watch Louise moving around the big mansion was a delight; she seemed to bring a glowing radiance wherever she went.

I have to get out of here! The thought took on new urgency as he pictured Louise in his mind, tall, slim, so graceful she seemed to float instead of to walk, with her hair a golden halo round her head. So lovely, so warm, so loving.

Massey's breath came in panicky harsh gasps now even though he fought for control over his rebellious lungs. There still was plenty of time, he told himself. Just get in the right position and lift. How much can a coffin-lid weigh anyway?

Plenty, came the answer, *if there's a ton of dirt holding it down.*

'No! It isn't so!' Massey shouted, and the booming sound ricocheted mockingly from the walls of his coffin. 'I'm not underground yet! I can still get out!'

He squirmed around on one hip after a good deal of wriggling, and put his shoulder to the coffin lid. He took a deep breath.

Now – lift!

He pushed upward, anchoring himself with his left hand and pressing up with his right shoulder, until it seemed that his left arm would buckle under the strain. Bands of pain coursed through his body, across his chest, down his back.

The lid would not budge.

Massey's calmness began to desert him. The air was so close it stank, now, stank with musty graveyard odours and with his own perspiration and with the killing dankness of the carbon dioxide that was rapidly replacing its oxygen. He began to laugh hysterically, suddenly, without warning. He threw his head back and laughed, not seeming to care that by so laughing he was consuming more of his precious remnant of breathable air.

It was all so funny! He remembered his last day of consciousness. Remembered Louise – in Henry Marshall's arms!

Henry Marshall had arrived on the scene in the first year of Massey's marriage to Louise. She had told Massey, one night, in that casual way of hers, 'I'm having a guest for dinner.'

'Oh? Anyone I know?'

'A boy named Henry Marshall. An old playmate of mine; I haven't seen him for years.'

Massey had smiled indulgently. Above all else, he wanted Louise to be happy, and never to fear that because she had married a husband nearly twice her age she was condemned to a life of solemn loneliness.

Henry Marshall arrived at the dot of six that night. He was a boy of about twenty-five, tall and handsome, with wavy blond hair and an easy, likable manner about him. Something in his very charm made Massey dislike him almost on sight. He was too casual, took things too much for granted. Massey noticed that Henry Marshall was dressed rather shabbily, too.

It was not a pleasant evening. Louise and Henry Marshall reminisced together, chuckled over old times that meant nothing to Massey, told stories of friends long since unseen. Henry Marshall stayed late, past eleven, and when he finally left and Massey held Louise tightly in the quiet of her bedroom he sensed a certain remoteness about her that he had never felt before. It was as if she were making love mechanically, not really caring.

Massey brooded about that in the days that followed, though he never spoke a word to Louise. And Henry Marshall became a frequent visitor at the Massey's, coming sometimes for dinner, occasionally remaining as a house guest for two and three days. Massey resented the younger man's presence, but, as always, he remained silent out of deference to his wife's happiness.

He had almost come to accept Marshall's regular visits, even though they were occurring more frequently now, twice a month where once they had been only once a month. But, thought Massey as he lay in the clammy darkness of the coffin where he had been interred alive, this final visit – only a few days ago, was it, or had years gone by? – this final visit had been too much.

Young Marshall had arrived on Friday night in time for dinner, as usual. By now he was well known among the servants, and they gave him his usual room in the north wing of the building. He was gay and amusing at dinner and afterwards.

Massey retired early that night, pleading a headache. But he lay awake, tossing restlessly in his bed, perturbed half by the problems involved in a large steel manoeuvre coming up on Monday, half by the presence of this flippant youngster under his own roof.

Half the sleepless night went by, and visions danced before him: Louise, lovely, tempting, belonging to him. A current of excitement rose in Massey. He left his bed, donned a housecoat, and made his way down the hallway to his wife's bedroom. The great clock in the corridor told him that the time was past three in the morning, and the big house was quiet.

Louise had left the 'do not disturb' sign on her bedroom door. Massey opened the door gently, silently, thinking that if she were asleep he would not waken her, but hoping that perhaps she, too, had tossed and turned this evening, and would welcome him into her bed, into her arms.

He tiptoed towards the canopied bed.

Louise was not asleep. She was looking up at him, eyes bright with fear (or was it defiance?).

Louise was not alone.

Henry Marshall lay beside her, an arm thrown negligently over her bare shoulders.

In one stunned instant of understanding. Massey saw confirmed what he had barely dared to suspect, these past years when Henry Marshall had visited them so many times. Louise was deceiving him!

A hot ribbon of pain coursed across the front of his body, centring like a cauterising knife just behind his ribs. He gasped in agony and confusion.

'Louise – I didn't know –'

They were sitting up in bed, both of them, smiling at him. They were unafraid.

'Well, now you *do* know,' Henry Marshall said. 'And it's been going on for years. What are you going to do about it, old boy?'

Massey's heart thundered agonisingly. He staggered, nearly fell, grabbed a bedpost to support himself. His arms and legs felt cold with a deadly chill.

Louise said quietly, 'You were bound to find out about us sooner or later. Henry and I have been in love for years – ever since we were nineteen. But we couldn't afford to marry – and he agreed to wait a few years, when I met you. Only a few years; that's what your doctor told me, privately. He didn't want you to know.'

Massey put his hands to the fiery ball of palpitating hell that his heart had abruptly become. He could almost feel the blood circulating through his body, pounding at his brain.

Louise said, 'Dr Robinson said you had a serious heart defect – any shock was likely to carry you off. But he didn't want you to know about it; he said your days were numbered anyway, so you might just as well live them out in peace. But *I* knew – and Henry knew! And now we'll inherit your money, James. We're both still young, and we'll have each other for years to come!'

Massey took two uncertain steps towards the couple in the bed. Red flashes of light were interfering with his vision now, and his legs were numb.

'Louise – it isn't so, Louise – this is all a dream, isn't it?'

'You're wide awake! It's actually happening! Why don't you die, you old fool? Die! Die!'

And then he had started to fall, toppling into the thick wine-red carpet of Louise's bedroom, lying there with his hands dug deep into the high pile rug, while eddies of pain rippled through him, and above him sounded their mocking laughter and Louise's repeated cry of 'Die, you old fool! Die! Die!'

So that was the way it had been. Massey recalled everything, now, and he understood. The shock of finding Louise and Henry Marshall that way had touched off the heart attack that had been inevitable for so long. He had lain on the floor in Louise's bedroom, unconscious, in a coma, perhaps, and somehow – somehow – the doctors had decided he was dead.

It was incredible. Had life indeed been flickering so feebly in him that the high-price medicos had failed to realise he still lived? Or – the thought chilled Massey there in the darkness – had Louise and her lover found some complacent doctor who, for a fee, would certify death when death had not really come? What if Louise had known he was still alive, though unconscious, and had knowingly placed him in this coffin and sent him to the darkness of the grave?

A terrible passion came to life in Massey. He *would* get out! He had won before, in corporation matters, in proxy fights, in struggles of every kind. He was a mild-mannered man on the surface, but this will was all-consuming once it was aroused.

He would free himself.

Somehow.

Massey vowed to escape from this grave, whether he lay under a ton of soil or not. He would return to life, come back from the grave. Punish Louise for her crime, make her atone for her mocking infidelity.

I'll get out, he swore to himself. *I won't die here like a trapped rat.*

The word 'rat' brought a new and even more ghastly thought to mind. He had heard legends of the graveyard rats, great slug-shaped creatures with blazing red eyes and tails like scaled serpents, who tunnelled under the graveyards and gnawed their way into the new graves to devour the flesh of recent corpses.

Suppose they came for him? Suppose, even now as he lay here, the graveyard beasts squatted in their unmentionable tunnels below his coffin, nibbling at the wood with yellowed teeth, gnawing, biting, scratching, boring ominously inward.

How the rats would rejoice when they found a living man within the coffin!

Massey had always had a vivid imagination. Now with darkness settled like a cloak about him, he found himself unable to make that imagination cease functioning. Sharply in the eye of his mind he saw the gleeful cascade of rats pouring through the breach in the coffin wall, saw dozens of the foul beasts launching themselves on him with more burrowing greedily in from all sides. He pictured the rats madly joyous at the discovery of a live being, of fresh meat.

He saw their bristly snouts nuzzling at the soft pink flesh of his throat. He could picture their razor-keen teeth meeting beneath his chin, while his outraged blood spurted out over them. He could feel the animals quarrelling with each other for the right to devour the tender morsels that were his eyes.

What was that? That sound?

A fitful champing and chewing sound, was it? As of hundreds of rats patiently gnawing at the sleek fresh wood of his coffin?

No, he thought. More imagination. There was no sound. Everything was utterly silent. It was, he thought, the silence of – of the grave.

Then he wondered how he could still retain a sense of humour. How, for that matter, he could still retain any shred of his sanity, trapped like this.

He could no longer preserve the fiction that he was still lying in state in some undertaker's parlour. Coffins do not normally have locks; the only reason why he had been unable to lift the lid was that he was already in the ground. No doubt Louise and her lover had rushed him into the ground as fast as they could.

They would be in for a surprise, Massey thought with calmness that surprised himself. Calmness was what he needed now. In the same way as he had piloted so many complicated financial manoeuvres, James Ronald Massey now set to work to think of a way to escape from the living grave to which he had been condemned.

Pushing at the lid was futile. He had already tried that a dozen unsuccessful times. But perhaps he could break the lid, claw his way upward through the dirt till he reached the surface.

He felt in the darkness for the satin lining of the coffin. The air hung like a moist cloth around him now. He realised he had no more than a few minutes' air left, and then the hideous slow death of stragulation would start.

Better that than the rats, he told himself. I don't want to be alive if the rats break into the coffin. I'd rather choke to death than be eaten alive. Yes. Much better to choke.

His hands clawed at the satin and ripped it away, shredding the expensive cloth. Now he could feel the smooth, cool pine boards from which his coffin had been made. The wood had been planed and sanded to a perfect finish. He laughed, a little wildly. Probably Louise had bought him the most expensive coffin that could be found. 'Nothing but the best for my poor dead darling husband,' she must have told the undertaker.

He began to pound at the wood, hoping he would hear it splinter. But the wood held. He gasped for breath, knowing just a bit of fresh air remained, that now the torture would begin. He could barely fill his lungs. He drew in a deep breath and nearly retched at the nauseous taste of the stale air.

Weirdly he wondered if perhaps they had laid him in his grave upside-down. Perhaps he did not face the sky, and perhaps he was really digging at the bottom of his coffin instead of the top. In that case, even if he did succeed in breaking through the solid wood he would be far from free.

Impossible, he thought. *A joke of my tired mind*. He had to keep trying. Couldn't give up now. Not now, when the air would be gone in minutes, and the rats lay waiting, waiting for him.

His hands, which had never done any kind of manual labour, now clawed and scraped desperately at the unyielding wood of the coffin lid. His nails raked the mocking pine boards again and again, as if he thought to dig his way through the wood splinter by splinter. His nails ripped away one by one and blood streamed down his fingers, and he felt the bright hotness of the terrible pain, but still he clawed.

And screamed.

'Help me! Can't you hear me? I'm buried alive in here! Alive! I'll give ten thousand dollars to any man who gets me out! Twenty thousand! Fifty thousand! Do you hear me, fifty thousand dollars!'

He might just as well have offered the moon and the stars. No one heard his call; no one answered him. The funeral was probably long since over, the mourners dispersed. At this moment perhaps Louise and Henry Marshall were making love and laughing to each other about the fortune that now was theirs.

'Help me! Help me!'

His broken fingers clawed futilely at the wooden barrier above him, clawed until his nerves were numbed by constant agony and he could feel no more pain. The air was all but gone, now.

Part of his mind was still clear. Part was still engaged in formulating plans. Break a hole in the coffin lid, he thought. Widen it. Claw through the dirt to the surface. The soil will still be loose and soft. You can push it to one side if you can only get out of this coffin. Get your head above air, breathe the fresh air again, call for help.

Then settle with Louise and Henry.

It was all so simple – all but the first step. He could not get a purchase on the wood. The air was a vile moist thing now, and he could feel the cold hand of asphyxiation tightening steadily round his throat. The staleness of the air was making thought more difficult; he could barely think clearly any more. And he seemed to hear the rats again, chewing tirelessly at the wood, as if they knew that a living being lay in the wooden box, as if they yearned to get to Massey while the warm blood still pulsed in his veins.

And his heart – the heart whose sudden failure had been mistaken for death – his heart now pounded wildly from his exertions, and the pain that shot through him was ten times the torment he had experienced that night in Louise's bedroom. He wondered how long he could stand the combined assault.

The rats . . . the rats coming to get me . . . and the air almost gone . . . the darkness . . . my heart, my heart! . . . I'll need a miracle to get out of here now . . . my heart! The pain!

The pain!

Suddenly tranquillity stole over Massey. He smiled, and realised that the pain had diminished. He felt calm and assured now.

How foolish he had been to work so hard to get out of his coffin! There was such an easier way to do it!

All he had to do was drift. He drifted upward, passed lightly through the sturdy wood he had failed to break, drifted up through five feet of dark earth, and stood once more on the surface of the green land.

Free!

It was mid-afternoon. The sun glinted brightly, the sun Massey had thought never to see again. Fifty feet away, a group of people were gathered round a marble headstone, placing a wreath. Massey shouted to them.

'I'm free! They buried me, but I escaped from the grave! Get the sexton! Tell him there's been a mistake, please!'

Curiously, they ignored him. They did not even turn around to see who called. Massey repeated his words, to no avail.

He took a deep breath – and discovered for the first time that he could not taste the spring-like freshness of the air. He felt no cool fragrance in his nostrils.

Massey looked down. Then, suddenly, it was as if the ground parted beneath him, and he could see clearly the coffin lying deep in the earth, and he could see into the coffin, where the dead body of a middle-aged man lay – his fingers torn and bloodied, his face mottled with the discoloration of asphyxiation and the redness of a sudden and fatal heart attack.

William Faulkner

A Rose for Emily

I

When Miss Emily Grierson died, our whole town went to her funeral: the men through a sort of respectful affection for a fallen monument, the women mostly out of curiosity to see the inside of her house, which no one save an old man-servant – a combined gardener and cook – had seen in at least ten years.

It was a big, squarish frame house that had once been white, decorated with cupolas and spires and scrolled balconies in the heavily lightsome style of the 'seventies, set on what had once been our most select street. But garages and cotton gins had encroached and obliterated even the august names of that neighbourhood; only Miss Emily's house was left, lifting its stubborn and coquettish decay above the cotton wagons and the petrol pumps – an eyesore among eyesores. And now Miss Emily had gone to join the representatives of those august names where they lay in the cedar-bemused cemetery among the ranked and anonymous graves of Union and Confederate soldiers who fell at the battle of Jefferson.

Alive, Miss Emily had been a tradition, a duty, and a care; a sort of hereditary obligation upon the town, dating from that day in 1894 when Colonel Sartoris, the mayor – he who fathered the edict that no Negro woman should appear on the streets without an apron – remitted her taxes, the dispensation dating from the death of her father on into perpetuity. Not that Miss Emily would have accepted charity. Colonel Sartoris invented an involved tale to the effect that Miss Emily's father had loaned money to the town, which the town, as a matter of business, preferred this way of repaying. Only a man of Colonel Sartoris's generation and thought could have invented it, and only a woman could have believed it.

When the next generation, with its more modern ideas, became mayors and aldermen, this arrangement created some little dissatisfaction. On the first of the year they mailed her a tax notice. February came, and there was no reply. They wrote her a formal letter asking her to call at the sheriff's office at her convenience. A week later the mayor wrote her himself, offering to call or to send his car for her, and received in reply a note on paper of an archaic shape, in a thin, flowing calligraphy in faded ink, to the effect that she no longer went out at all. The tax notice was also enclosed, without comment.

They called a special meeting of the Board of Aldermen. A deputation waited upon her, knocked at the door through which no visitor had passed since she ceased giving china-painting lessons eight or ten years earlier. They were admitted by the old Negro into a dim hall from which a stairway mounted into still more shadow. It smelled of dust and disuse – a close, dank smell. The Negro led them into the parlour. It was furnished in heavy, leather-covered furniture. When the Negro opened the blinds of one window, they could see that the leather was cracked; and when they sat down, a faint dust rose sluggishly about their thighs, spinning with slow motes in the single sun-ray. On a tarnished gilt easel before the fireplace stood a crayon portrait of Miss Emily's father.

They rose when she entered – a small, fat woman in black, with a thin gold chain descending to her waist and vanishing into her belt, leaning on an ebony cane with a tarnished gold head. Her skeleton was small and spare; perhaps that was why what would have been merely plumpness in another was obesity in her. She looked bloated, like a body long submerged in motionless water, and of that pallid hue. Her eyes, lost in the fatty ridges of her face, looked like two small pieces of coal pressed into a lump of dough as they moved from one face to another while the visitors stated their errand.

She did not ask them to sit. She just stood in the doorway and listened quietly until the spokesman came to a stumbling halt. Then they could hear the invisible watch ticking at the end of the gold chain.

Her voice was dry and cold. 'I have no taxes in Jefferson. Colonel Sartoris explained it to me. Perhaps one of you can gain access to the city records and satisfy yourselves.'

'But we have. We are the city authorities, Miss Emily. Didn't you get a notice from the sheriff, signed by him?'

'I received a paper, yes,' Miss Emily said. 'Perhaps he considers himself the sheriff. . . . I have no taxes in Jefferson.'

'But there is nothing on the books to show that, you see. We must go by the—'

'See Colonel Sartoris. I have no taxes in Jefferson.'

'But, Miss Emily—'

'See Colonel Sartoris.' (Colonel Sartoris had been dead almost ten years.) 'I have no taxes in Jefferson. Tobe!' The Negro appeared. 'Show these gentlemen out.'

II

So she vanquished them, horse and foot, just as she had vanquished their fathers thirty years before about the smell. That was two years after her father's death and a short time after her sweetheart – the one we believed would marry her – had deserted her. After her father's death she went out very little; after her sweetheart went away, people hardly saw her at all. A few of the ladies had the temerity to call, but were not received, and the only sign of life about the place was the Negro man – a young man then – going in and out with a market basket.

'Just as if a man – any man – could keep a kitchen properly,' the ladies said; so they were not surprised when the smell developed. It was another link between the gross, teeming world and the high and mighty Griersons.

A neighbour, a woman, complained to the mayor, Judge Stevens, eighty years old.

'But what will you have me do about it, madam?' he said.

'Why, send her word to stop it,' the woman said. 'Isn't there a law?'

'I'm sure that won't be necessary,' Judge Stevens said. 'It's probably just a snake or a rat that nigger of hers killed in the yard. I'll speak to him about it.'

The next day he received two more complaints, one from a man who came in diffident deprecation. 'We really must do something about it, Judge. I'd be the last one in the world to bother Miss Emily, but we've got to do something.' That night the Board of Aldermen met – three greybeards and one younger man, a member of the rising generation.

'It's simple enough,' he said. 'Send her word to have her place cleaned up. Give her a certain time to do it in, and if she don't . . .'

'Dammit, sir,' Judge Stevens said, 'will you accuse a lady to her face of smelling bad?'

So the next night, after midnight, four men crossed Miss Emily's lawn and slunk about the house like burglars, sniffing along the base of the brickwork and at the cellar openings, while one of them performed a regular sowing motion with his hand out of a sack slung from his shoulder. They broke open the cellar door and sprinkled lime there, and in all the outbuildings. As they recrossed the lawn, a window that had been dark was lighted and Miss Emily sat in it, the light behind her, and her upright torso motionless as that of an idol. They crept quietly across the lawn and into the shadow of the locusts that lined the street. After a week or two the smell went away.

That was when people had begun to feel really sorry for her. People in our town, remembering how Old Lady Wyatt, her great-aunt, had gone completely crazy at last, believed that the Griersons held themselves a little too high for what they really were. None of the young men was quite good enough to Miss Emily and such. We had long thought of them as a tableau: Miss Emily a slender figure in white in the background, her father a spraddled silhouette in the foreground, his back to her and clutching a horsewhip, the two of them framed by the back-flung front door. So when she got to be thirty and was still single, we were not pleased exactly, but vindicated; even with insanity in the family she wouldn't have turned down all of her chances if they had really materialised.

When her father died, it got about that the house was all that was left to her; and in a way, people were glad. At last they could pity Miss Emily. Being left alone, and a pauper, she had become humanised. Now she too would know the old thrill and the old despair of a penny more or less.

The day after his death all the ladies prepared to call at the house and offer condolence and aid, as is our custom. Miss Emily met them at the door, dressed as usual and with no trace of grief on her face. She told them that her father was not dead. She did that for three days, with the ministers calling on her, and the doctors, trying to persuade her to let them dispose of the body. Just as they were about to resort to law and force, she broke down, and they buried her father quickly.

We did not say she was crazy then. We believed she had to do that. We remembered all the young men her father had driven away, and we knew that, with nothing left, she would have to cling to that which had robbed her, as people will.

III

She was sick for a long time. When we saw her again, her hair was cut short, making her look like a girl, with a vague resemblance to those angels in coloured church windows – sort of tragic and serene.

The town had just let the contracts for paving the sidewalks, and in the summer after her father's death they began the work. The construction company came with niggers and mules and machinery, and a foreman named Homer Barron, a Yankee – a big, dark, ready man, with a big voice and eyes lighter than his face. The little boys would follow in groups to hear him cuss the niggers, and the niggers singing in time to the rise and fall of picks. Pretty soon he knew everybody in town.

Whenever you heard a lot of laughing anywhere about the square, Homer Barron would be in the centre of the group. Presently we began to see him and Miss Emily on Sunday afternoons driving in the yellow-wheeled buggy and the matched team of bays from the livery stable.

At first we were glad that Miss Emily would have an interest, because the ladies all said, 'Of course a Grierson would not think seriously of a Northerner, a day labourer.' But there were still others, older people, who said that even grief could not cause a real lady to forget *noblesse oblige* – without calling it *noblesse oblige*. They just said, 'Poor Emily. Her kinsfolk should come to her.' She had some kin in Alabama; but years ago her father had fallen out with them over the estate of Old Lady Wyatt, the crazy woman, and there was no communication between the two families. They had not even been represented at the funeral.

And as soon as the old people said, 'Poor Emily,' the whispering began. 'Do you suppose it's really so?' they said to one another. 'Of course it is. What else could . . .' This behind their hands; rustling of craned silk and satin behind jalousies closed upon the sun of Sunday afternoon as the thin, swift clop-clop-clop of the matched team passed: 'Poor Emily.'

She carried her head high enough – even when we believed that she was fallen. It was as if she demanded more than ever the recognition of her dignity as the last Grierson; as if it had wanted that touch of earthiness to reaffirm her imperviousness. Like when she bought the rat poison, the arsenic. That was over a year after they had begun to say 'Poor Emily,' and while the two female cousins were visiting her.

'I want some poison,' she said to the druggist. She was over thirty then, still a slight woman, though thinner than usual, with cold, haughty black eyes in a face the flesh of which was strained across the temples and about the eye-sockets as you imagine a lighthouse-keeper's face ought to look. 'I want some poison,' she said.

'Yes, Miss Emily. What kind? For rats and such? I'd recom—'

'I want the best you have. I don't care what kind.'

The druggist named several. 'They'll kill anything up to an elephant. But what you want is—'

'Arsenic,' Miss Emily said. 'Is that a good one?'

'Is . . . arsenic? Yes, ma'am. But what you want—'

'I want arsenic.'

The druggist looked down at her. She looked back at him, erect, her face like a strained flag. 'Why, of course,' the druggist said. 'If that's what you want. But the law requires you to tell what you are going to use it for.'

Miss Emily just stared at him, her head tilted back in order to look him eye for eye, until he looked away and went and got the arsenic and wrapped it up. The Negro delivery boy brought her the package; the

WILLIAM FAULKNER

druggist didn't come back. When she opened the package at home there was written on the box, under the skull and bones: 'For rats.'

IV

So the next day we all said, 'She will kill herself'; and we said it would be the best thing. When she had first begun to be seen with Homer Barron, we had said, 'She will marry him.' Then we said, 'She will persuade him yet,' because Homer himself had remarked – he liked men, and it was known that he drank with the younger men in the Elks' Club – that he was not a marrying man. Later we said, 'Poor Emily' behind the jalousies as they passed on Sunday afternoon in the glittering buggy, Miss Emily with her head high and Homer Barron with his hat cocked and a cigar in his teeth, reins and whip in a yellow glove.

Then some of the ladies began to say that it was a disgrace to the town and a bad example to the young people. The men did not want to interfere, but at last the ladies forced the Baptist minister – Miss Emily's people were Episcopal – to call upon her. He would never divulge what happened during that interview, but he refused to go back again. The next Sunday they again drove about the streets, and the following day the minister's wife wrote to Miss Emily's relations in Alabama.

So she had blood-kin under her roof again and we sat back to watch developments. At first nothing happened. Then we were sure that they were to be married. We learned that Miss Emily had been to the jeweller's and ordered a man's toilet set in silver, with the letters H. B. on each piece. Two days later we learned that she had bought a complete outfit of men's clothing, including a night-shirt, and we said, 'They are married.' We were really glad. We were glad because the two female cousins were even more Grierson than Miss Emily had ever been.

So we were not surprised when Homer Barron – the streets had been finished some time since – was gone. We were a little disappointed that there was not a public blowing-off, but we believed that he had gone on to prepare for Miss Emily's coming, or to give her a chance to get rid of the cousins. (By that time it was a cabal, and we were all Miss Emily's allies to help circumvent the cousins.) Sure enough, after another week they departed. And, as we had expected all along, within three days Homer Barron was back in town. A neighbour saw the Negro man admit him at the kitchen door at dusk one evening.

And that was the last we saw of Homer Barron. And of Miss Emily for some time. The Negro man went in and out with the market basket, but the front door remained closed. Now and then we would see her at a window for a moment, as the men did that night when they sprinkled the lime, but for almost six months she did not appear on the streets. Then we knew that this was to be expected too; as if that quality of her

484

father which had thwarted her woman's life so many times had been too virulent and too furious to die.

When we next saw Miss Emily, she had grown fat and her hair was turning grey. During the next few years it grew greyer and greyer until it attained an even pepper-and-salt iron-grey, when it ceased turning. Up to the day of her death at seventy-four it was still that vigorous iron-grey, like the hair of an active man.

From that time on her front door remained closed, save for a period of six or seven years, when she was about forty, during which she gave lessons in china-painting. She fitted up a studio in one of the downstairs rooms, where the daughters and granddaughters of Colonel Sartoris's contemporaries were sent to her with the same regularity and in the same spirit that they were sent to church on Sundays with a twenty-five cent piece for the collection plate. Meanwhile her taxes has been remitted.

Then the newer generation became the backbone and the spirit of the town, and the painting pupils grew up and fell away and did not send their children to her with boxes of colour and tedious brushes and pictures cut from the ladies' magazines. The front door closed upon the last one and remained closed for good. When the town got free postal delivery, Miss Emily alone refused to let them fasten the metal numbers above her door and attach a mail-box to it. She would not listen to them.

Daily, monthly, yearly we watched the Negro grow greyer and more stooped, going in and out with the market basket. Each December we sent her a tax notice, which would be returned by the post office a week later, unclaimed. Now and then we would see her in one of the downstairs windows – she had evidently shut up the top floor of the house – like the carven torso of an idol in a niche, looking or not looking at us, we could never tell which. Thus she passed from generation to generation – dear, inescapable, impervious, tranquil, and perverse.

And so she died. Fell ill in the house filled with dust and shadows, with only a doddering Negro man to wait on her. We did not even know she was sick; we had long since given up trying to get any information from the Negro. He talked to no one, probably not even to her, for his voice had grown harsh and rusty, as if from disuse.

She died in one of the downstairs rooms, in a heavy walnut bed with a curtain, her grey head propped on a pillow yellow and mouldy with age and lack of sunlight.

V

The Negro met the first of the ladies at the front door and let them in, with their hushed, sibilant voices, and their quick, curious glances, and then he disappeared. He walked right through the house and out the back and was not seen again.

The two female cousins came at once. They held the funeral on the second day, with the town coming to look at Miss Emily beneath a mass of bought flowers, with the crayon face of her father musing profoundly above the bier and the ladies sibilant and macabre; and the very old men – some in their brushed Confederate uniforms – on the porch and the lawn, talking of Miss Emily as if she had been a contemporary of theirs, believing that they had danced with her and courted her perhaps, confusing time with its mathematical progression, as the old do, to whom all the past is not a diminishing road but, instead, a huge meadow which no winter ever quite touches, divided from them now by the narrow bottle-neck of the most recent decade of years.

Already we knew that there was one room in that region above stairs which no one had seen in forty years, and which would have to be forced. They waited until Miss Emily was decently in the ground before they opened it.

The violence of breaking down the door seemed to fill this room with pervading dust. A thin, acrid pall as of the tomb seemed to lie everywhere upon this room decked and furnished as for a bridal: upon the valance curtains of faded rose colour, upon the rose-shaded lights, upon the dressing table, upon the delicate array of crystal and the man's toilet things backed with tarnished silver, silver so tarnished that the monogram was obscured. Among them lay a collar and tie, as if they had just been removed, which, lifted, left upon the surface a pale crescent in the dust. Upon a chair hung the suit, carefully folded; beneath it the two mute shoes and the discarded socks.

The man himself lay in the bed.

For a long while we just stood there, looking down at the profound and fleshless grin. The body had apparently once lain in the attitude of an embrace, but now the long sleep that outlasts love, that conquers even the grimace of love, had cuckolded him. What was left of him, rotted beneath what was left of the night-shirt, had become inextricable from the bed in which he lay; and upon him and upon the pillow beside him lay that even coating of the patient and biding dust.

Then we noticed that in the second pillow was the indentation of a head. One of us lifted something from it, and leaning forward, that faint and invisible dust, dry and acrid in the nostrils, we saw a long strand of iron-grey hair.

John Christopher

The Island of Bright Birds

The first time she heard him speak, he was describing how he made his own bread, a fairly ordinary subject for a Chelsea party of this kind. But there was something in the voice, a strength, which was not so usual, and she half turned from her own group to identify him.

He was a short, slenderly built man who yet contrived to look powerful. He was about fifty, she thought, with silver-gray hair and a clipped silver-gray mustache, and it was plain that he kept himself in good physical condition. He moved his head, as though conscious of her gaze, and their eyes met. His were very blue, and direct, and she was the first to look away.

Later he spoke to her, catching her skillfully between groups, and getting her to himself.

'My name's Merronish, Adrian Merronish,' he said. 'Friend of John's. We knew each other in the war.'

John and Helen Warrington were their hosts.

'I'm Angela Blake,' she said.

'I wanted to talk to you,' he said, 'because you are so beautiful. But also because you are happy. I should think you are in love.'

His sentences were short, but not clipped. Rather they carried an implication of flow, a wavelike hypnotic quality. What he said surprised but also pleased her. She said, laughing, 'The last part's true.'

'Is he here?'

She pointed. 'Over there. The tall one with the fair curly hair.'

He nodded in appraisal. 'You make a handsome pair.'

Peter, and her love for him, were the supremely important things in her life at that time.

'We are to be married next month,' she said. 'As soon as he has finished his present job, up in the wilds of Scotland. He's a development engineer.'

Merronish said, 'A development engineer. It sound like an exciting profession. I don't do anything but live on an island. An island full of bright birds. Someday you must visit it.'

She laughed again, glorying in a world that could offer islands and bright birds and her own true love.

'We'd love to,' she said.

She spoke of him to Peter, as they went home together.

'Yes, I know,' Peter said. 'A rather interesting chap.'

'Did he talk to you about his island?'

'Not much. He talked about my job mostly.' He paused, considering this. 'I suppose that's why I thought him interesting.'

'He goes to the root of things,' she said. 'He told me I was happy, because I was in love.'

Peter bent down to her, as a gust of breeze from the river ruffled the early summer leaves of the Embankment trees. With his mouth against her hair he asked her, 'True?'

She squeezed his arm with her two hands. 'So true.'

Merronish called on her two weeks after the funeral. She opened the door, saw and recognised him, and remembered what he had said at their first meeting. There was no danger, she thought bitterly, of anyone saying that now. She did not look much in mirrors these days, but she knew her hair was lank and untidy, her skin blotched from crying.

'What is it?' she said stiffly.

'May I come in?'

'If you like.'

He carried a great bunch of chrysanthemums and roses. She stood aside and he came in and put them on the hall table. He had the discreet solemnity of a professional mourner, she thought, but his blue eyes were still direct, seeking and holding.

'I saw John, and he told me,' he said. 'I'm sorry.'

'Thank you. For the flowers.' She stared at them, hoping she would not cry again. 'Can I get you a drink?'

She was sure he would say no, but he said yes, and took the seat she offered him. He sat there, watching patiently, while she got the drink; and afterward. He was waiting for her to talk. She had run from all company, even her family, since it happened, but now she felt it growing in her – the urge to tell her misery as once she had told her happiness.

She said, conscious of the dryness of her voice, 'I don't know how much John told you. It was a hit-and-run accident. There was a good trout stream near where he was working, and he used to go fishing in the evening. They found him dead by the side of the road. No one saw it happen – no one even saw the car. There was a bend in the road. No footpath, of course. The police said the car must have come round very fast, and hit from behind.'

She paused, seeing it again, as she had seen it so often. Merronish said, 'Go on,' in a gentle voice, and the tears came. She was alone again, in a melting universe of weeping, an ocean of which she could not remember the beginning or imagine the end.

At one point he gave her a handkerchief, but he might have been a robot serving her. When the outburst came to a sobbing, gasping end, she was almost surprised to find him still sitting there.

He waited until she was breathing steadily, and said, 'Now go and get yourself ready and I will take you out to dinner.'

She shook her head. 'No. It's kind of you, but no. I want to stay here.' She added petulantly, 'I'm not hungry.'

'Come all the same,' he said. 'Have a glass of wine while I eat. It will do you good not to be alone.'

She thought about that for a moment, and knew it was true. Obediently she got up and went to her bedroom to make up her face.

She learned things about herself during the next weeks and months, and about grief. The bouts of wild angry misery were fewer, but as time stretched between them she became aware of a new horror that in some ways was worse. The nearest description she could put to it was boredom, but it was boredom of a kind new to her, a yawning listless pointlessness that staled and fouled her very being. In it she contemplated suicide for the first time, but knew she could not command the energy even for that nihilistic resolve.

She had an overpowering need of something, anything, to distract her ears and eyes. She watched television in lethargic and fascinated irritation, and sometimes when the programmes had ended she found herself staring for long periods at the empty screen.

Merronish returned two weeks later, and after that at more or less weekly intervals. He would come up to London one day and go back the next; he would not leave his island for longer than that at one time. She was guarded at first, but soon was simply glad of his kindness and attention, his unfailing patience with her.

She was becoming aware again of other people in the world, but with more irritability than pleasure. They talked when she did not want them to talk, and were silent or vapid she when needed speech and comfort.

Merronish was the remarkable exception. He sensed her moods and responded to them, talking at the right time and listening with the right, unobtrusive attention. From being apathetic about his visits, she grew to welcome them, and at last began to count the days between them. Autumn blurred into winter, and there were times when, because of bad weather and rough seas, he was late in visiting her. Thrown back on the unsatisfactory others, and on contemplation of the wound of grief, which still could bleed, she found herself missing him quite sharply.

The great reassuring thing, of course, was that nothing that could remotely be called sexual came between them. If there had been the slightest hint of desire in his attitude, she would have been repelled and would have turned him away. But there were only kindness and patience. He never attempted even to kiss her good night, and scarcely touched her beyond a handshake. Once or twice she wondered about this, seeking a motive behind his kindness; but for the most part she was content to accept it. And to let it nourish her.

He talked a lot about the island, and a picture of it grew in her mind. Rose-pink granite rocks, lulled by blue or lashed by gray-green seas – rabbit-cropped grass burnt by long days of sun – a wood sparkling with rain after a shower, and echoing with birds. A place of peace and beauty, remote from the world's miseries, armoured by the waves against shock and change. And yet, she realised one day with a small tremor of surprise, she really knew very little about the island. His descriptions had been general, not particular. The thought whetted her curiosity; the next time he came, she would ask him questions.

But the answers she got were vague, and the picture remained as it had been – a mosaic of impressions, more a description of dream than reality. She could not be sure if it was a failure of communication or a deliberate evasiveness on his part. She even toyed with the idea that the island might not exist – might merely be some fantasy he had created for himself.

One day, on the telephone to Helen Warrington, she asked her about it, as tactfully as she could. Helen's reply was not helpful. No, she said, she did not know much about it. She and John had never been there. There had been talk of their going, but somehow it had never happened.

And Angela, putting down the telephone, realised that, although Merronish had talked of the place so much, he had never, since that first encounter, spoken of her visiting it.

It was spring again, the days lengthening and brightening, the earth stirring from its sleep, new green budding from old brown. She decided she would not ask him anymore, kept to her resolve, and as soon as he had gone away, regretted it. There were spring storms, and it was nearly three weeks before he came again. Almost as soon as she saw him, she said, 'The island – I would like to see it.'

He smiled at her. 'Of course.'

'How soon?'

'In the summer.' He brushed the silver-gray mustache down with the side of his finger. 'The summer is the best time to visit the island.'

As the train gathered speed leaving the station, she asked curiously, 'Do you always travel down by train?'

He nodded from the facing seat in the first-class compartment which they had to themselves.

'Invariably. Motoring is no longer a pleasure. Except for one occasion I haven't driven since the war.'

She looked out of the window. The sky was blue and empty over the sweltering city.

'It's a good day,' she said, 'to be leaving London.'

'Yes. A good day to be going to the island.'

'Tell me about it.'

'No. Seeing is best. And you will see it soon.'

'How soon? How long is the journey by boat?'

'Not much more than half an hour. We can do better than twenty knots on a day like this.'

'You have a speedboat?'

'A twin-engined diesel. "Hermes." '

'Do any other boats go to the island?'

'There's a young fisherman who brings over any heavy stuff I need. No one else.'

'Might people not go there while you're away?'

'It's unlikely. We're too far out for the small boats. And there's only one landing place, and that's a tricky one. Some nasty rocks, and the whole area's due for recharting.'

'So you preserve your isolation.'

'Yes. And hope to go on doing so.'

In the late afternoon there was some cloud in the sky, but it was still hot. England was a haze on the horizon; the sea was smooth and glassy except for the bubbling, widening furrow of their wake.

She stared at the island, which now lay full ahead. A hummock of pink and green rising out of the calm blue waters – the pink of rock, the green of trees and grass. So it was true. It existed. She had not been sure till now.

'It's strange,' she said.

'What?'

She raised her voice to be heard above the roar of the diesels. 'I don't see any gulls.'

'There are none.'

'Why is that?'

'You'll see.'

The landing place was round the other side and, as he had said, tricky. There was a tortuous and not very wide channel through rocks, and a short concrete jetty concealed behind a prow of granite. He handled the boat with a skill and confidence, bringing her in to bump her rubber fenders gently against the jetty wall. There was an iron ladder by which they climbed ashore. He tied up and they climbed the hill to the house.

It was built of the island's granite, and had been scarcely noticeable from the sea; as they approached she realised it was larger than she had expected – a rambling place with more than a dozen windows on this side. The immediate approach was through a garden, and one in surprisingly good heart for land which, in rough weather, would probably be touched by the salt spray blowing up from the inlet. She saw roses and honeysuckle, and a cabbage palm bursting into white spiky flower. They entered the house through a terrace where there were various flowering shrubs, and ropes of clematis dropping their large blue blossoms from a covering lattice.

The house, undistinguished from outside, was beautifully appointed within. The furniture was good, of several different periods but in harmony, and the decor was in quiet splendid taste. While he was getting them a drink, she rubbed the wallpaper gently with the back of her hand. It was heavy, silky stuff, the Regency stripes strongly embossed. There were paintings on the walls: a Stubbs, a Fragonard, and two of Russell Flint's studies of nude girls bathing.

There was a change in him, she thought, since they had come ashore, a quickening into enthusiasm. He did not let her sit down with her drink, but took her at once on a tour of the ground floor. There was a library, with three walls shelved and glassed, and behind the glass, gold leaf winking from dull greens and blues and reds of leather. Another fairly small room, looking out over the sea, was empty except for a few chairs, a table, and a harpsichord. The harpsichord was in light walnut, and the room was panelled to match. The kitchen, on the other hand, was all steel and plastic, with an electric mixer, a cooker, a deep-freeze, and a large blue refrigerator humming to itself.

'What about power?' she asked.

'A generator. I leave it on while I am away. It can run a week or more without attention.'

'And who cleans and tidies?'

'I do. Not difficult. I am a tidy person by nature.'

She said, 'It's a lovely house.'

He nodded, accepting this. 'Leave your glass there. I want to show you the rest of the island.'

She followed him obediently. They went up steps, along a path hemmed in by the blinding yellow of gorse and the white spears of sloe. The path branched and he pointed downward.

'My pool.'

It was a tiny cove, with a minuscule beach of golden sand. A wall, which had been built between the two enclosing arms of rock, held in the water – full tides would wash over and refresh it. It looked very blue. Beyond it, higher land seemed to have been cut away in an inverted saddle.

'It is open to the setting sun,' he said, 'but I wanted the sun in the morning, as well. One can swim at dawn and watch the sun rise.'

They took the upward path. The wood started farther up, but below it there was a place, about 50 by 100 yards, where the ground was level, covered with short grass and pocked with holes. In the centre of this small plateau a bird was perched on a padded hoop.

At the sight of it she exclaimed, 'An eagle?'

'A falcon, but not an eagle. The earl's bird. An eagle for an emperor, a peregrine for an earl. A tiercel.'

'Tiercel?'

'The male of the species. A third smaller than the female, but more powerful.'

'And you go away and leave him tethered?'

'His rein takes him to the edge of the wood.' He gestured toward the holes which she saw were littered with droppings. 'He gets at least one fat rabbit, morning and evening.'

'But why?' she asked. 'Why a falcon here?'

'For protection,' he said simply. 'To guard my bright birds.'

As they approached the wood she saw them – flashes of emerald, of blue, of yellow. She did not recognise them at first, but then their harsh chatter identified them. They were grass parakeets – budgerigars. She saw more and more, of many different colours and combinations of colours – turquoise, opaline, pearl-gray, mauve, olive, cobalt.

'They live here wild?'

'Yes. I have put up nesting boxes, and I give them seed. Apart from that they are on their own. The losses were heavy at first. Some died, some stupidly flew out to sea. I brought in more, and they adapted.'

'But I thought other birds attacked them?'

'There are no other birds.'

She realised that she had not seen any, that she had heard only the parakeets.

'They were attacked at the beginning,' he explained. 'That was when I brought the peregrine in. I tamed and trained him. He cleared the sky in a couple of months, and I restocked. Some gulls come in from time to time, and he kills them.'

They were in the wood, the path still winding up. The coloured birds flashed overhead.

'You killed them all?' she said in horror.

'It was the only thing to do.'

The wood was a tonsure round the island; its summit and centre were open. They came out into meadow grass. The birds were here, too, hanging onto the long grass and pecking at the seeds. There was a summerhouse, quite substantially built, with a veranda.

When he opened the door she saw that it was furnished with cushioned wicker chairs, a couch, a low table. He pressed a button just inside the door and to her amazement there was music, the precise ecstasy of a piano.

'*The Art of Fugue*,' he said. He smiled. 'No magic. A land line to a tape recorder in the house. I switched it on before I left.' He looked at her searchingly. 'Do you like my island?'

She said, 'It's . . . magnificent.'

'It wants one thing.' Their eyes were locked still. 'A mistress.'

She looked away.

After a pause he said, 'There is something else to show you.' But the enthusiasm had gone, his voice was cold. 'Over here.'

She followed him. It emerged suddenly from the high grass, which had concealed it. It was roughly square, its sides precipitously steep, a hole chiselled out of the the rocky core of the island. About twenty feet across, perhaps fifteen feet deep on the far side, twenty-five on this. The walls, like the floor, were granite.

'They got the stone from here,' he said, 'to build the house. Not long after Waterloo. The man who owned the island was a sea captain, and he had the use of French prisoners. Quite a few died.'

Imagining the past she averted her head.

'There is another story – something that happened fifty years later. The owner is said to have been in love with a beautiful girl. He brought her here by a trick, and when she defied him he had his servants put her down there. The story goes that, since she still would not yield, he sent down drugged wine, and when she was senseless he climbed down a rope ladder and violated her. If so, he was a crude and stupid man. Patience would have brought him to a better end. Privation, exposure, the place itself, would have tamed her.'

She stared into the barren granite hole. A little rainwater had collected in a hollow at one point. She could visualise the degradation of sucking at it, on hands and knees, with a face watching above, with the music of Bach faint on the air.

He said, 'The moment I saw you I knew you would crown the island.'

She could not look at him. She thought of his patient, hideous resolution. A hillock carved to let him see the dawn while he swam. Bird life destroyed to make way for his parakeets. Bach brought up to the island's crest for his pleasure. And so he had seen a woman, and wanted her.

What was it he had said in the train? 'Except for one occasion I haven't driven since the war.' One occasion. A hunting down, a waiting, and a car driven into a defenseless man on a lonely road . . . And then the slow, sexless wooing of a girl crazed by grief.

She turned to him, smiling, opening her arms. For a moment he was surprised, and then triumphant. He took her in his arms, felt her body melt toward his, and tried to guide her back to the summerhouse.

She shook her head.

'No, here,' she whispered. 'Here, Now!'

They lay in the grass, a foot or two from the lip of the granite hole. The sun slanted through the tops of the trees.

'Sleep,' she crooned. 'Be at rest, my darling. Sleep. Sleep.'

He was about twenty-five, dark, strong, with a stubble of beard, the local fisherman who had brought oil for the generator.

'Lucky there was plenty of food in the place,' he said. 'Of course, if you'd known how to handle the boat . . . But better not, I reckon. These are nasty waters for those that don't know them.'

She had led him up to the crest and they stood by the edge of the granite hole.

Looking down, he said, 'It's a long enough drop to kill anyone. You wouldn't think he would miss his footing, would you, knowing the place so well? But that's how it happens – you get over-confident.'

In three weeks the sun had bleached it and rain had rotted it. One could see the white gleam of bone.

'Funny that,' he said. 'The way he's fallen. He looks as though he's trying to climb out. Well, there's nothing we can do, I reckon.'

He looked around, at the waving empty grass, at the silent wood.

'Used to be full of budgies, this place,' he said. 'Lovebirds, you know. Hundreds of them.'

'They're dead.'

He looked at her, puzzled, 'Dead?'

'It was the falcon,' she said. 'I could not bear to see him tied, so I cut the tether. He killed them all, all the bright birds.'

Suddenly, uncontrollably, she began to weep. Sobbing she turned her face up toward the sky's bright blue. High up, almost invisible, the patient falcon hung, waiting.

Flannery O'Connor

The Comforts of Home

Thomas withdrew to the side of the window and with his head between the wall and the curtain he looked down on the driveway where the car had stopped. His mother and the little slut were getting out of it. His mother emerged slowly, stolid and awkward, and then the little slut's long slightly bowed legs slid out, the dress pulled above the knees. With a shriek of laughter she ran to meet the dog, who bounded, over-joyed, shaking with pleasure, to welcome her. Rage gathered throughout Thomas's large frame with a silent ominous intensity, like a mob assembling.

It was now up to him to pack a suitcase, go to the hotel, and stay there until the house should be cleared.

He did not know where a suitcase was, he disliked to pack, he needed his books, his typewriter was not portable, he was used to an electric blanket, he could not bear to eat in restaurants. His mother, with her daredevil charity, was about to wreck the peace of the house.

The back door slammed and the girl's laugh shot up from the kitchen, through the back hall, up the stairwell and into his room, making for him like a bolt of electricity. He jumped to the side and stood glaring about him. His words of the morning had been unequivocal: 'If you bring that girl back into this house, I leave. You can choose – her or me.'

She had made her choice. An intense pain gripped his throat. It was the first time in his thirty-five years ... He felt a sudden burning moisture behind his eyes. Then he steadied himself, overcome by rage. On the contrary: she had not made any choice. She was counting on his attachment to his electric blanket. She would have to be shown.

The girl's laughter rang upward a second time and Thomas winced. He saw again her look of the night before. She had invaded his room.

He had waked to find his door open and her in it. There was enough light from the hall to make her visible as she turned toward him. The face was like a comedienne's in a musical comedy – a pointed chin, wide apple cheeks and feline empty eyes. He had sprung out of his bed and snatched a straight chair and then he had backed her out the door, holding the chair in front of him like an animal trainer driving out a dangerous cat. He had driven her silently down the hall, pausing when he reached it to beat on his mother's door. The girl, with a gasp, turned and fled into the guest room.

In a moment his mother had opened her door and peered out apprehensively. Her face, greasy with whatever she put on it at night, was framed in pink rubber curlers. She looked down the hall where the girl had disappeared. Thomas stood before her, the chair still lifted in front of him as if he were about to quell another beast. 'She tried to get in my room,' he hissed, pushing in. 'I woke up and she was trying to get in my room.' He closed the door behind him and his voice rose in outrage. 'I won't put up with this! I won't put up with it another day!'

His mother, backed by him to her bed, sat down on the edge of it. She had a heavy body on which sat a thin, mysteriously gaunt and incongruous head.

'I'm telling you for the last time,' Thomas said, 'I won't put up with this another day.' There was an observable tendency in all of her actions. This was, with the best intentions in the world, to make a mockery of virtue, to pursue it with such a mindless intensity that everyone involved was made a fool of and virtue itself became ridiculous. 'Not another day,' he repeated.

His mother shook her head emphatically, her eyes still on the door.

Thomas put the chair on the floor in front of her and sat down on it. He leaned forward as if he were about to explain something to a defective child.

'That's just another way she's unfortunate,' his mother said. 'So awful, so awful. She told me the name of it but I forget what it is but it's something she can't help. Something she was born with. Thomas,' she said and put her hand to her jaw, 'suppose it were you?'

Exasperation blocked his windpipe. 'Can't I make you see,' he croaked, 'that if she can't help herself you can't help her?'

His mother's eyes, intimate but untouchable, were the blue of great distances after sunset. 'Nimpermaniac,' she murmured.

'Nymphomaniac,' he said fiercely. 'She doesn't need to supply you with any fancy names. She's a moral moron. That's all you need to know. Born without the moral faculty – like somebody else would be born without a kidney or a leg. Do you understand?'

'I keep thinking it might be you,' she said, her hand still on her jaw.

'If it were you, how do you think I'd feel if nobody took you in? What if you were a nimpermaniac and not a brilliant smart person and you did what you couldn't help and . . .'

Thomas felt a deep unbearable loathing for himself as if he were turning slowly into the girl.

'What did she have on?' she asked abruptly, her eyes narrowing.

'Nothing!' he roared. 'Now will you get her out of here!'

'How can I turn her out in the cold?' she said. 'This morning she was threatening to kill herself again.'

'Send her back to jail,' Thomas said.

'I would not send *you* back to jail, Thomas,' she said.

He got up and snatched the chair and fled the room while he was still able to control himself.

Thomas loved his mother. He loved her because it was his nature to do so, but there were times when he could not endure her love for him. There were times when it became nothing but pure idiot mystery and he sensed about him forces, invisible currents entirely out of his control. She proceeded always from the tritest of considerations – it was the *nice thing to do* – into the most foolhardly engagements with the devil, whom, of course, she never recognised.

The devil for Thomas was only a manner of speaking, but it was a manner appropriate to the situations his mother got into. Had she been in any degree intellectual, he could have proved to her from early Christian history that no excess of virtue is justified, that a moderation of good produces likewise a moderation in evil, that if Antony of Egypt had stayed at home and attended to his sister, no devils would have plagued him.

Thomas was not cynical and so far from being opposed to virtue, he saw it as the principle of order and the only thing that makes life bearable. His own life was made bearable by the fruits of his mother's saner virtues – by the well-regulated house she kept and the excellent meals she served. But when virtue got out of hand with her, as now, a sense of devils grew upon him, and these were not mental quirks in himself or the old lady, they were denizens with personalities, present though not visible, who might any moment be expected to shriek or rattle a pot.

The girl had landed in the county jail a month ago on a bad cheque charge and his mother had seen her picture in the paper. At the breakfast table she had gazed at it for a long time and then had passed it over the coffee pot to him. 'Imagine,' she said, 'only nineteen years old and in that filthy jail. And she doesn't look like a bad girl.'

Thomas glanced at the picture. It showed the face of a shrewd ragamuffin. He observed that the average age for ciminality was steadily lowering.

'She looks like a wholesome girl,' his mother said.

'Wholesome people don't pass bad cheques,' Thomas said.

'You don't know what you'd do in a pinch.'

'I wouldn't pass a bad cheque,' Thomas said.

'I think,' his mother said, 'I'll take her a little box of candy.'

If then and there he had put his foot down, nothing else would have happened. His father, had he been living, would have put his foot down at that point. Taking a box of candy was her favourite nice thing to do. When anyone within her social station moved to town, she called and took a box of candy; when any of her friend's children had babies or won a scholarship, she called and took a box of candy; when an old person broke his hip, she was at his bedside with a box of candy. He had been amused at the idea of her taking a box of candy to the jail.

He stood now in his room with the girl's laugh rocketing away in his head and cursed his amusement.

When his mother returned from the visit to the jail, she had burst into his study without knocking and had collapsed full-length on his couch, lifting her small swollen feet up on the arm of it. After a moment, she recovered herself enough to sit up and put a newspaper under them. Then she fell back again. 'We don't know how the other half lives,' she said.

Thomas knew that though her conversation moved from cliché to cliché there were real experiences behind them. He was less sorry for the girl's being in jail than for his mother having to see her there. He would have spared her all unpleasant sights. 'Well,' he said and put away his journal, 'you had better forget it now. The girl has ample reason to be in jail.'

'You can't imagine what all she's been through,' she said, sitting up again, 'listen.' The poor girl, Star, had been brought up by a stepmother with three children of her own, one an almost grown boy who had taken advantage of her in such dreadful ways that she had been forced to run away and find her real mother. Once found, her real mother had sent her to various boarding schools to get rid of her. At each of these she had been forced to run away by the presence of perverts and sadists so monstrous that their acts defied description. Thomas could tell that his mother had not been spared the details that she was sparing him. Now and again when she spoke vaguely, her voice shook and he could tell that she was remembering some horror that had been put to her graphically. He had hoped that in a few days the memory of all this would wear off, but it did not. The next day she returned to the jail with Kleenex and cold-cream and a few days later, she announced that she had consulted a lawyer.

It was at these times that Thomas truly mourned the death of his father though he had not been able to endure him in life. The old man would have had none of this foolishness. Untouched by useless compassion, he would (behind her back) have pulled the necessary strings with his crony, the sheriff, and the girl would have been packed off to the state penitentiary to serve her time. He had always been engaged in some enraged action until one morning when (with an angry glance at his wife as if she alone were responsible) he had dropped dead at the breakfast table. Thomas had inherited his father's reason without his ruthlessness and his mother's love of good without her tendency to pursue it. His plan for all practical action was to wait and see what developed.

The lawyer found that the story of the repeated atrocities was for the most part untrue, but when he explained to her that the girl was a psychopathic personality, not insane enough for the asylum, not criminal enough for the jail, not stable enough for society, Thomas's mother was more deeply affected than ever. The girl readily admitted that her story was untrue on account of her being a congenital liar; she lied, she said, because she was insecure. She had passed through the hands of several psychiatrists who had put the finishing touches to her education. She knew there was no hope for her. In the presence of such an affliction as this, his mother seemed bowed down by some painful mystery that nothing would make endurable but a redoubling of effort. To his annoyance, she appeared to look on *him* with compassion, as if her hazy charity no longer made distinctions.

A few days later she burst in and said that the lawyer had got the girl paroled – to her.

Thomas rose from his Morris chair, dropping the review he had been reading. His large bland face contracted in anticipated pain. 'You are not,' he said, 'going to bring that girl here!'

'No, no,' she said, 'calm yourself. Thomas.' She had managed with difficulty to get the girl a job in a pet shop in town and a place to board with a crotchety old lady of her acquaintance. People were not kind. They did not put themselves in the place of someone like Star who had everything against her.

Thomas sat down again and retrieved his review. He seemed just to have escaped some danger which he did not care to make clear to himself. 'Nobody can tell you anything,' he said, 'but in a few days that girl will have left town, having got what she could out of you. You'll never hear from her again.'

Two nights later he came home and opened the parlour door and was speared by a shrill depthless laugh. His mother and the girl sat close to the fireplace where the gas logs were lit. The girl gave the immediate impression of being physically crooked. Her hair was cut like a dog's or an elf's and she was dressed in the latest fashion. She was training on him a long familiar sparkling stare that turned after a second into an intimate grin.

'Thomas!' his mother said, her voice firm with the injunction not to bolt, 'this is Star you've heard so much about. Star is going to have supper with us.'

The girl called herself Star Drake. The lawyer had found that her real name was Sarah Ham.

Thomas neither moved nor spoke but hung in the door in what seemed a savage perplexity. Finally he said, 'How do you do, Sarah,' in a tone of such loathing that he was shocked at the sound of it. He reddened, feeling it beneath him to show contempt for any creature so pathetic. He advanced into the room, determined at least on a decent politeness and sat down heavily in a straight chair.

'Thomas writes history,' his mother said with a threatening look at him. 'He's president of the local Historical Society this year.'

The girl leaned forward and gave Thomas an even more pointed attention. 'Fabulous!' she said in a throaty voice.

'Right now Thomas is writing about the first settlers in this county,' his mother said.

'Fabulous!' the girl repeated.

Thomas by an effort of will managed to look as if he were alone in the room.

'Say, you know who he looks like?' Star asked, her head on one side, taking him in at an angle.

'Oh, someone very distinguished!' his mother said archly.

'This cop I saw in the movie I went to last night,' Star said.

'Star,' his mother said, 'I think you ought to be careful about the kind of movies you go to. I think you ought to see only the best ones. I don't think crime stories would be good for you.'

'Oh this was a crime-does-not-pay,' Star said, 'and I swear this cop looked exactly like him. They were always putting something over on the guy. He would look like he couldn't stand it a minute longer or he would blow up. He was a riot. And not bad looking,' she added with an appreciative leer at Thomas.

'Star,' his mother said, 'I think it would be grand if you developed a taste for music.'

Thomas sighed. His mother rattled on and the girl, paying no attention to her, let her eyes play over him. The quality of her look was such that it might have been her hands, resting now on his knees, now on his neck. Her eyes had a mocking glitter and he knew that she was well aware he could not stand the sight of her. He needed nothing to tell him he was in the presence of the very stuff of corruption, but blameless corruption because there was no responsible faculty behind it. He was

501

looking at the most unendurable form of innocence. Absently he asked himself what the attitude of God was to this, meaning if possible to adopt it.

His mother's behaviour throughout the meal was so idiotic that he could barely stand to look at her and since he could less stand to look at Sarah Ham, he fixed on the sideboard across the room a continuous gaze of disapproval and disgust. Every remark of the girl's his mother met as if it deserved serious attention. She advanced several plans for the wholesome use of Star's spare time. Sarah Ham paid no more attention to this advice than if it came from a parrot. Once when Thomas inadvertently looked in her direction, she winked. As soon as he had swallowed the last spoonful of dessert, he rose and muttered, 'I have to go, I have a meeting.'

'Thomas,' his mother said. 'I want you to take Star home on your way. I don't want her riding in taxis by herself at night.'

For a moment Thomas remained furiously silent. Then he turned and left the room. Presently he came back with a look of obscure determination on his face. The girl was ready, meekly waiting at the parlour door. She cast up at him a great look of admiration and confidence. Thomas did not offer his arm but she took it anyway and moved out of the house and down the steps, attached to what might have been a miraculously moving monument.

'Be good!' his mother called.

Sarah Ham snickered and poked him in the ribs.

While getting his coat he had decided that this would be his opportunity to tell the girl that unless she ceased to be a parasite on his mother, he would see to it, personally, that she was returned to jail. He would let her know that he understood what she was up to, that he was not an innocent and that there were certain things he would not put up with. At his desk, pen in hand, none was more articulate than Thomas. As soon as he found himself shut into the car with Sarah Ham, terror seized his tongue.

She curled her feet up under her and said, 'Alone at last,' and giggled.

Thomas swerved the car away from the house and drove fast toward the gate. Once on the highway, he shot forward as if he were being pursued.

'Jesus!' Sarah Ham said, swinging her feet off the seat, 'where's the fire?'

Thomas did not answer. In a few seconds he could feel her edging closer. She stretched, eased nearer, and finally hung her hand limply over his shoulder. 'Tomsee doesn't like me,' she said, 'but I think he's fabulously cute.'

Thomas covered the three and a half miles into town in a little over four minutes. The light at the first intersection was red but he ignored it. The old woman lived three blocks beyond. When the car screeched to a halt at the place, he jumped out and ran around to the girl's door and opened it. She did not move from the car and Thomas was obliged to wait. After a moment one leg emerged, then her small white crooked face appeared and stared up at him. There was something about the look of it that suggested blindness but it was the blindness of those who don't know that they cannot see. Thomas was curiously sickened. The empty eyes moved over him. 'Nobody likes me,' she said in a sullen tone. 'What if you were me and I couldn't stand to ride you three miles?'

'My mother likes you,' he muttered.

'Her!' the girl said. 'She's just about seventy-five years behind the times!'

Breathlessly Thomas said, 'If I find you bothering her again, I'll have you put back in jail.' There was a dull force behind his voice though it came out barely above a whisper.

'You and who else?' she said and drew back in the car as if now she did not intend to get out at all. Thomas reached into it, blindly grasped the front of her coat, pulled her out by it and released her. Then he lunged back to the car and sped off. The other door was still hanging open and her laugh, bodiless but real, bounded up the street as if it were about to jump in the open side of the car and ride away with him. He reached over and slammed the door and then drove toward home, too angry to attend his meeting. He intended to make his mother well-aware of his displeasure. He intended to leave no doubt in her mind. The voice of his father rasped in his head.

Numbskull, the old man said, put your foot down now. Show her who's boss before she shows you.

But when Thomas reached home, his mother, wisely, had gone to bed.

The next morning he appeared at the breakfast table, his brow lowered and the thrust of his jaw indicating that he was in a dangerous humour. When he intended to be determined, Thomas began like a bull that, before charging, backs with his head lowered and paws the ground. 'All right now listen,' he began, yanking out his chair and sitting down, 'I have something to say to you about that girl and I don't intend to say it but once.' He drew breath. 'She's nothing but a little slut. She makes fun of you behind your back. She means to get everything she can out of you and you are nothing to her.'

His mother looked as if she too had spent a restless night. She did not dress in the morning but wore her bathrobe and a gray turban around her head, which gave her face a disconcerting omniscient look. He might have been breakfasting with a sibyl.

'You'll have to use canned cream this morning,' she said, pouring his coffee. 'I forgot the other.'

'All right, did you hear me?' Thomas growled.

'I'm not deaf,' his mother said and put the pot back on the trivet. 'I know I'm nothing but an old bag of wind to her.'

'Then why do you persist in this foolhardy . . .'

'Thomas,' she said, and put her hand to the side of her face, 'it might be . . .'

'It is not me!' Thomas said, grasping the table leg at his knee.

She continued to hold her face, shaking her head slightly. 'Think of all you have,' she began. 'All the comforts of home. And morals, Thomas. No bad inclinations, nothing bad you were born with.'

Thomas began to breathe like someone who feels the onset of asthma. 'You are not logical,' he said in a limp voice. '*He* would have put his foot down.'

The old lady stiffened. 'You,' she said, 'are not like him.'

Thomas opened his mouth silently.

'However,' his mother said, in a tone of such subtle accusation that she might have been taking back the compliment, 'I won't invite her back again since you're so dead set against her.'

'I am not set against her,' Thomas said. 'I am set against your making a fool of yourself.'

As soon as he left the table and closed the door of his study on himself, his father took up a squatting position in his mind. The old man had had the countryman's ability to converse squatting, though he was no countryman but had been born and brought up in the city and only moved to a smaller place later to exploit his talents. With steady skill he had made them think him one of them. In the midst of a conversation on the courthouse lawn, he would squat and his two or three companions would squat with him with no break in the surface of the talk. By gesture he had lived his lie; he had never deigned to tell one.

Let her run over you, he said. You ain't like me. Not enough to be a man.

Thomas began vigorously to read and presently the image faded. The girl had caused a disturbance in the depths of his being, somewhere out of the reach of his power of analysis. He felt as if he had seen a tornado pass a hundred yards away and had an intimation that it would turn again and head directly for him. He did not get his mind firmly on his work until mid-morning.

Two nights later, his mother and he were sitting in the den after their supper, each reading a section of the evening paper, when the telephone began to ring with the brassy intensity of a fire alarm. Thomas reached for it. As soon as the receiver was in his hand, a shrill female voice screamed into the room, 'Come get this girl! Come get her! Drunk!

Drunk in my parlour and I won't have it! Lost her job and come back here drunk! I won't have it!'

His mother leapt up and snatched the receiver.

The ghost of Thomas's father rose before him. Call the sheriff, the old man prompted. 'Call the sheriff,' Thomas said in a loud voice. 'Call the sheriff to go there and pick her up.'

'We'll be right there,' his mother was saying. 'We'll come and get her right away. Tell her to get her things together.'

'She ain't in no condition to get nothing together,' the voice screamed. 'You shouldn't have put something like her off on me! My house is respectable!'

'Tell her to call the sheriff,' Thomas shouted.

His mother put the receiver down and looked at him. 'I wouldn't turn a dog over to that man,' she said.

Thomas sat in the chair with his arms folded and looked fixedly at the wall.

'Think of the poor girl, Thomas,' his mother said, 'with nothing. Nothing. And we have everything.'

When they arrived, Sarah Ham was slumped spraddle-legged against the banister on the boarding house front-steps. Her tam was down on her forehead where the old woman had slammed it and her clothes were bulging out of her suitcase where the old woman had thrown them in. She was carrying on a drunken conversation with herself in a low personal tone. A streak of lipstick ran up one side of her face. She allowed herself to be guided by his mother to the car and put in the back seat without seeming to know who the rescuer was. 'Nothing to talk to all day but a pack of goddamned parakeets,' she said in a furious whisper.

Thomas, who had not got out of the car at all, or looked at her after the first revolted glance, said, 'I'm telling you, once and for all, the place to take her is the jail.'

His mother, sitting on the back seat, holding girl's hand, did not answer.

'All right, take her to the hotel,' he said.

'I cannot take a drunk girl to a hotel, Thomas,' she said. 'You know that.'

'Then take her to a hospital.'

'She doesn't need a jail or a hotel or a hospital,' his mother said, 'she needs a home.'

'She does not need mine,' Thomas said.

'Only for tonight, Thomas,' the old lady sighed. 'Only for tonight.'

Since then eight days had passed. The little slut was established in the guest room. Every day his mother set out to find her a job and a place to board, and failed, for the old woman had broadcast a warning.

FLANNERY O'CONNOR

Thomas kept to his room or the den. His home was to him home, workshop, church, as personal as the shell of a turtle and as necessary. He could not believe that it could be violated in this way. His flushed face had a constant look of stunned outrage.

As soon as the girl was up in the morning, her voice throbbed out in a blues song that would rise and waver, then plunge low with insinuations of passion about to be satisfied and Thomas, at his desk, would lunge up and begin frantically stuffing his ears with Kleenex. Each time he started from one room to another, one floor to another, she would be certain to appear. Each time he was halfway up or down the stairs, she would either meet him and pass, cringing coyly, or go up or down behind him, breathing small tragic spearmint-flavoured sighs. She appeared to adore Thomas's repugnance to her and to draw it out of him every chance she got as if it added delectably to her martyrdom.

The old man – small, wasp-like, in his yellowed panama hat, his seersucker suit, his pink carefully-soiled shirt, his small string tie – appeared to have taken up his station in Thomas's mind and from there, usually squatting, he shot out the same rasping suggestion every time the boy paused from his forced studies. Put your foot down. Go to see the sheriff.

The sheriff was another edition of Thomas's father except that he wore a checkered shirt and a Texas type hat and was ten years younger. He was as easily dishonest, and he had genuinely admired the old man. Thomas, like his mother, would have gone far out of his way to avoid his glassy pale blue gaze. He kept hoping for another solution, for a miracle.

With Sarah Ham in the house, meals were unbearable.

'Tomsee doesn't like me,' she said the third or fourth night at the supper table and cast her pouting gaze across at the large rigid figure of Thomas, whose face was set with the look of a man trapped by insufferable odours. 'He doesn't want me here. Nobody wants me anywhere.'

'Thomas's name is Thomas,' his mother interrupted. 'Not Tomsee.'

'I made Tomsee up,' she said. 'I think it's cute. He hates me.'

'Thomas does not hate you,' his mother said. 'We are not the kind of people who hate,' she added, as if this were an inperfection that had been bred out of them generations ago.

'Oh, I know when I'm not wanted,' Sarah Ham continued. 'They didn't even want me in jail. If I killed myself I wonder would God want me?'

'Try it and see,' Thomas muttered.

The girl screamed with laughter. Then she stopped abruptly, her face puckered and she began to shake. 'The best thing to do,' she said, her

506

teeth clattering, 'is to kill myself. Then I'll be out of everybody's way. I'll go to hell and be out of God's way. And even the devil won't want me. He'll kick me out of hell, not even in hell . . .' she wailed.

Thomas rose, picked up his plate and knife and fork and carried them to the den to finish his supper. After that, he had not eaten another meal at the table but had had his mother serve him at his desk. At these meals, the old man was intensely present to him. He appeared to be tipping backwards in his chair, his thumbs beneath his galluses, while he said such things as, She never ran me away from my own table.

A few nights later, Sarah Ham slashed her wrists with a paring knife and had hysterics. From the den where he was closeted after supper, Thomas heard a shriek, then a series of screams, then his mother's scurrying footsteps through the house. He did not move. His first instant of hope that the girl had cut her throat faded as he realised she could not have done it and continue to scream the way she was doing. He returned to his journal and presently the screams subsided. In a moment his mother burst in with his coat and hat. 'We have to take her to the hospital,' she said. 'She tried to do away with herself. I have a tourniquet on her arm. Oh Lord, Thomas,' she said, 'imagine being so low you'd do a thing like that!'

Thomas rose woodenly and put on his hat and coat. 'We will take her to the hospital,' he said, 'and we will leave her there.'

'And drive her to despair again?' the old lady cried. 'Thomas!'

Standing in the centre of his room now, realising that he had reached the point where action was inevitable, that he must pack, that he must leave, that he must go, Thomas remained immovable.

His fury was directed not at the little slut but at his mother. Even though the doctor had found that she had barely damaged herself and had raised the girl's wrath by laughing at the tourniquet and putting only a streak of iodine on the cut, his mother could not get over the incident. Some new weight of sorrow seemed to have been thrown across her shoulders, and not only Thomas, but Sarah Ham was infuriated by this, for it appeared to be a general sorrow that would have found another object no matter what good fortune came to either of them. The experience of Sarah Ham had plunged the old lady into mourning for the world.

The morning after the attempted suicide, she had gone through the house and collected all the knives and scissors and locked them in a drawer. She emptied a bottle of rat poison down the toilet and took up the roach tablets from the kitchen floor. Then she came to Thomas's study and said in a whisper, 'Where is that gun of his? I want you to lock it up.'

'The gun is in my drawer,' Thomas roared, 'and I will not lock it up.

If she shoots herself, so much the better!'

'Thomas,' his mother said, 'she'll hear you!'

'Let her hear me!' Thomas yelled. 'Don't you know she has no intention of killing herself? Don't you know her kind never kill themselves? Don't you . . .'

His mother slipped out the door and closed it to silence him and Sarah Ham's laugh, quite close in the hall, came rattling into his room. 'Tomsee'll find out. I'll kill myself and then he'll be sorry he wasn't nice to me. I'll use his own lil gun, his own lil ol' pearl-handled revol-lervuh!' she shouted and let out a loud tormented-sounding laugh in imitation of a movie monster.

Thomas ground his teeth. He pulled out his desk drawer and felt for the pistol. It was an inheritance from the old man, whose opinion it had been that every house should contain a loaded gun. He had discharged two bullets one night into the side of a prowler, but Thomas had never shot anything. He had no fear that the girl would use the gun on herself and he closed the drawer. Her kind clung tenaciously to life and were able to wrest some histrionic advantage from every moment.

Several ideas for getting rid of her had entered his head but each of these had been suggestions whose moral tone indicated that they had come from a mind akin to his father's, and Thomas had rejected them. He could not get the girl locked up again until she did something illegal. The old man would have been able with no qualms at all to get her drunk and send her out on the highway in his car, meanwhile notifying the highway patrol of her presence on the road, but Thomas considered this below his moral stature. Suggestions continued to come to him, each more outrageous than the last.

He had not the vaguest hope that the girl would get the gun and shoot herself, but that afternoon when he looked in the drawer, the gun was gone. His study locked from the inside, not the out. He cared nothing about the gun, but the thought of Sarah Ham's hands sliding among his papers infuriated him. Now even his study was contaminated. The only place left untouched by her was his bedroom.

That night she entered it.

In the morning at breakfast, he did not eat and did not sit down. He stood beside his chair and delivered his ultimatum while his mother sipped her coffee as if she were both alone in the room and in great pain. 'I have stood this,' he said, 'for as long as I am able. Since I see plainly that you care nothing about me, about my peace or comfort or working conditions, I am about to take the only step open to me. I will give you one more day. If you bring the girl back into this house this afternoon, I leave. You can choose – her or me.' He had more to say but at that point his voice cracked and he left.

At ten o'clock his mother and Sarah Ham left the house.

At four he heard the car wheels on the gravel and rushed to the window. As the car stopped, the dog stood up, alert, shaking.

He seemed unable to take the first step that would set him walking to the closet in the hall to look for the suitcase. He was like a man handed a knife and told to operate on himself if he wished to live. His huge hands clenched helplessly. His expression was a turmoil of indecision and outrage. His pale blue eyes seemed to sweat in his broiling face. He closed them for a moment and on the back of his lids, his father's image leered at him. Idiot! the old man hissed, idiot! The criminal slut stole your gun! See the sheriff! See the sheriff!

It was a moment before Thomas opened his eyes. He seemed newly stunned. He stood where he was for at least three minutes, then he turned slowly like a large vessel reversing its direction and faced the door. He stood there a moment longer, then he left, his face set to see the ordeal through.

He did not know where he would find the sheriff. The man made his own rules and kept his own hours. Thomas stopped first at the jail where his office was, but he was not in it. He went to the courthouse and was told by a clerk that the sheriff had gone to the barber shop across the street. 'Yonder's the deppity,' the clerk said and pointed out the window to the large figure of a man in a checkered shirt, who was leaning against the side of a police car, looking into space.

'It has to be the sheriff,' Thomas said and left for the barber shop. As little as he wanted anything to do with the sheriff, he realised that the man was at least intelligent and not simply a mound of sweating flesh.

The barber said the sheriff had just left. Thomas started back to the courthouse and as he stepped onto the sidewalk from the street, he saw a lean, slightly stooped figure gesticulating angrily at the deputy.

Thomas approached with an aggressiveness brought on by nervous agitation. He stopped abruptly three feet away and said in an over-loud voice, 'Can I have a word with you?' without adding the sheriff's name, which was Farebrother.

Farebrother turned his sharp creased face just enough to take Thomas in, and the deputy did likewise, but neither spoke. The sheriff removed a very small piece of cigarette from his lip and dropped it at his feet. 'I told you what to do,' he said to the deputy. Then he moved off with a slight nod that indicated Thomas could follow him if he wanted to see him. The deputy slunk around the front of the police car and got inside.

Farebrother, with Thomas following, headed across the courthouse square and stopped beneath a tree that shaded a quarter of the front lawn. He waited, leaning slightly forward, and lit another cigarette.

FLANNERY O'CONNOR

Thomas began to blurt out his business. As he had not had time to prepare his words, he was barely coherent. By repeating the same thing over several times, he managed at length to get out what he wanted to say. When he finished, the sheriff was still leaning slightly forward, at an angle to him, his eyes on nothing in particular. He remained that way without speaking.

Thomas began again, slower and in a lamer voice, and Farebrother let him continue for some time before he said, 'We had her once.' He then allowed himself a slow, creased, all-knowing, quarter smile.

'I had nothing to do with that,' Thomas said. 'That was my mother.'

Farebrother squatted.

'She was trying to help the girl,' Thomas said. 'She didn't know she couldn't be helped.'

'Bit off more than she could chew, I reckon,' the voice below him mused.

'She has nothing to do with this,' Thomas said. 'She doesn't know I'm here. The girl is dangerous with that gun.'

'*He*,' the sheriff said, 'never let anything grow under his feet. Particularly nothing a woman planted.'

'She might kill somebody with that gun,' Thomas said weakly, looking down at the round top of the Texas type hat.

There was a long time of silence.

'Where's she got it?' Farebrother asked.

'I don't know. She sleeps in the guest room. It must be in there, in her suitcase probably,' Thomas said.

Farebrother lapsed into silence again.

'You could come search the guest room,' Thomas said in a strained voice. 'I can go home and leave the latch off the front door and you can come in quietly and go upstairs and search her room.'

Farebrother turned his head so that his eyes looked boldly at Thomas's knees. 'You seem to know how it ought to be done,' he said. 'Want to swap jobs?'

Thomas said nothing because he could not think of anything to say, but he waited doggedly. Farebrother removed the cigarette butt from his lips and dropped it on the grass. Beyond him on the courthouse porch a group of loiterers who had been leaning at the left of the door moved over to the right where a patch of sunlight had settled. From one of the upper windows a crumpled piece of paper blew out and drifted down.

'I'll come along about six,' Farebrother said. 'Leave the latch off the door and keep out of my way – yourself and them two women too.'

Thomas let out a rasping sound of relief meant to be 'Thanks,' and struck off across the grass like someone released. The phrase, 'them two

510

women,' stuck like a burr in his brain – the subtlety of the insult to his mother hurting him more than any of Farebrother's references to his own incompetence. As he got into his car, his face suddenly flushed. Had he delivered his mother over to the sheriff – to be a butt for the man's tongue? Was he betraying her to get rid of the little slut? He saw at once that this was not the case. He was doing what he was doing for her own good, to rid her of a parasite that would ruin their peace. He started his car and drove quickly home but once he had turned in the driveway, he decided it would be better to park some distance from the house and go quietly in by the back door. He parked on the grass and on the grass walked in a circle toward the rear of the house. The sky was lined with mustard-coloured streaks. The dog was asleep on the back doormat. At the approach of his master's step, he opened one yellow eye, took him in, and closed it again.

Thomas let himself into the kitchen. It was empty and the house was quiet enough for him to be aware of the loud ticking of the kitchen clock. It was a quarter to six. He tiptoed hurriedly through the hall to the front door and took the latch off it. Then he stood for a moment listening. From behind the closed parlour door, he heard his mother snoring softly and presumed that she had gone to sleep while reading. On the other side of the hall, not three feet from his study, the little slut's black coat and red pocketbook were slung on a chair. He heard water running upstairs and decided she was taking a bath.

He went into his study and sat down at his desk to wait, noting with distaste that every few moments a tremor ran through him. He sat for a minute or two doing nothing. Then he picked up a pen and began to draw squares on the back of an envelope that lay before him. He looked at his watch. It was eleven minutes to six. After a moment he idly drew the centre drawer of the desk out over his lap. For a moment he stared at the gun without recognition. Then he gave a yelp and leaped up. She had put it back!

Idiot! his father hissed, idiot! Go plant it in her pocketbook. Don't just stand there. Go plant it in her pocketbook!

Thomas stood staring at the drawer.

Moron! the old man fumed. Quick while there's time! Go plant it in her pocketbook.

Thomas did not move.

Imbecile! his father cried.

Thomas picked up the gun.

Make haste, the old man ordered.

Thomas started forward, holding the gun away from him. He opened the door and looked at the chair. The black coat and red pocketbook were lying on it almost within reach.

Hurry up, you fool, his father said.

From behind the parlour door the almost inaudible snores of his mother rose and fell. They seemed to mark an order of time that had nothing to do with the instants left to Thomas. There was no other sound.

Quick, you imbecile, before she wakes up, the old man said.

The snores stopped and Thomas heard the sofa springs groan. He grabbed the red pocketbook. It had a skin-like feel to his touch and as it opened, he caught an unmistakable odour of the girl. Wincing, he thrust in the gun and then drew back. His face burned an ugly dull red.

'What is Tomsee putting in my purse?' she called and her pleased laugh bounced down the staircase. Thomas whirled.

She was at the top of the stair, coming down in the manner of a fashion model, one bare leg and then the other thrusting out the front of her kimona in a definite rhythm. 'Tomsee is being naughty,' she said in a throaty voice. She reached the bottom and cast a possessive leer at Thomas whose face was now more gray than red. She reached out, pulled the bag open with her finger and peered at the gun.

His mother opened the parlour door and looked out.

'Tomsee put his pistol in my bag!' the girl shrieked.

'Ridiculous,' his mother said, yawning. 'What would Thomas want to put his pistol in your bag for?'

Thomas stood slightly hunched, his hands hanging helplessly at the wrists as if he had just pulled them up out of a pool of blood.

'I don't know what for,' the girl said, 'but he sure did it,' and she proceeded to walk around Thomas, her hands on her hips, her neck thrust forward and her intimate grin fixed on him fiercely. All at once her expression seemed to open as the purse had opened when Thomas touched it. She stood with her head cocked on one side in an attitude of disbelief. 'Oh boy,' she said slowly, 'is he a case.'

At that instant Thomas damned not only the girl but the entire order of the universe that made her possible.

'Thomas wouldn't put a gun in your bag,' his mother said. 'Thomas is a gentleman.'

The girl made a chortling noise. 'You can see it in there,' she said and pointed to the open purse.

You *found* it in her bag, you dimwit! the old man hissed.

'I found it in her bag!' Thomas shouted. 'The dirty criminal slut stole my gun!'

His mother gasped at the sound of the other presence in his voice. The old lady's sybil-like face turned pale.

'Found it my eye!' Sarah Ham shrieked and started for the pocketbook, but Thomas, as if his arm were guided by his father, caught it first and snatched the gun. The girl in a frenzy lunged at Thomas's throat and would actually have caught him around the neck had not his mother thrown herself forward to protect her.

Fire! the old man yelled.

Thomas fired. The blast was like a sound meant to bring an end to evil in the world. Thomas heard it as a sound that would shatter the laughter of sluts until all shrieks were stilled and nothing was left to disturb the peace of perfect order.

The echo died away in waves. Before the last one had faded, Farebrother opened the door and put his head inside the hall. His nose wrinkled. His expression for some few seconds was that of a man unwilling to admit surprise. His eyes were clear as glass, reflecting the scene. The old lady lay on the floor between the girl and Thomas.

The sheriff's brain worked instantly like a calculating machine. He saw the facts as if they were already in print: the fellow had intended all along to kill his mother and pin it on the girl. But Farebrother had been too quick for him. They were not yet aware of his head in the door. As he scrutinised the scene, further insights were flashed to him. Over her body, the killer and the slut were about to collapse into each other's arms. The sheriff knew a nasty bit when he saw it. He was accustomed to enter upon scenes that were not as bad as he had hoped to find them, but this one met his expectations.

Penelope Mortimer

The Skylight

The heat, as the taxi spiralled the narrow hill bends, became more violent. The road thundered between patches of shade thrown by overhanging rock. Behind the considerable noise of the car, the petulant hooting at each corner, the steady tick-tick of the cicadas spread through the woods and olive groves as though to announce their coming.

The woman sat so still in the back of the taxi that at corners her whole body swayed, rigid as a bottle in a jolting bucket, and sometimes fell against the five-year-old boy who curled, thumb plugged in his mouth, on the seat beside her. The woman felt herself disintegrate from heat. Her hair, tallow blonde, crept on her wet scalp. Her face ran off the bone like water off a rock – the bridges of nose, jaw and cheekbones must be drained of flesh by now. Her body poured away inside the too-tight cotton suit and only her bloodshot feet, almost purple in the torturing sandals, had any kind of substance.

'When are we there?' the boy asked.

'Soon.'

'In a minute will we be there?'

'Yes.'

A long pause. What shall we find, the mother asked herself. She wished, almost at the point of tears, that there were someone else to ask, and answer, this question.

'Are we at France now?'

For the sixth time since the plane had landed she answered, 'Yes, Johnny.'

The child's eyes, heavy-lidded, long-lashed, closed; the thumb stoppered his drooping mouth. Oh, no, she thought, don't let him, he mustn't go to sleep.

514

'Look. Look at the . . .' Invention failed her. They passed a shack in a stony clearing. 'Look at the chickens,' she said, pulling at the clamped stuff of her jacket. 'French chickens,' she added, long after they had gone by. She stared dully at the taxi-driver's back, the dark stain of sweat between his shoulder-blades. He was not the French taxi-driver she had expected. He was old and quiet and burly, driving his cab with care. The price he had quoted for this forty kilometre drive from the airport had horrified her. She had to translate all distances into miles and then apply them, a lumbering calculation, to England. How much she had wanted to ask, would an English taxi-driver charge to take us from London Airport to . . .? It was absurd. There was no one to tell her anything. Only the child asking his interminable questions, with faith.

'Where?' he demanded suddenly, sitting up.

She felt herself becoming desperate. It's too much for me, she thought. I can't face it. 'What do you mean – where?'

'The chickens.'

'Oh. They've gone. Perhaps there'll be some more, later on.'

'But when are we there?'

'Oh, *Jonathan* . . .' In her exasperation, she used his full name. He turned his head away, devouring his thumb, looking closely at the dusty rexine. When her hot, stiff body fell against him, he did not move. She tried to compose herself, to resume command.

It had seemed so sensible, so economical, to take this house for the summer. We all know, she had said (although she herself did not), what the French are – cheat you at every turn. And then, the horror of those Riviera beaches. We've found this charming little farmhouse up in the mountains – well, they say you can nip down to Golfe-Juan in ten minutes. In the car, of course. Philip will be driving the girls, but I shall take Johnny by air. I couldn't face those dreadful hotels with him. Expensive? But, my dear, you don't *know* what it cost us in Bournemouth last year, and I feel one owes them the sun. And then there's this dear old couple, the Gachets, thrown in so to speak. They'll have it all ready for us, otherwise of course I couldn't face arriving there alone with Johnny. As it is, we shall be nicely settled when Philip and the girls arrive. I envy us too. I couldn't face the prospect of those awful public meals with Johnny – no, I just couldn't face it.

And so on. It was a story she had made up in the cold, well-ordered English spring. She could hear herself telling it. Now it was real. She was inadequate. She was in pain from the heat, and not a little afraid. The child depended on her. I can't face it, she thought, anticipating the arrival at the strange house, the couple, the necessity of speaking French, the task of getting the child bathed and fed and asleep. Will there be hot water, mosquitoes, do they know how to boil an egg? Her head beat with worry. She looked wildly from side to side of the taxi, searching for some sign of life. The woods had ended, and there was now no relief from the sun. An ugly pink house with green shutters stood away from the road; it looked solid, like an enormous brick, in its plot of small vines. Can that be it? But the taxi drove on.

'I suppose he knows where he's going,' she said.

The child turned on his back, as though in bed, straddling his thin legs. Over the bunched hand his eyes regarded her darkly, unblinking.

'Do sit *up*,' she said. His eyelids drooped again. His legs, his feet in their white socks and disproportionately large brown sandals, hung limp. His head fell to one side. 'Poor baby,' she said softly. 'Tired baby.' She managed to put an arm round him. They sat close, in extreme discomfort.

Suddenly, without warning, the driver swung the taxi off the road. The woman fell on top of the child who struggled for a moment before managing to free himself. He sat up, alert, while his mother pulled and pushed, trying to regain her balance. A narrow, stony track climbed up into a bunch of olive trees. The driver played his horn round each bend. Then, on a perilous slope, the car stopped. The driver turned in his seat, searching back over his great soaked shoulder as though prepared, even expecting, to find his passengers gone.

'La Caporale,' he said.

The woman bent, peering out of the car windows. She could see nothing but stones and grass. The heat seized the stationary taxi, turning it into a furnace.

'But – where?'

He indicated something which she could not see, then hauled himself out of the driving seat, lumbered round and opened the door.

'*Ici?*' she asked, absolutely disbelieving.

He nodded, spoke, again waved an arm, pointing.

'*Mais . . .*' It was no good. 'He says we're here,' she told the child. 'We'd better get out.'

They stood on the stony ground, looking about them. There was a black barn, its doors closed. There was a wall of loose rocks piled together. The cicadas screeched. There was nothing.

'But where's the house?' she demanded. 'Where is the house? *Où est la maison?*'

The driver picked up their suitcases and walked away. She took the child's hand, pulling him after her. The high heels of her sandals twisted on the hard rubble; she hurried bent from the waist, as though on bound feet. Then, suddenly remembering, she stopped and pulled out of her large new handbag a linen hat. She fitted this, hardly glancing at him, on the child's head. 'Come on,' she said. 'I can't think where he's taking us.'

Round the end of the wall, over dead grass; and above them, standing on a terrace, was the square grey house, its shuttered windows set anyhow into its walls like holes in a warren. A small skylight, catching the sun, flashed from the mean slate roof.

They followed the driver up the steps on to the terrace. A few pots and urns stood about, suggesting that somebody had once tried to make a garden. A withered hosepipe lay on the ground as though it had died trying to reach the sparse geraniums. A chipped, white-painted table and a couple of wrought-iron chairs were stacked under a palm tree. A lizard skittered down the front of the house. The shutters and the door were of heavy black timber with iron bars and hinges. They were all closed. The heat sang with resonant hum of failing consciousness. The driver put the suitcases down outside the closed door and wiped his face and the back of his neck with a handkerchief.

'*Vous avez la clef, madame?*'

'*La clay? La clay?*'

He pursed and twisted his hand over the lock.

'Oh, the key. No. *Non*. Monsieur and Madame Gachet . . . the people who live in the house . . . *Ce n'est pas*,' she tried desperately, '*fermé*.'

The driver tried the door. It was firm. She knocked. There was no answer.

'*Vous n'avez la clef?*' He was beginning to sound petulant.

'*Non. Non. Parce que* . . . Oh *dear*.' She looked up at the blind face of the house. 'They must be out. Perhaps they didn't get my wire. Perhaps . . .' She looked at the man, who did not understand what she was saying; at the child, who was simply waiting for her to do something. 'I don't know *what* to do. Monsieur and Madame Gachet . . .' She pushed back her damp hair. 'But I wrote to them weeks ago. My husband wrote to them. They *can't* be out.'

She lifted the heavy knocker and again hammered it against the door. They waited, at first alertly, then slackening, the woman losing hope, the driver and the child losing interest. The driver spoke. She understood that he was going, and wished to be paid.

'But you can't leave us like this. Supposing they don't get back for hours? Can't you help us to get in?'

He looked at her stolidly. Furious with him, humiliated by his lack of chivalry, she ran to one of the windows and started trying to prise the shutters open. As she struggled, breaking a fingernail, looking about for some object she could use, running to her handbag and spilling it out for a nail file, a pair of scissors, finding nothing, trying again with her useless fingers, she spoke incessantly, her words coming in little gasps of anger and anxiety.

'Really, one would think that a great man like you could *do* something instead of just standing there, what do you think we shall *do*, just left here in the middle of nowhere after we've come all this way. I can tell you people don't behave like this in England, haven't you got a knife or something? *Un couteau? Un couteau*, for heaven's sake?'

She was almost hysterical. The driver became angry. He picked up her wallet, thrown out of the handbag, and shook it at her. He spoke very quickly. Frightened, she controlled herself. She snatched the wallet from him. She was trembling.

'Very well. Take your money and go.' She had not got the exact amount. She gave him two hundred francs. He nodded, looked over the house once more, shrugged his shoulders and moved away.

'The change!' she called. 'Change . . .' pronouncing the word, with little hope, in French. 'L'argent . . .'

'*Merci, madame*,' he said, raising his hand. '*Bonne chance.*' He disappeared down the steps. In a moment she saw him walking heavily, not hurrying, across the grass.

'Well,' she said, turning to the child. 'Well . . .' She paused, listening to the taxi starting up, the sound of its engine revving as it turned in the stony space, departing, diminishing – gone. The child looked at her. Suspicion, for the first time in his life, darkened and swelled his face. It became tumescent, the mouth trembling, the eyes dilated before the moment of tears.

'Let's have some chocolate,' she said. The half-bar fallen from her handbag had melted completely. 'We can't,' she said, with a little, brisk laugh. 'It's melted.'

'Want a drink?'

'A drink.' As though in a strange room, she looked round searching for the place where, quite certainly, there must be drink. 'Well, I don't know . . .' There was a rusty tap in the wall, presumably used for the hose. She pretended not to have seen it. Typhus or worse. She remembered the grapes – they looked far from ripe – that had hung on sagging wires over the steps. 'We'll get into the house,' she said, and added firmly, as though there was no question about it, 'We must get in.'

'Why can't we go into the house?'

'Because it's locked.'

'Where did the people put the key?'

She ran to the door and started searching in the creeper, along the ledge, her fingers recoiling from fear of snakes or lizards. She ran round to the side of the house, the child trotting after her. A makeshift straw roof had been propped up over an old kitchen table. A rusty oil stove stood against the wall of the house. She searched in its greasy oven. She tried the holes in the wall, the dangerous crevices of a giant cactus. The child leant against the table. He seemed now to be apathetic.

'We'll go round to the back,' she said. But at the back of the house there were no windows at all. A narrow gully ran between the house and a steep hill of brown grass. The hill, rising to dense woods, was higher than the roof of the house. She began to climb the hill.

'Don't come,' she called. 'Stay in the shade.'

She climbed backwards, shading her eyes against the unbearable sun. The child sat himself on the wall of the gully, swinging his legs and waiting for her. She looked down on the glistening roof and saw the small mouth of the skylight, open. She knew, even while she measured it with her eyes, imagined herself climbing through it, that it was inaccessible. Her mind gabbled unanswerable questions: how far is the nearest house? Telephone? How can we get back to Nice? Where does the road lead to? As she looked down at the house, something swift and black, large as a cat, streaked along the gutter, down the drainpipe and into the gully.

'Johnny!' she called. 'Johnny!' She began to run back down the hill. Her ankle twisted, she fell on the hard grass. She pulled off her sandals and ran barefoot. 'Get up from there! Don't sit there!'

'Why?'

'I saw . . .'

'What? What did you see?'

'Oh, nothing. I think we'll have to go back to that house we passed. Perhaps they know . . .'

'What did you see, though?'

'Nothing, nothing. The skylight's open.'

'What's a skylight?'

'A sort of window in the roof.'

'But what did you *see*?'

'If there was a ladder, perhaps we could . . .' She looked round in a worried way, but without conviction. It was to distract the child from the rat.

'There's a ladder.'

It was lying in the gully – a long, strong, new ladder. She looked at it hopelessly, disciplining herself to a blow from fate. 'No,' she said. 'I could never lift it.'

The child did not deny this. He asked: 'When are the people coming back?'

'I don't know.'

'I want some chocolate.'

'Oh, Johnny!'

'I want a drink.'

'Johnny – *please*!'

'I don't want to be at France. I want to go home now.'

'Please, Johnny, you're a big man, you've got to look after Mummy—'

'I don't *want* to—'

'Let's see if we can lift the ladder.'

She jumped down into the gully. The ladder was surprisingly light. As she lifted one end, propping the other against the gully wall, juggled it, hand over hand on the rungs, into position, she talked to the child as though he were helping her.

'That's right, it's not a bit heavy, after all, is it, now let's just get it straight, that's the way . . .'

Supposing, she thought, the Gachets came back and find me breaking into the house like this? You've paid the rent, she told herself. It's your house. It's scandalous, it's outrageous. One must do *something*.

'Are you going to climb up there?' the child asked, with interest.

She hesitated. 'Yes,' she said. 'Yes, I suppose so.'

'Can I go up the ladder too?'

'No, of course not.' She grasped the side of the ladder firmly, testing the bottom rung.

'But I *want* to . . .'

'Oh, *Jonathan*! Of course you can't!' she snapped, exasperated. 'What d'you think this is – a game? Please, Johnny, *please* don't start. Oh, my God . . .' I *can't* face it, she thought, as she stepped off the ladder, pulled herself up on to the grass, held his loud little body against her sweat-soaked blouse, took off his hat for him and stroked his stubbly hair, rocked him and comforted him, desperately wondered what bribe or reward she might have in her luggage, what prize she could offer. . . . She spoke to him quietly, telling him that if he would let her go up the ladder and get into the house she might find something, she would almost certainly find something, a surprise, a wonderful surprise.

'A toy.'

'Well, you never know.' She was shameless. 'Something really *lovely*.'

'A big toy,' he stated, knowing his strength.

'A big toy, and a lovely bath and a lovely boiled egg—'

'And a biscuit.'

'Of course. A chocolate biscuit. And a big glass of milk.'

'And two toys. One big and one little.'

'Yes, and then we'll go to sleep, and not tomorrow but the next day Daddy will come . . .' She felt, by the weight against her breast, that she was sending him to sleep. She put him away from her carefully. He lay down, without moving the curled position of his body, on the grass. He sucked his thumb, looking at her out of the corners of his bright eyes. 'So I'll climb the ladder. You watch. All right?'

He nodded. She jumped down into the gully again, pulled her tight skirt high above her knees, and started to climb. She kept her eyes away from the gutter. The fear of a rat running close to her made her sick, almost demented with fear. If I see a rat, she thought, I shall jump, I know I shall jump. I can't face it. She saw herself lying dead or unconscious in the gully, the child left completely alone. As she came level with the roof she heard a sound, a quick scuttering; her feet seemed steeped in hot glycerine, her hands weakened. She lay for a moment face downwards on the ladder, certain that when she opened her eyes she would be falling.

When she dared to look again, she was amazed to see how near she was to the skylight – little more than a yard. This distance, certainly, was over burning slate, much of it jagged and broken. But the gutter was firm, and the gradient of the roof very slight. In her relief, now edged with excitement, she did not assess the size of the skylight. The ladder, propped against the gully wall, was steady as a staircase. She mounted two more rungs and cautiously, with one foot, tested the gutter. Now all she had to do was to edge, then fling herself, forward; grasp the sill of the skylight and pull herself up. She did this with a new assurance, almost bravado. She was already thinking what a story it would be to tell her husband; that her daughters – strong, agile girls – would certainly admire her.

She lay on the roof and looked down through the skylight. It was barely eighteen inches wide – perhaps two feet long. She could no more get through it than a camel through a needle's eye. A child, a thin child, could have managed it. Her youngest daughter could have wormed through somehow. But for her it was impossible.

She looked down at the dusty surface of a chest of drawers. She could almost touch it. Pulling herself forward a little more she could see two doors – attics, no doubt – and a flight of narrow stairs descending into semi-darkness. In her frustration she tried to shake the solid sill of the skylight, as though it might give away. It's not fair, she cried to herself; it's not fair. For a moment she felt like bursting into tears, like sobbing her heart out on the high, hard shoulder of the house. Then, with a kind of delight, she thought – Johnny.

She could lower him through. He would only have to run down the stairs and unbolt one of the downstairs windows. A few weeks ago he had locked himself in the lavatory at home and seemed, for a time, inaccessible. But she had told him what to do, and he had eventually freed himself. Even so, I don't believe you can do this, she told herself. I don't believe you can risk it. At the same time, she knew that she had thought of the obvious – it seemed to her now the only – solution. Her confidence was overwhelming. She was dealing with the situation in a practical, courageous way. She was discovering initiative in herself, and ingenuity.

She came quickly, easily down the ladder. The boy was still curled as she had left him. As she approached, smacking the dust and grime from her skirt, he rolled on to his back, but did not question her. She realised with alarm that he was nearly asleep. A few minutes more and nothing would rouse him. She imagined herself carrying him for miles along the road. Already the heat was thinning. The cicadas, she noticed, were silent.

'Johnny,' she said. 'Would you like to climb the ladder?'

His eyes focused, but he continued to suck his thumb.

'You can climb the ladder, if you like,' she said carelessly.

'Now? Can I climb it now?'

'Yes, if you want to.'

'Can I get through the little window?'

She was delighted with him. 'Yes. Yes, you can. And, Johnny . . .'

'What?'

'When you've got through the little window, I want you to do something for me. Something very clever. Can you do something clever?'

He nodded, but looked doubtful.

She explained, very carefully, slowly. Then, taking his hand, she led him round to the front of the house. She chose a window so near the ground that he could have climbed through it without effort from the outside. She investigated the shutters, and made certain they that were only held by a hook and eyelet screw on the inside. She told him that he would have to go down two flights of stairs and turn to the right, and he would find the room with the window in it. She tied her handkerchief round his right wrist, so that he would know which way to turn when he got to the bottom of the stairs.

'And if you can't open the window,' she said, 'you're to come straight back up the stairs. Straight back. And I'll help you through the skylight again. You understand? If you can't open the window, you're to go *straight back* up the stairs. All right?'

'Yes,' he said. 'Can I climb the ladder now?'

'I'm coming with you. You must go slowly.'

But he scaled it like a monkey. She cautioned him, implored him, as she climbed carefully. 'Wait, Johnny. Johnny, don't go so fast. Hold on tightly. Johnny, be *careful* . . .' At the top, she realised that she should have gone first. She had to get around him in order to reach the skylight and pull him after her. She was now terribly frightened, and frightened that she would transmit her fear to him. 'Isn't it exciting?' she said, her teeth chattering. 'Aren't we high up? Now hold on very tightly, because I'm just going to . . .'

She stepped round him. It was necessary this time to put her full weight on the gutter. If I fall, she thought clearly, I must remember to let go of the ladder. The gutter held, and she pulled herself up, sitting quite comfortably on the edge of the skylight. In a moment she had pulled him to her. It was absurdly easy. She put her hands under his arms, feeling the small, separate ribs. He was light and pliable as a terrier.

'Remember what I told you.'

'Yes.' He was wriggling, anxious to go.

'What did I tell you?'

'Go downstairs and go that way and open the window.'

'And supposing you can't open the window?'

'Come back again.'

'And hurry. I'll count. I'll count a hundred. I'll go down and stand by the window. You be there when I've counted a hundred.'

'All right,' he said.

Holding him tightly in her hands, his legs dangling, his shoulders hunched, she lowered him until he stood safely on the chest of drawers. When she let go he shook himself and looked up at her.

'Can you get down?' she asked anxiously. 'Are you all right?'

He squatted, let his legs down, slid backwards on his stomach and landed with a little thud on the floor.

'It's dirty down here,' he said cheerfully.

'Is it all right, though?' She had a new idea, double security. 'Run down those stairs and come back, tell me what you see.'

Obediently, he turned and ran down the stairs. The moment he had gone, she was panic-stricken. She called, 'Johnny! Johnny!' her head through the skylight, her body helpless and unable to follow. 'Come back, Johnny! Are you all right?'

He came back almost immediately.

'There's stairs,' he said, 'going down. Shall I go and open the window now?'

'Yes,' she said. 'And hurry.'

'All right.'

'I'm beginning to count now!' And loudly, as she slid back to the ladder, she called, 'One . . . two . . . three . . . four . . .' Almost at the bottom, her foot slipped, she tore her skirt. She ran round to the front of the house, and as she came up to the window she began calling again in a bold voice, rough with anxiety. 'Forty-nine . . . fifty . . . fifty-one . . .' She hammered with her knuckles on the shutter, shouting, 'It's this window, Johnny! Here, Johnny! This one!'

Waiting, she could not keep still. She looked at the split in her skirt, pushed at her straggled hair; she banged again on the shutter; she glanced at her watch; she looked up again and again at the blank face of the house.

'Sixty-eight . . . sixty-nine . . . seventy . . . !'

She sucked the back of her hand, where there was a deep scratch; she folded her impatient arms and unfolded them; she knocked again, calling, 'Johnny! Johnny! It's this one!' and then, in a moment, 'I've nearly counted a hundred! Are you there, Johnny?'

It's funny, she thought, that the crickets should have stopped. The terrace was now almost entirely in shadow. It gets dark quickly, she remembered. It's not slow. The sun goes, and that's it: it's night-time.

'Ninety . . . ninety-one . . . ninety-two . . . Johnny? Come on. Hurry up!'

Give him time, she told herself. He's only five. He never can hurry. She went and sat on the low wall at the edge of the terrace. She watched the minute-hand of her watch creeping across the seconds. Five minutes. It must be five minutes. She stood up, cupping her hands round her mouth.

'A hundred!' she shouted. 'I've counted a hundred!'

An aeroplane flew high, high overhead, where the sky was the most delicate blue. It made no sound. There was no sound. As though she were suddenly deaf she reached, stretched her body, made herself entirely a receptacle for sound – a snapping twig, a bird hopping; even a fall of dust. The house stood in the front of her like a locked box. The sunlight at the end of the terrace went out.

'Joh-oh-oh-nny! I'm here! I'm down here!'

She managed to get two fingers in the chink between the shutters. She could see the rusty arm of the hook. But she could not reach it. The shutters had warped, and the aperture at the top was too small for anything but a knife, a nail file, a piece of tin.

'I'm going back up the ladder!' she shouted. 'Come back to the skylight! Do you hear me?'

One cicada began its noise again; only one. She ran round to the back of the house and for the third time climbed the ladder, throwing herself without caution on to the roof, dragging herself to the open skylight. There was a wide track in the dust, where he had slid off the chest of drawers.

'Johnny! Johnny! Where are you?'

Her voice deadened by the small, enclosed landing. It was like shouting into the earth. There was no volume to it, and no echo. Without realising it, she had begun to cry. Her head lowered into the almost total darkness, she sobbed, 'Johnny! Come up here! I'm here by the skylight, by the little window!'

In the silence she heard, quite distinctly, a tap dripping. A regular, metallic drip, like torture. She shouted directions to him, waiting between each one, straining to hear the slightest sound, the faintest answer. The tap dripped. The house seemed to be holding its breath.

'I'm going down again! I'm going back to the window!'

She wrestled once more with the shutters. She found a small stick, which broke. She poked with her latchkey, with a comb. She dragged the table across the terrace and tried, standing on it, to reach the first-floor windows. She climbed the ladder twice more, each time expecting to find him under the skylight, waiting for her.

It was now dark. Her strength had gone and her calls became feeble, delivered brokenly, like prayers. She ran round the house, uselessly searching and shouting his name. She threw a few stones at the upper windows. She fell on the front door, kicking it with her bare feet. She climbed the ladder again and this time lost her grip on the gutter and only just saved herself from falling. As she lay on the roof she became dizzy and frightened, in some part of her, that she was going to faint. The other part of her didn't care. She lay for a long time with her head through the skylight, weeping and calling, sometimes weakly, sometimes with an attempt at command; sometimes, with a desperate return of will, trying to force herself through the impossible opening.

For the last time, she beat on the shutters, her blows as puny as his would have been. It was three hours since she had lowered him through the skylight. What more could she do? There was nothing more she could do. At last she said to herself, something has happened to him, I must go for help.

It was terrible to leave the house. As she stumbled down the steps and across the grass, which cut into her feet like stubble, she kept looking back, listening. Once she imagined she heard a cry, and ran back a few yards. But it was only the cicada.

It took her a long time to reach the road. The moon had risen. She walked in little spurts, running a few steps, then faltering, almost loitering until she began to run again. She remembered the pink house in the vineyard. She did not know how far it was; only that it was before the woods. She was crying all the time now, but did not notice it, any more that she was aware of her curious, in fact alarming, appearance. 'Johnny!' she kept sobbing. 'Oh, Johnny.' She began to trot, keeping up an even pace. The road rose and fell; over each slope she expected to see the lights of the pink house. When she saw the headlamps of a car bearing down on her she stepped into the middle of the road and beat her arms up and down, calling, 'Stop! Stop!'

The car swerved to avoid her, skidded, drew up with a scream across the road. She ran towards it.

'Please! . . . Please! . . .'

The faces of the three men were shocked and hostile. They began to shout at her in French. Their arms whirled like propellers. One shook his fist.

'Please . . .' she gasped, clinging to the window. 'Do you speak English? Please do you speak English?'

One or the men said. 'A little.' The other two turned on him. There was uproar.

'Please, I beg of you. It's my little boy.' Saying the words, she began to weep uncontrollably.

'An accident?'

'Yes, yes. In the house, up there. I can't get into the house—'

It was a long, difficult time before they understood; each amazing fact had to be interpreted. If it had been their home, they might have asked her in; at least opened the door. She had to implore and harangue them through a half-open window. At last the men consulted together.

'My friends say we cannot . . . enter this house. They do not wish to go to prison.'

'But it's *my* house – I've paid for it!'

'That may be. We do not know.'

'Then take me to the police – take me to the British Consul—'

The discussion became more deliberate. It seemed that they were going to believe her.

'But how can we get in? You say the house is locked up. We have no tools. We are not—'

'A hammer would do – if you had a hammer and chisel—'

They shook their heads. One of them even laughed. They were now perfectly relaxed, sitting comfortably in their seats. The interpreter lit a cigarette.

'There's a farm back there,' she entreated. 'It's only a little way. Will you take me? Please, please, will you take me?'

The interpreter considered this, slowly breathing smoke, before even putting it to his friends. He looked at his flat, black-faced, illuminated watch. Then he threw the question to them out of the corner of his mouth. They made sounds of doubt, weighing the possibility, the inconvenience.

'Johnny may be dying,' she said. 'He must have fallen. He must be hurt badly. He may' – her voice rose, she shook the window – 'he may be dead . . .'

They opened the back door and let her into the car.

'Turn round,' she said. 'It's back there on the left. But it's away from the road, so you must look out.'

In the car, since there was nothing she could do, she began to shiver. She realised for the first time her responsibility. I may have murdered him. The feeling of the child as she lifted him through the skylight came back to her hands: his warmth. The men, embarrassed, did not speak.

'There it is! There!'

They turned off the road. She struggled from the car before it had stopped, and ran to the front door. The men in the car waited, not wishing to compromise themselves, but curious to see what was going to happen.

The door was opened by a small woman in trousers. She was struck by the barrage of words, stepped back from it. Then, with her myopic eyes, she saw the whole shape of distress – a person in pieces. 'My dear,' she said. 'My dear . . . what's happened? What's the matter?'

'You're English? Oh – you're English?'

'My name's Pat Jardine. Please come in, please let me do something for you—' Miss Jardine's handsome little face was overcast with pain. She could not bear suffering. Her house was full of cats; she made splints for sparrows out of match-sticks. If her friend Yvonne killed a wasp, Miss Jardine turned away, shutting her eyes tight and whispering, 'Oh, the poor darling.' As she listened to the story her eyes filled with tears, but her mind with purpose.

'We have a hammer, chisel, even a crowbar,' she said. 'But the awful thing is, we haven't a man. I mean, of course we can try – we *must* try – but it would be useful to have a man. Now who can I—?'

'There are three men in the car, but they don't speak English and they don't—'

Miss Jardine hurried to the car. She spoke quietly but passionately, allowing no interruption. Another woman appeared, older, at first suspicious.

'Yvonne,' Miss Jardine said, breathlessly introducing her. 'Get the crowbar, dear, and the hammer – and perhaps the axe, yes, get the axe—' At the same time she poured and offered a glass of brandy. 'Drink this. What else do we need? Blankets. First-aid box. You never know.'

'Thank you. Thank you.'

'Nonsense, I'm only glad you came to us. Now we must go. Yvonne? Have you got the axe, dear?'

The three men had got out of the car and were standing about. They looked, in their brilliant shirts and pointed shoes, their slight glints of gold and chromium, like women on a battlefield – at a loss. Yvonne and Miss Jardine clattered the great tools into the boot. Miss Jardine hurried away for a rope. The men murmured together, and laughed quietly and self-consciously. When everything was ready they got into the car. The three women squeezing into the back.

On the way, driving fast, eating up the darkness, Miss Jardine said, 'But I simply don't understand the Gachets. If they knew you were coming today. I mean, it's simply scandalous.'

'They are decadent people,' Yvonne said slowly. 'They have been spoiled, pigging it in that house all winter. The owners take no interest, now their children are grown up. The Gachets did not wish to work for you, obviously.'

'But at least they could have *said*—'

'They are decadent people,' Yvonne repeated. After a half a mile, she added, 'Gachet drinks two litres of wine a day. His wife is Italian.'

Now there were so many people. The hours of being alone were over. But she could not speak. She sat forward on the seat, her hands tightly clasped, her face shrivelled. When they came to the turning she opened her lips and took a breath, but Miss Jardine had already directed them. They lurched and bumped up the lane, screamed to a stop in front of the black barn doors.

'Is that locked too?' Yvonne asked.

There was no answer. They clambered out. Yvonne gave the tools and the rope to the men. Yvonne and Miss Jardine carried the blankets and the first-aid box. The moonlight turned the grass into lava.

'A torch,' Miss Jardine said. 'Blast!'

'We have a light,' the interpreter said. 'Although it does not seem necessary.'

'Good. Then let's go.'

She ran in front of them, although there was no purpose in reaching the house first. It was clear in the moonlight that she could see the things spilled out of her handbag, the mirror of her powder compact, the brass catch of her purse. Before she was up the steps she began to call again, 'Johnny? Johnny?' The others, coming more slowly behind her with their burdens, felt pity, reluctance and dread.

'What shall we try first? The door?'

'No, we'll have to break a window. The door's too solid.'

'Which of you can use an axe?'

The men glanced at each other. Finally the interpreter shrugged his shoulders and took the axe, weighing it. Yvonne spoke contemptuously to him, making as though to take the axe herself. He went up to the window, raised the axe and smashed it into the shutters. Glass and wood splintered. It had only needed one blow.

She was at the window, tugging at the jagged edges of the glass. The interpreter pushed her out of the way. He undid the catch of the window and stood back, examining a small scratch on his wrist and shaking his hand in the air as though to relieve some intolerable hurt. She was through the window, blundering across a room, while she heard Miss Jardine calling, 'Open the front door if you can! We're coming!'

They did not exist for her any longer. She did not look for light switches. The stairs were brilliant.

'Johnny?' she called. 'Johnny? Where are you?'

A door on the first-floor landing was wide open. She ran to the doorway and her hands, without any thought from herself, flew out and caught the lintel on either side, preventing her entrance.

He was lying on the floor. He was lying in exactly the same position in which he had curled on the grass outside, except that his thumb had fallen from his mouth; but it was still upright, still wet. His small snores came rhythmically, with a slight click at the end of each snore. Surrounding him was a confusion, a Christmas of toys. In his free hand he had been holding a wooden soldier; it was still propped inside the lax, curling fingers. She was aware, in a moment of absolute detachment, that the toys were very old; older, possibly, than herself. Then she stopped thinking. She walked forward.

Kneeling, she touched him. He mumbled, but did not wake up. She shook him, quite gently. He opened his eyes directly on to her awful, hardly recognisable face.

'I like the toys,' he said. His thumb went back into his mouth. His eyelids sank. His free hand gripped the soldier, then loosened.

'*Jonathan!*'

With one hand she pushed him upright. With the other, she hit him. She struck him so hard that her palm stung.

One of the women started screaming. 'Oh, no! . . . No!'

She struggled to her feet and pushed past the blurred, obstructing figures in the doorway. She stumbled down the stairs. The child was crying. The dead house was full of sound. She flung herself into a room. 'Oh, thank God,' she whispered. 'Oh, thank God . . .' She crouched with her head on her knees, her arms wrapped round her own body, her body rocking with the pain of gratitude.

Roald Dahl

Pig

I

Once upon a time, in the City of New York, a beautiful baby boy was born into this world, and the joyful parents named him Lexington.

No sooner had the mother returned home from the hospital carrying Lexington in her arms than she said to her husband, 'Darling, now you must take me out to a most marvellous restaurant for dinner so that we can celebrate the arrival of our son and heir.'

Her husband embraced her tenderly and told her that any woman who could produce such a beautiful child as Lexington deserved to go absolutely anywhere she wanted. But was she strong enough yet, he enquired, to start running around the city late at night?

'No,' she said, she wasn't. But what the hell.

So that evening they both dressed themselves up in fancy clothes, and leaving little Lexington in care of a trained infant's nurse who was costing them twenty dollars a day and was Scottish into the bargain, they went out to the finest and most expensive restaurant in town. There they each ate a giant lobster and drank a bottle of champagne between them, and after that, they went on to a nightclub, where they drank another bottle of champagne and then sat holding hands for several hours while they recalled and discussed and admired each individual physical feature of their lovely newborn son.

They arrived back at their house on the East Side of Manhattan at around two o'clock in the morning and the husband paid off the taxi driver and then began feeling in his pockets for the key to the front door. After a while, he announced that he must have left it in the pocket of his other suit, and he suggested they ring the bell and get the nurse to come down and let them in. An infant's nurse at twenty dollars a day must expect to be hauled out of bed occasionally in the night, the husband said.

So he rang the bell. They waited. Nothing happened. He rang it again, long and loud. They waited another minute. Then they both stepped back on to the street and shouted the nurse's name (McPottle) up at the nursery windows on the third floor, but there was still no response. The house was dark and silent. The wife began to grow apprehensive. Her baby was imprisoned in this place, she told herself. Alone with McPottle. And who was McPottle? They had known her for two days, that was all, and she had a thin mouth, a small disapproving eye, and a starchy bosom, and quite clearly she was in the habit of sleeping too soundly for safety. If she couldn't hear the front-door bell, then how on earth did she expect to hear a baby crying? Why, this very second the poor thing might be swallowing its tongue or suffocating on its pillow.

'He doesn't use a pillow,' the husband said. 'You are not to worry. But I'll get you in if that's what you want.' He was feeling rather superb after all the champagne, and now he bent down and undid the laces of one of his black patent-leather shoes, and took it off. Then, holding it by the toe, he flung it hard and straight through the dining-room window on the ground floor.

'There you are,' he said, grinning. 'We'll deduct it from McPottle's wages.'

He stepped forward and very carefully put a hand through the hole in the glass and released the catch. Then he raised the window.

'I shall lift you in first, little mother,' he said, and he took his wife around the waist and lifted her off the ground. This brought her big red mouth up level with his own, and very close, so he started kissing her. He knew from experience that women like very much to be kissed in this position, with their bodies held tight and their legs dangling in the air, so he went on doing it for quite a long time, and she wiggled her feet, and made loud gulping noises down in her throat. Finally, the husband turned her round and began easing her gently through the open window into the dining-room. At this point, a police patrol car came nosing silently along the street towards them. It stopped about thirty yards away, and three cops of Irish extraction leaped out of the car and started running in the direction of the husband and wife, brandishing revolvers.

'Stick 'em up!' the cops shouted. 'Stick 'em up!' But it was impossible for the husband to obey this order without letting go of his wife, and had he done this she would either have fallen to the ground or would have been left dangling half in and half out of the house, which is a terribly uncomfortable position for a woman; so he continued gallantly to push her upwards and inwards through the window. The cops, all of whom had received medals before for killing robbers, opened fire immediately, and although they were still running, and although the wife in particular was presenting them with a very small target indeed, they succeeded in scoring several direct hits on each body – sufficient anyway to prove fatal in both cases.

Thus, when he was no more than twelve days old, little Lexington became an orphan.

II

The news of this killing, for which the three policemen subsequently received citations, was eagerly conveyed to all relatives of the deceased couple by newspaper reporters, and the next morning, the closest of these relatives, as well as a couple of undertakers, three lawyers, and a priest, climbed into taxis and set out for the house with the broken window. They assembled in the living-room, men and women both, and they sat around in a circle on the sofas and armchairs, smoking cigarettes and sipping sherry and debating what on earth should be done now with the baby upstairs, the orphan Lexington.

It soon became apparent that none of the relatives was particularly keen to assume responsibility for the child, and the discussions and arguments continued all through the day. Everybody declared an enormous, almost an irresistible desire to look after him, and would have done so with the greatest of pleasure were it not for the fact that their apartment was too small, or that they already had one baby and couldn't possibly afford another, or that they wouldn't know what to do with the poor little thing when they went abroad in the summer, or that they were getting on in years, which surely would be most unfair to the boy when he grew up, and so on and so forth. They all knew, of course, that the father had been heavily in debt for a long time and that the house was mortgaged and that consequently there would be no money at all to go with the child.

They were still arguing like mad at six in the evening when suddenly, in the middle of it all an old aunt of the deceased father (her name was Glosspan) swept in from Virginia, and without even removing her hat and coat, not even pausing to sit down, ignoring all offers of a martini, a whisky, a sherry, she announced firmly to the assembled relatives that she herself intended to take sole charge of the infant boy from then on. What was more, she said, she would assume full financial responsibility on all counts, including education, and everyone else could go back home where they belonged and give their consciences a rest. So saying, she trotted upstairs to the nursery and snatched Lexington from his cradle and swept out of the house with the baby clutched tightly in her arms, while the relatives simply sat and stared and smiled and looked relieved, and McPottle the nurse stood stiff with disapproval at the head of the stairs, her lips compressed, her arms folded across her starched bosom.

And thus it was that the infant Lexington, when he was thirteen days old, left the City of New York and travelled southward to live with his Great Aunt Glosspan in the State of Virginia.

III

Aunt Glosspan was nearly seventy when she became guardian to Lexington, but to look at her you would never have guessed it for one minute. She was as sprightly as a woman half her age, with a small, wrinkled, but still quite beautiful face and two lovely brown eyes that sparkled at you in the nicest way. She was also a spinster, though you would never have guessed that either, for there was nothing spinsterish about Aunt Glosspan. She was never bitter or gloomy or irritable; she didn't have a moustache; and she wasn't in the least bit jealous of other people, which in itself is something you can seldom say about either a spinster or a virgin lady, although of course it is not known for certain whether Aunt Glosspan qualified on both counts.

But she was an eccentric old woman, there was no doubt about that. For the past thirty years she had lived a strange isolated life all by herself in a tiny cottage high up on the slopes of the Blue Ridge Mountains, several miles from the nearest village. She had five acres of pasture, a plot for growing vegetables, a flower garden, three cows, a dozen hens, and a fine cockerel.

And now she had little Lexington as well.

She was a strict vegetarian and regarded the consumption of animal flesh as not only unhealthy and disgusting, but horribly cruel. She lived upon lovely clean foods like milk, butter, eggs, cheese, vegetables, nuts, herbs, and fruit, and she rejoiced in the conviction that no living creature would be slaughtered on her account, not even a shrimp. Once, when a brown hen of hers passed away in the prime of life from being egg-bound, Aunt Glosspan was so distressed that she nearly gave up egg-eating altogether.

She knew not the first thing about babies, but that didn't worry her in the least. At the railway station in New York, while waiting for the train that would take her and Lexington back to Virginia, she bought six feeding-bottles, two dozen diapers, a box of safety pins, a carton of milk for the journey, and a small paper-covered book called *The Care of Infants*. What more could anyone want? And when the train got going, she fed the baby some milk, changed its nappies after a fashion, and laid it down on the seat to sleep. Then she read *The Care of Infants* from cover to cover.

'There is no problem here,' she said, throwing the book out of the window. 'No problem at all.'

And curiously enough there wasn't. Back home in the cottage everything went just as smoothly as could be. Little Lexington drank his milk and belched and yelled and slept exactly as a good baby should, and Aunt Glosspan glowed with joy whenever she looked at him, and showered him with kisses all day long.

IV

By the time he was six years old, young Lexington had grown into a most beautiful boy with long golden hair and deep blue eyes the colour of cornflowers. He was bright and cheerful, and already he was learning to help his old aunt in all sorts of different ways around the property, collecting the eggs from the chicken house, turning the handle of the butter churn, digging up potatoes in the vegetable garden, and searching for wild herbs on the side of the mountain. Soon Aunt Glosspan told herself, she would have to start thinking about his education.

But she couldn't bear the thought of sending him away to school. She loved him so much now that it would kill her to be parted from him for any length of time. There was, of course, that village school down in the valley, but it was a dreadful-looking place, and if she sent him there she just knew they would start forcing him to eat meat the very first day he arrived.

'You know what, my darling?' she said to him one day when he was sitting on a stool in the kitchen watching her make cheese. 'I don't really see why I shouldn't give you your lessons myself.'

The boy looked up at her with his large blue eyes, and gave her a lovely trusting smile. 'That would be nice,' he said.

'And the very first thing I should do would be to teach you how to cook.'

'I think I would like that, Aunt Glosspan.'

'Whether you like it or not, you're going to have to learn some time,' she said. 'Vegetarians like us don't have nearly so many foods to choose from as ordinary people, and therefore they must learn to be doubly expert with what they have.'

'Aunt Glosspan,' the boy said, 'what *do* ordinary people eat that we don't?'

'Animals,' she answered, tossing her head in disgust.

'You mean *live* animals?'

'No,' she said. 'Dead ones.'

The boy considered this for a moment.

'You mean when they die they *eat* them instead of *burying* them?'

'They don't wait for them to die, my pet. They kill them.'

'How do they kill them, Aunt Glosspan?'

'They usually slit their throats with a knife.'

'But what *kind* of animals?'

'Cows and pigs mostly, and sheep.'

'Cows!' the boy cried. 'You mean like Daisy and Snowdrop and Lily?'

'Exactly, my dear.'

'But *how* do they eat them, Aunt Glosspan?'

'They cut them up into bits and they cook the bits. They like it best when it's all red and bloody and sticking to the bones. They love to eat lumps of cow's flesh with the blood oozing out of it.'

'Pigs too?'

'They adore pigs.'

'Lumps of bloody pig's meat,' the boy said. 'Imagine that. What else do they eat, Aunt Glosspan?'

'Chickens.'

'Chickens!'

'Millions of them.'

'Feathers and all?'

'No, dear, not the feathers. Now run along outside and get Aunt Glosspan a bunch of chives, will you, my darling?'

Shortly after that, the lessons began. They covered five subjects, reading, writing, geography, arithmetic, and cooking, but the latter was by far the most popular with both teacher and pupil. In fact, it very soon became apparent that young Lexington possessed a truly remarkable talent in this direction. He was a born cook. He was dexterous and quick. He could handle his pans like a juggler. He could slice a single potato into twenty paper-thin slivers in less time than it took his aunt to peel it. His palate was exquisitely sensitive, and he could taste a pot of strong onion soup and immediately detect the presence of a single tiny leaf of sage. In so young a boy, all this was a bit bewildering to Aunt Glosspan, and to tell the truth she didn't quite know what to make of it. But she was proud as proud could be, all the same, and predicted a brilliant future for the child.

'What a mercy it is,' she said, 'that I have such a wonderful little fellow to look after me in my dotage.' And a couple of years later, she retired from the kitchen for good, leaving Lexington in sole charge of all household cooking. The boy was now ten years old, and Aunt Glosspan was nearly eighty.

V

With the kitchen to himself, Lexington straight away began experimenting with dishes of his own invention. The old favourites no longer interested him. He had a violent urge to create. There were hundreds of fresh ideas in his head. 'I will begin,' he said, 'by devising a chestnut soufflé.' He made it and served it up for supper that very night. It was terrific. 'You are a genius!' Aunt Glosspan cried, leaping up from her chair and kissing him on both cheeks. 'You will make history.'

From then on, hardly a day went by without some new delectable creation being set upon the table. There was Brazilnut soup, hominy cutlets, vegetable ragout, dandelion omelette, cream-cheese fritters, stuffed-cabbage surprise, stewed foggage, shallots à la bonne femme, beetroot mousse piquant, prunes Stroganoff, Dutch rarebit, turnips on horseback, flaming spruce-needle tarts, and many many other beautiful compositions. Never before in her life, Aunt Glosspan declared, had she tasted such food as this; and in the mornings, long before lunch was due, she would go out on to the porch and sit there in her rocking-chair, speculating about the coming meal, licking her chops, sniffing the aromas that came wafting out through the kitchen window.

'What's that you're making in there today, boy?' she would call out.

'Try to guess, Aunt Glosspan.'

'Smells like a bit of salsify fritters to me,' she would say, sniffing vigorously.

Then out he would come, this ten-year-old child, a little grin of triumph on his face, and in his hands a big steaming pot of the most heavenly stew made entirely of parsnips and lovage.

'You know what you ought to do,' his aunt said to him, gobbling the stew. 'You ought to set yourself down this very minute with paper and pencil and write a cooking-book.'

He looked at her across the table, chewing his parsnips slowly.

'Why not?' she cried. 'I've taught you how to write and I've taught you how to cook and now all you've got to do is put the two things together. You write a cooking-book, my darling, and it'll make you famous the whole world over.'

'All right,' he said. 'I will.'

And that very day, Lexington began writing the first page of that monumental work which was to occupy him for the rest of his life. He called it *Eat Good and Healthy*.

VI

Seven years later, by the time he was seventeen, he had recorded over nine thousand different recipes, all of them original, all of them delicious.

But now, suddenly, his labours were interrupted by the tragic death of Aunt Glosspan. She was afflicted in the night by a violent seizure, and Lexington, who had rushed into her bedroom to see what all the noise was about, found her lying on her bed yelling and cussing and twisting herself up into all manner of complicated knots. Indeed, she was a terrible sight to behold, and the agitated youth danced around her in his pyjamas, wringing his hands, and wondering what on earth he should do. Finally, in an effort to cool her down, he fetched a bucket of water from the pond in the cow field and tipped it over her head, but this only intensified the paroxysms, and the old lady expired within the hour.

'This is really too bad,' the poor boy said, pinching her several times to make sure that she was dead. 'And how sudden! How quick and sudden! Why only a few hours ago she seemed in the very best of spirits. She even took three large helpings of my most recent creation, devilled mushroom-burgers, and told me how succulent it was.'

After weeping bitterly for several minutes, for he had loved his aunt very much, he pulled himself together and carried her outside and buried her behind the cowshed.

The next day, while tidying up her belongings, he came across an envelope that was addressed to him in Aunt Glosspan's handwriting. He opened it and drew out two fifty-dollar bills and a letter. *Darling boy*, the letter said, *I know that you have never yet been down the mountain since you were thirteen days old, but as soon as I die you must put on a pair of shoes and a clean shirt and walk down to the village and find the doctor. Ask the doctor to give you a death certificate to prove that I am dead. Then take this certificate to my lawyer, a man called Mr Samuel Zuckermann, who lives in New York City and who has a copy of my will. Mr Zuckermann will arrange everything. The cash in this envelope is to pay the doctor for the certificate and to cover the cost of your journey to New York. Mr Zuckermann will give you more money when you get there, and it is my earnest wish that you use it to further your researches into culinary and vegetarian matters, and that you continue to work upon the great book of yours until you are satisfied that it is complete in every way. Your loving aunt – Glosspan.*

Lexington, who had always done everything his aunt told him, pocketed the money, put on a pair of shoes and a clean shirt, and went down the mountain to the village where the doctor lived.

'Old Glosspan?' the doctor said. 'My God, is *she* dead?'

'Certainly she's dead,' the youth answered. 'If you will come back home with me now I'll dig her up and you can see for yourself.'

'How deep did you bury her?' the doctor asked.

'Six or seven feet down, I should think.'

'And how long ago?'

'Oh, about eight hours.'

'Then she's dead,' the doctor announced. 'Here's the certificate.'

VII

Our hero now set out for the City of New York to find Mr Samuel Zuckermann. He travelled on foot, and he slept under hedges, and he lived on berries and wild herbs, and it took him sixteen days to reach the metropolis.

'What a fabulous place this is!' he cried as he stood at the corner of Fifty-seventh Street and Fifth Avenue, staring around him. 'There are no cows or chickens anywhere, and none of the women looks in the least like Aunt Glosspan.'

As for Mr Samuel Zuckermann, he looked like nothing that Lexington had ever seen before.

He was a small spongy man with livid jowls and a huge magenta nose, and when he smiled, bits of gold flashed at you marvellously from lots of different places inside his mouth. In his luxurious office, he shook Lexington warmly by the hand and congratulated him upon his aunt's death.

'I suppose you knew that your dearly beloved guardian was a woman of considerable wealth?' he said.

'You mean the cows and the chickens?'

'I mean half a million bucks,' Mr Zuckermann said.

'How much?'

'Half a million dollars, my boy. And she's left it all to you.' Mr Zuckermann leaned back in his chair and clasped his hands over his spongy paunch. At the same time, be began secretly working his right forefinger in through his waistcoat and under his shirt so as to scratch the skin around the circumference of his navel – a favourite exercise of his, and one that gave him a peculiar pleasure. 'Of course, I shall have to deduct fifty per cent for my services,' he said, 'but that still leaves you with two hundred and fifty grand.'

'I am rich!' Lexington cried. 'This is wonderful! How soon can I have the money?'

'Well,' Mr Zuckermann said, 'luckily for you, I happen to be on rather cordial terms with the tax authorities around here, and I am confident that I shall be able to persuade them to waive all death duties and back taxes.'

'How kind you are,' murmured Lexington.

'I should naturally have to give somebody a small honorarium.'

'Whatever you say, Mr Zuckermann.'

'I think a hundred thousand would be sufficient.'

'Good gracious, isn't that rather excessive?'

'Never undertip a tax inspector or a policeman,' Mr Zuckermann said. 'Remember that.'

'But how much does it leave for me?' the youth asked meekly.

'One hundred and fifty thousand. But then you've got the funeral expenses to pay out of that.'

'*Funeral* expenses?'

'You've got to pay the funeral parlour. Surely you know that?'

'But I buried her myself, Mr Zuckermann, behind the cowshed.'

'I don't doubt it,' the lawyer said. 'So what?'

'I never used a funeral parlour.'

'Listen,' Mr Zuckermann said patiently. 'You may not know it, but there is a law in this State which says that no beneficiary under a will may receive a single penny of his inheritance until the funeral parlour has been paid in full.'

'You mean that's a *law*?'

'Certainly it's a law, and a very good one it is, too. The funeral parlour is one of our great national institutions. It must be protected at all cost.'

Mr Zuckermann himself, together with a group of public-spirited doctors, controlled a corporation that owned a chain of nine lavish funeral parlours in the city, not to mention a casket factory in Brooklyn and a postgraduate school for embalmers in Washington Heights. The celebration of death was therefore a deeply religious affair in Mr Zuckermann's eyes. In fact, the whole business affected him profoundly, almost as profoundly, one might say, as the birth of Christ affected the shopkeeper.

'You had no right to go out and bury your aunt like that,' he said. 'None at all.'

'I'm very sorry, Mr Zuckermann.'

'Why, it's downright subversive.'

'I'll do whatever you say, Mr Zuckermann. All I want to know is how much I'm going to get in the end, when everything's paid.'

There was a pause. Mr Zuckermann sighed and frowned and continued secretly to run the tip of his finger around the rim of his navel.

'Shall we say fifteen thousand?' he suggested, flashing a big gold smile. 'That's a nice round figure.'

'Can I take it with me this afternoon?'

'I don't see why not.'

So Mr Zuckermann summoned his chief cashier and told him to give Lexington fifteen thousand dollars out of the petty cash, and to obtain a receipt. The youth, who by this time was delighted to be getting anything at all, accepted the money gratefully and stowed it away in his knapsack. Then he shook Mr Zuckermann warmly by the hand, thanked him for all his help, and went out of the office.

'The whole world is before me!' our hero cried as he emerged into the street. 'I now have fifteen thousand dollars to see me through until my book is published. And after that, of course, I shall have a great deal more.' He stood on the pavement, wondering which way to go. He turned left and began strolling slowly down the street, staring at the sights of the city.

'What a revolting smell,' he said, sniffing the air. 'I can't stand this.' His delicate olfactory nerves, tuned to receive only the most delicious kitchen aromas, were being tortured by the stench of the diesel-oil fumes pouring out of the backs of the buses.

'I must get out of this place before my nose is ruined altogether,' he said. 'But first, I've simply got to have something to eat. I'm starving.' The poor boy had had nothing but berries and wild herbs for the past two weeks, and now his stomach was yearning for solid food. I'd like a nice hominy cutlet, he told himself. Or maybe a few juicy salsify fritters.

He crossed the street and entered a small restaurant. The place was hot inside, and dark and silent. There was a strong smell of cooking-fat and cabbage water. The only other customer was a man with a brown hat on his head, crouching intently over his food, who did not look up as Lexington came in.

Our hero seated himself at a corner table and hung his knapsack on the back of his chair. This, he told himself, is going to be most interesting. In all my seventeen years I have tasted only the cooking of two people, Aunt Glosspan and myself – unless one counts Nurse McPottle, who must have heated my bottle a few times when I was an infant. But I am now about to sample the art of a new chef altogether, and perhaps, if I am lucky, I may pick up a couple of useful ideas for my book.

A waiter approached out of the shadows at the back, and stood beside the table.

'How do you do,' Lexington said. 'I should like a large hominy cutlet please. Do it twenty-five seconds each side, in a very hot skillet with sour cream, and sprinkle a pinch of lovage on it before serving – unless of course your chef knows of a more original method, in which case I should be delighted to try it.'

The waiter laid his head over to one side and looked carefully at his customer. 'You want the roast pork and cabbage?' he asked. 'That's all we got left.'

'Roast what and cabbage?'

The waiter took a soiled handkerchief from his trouser pocket and shook it open with a violent flourish, as though he were cracking a whip. Then he blew his nose loud and wet.

'You want it or don't you?' he said, wiping his nostrils.

'I haven't the foggiest idea what it is,' Lexington replied, 'but I should love to try it. You see, I am writing a cooking-book and . . .'

'One pork and cabbage!' the waiter shouted, and somewhere in the back of the restaurant, far away in the darkness, a voice answered him.

The waiter disappeared. Lexington reached into his knapsack for his personal knife and fork. These were a present from Aunt Glosspan, given him when he was six years old, made of solid silver, and he had never eaten with any other instruments since. While waiting for the food to arrive, he polished them lovingly with a piece of soft muslin.

Soon the waiter returned carrying a plate on which there lay a thick greyish-white slab of something hot. Lexington leaned forward anxiously to smell it as it was put down before him. His nostrils were wide open now to receive the scent, quivering and sniffing.

'But this is absolute heaven!' he exclaimed. 'What an aroma! It's tremendous!'

The waiter stepped back a pace, watching his customer carefully.

'Never in my life have I smelled anything as rich and wonderful as this!' our hero cried, seizing his knife and fork. 'What on earth is it made of?'

The man in the brown hat looked around and stared, then returned to his eating. The waiter was backing away towards the kitchen.

Lexington cut off a small piece of the meat, impaled it on his silver fork, and carried it up to his nose so as to smell it again. Then he popped it into his mouth and began to chew it slowly, his eyes half closed, his body tense.

'This is fantastic!' he cried. 'It is a brand-new flavour! Oh, Glosspan, my beloved Aunt, how I wish you were with me now so you could taste this remarkable dish! Waiter! Come here at once! I want you!'

The astonished waiter was now watching from the other end of the room, and he seemed reluctant to move any closer.

'If you will come and talk to me I will give you a present,' Lexington said, waving a hundred-dollar bill. 'Please come over here and talk to me.'

The waiter sidled cautiously back to the table, snatched away the money, and held it up close to his face, peering at it from all angles. Then he slipped it quickly into his pocket.

'What can I do for you, my friend?' he asked.

'Look,' Lexington said. 'If you will tell me what this delicious dish is made of, and exactly how it is prepared, I will give you another hundred.'

'I already told you,' the man said. 'It's pork.'

'And what exactly is pork?'

'You never had roast pork before?' the waiter asked, staring.

'For heaven's sake, man, tell me what it is and stop keeping me in suspense like this.'

'It's pig,' the waiter said. 'You just bung it in the oven.'

'*Pig!*'

'All pork is pig. Didn't you know that?'

'You mean *this* is *pig's meat*?'

'I guarantee it.'

'But . . . but . . . that's impossible,' the youth stammered. 'Aunt

Glosspan, who knew more about food than anyone else in the world, said that meat of any kind was disgusting, revolting, horrible, foul, nauseating, and beastly. And yet this piece that I have here on my plate is without doubt the most delicious thing that I have ever tasted. Now how on earth do you explain that? Aunt Glosspan certainly wouldn't have told me it was revolting if it wasn't.'

'Maybe your aunt didn't know how to cook it,' the waiter said.

'Is that possible?'

'You're damned right it is. Especially with pork. Pork has to be very well done or you can't eat it.'

'Eureka!' Lexington cried. 'I'll bet that's exactly what happened! She did it wrong!' He handed the man another hundred-dollar bill. 'Lead me to the kitchen,' he said. 'Introduce me to the genius who prepared this meat.'

Lexington was at once taken into the kitchen, and there he met the cook who was an elderly man with a rash on one side of his neck.

'This will cost you another hundred,' the waiter said.

Lexington was only too glad to oblige, but this time he gave the money to the cook. 'Now listen to me,' he said. 'I have to admit that I am really rather confused by what the waiter has just been telling me. Are you quite positive that the delectable dish which I have just been eating was prepared from pig's flesh?'

The cook raised his right hand and began scratching the rash on his neck.

'Well,' he said, looking at the waiter and giving him a sly wink, 'all I can tell you is that I *think* it was pig's meat.'

'You mean you're not sure?'

'One can't ever be sure.'

'Then what else could it have been?'

'Well,' the cook said, speaking very slowly and still staring at the waiter. 'There's just a chance, you see, that it might have been a piece of human stuff.'

'You mean a man?'

'Yes.'

'Good heavens.'

'Or a woman. It could have been either. They both taste the same.'

'Well – now you really do surprise me,' the youth declared.

'One lives and learns.'

'Indeed one does.'

'As a matter of fact, we've been getting an awful lot of it just lately from the butcher's in place of pork,' the cook declared.

'Have you really?'

'The trouble is, it's almost impossible to tell which is which. They're both very good.'

'The piece I had just now was simply superb.'

'I'm glad you liked it,' the cook said. 'But to be quite honest, I think that was a bit of pig. In fact, I'm almost sure it was.'

'You are?'

'Yes, I am.'

'In that case, we shall have to assume that you are right,' Lexington said. 'So now will you please tell me – and here is another hundred dollars for your trouble – will you please tell me precisely how you prepared it?'

The cook, after pocketing the money, launched out upon a colourful description of how to roast a loin of pork, while the youth, not wanting to miss a single word of so great a recipe, sat down at the kitchen table and recorded every detail in his notebook.

'Is that all?' he asked when the cook had finished.

'That's all.'

'But there must be more to it than that, surely?'

'You got to get a good piece of meat to start off with,' the cook said. 'That's half the battle. It's got to be a good hog and it's got to be butchered right, otherwise it'll turn out lousy which ever way you cook it.'

'Show me how,' Lexington said. 'Butcher me one now so I can learn.'

'We don't butcher pigs in the kitchen,' the cook said. 'That lot you just ate came from a packing-house over in the Bronx.'

'Then give me the address!'

The cook gave him the address, and our hero, after thanking them both many times for all their kindnesses, rushed outside and leapt into a taxi and headed for the Bronx.

VIII

The packing-house was a big four-storey brick building, and the air around it smelled sweet and heavy, like musk. At the main entrance gates, there was a large notice which said VISITORS WELCOME AT ANY TIME, and thus encouraged, Lexington walked through the gates and entered a cobbled yard which surrounded the building itself. He then followed a series of signposts (THIS WAY FOR THE GUIDED TOURS), and came eventually to a small corrugated-iron shed set well apart from the main building (VISITORS' WAITING-ROOM). After knocking politely on the door, he went in.

There were six other people ahead of him in the waiting-room. There was a fat mother with her two little boys aged about nine and eleven. There was a bright-eyed young couple who looked as though they might be on their honeymoon. And there was a pale woman with long white gloves, who sat very upright, looking straight ahead, with her hands folded on her lap. Nobody spoke. Lexington wondered whether they were all writing cooking-books, like himself, but when he put this question to them aloud, he got no answer. The grown-ups merely smiled mysteriously to themselves and shook their heads, and the two children stared at him as though they were seeing a lunatic.

Soon, the door opened and a man with a merry pink face popped his head into the room and said, 'Next, please.' The mother and the two boys got up and went out.

About ten minutes later, the same man returned. 'Next, please,' he said again, and the honeymoon couple jumped up and followed him outside.

Two new visitors came in and sat down – a middle-aged husband and a middle-aged wife, the wife carrying a wicker shopping-basket containing groceries.

'Next, please,' said the guide, and the woman with the long white gloves got up and left.

Several more people came in and took their places on the stiff-backed wooden chairs.

Soon the guide returned for the third time, and now it was Lexington's turn to go outside.

'Follow me, please,' the guide said, leading the youth across the yard towards the main building.

'How exciting this is!' Lexington cried, hopping from one foot to the other. 'I only wish that my dear Aunt Glosspan could be with me now to see what I am going to see.'

'I myself only do the preliminaries,' the guide said. 'Then I shall hand you over to someone else.'

'Anything you say,' cried the ecstatic youth.

First they visited a large penned-in area at the back of the building where several hundred pigs were wandering around. 'Here's where they start,' the guide said. 'And over there's where they go in.'

'Where?'

'Right there.' The guide pointed to a long wooden shed that stood against the outside wall of the factory. 'We call it the shackling-pen. This way, please.'

Three men wearing long rubber boots were driving a dozen pigs into the shackling-pen just as Lexington and the guide approached, so they all went in together.

'Now,' the guide said, 'watch how they shackle them.'

Inside, the shed was simply a bare wooden room with no roof, but there was a steel cable with hooks on it that kept moving slowly along the length of one wall, parallel with the ground, about three feet up. When it reached the end of the shed, this cable suddenly changed direction and climbed vertically upward through the open roof towards the top floor of the main building.

The twelve pigs were huddled together at the far end of the pen, standing quietly, looking apprehensive. One of the men in rubber boots pulled a length of metal chain down from the wall and advanced upon the nearest animal, approaching it from the rear. Then he bent down and quickly looped one end of the chain around one of the animal's hind legs. The other end he attached to a hook on the moving cable as it went by. The cable kept moving. The chain tightened. The pig's leg was pulled up and back, and then the pig itself began to be dragged backwards. But it didn't fall down. It was rather a nimble pig, and somehow it managed to keep its balance on three legs, hopping from foot to foot and struggling against the pull of the chain, but going back and back all the time until at the end of the pen where the cable changed direction and went vertically upward, the creature was suddenly jerked off its feet and borne aloft. Shrill protests filled the air.

'Truly a fascinating process,' Lexington said. 'But what was that funny cracking noise it made as it went up?'

'Probably the leg,' the guide answered. 'Either that or the pelvis.'

'But doesn't that matter?'

'Why should it matter?' the guide asked. 'You don't eat the bones.'

The rubber-booted men were busy shackling the rest of the pigs, and one after another they were hooked to the moving cable and hoisted up through the roof, protesting loudly as they went.

'There's a good deal more to this recipe than just picking herbs,' Lexington said. 'Aunt Glosspan would never have made it.'

At this point, while Lexington was gazing skyward at the last pig to go up, a man in rubber boots approached him quietly from behind and looped one end of a chain around the youth's own ankle, hooking the other end to the moving belt. The next moment, before he had time to realise what was happening, our hero was jerked off his feet and dragged backwards along the concrete floor of the shackling-pen.

'Stop!' he cried. 'Hold everything! My leg is caught!'

But nobody seemed to hear him, and five seconds later, the unhappy young man was jerked off the floor and hoisted vertically upward through the open roof of the pen, dangling upside down by one ankle, and wriggling like a fish.

'Help!' he shouted. 'Help! There's been a frightful mistake! Stop the engines! Let me down!'

The guide removed a cigar from his mouth and looked up serenely at the rapidly ascending youth, but he said nothing. The men in rubber boots were already on their way out to collect the next batch of pigs.

'Oh, save me!' our hero cried. 'Let me down! Please let me down!'

But he was now approaching the top floor of the building where the moving belt curled over like a snake and entered a large hole in the wall, a kind of doorway without a door; and there, on the threshold, waiting to greet him, clothed in a dark-stained yellow rubber apron, and looking for all the world like Saint Peter at the Gates of Heaven, the sticker stood.

Lexington saw him only from upside down, and very briefly at that, but even so he noticed at once the expression of absolute peace and benevolence on the man's face, the cheerful twinkle in the eyes, the little wistful smile, the dimples in his cheeks – and all this gave him hope.

'Hi there,' the sticker said, smiling.

'Quick! Save me!' our hero cried.

'With pleasure,' the sticker said, and taking Lexington gently by one ear with his left hand, he raised his right hand and deftly slit open the boy's jugular vein with a knife.

The belt moved on. Lexington went with it. Everything was still upside down and the blood was pouring out of his throat and getting into his eyes, but he could still see after a fashion, and he had a blurred impression of being in an enormously long room, and at the far end of the room there was a great smoking cauldron of water, and there were dark figures, half hidden in the steam, dancing around the edge of it, brandishing long poles. The conveyor-belt seemed to be travelling right over the top of the cauldron, and the pigs seemed to be dropping down one by one into the boiling water, and one of the pigs seemed to be wearing long white gloves on its front feet.

Suddenly our hero started to feel very sleepy, but it wasn't until his good strong heart had pumped the last drop of blood from his body that he passed on out of this, the best of all possible worlds, into the next.

Stanley Ellin

Robert

The windows of the Sixth Grade classroom were wide open to the June afternoon, and through them came all the sounds of the departing school: the thunder of bus motors warming up, the hiss of gravel under running feet, the voices raised in cynical fervour.

> 'So we sing all hail to thee,
> District Schoo-wull Number Three . . .'

Miss Gildea flinched a little at the last high, shrill note, and pressed her fingers to her aching forehead. She was tired, more tired than she could ever recall being in her thirty-eight years of teaching, and, as she told herself, she had reason to be. It had not been a good term, not good at all, what with the size of the class, and the Principal's insistence on new methods, and then her mother's shocking death coming right in the middle of everything.

Perhaps she had been too close to her mother, Miss Gildea thought; perhaps she had been wrong, never taking into account that some day the old lady would have to pass on and leave her alone in the world. Well, thinking about it all the time didn't make it any easier. She should try to forget.

And, of course, to add to her troubles, there had been during the past few weeks this maddening business of Robert. He had been a perfectly nice boy, and then, out of a clear sky, had become impossible. Not bothersome or noisy really, but sunk into an endless daydream from which Miss Gildea had to sharply jar him a dozen times a day.

She turned her attention to Robert who sat alone in the room at the desk immediately before hers, a thin boy with neatly combed, colourless

547

hair bracketed between large ears; mild blue eyes in a pale face fixed solemnly on hers.

'Robert.'

'Yes, Miss Gildea.'

'Do you know why I told you to remain after school, Robert?'

He frowned thoughtfully at this, as if it were some lesson he was being called on for, but had failed to memorise properly.

'I suppose for being bad,' he said, at last.

Miss Gildea sighed.

'No, Robert, that's not it at all. I know a bad boy when I see one, Robert, and you aren't one like that. But I do know there's something troubling you, something on your mind, and I think I can help you.'

'There's nothing bothering me, Miss Gildea. Honest, there isn't.'

Miss Gildea found the silver pencil thrust into her hair and tapped it in a nervous rhythm on her desk.

'Oh, come, Robert. During the last month every time I looked at you your mind was a million miles away. Now, what is it? Just making plans for vacation, or, perhaps, some trouble with the boys?'

'I'm not having trouble with anybody, Miss Gildea.'

'You don't seem to understand, Robert, that I'm not trying to punish you for anything. Your homework is good. You've managed to keep up with the class, but I do think your inattentiveness should be explained. What, for example, were you thinking this afternoon when I spoke to you directly for five minutes, and you didn't hear a word I said?'

'Nothing, Miss Gildea.'

She brought the pencil down sharply on the desk. 'There must have been *something*, Robert. Now, I insist that you think back, and try to explain yourself.'

Looking at his impassive face she knew that somehow she herself had been put on the defensive, that if any means of graceful retreat were offered now she would gladly take it. Thirty-eight years, she thought grimly, and I'm still trying to play mother-hen to ducklings. Not that there wasn't a bright side to the picture. Thirty-eight years passed meant only two more to go before retirement, the half-salary pension the chance to putter around the house, tend to the garden properly. The pension wouldn't buy you furs and diamonds, sure enough, but it could buy the right to enjoy your own home for the rest of your days instead of a dismal room in the County Home for Old Ladies. Miss Gildea had visited the County Home once, on an instructional visit, and preferred not to think about it.

'Well, Robert,' she said wearily, 'have you remembered what you were thinking?'

'Yes, Miss Gildea.'

'What was it?'

'I'd rather not tell, Miss Gildea.'

'I insist!'

'Well,' Robert said gently, 'I was thinking I wished you were dead, Miss Gildea. I was thinking I wished I could kill you.'

Her first reaction was simply blank incomprehension. She had been standing not ten feet away when that car had skidded up on the sidewalk and crushed her mother's life from her, and Miss Gildea had neither screamed nor fainted. She had stood there dumbly, because of the very unreality of the thing. Just the way she stood in court where they explained that the man got a year in jail, but didn't have a dime to pay for the tragedy he had brought about. And now the orderly ranks of desks before her, the expanse of blackboard around her, and Robert's face in the midst of it all were no more real. She found herself rising from her chair, walking toward Robert who shrank back, his eyes wide and panicky, his elbow half lifted as if to ward off a blow.

'Do you understand what you've just said?' Miss Gildea demanded hoarsely.

'No, Miss Gildea! Honest, I didn't mean anything.'

She shook her head unbelievingly. 'Whatever made you say it? Whatever in the world could make a boy say a thing like that, such a wicked, terrible thing!'

'You wanted to know! You kept asking me!'

The sight of that protective elbow raised against her cut as deep as the incredible words had.

'Put that arm down!' Miss Gildea said shrilly, and then struggled to get her voice under control. 'In all my years I've never struck a child, and I don't intend to start now!'

Robert dropped his arm and clasped his hands together on his desk, and Miss Gildea looking at the pinched white knuckles realised with surprise that her own hands were shaking uncontrollably. 'But if you think this little matter ends here, young-feller-me-lad,' she said, 'you've got another thought coming. You get your things together, and we're marching right up to Mr Harkness. He'll be very much interested in all this.'

Mr Harkness was the Principal. He had arrived only the term before, and but for his taste in eyeglasses (the large, black-rimmed kind which, Miss Gildea privately though, looked actorish) and his predilection for the phrase 'modern pedagogical methods' was, in her opinion, a rather engaging young man.

He looked at Robert's frightened face and then at Miss Gildea's pursed lips. 'Well,' he said pleasantly, 'what seems to be the trouble here?'

'That,' said Miss Gildea, 'is something I think Robert should tell you about.'

She placed a hand on Robert's shoulder, but he pulled away and backed slowly toward Mr Harkness, his breath coming in loud, shuddering sobs, his eyes riveted on Miss Gildea as if she were the only thing in the room beside himself. Mr Harkness put an arm around Robert and frowned at Miss Gildea.

'Now, what's behind all this, Miss Gildea? The boy seems frightened to death.'

Miss Gildea found herself sick of it all, anxious to get out of the room, away from Robert. 'That's enough, Robert,' she commanded. 'Just tell Mr Harkness exactly what happened.'

'I said the boy was frightened to death, Miss Gildea,' Mr Harkness said brusquely. 'We'll talk about it as soon as he understands we're his friends. Won't we, Robert?'

Robert shook his head vehemently. 'I didn't do anything bad! Miss Gildea said I didn't do anything bad!'

'Well, then!' said Mr Harkness triumphantly. 'There's nothing to be afraid of, is there?'

Robert shook his head again. 'She said I had to stay in after school.'

Mr Harkness glanced sharply at Miss Gildea. 'I suppose he missed the morning bus, is that it? And after I said in a directive that the staff was to make allowances—'

'Robert doesn't use a bus,' Miss Gildea protested. 'Perhaps I'd better explain all this, Mr Harkness. You see—'

'I think Robert's doing very well,' Mr Harkness said, and tightened his arm around Robert who nodded shakily.

'She kept me in,' he said, 'and then when we were alone she came up close to me and she said, "I know what you're thinking. You're thinking you'd like to see me dead! You're thinking you'd like to kill me, aren't you?"'

Robert's voice had dropped to an eerie whisper that bound Miss Gildea like a spell. It was broken only when she saw the expression on Mr Harkness's face.

'Why, that's a lie!' she cried. 'That's the most dreadful lie I ever heard any boy dare—'

Mr Harkness cut in abruptly. 'Miss Gildea! I *insist* you let the boy finish what he has to say.'

Miss Gildea's voice fluttered. 'It seems to me, Mr Harkness, that he has been allowed to say quite enough already!'

'Has he?' Mr Harkness asked.

'Robert has been inattentive lately, especially so this afternoon. After class I asked him what he had been thinking about, and he dared to say he was thinking how he wished I were dead! How he wanted to kill me!'

'Robert said that?'

'In almost those exact words. And I can tell you, Mr Harkness, that I was shocked, terribly shocked, especially since Robert always seemed like such a nice boy.'

'His record—?'

'His record is quite good. It's just—'

'And his social conduct?' asked Mr Harkness in the same level voice.

'As far as I know, he gets along with the other children well enough.'

'But for some reason,' persisted Mr Harkness, 'you found him annoying you.'

Robert raised his voice. 'I didn't! Miss Gildea said I didn't do anything bad. And I always liked her. I like her better than *any* teacher!'

Miss Gildea fumbled blindly in her hair for the silver pencil, and failed to find it. She looked around the floor distractedly.

'Yes?' said Mr Harkness.

'My pencil,' said Miss Gildea on the verge of tears. 'It's gone.'

'Surely, Miss Gildea,' said Mr Harkness in a tone of mild exasperation. 'This is not quite the moment—'

'It was very valuable,' Miss Gildea tried to explain hopelessly. 'It was my mother's.' In the face of Mr Harkness's stony surveillance she knew she must look a complete mess. Hems crooked, nose red, hair all dishevelled. 'I'm all upset, Mr Harkness. It's been a long term and now all this right at the end of it. I don't know what to say.'

Mr Harkness's face fell into sympathetic lines.

'That's quite all right, Miss Gildea. I know how you feel. Now, if you want to leave, I think Robert and I should have a long, friendly talk.'

'If you don't mind—'

'No, no,' Mr Harkness said heartily. 'As a matter of fact, I think that would be the best thing all around.'

After he had seen her out he closed the door abruptly behind her, and Miss Gildea walked heavily up the stairway and down the corridor to the Sixth Grade room. The silver pencil was there on the floor at Robert's desk, and she picked it up and carefully polished it with her handkerchief. Then she sat down at her desk with the handkerchief to her nose and wept soundlessly for ten minutes.

That night when the bitter taste of humiliation had grown faint enought to permit it, Miss Gildea reviewed the episode with all the honesty at her command. Honesty with oneself had always been a major point in her credo, had, in fact, been passed on through succeeding classes during the required lesson on The Duties of An American Citizen, when Miss Gildea, to sum up the lesson, would recite: 'This above all, To thine ownself be true . . .' while thumping her fist on her desk as an accompaniment to each syllable.

Hamlet, of course, was not in the syllabus of the Sixth Grade, whose reactions over the years never deviated from a mixed bewilderment and indifference. But Miss Gildea, after some prodding of the better minds into a discussion of the lines, would rest content with the knowledge that she had sown good seed on what, she prayed, was fertile ground.

Reviewing the case of Robert now, with her emotions under control, she came to the unhappy conclusion that it was she who had committed the injustice. The child had been ordered to stay after school, something that to him could mean only a punishment. He had been ordered to disclose some shadowy, childlike thoughts that had drifted through his mind hours before, and, unable to do so, either had to make up something out of the whole cloth, or blurt out the immediate thought in his immature mind.

It was hardly unusual, reflected Miss Gildea sadly, for a child badgered by a teacher to think what Robert had; she could well remember her own feelings toward a certain pompadoured harridan who still haunted her dreams. And the only conclusion to be drawn, unpleasant though it was, was that Robert, and not she, had truly put into practice those beautiful words from Shakespeare.

It was this, as well as the sight of his pale accusing face before her while she led the class through the morning session next day, which prompted her to put Robert in charge of refilling the water pitcher during recess. The duties of the water pitcher monitor were to leave the playground a little before the rest of the class and clean and refill the pitcher on her desk, but since the task was regarded as an honour by the class, her gesture, Miss Gildea felt with some self-approval, carried exactly the right note of conciliation.

She was erasing the blackboard at the front of the room near the end of the recess when she heard Robert approaching her desk, but much as she wanted to she could not summon up courage enough to turn and face him. As if, she thought, he were the teacher, and I were afraid of him. And she could feel her cheeks grow warm at the thought.

He re-entered the room on the sound of the bell that marked the end of recess, and this time Miss Gildea plopped the eraser firmly into its place beneath the blackboard and turned to look at him. 'Thank you very much, Robert,' she said as he set the pitcher down and neatly capped it with her drinking glass.

'You're welcome, Miss Gildea,' Robert said politely. He drew a handkerchief from his pocket, wiped his hands with it, then smiled gently at Miss Gildea. 'I bet you think I put poison or something into that water,' he said gravely, 'but I wouldn't do anything like that, Miss Gildea. Honest, I wouldn't.'

Miss Gildea gasped, then reached out a hand toward Robert's shoulder. She withdrew it hastily when he shrank away with the familiar panicky look in his eyes.

'Why did you say that, Robert?' Miss Gildea demanded in a terrible voice. 'That was plain impudence, wasn't it? You thought you were being smart, didn't you?'

At that moment the rest of the class surged noisily into the room, but Miss Gildea froze them into silence with a commanding wave of the hand. Out of the corner of her eye she noted the cluster of shocked and righteous faces allied with her in condemnation, and she felt a quick little sense of triumph in her position.

'I was talking to you, Robert,' she said. 'What do you have to say for yourself?'

Robert took another step backward and almost tumbled over a schoolbag left carelessly in the aisle. He caught himself, then stood there helplessly, his eyes never leaving Miss Gildea's.

'Well, Robert!'

He shook his head wildly. 'I didn't do it!' he cried. 'I didn't put anything in your water, Miss Gildea! I told you I didn't!'

Without looking Miss Gildea knew that the cluster of accusing faces had swung toward her now, felt her triumph turn to a sick bewilderment inside her. It was as if Robert, with his teary eyes and pale, frightened face and too large ears, had turned into a strange jelly-like creature that could not be pinned down and put in its place. As if he were retreating further and further down some dark, twisting path, and leading her on with him. And, she thought desperately, she had to pull herself free before she did something dreadful, something unforgivable.

She couldn't take the boy to Mr Harkness again. Not only did the memory of that scene in his office the day before make her shudder, but a repeated visit would be an admission that after thirty-eight years of teaching she was not up to the mark as a disciplinarian.

But for her sake, if for nothing else, Robert had to be put in his place. With a gesture, Miss Gildea order the rest of the class to their seats and turned to Robert who remained standing.

'Robert,' said Miss Gildea, 'I want an apology for what has just happened.'

'I'm sorry, Miss Gildea,' Robert said, and it looked as if his eyes would be brimming with tears in another moment.

Miss Gildea hardened her heart to this. '*I apologise, Miss Gildea, and it will not happen again,*' she prompted.

Miraculously, Robert contained his tears. 'I apologise, Miss Gildea, and it will not happen again,' he muttered and dropped limply into his seat.

'Well!' said Miss Gildea, drawing a deep breath as she looked around at the hushed class. 'Perhaps that will be a lesson to us all.'

The classroom work did not go well after that, but, as Miss Gildea told herself, there were only a few days left to the end of term, and after that, praise be, there was the garden, the comfortable front porch of the old house to share with neighbours in the summer evenings, and then next term a new set of faces in the classroom, with Robert's not among them.

Later, closing the windows of the room after the class had left, Miss Gildea was brought up short by the sight of a large group gathered on the sidewalk near the parked buses. It was Robert, she saw, surrounded by most of the Sixth Grade, and obviously the centre of interest. He was nodding emphatically when she put her face to the window, and she drew back quickly at the sight, moved by some queer sense of guilt.

Only a child, she assured herself, *he's only a child*, but that thought did not in any way dissolve the anger against him that stuck like a lump in her throat.

That was on Thursday. By Tuesday of the next week, the final week of the term, Miss Gildea was acutely conscious of the oppressive atmosphere lying over the classroom. Ordinarily, the awareness of impending vacation acted on the class like a violent agent dropped into some inert liquid. There would be ferment and seething beneath the surface, manifested by uncontrollable giggling and whispering, and this would grow more and more turbulent until all restraint and discipline was swept away in the general upheaval of excitement and good spirits.

That, Miss Gildea thought, was the way it always had been, but it was strangely different now. The Sixth Grade, down to the most irrepressible spirits in it, acted as if it had been turned to a set of robots before her startled eyes. Hands tightly clasped on desks, eyes turned toward her with an almost frightening intensity, the class responded to her mildest requests as if they were shouted commands. And when she walked down the aisles between them, one and all seemed to have adopted Robert's manner of shrinking away fearfully at her approach.

Miss Gildea did not like to think of what all this might mean, but valiantly forced herself to do so. Can it mean, she asked herself, that all think as Robert does, are choosing this way of showing it? And, if they knew how cruel it was, would they do it?

Other teachers, Miss Gildea knew, sometimes took problems such as this to the Teachers' Room where they could be studied and answered by those who saw them in an objective light. It might be that the curious state of the Sixth Grade was being duplicated in other classes. Perhaps she herself was imagining the whole thing, or, frightening thought looking back, as people will when they grow old, on the sort of past that never really did exist. Why, in that case – and Miss Gildea had to laugh at herself with a faint merriment – she would just find herself reminiscing about her thirty-eight years of teaching to some bored young woman who didn't have the fraction of experience she did.

But underneath the current of these thoughts, Miss Gildea knew there was one honest reason for not going to the Teachers' Room this last week of the term. She had received no gifts, not one. And the spoils from each grade heaped high in a series of pyramids against the wall. The boxes of fractured cookies, the clumsily wrapped jars of preserves, the scarves, the stockings, the handkerchiefs, infinite, endless boxes of handkerchiefs, all were there to mark the triumph of each teacher. And Miss Gildea, who in all her years at District School Number Three had been blushingly proud of the way her pyramid was highest at the end of each term, had not yet received a single gift from the Sixth Grade class.

After the class was dismissed that afternoon, however the spell was broken. Only a few of her pupils still loitered in the hallway near the door, Miss Gildea noticed, but Robert remained in his seat. Then, as she gathered together her belongings Robert approached her with a box outheld in his hand. It was, from its shape, a box of candy, and, as Miss Gildea could tell from the wrapping, expensive candy. Automatically, she reached a hand out, then stopped herself short. He'll never make-up to me for what he's done, she told herself furiously; I'll never let him.

'Yes, Robert?' she said coolly.

'It's a present for you, Miss Gildea,' Robert said, and then as Miss Gildea watched in fascination he began to strip the wrappings from it. He laid the paper neatly on the desk and lifted the cover of the box to display the chocolates within. 'My mother said that's the biggest box they had,' he said wistfully. 'Don't you even want them, Miss Gildea?'

Miss Gildea weakened despite herself. 'Did you think I would, after what's happened, Robert?' she asked.

Robert reflected a moment. 'Well,' he said at last, 'if you want me to, I'll eat one right in front of you, Miss Gildea.'

Miss Gildea recoiled as if at a faraway warning. *Don't let him say any more*, something inside her cried; *he's only playing a trick, another horrible trick*, and then she was saying, 'Why would I want you to do that, Robert?'

'So you'll see they're not poison or anything, Miss Gildea,' Robert said. 'Then you'll believe it, won't you, Miss Gildea?'

She had been prepared. Even before he said the words, she had felt her body drawing itself tighter and tighter against what she knew was coming. But the sound of the words themselves only served to release her like a spring coiled too tightly.

'You little monster!' sobbed Miss Gildea and struck wildly at the proffered box which flew almost to the far wall, while chocolates cascaded stickily around the room. 'How dare you!' she cried. 'How dare you!' and her small bony fists beat at Robert's cowering shoulders and back as he tried to retreat.

He half turned in the aisle, slipped on a piece of chocolate, and went down to his knees, but before he could recover himself Miss Gildea was on him again, her lips drawn back, her fists pummelling him as if they were a pair of tireless mallets. Robert had started to scream at the top of his lungs from the first blow, but it was no more than a remote buzzing in Miss Gildea's ears.

'Miss Gildea!'

That was Mr Harkness's voice, she knew, and those must be Mr Harkness's hands which pulled her away so roughly that she had to keep herself from falling by clutching at her desk. She stood there weakly, feeling the wild fluttering of her heart, feeling the sick churning of shame and anguish in her while she tried to bring the room into focus again. There was the knot of small excited faces peering through the open doorway, they must have called Mr Harkness, and Mr Harkness himself listening to Robert who talked and wept alternately, and there was a mess everywhere. Of course, thought Miss Gildea dazedly, those must be chocolate stains. Chocolate stains all over my lovely clean room.

Then Robert was gone, the faces at the door were gone, and the door itself was closed behind them. Only Mr Harkness remained, and Miss Gildea watched him as he removed his glasses, cleaned them carefully, and then held them up at arm's length and studied them before settling them once more on his nose.

'Well, Miss Gildea,' said Mr Harkness as if he were speaking to the glasses rather than to her, 'this is a serious business.'

Miss Gildea nodded.

'I am sick,' Mr Harkness said quietly, 'really sick at the thought that somewhere in this school, where I tried to introduce decent pedagogical standards, corporal punishment is still being practised.'

'That's not fair at all, Mr Harkness,' Miss Gildea said shakily. 'I hit the boy, that's true, and I know I was wrong to do it, but that is the first time in all my life I raised a finger against any child. And if you knew my feelings—'

'Ah,' said Mr Harkness, 'that's exactly what I would like to know, Miss Gildea.' He nodded to her chair, and she sat down weakly. 'Now, just go ahead and explain everything as you saw it.'

It was a difficult task, made even more difficult by the fact that Mr Harkness chose to stand facing the window. Forced to address his back this way, Miss Gildea found that she had the sensation of speaking in a vacuum, but she mustered the facts as well as she could, presented them with strong emotion, and then sank back in the chair quite exhausted.

Mr Harkness remained silent for a long while, then slowly turned to face Miss Gildea. 'I am not a practising psychiatrist,' he said at last, 'although as an educator I have, of course, taken a considerable interest in that field. But I do not think it needs a practitioner to tell what a clearcut and obvious case I am facing here. Nor,' he added sympathetically, 'what a tragic one.'

'It might simply be,' suggested Miss Gildea, 'that Robert—'

'I am not speaking about Robert,' said Mr Harkness soberly, quietly.

It took an instant for this to penetrate, and then Miss Gildea felt the blood run cold in her.

'Do you think I'm lying about all this?' she cried increduously. 'Can you possibly—'

'I am sure,' Mr Harkness replied soothingly, 'that you were describing things exactly as you saw them, Miss Gildea. But – have you ever heard the phrase "persecution complex"? Do you think you could recognise the symptoms of that condition if they were presented objectively? I can, Miss Gildea. I assure you, I can.'

Miss Gildea struggled to speak, but the words seemed to choke her. 'No,' she managed to say, 'you couldn't! Because some mischievous boy chooses to make trouble—'

'Miss Gildea, no child of eleven, however mischievous, could draw the experiences Robert has described to me out of his imagination. He has discussed these experiences with me at length; now I have heard your side of the case. And the conclusions to be drawn, I must say, are practically forced on me.'

The room started to slip out of focus again, and Miss Gildea frantically tried to hold it steady.

'But that just means you're taking his word against mine!' she said fiercely.

'Unfortunately, Miss Gildea, not his word alone. Last weekend, a delegation of parents met the School Board and made it quite plain that they were worried because of what their children told them of your recent actions. A dozen children in your class described graphically at that meeting how you had accused them of trying to poison your drinking water, and how you had threatened them because of this. And Robert, it may interest you to know, was not even one of them.

'The School Board voted your dismissal then and there, Miss Gildea, but in view of your long years of service it was left for me to override that decision if I wished to on my sole responsibility. After this episode, however, I cannot see that I have any choice, I must do what is best.'

'Dismissal?' said Miss Gildea vaguely. 'But they can't. I only have two more years to go. They can't do that, Mr Harkness; all they're trying to do is trick me out of my pension!'

'Believe me,' said Mr Harkness gently, 'they're not trying to do anything of the sort, Miss Gildea. Nobody in the world is trying to hurt you. I give you my solemn word that the only thing which has entered into consideration of this case from first to last has been the welfare of the children.'

The room swam in sunlight, but under it Miss Gildea's face was grey and lifeless. She reached forward to fill her glass with water, stopped short, and seemed to gather herself together with a sudden brittle determination. 'I'll just have to speak to the Board myself,' she said in a high breathless voice. 'That's the only thing to do, go there and explain the whole thing to them!'

'That would not help,' said Mr Harkness pityingly. 'Believe me, Miss Gildea, it would not.'

Miss Gildea left her chair and came to him, her eyes wide and frightened. She laid a trembling hand on his arm and spoke eagerly, quickly, trying to make him understand. 'You see,' she said, 'that means I won't get my pension. I must have two more years for that, don't you see? There's the payment on the house, the garden – no, the garden is part of the house, really – but without the pension—'

She was pulling furiously at his arm with every phrase as if she could drag him bodily into a comprehension of her words, but he stood unyielding and only shook his head pityingly. 'You must control yourself, Miss Gildea,' he pleaded. 'You're not yourself, and it's impossible—'

'No!' she cried in a strange voice. 'No!'

When she pulled away he knew almost simultaneously what she intended to do, but the thought froze him to the spot, and when he moved it was too late. He burst into the corridor through the door she had flung open, and almost threw himself down the stairway to the main hall. The door to the street was just swinging shut and he ran toward it, one hand holding the rim of his glasses, a sharp little pain digging into his side, but before he could reach the door he heard the screech of brakes, the single agonised scream, and the horrified shout of a hundred shrill voices.

He put his hand on the door, but could not find the strength to open it. A few minutes later, a cleaning women had to sidle around him to get outside and see what all the excitement was about.

Miss Reardon, the substitute, took the Sixth Grade the next day, and, everything considered, handled it very well. The single ripple in the even current of the session came at its very start when Miss Reardon explained her presence by referring to the 'sad accident that happened to dear Miss Gildea'. The mild hubbub which followed this contained several voices, notably in the back of the room, which protested plaintively, 'It was *not* an accident, Miss Reardon; she ran right in front of that bus,' but Miss Reardon quickly brought order to the room with a few sharp raps of her ruler, and after that, classwork was carried on in a pleasant and orderly fashion.

Robert walked home slowly that afternoon, swinging his schoolbag placidly at his side, savouring the June warmth soaking into him, the fresh green smell in the air, the memory of Miss Reardon's understanding face so often turned toward his in eager and friendly interest. His home was identical with all the others on the block, square white boxes with small lawns before them, and its only distinction was that all its blinds were drawn down. After he had closed the front door very quietly behind him, he set his schoolbag down in the hallway, and went into the stuffy half-darkness of the living room.

Robert's father sat in the big armchair in his bathrobe, the way he always did, and Robert's mother was bent over him holding a glass of water.

'No!' Robert's father said. 'You just want to get rid of me, but I won't let you! I know what you put into it, and I won't drink it! I'll die before I drink it!'

'Please,' Robert's mother said, 'please take it. I swear it's only water. I'll drink some myself if you don't believe me.' But when she drank a little and then held the glass to his lips, Robert's father only tossed his head from side to side.

Robert stood there watching the scene with fascination, his lips moving in silent mimicry of the familiar words. Then he cleared his throat.

'I'm home, mama,' Robert said softly. 'Can I have some milk and cookies, please?'

Stanley Ellin

The Question

I am an electrocutioner . . . I prefer this word to executioner; I think words make a difference. When I was a boy, people who buried the dead were undertakers, and then somewhere along the way they became morticians and are better off for it.

Take the one who used to be the undertaker in my town. He was a decent, respectable man, very friendly if you'd let him be, but hardly anybody would let him be. Today, his son – who now runs the business – is not an undertaker but a mortician, and is welcome everywhere. As a matter of fact, he's an officer in my Lodge and is one of the most popular members we have. And all it took to do that was changing one word to another. The job's the same but the word is different, and people somehow will always go by words rather than meanings.

So, as I said, I am an electrocutioner – which is the proper professional word for it in my state where the electric chair is the means of execution.

Not that this is my profession. Actually, it's a sideline, as it is for most of us who perform executions. My real business is running an electrical supply and repair shop just as my father did before me. When he died I inherited not only the business from him, but also the position of state's electrocutioner.

We established a tradition, my father and I. He was running the shop profitably even before the turn of the century when electricity was a comparatively new thing, and he was the first man to perform a successful electrocution for the state. It was not the state's first electrocution, however. That one was an experiment and was badly bungled by the engineer who installed the chair in the state prison. My father, who had helped install the chair, was the assistant at the electrocution, and he told me that everything that could go wrong that day did go wrong.

The current was eccentric, his boss froze on the switch, and the man in the chair was alive and kicking at the same time he was being burned to a crisp. The next time, my father offered to do the job himself, rewired the chair, and handled the switch so well that he was offered the job of official electrocutioner.

I followed in his footsteps, which is how a tradition is made, but I am afraid this one ends with me. I have a son, and what I said to him and what he said to me is the crux of the matter. He asked me a question – well, in my opinion, it was the kind of question that's at the bottom of most of the world's troubles today. There are some sleeping dogs that should be left to lie; there are some questions that should not be asked.

To understand all this, I think you have to understand me, and nothing could be easier. I'm sixty, just beginning to look my age, a little over-weight, suffer sometimes from arthritis when the weather is damp. I'm a good citizen, complain about my taxes but pay them on schedule, vote for the right party, and run my business well enough to make a comfortable living from it.

I've been married thirty-five years and never looked at another woman in all that time. Well, looked maybe, but no more than that. I have a married daughter and a grand-daughter almost a year old, and the prettiest, smilingest baby in town. I spoil her and don't apologise for it, because in my opinion that is what grandfathers were made for – to spoil their grandchildren. Let mama and papa attend to the business; grandpa is there for the fun.

And beyond all that I have a son who asks questions. The kind that shouldn't be asked.

Put the picture together, and what you get is someone like yourself. I might be your next-door neighbour, I might be your old friend, I might be the uncle you meet whenever the family gets together at a wedding or a funeral. I'm like you.

Naturally, we all look different on the outside but we can still recognise each other on sight as the same kind of people. Deep down inside where it matters we have the same feelings, and we know that without any questions being asked about them.

'But,' you might say, 'there is a difference between us. You're the one who performs the executions, and I'm the one who reads about them in the papers, and that's a big difference, no matter how you look at it.'

Is it? Well, look at it without prejudice, look at it with absolute honesty, and you'll have to admit that you're being unfair,

Let's face the facts, we're all in this together. If an old friend of yours happens to serve on a jury that finds a murderer guilty, you don't lock the door against him, do you? More than that: if you could get an introduction to the judge who sentences that murderer to the electric chair, you'd be proud of it, wouldn't you? You'd be honoured to have him sit at your table, and you'd be quick enough to let the world know about it.

And since you're so willing to be friendly with the jury that convicts and the judge that sentences, what about the man who has to pull the switch? He's finished the job you wanted done, he's made the world a better place for it. Why must he go hide away in a dark corner until the next time he's needed?

There's no use denying that nearly everybody feels he should, and there's less use denying that it's a cruel thing for anyone in my position to face. If you don't mind some strong language, it's a damned outrage to hire a man for an unpleasant job, and then despise him for it. Sometimes it's hard to abide such righteousness.

How do I get along in the face of it? The only way possible – by keeping my secret locked up tight and never being tempted to give it away. I don't like it that way, but I'm no fool about it.

The trouble is that I'm naturally easygoing and friendly. I'm the sociable kind. I like people, and I want them to like me. At Lodge meetings or in the clubhouse down at the golf course I'm always the centre of the crowd. And I know what would happen if at any such time I ever opened my mouth and let that secret out. A five-minute sensation, and after that the slow chill setting in. It would mean the end of my whole life then and there, the kind of life I want to live, and no man in his right mind throws away sixty years of his life for a five-minute sensation.

You can see I've given the matter a lot of thought. More than that, it hasn't been idle thought. I don't pretend to be an educated man, but I'm willing to read books on any subject that interests me, and execution has been one of my main interests ever since I got into the line. I have the books sent to the shop where nobody takes notice of another piece of mail, and I keep them locked in a bin in my office so that I can read them in private.

There's a nasty smell about having to do it this way – at my age you hate to feel like a kid hiding himself away to read a dirty magazine – but I have no choice. There isn't a soul on earth outside of the warden at the state's prison and a couple of picked guards there who know I'm the one pulling the switch at an execution, and I intend it to remain that way.

Oh, yes, my son knows now. Well, he's difficult in some ways, but he's no fool. If I wasn't sure he would keep his mouth shut about what I told him, I wouldn't have told it to him in the first place.

Have I learned anything from those books? At least enough to take a pride in what I'm doing for the state and the way I do it. As far back in history as you want to go there have always been executioners. The day that men first made laws to help keep peace among themselves was the day the first executioner was born. There have always been law-breakers; there must always be a way of punishing them. It's as simple as that.

The trouble is that nowadays there are too many people who don't want it to be as simple as that. I'm no hypocrite, I'm not one of those narrow-minded fools who thinks that every time a man comes up with a generous impulse he's some kind of crackpot. But he can be mistaken. I'd put most of the people who are against capital punishment in that class. They are fine, high-minded citizens who've never in their lives been close enough to a murderer or rapist to smell the evil in him. In fact, they're so fine and high-minded that they can't imagine anyone in the world not being like themselves. In that case, they say anybody who commits murder or rape is just a plain, ordinary human being who's had a bad spell. He's no criminal, they say, he's just sick. He doesn't need the electric chair; all he needs is a kindly old doctor to examine his head and straighten out the kinks in his brain.

In fact, they say there is no such thing as a criminal at all. There are only well people and sick people, and the ones who deserve all your worry and consideration are the sick ones. If they happen to murder or rape a few of the well ones now and then, why, just run for the doctor.

This is the argument from beginning to end, and I'd be the last one to deny that it's built on honest charity and good intentions. But it's a mistaken argument. It omits the one fact that matters. When anyone commits murder or rape he is no longer in the human race. A man has a human brain and a God-given soul to control his animal nature. When the animal in him takes control he's not a human being any more. Then he has to be exterminated the way any animal must be if it goes wild in the middle of helpless people. And my duty is to be the exterminator.

It could be that people just don't understand the meaning of the word *duty* any more. I don't want to sound old-fashioned, God forbid, but when I was a boy things were more straight-forward and clear-cut. You learned to tell right from wrong, you learned to do what had to be done, and you didn't ask questions every step of the way. Or if you had to ask any questions, the ones that mattered were *how* and *when*.

Then along came psychology, along came the professors, and the main question was always *why*. Ask yourself *why, why, why* about everything you do, and you'll end up doing nothing. Let a couple of generations go along that way, and you'll finally have a breed of people who sit around in trees like monkeys, scratching their heads.

Does this sound far-fetched? Well, it isn't. Life is a complicated thing to live. All his life a man finds himself facing one situation after another, and the way to handle them is to live by the rules. Ask yourself *why* once too often, and you can find yourself so tangled up that you go under. The show must go on. Why? Women and children first. Why? My country, right or wrong. Why? Never mind your duty. Just keep asking *why* until it's too late to do anything about it.

Around the time I first started going to school my father gave me a dog, a collie pup named Rex. A few years after Rex suddenly became unfriendly, the way a dog will sometimes, and then vicious, and then one day he bit my mother when she reached down to pat him.

The day after that I saw my father leaving the house with his hunting rifle under his arm and with Rex on a leash. It wasn't the hunting season, so I knew what was going to happen to Rex and I knew why. But it's forgivable in a boy to ask things that a man should be smart enough not to ask.

'Where are you taking Rex?' I asked my father. 'What are you going to do with him?'

'I'm taking him out back of town,' my father said. 'I'm going to shoot him.'

'But why?' I said, and that was when my father let me see that there is only one answer to such a question.

'Because it has to be done,' he said.

I never forgot that lesson. It came hard; for a while I hated my father for it, but as I grew up I came to see how right he was. We both knew why the dog had to be killed. Beyond that, all questions would lead nowhere. Why the dog had become vicious, why God had put a dog on earth to be killed this way – these are the questions that you can talk out to the end of time, and while you're talking about them you still have a vicious dog on your hands.

It is strange to look back and realise now that when the business of the dog happened, and long before it and long after it, my father was an electrocutioner, and I never knew it. Nobody knew it, not even my mother. A few times a year my father would pack his bag and a few tools and go away for a couple of days, but that was all any of us knew. If you asked him where he was going he would simply say he had a job to do out of town. He was not a man you'd ever suspect of philandering or going off on a solitary drunk, so nobody gave it a second thought.

It worked the same way in my case. I found out how well it worked when I finally told my son what I had been doing on those jobs out of town, and that I had gotten the warden's permission to take him on as an assistant and train him to handle the chair himself when I retired. I could tell from the way he took it that he was as thunderstruck at this as I had been thirty years before when my father had taken me into his confidence.

'Electrocutioner?' said my son. 'An *electrocutioner?*'

'Well, there's no disgrace to it,' I said. 'And since it's got to be done, and somebody has to do it, why not keep it in the family? If you knew anything about it, you'd know it's a profession that's often passed down in a family from generation to generation. What's wrong with a good, sound tradition? If more people believed in tradition you wouldn't have so many troubles in the world today.'

It was the kind of argument that would have been more than enough to convince me when I was his age. What I hadn't taken into account was that my son wasn't like me, much as I wanted him to be. He was a grown man in his own right, but a grown man who had never settled down to his responsibilities. I had always kept closing my eyes to that. I had always seen him the way I wanted to and not the way he was.

When he left college after a year, I said, all right, there are some people who aren't made for college, I never went there, so what difference does it make. When he went out with one girl after another and could never make up his mind to marrying any of them, I said, well, he's young, he's sowing his wild oats, the time will come soon enough when he's ready to take care of a home and family. When he sat day-dreaming in the shop instead of tending to business I never made a fuss about it. I knew when he put his mind to it he was as good an electrician as you could ask for, and in these soft times people are allowed to do a lot more dreaming and a lot less working than they used to.

The truth was that the only thing that mattered to me was being his friend. For all his faults he was a fine-looking boy with a good mind. He wasn't much for mixing with people, but if he wanted to he could win anyone over. And in the back of my mind all the while he was growing up was the thought that he was the only one who would learn my secret some day, and would share it with me, and make it easier to bear. I'm not secretive by nature. A man like me needs a thought like that to sustain him.

So when the time came to tell him he shook his head and said no. I felt that my legs had been kicked out from under me. I argued with him and he still said no, and I lost my temper.

'Are you against capital punishment?' I asked him. 'You don't have to apologise if you are. I'd think all the more of you, if that's your only reason.'

'I don't know if it is,' he said.

'Well, you ought to make up your mind one way or the other,' I told him. 'I'd hate to think you were like every other hypocrite around who says it's all right to condemn a man to the electric chair and all wrong to pull the switch.'

'Do I have to be the one to pull it?' he said. 'Do you?'

'Somebody has to do it. Somebody always has to do the dirty work for the rest of us. It's not like the Old Testament days when everybody did it for himself. Do you know how they executed a man in those days? They laid him on the ground tied hand and foot, and everybody around had to heave rocks on him until he was crushed to death. They didn't invite anybody to stand around and watch. You wouldn't have had much choice then, would you?'

'I don't know,' he said. And then because he was as smart as they come and knew how to turn your words against you, he said, 'After all, I'm not without sin.'

'Don't talk like a child,' I said. 'You're without the sin of murder on you or any kind of sin that calls for execution. And if you're so sure the Bible has all the answers, you might remember that you're supposed to render unto Caesar the things that are Caesar's.'

'Well,' he said, 'in this case I'll let you do the rendering.'

I knew then and there from the way he said it and the way he looked at me that it was no use trying to argue with him. The worst of it was knowing that we had somehow moved far apart from each other and would never really be close again. I should have had sense enough to let it go at that. I should have just told him to forget the whole thing and keep his mouth shut about it.

Maybe if I had ever considered the possibility of his saying no, I would have done it. But because I hadn't considered any such possibility I was caught off balance. I was too much upset to think straight. I will admit it now. It was my own fault that I made an issue of things and led him to ask the one question he should never have asked.

'I see,' I told him. 'It's the same old story, isn't it? Let somebody else do it. But if they pull your number out of a hat and you have to serve on a jury and send a man to the chair, that's all right with you. At least, it's all right as long as there's somebody else to do the job that you and the judge and every decent citizen wants done. Let's face the facts, boy, you don't have the guts. I'd hate to think of you even walking by the death house. The shop is where you belong. You can be nice and cosy there, wiring up fixtures and ringing the cash register. I can handle my duties without your help.'

It hurt me to say it. I had never talked like that to him before, and it hurt. The strange thing was that he didn't seem angry about it; he only looked at me that way puzzled.

'Is that all it is to you?' he said. 'A duty?'

'Yes.'

'But you get paid for it, don't you?'

'I get paid little enough for it.'

He kept looking at me that way. 'Only a duty?' he said, and never took his eyes off me. 'But you enjoy it, don't you?'

That was the question he asked.

You enjoy it, don't you? You stand there looking through a peephole in the wall at the chair. In thirty years I have stood there more than a hundred times looking at that chair. The guards bring somebody in. Usually he is in a daze; sometimes he screams, throws himself around and fights. Sometimes it is a woman, and a woman can be as hard to handle as a man when she is led to the chair. Sooner or later, whoever it is is strapped down and the black hood is dropped over his head. Now your hand is on the switch.

The warden signals, and you pull the switch. The current hits the body like a tremendous rush of air suddenly filling it. The body leaps out of the chair with only the straps holding it back. The head jerks, and a curl of smoke comes from it. You release the switch and the body falls back again.

You do it once more, do it a third time to make sure. And whenever your hand presses the switch you can see in your mind what the current is doing to that body and what the face under the hood must look like.

Enjoy it?

That was the question my son asked me. That was what he said to me, as if I didn't have the same feelings deep down in me that we all have.

Enjoy it?

But, my God, how could anyone *not* enjoy it!

Frank Baker

In the Steam Room

In the steam room the physical body is wrung out of you, and yet you become most painfully aware of it. As you open the door to the dank lobby which leads to the inner door and pause there a moment before approaching this forbidden threshold, you are aware of a sense of the ridiculous, standing there naked, already drenched in your own sweat, your skin flabby and salmon pink, yet asking for more. You wonder what made you pay your money for the ambiguous luxury of a Turkish Bath. You almost turn back from that second door. It is not exactly inviting; and the earlier part of the ceremonial debilitation of your winter-weakened body has been more of an undermining of your whole nervous system than anything else, only serving to emphasise the naked fact that this body which you so cherish is doomed to extinction, whatever manner of ending is to embrace it. No: it is not altogether a pleasant experience, wandering with a neutral linen cloth round your middle (or discarding it if you so wish) from room to room where other unclothed men, mostly middle-aged, sprawl inertly in steel deck chairs, lie out on benches, pad about like neurotic leopards on the hot stone floor, or go to the showers to wash away the grey sweat which has been sucked out of their pores. Not altogether pleasant, but oddly fascinating; and it is this fascination, this unholy masochism which finally drives you towards the second door, and the steam room.

Such thoughts passed in my mind as I faced that door. I was really rather weary of this body of mine by now. Outside, a superb morning of early spring was blooming; one ought to be walking high in the hills or lying in the sun, not stuck in a clammy town and going through this almost obscene performance of trying to restore a body which was well past its prime. About ready for the knacker's yard, that's what I am,

I told myself. And then I pushed open the heavy door and entered the steam room. I was, so to speak, in the condemned cell.

Ferocious whirling clouds of saturating steam made it impossible at first to see anything at all. For a few moments it seemed unbearable and I nearly gave it up. The steam coiled and eddied, lapping at the substance of the solid square room and at once snaking at me as though to macerate me deep in its own essence. The door closed behind me, and I was alone – or thought that I was alone. Because at first I did not see the one other inmate; and even when I did begin to see him, lying belly down on the slatted bench along by one wall, I was still alone. In the steam room, even when there are others present, you are always strangely alone. It is quite impossible to imagine holding a conversation with anyone in there. Even Socrates would have dried up. The silence is unbreakable and any desire to break it is soon quelled by the very weight of the heat which presses down on you and by the sinuous vapours which churn your body and seem to choke out your entire personality. At first I stood near the door, wondering how I was able to breathe at all. Every breath became more of an effort. I bent forward, resting my hands on my knees, and opening my mouth felt the moisture dripping down my body. Then I touched the end of the bench nearest to me, and drew my fingers sharply away. Surely, not even a glutton for punishment could sit on this? The heat seemed intolerable, and yet, in fact, it was tolerable; and after a moment or two I did sit, leaning forward and staring into the vapourised mobility of the room. It was then I saw, on the far side, a tattooed arm hanging down from the bench, and gradually there came into misty view the rest of the other man's body, a large clumsy body with streaks of wet grey hair on its back. I looked at the other benches, but all were empty; there was only this one occupant, and myself. I was glad to feel his presence; I might have been uneasier without him. I tried to lie on my back, but the heat was too much and I felt if I so much as touched the stone wall I would sizzle and shrink to a wet cinder. I half expected to see the electric chair rise up from a trap door in the centre of the room. I saw a block of what looked like iron scooped out to make a neck rest, and similar blocks on the other benches. But I did not dare to touch it, feeling it would be red hot. I began to expect the skin to peel off my body layer by layer, until a raw piece of sinewy meat would be all that was left of me. And then I wondered how much of this it was wise to take; whether a point would be reached when it would be impossible for me to make the supreme effort to reach the door and get out. Sense of time began to waver; had I been in here one minute, two, or even ten? And what was the longset span of time one could endure with safety? An odd pride began to govern the me who seemed to have become a distillation of the body I had brought in, and was now floating around in this gyration of steam – a pride which told me I must not weaken till the other man had gone. But he had not moved so far as I could judge; he was still in the same position. By now I could see the pink soles of his feet, the fat and flattened thighs, the wrinkled buttocks, the hairy back, and the neck crouched in upon the block. How could he bear it? For how long had he been roasting? Probably he was well accustomed to the tyrannies of the Turkish Bath and knew just how much of the steam room he could take, unlike myself who had only used it once before in my life, and then not here. An ardent balneologist, perhaps, given to boasting of his experience. No. I was not going to be beaten by this man; what he could suffer I could suffer. And so, gingerly, with a great deal of trepidation, I offered my back to the wood slats, stretched out my legs, and closed my eyes.

I began then to think of death. At the age of fifty-six you do think of death rather more often than you wish, and it can become disquieting. How would the end come? Always assuming it was an end. . . . Peacefully, with those I loved and who loved me, at my bedside Absolution given, the Host on my tongue, the prayers for the dying distant in my ears? After a stroke, with limbs paralysed, speech distorted, vision impaired? Aided by merciful drugs to lose the pain of a cancer? Alone, struggling to find the way home in a snow drift? Dragged down by the crash of a wave, or hurled broken on a spine of rock? The operative figure in a bedraggled and shameful procession to the gallows? Crushed to a raw bleeding mess by a nose to nose meeting of car and lorry? Falling from the triforium of a cathedral and knowing, in the air, that the flagstones were bound to be splashed and spattered by blood and brains? On the operating table, intestines laid indecently bare, the surgeon cutting through to an enlarged appendix? Drifting to a fog of remorse after a supper of barbiturate and whisky? The roof of the mouth blown to bits by my own gun? Licked by tongues of fire in a top storey hotel room? Dragging the unwanted old body to some rank dustbin with mildewed bread crushed down on top of a mush of tea-leaves soggy in newspaper? By axe, knife, or guile of poisoner? Fallen forward on the lavatory seat in one last defeated effort to evacuate bowels? By interior haemorrhage, the crash of a fist, or broken bottle splintered in the eyes? Slowly, unknowingly, face upwards in a hot bath? Or face downwards in. . . .

There were as many ways of dying as there were of living, and, for all I knew, one of those ways might now have come to me unless I could urge my palpitating body up from this blistering bench towards the door. There were ways of dying which perhaps had never yet been imagined, unimaginable as once had been the searing pains which ate into Hiroshima, and slower than the unfolding of the glory of spring. Slow, too slow; and again – quick, too quick – as when the hands of a murderer both lost and took control, and smothered you head downwards on a wooden bench in the steam room of a Turkish Bath; then, having attacked unseen, left you to rot away in the heat with the door locked, left your carcase to be found hours later and taken from hence to the cold slab of the mortuary, there to suffer the final humiliation of identification.

I forced my stupefied nine stone up from the bench, hideously fascinated by these images (of the ways of dying). It was dreadfully true that I could not with certainty declare that my way out would not be one of these ways. But one way I would not go; not in the steam room, the breath pumped out of me, the lungs bursting. It was possible to avoid that.

Yet, suppose the door would not open? Suppose it had been locked on the other side because of some fault in the mechanism of the heating – and why not? for no one had seen me enter so far as I knew. I remembered that there were few others in the Baths that morning. And now the silence, smothered by the confluence of steam, burst and gurgled in my ears, my throat was rough as sandpaper, my eyes streaked with sweat that seemed the colour of blood. I dragged myself up, sat, and looked down at my legs. They seemed to taper away to slimy strands of seaweed in a dank cave. With all that foetid heat I yet felt cold. I *was* cold; and I was trembling. And I crouched forward as though to begin a race – a race I must make to the door.

I don't exaggerate these fancies; and I don't exaggerate the horrible relish with which I indulged such images and then, with a pent-up sigh of relief, turned to look to the other bench, determined to make some remark, merely in order to have the consolation of a response from my companion. It was an absurd comfort to know he was there, probably dreaming of past pleasures, of lovers who had shared their younger bodies with his, of luxurious meals and rare wines; perhaps, even now, ageing as he was, contemplating richer pastures. If the door were locked, had been locked in error, with his company this could be lightly met. We would both shout, and bang, and bang again, till one of the attendants would come, full of apologies; and I would be able to tell the story of how I was nearly stifled to my end in the steam room and was only saved by a sense of humour which I and the other man found we both shared. Perhaps I would come to know him well, we might even become close friends, and in extreme old age take a delight in recalling the oddity of our first encounter with one another.

I think I tried humour. I think I said 'What don't you turn over and roast the other side' (thinking of the Roman Martyr Lawrence, on the grid-iron). But whatever I said, no answer came. I looked across to the arm hanging down, with the finger tips nearly to the floor. And then I seemed to see something else: a thin red trickle coming slowly from the slats by his head. And there was a smell in the place, a smell of sickly corruption.

I moved a little closer, then suddenly stopped. I realised there were no feet displayed on the bench; no spread-eagled thighs, no buttocks, back, neck, or head. . . .

I was alone in the steam room. The door had not opened since I came in. I had been alone all the time.

Of course the door was not locked, and of course I got out, panting, weakened by the sweat which blinded me, and moving on legs which seemed to have shrivelled to sticks. Falling into one of the deck chairs in the adjoining chamber I tried to admit a sense of relief into me. But it would not come. My heart thumped and stuttered, and I began to want to return to the steam room to certify what I had not seen; what, it appeared, I must have imagined. But too vividly I remembered the coiling scarlet streak of colour on the floor of the colourless engulfing room (like a painting by Francis Bacon); something which had been dribbling from the head of the man I had seen, or thought I had seen, lying face down on the bench. Very good, then: so there had been blood. I had imagined that too. Macabre inventions fester in the mind easily when the body is weakened; and I had come to the Baths in a weak condition, tired and burdened by worries. I had hoped to lose them here. But it had been a mistake – one that I warn others never to make.

But *had* there been another man there? And had I merely never heard him leave as I lay, muted and steamed, on the slats? Or had my desire for company embodied him in my imagination? Either was possible; and now I began to watch the outer door to the steam room, hoping that the other inmate would emerge, if there had been another – and I hoped so; it would be more comfortable if this were so.

Nobody came out. Perhaps three minutes passed. A thin lank man, almost altogether hairless, passed me and went towards the shampoo room; and a short paunchy man with a Jewish face fell into the chair next to mine with a grunt of satisfaction. Both were in their fifties. It was impossible to place them, except that by their lack of muscle, it was clear they did not do heavy manual labour. One might have been a bishop, the other an accountant. It didn't matter; they were only flesh and blood here, and male. I looked at the key of my cubicle, attached to my wrist by its strap, and thought with deliberate pleasure of the soothing rest I would soon have on the cubicle bed, after massage in the shampoo room, the final shower, the cold refreshing dip and the rough invigoration of the outsize bath towel I would take from the attendant's office. But this pleasurable thought was beaten down by renewed apprehension. I could not relax until I had been again to the steam room to find out if there was another man there, or not. And I began to dread that second visit. What would I really find?

There was movement in front of me. I looked up. Somebody was going towards the steam room. I did not see his face as he disappeared into the lobby; but he was a tall cumbersome man and I had seen his back. It was covered with hair. And his arms were tattooed.

Now it is a fact about the male of the species that he grows hair almost anywhere, but not so commonly on his back, between the shoulder blades. It was certain that this man was the one I had seen, or thought I had seen, in there a few moments ago. Was he so soon going in for a further steaming? I wanted to make some remark to the man next to me; but he was snoring, and it is not good etiquette to address a stranger in the Turkish Bath. The word 'Silence' is displayed everywhere, and it is generally respected. So I waited, tensed now, disliking every second. I longed to leave the place and get out into the March sun; the experience had become tainted. But there was something I had to see through. I waited.

In another half minute a second man passed me and also went towards the lobby. I would have recognised him without the scarlet slip he wore on his nakedness; he was one of the attendants, who had taken my ticket and shown me to cubicle number seven: a man of powerful build, with a waxy military moustache, hectic colouring on his cheekbones, a curiously theatrical figure. Ex-R.S.M., perhaps. And he had seemed to me in some way like a Turk – the genius of the Bath – its familiar. A pantomime being, with something of clockwork in his movements; and in his fixed unnatural smile too much show of very white teeth. One of those men who overdo the body business. His chest was tattooed. And his body was taut with muscle, his hands very large and white, yet with red protuberant knuckles.

He opened the door labelled 'steam room' and passed out of view. I closed my eyes, trying to become detached from action which, I told myself, had nothing to do with me. But all the time I was invaded by fears I could not rightly interpret. I tried to pull myself out of the chair to go to the steam room again. But it could not be done. I stayed, eyes closed, seeing again that scarlet rivulet on the stone floor.

Again I was aware of movement. The paunchy man next to me was reading a newspaper, his left hand picking at the softened skin on his left heel. I saw the attendant coming out from the steam room. He walked quickly and silently past me.

I got up suddenly. The whole thing had now become absurd; why should I feel this involvement? Why accept it? Stifling questions, blacking out images, I went back to the showers I had already used when I first came in. I washed myself down from head to foot with soap, feeling like Pontius Pilate after he had given Barabbas to the crowd. Then I went quickly towards the shampoo room. The quicker I got out of this place the better, I said. But I had to have my money's worth; and I greatly looked forward to the massaging of my flaccid body. Perhaps it would erase the discomfiture which had fallen, unbidden, upon me.

I lay on my back on the stone slab in the shampoo room and rested my head on the scooped-out head-rest. I closed my eyes. This was the essential pleasure of the Turkish Bath and I gave myself to it unreservedly. Outwardly as cleansed as by the first lavation after birth, I waited for the therapy of the masseur. He came almost immediately to me, and I did not open my eyes as he began to soap me, then work his strong pliable fingers along my tired and relaxed body. This was altogether an impersonal act, but I permitted myself the words 'marvellous weather.' He made no verbal response. But suddenly his fingers became tensed. For a moment he stopped. I smelt his breath, very close to me. It was slightly sour. I opened my eyes.

I was looking up to the moustached raw face of the attendant who had gone into the steam room. This was a shock, because I had not realised he was also one of the masseurs. But this was not, I knew, the only reason why his ministration came as a shock. When I saw his white teeth and felt his strong fingers working round my ribs I knew that presently he would ask me to turn over. I said something. I said, 'The heat in the steam room was almost more than I could take to-day.' (And I added 'to-day' as if to make it clear that I was a practised devotee of the rituals of the Turkish Bath). To this, he made no comment. With a fixed expression, he only said, 'Turn over, will you please, sir?'

I did. And as his hands began to knead down my back to my loins a sudden rising sickness glotted in my throat. I swallowed. 'Stop a second,' I said. 'I'm not comfortable.' He stopped. I moved my head a little. He asked, 'Ready now, sir?' I murmured yes, I was ready. And now his hands smoothed and slid over my thighs and buttocks, then to my shoulder blades, curving round the nape of my neck. The nausea seeped up in me again. I felt his thumbs. My face was pressed close down to the slab and I could not get into an easy position. I again asked him to stop. But he took no notice; and as I tried to yield my body to his manipulation I felt a horrifying sense of urgency, in him and in myself. From him – an intuition that he was playing for time, that he had to keep me here; in myself, fear which became terror. For what did I know about this man, who now had mastery of my body? What did I know of his past? Of the earlier activities of those hands?

His hands were now pressing at the top of my spine. Then he thumped me lightly, several times. He was hurting me. I tried to assure myself this could not be helped; it would be ridiculous to complain. After all, the man was a professional; he knew precisely how to deal with the pains of middle-age. Perhaps too precisely . . .

My head swam. Into my imagination lurched back the man in the steam room, the blood from the inert head. There was a harsh dryness in my nostrils and throat. Death could come quickly, yet never quickly enough under certain conditions. And death was not so much the enemy as was the manner in which it chose to come, seizing as its means a chance encounter with one whose dreadful deed had so nearly been witnessed. Did he know that I knew? And had there been other victims before the man who, dead or alive, might now be still in the steam room?

I heard someone speaking. 'Jake, I can't get into the steam room. Has something gone wrong with the door?'

The hands were lifted suddenly away. I gasped, and an intense relief filled me. I turned over, pulled myself up.

'I'm sorry, sir.' Jake spoke. Another man was standing beside him, the man who had sat in the chair next to me just now. 'I had to lock it. Something wrong with the regulator – or ventilation blocked, maybe. I was just going to tell the other gents.'

'Damn' nuisance! Reckon we should have a rebate on this – don't you agree?' He had addressed me.

'I used the room,' I said. 'It was – certainly – very hot.'

The other man moved away. I forced myself to look at the attendant. 'Someone went in,' I said, 'just after me.'

'Yes, sir.' His eyes were an unreflecting blue, cold as stones; his words were on one level note. 'I found the gent and saw he wasn't comfortable. So I called him out, and locked up till I can put it right.'

He moved away from me. 'Kindly take a shower, sir,' he said, 'if you intend to use the cold bath.'

I took the shower, and washed away the pressure of his hands. Quickly I plunged my body into the cold pool in the adjoining room. But there was none of the relaxed exhilaration this should have given me. I went back to the long rest room, found a towel and dried myself. I looked at the half dozen or so men who reclined in the arm-chairs. None of them had tattoos on their arms . . .

I heard Jake talking to a colleague. 'I'll slip down to the boiler room and see if I can fix it.' He was pulling on a sweater over his shirt. I saw him go out. A few moments later I left too, glad to find the sun and breathe even the petrol fumes of the city.

Jake did not return, nor was the steam room used. When the door was unlocked an Italian, who had recently opened a restaurant in the city, was found dead, lying face downwards on a bench, his nose blocked with blood. He had been suffocated by pressure on his neck from behind, his face forced down to the slats.

Some days later the body of the attendant was dragged from the river. He had lived alone, a bachelor and ex-seaman, and although no motive for the crime was discovered it was openly surmised that he had been responsible, since it was found that there was no defect in the steam room. It was also found that he and the Italian had been at sea together twenty years earlier.

I shall never know whether I actually saw the body, dead or alive, in that place. I only know that the place smelt of death by violence, that the steam was fouled by coiling wreaths of the lust to kill, and that the hands of the killer pressed down upon my own body. The horror of the minutes I spent under the hands of the attendant never really leaves me.

And when I think, as I often do, of how my end might come, I tell myself I am certain of only one thing: it will not come, at the hand of a masseur, in the steam room of a Turkish Bath.

Edmund Crispin

The Pencil

It was not until the third night that they came for Eliot. He had expected them sooner, and in his cold withdrawn fashion had resented and grown impatient at the delay – for although his tastes had never been luxurious, the squalid bedroom which he had rented in the Clerkenwell boarding-house irked him. Now, listening impassively to the creak of their furtive steps on the staircase, he glanced at his gun-metal wrist-watch and made certain necessary adjustments in the hidden thing that he carried on him. Then quite deliberately he turned his chair so that his back was towards the door.

His belated dive for his revolver, after they had crept up behind him, was convincing enough to draw a gasp from one of them before they pinioned his arms, thrusting a gun-muzzle inexpertly at the back of his neck. Petty crooks, thought Eliot contemptuously as he feigned a struggle. And, 'petty crooks', again, as they searched him and hustled him down to the waiting car. Yet his scorn was not vainglorious. The hard knot into which his career of professional killing had twisted his emotions left no room even for that. Only once had Eliot killed on his own account – and that was when they had nearly caught him. He was not proposing to repeat the mistake.

It was a little after midnight, and the narrow street was deserted. The big car moved off smoothly and quietly. Presently it stopped by an over-grown bomb site, blanched under the moon, and the blinds were drawn down. There they gagged Eliot, and blindfolded him, and tied his hands behind his back. When they found him submissive, their confidence perceptibly grew. Between them and Addison's lot, Eliot reflected as the car moved off again, there was little or nothing to choose: petty crooks all of them, petty warehouse thieves whose spheres of operation had happened to collide. That was why he was here.

He made no attempt to chart mentally the car's progress. He had not been asked to do that – and it was Eliot's great merit as a hireling murderer that he was incurious, never going beyond the letter of his commission. Leaning back against the cushions, he reconsidered his instructions as the car purred on through London, through the night.

'Holden's people are getting to be a nuisance,' Addison had said – Addison the young boss with his swank and his oiled hair and his Hollywood mannerisms. 'But if Holden dies, they'll fall to pieces. That's your job – to kill Holden.'

Eliot had only nodded. Explanations bored him.

'But the trouble is,' Addison had continued, 'that we can't find Holden. We don't know where his hide-out is. That means we've got to fix things so that they lead us to it themselves. My idea is to make you the bait.' He had grinned. 'Poisoned bait.'

With that he had gone on to explain how Eliot was to be represented as a new and shaky recruit to the Addison mob; how it was to be made to seem that Eliot possessed information which Holden would do much to get. Eliot had listened to what concerned him directly and ignored the rest. It was thorough, certainly. They ought to fall for it. . . .

And to judge from his present situation, they had.

It seemed a long drive. The one thing above all others that Holden's men wanted to avoid was the possibility of being followed, the possibility that he, Eliot, might pick up some clue to the hideout's whereabouts. So whatever route they were taking, it certainly wasn't the most direct. At last they arrived. Eliot was pushed upstairs and through a door, was thrust roughly on to a bed. A bed, he thought: good. That meant that Holden had only this one musty-smelling room. All the more chance, therefore, that the job would come off.

He let them hit him a few times before he talked: his boyhood had inured him to physical pain, and he was being well paid. Then he told them what they wanted to know – the story Addison had given him, the story with just enough truth in it to be convincing. Eliot enjoyed the acting: he was good at it. And they were at a disadvantage, of course, in that having left the blindfold on they were unable to watch his eyes.

In any case, Holden – who to judge from his voice was a nervous elderly Cockney – seemed satisfied. And Holden was the only one of them who mattered. . . . Before long, Eliot knew, the police would get Holden and Addison too, and their small-time wrangling for the best cribs would be done with for good and all. That, however, was of no consequence to Eliot. All he had to do was to say his lesson nicely and leave his visiting-card and collect his fee.

And here it was at last: the expected, the inevitable offer. Yes, all right, Eliot said smoothly after a few moments' apparent hesitation, he didn't mind being their stool-pigeon so long as they paid him enough. And they were swallowing that, too, telling him what they wanted him to find out about Addison's plans, sticking a cigarette between his bruised lips and lighting it for him. He almost laughed. They weren't taking off the blindfold, though: they didn't trust him enough for that. They were going to let him go, but in case he decided not to play ball with them, after all, they weren't risking his carrying away any important news about them.

They were going to let him go. This is it, Eliot thought. And delicately, as he lay sprawled on the bed, his fingers moved under the hem of his jacket, so that, hidden from his interrogators, something slim and smooth rolled out on to the bed-clothes.

Fractionally he shifted his position, thrusting the object, to the limit that the rope round his wrists would allow, underneath the pillow. It was a nice little thing, and Eliot was sorry to lose it: in appearance, nothing more than an ordinary propelling pencil, but with a time-fuse inside it and a powerful explosive charge. Addison had told him that it was one of the many innocent-looking objects supplied to French saboteurs during the Occupation, to be deposited on the desks of German military commanders or in other such strategic places. And Eliot, who cared nothing for the war but who was interested in any destructive weapon, had appreciated its potentialities. As a means of murder it was chancy, of course: this one might kill Holden, or on the other hand it might kill a maidservant making up the bed. . . .

But that was none of Eliot's business. He was doing what he had been told to do, and whether it succeeded or not, he was going to collect.

The return drive was a replica of the first. At the bomb site the gag and bonds and blindfold were taken off, and presently Eliot was back at his lodging-house door, in the grey light of early dawn, watching Holden's car drive rapidly away. He mounted to his room, examined his damaged face without resentment in the mirror, on an impulse started to pack. Then, tiring suddenly, he lay down on the bed and slept. The pencil had been set to explode at eight.

It was a quarter to eight when Eliot woke, and the full light had come. Finish packing first, he thought; then see Addison and report. The early editions of the evening papers would tell him, before he caught the boat-train, whether Holden was dead or not. . . .

So he was shifting the pillows, to make more room on the bed for his big shabby suitcase, just as the clock of St John's struck the hour.

And that was when he saw the pencil.

For a second he stared at it in simple incomprehension. Then understanding came. Of course, thought Eliot dully, of course. They weren't risking the secret of their precious hide-out. This is where they brought me to, after driving me round and round the streets. This is where they questioned me – here in my own room. . . .

Panic flooded him. He ran. From the bedside to the door was a distance of no more than three paces.

But the explosion had caught and killed him before his fingers even touched the knob.

Olaf Ruhen

The Dark of the Moon

Tombo's corpse was the first that Eve Maybrick had seen; but it was not that of itself which shocked her so deeply. It was the agony of the face, lined and drawn and strangely swollen under the chin, the eyes wide and staring in an excess of disbelief and terror.

The limbs were not at all discomposed, except as the villagers had put them, with the arms folded, the knees drawn up on the bamboo stretcher, for Tombo had been a long time dying. He had been six days dying, six days in which his death was written; but the gaunt waste that had been Tombo's fine and well-developed body less than a week before shocked her, too.

She turned to her companion while the wailing women watched her from the corners of their weeping eyes, their heads bent over their nursing children, their hands touching the corpse, as many as could manage.

'Well, that's what witchcraft can do,' Sommers said. 'Let's get out of here.'

They passed by the men, weeping a little apart from the women, and covering their greased bodies with the white wood-ashes from the cooking-fires in token of their mourning, and walked over towards the parsonage.

Maybrick was waiting on the veranda, his puny body covered completely in the heat with long khaki trousers and a white shirt done up at collar and cuffs.

The two men looked like members of alien races – Sommers tall, heavy for his height, soldier-straight, unshaved yet unable even to stand without a mental swagger; Maybrick delicate and tender-fleshed, a small man with a high-domed forehead, chubby cheeks; a man personable enough and friendly, but a pale wraith of a messenger to carry the word of God into the wild hills.

Maybrick said, 'Hello, Mr Sommers. We've seen nothing of you for months. You've been seeing about your houseboy – very sad. We did what we could, but it had no effect. A most mysterious thing. The people say witchcraft. Everything is witchcraft. Sanguma, sanguma, they say. I thought I had a convert in your Tombo. I thought he had a true belief, but he died. He's been here a week; and I couldn't do anything. He came last Wednesday.'

'They kill themselves,' Sommers said.

'Yes; well, it's nearly a week ago he came in. I spoke to him, and it was just as if he couldn't hear me. He seemed to be trying to say something, but he couldn't talk. He just got worse and worse, and yesterday he died. I thought you might have come over earlier. I thought you might know what to do.'

'Nothing you can do,' said Sommers. 'These coons kill themselves. I thought Tombo was safe. He's from Aitape, and I thought he wouldn't know the local conventions yet. But they die just the same. Just scare themselves to death.'

Eve shuddered, remembering the vacuous stare that still mirrored the utmost in horror in the dead man's face.

'What was he doing to walk in the dark of the moon?' she asked.

'Do you think that had anything to do with it?' Sommers countered. 'As a matter of fact he was doing something for me. I sent him on a message. I could feel a bit guilty, I suppose. If it were witchcraft he died of.'

'It's the same story they told us when we came,' Eve said. 'They told us no one could walk in the dark of the moon. And on the night of the new moon. They said the sanguma would get anyone who did. They said he would return to the village on the next night but he wouldn't talk. That he would be tired but couldn't sleep. That he would have things to say but couldn't talk. He would be hungry and couldn't eat; and he would seek comfort and couldn't listen. And that he would die within a week. That's exactly what they told us. And that's exactly what Tombo did. It was horrible.'

'Oh, well . . .' Sommers said. But Eve cut in again quickly. Normally she didn't talk much. This was a flood to drown her feelings.

'I saw him the first day when he came in the late afternoon,' she said. 'He was walking like a man in a trance. He didn't take any notice of anything, but once or twice he would walk up to some of the men. They were in groups you know; standing round; and everyone was very silent. He would shake his head from side to side, and his eyes were staring, and he would say nothing. The men would watch him and say nothing.

'And I was watching once when he stooped and put an arm round young Ratu. Ratu is Joanna's child. He's about three. And Ratu screamed and ran. And Tombo stayed there, just the way he was with his arm outstretched, and he looked puzzled and horrified and worn out all at once. He looked terrible. But his body was fit and well. He was drawn about the face, but that corpse doesn't even look like him. And that was only five-six days ago.'

'He was a fine build of a man,' Sommers said: 'I brought him and his wife from Aitape. It's not my area, of course, but I signed him up while I was there. It pays to have a boy from outside. And I thought he would be safe from this sort of thing. He doesn't know the local conventions. But just the same he died of them.'

A maid came out with a tray of tea-things, her roly-poly brown face beaming above a spotless white Mother Hubbard that was pushed most absurdly out of shape by her strong and well-formed breasts.

Eve busied herself with a small cane table, and Sommers watched her. He was a lusty man; and Eve satisfied his eye. Her red-brown hair, her green eyes, pale skin, trim figure were appetisers to his hunger, and her movements were rhythmic, wasting no effort. She caught his look and flushed, but Sommers didn't turn away. There was nothing sensitive about him.

He excused himself after a while, and despite protests from Maybrick, readied himself for the long walk back to his house.

Maybrick sounded over-enthusiastic with his invitations to stay the night, Eve thought. She supported him in them only to the extent that politeness demanded, hoping fervently that Sommers wouldn't accept; and also that his infrequent visits would never coincide with her husband's self-imposed patrols which took him away sometimes for a week or more.

But Maybrick's self-reliance, never firmly founded, had received a jolt from the outbreak of witchcraft in the village which he thought he had made a little stronghold of Methodism. He craved male companionship, sub-consciously seeking a lead he could follow.

Nearby all his tiny flock were paying their pagan homage to the corpse and its destroyer, swept at a blow from their newer religious solace, of which the visible symbol was the great kunai-grass barn of a church that Maybrick had erected: a barn too ambitious for the materials of its making, for it lurched drunkenly now by the side of the village road.

'Come again soon, Mr Sommers,' Maybrick called as his visitor opened the picket-gate. 'And stay a while. The house is yours at any time.'

Sommers waved a farewell with his stick, and set out along the path, striding heel-and-toe like a city hiker in the freshness of early morning.

It was dark when he reached his own house, but the lamps were lit. Tombo's wife, a pretty little dark girl, squatted on the floor by an inner door, dealing a tattered pack of cards to two youngsters. Unlike Maybrick's servants, she wore only a lap-lap; and her bared breasts were pleasant to look at. She got up hurriedly as Sommers came in, and went out to the kitchen. The two boys stayed on the floor.

She came out almost immediately with a bottle of rum, a jug of water and a tray of ice. Sommers mixed himself a drink and took it out on the veranda.

The house lay at the top of his domain, a section of steeply sloping hillside. Sommers had bought it from the natives at the cost of a few years' time and infinite patience in negotiation.

Some day he planned a tea plantation. In the meantime he had only the house, and he supported himself by recruiting-trips among the natives. He had several ways of handling natives. They served him for one thing. And the headman found it politic to keep in with him. So he did a steady trade in labour for the plantations, and made sufficient money for his wants.

The new plantation could wait. It needed capital for drying-sheds and packaging and shipping equipment; but some day it would be a winner.

He watched the hillside under the young moon, deliberately turning his thoughts towards tea. But in spite of himself they turned towards the missionary's wife.

'Beba,' he called; and a voice answered from the two huts clustered against the thin mountain bush at the edge of the clearing.

'Yes, master. Coming, master.'

The boy hurried to the veranda.

'Come here,' Sommers said. And waited till the boy mounted the steps and stood behind his chair.

'You've got a lot of friends along at the village, Beba,' Sommers said, speaking a fluent pidgin in the fast native fashion. 'Suppose you waited for something you wanted to know. Now a friend with a flute or a drum could let you know – not a big drum that would tell everyone. A little drum; that no one else would know the meaning of. Right?'

'Yes, master,' Beba said.

'Well, suppose the missionary goes away for a walkabout – a long walkabout, two, three days, a week; I'd like to know. You must tell me, without fail. But don't stay at the village yourself – I want you here. You find a friend in the village to let me know. Understand?'

'Yes, master.'

'Now this isn't a thing for talking about. I want no talk in the village. And I want no talk here. Especially no talk to Kardu. Not now or after. Otherwise . . .' He lifted up his fist in front of his face and clenched it.

Beba just said: 'Yes, master,' again, in a matter-of-fact way, and waited.
'That's all,' said Sommers. 'Now get.'

He watched Beba back to his hut and raised his voice again.
'Kardu.'

After a moment the little dark girl was at his side, silently.

He looked at her keenly. 'You're still playing "Lucky"?'

'Yes, master.'

'Get me some more ice, and then get to bed. I'll be in when the moon goes down.'

Kardu turned without a word, and without a change of expression. Sommers knew that he would find her lying awake on the floor beneath his bed, waiting for his next call. She was very amenable, and she put on none of the airs most native girls gave themselves when they were elevated to the position of a white man's mistress.

But for the first time since he had stolen her from his houseboy he could find no interest in Kardu that night. She had intrigued him in the past to the point where he had sent Tombo off on a fruitless errand – as it happened, to his death – but that part of it was purely accidental. And he had been firm about allowing that death to play no part at all in his continuing relations with the girl.

Quite suddenly now, within a week, he had lost all interest in her. It was the white woman. He wanted her; and he would do a lot to get her.

Beba brought him no message in the days that followed, and his desire was growing mightily. Sommers called a couple of times at the village, and fancied he was making progress. Maybrick liked him – that was obvious. And Eve seemed to be glad of his additional company.

He thought the time to strike was soon. In the meantime his temper was shortening, and the little Kardu took the brunt of it uncomplainingly.

It was three weeks before he found Beba by his chair one night. He had heard nothing. No sounds of drums or flute. But Beba was there.

'Master?'

'What it is?'

'The drums talked, master. The parson has gone. He has gone up the valley and will be gone tomorrow and the next day. Perhaps half a day more; perhaps not.'

'Right,' said Sommers. 'Now get out.'

He got up quickly and went into the house. He picked up his revolver-belt and a flashlight; and came out strapping the belt round his waist. Beba was still by the steps.

'Master?'

'Something else?'

'Master, the moon is dark again. This is the first night of the dark of the moon.'

It was unexpected, and Sommers hesitated. But only for a moment.

'I've got eyes in my head,' he said. 'Now go, if you haven't anything else to say.'

Beba walked across to the huts without a word, and Sommers cut down into the track and plunged into the thick gloom of the bush. He knew the trail, but he used the flashlight fairly constantly. He was ten minutes from the clearing where the house stood when he heard two clear notes of a flute. The sound seemed to come from the clearing; and from somewhere it was answered. Sommers stood stock-still a moment, unreasonably angry that anyone should keep a check on his movements – if the two notes represented a message, as seemed likely. He hadn't heard any flute before, and there must have been a purpose in the call and the answer. But he had no desire to retrace his steps up the steep hill, and after a moment he went on.

When he got down to creek-level and crossed the swingbridge the bush changed character. Taro grew above the bank; and in the air was the faint sweet scent of gora-gora, the ginger-lily, which stood in clumps eight feet high. The bush was more tangled and diverse, broken here and there by clumps of the giant bamboo, now whispering in the light breeze. The creepers reached down into the water of the creek, and there were stirrings amongst the leaves. The bush grew darker, and Sommers kept his flashlight on constantly; more acutely conscious with every moment of the noises of the night.

But there's no noise in the bush that says, 'Master'.

It was soft and sibilant. But it was an order, not a supplication. Sommers swung in his tracks, and played the flashlight along the way he had come. His revolver had leapt to his hand. He slipped the safety-catch off and fingered the trigger, feeling comfort in it; almost fondling it, as a baby will fondle fur.

Now the sound was ahead of him. Soft yet sharp. And in the same . . . or in another voice? He swung again, and this time he fancied he saw the movement of a shadow and fired immediately. The night noises ceased, and to the right of him a voice said, 'Master'.

He started to walk on down the track, and a blunt-headed arrow took the flashlight from his hand. He yelled and swung and shot, then scrambled frantically for the flashlight.

And as he picked it up a voice in front of him said, 'Master'.

He fired three shots quickly then. But it must have been half an hour before he fired the last. He was at screaming-pitch then.

And all that answered him was the same whisper, 'Master'. But as the last shot belted into a tree-trunk he went down under a rush of soft brown bodies.

He went down and he went out. He could not have been out for long:
but when he came to he was in a strange clearing. It did not lie on the
track, and he had never seen it before.

There was a small fire burning in the clearing, and there were men
about him, and some carried torches of the fronds of coconut-palms.
What men they were he didn't know. They wore painted bark-masks
over their faces, and little else. They were armed and ornamented, and
they were silent.

He himself was naked, and unmarked. There was not a stitch of his
clothes anywhere; nor did anyone have his revolver or his flashlight, so
far as he could see.

He didn't take much stock of his situation, because he was in an
excess of terror and because the moment that his eyes opened the voices
began.

This time they said, 'Dance, master'.

They were the same voices, and they came at him the same way as
they had in the dark, now from this side of the circle, now from that.
His arms were still bound, and he hesitated.

An arrow thudded into the ground by his foot, and from the other
side of the circle a voice said, 'Dance, master'.

He lifted his foot, and danced in the native way, but shuffling. And
the natives danced; and when he hesitated and slowed down they said,
'Dance, master', but otherwise they were silent. There was a throbbing
that he thought was drums, but it seemed more a vibration than a sound.
And he danced – and danced.

In the dance from time to time they practised indignities on him, of
several kinds. But he had lost all cohesion in his mind. He couldn't even
promise revenge to himself because somehow he knew there would be
no revenge.

The indignities and the upsurge of his feelings tired him, and he felt
consciousness leaving him as he toppled. But when he came back to life
again he was on his feet. And his feet were dancing. Some time later he
discovered that his arms were not bound.

The tempo of the dance was terrific. He was caught up in it. But from
time to time great waves of blackness seemed to engulf him, sometimes
not quite, and sometimes utterly.

It was from one of these blackouts that he awoke to find himself in
the village street. There was no dance, no drumbeat. He was staggering
like a man dying of thirst in a desert, or as such a man is pictured, and
it was a dead and unreal world.

He couldn't even think it was the village. The thing had the qualities
of a nightmare. There was no sound at all, a complete and utter absence
of sound. There was sight, unreal vision which seemed to have no depth.

But there was no sound.

The boys were standing in groups, looking at him; and they looked as though they, too, were horrified.

He went up to the nearest group to speak to them. He did speak, but his tongue was motionless in his mouth, and no sound came. He put his hand on the nearest man's chest, and it was warm and living. The man was shrinking back and he slapped the chest hard, but the slap gave no sound.

He wandered from one group to another. He stopped still and looked at himself. He was naked still. His feet were bleeding, not badly. His hands and wrists and shoulders and his belly were all scratched, and here and there bleeding slightly. These were all wounds from the creepers in the bush. Except for them he had no mark on him.

Yet he was a living pain: dead-tired and racked with pain. He was not sure that he could remember the village. He was not sure that he was in it; or that it was not nightmare. He couldn't really remember himself: who he was, or what he did. He could remember there was something he wanted in this silent village, and he staggered on, aimlessly, in circles.

Then he saw the church, reeling on its piles by the flower-bordered road, and it reminded him of something, and he went inside.

It was there that Eve Maybrick found him: a zombie, another Tombo, one of the walking dead.

'Six days,' she thought. 'I've got six days.'

Not once did it occur to her that that was an abnegation of her faith. She sent a messenger after Maybrick; but he would be already on his return by the time the messenger reached him. And she sent another down the valley to the settlement; but that was a week's walk.

Maybrick came back in two more days.

As it happened, Sommers didn't have six days. He had little more than three. After Maybrick came back he prayed for Sommers. That was all he could do. And on the following night at midnight Sommers died.

The Maybricks are good religious people who hold to their faith, but at their mission they do not walk about in the dark of the moon. And they avoid the subject of witchcraft.

For in all the three days Sommers didn't speak. So he couldn't tell them of the little brown men in the masks who ruled the dark nights.

And not even he knew of the sago spines – the two-inch needles administered mercifully under the anaesthetic of exhaustion. He was buried with them – two in his ears that had pierced his eardrums so he couldn't hear; two through the base of his tongue so he couldn't talk; and two under the scratched skin of his belly so that he would die within a week.

William Brittain

Falling Object

Edmund Plummer stood on the roof of the Talmadge Building and peered over the parapet. He could see the flat stainless-steel-and-glass side of the building seeming to become smaller as his gaze travelled downwards to the street twenty stories below. There were no setbacks, no architectural gewgaws to break the edifice's severe rectangular lines; it was a triumph of modern efficiency, providing the maximum of office space with the minimum of materials.

But Plummer thought he had discovered something unusual about the building. If true it might make necessary a revision of his original set of equations. He raised his bifocal glasses and bent forward to peer once again through the telescope of the surveyor's transit he had set up on the roof. Then he checked the measurement gauges on the instrument and jotted some figures into a notebook in neat precise columns.

There could be no question about it. Instead of rising at a precise right angle from the pavement below, the sides of the Talmadge Building leaned to the south almost three inches – two and seven-eighths inches, to be exact.

Edmund Plummer wished to be exact.

He looked at his watch, startled that his time on the roof had passed so quickly. Down below, on the fourteenth floor, men and women would be leaving their offices to go home. Then it would be Plummer's job to sweep and mop and carry away the mountainous pile of wastepaper and other debris created each day in order to keep a few of the wheels in that remarkable machine called American Business running properly.

Plummer neither liked nor disliked his job as a cleaning man. He had felt the same way about his previous job as a dishwasher and the one before that when he went from door to door handing out advertising leaflets for a chain of department stores. They were ways to keep alive, that was all. And even in these menial occupations, sooner or later he would have to quit and move on. Eventually, no matter where he was or what he did, someone would recognise him as the man whom the law had freed but whom everyone knew to be a—

Plummer tried to keep the word out of his mind. But it was impossible. Besides, it was all down in the official government records, which were now probably yellowing and gathering dust in a warehouse somewhere.

He managed to smile to himself, wondering what the secretaries on the fourteenth floor, who were so pleasant and so condescending to him, would think if they ever found out that the odd little man who emptied their ashtrays and dusted their desks and smiled vacantly at them had received his Ph.D. in physics at the age of twenty-three. Would they still giggle and call him 'Plumsy' if they became aware that during the fall of 1942 and the spring of '43, at the height of World War II, he had been considered potentially more valuable to the Allies than a squadron of bombers?

And what would their reaction be if they discovered that their genial janitor had once stood in the dock of justice accused of being a traitor?

There was nothing thrilling or sensational about what had happened to Plummer; the whole grubby business had been a tragedy of errors from beginning to end. During October of 1942 – at about the time that British bombers were stepping up their incessant pounding of the German industrial cities – Plummer was hard at work on a device of his own invention. It was an improved bombsight.

As any bomber pilot of that time could testify, the most dangerous part of a mission was the 'bombing run' – the approach to the target. At that point the plane had to be kept straight and level for a period of approximately thirty seconds, allowing the bombardier to adjust his sight, make the correct allowances for speed, direction, and altitude, then release his bombs. During that thirty-second period the plane was a sitting duck at the not-so-tender mercies of both the cruelly accurate anti-aircraft batteries on the ground and the best fliers the German Luftwaffe could put into the air. Men who have been through it are willing to swear that the thirty seconds over the target really lasted thirty years.

Plummer's new bombsight was designed to reduce that period of time by a full seven seconds. Seven seconds – the entire R.A.F. would have been willing to sell its collective soul to obtain seven seconds of grace on their flights through the shrapnel-filled hell.

But the device was never to reach the men who so desperately needed it.

Near the end of October 1942 certain 'bugs' started cropping up in the new bombsight. On several occasions, problems that had seemed near solution proved to be more complicated than was first supposed, forcing not only Plummer but his entire staff to spend valuable time readjusting their theories to fit cold, hard, unyielding facts.

At about the same time Plummer received a visitor at his small apartment near the Baltimore research centre. The visitor gave his name as Norman Gant. He had heard of Plummer's work on the bombsight, and he wondered if he might discuss – no, of course not. The government would be keeping close watch on the progress of such an important device. Still, Gant explained, there were those who were interested in seeing that such an invention did not come into use *too* soon. Perhaps certain problems that Plummer was having might delay final production for a year, maybe longer. Those whom Gant represented would be willing to pay a huge sum for such delay.

Plummer had thrown the man out of the apartment.

But unfortunately he had neglected to report the offer of a bribe. And even more unfortunately the progress on the bombsight came almost to a halt. First, the optical system had to be scrapped; then the unit refused to function reliably at any altitude above 100 feet; and the focusing gauge tended to jam in wet weather. Everything that could possibly go wrong seemed to do so.

And in April of the following year, during a raid on an apartment suspected of harbouring German nationals, the man who called himself Gant was picked up by the F.B.I. He was quickly identified as Josef Schissel, a former guard at one of the Vernichtungslager – the Nazi extermination camps. Having spent several years in the United States as a youth, Schissel spoke English without an accent, and in addition he was familiar with American slang. The Abwehr, the German Intelligence Bureau, had received word of the device on which Plummer was working, and Schissel had been smuggled into the United States by way of Mexico for the sole purpose of rendering the new bombsight project ineffectual. This Schissel proceeded to do – simply by swearing that the young scientist had indeed accepted money from him to slow down work on the bombsight. Schissel's confession, coupled with the almost total lack of progress on the device itself, was enough to make the authorities gravely suspicious that Plummer had sold out his country.

At the ensuing trial Plummer was pitifully unable to refute the circumstantial evidence against him. Why, it was asked, hadn't he reported his meeting with Schissel immediately? His answer – that he considered the man just another anti-war crackpot – was the object of derisive laughter by the prosecuting attorney. Plummer pointed out that his standard of living hadn't changed a bit since the supposed pay-off. The prosecution, however, took the position that a man as intelligent as Plummer would be far too clever to begin spending the money immediately. Secret Swiss bank accounts were hinted at. And yet the government could produce no real evidence of anything more serious than poor judgment. Plummer might even have convinced everyone of his innocence – except for Schissel's testimony.

When the small clean-shaven German was placed on the witness stand he requested and was granted the privilege of making a statement to the court. Everyone present expected him to scream curses at the government which was holding him captive. The judge held his gavel ready to hammer down any such attempt.

Instead, Schissel began by thanking the court as well as his captors for the extreme courtesy they had shown to him, an enemy agent. He commended the judge for his fairness. Under the circumstances, Schissel went on, he was sorry to have placed the judge in such a difficult position. He realised that the judge would find it necessary to declare Plummer innocent because of the value of his brain to the Allies.

'You must find him innocent because the government forces you to do so,' Schissel concluded in a low voice. 'It is a pity that the law must yield to expediency.' Stretching out his hand, Schissel pointed dramatically at Plummer. 'Nevertheless, that man is a traitor to his country.'

It may have been that Judge Randall Barth felt compelled to prove that in his courtroom the law still reigned supreme; perhaps Schissel's humble manner and his obvious willingness to take the entire punishment on his own shoulders evoked some sympathetic vibration in the judicial conscience. Whatever the reason, the fact remains that the enemy agent's words had an astounding effect. 'That agent really got under Judge Barth's skin,' one reporter was overheard to tell another. 'The old man's liable to set Schissel free and hang Plummer instead.'

In his final summation Judge Barth left no doubt that he considered Plummer to be the lowest form of human scum. He stated that he would personally see to it that the complete testimony of the trial was made available to any prospective employer foolish enough even to consider giving employment to such a person. Nevertheless, on the basis of the evidence alone—

Forcing each word through teeth clenched in anger the judge pronounced the accused not guilty. The reporters rushed from the building to file their stories.

In the court of law Plummer was innocent. But public opinion does not operate by rules of evidence. In a world of defence contracts and top-secret information Plummer found himself an outcast. His fiancée returned his ring; there was no note attached. He learned that while a rising young physicist attracts friends as honey attracts bees, a suspected traitor attracts only curses and looks of scorn and disgust. The two years in which he went without work wiped out his small savings. And then began the series of pointless, dead-end, menial jobs. He didn't live; he merely existed from day to day.

Then one morning in 1956 he found a cast-off newspaper on a park bench. He was about to pass it by when his eye was attracted by a small headline containing a familiar name. After thirteen years of imprisonment, the article stated, Josef Schissel, a spy for the Nazis during World War II, was to be released.

Schissel would be free. And Plummer resolved to kill him.

There followed for Plummer several years of keeping painstaking records on Schissel's whereabouts. He was returned to Germany. There he was influential in the exposure of three major Nazi war criminals. A general, grateful for Schissel's assistance in rounding up the wanted men, pulled some political strings to obtain a visa to enable the former spy to revisit the United States. The visa was twice renewed. Finally, in 1965, Schissel was granted permission to live permanently in the United States. Three years later he bought a small delicatessen only a couple of blocks from the Talmadge Building. Within a few months word of his delicious coffee and generously large slices of rich pastries had been passed to several of the secretaries in the building, and Schissel was commissioned to make daily deliveries for the morning coffee breaks.

It was then that Plummer applied for a job in the Talmadge Building as a janitor. He was hired.

At that time Plummer had no idea which method he would use to kill Schissel. It was enough to have finally located the man who had ruined his life.

During his first day on the job Plummer found out that the coffee-break items were delivered by Schissel himself; the Talmadge Building provided the major part of his income, and he did not trust any of his helpers to make the deliveries properly. But try as he might, for the first week on the job, Plummer could not catch sight of his intended victim. He began to wonder what changes twenty-five years had made in Schissel's appearance.

During the second week Plummer was sent to the roof of the building to clean away a pile of debris left by some workmen. It was hard work, and when he finally finished, he leaned against the parapet, enjoying the cooling breeze which never reached the sidewalk far below. He saw a panel truck pull up to the curb in the alley next to the building. A man wearing a white apron got out. From where Plummer was standing, the figure was curiously foreshortened. The man, who from that distance resembled a tiny white insect, opened the rear of the truck, took out a small wheeled cart, and began to fill it with coffee urns and trays wrapped in white paper. Then the man wheeled the cart around the corner to the building's front entrance. There the doorman greeted him cordially and even opened the door for him. It was several seconds after the man had entered that Plummer realised who he must be.

Schissel! There below him in the street, the man whose lies had made Plummer's existence a living hell was calmly making his daily delivery. Heart pounding furiously, Plummer raced down the stairs from the roof. He ran to the door of the service elevator and was about to punch the button when he stopped. As he withdrew his hand he smiled grimly.

He knew now how Schissel would die.

A few days later, from his meagre savings, Plummer purchased a small but heavy steel strongbox. By going without lunches for several weeks he saved enough money to buy a second-hand surveyor's transit, complete with tripod, from the pawnshop around the corner from the shabby room in which he lived. The following Sunday he carried the transit to several points within two blocks of the Talmadge Building. From each of these spots the entire height of the structure was visible, and at each he took readings with his transit.

Then Plummer began his calculations. They were comparatively simple for a man who had once designed a bombsight. The Talmadge Building was 242 feet high. Five feet, eight inches – he guessed that to be Schissel's height – would have to be subtracted from that, making the distance $236\frac{1}{3}$ feet. Weight, of course, was not important. It was the mass that counted, barring the negligible effect of the air itself. Wind needed to be taken into consideration, so he would choose a calm day. A rate of acceleration of 32.2 feet per second (approximately) meant a distance of 16 feet the first second (approximately) and – no! Approximations were not good enough. The figures had to be exact. But Plummer was trained to be exact.

And he knew that a heavy strongbox, dropped from the roof of the Talmadge Building at precisely the correct instant, would smash into the head of Josef Schissel on the sidewalk below with the velocity of a cannonball. Even if it were to hit only Schissel's shoulder or back it would most certainly kill him.

There was one further aspect of the problem that Plummer found intriguing. Schissel certainly wasn't going to just stand there and wait for the box to hit him. No, Schissel would be moving too. But this did not disturb Plummer. With the exception of the fact that the target as well as the 'bomb' was in motion, these were the same calculations that bombardiers had performed over enemy factories. It was merely necessary to see that the target and the bomb collided at the same place at the same time.

From one of the secretaries on the fourteenth floor Plummer borrowed a stop watch. Each day, just before the coffee break, he went to the roof and observed Schissel unloading his trays and urns, wheeling them around the corner of the building, and entering through the front door. The time it took Schissel to push the cart from his truck to the front entrance varied only because he was not always able to park his truck in the same place. Plummer began measuring the time from the moment Schissel passed a fire hydrant and he noted that the man could be depended on not to change his pace. His movements were as regular as clockwork.

The strongbox would be released to hit Schissel's head just as the man reached the corner of the building, since at that spot he cut the corner sharply, coming within two feet of the side of the building.

As a final step in his preparations Plummer managed 'accidentally' to spill a blob of white paint on the sidewalk several yards down the alley from the corner. The spot had been chosen after several days of observation and calculations. When Schissel reached the blob of paint, the box would be dropped; Schissel would continue to walk ahead, and at the precise moment he arrived at the corner, the plummeting heavy metal box would have reached a point five feet, six inches, above the pavement. Finis.

And now Plummer had discovered that the Talmadge Building leaned two and seven-eighths inches to the south.

For a moment he wondered if it would be necessary to revise his entire plan. Then he shook his head. No, there was really no need for it. He would merely hold the box a bit farther out from the parapet before dropping it. A larger object than the box would, of course, be desirable in reducing the margin for error, but something heavy and yet small enough to be smuggled up to the roof was essential. The strongbox would do admirably. Besides, Plummer had another use for it.

Before dropping it on Schissel's head Plummer planned to fill the box with all the newspaper clippings he had saved concerning the German so the world might fully understand the reasons why he had to die.

The following day was rainy. The day after that a high wind sprang up early in the morning, and the same evening a grey mass of fog settled in, remaining for forty-eight hours. Plummer wondered if he would ever be able to put his murder plan into operation.

Friday morning arrived, sunny and cool and without a breath of wind. Looking through the window of his dingy room, Plummer smiled and hummed a happy tune to himself. It was a perfect day for walking with a girl in the park, for lying on the grass and watching the sky, for taking a trip to the country – and for murder.

Now that the time had come to carry out his plan, Plummer found himself curiously at ease. He whistled gaily at his image in the shaving mirror. He decided to skip breakfast, using the time instead to thumb through his thick packet of newspaper clippings for a last time. The earliest ones, dated April 1943, he handled gingerly. They were brittle with age but still quite readable. SUSPECT GOVERNMENT SCIENTIST OF SELL-OUT read the one on the top of the pile.

Replacing the clippings in their envelope, he crammed it into a jacket pocket and left the room. As he reached the sidewalk he remembered that he had forgotten to lock the door. He considered going back and then decided against it. There was nothing he possessed that was worth stealing.

He was six minutes late getting to work. In the basement of the Talmadge Building he went to his locker and changed into his blue coveralls, his mind on the steel strongbox waiting on a shelf of the broom closet on the fourteenth floor.

At 9.40 Plummer was on a stepladder, busily polishing the globes of the lights in a hallway on the fourteenth floor. Only twenty more minutes, he thought to himself. At ten o'clock. Then I'll put away the ladder in the closet, take the box, and go to the roof. Schissel will drive his truck up to the curb at 10.15, just as he always does. But he'll never make it to the front door. All these years I've spent waiting for this chance, and now there's just a few more minutes to—

'Plummer?'

It was Ed Malenski, who worked on the floor above. He must have come down the stairs; Plummer hadn't seen anyone get out of the service elevator. 'Yeah, Ed,' he answered.

'Dandridge wants to see you in his office right away. He couldn't reach you on the phone, so he called me and told me to let you know.'

Jerome Dandridge was the head of the maintenance department of the Talmadge Building. Plummer supposed he was going to be reprimanded for being late. He didn't mind. Just as long as it didn't take too long. He rode the service elevator to the basement, got out, and knocked softly on the door of Dandridge's office.

'Come in.' Plummer opened the door. Dandridge was sitting at his desk, and another man, conservatively dressed, stood beside him. The second man was a stranger to Plummer, and Dandridge made no attempt to introduce him.

'Mr Dandridge, I'm sorry about being late, but—'

'That's not why I wanted to see you,' Dandridge rumbled. 'How long you been with us, Plummer?'

'About four months.'

'And before that? What did you do before that?'

'Dishwasher – other things,' Plummer replied. 'It's all in my application. Why?'

Without answering, Dandridge turned to the other man and picked up a paper from his desk. 'Says here he never completed high school,' he muttered. 'What d'ya think, Mr Ross?'

'Hard to tell,' was the answer. 'A long time has gone by since then. People change.'

The man called Ross turned to Plummer. He reached into a pocket and pulled out a leather folder. 'Mr Plummer,' he began, 'I'm Joseph Ross. I'm with the F.B.I., and—'

Plummer was only half listening. Something had fallen from Ross's pocket when the agent had produced his identification. It was a small yellowed piece of paper with print on it. Automatically Plummer bent down to pick it up. His eyes widened. The black print screamed at him from the newspaper clipping.

SUSPECT GOVERNMENT SCIENTIST OF SELL-OUT.

They knew who he was! It wasn't fair. Not today. Not after all these weeks of planning.

'No! Not now!' he shouted. Running to the office door he dashed through it, slamming it behind him. Across the hall was the service elevator, its doors open. He scurried inside and punched the button for the top floor. As the doors slid shut he had just time to see Ross and Dandridge burst out of the office in a vain attempt to halt the elevator.

The car rose swiftly to the twentieth floor. Plummer stepped into the corridor and looked around. It was empty. They were probably waiting in the basement for the indicator to show which floor he had stopped at. He had only a few seconds before—

Behind him the elevator doors closed and he could hear the car starting downwards.

He ran to the stairway leading to the roof and pounded up the steps. Opening the thick door with his pass key, he moved out into the sunlight. Inserting the key into the outer lock, he turned it hard in the wrong direction. The key snapped off. Perhaps that would be enough to jam the lock. To make doubly sure he inserted some small pieces of wood at the edges of the door, forcing them into place with the heel of his hand.

How much time? He glanced at his watch. Three minutes, ten seconds, before Schissel was scheduled to arrive. Please, please let the door to the roof hold for a few minutes. Just until he had enough time to drop—

The steel box! He had forgotten to take the box. It was still on the fourteenth floor, in the broom closet.

There had to be something else. A brick. That was it, a brick. He scanned the entire roof.

There was nothing but tiny scraps of wood which the slightest movement of air would blow off course. Even if they were to fall perfectly straight, Schissel would hardly feel them when they struck. He had to find something heavy.

There was nothing.

Plummer heard a pounding on the door to the roof. The lock rattled, but the thick iron door remained closed. 'Plummer! Open up!' called a muffled voice.

Far below he could see the sunlight glinting off the top of a panel truck as it moved up the alley at the side of the building. A tiny ant-like figure got out and opened the rear doors. The cart was piled high with trays. The coffee urns were put into place.

And in that instant Plummer found the weapon that would kill Schissel. It was one he should have thought of long ago – so much better than the strongbox. He removed the packet of clippings from his pocket and grasped them tightly in his hand.

Behind Plummer, Ross and Dandridge had managed to open the door a scant two inches before a wooden wedge at its base again jammed it. 'Plummer, listen!' shouted Ross through the opening. 'The army just located a report that Schissel sent to his superiors back in '43. That's why I'm here. It only landed on my desk two days ago and—'

But Plummer, deep in concentration, did not hear. Down below, Josef Schissel closed the doors of his truck and gripped the handle of his cart. He took a step forward – two – three –

'Open up, Plummer. The government's willing to do anything in its power to make amends. You're cleared! You're inno—'

The front wheels of Schissel's cart glided over a white paint stain on the sidewalk. The rear wheels followed. And then Schissel's right foot came down on the white spot.

With the soles of his heavy work shoes poised on the parapet $236\frac{1}{2}$ feet above Schissel's head, Edmund Plummer folded his arms tightly across his chest, smiled through the tears streaming down his cheeks, and stepped off the parapet and out into space.

Patricia Highsmith

The Terrapin

Victor heard the elevator door open, his mother's quick footsteps in the hall, and he flipped his book shut. He shoved it under the sofa pillow out of sight, and winced as he heard it slip between sofa and wall and fall to the floor with a thud. Her key was in the lock.

'Hello, Vee-ector-r!' she cried, raising one arm in the air. Her other arm circled a big brown paper bag, her hand held a cluster of little bags. 'I have been to my publisher and to the market and also to the fish market,' she told him. 'Why aren't you out playing? It's a lovely, lovely day!'

'I was out,' he said. 'For a little while. I got cold.'

'Ugh!' She was unloading the grocery bag in the tiny kitchen off the foyer. 'You are seeck, you know that? In the month of October, you are cold? I see all kinds of children playing on the sidewalk. Even, I think, that boy you like. What's his name?'

'I don't know,' Victor said. His mother wasn't really listening, anyway. He pushed his hands into the pockets of his short, too small shorts, making them tighter than ever, and walked aimlessly around the living-room, looking down at his heavy, scuffed shoes. At least his mother had to buy him shoes that fit him, and he rather liked these shoes, because they had the thickest soles of any he had ever owned, and they had heavy toes that rose up a little, like mountain climbers' shoes. Victor paused at the window and looked straight out at a toast-coloured apartment building across Third Avenue. He and his mother lived on the eighteenth floor, next to the top floor where the penthouses were. The building across the street was even taller than this one. Victor had liked their Riverside Drive apartment better. He had liked the school he had gone to there better. Here they laughed at his clothes. In the other school,

599

they had finally got tired of laughing at them.

'You don't want to go out?' asked his mother, coming into the living-room, wiping her hands briskly on a paper bag. She sniffed her palms. 'Ugh! That stee-enk!'

'No, Mama,' Victor said patiently.

'Today is Saturday.'

'I know.'

'Can you say the days of the week?'

'Of course.'

'Say them.'

'I don't want to say them. I know them.' His eyes began to sting around the edges with tears. 'I've known them for years. Years and years. Kids five years old can say the days of the week.'

But his mother was not listening. She was bending over the drawing-table in the corner of the room. She had worked late on something last night. On his sofa bed in the opposite corner of the room, Victor had not been able to sleep until two in the morning, when his mother had gone to bed on the studio couch.

'Come here, Veector. Did you see this?'

Victor came on dragging feet, hands still in his pockets. No, he hadn't even glanced at her drawing-board this morning, hadn't wanted to.

'This is Pedro, the little donkey. I invented him last night. What do you think? And this is Miguel, the little Mexican boy who rides him. They ride and ride all over Mexico, and Miguel thinks they are lost, but Pedro knows the way home all the time, and . . .'

Victor did not listen. He deliberately shut his ears in a way he had learned to do from many years of practice, but boredom, frustration – he knew the word frustration, had read all about it – clamped his shoulders, weighed like a stone in his body, pressed hatred and tears up to his eyes, as if a volcano were churning in him. He had hoped his mother might take a hint from his saying that he was cold in his silly short shorts. He had hoped his mother might remember what he had told her, that the fellow he had wanted to get acquainted with downstairs, a fellow who looked about his own age, eleven, had laughed at his short pants on Monday afternoon. *They make you wear your kid brother's pants or something?* Victor had drifted away, mortified. What if the fellow knew he didn't even own any longer pants, not even a pair of knickers, much less *long* pants, even blue jeans! His mother, for some cock-eyed reason, wanted him to look 'French', and made him wear short shorts and stockings that came to just below his knees, and dopey shirts with round collars. His mother wanted him to stay about six years old, for ever, all his life. She liked to test out her drawings on him. *Veector is my sounding board*, she sometimes said to her friends. *I show my drawings to Veector and I know if children will like them.* Often Victor said he liked stories that he did not like, or drawings that he was indifferent to, because he felt sorry for his mother and because it put her in a better mood if he said he liked them. He was quite tired now of children's book illustrations, if he had ever in his life liked them – he really couldn't remember – and now he had two favourites: Howard Pyle's illustrations in some of Robert Louis Stevenson's books and Cruikshank's in Dickens. It was too bad, Victor thought, that he was absolutely the last person of whom his mother should have asked an opinion, because he simply *hated* children's illustrations. And it was a wonder his mother didn't see this, because she hadn't sold any illustrations for books for years and years, not since *Wimple-Dimple,* a book whose jacket was all torn and turning yellow now from age, which sat in the centre of the bookshelf in a little cleared spot, propped up against the back of the bookcase so everyone could see it. Victor had been seven years old when that book was printed. His mother liked to tell people and remind him, too, that he had told her what he wanted to see her draw, had watched her make every drawing, had shown his opinion by laughing or not, and that she had been absolutely guided by him. Victor doubted this very much, because first of all the story was somebody else's and had been written before his mother did the drawings, and her drawings had had to follow the story, naturally. Since then, his mother had done only a few illustrations now and then for magazines for children, how to make paper pumpkins and black paper cats for Hallowe'en and things like that, though she took her portfolio around to publishers all the time. Their income came from his father, who was a wealthy businessman in France, an exporter of perfumes. His mother said he was very wealthy and very handsome. But he had married again, he never wrote, and Victor had no interest in him, didn't even care if he never saw a picture of him, and he never had. His father was French with some Polish, and his mother was Hungarian with some French. The word Hungarian made Victor think of gypsies, but when he had asked his mother once, she had said emphatically that she hadn't any gypsy blood, and she had been annoyed that Victor brought the question up.

And now she was sounding him out again, poking him in the ribs to make him wake up, as she repeated:

'Listen to me! Which do you like better, Veector? "In all Mexico there was no bur-r-ro as wise as Miguel's Pedro," or "Miguel's Pedro was the wisest bur-r-ro in all Mexico."?'

'I think – I like it the first way better.'

'Which way is that?' demanded his mother, thumping her palm down on the illustration.

Victor tried to remember the wording, but realised he was only staring at the pencil smudges, the thumbprints on the edges of his mother's illustration board. The coloured drawing in the centre did not interest him at all. He was not-thinking. This was a frequent, familiar sensation to him now, there was something exciting and important about not-thinking, Victor felt, and he thought one day he would find something about it – perhaps under another name – in the Public Library or in the psychology books around the house that he browsed in when his mother was out.

'Veec-tor! What are you doing?'

'Nothing, Mama!'

'That is exactly it! Nothing! Can you not even *think*?'

A warm shame spread through him. It was as if his mother read his thoughts about not-thinking. 'I am thinking,' he protested. 'I'm thinking about *not*-thinking.' His tone was defiant. What could she do about it, after all?

'About what?' Her black, curly head tilted, her mascaraed eyes narrowed at him.

'Not-thinking.'

His mother put her jewelled hands on her hips. 'Do you know, Veector, you are a little bit strange in the head?' She nodded. 'You are seeck. Psychologically seeck. And retarded, do you know that? You have the behaviour of a leetle boy five years old,' she said slowly and weightily. 'It is just as well you spend your Saturdays indoors. Who knows if you would not walk in front of a car, eh? But that is why I love you, little Veector.' She put her arm around his shoulders, pulled him against her and for an instant Victor's nose pressed into her large, soft bosom. She was wearing her flesh-coloured dress, the one you could see through a little where her breast stretched it out.

Victor jerked his head away in a confusion of emotions. He did not know if he wanted to laugh or cry.

His mother was laughing gaily, her head back. 'Seeck you are! Look at you! My lee-tle boy still, lee-tle short pants – Ha! Ha!'

Now the tears showed in his eyes, he supposed, and his mother acted as if she were enjoying it! Victor turned his head away so she would not see his eyes. Then suddenly he faced her. 'Do you think I like these pants? *You* like them, not me, so why do you have to make fun of them?'

'A lee-tle boy who's crying!' she went on, laughing.

Victor made a dash for the bathroom, then swerved away and dived onto the sofa, his face towards the pillows. He shut his eyes tight and opened his mouth, crying but not-crying in a way he had learned through practice also. With his mouth open, his throat tight, not breathing for nearly a minute, he could somehow get the satisfaction of crying, screaming even, without anybody knowing it. He pushed his nose, his open mouth, his teeth, against the tomato-red sofa pillow, and though his mother's voice went on in a lazily mocking tone, and her laughter went on, he imagined that it was getting fainter and more distant from him. He imagined, rigid in every muscle, that he was suffering the absolute worst that any human being could suffer. He imagined that he was dying. But he did not think of death as an escape, only as a concentrated and painful incident. This was the climax of his not-crying. Then he breathed again, and his mother's voice intruded:

'Did you hear me? – *Did you hear me?* Mrs Badzerkian is coming for tea. I want you to wash your face and put on a clean shirt. I want you to recite something for her. Now what are you going to recite?'

'In winter when I go to bed,' said Victor. She was making him memorise every poem in *A Child's Garden of Verses*. He had said the first one that came into his head, and now there was an argument, because he had recited that one the last time. 'I said it, because I couldn't think of any other one right off the bat!' Victor shouted.

'Don't yell at me!' his mother cried, storming across the room at him. She slapped his face before he knew what was happening.

He was up on one elbow on the sofa, on his back, his long, knobby-kneed legs splayed out in front of him. All right, he thought, if that's the way it is, that's the way it is. He looked at her with loathing. He would not show the slap had hurt, that it still stung. No more tears for today, he swore, no more even not-crying. He would finish the day, go through the tea, like a stone, like a soldier, not wincing. His mother paced around the room, turning one of her rings round and round, glancing at him from time to time, looking quickly away from him. But his eyes were steady on her. He was not afraid. She could even slap him again and he wouldn't care.

At last, she announced that she was going to wash her hair, and she went into the bathroom.

Victor got up from the sofa and wandered across the room. He wished he had a room of his own to go to. In the apartment on Riverside Drive, there had been three rooms, a living-room and his and his mother's rooms. When she was in the living-room, he had been able to go into his bedroom and vice versa, but here . . . They were going to tear down the old building they had lived in on Riverside Drive. It was not a pleasant thing for Victor to think about. Suddenly remembering the book that had fallen, he pulled out the sofa and reached for it. It was Menninger's *The Human Mind*, full of fascinating case histories of people. Victor put it back on the bookshelf between an astrology book and *How to Draw*. His mother did not like him to read psychology books, but Victor loved them, especially ones with case histories in them. The people in the case histories did what they wanted to do. They were natural. Nobody bossed them. At the local branch library, he spent hours browsing through the psychology shelves. They were in the adults' section, but the librarian did not mind his sitting at the tables there, because he was quiet.

Victor went into the kitchen and got a glass of water. As he was standing there drinking it, he heard a scratching noise coming from one of the paper bags on the counter. A mouse, he thought, but when he moved a couple of the bags, he didn't see any mouse. The scratching was coming from inside one of the bags. Gingerly, he opened the bag with his fingers, and waited for something to jump out. Looking in, he saw a white paper carton. He pulled it out slowly. Its bottom was damp. It opened like a pastry box. Victor jumped in surprise. It was a turtle on its back, a live turtle. It was wriggling its legs in the air, trying to turn over. Victor moistened his lips, and frowning with concentration, took the turtle by its sides with both hands, turned him over and let him down gently into the box again. The turtle drew in its feet then, and its head stretched up a little and it looked straight at him. Victor smiled. Why hadn't his mother told him she'd brought him a present? A live turtle. Victor's eyes glazed with anticipation as he thought of taking the turtle down, maybe with a leash around its neck, to show the fellow who'd laughed at his short pants. He might change his mind about being friends with him, if he found he owned a turtle.

'Hey, Mama! Mama!' Victor yelled at the bathroom door. 'You brought me a tur-rtle?'

'A what?' The water shut off.

'A turtle! In the kitchen!' Victor had been jumping up and down in the hall. He stopped.

His mother had hesitated, too. The water came on again, and she said in a shrill tone, 'C'est une terrapène! Pour un ragoût!'

Victor understood, and a small chill went over him because his mother had spoken in French. His mother addressed him in French when she was giving an order that had to be obeyed, or when she anticipated resistance from him. So the terrapin was for a stew. Victor nodded to himself with a stunned resignation, and went back to the kitchen. For a stew. Well, the terrapin was not long for this world, as they say. What did a terrapin like to eat? Lettuce? Raw bacon? Boiled potato? Victor peered into the refrigerator.

He held a piece of lettuce near the terrapin's horny mouth. The terrapin did not open its mouth, but it looked at him. Victor held the lettuce near the two little dots of its nostrils, but if the terrapin smelled it, it showed no interest. Victor looked under the sink and pulled out a large wash pan. He put two inches of water into it. Then he gently dumped the terrapin into the pan. The terrapin paddled for a few seconds, as if it had to swim, then finding that its stomach sat on the bottom of the pan, it stopped, and drew its feet in. Victor got down on his knees and studied the terrapin's face. Its upper lip overhung the lower, giving it a rather stubborn and unfriendly expression, but its eyes – they were bright and shining. Victor smiled when he looked hard at them.

'Okay, monsieur terrapène,' he said, 'just tell me what you'd like to eat and we'll get it for you! – Maybe some tuna?'

They had had tuna fish salad yesterday for dinner, and there was a small bowl of it left over. Victor got a little chunk of it in his fingers and presented it to the terrapin. The terrapin was not interested. Victor looked around the kitchen, wondering, then seeing the sunlight on the floor of the living-room, he picked up the pan and carried it to the living-room and set it down so the sunlight would fall on the terrapin's back. All turtles liked sunlight, Victor thought. He lay down on the floor on his side, propped up on an elbow. The terrapin stared at him for a moment, then very slowly and with an air of forethought and caution, put out its legs and advanced, found the circular boundary of the pan, and moved to the right, half its body out of the shallow water. It wanted out, and Victor took it in one hand, by the sides, and said:

'You can come out and have a little walk.'

He smiled as the terrapin started to disappear under the sofa. He caught it easily, because it moved so slowly. When he put it down on the carpet, it was quite still, as if it had withdrawn a little to think what it should do next, where it should go. It was a brownish green. Looking at it, Victor thought of river bottoms, of river water flowing. Or maybe oceans. Where did terrapins come from? He jumped up and went to the dictionary on the bookshelf. The dictionary had a picture of a terrapin, but it was a dull, black and white drawing, not so pretty as the live one. He learned nothing except that the name was of Algonquian origin, that the terrapin lived in fresh or brackish water, and that it was edible. Edible. Well, that was bad luck, Victor thought. But he was not going to eat any terrapène tonight. It would be all for his mother, that ragoût, and even if she slapped him and made him learn an extra two or three poems, he would not eat any terrapin tonight.

His mother came out of the bathroom. 'What are you doing there? – Veector?'

Victor put the dictionary back on the shelf. His mother had seen the pan. 'I'm looking at the terrapin,' he said, then realised the terrapin had disappeared. He got down on hands and knees and looked under the sofa.

'Don't put him on the furniture. He makes spots,' said his mother. She was standing in the foyer, rubbing her hair vigorously with a towel.

Victor found the terrapin between the wastebasket and the wall. He put him back in the pan.

'Have you changed your shirt?' asked his mother.

Victor changed his shirt, and then at his mother's order sat down on the sofa with *A Child's Garden of Verses* and tackled another poem, a brand new one for Mrs Badzerkian. He learned two lines at a time, reading it aloud in a soft voice to himself, then repeating it, then putting two, four and six lines together, until he had the whole thing. He recited it to the terrapin. Then Victor asked his mother if he could play with the terrapin in the bathtub.

'No! And get your shirt all splashed?'

'I can put on my other shirt.'

'No! It's nearly four o'clock now. Get that pan out of the living-room!'

Victor carried the pan back to the kitchen. His mother took the terrapin quite fearlessly out of the pan, put it back into the white paper box, closed its lid, and stuck the box in the refrigerator. Victor jumped a little as the refrigerator door slammed. It would be awfully cold in there for the terrapin. But then, he supposed, fresh or brackish water was cold now and then, too.

'Veector, cut the lemon,' said his mother. She was preparing the big round tray with cups and saucers. The water was boiling in the kettle.

Mrs Badzerkian was prompt as usual, and his mother poured the tea as soon as she had deposited her coat and pocketbook on the foyer chair and sat down. Mrs Badzerkian smelled of cloves. She had a small, straight mouth and a thin moustache on her upper lip which fascinated Victor, as he had never seen one on a woman before, not one at such short range, anyway. He never had mentioned Mrs Badzerkian's moustache to his mother, knowing it was considered ugly, but in a strange way, her moustache was the thing he liked best about her. The rest of her was dull, uninteresting, and vaguely unfriendly. She always pretended to listen carefully to his poetry recitals, but he felt that she fidgeted, thought of other things while he spoke, and was glad when it was over. Today, Victor recited very well and without any hesitation, standing in the middle of the living-room floor and facing the two women, who were then having their second cups of tea.

'Très bien,' said his mother. 'Now you may have a cookie.'

Victor chose from the plate a small round cookie with a drop of orange goo in its centre. He kept his knees close together when he sat down. He always felt Mrs Badzerkian looked at his knees and with distaste. He often wished she would make some remark to his mother about his being old enough for long pants, but she never had, at least not within his hearing. Victor learned from his mother's conversation with Mrs Badzerkian that the Lorentzes were coming for dinner tomorrow evening. It was probably for them that the terrapin stew was going to be made. Victor was glad that he would have the terrapin one more day to play with. Tomorrow morning, he thought, he would ask his mother if he could take the terrapin down on the sidewalk for a while, either on a leash or in the paper box, if his mother insisted.

'—like a chi-ild!' his mother was saying, laughing, with a glance at him, and Mrs Badzerkian smiled shrewdly at him with her small, tight mouth.

Victor had been excused, and was sitting across the room with a book on the studio couch. His mother was telling Mrs Badzerkian how he had played with the terrapin. Victor frowned down at his book, pretending not to hear. His mother did not like him to open his mouth to her or her guests once he had been excused. But now she was calling him her 'lee-tle ba-aby Veec-tor . . .'

He stood up with his finger in the place in his book. 'I don't see why it's childish to look at a terrapin!' he said, flushing with sudden anger. 'They are very interesting animals, they—'

His mother interrupted him with a laugh, but at once the laugh disappeared and she said sternly, 'Veector, I thought I had excused you. Isn't that correct?'

He hesitated, seeing in a flash the scene that was going to take place when Mrs Badzerkian had left. 'Yes, Mama. I'm sorry,' he said. Then he sat down and bent over his book again.

Twenty minutes later, Mrs Badzerkian left. His mother scolded him for being rude, but it was not a five- or ten-minute scolding of the kind he had expected. It lasted hardly two minutes. She had forgotten to buy heavy cream, and she wanted Victor to go downstairs and get some. Victor put on his grey woollen jacket and went out. He always felt embarrassed and conspicuous in the jacket, because it came just a little bit below his short pants, and he looked as if he had nothing on underneath the coat.

Victor looked around for Frank on the sidewalk, but he didn't see him. He crossed Third Avenue and went to a delicatessen in the big building that he could see from the living-room window. On his way back, he saw Frank walking along the sidewalk, bouncing a ball. Now Victor went right up to him.

'Hey,' Victor said. 'I've got a terrapin upstairs.'

'A what?' Frank caught the ball and stopped.

'A terrapin. You know, like a turtle. I'll bring him down tomorrow morning and show you, if you're around. He's pretty big.'

'Yeah? – Why don't you bring him down now?'

'Because we're gonna eat now,' said Victor. 'See you.' He went into his building. He felt he had achieved something. Frank had looked really interested. Victor wished he could bring the terrapin down now, but his mother never liked him to go out after dark, and it was practically dark now.

When Victor got upstairs, his mother was still in the kitchen. Eggs were boiling and she had put a big pot of water on a back burner. 'You took him out again!' Victor said, seeing the terrapin's box on the counter.

'Yes, I prepare the stew tonight,' said his mother. 'That is why I need the cream.'

Victor looked at her. 'You're going to – You have to kill it tonight?'

'Yes, my little one. Tonight.' She jiggled the pot of eggs.

'Mama, can I take him downstairs to show Frank?' Victor asked quickly. 'Just for five minutes, Mama. Frank's down there now.'

'Who is Frank?'

'He's that fellow you asked me about today. The blond fellow we always see. Please, Mama.'

His mother's black eyebrows frowned. 'Take the terrapène downstairs? Certainly not. Don't be absurd, my baby! The terrapène is not a toy!'

Victor tried to think of some other lever of persuasion. He had not removed his coat. 'You wanted me to get acquainted with Frank—'

'Yes. What has that got to do with a terrapin?'

The water on the back burner began to boil.

'You see, I promised him I'd—' Victor watched his mother lift the terrapin from the box, and as she dropped it into the boiling water, his mouth fell open. '*Mama!*'

'What is this? What is this noise?'

Victor, open-mouthed, stared at the terrapin whose legs were now racing against the steep sides of the pot. The terrapin's mouth opened, its eyes looked directly at Victor for an instant, its head arched back in torture, the open mouth sank beneath the seething water – and that was the end. Victor blinked. It was dead. He came closer, saw the four legs and the tail stretched out in the water, its head. He looked at his mother.

She was drying her hands on a towel. She glanced at him, then said, 'Ugh!' She smelled her hands, then hung the towel back.

'Did you have to kill him like that?'

'How else? The same way you kill a lobster. Don't you know that? It doesn't hurt them.'

He stared at her. When she started to touch him, he stepped back. He thought of the terrapin's wide open mouth, and his eyes suddenly flooded with tears. Maybe the terrapin had been screaming and it hadn't been heard over the bubbling of the water. The terrapin had looked at him, wanting him to pull him out, and he hadn't moved to help him. His mother had tricked him, done it so fast, he couldn't save him. He stepped back again. 'No, don't touch me!'

His mother slapped his face, hard and quickly.

Victor set his jaw. Then he about-faced and went to the closet and threw his jacket onto a hanger and hung it up. He went into the living-room and fell down on the sofa. He was not crying now, but his mouth opened against the sofa pillow. Then he remembered the terrapin's mouth and he closed his lips. The terrapin had suffered, otherwise it would not have moved its legs so terribly fast to get out. Then he wept, soundlessly as the terrapin, his mouth open. He put both hands over his face, so as not to wet the sofa. After a long while, he got up. In the kitchen, his mother was humming, and every few minutes he heard her quick, firm steps as she went about her work. Victor had set his teeth again. He walked slowly to the kitchen doorway.

The terrapin was out on the wooden chopping board, and his mother, after a glance at him, still humming, took a knife and bore down on its blade, cutting off the terrapin's little nails. Victor half closed his eyes, but he watched steadily. The nails, with bits of skin attached to them, his mother scooped off the board into her palm and dumped into the garbage bag. Then she turned the terrapin onto its back and with the same sharp, pointed knife, she began to cut away the pale bottom shell. The terrapin's neck was bent sideways. Victor wanted to look away, but still he stared. Now the terrapin's insides were all exposed, red and white and greenish. Victor did not listen to what his mother was saying, about cooking terrapins in Europe, before he was born. Her voice was gentle and soothing, not at all like what she was doing.

'All right, don't look at me like that!' she suddenly threw at him, stomping her foot. 'What's the matter with you? Are you crazy? Yes, I think so! You are seeck, you know that?'

Victor could not touch any of his supper, and his mother could not force him to, even though she shook him by the shoulders and threatened to slap him. They had creamed chipped beef on toast. Victor did not say a word. He felt very remote from his mother, even when she screamed right into his face. He felt very odd, the way he did sometimes when he was sick at his stomach, but he was not sick at his stomach. When they went to bed, he felt afraid of the dark. He saw the terrapin's face very large, its mouth open, its eyes wide and full of pain. Victor wished he could walk out the window and float, go anywhere he wanted to, disappear, yet be everywhere. He imagined his mother's hands on his shoulders, jerking him back, if he tried to step out the window. He hated his mother.

He got up and went quietly into the kitchen. The kitchen was absolutely dark, as there was no window, but he put his hand accurately on the knife rack and felt gently for the knife he wanted. He thought of the terrapin, in little pieces now, all mixed up in the sauce of cream and egg yolks and sherry in the pot in the refrigerator.

His mother's cry was not silent; it seemed to tear his ears off. His second blow was in her body, and then he stabbed her throat again.

Only tiredness made him stop, and by then people were trying to bump the door in. Victor at last walked to the door, pulled the chain bolt back, and opened it for them.

He was taken to a large, old building full of nurses and doctors. Victor was very quiet and did everything he was asked to do, and answered the questions they put to him, but only those questions, and since they didn't ask him anything about a terrapin, he did not bring it up.

Eddy C. Bertin

The Taste of Your Love

That night he decided to pick one up in Riccione. The last one he had had been in Bellariva, three weeks ago, and he'd had a hell of a job getting rid of the body. A pretty one, that girl had been, a small blonde German tourist with well-formed legs. Of course, she had been only a small parcel of selected items, after he'd finished making love to her, in his own way. It was not quite what he had expected. She was so soft, she had already fainted the first time, and she had been dead before he had been able to make five cuts; but he'd enjoyed it all the same. The night had been beautiful afterwards, after he had disposed of the parcel in the sea, and he had walked on the beach for a long time. He had looked up at the sky, and almost felt himself crushed by the coldness and depth of the eternity above him. He had felt very small, and thankful for the joys life and love had brought him.

He had been very careful, and though he needed love very badly, he had kept away from it for three weeks. Then the hunger, the desperate need for love became too much to bear alone any longer. He was a man who needed people, as much as food and drink. He liked to walk among people, masses of people, unnoticed; a man in the crowd, wondering about the others, who they really were deep inside, the very insides of their narrow minds. Each one had another face; another world from which he was excluded. Sometimes he wished to be able to read their faces as if they were so many open books, not out of an unhealthy curiosity to pry into their tiny secrets, but to really feel like them, understand them.

After those three weeks, he couldn't wait any longer. That afternoon he had been lying on the beach; the sand scratching his back, his mind a kaleidoscope of tumbling memories, like the first time he had caught an alley cat and cut its belly open with a piece of a broken bottle. He remembered the first girl he had, a tiny built brunette, who lived two blocks away. It had been a very fumbling attempt, but they both liked it very much, till she suddenly became frightened and tried to get away from him. He had been mad, and his hands were around her throat of their own accord. Orgasm came just as her eyes turned upwards and her swollen tongue came lolling out between her purple lips. He still heard the gurgling sounds she had made in his ears. Then somebody had come up behind him, just in time they later said, and he had been kept in another place for several years before they set him free again.

He was of legal age then, his mind cured, and with some pocket money on him. With the money he bought a long butcher's knife, went to a brothel, and strangled the prostitute in her room. He possessed her, then hung her body on a strong clasp in the wall and made a work of art out of her body. He had to cut away several parts before she was the shape he desired. Then he painted a landscape on the walls with the red stickiness which was everywhere by the time he had finished, cleaned himself and left the country. He had been travelling all over Europe ever since, working here and there a bit. He had also perfected his love-making techniques during those years, and discovered quite a number of unusual enjoyments.

He had been dozing on the sand, and when he opened his eyes, the sun burned deep into them. Through the coloured dots and circles he saw a pair of shapely legs walking by, and the burning hunger in his insides told him that he needed a woman's love, and badly.

He rented a new room in Rimini, and took the bus to Riccione. The driver took his one hundred lira, and he found a place for himself among the packed mass of humanity. It was only a short drive, in fact he could have walked the distance in less than half an hour, but he just didn't feel like walking. It was an evening for driving, with the sound of the big motor a steady roar, the ground drumming under his feet like the membrane of a heavy drum, a strong beating heart. In fact there were too many people, and he could hardly see the numbers of the stops, very inconveniently placed between trees beside the road. He went too far, and had to return one stop by foot.

After walking through some of the small streets, he decided on one of the lesser known clubs. He paid his entrance fee, and stepped from the lamp-lit darkness outside into the soft-red and blue miniature world inside. The loud music bombarded him at the entrance, deafening his ears for a few seconds. The dancing floor was small and filled with a mass of humanity, slowly moving like a lazy dinosaur on the moors, to the sound of hard rock. Funny, he thought, how Italians dance slowly to every damn kind of music; it was in strange contrast with their hurried movements and speech to see them dancing, never leaving the square stone on which they're standing.

He found a table beside the dancing floor and ordered a bottle of cheap white wine, experience having taught him the horrible prices they considered normal for a glass of beer. Slowly he adjusted to the music, letting the rhythm build up inside his blood together with the crawling need in him. He adapted his senses to the hard electronic sounds and tried without success to hear the voice of the singer amid the music. He liked discotheques, they had a special atmosphere of intimacy. They were apart from the outside world, small worlds by themselves in which people and love affairs are born and die, in the space of one evening. They also were ideal hunting grounds.

He danced a few times, but didn't find what he was looking for. Most Italian girls were with their steady boy friends, and most of the foreign girls were with tourist groups or holiday lovers. He danced with a young French girl with a delicious accent and long legs, and then with a smaller German woman whose breasts were too large for her figure and too hard to be real. But both left him cold. They were not his type.

Then he noticed her. He couldn't have seen her before, because she was like a painting on the wall. One sees it but somehow doesn't really notice it. She moved shadow-like, slowly, observing yet unobserved herself. He first noticed her hair, long and dark, neither brown nor black, which lay flat against her shoulders. Then she passed under one of the few lights, her face turning into a black and white ink sketch, finely drawn features and dark lonely eyes.

She attracted him immediately, there was something in her way of walking, something in her whole posture, not exciting or inviting but rather the opposite, a coldness. He knew that he needed that girl tonight. He took note of where she sat down, then simply went over and asked her for the next dance.

She accepted without words. She had a very small waist, his arms almost completely circling her. He said a few things, unimportant small talk one says to a stranger. When she didn't answer, he tried a few other languages. Finally she responded in a weird combination of broken English and a few snatches of an unknown language. It could have been Greek, but he wasn't sure. He tried to find out where she was from, but she only answered with a slight smile, more a lifting of her lips, half-sad and half-mocking. He was strongly aware of her apartness, which surrounded her like a cloak. The dancing couples around them formed a fog of chaotic lights, swimming among colour waves, their heads and shoulders submerged in the flowing waves of music and movement.

They were dancing apart at first, his one arm around her shoulders. There was the faintest touch of her hair against his face, and a soft smell of perfume, sweet and unoffending. He felt the desire, the burning need for her love growing in him. Deliberately he pulled her closer, and they danced cheek to cheek, her flesh a warm and soothing softness next to his face. They had exactly the same time-sense and rhythm. They rode the music, something which rarely happens, two complete strangers adapting to each other's way of dancing fully.

After the dance, he brought her back to her table and joined her. She didn't protest, but there was not much to talk about except senseless small things. He noticed the way her hair fell half over her left cheek, and saw to his surprise that her hair was fastened to her dress, so it always covered that cheek. She had hollows under her eyes, he also noticed, as if she'd been awake for a long time. Maybe he wouldn't use the scalpel right away this time. Why not start with the pins? It was years since he had used them.

She took a sip of her drink, and he noticed with pleasure that she wore no ornaments, no rings, no watch, only a very small silver bracelet which seemed very old. It was best that way. Once he had made love to an older Belgian woman who had refused to part with her ornaments, and he had broken one of his best knives on her wrist watch during love play. He drank in the dark wine of her presence, fondly making comparisons with his earlier loves. Her breasts would be small and pointed, he thought. Yes, he would start with the breasts and use a small scalpel after all, the one he had used for detail work. He would have to truss her up well, of course, and gag her strongly, so that she would only be able to make the little throaty sounds which excited him so strongly. He would start at the nipples, slowly working in circles around her breasts, going downwards, drawing red patterns towards her navel. Only then he would start using the pins, the wooden ones which he could drive into her sides, slowly.

They danced again and again, sometimes staying on the dance floor for many minutes, pressing closer to each other, her hair against his hot cheek. He nibbled her ear and tried to kiss the corners of her mouth, but she turned away. 'Not here, not now,' she said. 'Later.' 'Why not?' he asked mockingly. 'I want you. I need your love.' She smiled, that half-mocking drawing of her lips. 'I will taste your love tonight,' she answered. Indeed you will, my dear, he thought, you'll never forget how my love tastes. Not in the short time you have left in this world. Maybe he could mix pleasures tonight? First the knives and the pins, and then conclude with the cord? If she was weak enough after his love making, and there was a hook in the wall strong enough to hold her, he could even watch her dangling, her body arching itself in spasmodic movements, her legs jerking like a spider's. Yes, he would have a wonderful night. He felt sure of that.

THE TASTE OF YOUR LOVE

The band broke up at closing time, and he got her coat from the checkroom. She wanted to wait for one of the late buses at first, but he convinced her that it was only a short walk. She followed him into his room without questions, and he locked the door carefully behind him. 'Please wait here,' she whispered, and went into the bathroom. He put on the bedside lamp, and put his love instruments into the pockets of his pyjamas, and the strong cord to tie her with. There was a hook in the wall, he noticed, quite high enough. Then the bathroom door opened and she came in.

The soft light played as a lover's hands over her youthful body, well-built and yet fragile looking, with slightly sagging breasts and a dark-shadowed navel. Her long hair hung loose now, still covering half of her face. She came over to him hurriedly, and pressed her body strongly against his. There was a look of fierce hunger in her eyes as their tongues met, and he felt desire rising in him, pumping in his blood. He tried to bring his left hand up along her spine, while the other searched for the cord, and suddenly found that he couldn't. Her arms were like steel, pinning down his own against his sides, unable to move. Her eyes smiled at him, and for the first time he noticed their glow. 'Now, my dear,' she whispered, 'I will taste your love', and with a sharp movement of her head, she tossed her hair away and uncovered the left part of her face. The scream bubbled up in his throat, but was never voiced, because her tongue erupted like a burning volcano in his mouth. Unable to move, unable to shriek, he saw the slimy, dark-haired, proboscis-like thing which covered half of her face uncoil itself as a tentacle, the many teeth-less mouths on it opening and closing. It moved along her lips, and then it was in his mouth, wet, slimy and sickly, moving and sucking, while blood-red pain tore his mind apart into a million silently screaming shards.

The landlady had seen the girl leaving the room in the middle of the night, and she had decided to throw her lodger out. After all, this was a respectable house, and she wanted nothing to do with things like that happening under her roof. She was very surprised that she didn't find her tenant in his rooms. The only things she saw were his clothes, lying in disorder on the floor, and a big plastic bag on the bed. Angrily she picked up the bag, and it felt wet and sticky and had red spots on it. The bag rattled, and she peered more closely and saw the bones through the plastic. But she definitely started to scream when she saw that part of the bag had the flattened form of a man's face.

Leonard Tushnet

Aunt Jennie's Tonic

Aunt Jennie was a witch or a saint. Or an ignorant old woman. The first two descriptions were subjective, depending on your dealings with her. The last was more objective, except for the 'ignorant' part.

Aunt Jennie was nobody's aunt, as far as I know. The title was purely honorific, given in recognition of her advanced age, 108 the year she died an untimely death. She would have been called 'Grandma' if she'd had children. I was the closest thing to offspring that she had. I recall her as an old woman, rambling in her talk, going back and forth in time and space, giving irrelevant details and omitting important ones, getting side-tracked into reminiscences and then skipping ahead so much that I got lost and had to have her repeat herself.

That often made her angry. Once she sneered at my notebook on the kitchen table. 'You went to college and you can't remember from here to there. Me, I never learned even the Aleph-Beth and I could recite out of my head books and books you would take twenty years to write down.'

She was probably right. Unfortunately for me, I had double trouble in my interviews with her. I had to mentally translate her barbarous Yiddish dialect, interlarded as it was with Hungarian and Slovak words, and then retranslate it into anatomical and chemical terms before putting it down on paper.

Those people who called Aunt Jennie a witch used the word metaphorically. They disbelieved in her charmed potions. They were rational doctors, rabbis, social workers. They railed at her followers as superstitious fools. They tried to influence the Board of Health, the City Law Department, and the Jewish Community Council to have her put away in a nice safe place like the Home for the Aged.

They were unsuccessful because those who called her a saint meant what they said. The parents of girls 'in trouble', the relatives of lunatics, the senior citizens who came to her for tonics were grateful. They saw to it that her frame house on Avenue K near the abattoirs was fireproofed and a sprinkler system installed; they provided her with matzos for Passover; they arranged for weekly deliveries of food.

Aunt Jennie was old, very old. She was small, her neck bent by arthritis, her hands gnarled. She kept a coal stove going winter and summer in her little three-room house with its bedroom, a large kitchen, and another room whose door was always locked. She wore a babushka that hid her dark-brown hair, a shawl, a shapeless cardigan sweater buttoned up to the neck, and a heavy woollen skirt over several petticoats. She was never without an apron, and she never wore shoes but padded about in heavy felt slippers.

She was really 108 years old when she died, give or take a year. I know because my great-grandmother was eight years old when she came to this country in 1873. The ticket of entry at Philadelphia from Trieste is still in the family scrapbook. My great-grandmother was born in Homona (then Hungary, now Slovakia). She was orphaned in one of the epidemics that periodically swept the outlying areas of Franz Josef's empire. She was sent for by a well-to-do relative in Newark who also sent enough money for a travelling companion. That companion was Aunt Jennie. Great-grandma's ticket says 'in charge of Shaindel Weiss', giving Shaindel's age as twenty. My great-grandmother died at 96, active, bright, alert, not a white hair on her head, her skin rosy and smooth as a teenager's. Her death was by accident – she tripped over a toy left on the stairs by one of my cousin's children, fell downstairs, and broke her neck.

Aunt Jennie died only a month later, not by accident. She was killed, not surprising in view of where she lived. The kids who killed her were caught when they tried to spend the mutilated gold pieces and the silver dollars. They hadn't meant to suffocate her, they said. They just wanted to keep her quiet while they searched her house for the fortune she was supposed to have. But the gag they used was a rag she had in her hand, saturated with metal polish, and they stuffed it too far down her throat.

The first time I saw Aunt Jennie I was already in college. I'd heard of her as part of the family lore, spoken of with respect, except by Dr Allan, Aunt Rose's husband. He pooh-poohed her 'miracles' as the results of suggestion therapy, quoting Freud's statement: 'There are more cures effected at Lourdes than by psychoanalysis.' The family paid no attention to him. They told of Mollie Frohlich, a violent maniac until Aunt Jennie took her in hand, and of Lawyer Greenbaum's son who didn't grow until he followed Aunt Jennie's advice, and of Sarah Miller, given up by doctors but brought back to health by Aunt Jennie. I also heard whisperings about other treatments Aunt Jennie gave, treatments adjudged unfit for children to hear about.

My great-grandmother attributed her own good health to Aunt Jennie's tonic, a thick brown-black foul-smelling liquid. Every Friday night, after she lit the candles, great-grandma would take a tablespoonful of her tonic, shudder, and quickly chew on celery to get the taste out of her mouth. Then she'd lament, 'Ai, if my husband (let him rest in peace!) wouldn't have been so stubborn he would be here today! But he was an Apikouros.' Epicurean is the generic Yiddish word for an atheist, an unbeliever. In this case, an unbeliever in Aunt Jennie's tonic. Great-grandma's four sons, my great-uncles and my grandfather also took the tonic. My grandmother never had; she died in childbirth. My father, an Apikouros too, refused it; he said he preferred grey hairs to a sick stomach.

The tonic came in a one-ounce bottle, enough for a month. When the bottle was empty, Aunt Jennie would refill it at a cost of a bottle of cherry brandy, one of almond extract, and a five-dollar gold piece. Five-dollar gold pieces became worth much more than their face value, but Aunt Jennie refused other payment. The family grumbled but paid up when my grandfather or his brothers asked rhetorically, 'Will it be cheaper for you if I were like old man Abramowitz in the Daughters of Israel Home or like Hochberg laying in bed, filthy like an animal and blind? Or like poor Mrs Weinstein, wandering around the streets the police always have to bring her home and you'll have to tip them?'

One day there was nobody to go for great-grandma's tonic but me. A big blue Cadillac was parked outside Aunt Jennie's house. I knocked at the door, was told to enter, and saw an astonishing scene. Aunt Jennie was holding a brown paper bag, and a middle-aged well-dressed man was interpreting her instructions to the mayor and his wife. (I recognised them from newspaper pictures.) 'Everything will continue to be good,' Aunt Jennie was saying. 'Don't forget – no salt in his food and no food made with salt. Let him take every night one teaspoon of the powder mixed with pure spring water.' Mrs Callaghan dropped to her knees and kissed Aunt Jennie's hand. 'May the Holy Mother and all the saints in Heaven watch over you!' Mayor Callaghan, tears streaming down his face, handed Aunt Jennie a little cloth bag. 'I can't thank you enough. You've saved us all.' Aunt Jennie hefted the bag. 'It's all there,' he went on, 'and all in gold, and if you want twice as much, just let me know. I'll clean out every coin store in town for you. And if anybody ever bothers you about anything, just let me know.' The interpreter looked at me, shrugged, and then translated only the mayor's remarks.

The Callaghans left. I grabbed the interpreter's arm. 'What's this all about?' I asked.

'They have a son, he was *meshuga*, she cured him,' he answered.

I introduced myself to Aunt Jennie. She grimaced in what she supposed was a smile. 'So you're Tsilli's great-grandson? And for what are you studying?' (Studying was taken for granted in one of my age.)

'To be a chemist.' I explained to her what a chemist did.

She kept nodding but I didn't think she was listening. When I finished, she said, 'You speak a beautiful Yiddish. So many young people come here they don't know a word.'

I told her my Yiddish was the result of six years at a Sholem Aleichem school. I didn't tell her I was forced to go there by my father, a rabid secularist who equated Hebrew with the synagogue.

She patted my hand. 'It's good to learn the mother tongue. Sit down a while and talk to me. People come but they run right away. All they want is my medicines.'

I sat down. While she carefully filled the little bottle I asked, 'What was the mayor so happy about?'

Aunt Jennie screwed the cap on the bottle. 'He has a son, went crazy like a dybbuk was in him. With my powders he's now better.' She looked at me shrewdly. 'My child, I'm a bit of a chemist, too. I make special medicines. Only a few, but good. I learned from a wise man in Nagy Arok the time I ran away from home.' She rambled on with a very romantic tale of a betrothal when she was fourteen to a man she didn't like. It was interesting at first, but the unnecessary details with which she embroidered her story became boring after a while. I got up and excused myself, saying I had to go on other errands for my great-grandmother.

'Go, then,' she said. 'You're a good boy to do what your elders want. Come again next month.'

I didn't see her for several months. That time I met in her kitchen a weeping girl with her embittered mother. The mother was arguing with Aunt Jennie. 'Ten silver dollars! There's no bank open now. Where will I get silver dollars? Here's a twenty-dollar bill. Take it and give me the pill.'

Aunt Jennie shook her head. 'Not for fifty pieces of paper like that.' The woman flounced out, dragging the girl with her.

I was curious. 'Why didn't you take the twenty dollars?' I asked.

'Because I need the silver. And the gold. You're a chemist. You should know. Can you use paper when you need metal?' We chatted. She asked about great-grandma and her friend, Mr Gottfried, and complained that nobody came to visit with her any more. 'With automobiles they're afraid. With horses and wagons they didn't worry about the bad street.' Indeed, Avenue K was in poor shape. Rubble from the buildings demolished to make way for the new skyway lay all around, and trucks from the nearby slaughterhouses had rutted the streets. Everyone but

Aunt Jennie had already left the neighbourhood.

She took a liking to me. She made coffee and gave me sweet hard cinnamon cookies. She told about her life with the wise man of Nagy Arok. 'What he had in his little finger a dozen professors don't have in their heads.' I was polite, not letting Aunt Jennie know what I thought she was – a herb doctor convinced of the efficacy of her concoctions and mysterious enough to convince others.

I didn't see her for a long time. I got my degree, my Master's, and then my Ph.D. I got married. I had a son. Aunt Jennie, great-uncle Bernard said, often inquired about me and was pleased with my progress.

Shortly after I began work as a junior pharmacologist at Reinhard and Kessel, my cousin Estelle attempted suicide. This was her fourth try; and when she got out of her depression, she promptly entered the manic stage of her psychosis. The doctors advised commitment to an institution. Great-grandma intervened. 'You've spent a fortune already and no results. Why don't you try Aunt Jennie?' Aunt Bessie hopelessly agreed.

Estelle's cure was the talk of the family circle. 'She was better in one week,' Aunt Bessie said. 'In one week! And just from a no-salt diet and a plain white powder! We get spring water delivered for Estelle from the health-foods store.'

I paid little attention to the talk. I'm not a physician, not a psychiatrist, but I knew that patients with manic-depressive psychosis could have long periods of normal behaviour between their swings of mood. But less than a year later came the word that lithium salts were very effective in the treatment of mania. I recalled the Callaghan episode. I begged a little of the powder from Aunt Bessie and analysed it. It was an impure lithium salicylate.

I was a scientist, and an ambitious man. Not stupid, either. Paracelsus had said that the best *materia medica* came from herbalists, wise women, and shepherds. I knew of the drugs that had entered therapeutics through folk medicine: the Peruvian bark for malaria, ephedrine from the Chinese *Ma Huang* for asthma, the tranquilliser reserpine from the Indian snakeroot, and many others. I knew that witch doctors and herb healers would not have achieved their eminence in primitive societies had their remedies been totally worthless.

Here was an opportunity to advance science – and myself. Aunt Jennie knew that lithium salts were effective in mania. How did she get her powder? What else did she know?

I wasn't dishonest with her. She was too clever not to see through any dissembling I could try. I told her straightforwardly, 'Aunt Jennie, may you live and be well, but accidents happen to all of us, like with my neighbour who was run over by a car. Who is going to carry on after you're gone? Who is going to help these poor people who come to you?

I want to become your pupil. You teach me what you know so that your wisdom won't be lost with you.'

Aunt Jennie was flattered. 'You want an old woman like me to teach you? And you went to a university?'

'Some things we don't learn in school. Some things we learn from people like you.' And I told her of how quinine was developed from chinchona and of how right now doctors at the National Cancer Institute were investigating a plant from Guatemala that the natives there used to cure cancer.

Aunt Jennie shook her head in amazement. 'Is that so? Big doctors in Washington listen to people like me? A blessing on Columbus!' She got excited. 'I can tell you how to make a pill that will bring on a woman's time, and a powder for weak blood, and another for lunatics, and a medicine to make boys into men, and one to make barren women bear, and another to straighten crooked bones and another to stop hair from getting grey, and another for a bad cough, and another for swelling of the feet, and salves for all kinds of sores, and—'

I held up my hand. 'One at a time, Aunt Jennie, one at a time, Aunt Jennie, one at a time! Let's start with the powder for lunatics.' I figured that would be a touchstone. If she'd made the lithium salicylate by chance, then her folk knowledge would be worthless to me, but if she knew what she was doing, well. . . .

'Come.' She unlocked the door to the third room. Shelves filled with jars were on the far wall. On the right was a large table on which lay cigar boxes and piles of drying herbs, flowers, and grasses. On the left was a heap of what appeared to be a crystalline gravel. The odour in the room was a mixture of aromatics, decay, must and dust. Near the door were several large earthenware crocks. Aunt Jennie lifted the lid off one of them. I smelled vinegar. 'That's where I age my gold and silver.'

Woe is me! I thought to myself. I'm wasting my time. Gold doesn't age or combine with acetic acid, and silver acetate can't be prepared by pickling.

Aunt Jennie picked up a handful of the glittering coarse stones. 'Now I'll show you how I make the powder.' In the kitchen she had me pound the stones with a brass pestle in a mortar, the kind we have as a showpiece at home. She went back into the little room and returned with two bottles clearly labelled, one OIL OF WINTERGREEN and the other OIL OF VITRIOL. I kept a straight face. My herb doctor was an amateur chemist!

She poured the now fine powder into a glass pie plate and added the sulphuric acid slowly, stirring it into the powder with a glass rod. She shook up her stove and carefully lowered the plate on to the red-hot coals. 'Now I say the words.' She muttered some garbled Hebrew for a few minutes. She lifted out the pie plate with two pairs of tongs and set it at the back of the stove. She covered her eyes and repeated the incantation. She had a gallon jug of spring water under the sink. From it she poured a glassful and slowly, very slowly, dropped the water on the plate. The drops sizzled and danced, but soon the plate was cool enough for her to bring back to the table. From a cupboard drawer she took a linen handkerchief, fitted it into another glass, and poured the cloudy liquid from the plate into it. 'Linen it must be, not cotton,' she warned me. 'I forgot to tell you the prayer was the one for bedtime.' The crude filtration over, there was left not quite an ounce of an almost clear liquid in the glass. She added a few drops of the oil of wintergreen and a teaspoonful of milk and then set the glass far back on the coolest part of the stove. 'Now it sits a day, a night, and a day before all the water goes away and the powder is left. I'll save this for you when you come again.' I asked her if I could have some of the stones. 'Why not? You can practise making the powder.'

I had the stones analysed and got a surprise. They were specimens of amblygonite, a compound phosphate rock bearing iron, aluminium, and lithium. I looked up the literature on the preparation of lithium salts, and sure enough! – Aunt Jennie had followed a standard procedure. But there was no amblygonite, according to the geologists, in this part of the country.

You have no idea how long it took me to get the details from Aunt Jennie with all her irrelevant remarks and side comments. The amblygonite was brought to her by Anton Kiss, 'a Gentile, but a fine man', from a quarry pit near the Passaic River. (The geologists didn't know everything, it seems.) Kiss brought a load whenever he came for his tonic. I saw him once, a strapping Magyar with a black handle-bar moustache, hale and hearty at seventy-nine. The oil of vitriol and the oil of wintergreen were supplied by Levine the druggist, still active in his store at eighty-one and a patron of Aunt Jennie's.

Of course, the incantations were meaningless in the preparation of lithium salicylate. Aunt Jennie thought they were necessary, and I didn't dare suggest they weren't. She was not rigid, however, about her apparatus. She used Pyrex and Corning ware, I discovered, as a modern advance over her old utensils.

Lithium for mania was interesting but of no moment to me. What was the use of rediscovering America? Now what I wanted to know was what was in Aunt Jennie's other medications. What did she have that, sans mysticism, would benefit mankind – and me?

Disappointment after disappointment. The medicine for straightening crooked bones was nonsense, merely a calcium mixture. She had three salves for skin ulcers: one was common zinc oxide in a rendered chicken-fat base; one was bread mould, the penicillin being suspended in clarified butter; one was made up of a watery suspension of gold shaved from the milled coins, a poor substitute for the gold-leaf treatment reported in the medical literature. The potion for dropsy was pounded foxglove mixed with cherry brandy, a novel and uneconomical way to prepare tincture of digitalis.

I've omitted all Aunt Jennie's mumbo jumbo: one salve had to be made only on a dark night, another at dawn, and the digitalis had to take ten days, each day stirred with a silver spoon, *mazel tov* being said ten times. I pretended to copy down the charms. Aunt Jennie looked at my note-book and marvelled. 'And even in English you can write the sacred tongue? Such wonders in America!'

I had to go slowly. I was dependent on Aunt Jennie's whims. I could neither cut short her reminiscences nor ask her for specific medications. Anne, my wife, complained that I was away from home too much. I missed playing with my boy. But I was willing to make sacrifices. I was certain that sooner or later amidst all the magical charms I'd find something spectacular.

One evening when I came, Aunt Jennie handed me a chopping knife and a wooden bowl. 'Here. Chop. Chop even finer than for gefilte fish.' She had ready a pile of salted meat. 'Lazar the butcher brought me a fresh supply. I'll trim the meat and you'll chop it. We're going to make some new medicines.'

I discovered why she lived so near to the slaughterhouses. Aunt Jennie made endocrine preparations: estrogens from minced ovaries soaked in almond extract; androgens from testes marinated in a mixture of roasted cattails (the plant type, not the animal), oil, garlic, and vinegar; desiccated thyroid from calves' thyroids blended with cinnamon and chopped cabbage leaves and dried in the oven. Her famed remedy for anaemia was, as I'd expected, liver extract. Beef liver ('from pigs is better but pigs are not kosher') finely ground with kidneys and spleen, saturated with cherry brandy, evaporated in the sun, and then pounded in the mortar and pestle to a coarse powder. What good was all that to me?

One more try, I resolved, and then I'd give up the whole silly project. I got Aunt Jennie to give me the recipe for her abortifacient. That was very complicated. 'Only from bulls can this be made and you need to have an expert butcher, not a plain slaughterer. He must cut out for you the bladder, the testicles, and all the parts around. Before, you had to make the pill the same day you got the parts but now, with freezers, you can keep them until you've got time. Grind everything in a meat grinder. Stir in a few drops of cherry brandy at a time and recite these three psalms' – and King David would turn over in his grave if he heard what Aunt Jennie called psalms – 'and then throw in the pot a silver dollar.

Wait until night, then take out the silver and rub it on this hand grindstone until the stone turns grey from the silver. Then put the grindstone in the pot and let it stand off the stove until it's cool. . . .' A few more complicated, weird steps and 'What's left looks like glue, only black, and you mix it with dough to make a pill.'

I had a sinking suspicion that I knew what Aunt Jennie made 'to bring a woman around.' I took one of the pills for analysis. I was right. Prostaglandin B, now in commercial production by a more rational method.

There was no question but that Aunt Jennie's remedies were effective. There was equally no question but that they were already well known and already preparable without voodoo and in less time. Aunt Jennie was a cook-book pharmacologist using materials without knowledge of the rationale for their use. The silver was bactericidal, for example, and the cherry brandy a mode of alcohol extraction, but all the mumbling and chanting was nonsense totally unscientific. Modern chemistry had anticipated the crude formulas she had given me.

I went to see her for what I thought was the last time, bringing her a bottle of sweet wine as a gift. She insisted on having a glass with me and became garrulous. 'The next thing we'll make is the medicine for grey hair, the one Tsilli, your great-grandma takes. I take it myself and see – my hair is as brown as the day I landed in America.'

Fool that I was! I suddenly realized that Aunt Jennie's tonic was what I'd been looking for all the time. Anything that would prevent grey hair would make me a fortune. Grey hair was commoner than anaemia or mania or unwanted pregnancies. The cosmetics industry was enormous. And Aunt Jennie's tonic was certainly effective. All the old men and women I knew of who took the tonic had not a grey hair in their heads.

'Let's start,' I said enthusiastically.

She patted my hand. 'Don't be in a hurry. We have to wait until Thursday for the new moon. Meanwhile I'll give you a little bottle you can test, like you say you do where you work.' She handed me the familiar one-ounce bottle. 'Only don't waste it. It's too hard to make. And don't take any yourself. You don't need it.'

I had no intention of taking any although I knew great-grandma swallowed it with impunity. When I got home, I had an idea. Scotty, our Airedale, was thirteen years old, sluggish, his black and tan hair totally grey, cataracts filming his eyes; I knew his end was near but sentiment kept me from bringing him to the vet's to be put to sleep. I decided to see if the tonic was effective only in humans. I held Scotty's jaws apart and gave him a tablespoonful.

That was Sunday. On Tuesday Anne said, 'Look at Scotty. He's actually getting frisky again.' He was. He no longer lay apathetically near the radiator but roamed about the house sniffing and growling. He looked dirty, but I saw that the colour was due to the darkening of the hair near the skin. On Wednesday I thought I noted an improvement in his vision. I got excited. I had him shorn. I gave him another table-spoonful of the tonic, all I had left. I had begun the analysis of the rest in my laboratory.

I was at Aunt Jennie's just before sunset on Thursday. I helped her clean up her supper dishes and set up her apparatus. And I made very careful notes.

She had a pile of meat she had taken from the freezer earlier. The meat was well thawed out, soft and mushy. She stripped a liver and three spleens of their outer membranes, chopped them finely, added dill and saffron, and covered the mixture with cherry brandy. She took other organs, among which I recognised only sweetbreads and brains, ground them up, added seven teaspoonfuls of almond extract ('no more, no less'), four or five varied spices, and put them into a separate iron pot. She rubbed a gold piece with a lump of charcoal and then on a coarse grater. Fine shavings of the soft metal fell into the wooden bowl under the grater. 'Enough to cover two thumbnails,' she said. 'You could use more but it's a waste.' She stirred the shaved gold into the first pot, added more cherry brandy, and again stirred vigorously. 'First comes the prayer, *Foruch Hai Ha-Olamin*; next, the *Shomer*; next, the *Shemai*. . . .' I didn't dare interrupt her by telling that I knew no Hebrew prayers, that I was an unbeliever. 'All ten you must say while you're stirring.' She looked out of the window. 'Aha! There's the new moon. We're lucky there are no clouds. Otherwise we'd have to wait a whole day. Now the *Rosh Chodesh*, and we're ready.' She mumbled the prayer to be said on seeing a new moon, and washed her hands afterwards. 'Also never forget the prayer for the washing of the hands.' She combined the contents of the two pots. 'Stir only with a wooden spoon.' Then she took a very large linen napkin and ladled the mixture into it bit by bit over another wooden bowl. She tied the four corners of the napkin together and expressed the juice. 'You're stronger. You squeeze.' The filtering finished with about eight ounces of a dark brown alcoholic liquid, which she put into a pottery jug with a lump of charcoal. 'Done! Now we have to wait until only half the juice is left. In Hungary we used to put it in a dark cool place and cover it with a heavy sheepskin, but here in America are iceboxes; so I just cover it with a clean rag and keep it in the icebox. It takes about ten days, sometimes two weeks, and the tonic is ready. Then you put it in a small bottle with a tight top and don't let air get at it until you're ready to use it. It can stay like that for a year on a shelf in the pantry.'

Lots of mumbo jumbo, you see, with a little science; charcoal for clarification, evaporation of the alcohol, avoidance of air to prevent contamination, and the use of animal organs of high cellular content. But, and a big but, the tonic was effective. I cajoled another ounce from Aunt Jennie for more extensive analysis.

I got nowhere fast. The tonic was rich in sulphur, potassium, and phosphorus. The organic chains were complex unstable amides and amines. The proteins did not correspond to those that normally would be present in the organs Aunt Jennie used. I needed more data. I waited impatiently for the next new moon.

Meanwhile, Scotty's eyes began to clear; his hair grew back black and tan; he frolicked like a young pup. My wife and son were delighted with him. So was I. I brought him to the vet for a checkup. The vet wouldn't believe he was thirteen years old. He shrugged. 'Well, Dr Ross, I suppose if Moses could live to be a hundred and twenty, maybe your dog will live to be twenty.' All he found was atrophy of the testicles, not abnormal at Scotty's age.

At the next new moon I asked Aunt Jennie for pieces of the organs she used. I painfully transliterated the prayers she chanted. She chuckled. 'You know, my child, it took me too a long time to learn. I kept mixing up the prayers, putting the third before the first, and the fifth before the second, until I thought my brains would cook before I got them right. I couldn't write like you. With you it'll be easier.'

It wasn't. I found that, besides the liver, brains, pancreas, and spleens I'd recognised, Aunt Jennie used adrenals and calves' thymus. Gold, naturally, was not in the final mixture; if it had any effect, it could only have been as a catalyst, which was highly unlikely. The proteins were again unclassifiable.

I worked on the tonic in my own time. I could have asked for advice and help from my superiors, but I wanted to keep the secret to myself. I dreamed of getting the Nobel Prize, once I had patented the basic ingredient and published my findings, as the man who would go down in history as the discoverer of the veritable elixir of youth.

For I knew that the tonic not only restored grey hair to its normal colour. It had made Scotty young again. It kept my great-grandmother and my great-uncles and my grandfather hale and hearty at their advanced ages. It kept Lazar the butcher and Levine the druggist and Lawyer Greenbaum and Mrs Schoenfeld and Mr Gottfried and Zoltan Kovacs, the family handyman, from becoming senile. It was why Aunt Jennie had so many followers.

I tried everything in the books, but I could come to no definitive analysis. I started the other way around. I made alcoholic extracts of the various organs and combined them in several ways. No good. My experiments with aged dogs got nowhere. Only Aunt Jennie's tonic, prepared her own way, worked on them.

Aunt Jennie herself was no help to me. Why cherry brandy? Why not plum brandy? 'Cherry brandy. That's all you can use.' She let herself be persuaded once to use a fine French brandy. The resultant tonic looked and smelled different and was completely worthless. Why almond extract? 'You don't need almond extract. The wise man, my teacher, squeezed from out of ground up kernels of peaches a kind of oil, but I found here in the stores you can buy the same thing, only from almonds, so why go through the forest when you can float down the river?' Why the gold, the iron pots, the wooden spoon? 'You'll make me crazy yet with your questions. That's the way it was, that's the way it is, and that's the way it will be.'

She was pleased, however, that I was such an earnest pupil. At great-grandma's funeral she told the family, 'Lawyer Greenbaum wrote out a paper so Albert can have all my medicines when I'm gone.' She was unaware that her tonic conferred longevity on its takers. She attributed her and her patrons' old age to the will of God.

I decided to systematise and rationalise Aunt Jennie's technique. I set up a laboratory in our basement and made contact with an abattoir to provide me with the necessary organs.

And then Aunt Jennie was killed. I was her heir. There was nothing she had that I wanted except her tonic. Of that she had exactly thirteen one-ounce bottles. I put them into a little house safe that I bought. They were my ace in the hole for my own use in case I couldn't duplicate the tonic.

I know that what I did then sounds callous. I used Aunt Jennie's patrons (including my own family) as experimental animals. I was driven by my ambition. I made variations and substitutions in preparing the tonic, trying to simplify the procedure and get at the basic substance.

New moons were ridiculous, a superstitious touch; the tonic should be preparable at any time. The prayers (taught me by a pious friend) were also unnecessary; they were purely a timing mechanism to denote the completion of the extractive process. My first batch of tonic made without the hocus-pocus was effective in dogs and humans.

I began to omit one ingredient at a time. The gold went first. The tonic seemed to be the same, but wasn't. It took me a month before I realised that my grandfather's death from pneumonia following a broken hip was not adventitious. Scotty's eyes began to film over and his hair turned grey. I tried substituting various gold salts. No go. My great-uncle Bernard failed rapidly. 'Listen, what can you expect?' said my cousins. 'He's seventy-five.' Mrs Schoenfeld died. So did Lawyer Greenbaum. I tried colloidal gold. Success! But now Scotty was dead, too.

Now I omitted first the dill and then the saffron. The absence of dill made no difference, but the tonic made without saffron had no value.

The proportions of the four or five spices in the second pot could not be varied and all had to be used. I discovered that calves' thymus was essential; the source of the other organs (swine, beef, lamb) was unimportant. Zoltan Kovacs died of debility; I read Anton Kiss's obituary. I omitted first the liver, then the brains, and so on down the list. Brains, adrenals, thymus, and spleen were all I needed. Mr Gottfried died of old age, and so did one by one my great-uncles. My experiments, you see, had to be confirmed by biological testing, and evidently the effects of the tonic wore off in a week.

At last I was ready to return to the analytic phase of my investigation. There were many tantalizing clues in the fabulous tonic. The inhibition of ageing was probably not its only function. Take the spleen, for instance. The spleen was involved in immunological processes; maybe the tonic would solve the problem of tissue rejection in transplants. And saffron came from a crocus related to the variety which yields colchicine, a compound with strong chromosomal effects. And the adrenals were significant endocrine glands.

I'd had a series of colds. I decided to try the effect of the tonic to build up my resistance. I took a tablespoonful.

The next day I was full of pep. My mind seemed to be working at top speed. I developed a new procedure for the synthesis of thiouracil and ran the preliminary tests. A couple of days later I was able to show my boss, Dr Heinrichs, the result. He was enthusiastic. He shook my hand. He said I was brilliant. He assigned me to his stalled steroid project.

To make sure I'd live up to his expectations, that night I took another tablespoonful of the tonic. I slept like a baby, woke up singing, and realised that the tonic was a better stimulant than any of the amphetamines.

In twenty-four hours I solved Dr Heinrichs' problem. He took me to see Dr Kessel, the president, and demanded that I get a new contract with a substantial rise lest I be lured away by another company.

From then on I took no chances. Every week I took a dose of Aunt Jennie's tonic. I put away my note-books for my own experiments. I could make the tonic anytime now, and I had lots of time before me. I calculated that if my present acuity and originality of invention continued at the same rate, in a couple of years I'd be able to set my own terms as a pharmacologist and have my own laboratory with a staff of Ph.D.s to help in the analysis of the tonic.

I was amazed at my own successes. I had brilliant intuitions and pragmatic ability. Every project was a challenging game. I got a bonus at the end of three months and another six months later.

The first intimation I had of trouble was with my sex life. My libido was definitely lessened. I attributed that to my working so hard and to fatigue. I was peppy all day long, but by eight o'clock I was ready for sleep. Then suddenly I became impotent. That upset me. I went to a urologist. He found nothing wrong with me and said the impotence was psychogenic.

I didn't believe him. I suspected the tonic was the cause. I didn't take it for a month. No change, except that I lost the sparkle and initiative and flashes of genius that had made my work so outstanding. As soon as I started the tonic again, my work improved.

Not my home life. To the silent reproach caused by my impotence was now added open marital discord. Anne and I quarrelled constantly. She accused me of extravagance, of flaring up over trivialities, of lack of interest in my son. She was right, not that I cared to correct myself. I was having too much fun. I was taking an active interest in sports as a participant, not as a spectator. I spent hours in the gym, on the tennis courts, and joined a Celtic soccer team across the river.

I lost my job because of my sports activities. Dr Heinrichs cautioned me one day: 'Albert, you're the head of a section now, but Dr Kessel is very dissatisfied with the work going on there now. Not enough supervision, too much camaraderie, too many practical jokes that could turn out to be dangerous. And you've been taking – too much time off.' I gave him the Bronx cheer and resigned.

When I told Anne what I'd done, she burst into tears. 'You ought to see a psychiatrist, Albert. You're not the same man I married.'

She was wrong. I was the same. She wasn't. She had grown older. I hadn't, thanks to Aunt Jennie's tonic.

She left me two weeks later, saying she couldn't stand my irresponsibility and my childish rages. I wasn't affected by her departure. The way I saw it was – marriage was a convenient way of having sex, and sex was no longer a concern of mine. I had no doubt that if I stopped the tonic long enough my sex urge would return, but between incredible longevity and brief ecstasies, who wouldn't choose long life?

About that time I noted that my scrotal sac was shrinking, my testicles were smaller, and my axillary hair was thinning out. I went back to shaving only twice a week. But my belly became flat and hard, and my muscles developed tremendously.

I became a boxer. Amateur, of course. But willing to pick a fight with a casual stranger and knock him out with a quick blow to the jaw, like in the movies. I became known to the police as a brawler.

I skipped support for my wife and son for a few months. Her brother, an attorney, hailed me into court and wanted me declared incompetent so that Anne could be appointed my guardian and have full charge of whatever funds I had. The court-appointed psychiatrists said I was not crazy, merely immature.

My money was running low. I made up a batch of the tonic and put an ad in a man's magazine: GREY HAIR RESTORED TO NORMAL WITHOUT DYE. The response was fantastic. I sold two quarts (all I had) at ten dollars an ounce, and then made several gallons.

That one ad was enough. I had a steady clientele and they told their friends. I raised the price to twenty dollars and then to twenty-five and didn't lose a customer. I had grandiose ideas of taking over a factory to produce the tonic, of a big advertising campaign, and of being on Easy Street in no time without sweat.

I ran afoul of the Food and Drug Administration. Their chemists reported that the tonic was made up of organic extracts that could not possibly have an effect on grey hair. I was ordered to cease its distribution. I took a trip to Washington, showed my credentials as a pharmacologist, carried on and shouted at those stupid bureaucrats, demanded that they experiment with the tonic on aged animals, and made such a scene that I ended up in a hospital under observation with a diagnosis of possible paranoid psychosis.

I probably would have been released in two weeks had I not been so frightened at the prospect of being without the tonic. I raged and fought with the doctors and was formally committed to an insane asylum. Anne came down and had me transferred to an institution in New Jersey.

She refused to sign for my temporary release. 'Get some treatment first, Albert. I'm going to wait until all those people who keep sending money for the hair tonic get discouraged. I'm kept busy returning the cheques and cash.'

The doctors made me furious. 'A classic well-constructed paranoid delusion,' they said. 'Belief in the possession of an elixir of life is not uncommon.'

All my pleadings were in vain. The doctors, smug as only doctors can be, paid no attention when I said that I was not a crackpot, that I really had a formula that prolonged life. I lost control of myself. I hit out at the attendants and refused to take the sedatives prescribed for me. The doctors had an answer for that – electro-shock therapy.

After a dozen shocks I had enough sense left to recognise that I was being an idiot. The shock treatments not only left me sore physically but they also induced amnesia. I resigned myself to being a good calm patient. I stopped talking about the tonic. I made a silent resolve to reform. As soon as I got out, I'd go back to my original plan of analysing the tonic and publishing my findings. I now understood why Aunt Jennie had said that the tonic was not for me but only for other men and women. Its longevity effect came presumably after sex hormone production was at a low level. Before that time it was a stimulant, actually a true rejuvenator, but juvenility was a menace, not a help, to normal adults. It had been so to me, at least, judging from the way I'd been acting.

Most of the amnesia disappeared fairly rapidly, but there were a number of things I couldn't recall. I didn't worry too much about that. Chemical formulas, names of drugs, salting-out procedures – I could find them in text-books any time. I had also forgotten some parts of Aunt Jennie's recipe for the tonic, but fortunately the rationalised version was safely in my note-books in the desk in the laboratory at home.

Anne came to see me regularly. She was pleased at my so-called improvement. 'I took the liberty of speaking to Dr Heinrichs,' she said, 'and he assured me your old job is open to you.' I nodded and said nothing about the tonic.

The day I was discharged she came for me. 'I have a surprise for you. I didn't know how long you'd be in that place; so I sold the house and took an apartment. It's very nice. You'll like it.'

A chill went through me. 'What did you do with the laboratory set-up?' I asked.

'I put everything in storage,' she replied. 'All the apparatus, I mean. I threw out a lot of junk you had there, though.'

Correct. Along with the old insurance policies and invoices for chemicals, she'd thrown out my note-books.

I'm working again as a junior pharmacologist. About once a month I make up a batch of Aunt Jennie's tonic, but it's no good. It has no effect on aged dogs. There's something I just can't recall. Those four or five, maybe six, spices she added to the second pot. So far I've tried dozens of spices and herbs. No luck.

But I'm not discouraged. I have hope. Just last week I read about cyanins being used to stimulate the growth of tissue cultures in vitro. And cyanins are present in almonds. Any day now I'm sure to remember those spices.

Daphne du Maurier

Not after Midnight

I am a schoolmaster by profession. Or was. I handed in my resignation
to the Head before the end of the summer term in order to forestall inevitable dismissal. The reason I gave was true enough – ill-health, caused
by a wretched bug picked up on holiday in Crete, which might necessitate a stay in hospital of several weeks, various injections, etc. I did not
specify the nature of the bug. He knew, though, and so did the rest of
the staff. And the boys. My complaint is universal, and has been so
through the ages, an excuse for jest and hilarious laughter from earliest
times, until one of us oversteps the mark and becomes a menace to
society. Then we are given the boot. The passer-by averts his gaze, and
we are left to crawl out of the ditch alone, or stay there and die.

If I am bitter, it is because the bug I caught was picked up in all
innocence. Fellow-sufferers of my complaint can plead predisposition,
poor heredity, family trouble, excess of the good life, and, throwing
themselves on a psychoanalyst's couch, spill out the rotten beans within
and so effect a cure. I can do none of this. The doctor to whom I endeavoured to explain what had happened listened with a superior smile,
and then murmured something about emotionally destructive identification coupled with repressed guilt, and put me on a course of pills. They
might have helped me if I had taken them. Instead I threw them down
the drain and became more deeply imbued with the poison that seeped
through me, made worse of course by the fatal recognition of my condition by the youngsters I had believed to be my friends, who nudged
one another when I came into class, or, with stifled laughter, bent their
loathsome little heads over their desks – until the moment arrived when
I knew I could not continue, and took the decision to knock on the
headmaster's door.

Well, that's over, done with, finished. Before I take myself to hospital or alternatively, blot out memory, which is a second possibility, I want to establish what happened in the first place. So that, whatever becomes of me, this paper will be found, and the reader can make up his mind whether, as the doctor suggested, some want of inner balance made me an easy victim of superstitious fear, or whether, as I myself believe, my downfall was caused by an age-old magic, insidious, evil, its origins lost in the dawn of history. Suffice to say that he who first made the magic deemed himself immortal, and with unholy joy infected others, sowing in his heirs, throughout the world and down the centuries, the seeds of self-destruction.

To return to the present. The time was April, the Easter holidays. I had been to Greece twice before, but never Crete. I taught classics to the boys at the preparatory school, but my reason for visiting Crete was not to explore the sites of Knossos or Phaestus but to indulge a personal hobby. I have a minor talent for painting in oils, and this I find all-absorbing, whether on free days or in the school holidays. My work has been praised by one or two friends in the art world, and my ambition was to collect enough paintings to give a small exhibition. Even if none of them sold, the holding of a private show would be a happy achievement.

Here, briefly, a word about my personal life. I am a bachelor. Age forty-nine. Parents dead. Educated at Sherborne and Brasenose, Oxford. Profession, as you already know, schoolmaster. I play cricket and golf, badminton, and rather poor bridge. Interests, apart from teaching, art, as I have already said, and occasional travel, when I can afford it. Vices, up to the present, literally none. Which is not being self-complacent, but the truth is that my life has been uneventful by any standard. Nor has this bothered me. I am probably a dull man. Emotionally I have had no complications. I was engaged to a pretty girl, a neighbour, when I was twenty-five, but she married somebody else. It hurt at the time, but the wound healed in less than a year. One fault, if fault it is, I have always had, which perhaps accounts for my hitherto monotonous life. This is an aversion to becoming involved with people. Friends I possess, but at a distance. Once involved, trouble occurs, and too often disaster follows.

I set out for Crete in the Easter holidays with no encumbrance but a fair-sized suitcase and my painting gear. A travel agent had recommended a hotel overlooking the Gulf of Mirabello on the eastern coast, after I had told him I was not interested in archaeological sights but wanted to paint. I was shown a brochure which seemed to meet my requirements. A pleasantly situated hotel close to the sea, and chalets by the water's edge where one slept and breakfasted. Clientele well-to-do, and although I count myself no snob I cannot abide paper-bags and orange-peel. A couple of pictures painted the previous winter – a view of St Paul's Cathedral under snow, and another one of Hampstead Heath, both sold to an obliging female cousin – would pay for my journey, and I permitted myself an added indulgence, though it was really a necessity the hiring of a small Volkswagen on arrival at the airport of Herakleion.

The flight, with an overnight stop in Athens, was pleasant and un-eventful, the forty-odd miles' drive to my destination somewhat tedious, for being a cautious driver I took it slowly, and the twisting road, once I reached the hills, was decidedly hazardous. Cars passed me, or swerved towards me, hooting loudly. Also, it was very hot, and I was hungry. The sight of the blue Gulf of Mirabello and the splendid mountains to the east acted as a spur to sagging spirits, and once I arrived at the hotel, set delightfully in its own grounds, with lunch served to me on the terrace despite the fact that it was after two in the afternoon – how different from England! – I was ready to relax and inspect my quarters. Disappoint-ment followed. The young porter led me down a garden path flagged on either side by brilliant geraniums to a small chalet bunched in by neigh-bours on either side, and overlooking, not the sea, but a part of the garden laid out for mini-golf. My next-door neighbours, an obviously English mother and her brood, smiled in welcome from their balcony, which was strewn with bathing-suits drying under the sun. Two middle-aged men were engaged in mini-golf. I might have been in Maidenhead.

'This won't do,' I said, turning to my escort. 'I have come here to paint. I must have a view of the sea.'

He shrugged his shoulders, murmuring something about the chalets beside the sea being fully booked. It was not his fault, of course. I made him trek back to the hotel with me, and addressed myself to the clerk at the reception desk.

'There has been some mistake,' I said. 'I asked for a chalet overlooking the sea, and privacy above all.'

The clerk smiled, apologised, began ruffling papers, and the inevitable excuses followed. My travel agent had not specifically booked a chalet overlooking the sea. These were in great demand, and were fully booked. Perhaps in a few days there might be some cancellations, one never could tell, in the meantime he was sure I should be very comfortable in the chalet that had been allotted to me. All the furnishings were the same, my breakfast would be served me, etc., etc.

I was adamant. I would not be fobbed off with the English family and the mini-golf. Now having flown all those miles at considerable expense. I was bored by the whole affair, tired, and considerably annoyed.

'I am a professor of art,' I told the clerk. 'I have been commissioned to execute several paintings while I am here, and it is essential that I should have a view of the sea, and neighbours who will not disturb me.'

(My passport states my occupation as professor. It sounds better than schoolmaster or teacher, and usually arouses respect in the attitude of reception clerks.)

The clerk seemed genuinely concerned, and repeated his apologies. He turned again to the sheaf of papers before him. Exasperated, I strode across the spacious hall and looked out of the door on to the terrace down to the sea.

'I cannot believe,' I said, 'that every chalet is taken. It's too early in the season. In summer, perhaps, but not now.' I waved my hand towards the western side of the bay. 'That group over there,' I said, 'down by the water's edge. Do you mean to say every single one of them is booked?'

He shook his head and smiled. 'We do not usually open those until mid-season. Also, they are more expensive. They have a bath as well as a shower.'

'How much more expensive?' I hedged.

He told me. I made a quick calculation. I could afford it if I cut down on all other expenses. Had my evening meal in the hotel, and went without lunch. No extras in the bar, not even mineral water.

'Then there is no problem,' I said grandly. 'I will willingly pay more for privacy. And, if you have no objection, I should like to choose the chalet which would suit me best. I'll walk down to the sea now and then come back for the key, and your porter can bring my things.'

I gave him no time to reply, but turned on my heel and went out on to the terrace. It paid to be firm. One moment's hesitation, and he would have fobbed me off with the stuffy chalet overlooking the mini-golf. I could imagine the consequences. The chattering children on the balcony next door, the possibly effusive mother, and the middle-aged golfers urging me to have a game. I could not have borne it.

I walked down through the garden to the sea, and as I did so my spirits rose. For this, of course, was what had been so highly coloured on the agent's brochure, and why I had flown so many miles. No exaggeration, either. Little white-washed dwellings, discreetly set apart from one another, the sea washing the rocks below. There was a beach, from which doubtless people swam in high season, but no one was on it now, and, even if they should intrude, the chalets themselves were well to the left, inviolate, private. I peered at each in turn, mounting the steps, standing on the balconies. The clerk must have been telling the truth about none of them being let before full season, for all had their windows shuttered. All except one. And directly I mounted the steps and stood on the balcony I knew that it must be mine. This was the view I had imagined. The sea beneath me, lapping the rocks, the bay widening into the gulf itself, and beyond the mountains. It was perfect. The chalets to the east of the hotel, which was out of sight anyway, could be ignored.

One, close to a neck of land, stood on its own like a solitary outpost with a landing-stage below, but this would only enhance my picture when I came to paint it. The rest were mercifully hidden by rising ground. I turned, and looked through the open windows to the bedroom within. Plain white-washed walls, a stone floor, a comfortable divan bed with rugs upon it. A bedside table with a lamp and telephone. But for these last it had all the simplicity of a monk's cell, and I wished for nothing more.

I wondered why this chalet, and none of its neighbours, was un-shuttered, and stepping inside I heard from the bathroom beyond the sound of running water. Not further disappointment, and the place booked after all? I put my head round the open door, and saw that it was a little Greek maid swabbing the bathroom floor. She seemed startled at the sight of me. I gestured, pointed, said, 'Is this taken?' She did not understand, but answered me in Greek. Then she seized her cloth and pail and, plainly terrified, brushed past me to the entrance, leaving her work unfinished.

I went back into the bedroom and picked up the telephone, and in a moment the smooth voice of the reception clerk answered.

'This is Mr Grey,' I told him, 'Mr Timothy Grey. I was speaking to you just now about changing my chalet.'

'Yes, Mr Grey,' he replied. He sounded puzzled. 'Where are you speaking from?'

'Hold on a minute,' I said. I put down the receiver and crossed the room to the balcony. The number was above the open door. It was 62. I went back to the telephone. 'I'm speaking from the chalet I have chosen,' I said. 'It happened to be open – one of the maids was cleaning the bathroom, and I'm afraid I scared her away. This chalet is ideal for my purpose. It is No. 62.'

He did not answer immediately, and when he did he sounded doubt-ful. 'No. 62?' he repeated. And then, after a moment's hesitation, 'I am not sure if it is available.'

'Oh, for heaven's sake . . .' I began, exasperated, and I heard him talking in Greek to someone beside him at the desk. The conversation went back and forth between them; there was obviously some difficulty, which made me all the more determined.

'Are you there?' I said. 'What's the trouble?'

More hurried whispers, and then he spoke to me again. 'No trouble, Mr Grey. It is just that we feel you might be more comfortable in No. 57, which is a little nearer to the hotel.'

'Nonsense,' I said, 'I prefer the view from here. What's wrong with No. 62? Doesn't the plumbing work?'

'Certainly the plumbing works,' he assured me, while the whispering started again. 'There is nothing wrong with the chalet. If you have made up your mind I will send down the porter with your luggage and the key.'

He rang off, possibly to finish his discussion with the whisperer at his side. Perhaps they were going to step up the price. If they did, I would have further argument. The chalet was no different from its empty neighbours, but the position, dead centre to sea and mountains, was all I had dreamed and more. I stood on the balcony, looking out across the sea and smiling. What a prospect, what a place! I would unpack and have a swim, then put up my easel and do a preliminary sketch before starting serious work in the morning.

I heard voices, and saw the little maid staring at me from half-way up the garden path, cloth and pail still in hand. Then, as the young porter advanced downhill bearing my suitcase and painting gear, she must have realised that I was to be the occupant of No. 62, for she stopped him mid-way, and another whispered conversation began. I had evidently caused a break in the smooth routine of the hotel. A few moments later they climbed the steps to the chalet together, the porter to set down my luggage, the maid doubtless to finish her swabbing of the bathroom floor. I had no desire to be on awkward terms with either of them, and, smiling cheerfully, placed coins in both their hands.

'Lovely view,' I said loudly, pointing to the sea. 'Must go for a swim,' and made breast-stroke gestures to show my intent, hoping for the ready smile of the native Greek, usually so responsive to goodwill.

The porter evaded my eyes and bowed gravely, accepting my tip nevertheless. As for the little maid, distress was evident in her face, and forgetting about the bathroom floor she hurried after him. I could hear them talking as they walked up the garden path together to the hotel.

Well, it was not my problem. Staff and management must sort out their troubles between them. I had got what I wanted, and that was all that concerned me. I unpacked and made myself at home. Then slipping, on bathing trunks, I stepped down to the ledge of rock beneath the balcony, and ventured a toe into the water. It was surprisingly chill, despite the hot sun that had been upon it all day. Never mind. I must prove my mettle, if only to myself. I took the plunge and gasped, and being a cautious swimmer at the best of times, especially in strange waters, swam round and round in circles rather like a sea-lion pup in a zoological pool.

Refreshing, undoubtedly, but a few minutes were enough, and as I climbed out again on to the rocks I saw that the porter and the little maid had been watching me all the time from behind a flowering bush up the garden path. I hoped I had not lost face. And anyway, why the interest? People must be swimming every day from the other chalets.

The bathing-suits on the various balconies proved it. I dried myself on the balcony, observing how the sun, now in the western sky behind my chalet, made dappled patterns on the water. Fishing-boats were returning to the little harbour port a few miles distant, the chug-chug engines making a pleasing sound.

I dressed, taking the precaution of having a hot bath, for the first swim of the year is always numbing, and then set up my easel and instantly became absorbed. This was why I was here, and nothing else mattered. I worked for a couple of hours, and as the light failed, and the colour of the sea deepened and the mountains turned a softer purple blue, I rejoiced to think that tomorrow I should be able to seize this after-glow in paint instead of charcoal, and the picture would begin to come alive.

It was time to stop. I stacked away my gear, and before changing for dinner and drawing the shutters – doubtless there were mosquitoes, and I had no wish to be bitten – watched a motor-boat with gently purring engine draw in softly to the eastward point with the landing-stage away to my right. Three people aboard, fishing enthusiasts no doubt, a woman amongst them. One man, a local, probably, made the boat fast, and stepped on the landing-stage to help the woman ashore. Then all three stared in my direction, and the second man, who had been standing in the stern, put up a pair of binoculars and fixed them on me. He held them steady for several minutes, focusing, no doubt, on every detail of my personal appearance, which is unremarkable enough, heaven knows, and would have continued had I not suddenly become annoyed and withdrawn into the bedroom, slamming the shutters to. How rude can you get, I asked myself? Then I remembered that these western chalets were all unoccupied, and mine was the first to open for the season. Possibly this was the reason for the intense interest I appeared to cause, beginning with members of the hotel staff and now embracing guests as well. Interest would soon fade. I was neither pop star nor millionaire. And my painting efforts, however pleasing to myself, were hardly like to draw a fascinated crowd.

Punctually at eight o'clock I walked up the garden path to the hotel and presented myself in the dining-room for dinner. It was moderately full and I was allotted a table in the corner, suitable to my single status, close to the screen dividing the service entrance from the kitchens. Never mind. I preferred this position to the centre of the room, where I could tell immediately that the hotel clientele were on what my mother used to describe as an 'all fellows to football' basis.

I enjoyed my dinner, treated myself – despite my de luxe chalet – to half a bottle of domestica wine, and was peeling an orange when an almighty crash from the far end of the room disturbed us all. Waiters hurried to the scene. Heads turned, mine amongst them. A hoarse American voice, hailing from the deep South, called loudly, 'For God's sake clear up this Goddarn mess!' It came from a square-shouldered man of middle age, whose face was so swollen and blistered by exposure to the sun that he looked as if he had been stung by a million bees. His eyes were sunk into his head, which was bald on top, with a grizzled thatch on either side, and the pink crown had the appearance of being tightly stretched, like the skin of a sausage about to burst. A pair of enormous ears the size of clams gave further distortion to his appearance, while a drooping wisp of moustache did nothing to hide the protruding underlip, thick as blubber and about as moist. I have seldom set eyes on a more unattractive individual. A woman, I suppose his wife, sat beside him, stiff and bolt upright, apparently unmoved by the debris on the floor, which appeared to consist chiefly of bottles. She was likewise middle-aged, with a mop of tow-coloured hair turning white, and a face as sunburnt as her husband's, but mahogany brown instead of red.

'Let's get the hell out of here and go to the bar!' The hoarse strains echoed across the room. The guests at the other tables turned discreetly back to their own dinner, and I must have been the only one to watch the unsteady exit of the bee-stung spouse and his wife – I could see the deaf-aid in her ear, hence possibly her husband's rasping tones – as he literally rolled past me to the bar, a lurching vessel in the wake of his steady partner. I silently commended the efficiency of the hotel staff, who made short work of clearing the wreckage.

The dining-room emptied. 'Coffee in the bar, sir,' murmured my waiter. Fearing a crush and loud chatter I hesitated before entering, for the camaraderie of hotel bars has always bored me, but I hate going without my after-dinner coffee. I need not have worried. The bar was empty, apart from the white-coated server behind the bar, and the American sitting at a table with his wife. Neither of them was speaking. There were three empty beer bottles already on the table before him. Greek music played softly from some lair behind the bar. I sat myself on a stool and ordered coffee.

The bar-tender, who spoke excellent English, asked if I had spent a pleasant day. I told him yes, I had had a good flight, found the road from Herakleion hazardous, and my first swim rather cold. He explained that it was still early in the year. 'In any case,' I told him, 'I have come to paint, and swimming will take second place. I have a chalet right on the water-front, No. 62, and the view from the balcony is perfect.'

Rather odd. He was polishing a glass, and his expression changed. He seemed about to say something, then evidently thought better of it, and continued with his work.

'Turn that God-damn record off!'

The hoarse, imperious summons filled the empty room. The bar-man made at once for the gramophone in the corner and adjusted the switch. A moment later the summons rang forth again.

'Bring me another bottle of beer!'

Now, had I been the bar-tender I should have turned to the man and, like a parent to a child, insisted that he said please. Instead, the brute was promptly served, and I was just downing my coffee when the voice from the table echoed through the room once more.

'Hi, you there, chalet No. 62. You're not superstitious?'

I turned on my stool. He was staring at me, glass in hand. His wife looked straight in front of her. Perhaps she had removed her deaf-aid. Remembering the maxim that one must humour madmen and drunks, I replied courteously enough.

'No,' I said, 'I'm not superstitious. Should I be?'

He began to laugh, his scarlet face creasing into a hundred lines.

'Well, God darn it, I would be,' he answered. 'The fellow from that chalet was drowned only two weeks ago. Missing for two days, and then his body brought up in a net by a local fisherman, half-eaten by octopuses.'

He began to shake with laughter, slapping his hand on his knee. I turned away in disgust, and raised my eyebrows in enquiry to the bartender.

'An unfortunate accident,' he murmured. 'Mr Gordon such a nice gentleman. Interested in archaeology. It was very warm the night he disappeared, and he must have gone swimming after dinner. Of course the police were called. We were all most distressed here at the hotel. You understand, sir, we don't talk about it much. It would be bad for business. But I do assure you that bathing is perfectly safe. This is the first accident we have ever had.'

'Oh, quite,' I said.

Nevertheless . . . It was rather off-putting, the fact that the poor chap had been the last to use my chalet. However, it was not as though he had died in the bed. And I was not superstitious. I understood now why the staff had been reluctant to let the chalet again so soon, and why the little maid had been upset.

'I tell you one thing,' boomed the revolting voice. 'Don't go swimming after midnight, or the octopuses will get you too.' This statement was followed by another outburst of laughter. Then he said, 'Come on, Maud. We're for bed,' and he noisily shoved the table aside.

I breathed more easily when the room was clear and we were alone.

'What an impossible man,' I said. 'Can't the management get rid of him?'

The bar-tender shrugged. 'Business is business. What can they do?

The Stolls have plenty of money. This is their second season here, and they arrived when we opened in March. They seem to be crazy about the place. It's only this year, though, that Mr Stoll has become such a heavy drinker. He'll kill himself if he goes on at this rate. It's always like this, night after night. Yet his day must be healthy enough. Out at sea fishing from early morning until sundown.'

'I dare say more bottles go over the side than he catches fish,' I observed.

'Could be,' the bar-tender agreed. 'He never brings his fish to the hotel. The boatman takes them home, I dare say.'

'I feel sorry for the wife.'

The bar-tender shrugged. 'She's the one with the money,' he replied sotto voce, for a couple of guests had just entered the bar, 'and I don't think Mr Stoll has it all his own way. Being deaf may be convenient to her at times. But she never leaves his side, I'll grant her that. Goes fishing with him every day. Yes, gentlemen, what can I get for you?'

He turned to his new customers, and I made my escape. The cliché that it takes all sorts to make a world passed through my head. Thank heaven it was not my world, and Mr Stoll and his deaf wife could burn themselves black under the sun all day at sea as far as I was concerned, and break beer bottles every evening into the bargain. In any event, they were not neighbours. No. 62 may have had the unfortunate victim of a drowning accident for its last occupant, but at least this had insured privacy for its present tenant.

I walked down the garden path to my abode. It was a clear starlit night. The air was balmy, and sweet with the scent of the flowering shrubs planted thickly in the red earth. Standing on my balcony I looked out across the sea towards the distant shrouded mountains and the harbour lights from the little fishing port. To my right winked the lights of the other chalets, giving a pleasing, almost fairy impression, like a clever backcloth on a stage. Truly a wonderful spot, and I blessed the travel agent who had recommended it.

I let myself in through my shuttered doorway and turned on the bed-side lamp. The room looked welcoming and snug; I could not have been better housed. I undressed, and before getting into bed remembered I had left a book I wanted to glance at on the balcony. I opened the shutters and picked it up from the deck-chair where I had thrown it, and once more, before turning in, glanced out at the open sea. Most of the fairy lights had been extinguished, but the chalet that stood on its own on the extreme point still had its light burning on the balcony. The boat, tied to the landing-stage, bore a riding-light. Seconds later I saw something moving close to my rocks. It was the snorkel of an underwater swimmer. I could see the narrow pipe, like a minute periscope, move steadily across the still, dark surface of the sea. Then it disappeared to the far left out of sight. I drew my shutters and went inside.

I don't know why it was, but the sight of that moving object was somehow disconcerting. It made me think of the unfortunate man who had been drowned during a midnight swim. My predecessor. He too, perhaps, had sallied forth one balmy evening such as this, intent on under-water exploration, and by so doing lost his life. One would imagine the unhappy accident would scare off other hotel visitors from swimming alone at night. I made a firm decision never to bathe except in broad daylight, and – chicken-hearted, maybe – well within my depth.

I read a few pages of my book, then, feeling ready for sleep, turned to switch out my light. In doing so I clumsily bumped the telephone, which fell to the floor. I bent over, picked it up, luckily no damage done, and saw that the small drawer that was part of the fixture had fallen open. It contained a scrap of paper, or rather card, with the name Charles Gordon upon it, and an address in Bloomsbury. Surely Gordon had been the name of my predecessor? The little maid, when she cleaned the room, had not thought to open the drawer. I turned the card over. There was something scrawled on the other side, the words 'Not after midnight'. And then, maybe as an afterthought, the figure 38. I replaced the card in the drawer and switched off the light. Perhaps I was over-tired after the journey, but it was well past two before I finally got off to sleep. I lay awake for no rhyme or reason, listening to the water lapping against the rocks beneath my balcony.

I painted solidly for three days, never quitting my chalet except for the morning swim and my evening meal at the hotel. Nobody bothered me. An obliging waiter brought my breakfast, from which I saved rolls for midday lunch, the little maid made my bed and did her chores without disturbing me, and when I had finished my impressionistic scene on the afternoon of the third day I felt quite certain it was one of the best things I had ever done. It would take pride of place in the planned exhibition of my work. Well satisfied, I could now relax, and I determined to explore along the coast the following day, and discover another view to whip up inspiration. The weather was glorious. Warm as a good English June. And the best thing about the whole site was the total absence of neighbours. The other guests kept to their side of the domain, and, apart from bows and nods from adjoining tables as one entered the dining-room for dinner, no one attempted to strike up acquaintance. I took good care to drink my coffee in the bar before the obnoxious Mr Stoll had left his table.

I realised now that it was his boat which lay anchored off the point.

They were away too early in the morning for me to watch their de-parture, but I used to spot them returning in the late afternoon; his square, hunched form was easily recognisable, and the occasional hoarse shout to the man in charge of the boat as they came to the landing-stage. Theirs, too, was the isolated chalet on the point, and I wondered if he had picked it purposely in order to soak himself into oblivion out of sight and earshot of his nearest neighbours. Well, good luck to him, as long as he did not obtrude his offensive presence upon me.

Feeling the need of gentle exercise, I decided to spend the rest of the afternoon taking a stroll to the eastern side of the hotel grounds. Once again I congratulated myself on having escaped the cluster of chalets in this populated quarter. Mini-golf and tennis were in full swing, and the little beach was crowded with sprawling bodies on every available patch of sand. But soon the murmur of the world was behind me, and screened and safe behind the flowering shrubs I found myself on the point to the landing-stage. The boat was not yet at its mooring, nor even in sight out in the gulf.

A sudden temptation to peep at the unpleasant Mr Stoll's chalet swept upon me. I crept up the little path, feeling as furtive as a burglar on the prowl, and stared up at the shuttered windows. It was no different from its fellows, or mine for that matter, except for a tell-tale heap of bottles lying in a corner of the balcony. Brute . . . Then something else caught my eye. A pair of frog-feet, and a snorkel. Surely, with all that liquor inside him, he did not venture his carcass under water? Perhaps he sent the local Greek whom he employed as crew to seek for crabs. I remem-bered the snorkel on my first evening, close to the rocks, and the riding-light in the boat.

I moved away, for I thought I could hear someone coming down the path and did not want to be caught prying, but before doing so I glanced up at the number of the chalet. It was 38. The figure had no particular significance for me then, but later on, changing for dinner, I picked up the tie-pin I had placed on my bedside table, and on sudden impulse opened the drawer beneath the telephone to look at my predecessor's card again. Yes, I thought so. The scrawled figure *was* 38. Pure co-incidence, of course, and yet . . . 'Not after midnight'. The words sud-denly had meaning. Stoll had warned me about swimming late on my first evening. Had he warned Gordon too? And Gordon had jotted down the warning on his card with Stoll's chalet-number underneath? It made sense, but obviously poor Gordon had disregarded the advice. And so, apparently, did one of the occupants of Chalet 38.

I finished changing, and instead of replacing the card in the telephone drawer put it in my wallet. I had an uneasy feeling that it was my duty to hand it in to the reception desk in case it threw any light on my unfortunate predecessor's demise. I toyed with the thought through dinner, but came to no decision. The point was, I might become involved, questioned by the police. And as far as I knew the case was closed. There was little point in my suddenly coming forward with a calling-card lying forgotten in a drawer that probably had no significance at all.

It so happened that the people seated to the right of me in the dining-room appeared to have gone, and the Stoll's table in the corner now came into view without my being obliged to turn my head. I could watch them without making it too obvious, and I was struck by the fact that he never once addressed a word to her. They made an odd contrast. She stiff as a ramrod, prim-looking, austere, forking her food to her mouth like a Sunday school teacher on an outing, and he, more scarlet than ever, like a great swollen sausage, pushing aside most of what the waiter placed before him after the first mouthful, and reaching out a pudgy, hairy hand to an ever-emptying glass.

I finished my dinner and went through to the bar to drink my coffee. I was early, and had the place to myself. The bar-tender and I exchanged the usual pleasantries and then, after an allusion to the weather, I jerked my head in the direction of the dining-room.

'I noticed our friend Mr Stoll and his lady spent the whole day at sea as usual,' I said.

The bar-tender shrugged. 'Day after day, it never varies,' he replied, 'and mostly in the same direction, westward out of the bay into the gulf. It can be squally, too, at times, but they don't seem to care.'

'I don't know how she puts up with him,' I said. 'I watched them at dinner – he didn't speak to her at all. I wonder what the other guests make of him.'

'They keep well clear, sir. You saw how it was for yourself. If he ever does open his mouth it's only to be rude. And the same goes for the staff. The girls dare not go in to clean the chalet until he's out of the way. And the smell!' He grimaced, and leant forward confidentially. 'The girls say he brews his own beer. He lights the fire in the chimney, and has a pot standing, filled with rotting grain, like some sort of pig swill! Oh, yes, he drinks it right enough. Imagine the state of his liver, after what he consumes at dinner and afterwards here in the bar!'

'I suppose,' I said, 'that's why he keeps his balcony light on so late at night. Drinking pig-swill until the small hours. Tell me, which of the hotel visitors is it who goes under-water swimming?'

The bar-tender looked surprised. 'No one, to my knowledge. Not since the accident, anyway. Poor Mr Gordon liked a night swim, at least so we supposed. He was one of the few visitors who ever talked to Mr Stoll, now I think of it. They had quite a conversation here one evening in the bar.'

'Indeed?'

'Not about swimming, though, or fishing either. They were discussing antiquities. There's a fine little museum here in the village, you know, but it's closed at present for repairs. Mr Gordon had some connection with the British Museum in London.'

'I wouldn't have thought,' I said, 'that would interest friend Stoll.'

'Ah,' said the bar-tender, 'you'd be surprised. Mr Stoll is no fool. Last year he and Mrs Stoll used to take the car and visit all the famous sites, Knossos, Mallia, and other places not so well known. This year it's quite different. It's the boat and fishing every day.'

'And Mr Gordon,' I pursued, 'did he ever go fishing with them?'

'No, sir. Not to my knowledge. He hired a car, like you, and explored the district. He was writing a book, he told me, on archaeological finds in eastern Crete, and their connection with Greek mythology.'

'Mythology?'

'Yes, I understood him to tell Mr Stoll it was mythology, but it was all above my head, you can imagine, nor did I hear much of the con-versation – we were busy that evening in the bar. Mr Gordon was a quiet sort of gentleman, rather after your own style, if you'll excuse me, sir, seeming very interested in what they were discussing, all to do with the old gods. They were at it for over an hour.'

H'm . . . I thought of the card in my wallet. Should I, or should I not, hand it over to the reception clerk at the desk? I said goodnight to the bar-tender and went back through the dining-room to the hall. The Stolls had just left their table and were walking ahead of me. I hung back until the way was clear, surprised that they had turned their backs upon the bar and were making for the hall. I stood by the rack of post-cards, to give myself an excuse for loitering, but out of their range of vision, and watched Mrs Stoll take her coat from a hook in the lobby near the entrance, while her unpleasant husband visited the cloakroom, and then the pair of them walked out of the front door which led direct to the car park. They must be going for a drive. With Stoll at the wheel in his condition?

I hesitated. The reception clerk was on the telephone. It wasn't the moment to hand over the card. Some impulse, like that of a small boy playing detective, made me walk to my own car, and when Stoll's tail-light was out of sight – he was driving a Mercedes – I followed in his wake. There was only the one road, and he was heading east towards the village and the harbour lights. I lost him, inevitably, on reaching the little port, for, instinctively making for the quayside opposite what appeared to be a main café, I thought he must have done the same. I parked the Volkswagen, and looked around me. No sign of the Mercedes. Just a sprinkling of other tourists like myself, and local inhabitants, strolling, or drinking in front of the café.

Oh well, forget it, I'd sit and enjoy the scene, have a lemonade. I must have sat there for over half-an-hour, savouring what is known as 'local colour', amused by the passing crowd, Greek families taking the air, pretty, self-conscious girls eyeing the youths, who appeared to stick together, practising a form of segregation, a bearded Orthodox priest who smoked incessantly at the table next to me, playing some game of dice with a couple of very old men, and of course the familiar bunch of hippies from my own country, considerably longer-haired than anybody else, dirtier, and making far more noise. When they switched on a transistor and squatted on the cobbled stones behind me, I felt it was time to move.

I paid for my lemonade, and strolled to the end of the quay and back – the line upon line of fishing-boats would be colourful by day, and possibly the scene worth painting – and then I crossed the street, my eye caught by a glint of water inland, where a side-road appeared to end in a cul-de-sac. This must be the feature mentioned in the guidebook as the Bottomless Pool, much frequented and photographed by tourists in the high season. It was larger than I had expected, quite a sizeable lake, the water full of scum and floating debris, and I did not envy those who had the temerity to use the diving-board at the further end of it by day.

Then I saw the Mercedes. It was drawn up opposite a dimly-lit café, and there was no mistaking the hunched figure at the table, beer-bottles before him, the upright lady at his side, but to my surprise, and I may add disgust, he was not imbibing alone but appeared to be sharing his after-dinner carousal with a crowd of raucous fishermen at the adjoining table.

Clamour and laughter filled the air. They were evidently mocking him, Greek courtesy forgotten in their cups, while strains of song burst forth from some younger member of the clan, and suddenly he put out his hand and swept the empty bottles from his table on to the pavement, with the inevitable crash of broken glass and the accompanying cheers of his companions. I expected the local police to appear at any moment and break up the party, but there was no sign of authority. I did not care what happened to Stoll – a night in gaol might sober him up – but it was a wretched business for his wife. However, it wasn't my affair, and I was turning to go back to the quay when he staggered to his feet, applauded by the fishermen, and, lifting the remaining bottle from his table, swung it over his head. Then, with amazing dexterity for one in his condition, he pitched it like a discus-thrower into the lake. It must have missed me by a couple of feet, and he saw me duck. This was too much. I advanced towards him, livid with rage.

'What the hell are you playing at?' I shouted.

He stood before me, swaying on his feet. The laughter from the café ceased as his cronies watched with interest. I expected a flood of abuse, but Stoll's swollen face creased into a grin, and he lurched forward and patted me on the arm.

'Know something?' he said. 'If you hadn't been in the way I could have lobbed it into the centre of the God-damn pool. Which is more than any of those fellows could. Not a pure-blooded Cretan amongst them. They're all of them God-damn Turks.'

I tried to shake him off, but he clung on to me with the effusive affection of the habitual drunkard who has suddenly found, or imagines he has found, a life-long friend.

'You're from the hotel, aren't you?' he hiccoughed. 'Don't deny it, buddy boy, I've got a good eye for faces. You're the fellow who paints all day on his God-damn porch. Well, I admire you for it. Know a bit about art myself. I might even buy your picture.'

His bonhomie was offensive, his attempt at patronage intolerable.

'I'm sorry,' I said stiffly, 'the picture is not for sale.'

'Oh, come off it,' he retorted. 'You artists are all the same. Play hard to get until someone offers 'em a darn good price. Take Charlie Gordon now . . .' He broke off, peering slyly into my face. 'Hang on, you didn't meet Charlie Gordon, did you?'

'No,' I said shortly, 'he was before my time.'

'That's right, that's right,' he agreed, 'poor fellow's dead. Drowned in the bay there right under your rocks. At least, that's where they found him.'

His slit eyes were practically closed in his swollen face, but I knew he was watching for my reaction.

'Yes,' I said, 'so I understand. He wasn't an artist.'

'An artist?' Stoll repeated the word after me, then burst into a guffaw of laughter. 'No, he was a connoisseur, and I guess that means the same God-damn thing to a chap like me. Charlie Gordon, connoisseur. Well, it didn't do him much good in the end, did it?'

'No,' I said, 'obviously not.'

He was making an effort to pull himself together, and still rocking on his feet he fumbled for a packet of cigarettes and a lighter. He lit one for himself, then offered me the packet. I shook my head, telling him I did not smoke. Then, greatly daring, I observed, 'I don't drink either.'

'Good for you,' he answered astonishingly, 'neither do I. The beer they sell you here is all piss anyway, and the wine is poison.' He looked over his shoulder to the group at the café and with a conspiratorial wink dragged me to the wall beside the pool.

'I told you all those bastards are Turks, and so they are,' he said, 'wine-drinking, coffee-drinking Turks. They haven't brewed the right stuff here for over five thousand years. They knew how to do it then.'

I remembered what the bar-tender had told me about the pig-swill in his chalet. 'Is that so?' I enquired.

He winked again, and then his slit eyes widened, and I noticed that they were naturally bulbous and protuberant, a discoloured muddy brown with the whites red-flecked. 'Know something?' he whispered hoarsely. 'The scholars have got it all wrong. It was beer the Cretans drank here in the mountains, brewed from spruce and ivy, long before wine. Wine was discovered centuries later by the God-damn Greeks.'

He steadied himself, one hand on the wall, the other on my arm. Then he leant forward and was sick into the pool. I was very nearly sick myself.

'That's better,' he said, 'gets rid of the poison. Doesn't do to have poison in the system. Tell you what, we'll go back to the hotel and you shall come along and have a night-cap at our chalet. I've taken a fancy to you, Mr What's-your-Name. You've got the right ideas. Don't drink, don't smoke, and you paint pictures. What's your job?'

It was impossible to shake myself clear, and I was forced to let him tow me across the road. Luckily the group at the café had now dispersed, disappointed, no doubt, because we had not come to blows, and Mrs Stoll had climbed into the Mercedes and was sitting in the passenger seat in front.

'Don't take any notice of her,' he said. 'She's stone-deaf unless you bawl at her. Plenty of room at the back.'

'Thank you,' I said, 'I've got my own car on the quay.'

'Suit yourself,' he answered. 'Well, come on, tell me, Mr Artist, what's your job? An academician?'

I could have left it at that, but some pompous strain in me made me tell the truth, in the foolish hope that he would then consider me too dull to cultivate.

'I'm a teacher,' I said, 'in a boys' preparatory school.'

He stopped in his tracks, his wet mouth open wide in a delighted grin. 'Oh, my God,' he shouted, 'that's rich, that's really rich. A God-damn tutor, a nurse to babes and sucklings. You're one of us, my buddy, you're one of us. And you've the nerve to tell me you've never brewed spruce and ivy!'

He was raving mad, of course, but at least this sudden burst of hilarity had made him free my arm, and he went on ahead of me to his car, shaking his head from side to side, his legs bearing his cumbersome body in a curious jog-trot, one-two . . . one-two . . . like a clumsy horse.

I watched him climb into the car beside his wife, and then I moved swiftly away to make for the safety of the quayside, but he had turned his car with surprising agility, and had caught up with me before I reached the corner of the street. He thrust his head out of the window, smiling still.

'Come and call on us, Mr Tutor, any time you like. You'll always find a welcome. Tell him so, Maud. Can't you see the fellow's shy?'

His bawling word of command echoed through the street. Strolling passers-by looked in our direction. The stiff, impassive face of Mrs Stoll peered over her husband's shoulder. She seemed quite unperturbed, as if nothing was wrong, as if driving in a foreign village beside a drunken husband was the most usual pastime in the world.

'Good evening,' she said in a voice without any expression. 'Pleased to meet you, Mr Tutor. Do call on us. Not after midnight. Chalet 38 . . .'

Stoll waved his hand, and the car went roaring up the street to cover the few kilometres to the hotel, while I followed behind, telling myself that this was one invitation I should never accept if my life depended on it.

It would not be true to say the encounter cast a blight on my holiday and put me off the place. A half-truth, perhaps. I was angry and disgusted, but only with the Stolls. I awoke refreshed after a good night's sleep to another brilliant day, and nothing seems so bad in the morning. I had only the one problem, which was to avoid Stoll and his equally half-witted wife. They were out in their boat all day, so this was easy. By dining early I could escape them in the dining-room. They never walked about the grounds, and meeting them face to face in the garden was not likely. If I happened to be on my balcony when they returned from fishing in the evening, and he turned his field-glasses in my direction, I would promptly disappear inside my chalet. In any event, with luck, he might have forgotten my existence, or, if that was too much to hope for, the memory of our evening's conversation might have passed from his mind. The episode had been unpleasant, even, in a curious sense, alarming, but I was not going to let it spoil the days that remained to me.

The boat had left its landing-stage by the time I came on to my balcony to have breakfast, and I intended to carry out my plan of exploring the coast with my painting gear, and, once absorbed in my hobby, could forget all about them. And I would not pass on to the management poor Gordon's scribbled card. I guessed now what had happened. The poor devil, without realising where his conversation in the bar would lead him, had been intrigued by Stoll's smattering of mythology and nonsense about ancient Crete, and, as an archaeologist, had thought further conversation might prove fruitful. He had accepted an invitation to visit Chalet 38 – the uncanny similarity of the words on the card and those spoken by Mrs Stoll still haunted me – though why he had chosen to swim across the bay instead of walking the slightly longer way by the rock path was a mystery. A touch of bravado, perhaps? Who knows? Once in Stoll's chalet he had been induced, poor victim, to drink some of the hell-brew offered by his host, which must have knocked all sense and judgement out of him, and when he took to the water once again, the carousal over, what followed was bound to happen. I only hoped he had been too far gone to panic, and sank instantly. Stoll had never come forward to give the facts, and that was that. Indeed, my theory of what had happened was based on intuition alone, coincidental scraps that appeared to fit, and prejudice. It was time to dismiss the whole thing from my mind and concentrate on the day ahead.

Or rather, days. My exploration along the coast westward, in the opposite direction from the harbour, proved even more successful than I had anticipated. I followed the winding road to the left of the hotel, and having climbed for several kilometres descended again from the hills to sea level, where the land on my right suddenly flattened out to what seemed to be a great stretch of dried marsh, sun-baked, putty-coloured, the dazzling blue sea affording a splendid contrast as it lapped the stretch of land on either side. Driving closer I saw that it was not marsh at all but salt flats, with narrow causeways running between them, the flats themselves contained by walls intersected by dykes to allow the sea-water to drain, leaving the salt behind. Here and there were the ruins of abandoned windmills, their rounded walls like castle keeps, and in a rough patch of ground a few hundred yards distant, and close to the sea, was a small church – I could see the minute cross on the roof shining in the sun. Then the salt flats ended abruptly, and the land rose once more to form the long, narrow isthmus of Spinalongha beyond.

I bumped the Volkswagen down to the track leading to the flats. The place was quite deserted. This, I decided, after viewing the scene from every angle, would be my pitch for the next few days. The ruined church in the foreground, the abandoned windmills beyond, the salt-flats on the left, and blue water rippling to the shore of the isthmus on my right.

I set up my easel, planted my battered felt hat on my head, and forgot everything but the scene before me. Those three days on the salt-flats – for I repeated the expedition on successive days – were the high-spot of my holiday. Solitude and peace were absolute. I never saw a single soul. The occasional car wound its way along the coast road in the distance and then vanished. I broke off for sandwiches and lemonade, which I'd brought with me, and then, when the sun was hottest, rested by the ruined windmill. I returned to the hotel in the cool of the evening, had an early dinner, and then retired to my chalet to read until bedtime. A hermit at his prayers could not have wished for greater seclusion.

The fourth day, having completed two separate paintings from different angles, yet loath to leave my chosen territory, which had now become a personal stamping ground, I stacked my gear in the car and struck off on foot to the rising terrain of the isthmus, with the idea of choosing a new site for the following day. Height might give an added advantage. I toiled up the hill, fanning myself with my hat, for it was extremely hot, and was surprised when I reached the summit to find how narrow was the isthmus, no more than a long neck of land with the sea immediately below me. Not the calm water that washed the salt-flats I had left behind, but the curling crests of the outer gulf itself, whipped by a northerly wind that nearly blew my hat out of my hand. A genius might have caught those varying shades on canvas – turquoise blending into Aegean blue with wine-deep shadows beneath – but not an amateur like myself. Besides, I could hardly stand upright. Canvas and easel would have instantly blown away.

I climbed downwards towards a clump of broom affording shelter, where I could rest for a few minutes and watch that curling sea, and it was then that I saw the boat. It was moored close to a small inlet where the land curved and the water was comparatively smooth. There was no mistaking the craft: it was theirs all right. The Greek they employed as crew was seated in the bows, with a fishing-line over the side, but from his lounging attitude the fishing did not seem to be serious, and I judged he was taking his siesta. He was the only occupant of the boat. I glanced directly beneath me to the spit of sand along the shore, and saw there was a rough stone building, more or less ruined, built against the cliff-face, possibly used at one time as a shelter for sheep or goats. There was a haversack and a picnic-basket lying by the entrance, and a coat. The Stolls must have landed earlier from the boat, although nosing the bows of the craft on to the shore must have been hazardous in the running sea, and were now taking their ease out of the wind. Perhaps Stoll was even brewing his peculiar mixture of spruce and ivy, with some goat-dung added for good measure, and this lonely spot on the isthmus of Spinalongha was his 'still'.

Suddenly the fellow in the boat sat up, and winding in his line he moved to the stern and stood there, watching the water. I saw something move, a form beneath the surface, and then the form itself emerged, head-piece, goggles, rubber suiting, aqualung and all. Then it was hidden from me by the Greek bending to assist the swimmer to remove his top-gear, and my attention was diverted to the ruined shelter on the shore. Something was standing in the entrance. I say 'something' because doubtless owing to a trick of light, it had at first the shaggy appearance of a colt standing on its hind legs. Legs and even rump were covered with hair, and then I realised that it was Stoll himself, naked, his arms and chest as hairy as the rest of him. Only his swollen scarlet face proclaimed him for the man he was, with the enormous ears like saucers standing out from either side of his bald head. I had never in all my life seen a more revolting sight. He came out into the sunlight and looked towards the boat, and then, as if well pleased with himself and his world, strutted forward, pacing up and down the spit of sand before the ruined shelter with that curious movement I had noticed earlier in the village, not the rolling gait of a drunken man but a stumping jog-trot, arms akimbo, his chest thrust forward, his backside prominent behind him.

The swimmer, having discarded goggles and aqualung, was now coming into the beach with long leisurely strokes, still wearing flippers – I could see them thrash the surface like a giant fish. Then, flippers cast aside on the sand, the swimmer stood up, and despite the disguise of the rubber suiting I saw, with astonishment, that it was Mrs Stoll. She was carrying some sort of bag around her neck, and advancing up the sand to meet her strutting husband she lifted it over her head and gave it to him. I did not hear them exchange a word, and they went together to the hut and disappeared inside. As for the Greek, he had gone once more to the bows of the boat to resume his idle fishing.

I lay down under cover of the broom and waited. I would give them twenty minutes, half-an-hour, perhaps, then make my way back to the salt-flats and my car. As it happened, I did not have to wait so long. It was barely ten minutes before I heard a shout below me on the beach, and peering through the broom I saw that they were both standing on the spit of sand, haversack, picnic-basket and flippers in hand. The Greek was already starting the engine, and immediately afterwards he began to pull up the anchor. Then he steered the boat slowly inshore, touching it beside a ledge of rock where the Stolls had installed themselves. They climbed aboard, and in another moment the Greek had turned the boat, and it was heading out to sea away from the sheltered inlet and into the gulf. Then it rounded the point and was out of my sight.

Curiosity was too much for me. I scrambled down the cliff on to the sand and made straight for the ruined shelter. As I thought, it had been a haven for goats; the muddied floor reeked, and their droppings were everywhere. In a corner, though, a clearing had been made, and there were planks of wood, forming a sort of shelf. The inevitable beer bottles were stacked beneath this, but whether they had contained the local brew or Stoll's own poison I could not tell. The shelf itself held odds and ends of pottery, as though someone had been digging in a rubbish dump and had turned up broken pieces of discarded household junk. There was no earth upon them, though; they were scaled with barnacles, and some of them were damp, and it suddenly occurred to me that these were what archaeologists call 'sherds', and came from the sea-bed. Mrs Stoll had been exploring, and exploring underwater, whether for shells or for something of greater interest I did not know, and these pieces scattered here were throwouts, of no use, and so neither she nor her husband had bothered to remove them. I am no judge of these things, and after looking around me, and finding nothing of further interest, I left the ruin.

The move was a fatal one. As I turned to climb the cliff I heard the throb of an engine, and the boat had returned once more, to cruise along the shore, so I judged from its position. All three heads were turned in my direction, and inevitably the squat figure in the stern had field-glasses poised. He would have no difficulty, I feared, in distinguishing who it was that had just left the ruined shelter and was struggling up the cliff to the hill above.

I did not look back but went on climbing, my hat pulled down well over my brows in the vain hope that it might afford some sort of conceal-ment. After all, I might have been any tourist who had happened to be at that particular spot at that particular time. Nevertheless, I feared recognition was inevitable. I tramped back to the car on the salt-flats, tired, breathless and thoroughly irritated. I wished I had never decided to explore the further side of the peninsula. The Stolls would think I had been spying upon them, which indeed was true. My pleasure in the day was spoilt. I decided to pack it in and go back to the hotel. Luck was against me, though, for I had hardly turned on to the track leading from the marsh to the road when I noticed that one of my tyres was flat. By the time I had put on the spare wheel – for I am ham-fisted at all mechanical jobs – forty minutes had gone by.

My disgruntled mood did not improve, when at last I reached the hotel, to see that the Stolls had beaten me to it. Their boat was already at its moorings beside the landing-stage, and Stoll himself was sitting on his balcony with field-glasses trained upon my chalet. I stumped up the steps feeling as self-conscious as someone under a television camera and went into my quarters, closing the shutters behind me. I was taking a bath when the telephone rang.

'Yes?' Towel round the middle, dripping hands, it could not have rung at a more inconvenient moment.

'That you, Mr Tutor-boy?'

The rasping, wheezing voice was unmistakable. He did not sound drunk, though.

'This is Timothy Grey,' I replied stiffly.

'Grey or Black, it's all the same to me,' he said. His tone was un-pleasant, hostile. 'You were out on Spinalongha this afternoon. Correct?'

'I was walking on the peninsula,' I told him. 'I don't know why you should be interested.'

'Oh, stuff it up,' he answered, 'you can't fool me. You're just like the other fellow. You're nothing but a God-damn spy. Well, let me tell you this. The wreck was clean-picked centuries ago.'

'I don't know what you're talking about,' I said. 'What wreck?'

There was a moment's pause. He muttered something under his breath, whether to himself or to his wife I could not tell, but when he resumed speaking his tone had moderated, something of pseudo-bonhomie had returned.

'O.K. . . . O.K. Tutor-boy,' he said. 'We won't argue the point. Let us say you and I share an interest. Schoolmasters, university professors, college lecturers, we're all alike under the skin, and above it too sometimes.' His low chuckle was offensive. 'Don't panic, I won't give you away,' he continued. 'I've taken a fancy to you, as I told you the other night. You want something for your God-darn school museum, correct? Something you can show the pretty lads and your colleagues, too? Fine. Agreed. I've got just the thing. You call round here later this evening, and I'll make you a present of it. I don't want your God-damn money . . .'

He broke off, chuckling again, and Mrs Stoll must have made some remark, for he added, 'That's right, that's right. We'll have a cosy little party, just the three of us. My wife's taken quite a fancy to you too.'

The towel round my middle slipped to the floor, leaving me naked. I felt vulnerable for no reason at all. And the patronising, insinuating voice infuriated me.

'Mr Stoll,' I said, 'I'm not a collector for schools, colleges or museums. I'm not interested in antiquities. I am here on holiday to paint, for my own pleasure, and quite frankly I have no intention of calling upon you or any other visitor at the hotel. Good evening.'

I slammed down the receiver and went back to the bathroom. Infernal impudence. Loathsome man. The question was, would he now leave me alone, or would he keep his glasses trained on my balcony until he saw me go up to the hotel for dinner, and then follow me, wife in tow, to the dining-room? Surely he would not dare to resume the conversation in front of waiters and guests? If I guessed his intentions aright, he wanted to buy my silence by fobbing me off with some gift. Those day-long fishing expeditions of his were a mask for under-water exploration – hence his allusion to a wreck – during which he hoped to find, possibly had found already, objects of value that he intended to smuggle out of Crete. Doubtless he had succeeded in doing this the preceding year, and the Greek boatman would be well paid for holding his tongue.

This season, however, it had not worked to plan. My unfortunate predecessor at Chalet 62, Charles Gordon, himself an expert in antiquities, had grown suspicious. Stoll's allusion, 'You're like the other fellow. Nothing but a God-damn spy', made this plain. What if Gordon had received an invitation to Chalet 38, not to drink the spurious beer but to inspect Stoll's collection and be offered a bribe for keeping silent? Had he refused, threatening to expose Stoll? Did he really drown accidentally, or had Stoll's wife followed him down into the water in her rubber-suit and mask and flippers, and then, once beneath the surface . . .?

My imagination was running away with me. I had no proof of anything. All I knew was that nothing in the world would get me to Stoll's chalet, and indeed, if he attempted to pester me again, I should have to tell the whole story to the management.

I changed for dinner, then opened my shutters a fraction and stood behind them, looking out towards his chalet. The light shone on his balcony, for it was already dusk, but he himself had disappeared. I stepped outside, locking the shutters behind me, and walked up the garden to the hotel.

I was just about to go through to the reception hall from the terrace when I saw Stoll and his wife sitting on a couple of chairs inside, guarding, as it were, the passage-way to lounge and dining-room. If I wanted to eat I had to pass them. Right, I thought. You can sit there all evening waiting. I went back along the terrace, and circling the hotel by the kitchens went round to the car park and got into the Volkswagen. I would have dinner down in the village, and damn the extra expense. I drove off in a fury, found an obscure taverna well away from the harbour itself, and instead of the three-course hotel meal I had been looking forward to on my en pension terms – for I was hungry after my day in the open and meagre sandwiches on the salt-flats – I was obliged to content myself with an omelette, an orange and a cup of coffee.

It was after ten when I arrived back in the hotel. I parked the car, and skirting the kitchen quarters once again made my way furtively down the garden path to my chalet, letting myself in through the shutters like a thief. The light was still shining on Stoll's balcony, and by this time he was doubtless deep in his cups. If there was any trouble with him the next day I would definitely go to the management.

I undressed and lay reading in bed until after midnight, then, feeling sleepy, switched out my light and went across the room to open the shutters, for the air felt stuffy and close. I stood for a moment looking out across the bay. The chalet lights were all extinguished except for one. Stoll's of course. His balcony light cast a yellow streak on the water beside his landing-stage. The water rippled, yet there was no wind. Then I saw it. I mean, the snorkel. The little pipe was caught an instant in the yellow gleam, but before I lost it I knew that it was heading in a direct course for the rocks beneath my chalet. I waited. Nothing happened, there was no sound, no further ripple on the water. Perhaps she did this every evening. Perhaps it was routine, and while I was lying on my bed reading, oblivious of the world outside, she had been treading water close to the rocks. The thought was discomforting, to say the least of it, that regularly after midnight she left her besotted husband asleep over his hell-brew of spruce and ivy and came herself, his under-water-partner, in her black-seal rubber suit, her mask, her flippers, to spy upon Chalet 62. And on this night in particular, after the telephone conversation and my refusal to visit them, coupled with my new theory as to the fate of my predecessor, her presence in my immediate vicinity was more than ominous, it was threatening.

Suddenly, out of the dark stillness to my right, the snorkel-pipe was caught in a finger-thread of light from my own balcony. Now it was almost immediately below me. I panicked, turned, and fled inside my room, closing the shutters fast. I switched off the balcony light and stood against the wall between my bedroom and bathroom, listening. The soft air filtered through the shutters beside me. It seemed an eternity before the sound I expected, dreaded, came to my ears. A kind of swishing movement from the balcony, a fumbling of hands, and heavy breathing. I could see nothing from where I stood against the wall, but the sounds came through the chinks in the shutters, and I knew she was there. I knew she was holding on to the hasp, and the water was dripping from the skin-tight rubber suit, and that even if I shouted, 'What do you want?' she would not hear. No deaf-aids under water, no mechanical device for soundless ears. Whatever she did by night must be done by sight, by touch.

She began to rattle on the shutters. I took no notice. She rattled again. Then she found the bell, and the shrill summons pierced the air above my head with all the intensity of a dentist's drill upon a nerve. She rang three times. Then silence. No more rattling of the shutters. No more breathing. She might yet be crouching on the balcony, the water dripping from the black rubber suit, waiting for me to lose patience, to emerge.

I crept away from the wall and sat down on the bed. There was not a sound from the balcony. Boldly I switched on my bedside light, half expecting the rattling of the shutters to begin again, or the sharp ping of the bell. Nothing happened, though. I looked at my watch. It was half-past twelve. I sat there hunched on my bed, my mind that had been so heavy with sleep now horribly awake, full of foreboding, my dread of that sleek black figure increasing minute by minute so that all sense and reason seemed to desert me, and my dread was the more intense and irrational because the figure in the rubber suit was female. What did she want?

I sat there for an hour or more until reason took possession once again. She must have gone. I got up from the bed and went to the shutters and listened. There wasn't a sound. Only the lapping of water beneath the rocks. Gently, very gently, I opened the hasp and peered through the shutters. Nobody was there. I opened them wider and stepped on to the balcony. I looked out across the bay, and there was no longer any light shining from the balcony of No. 38. The little pool of water beneath my shutters was evidence enough of the figure that had stood there an hour ago, and the wet footmarks leading down the steps towards the rocks suggested she had gone the way she came. I breathed a sigh of relief. Now I could sleep in peace.

It was only then that I saw the object at my feet, lying close to the shutter's base. I bent and picked it up. It was a small package, wrapped in some sort of waterproof cloth. I took it inside and examined it, sitting on the bed. Foolish suspicions of plastic bombs came to my mind, but surely a journey underwater would neutralise the lethal effect? The package was sewn about with twine, criss-crossed. It felt quite light. I remembered the old classical proverb, 'Beware of the Greeks when they bear gifts'. But the Stolls were not Greeks, and, whatever lost Atlantis they might have plundered, explosives did not form part of the treasure-trove of that vanished continent.

I cut the twine with a pair of nail-scissors, then unthreaded it piece by piece and unfolded the waterproof wrapping. A layer of finely-meshed net concealed the object within, and, this unravelled, the final token itself lay in my open hand. It was a small jug, reddish in colour, with a handle on either side for safe holding. I had seen this sort of object before – the correct name, I believe, is rhyton – displayed behind glass cases in museums. The body of the jug had been shaped cunningly and brilliantly into a man's face, with upstanding ears like scallop-shells, while pro-truding eyes and bulbous nose stood out above the leering, open mouth, the moustache drooping to the rounded beard that formed the base. At the top, between the handles, were the upright figures of three strutting men, their faces similar to that upon the jug, but here human resemblance ended, for they had neither hands nor feet but hooves, and from each of their hairy rumps extended a horse's tail.

I turned the object over. The same face leered at me from the other side. The same three figures strutted at the top. There was no crack, no blemish that I could see, except a faint mark on the lip. I looked inside the jug and saw a note lying on the bottom. The opening was too small for my hand, so I shook it out. The note was a plain white card, with words typed upon it. It read: 'Silenos, earth-born satyr, half-horse, half-man, who, unable to distinguish truth from falsehood, reared Dionysus, god of intoxication, as a girl in a Cretan cave, then became his drunken tutor and companion.'

That was all. Nothing more. I put the note back inside the jug, and the jug on the table at the far end of the room. Even then the lewd mocking face leered back at me, and the three strutting figures of the horsemen stood out in bold relief across the top. I was too weary to wrap it up again. I covered it with my jacket and climbed back into bed. In the morning I would cope with the laborious task of packing it up and getting my waiter to take it across to Chalet 38. Stoll could keep his rhyton – heaven knew what the value might be – and good luck to him. I wanted no part of it.

Exhausted, I fell asleep, but, oh God, to no oblivion. The dreams which came, and from which I struggled to awaken, but in vain, belonged to some other unknown world horribly intermingled with my own. Term had started, but the school in which I taught was on a mountain top hemmed in by forest, though the school buildings were the same and the classroom was my own. My boys, all of them familiar faces, lads I knew, wore vine-leaves in their hair, and had a strange, unearthly beauty both endearing and corrupt. They ran towards me, smiling, and I put my arms about them, and the pleasure they gave me was insidious and sweet, never before experienced, never before imagined, the man who pranced in their midst and played with them was not myself, not the self I knew, but a demon shadow emerging from a jug, strutting in his conceit as Stoll had done upon the spit of sand at Spinalongha.

I awoke after what seemed like centuries of time, and indeed broad daylight seeped through the shutters, and it was a quarter to ten. My head was throbbing. I felt sick, exhausted. I rang for coffee, and looked out across the bay. The boat was at its moorings. The Stolls had not gone fishing. Usually they were away by nine. I took the jug from under my coat, and with fumbling hands began to wrap it up in the net and waterproof packing. I had made a botched job of it when the waiter came on to the balcony with my breakfast tray. He wished me good morning with his usual smile.

'I wonder,' I said, 'if you would do me a favour.'

'You are welcome, sir,' he replied.

'It concerns Mr Stoll,' I went on. 'I believe he has Chalet 38 across the bay. He usually goes fishing every day, but I see his boat is still at the landing-stage.'

'That is not surprising,' the waiter smiled. 'Mr and Mrs Stoll left this morning by car.'

'I see. Do you know when they will be back?'

'They will not be back, sir. They have left for good. They are driving to the airport en route for Athens. The boat is probably vacant now if you wish to hire it.'

He went down the steps into the garden, and the jar in its waterproof packing was still lying beside the breakfast tray.

The sun was already fierce upon my balcony. It was going to be a scorching day, too hot to paint. And anyway, I wasn't in the mood. The events of the night before had left me tired, jaded, with a curious sapped feeling due not so much to the intruder beyond my shutters as to those interminable dreams. I might be free of the Stolls themselves, but not of their legacy.

I unwrapped it once again and turned it over in my hands. The leering, mocking face repelled me; its resemblance to the human Stoll was not pure fancy but compelling, sinister, doubtless his very reason for palming it off on me – I remembered the chuckle down the telephone – and if he possessed treasures of equal value to this rhyton, or even greater, then one object the less would not bother him. He would have a problem getting them through Customs, especially in Athens. The penalties were enormous for this sort of thing. Doubtless he had his contacts, knew what to do.

I stared at the dancing figures near the top of the jar, and once more I was struck by their likeness to the strutting Stoll on the shore of Spinalongha, his naked, hairy form, his protruding rump. Part man, part horse, a satyr . . . 'Silenos, drunken tutor to the god Dionysus.'

The jar was horrible, evil. Small wonder that my dreams had been distorted, utterly foreign to my nature. But not perhaps to Stoll's? Could it be that he too had realised its bestiality, but not until too late? The bar-tender had told me that it was only this year he had gone to pieces, taken to drink. There must be some link between his alcoholism and the finding of the jar. One thing was very evident, I must get rid of it – but how? If I took it to the management questions would be asked. They might not believe my story about its being dumped on my balcony the night before; they might suspect that I had taken it from some archaeological site, and then had second thoughts about trying to smuggle it out of the country or dispose of it somewhere on the island. So what? Drive along the coast and chuck it away, a rhyton centuries old and possibly priceless?

I wrapped it carefully, put it in my jacket pocket and walked up the garden to the hotel. The bar was empty, the bar-tender behind his counter polishing glasses. I sat down on a stool in front of him and ordered a mineral water.

'No expedition today, sir?' he enquired.

'Not yet,' I said. 'I may go out later.'

'A cool dip in the sea and a siesta on the balcony,' he suggested, 'and by the way, sir, I have something for you.'

He bent down and brought out a small screw-topped bottle filled with what appeared to be bitter lemon.

'Left here last evening with Mr Stoll's compliments,' he said. 'He waited for you in the bar until nearly midnight, but you never came.

So I promised to hand it over when you did.'

I looked at it suspiciously. 'What is it?' I asked.

The bar-tender smiled. 'Some of his chalet home-brew,' he said. 'It's quite harmless, he gave me a bottle for myself and my wife. She says it's nothing but lemonade. The real smelling stuff must have been thrown away. Try it.' He had poured some into my mineral water before I could stop him.

Hesitant, wary, I dipped my finger into the glass and tasted it. It was like the barley-water my mother used to make when I was a child. And equally tasteless. And yet . . . it left a sort of aftermath on the palate and the tongue. Not as sweet as honey nor as sharp as grapes, but pleasant, like the smell of raisins under the sun, curiously blended with the ears of ripening corn.

'Oh well,' I said, 'here's to the improved health of Mr Stoll,' and I drank my medicine like a man.

'I know one thing,' said the bar-tender, 'I've lost my best customer. They were away early this morning.'

'Yes,' I said, 'so my waiter informed me.'

'The best thing Mrs Stoll could do would be to get him into hospital,' the bar-tender continued. 'Her husband's a sick man, and it's not just the drink.'

'What do you mean?'

He tapped his forehead. 'Something wrong up here,' he said. 'You could see for yourself how he acted. Something on his mind. Some sort of obsession. I rather doubt we shall see them again next year.'

I sipped my mineral water, which was undoubtedly improved by the barley taste.

'What was his profession?' I asked.

'Mr Stoll? Well, he told me he had been professor of classics in some American university, but you never could tell if he was speaking the truth or not. Mrs Stoll paid the bills here, hired the boatman, arranged everything. Though he swore at her in public he seemed to depend on her. I sometimes wondered, though . . .'

He broke off.

'Wondered what?' I enquired.

'Well . . . She had a lot to put up with. I've seen her look at him sometimes, and it wasn't with love. Women of her age must seek some sort of satisfaction out of life. Perhaps she found it on the side while he indulged his passion for liquor and antiques. He had picked up quite a few items in Greece, and around the islands and here in Crete. It's not too difficult if you know the ropes.'

He winked. I nodded, and ordered another mineral water. The warm atmosphere in the bar had given me a thirst.

'Are there any lesser known sites along the coast?' I asked. 'I mean, places they might have gone ashore to from the boat?'

It may have been my fancy, but I thought he avoided my eye.

'I hardly know, sir,' he said. 'I dare say there are, but they would have custodians of some sort. I doubt if there are any places the authorities don't know about.'

'What about wrecks?' I pursued. 'Vessels that might have been sunk centuries ago, and are now lying on the sea bottom?'

He shrugged his shoulders. 'There are always local rumours,' he said casually, 'stories that get handed down through generations. But it's mostly superstition. I've never believed in them myself, and I don't know anybody with education who does.'

He was silent for a moment, polishing a glass. I wondered if I had said too much. 'We all know small objects are discovered from time to time,' he murmured, 'and they can be of great value. They get smuggled out of the country, or if too much risk is involved they can be disposed of locally to experts and a good price paid. I have a cousin in the village connected with the local museum. He owns the café opposite the Bottomless Pool. Mr Stoll used to patronise him. Papitos is the name. As a matter of fact, the boat hired by Mr Stoll belongs to my cousin; he lets it out on hire to the visitors here at the hotel.'

'I see.'

'But there . . . You are not a collector, sir, and you're not interested in antiques.'

'No,' I said, 'I am not a collector.'

I got up from the stool and bade him good morning. I wondered if the small package in my pocket made a bulge.

I went out of the bar and strolled on to the terrace. Nagging curiosity made me wander down to the landing-stage below the Stolls' chalet. The chalet itself had evidently been swept and tidied, the balcony cleared, the shutters closed. No trace remained of the last occupants. Before the day was over, in all probability, it would be opened for some English family who would strew the place with bathing-suits.

The boat was at its moorings, and the Greek hand was swabbing down the sides. I looked out across the bay to my own chalet on the opposite side and saw it, for the first time, from Stoll's viewpoint. As he stood there, peering through his field-glasses, it seemed clearer to me than ever before that he must have taken me for an interloper, a spy – possibly, even someone sent out from England to enquire into the true circumstances of Charles Gordon's death. Was the gift of the jar, the night before departure, a gesture of defiance? A bribe? Or a curse?

Then the Greek fellow on the boat stood up and faced towards me. It was not the regular boatman, but another one. I had not realised this before when his back was turned. The man who used to accompany the Stolls had been younger, dark, and this was an older chap altogether. I remembered what the bar-tender had told me about the boat belonging to his cousin, Papitos, who owned the café in the village by the Bottom-less Pool.

'Excuse me,' I called, 'are you the owner of the boat?'

The man climbed on to the landing-stage and stood before me.

'Nicolai Papitos is my brother,' he said. 'You want to go for trip round the bay? Plenty good fish outside. No wind today. Sea very calm.'

'I don't want to fish,' I told him. 'I wouldn't mind an outing for an hour or so. How much does it cost?'

He gave me the sum in drachmae, and I did a quick reckoning and made it out to be not more than two pounds for the hour, though it would doubtless be double that sum to round the point and go along the coast as far as that spit of sand on the isthmus of Spinalongha. I took out my wallet to see if I had the necessary notes or whether I should have to return to the reception desk and cash a traveller's cheque.

'You charge to hotel,' he said quickly, evidently reading my thoughts. 'The cost go on your bill.'

This decided me. Damn it all, my extras had been moderate to date.

'Very well,' I said, 'I'll hire the boat for a couple of hours.'

It was a curious sensation to be chug-chugging across the bay as the Stolls had done so many times, the line of chalets in my wake, the harbour astern on my right and the blue waters of the open gulf ahead. I had no clear plan in mind. It was just that, for some inexplicable reason, I felt myself drawn towards that inlet near the shore where the boat had been anchored on the previous day. 'The wreck was picked clean centuries ago . . .' Those had been Stoll's words. Was he lying? Or could it be that day after day, through the past weeks, that particular spot had been his hunting-ground, and his wife, diving, had brought the dripping treasure from its sea-bed to his grasping hands? We rounded the point, and inevitably, away from the sheltering arm that had hitherto en-compassed us, the breeze appeared to freshen, the boat became more lively as the bows struck the short curling seas.

The long isthmus of Spinalongha lay ahead of us to the left, and I had some difficulty in explaining to my helmsman that I did not want him to steer into the comparative tranquillity of the waters bordering the salt-flats, but to continue along the more exposed outward shores of the isthmus bordering the open sea.

'You want to fish?' he shouted above the roar of the engine. 'You find very good fish in there,' pointing to my flats of yesterday.

'No, no,' I shouted back, 'further on along the coast.'

He shrugged. He couldn't believe I had no desire to fish, and I wondered, when we reached our destination, what possible excuse I could make for heading the boat inshore and anchoring, unless – and this seemed plausible enough – I pleaded that the motion of the boat was proving too much for me.

The hills I had climbed yesterday swung into sight above the bows, and then, rounding a neck of land, the inlet itself, the ruined shepherd's hut close to the shore.

'In there,' I pointed. 'Anchor close to the shore.'

He stared at me, puzzled, and shook his head. 'No good,' he shouted, 'too many rocks.'

'Nonsense,' I yelled. 'I saw some people from the hotel anchored here yesterday.'

Suddenly he slowed the engine, so that my voice rang out foolishly on the air. The boat danced up and down in the troughs of the short seas.

'Not a good place to anchor,' he repeated doggedly. 'Wreck there, fouling the ground.'

So there was a wreck. . . . I felt a mounting excitement, and I was not to be put off.

'I don't know anything about that,' I replied, with equal determination, 'but this boat did anchor here, just by the inlet, I saw it myself.'

He muttered something to himself, and made the sign of the cross.

'And if I lose the anchor?' he said. 'What do I say to my brother Nicolai?'

He was nosing the boat gently, very gently, towards the inlet, and then, cursing under his breath, he went forward to the bows and threw the anchor overboard. He waited until it held, then returned and switched off the engine.

'If you want to go in close, you must take the dinghy,' he said sulkily. 'I blow it up for you, yes?'

He went forward once again, and dragged out one of those inflatable rubber affairs they use on air–sea rescue craft.

'Very well,' I said, 'I'll take the dinghy.'

In point of fact, it suited my purpose better. I could paddle close inshore, and would not have him breathing over my shoulder. At the same time, I couldn't forbear a slight prick to his pride.

'The man in charge of the boat yesterday anchored further in without mishap,' I told him.

My helmsman paused in the act of inflating the dinghy.

'If he like to risk my brother's boat that is his affair,' he said shortly. 'I have charge of it today. Other fellow not turn up for work this morning, so he lose his job. I do not want to lose mine.'

I made no reply. If the other fellow had lost his job it was probably because he had pocketed too many tips from Stoll.

The dinghy inflated and in the water, I climbed into it gingerly and began to paddle myself towards the shore. Luckily there was no run upon the spit of sand, and I was able to land successfully and pull the dinghy after me. I noticed that my helmsman was watching me with some interest from his safe anchorage, then, once he perceived that the dinghy was unlikely to come to harm, he turned his back and squatted in the bows of the boat, shoulders humped in protest, meditating no doubt, upon the folly of English visitors.

My reason for landing was that I wanted to judge, from the shore, the exact spot where the boat had anchored yesterday. It was as I thought. Perhaps a hundred yards to the left of where we had anchored today, and closer inshore. The sea was smooth enough, I could navigate it perfectly in the rubber dinghy. I glanced towards the shepherd's hut, and saw my footprints of the day before. There were other footprints too. Fresh ones. The sand in front of the hut had been disturbed. It was as though something had lain there, and then been dragged to the water's edge where I stood now. The goatherd himself perhaps, had visited the place with his flock earlier that morning.

I crossed over to the hut and looked inside. Curious . . . The little pile of rubble, odds and ends of pottery, had gone. The empty bottles still stood in the far corner, and three more had been added to their number, one of them half-full. It was warm inside the hut, and I was sweating. The sun had been beating down on my bare head for nearly an hour – like a fool I had left my hat back in the chalet, not having prepared myself for this expedition – and I was seized with an intolerable thirst. I had acted on impulse, and was paying for it now. It was, in retrospect, an idiotic thing to have done. I might become completely dehydrated, pass out with heat-stroke. The half-bottle of beer would be better than nothing.

I did not fancy drinking from it after the goatherd, if it was indeed he who had brought it here; these fellows were none too clean. Then I remembered the jar in my pocket. Well, it would at least serve a purpose. I pulled the package out of its wrappings and poured the beer into it. It was only after I had swallowed the first draught that I realised it wasn't beer at all. It was barley-water. It was the same home-brewed stuff that Stoll had left for me in the bar. Did the locals, then, drink it too? It was innocuous enough, I knew that; the bar-tender had tasted it himself, and so had his wife.

When I had finished the bottle I examined the jar once again. I don't know how it was, but somehow the leering face no longer seemed so lewd. It had a certain dignity that had escaped me before. The beard, for instance. The beard was shaped to perfection around the base – whoever had fashioned it was a master of his craft. I wondered whether

Socrates had looked thus when he strolled in the Athenian agora with his pupils and discoursed on life. He could have done. And his pupils may not necessarily have been the young men whom Plato said they were, but of a tenderer age, like my lads at school, like those youngsters of eleven and twelve who had smiled upon me in my dreams last night.

I felt the scalloped ears, the rounded nose, the full soft lips of the tutor Silenos upon the jar, the eyes no longer protruding but questioning, appealing, and even the naked horsemen on the top had grown in grace. It seemed to me now they were not strutting in conceit but dancing with linked hands, filled with a gay abandon, a pleasing, wanton joy. It must have been my fear of the midnight intruder that had made me look upon the jar with such distaste.

I put it back in my pocket, and walked out of the hut and down the spit of beach to the rubber dinghy. Supposing I went to the fellow Papitos who had connections with the local museum, and asked him to value the jar? Supposing it was worth hundreds, thousands, and he could dispose of it for me, or tell me of a contact in London? Stoll must be doing this all the time, and getting away with it. Or so the bar-tender had hinted. . . . I climbed into the dinghy and began to paddle away from the shore, thinking of the difference between a man like Stoll, with all his wealth, and myself. There he was, a brute with a skin so thick you couldn't pierce it with a spear, and his shelves back at home in the States loaded with loot. Whereas I . . . Teaching small boys on an in-adequate salary, and all for what? Moralists said that money made no difference to happiness, but they were wrong. If I had a quarter of the Stolls' wealth I could retire, live abroad, on a Greek island, perhaps, and winter in some studio in Athens or Rome. A whole new way of life would open up, and just at the right moment too, before I touched middle-age.

I pulled out from the shore and made for the spot where I judged the boat to have anchored the day before. Then I let the dinghy rest, pulled in my paddles and stared down into the water. The colour was pale green, translucent, yet surely fathoms deep, for, as I looked down to the golden sands beneath, the sea-bed had all the tranquillity of another world, remote from the one I knew. A shoal of fish, silver-bright and gleaming, wriggled their way towards a tress of coral hair that might have graced Aphrodite, but was seaweed moving gently in whatever currents lapped the shore. Pebbles that on land would have been no more than rounded stones were brilliant here as jewels. The breeze that rippled the gulf beyond the anchored boat would never touch these depths, but only the surface of the water, and as the dinghy floated on, circling slowly without pull of wind or tide, I wondered whether it was the motion in itself that had drawn the unhearing Mrs Stoll to underwater swimming. Treasure was the excuse, to satisfy her husband's greed, but down there, in the depths, she would escape from a way of life that must have been unbearable.

Then I looked up at the hills above the retreating spit of sand, and I saw something flash. It was a ray of sunlight upon glass, and the glass moved. Someone was watching me through field-glasses. I rested upon my paddles and stared. Two figures moved stealthily away over the brow of the hill, but I recognised them instantly. One was Mrs Stoll, the other the Greek fellow who had acted as their crew. I glanced over my shoulder to the anchored boat. My helmsman was still staring out to sea. He had seen nothing.

The footsteps outside the hut were now explained. Mrs Stoll, the boatman in tow, had paid a final visit to the hut to clear the rubble, and now, their mission accomplished, they would drive on to the airport to catch the afternoon 'plane to Athens, their journey made several miles longer by the detour along the coast-road. And Stoll himself? Asleep, no doubt, at the back of the car upon the salt-flats, awaiting their return.

The sight of that woman once again gave me a profound distaste for my expedition. I wished I had not come. And my helmsman had spoken the truth; the dinghy was now floating above rock. A ridge must run out here from the shore in a single reef. The sand had darkened, changed in texture, become grey. I peered closer into the water, cupping my eyes with my hands, and suddenly I saw the vast encrusted anchor, the shells and barnacles of centuries upon its spikes, and as the dinghy drifted on the bones of the long-buried craft itself appeared, broken, sparless, her decks, if decks there had been, long since dismembered or destroyed.

Stoll had been right: her bones had been picked clean. Nothing of any value could now remain upon that skeleton. No pitchers, no jars, no gleaming coins. A momentary breeze rippled the water, and when it became clear again and all was still I saw the second anchor by the skeleton bows, and a body, arms outstretched, legs imprisoned in the anchor's jaws. The motion of the water gave the body life, as though, in some desperate fashion, it still struggled for release, but, trapped as it was, escape would never come. The days and nights would follow, months and years, and slowly the flesh would dissolve, leaving the frame impaled upon the spikes.

The body was Stoll's, head, trunk, limbs grotesque, inhuman, as they swayed backwards and forwards at the bidding of the current.

I looked up once more to the crest of the hill, but the two figures had long since vanished, and in an appalling flash of intuition a picture of what had happened became vivid: Stoll strutting on the spit of sand, the half-bottle raised to his lips, and then they struck him down and dragged him to the water's edge, and it was his wife who towed him, drowning, to his final resting-place beneath the surface, there below me, impaled on the crusted anchor. I was sole witness to his fate, and no matter what lies she told to account for his disappearance I would remain silent; it was not my responsibility; guilt might increasingly haunt me, but I must never become involved.

I heard the sound of something choking beside me – I realise now it was myself, in horror and in fear – and I struck at the water with my paddles and started pulling away from the wreck back to the boat. As I did so my arm brushed against the jar in my pocket, and in sudden panic I dragged it forth and flung it overboard. Even as I did so, I knew the gesture was in vain. It did not sink immediately but remained bobbing on the surface, then slowly filled with that green translucent sea, pale as the barley liquid laced with spruce and ivy. Not innocuous but evil, stifling conscience, dulling intellect, the hell-brew of the smiling god Dionysus, which turned his followers into drunken sots, would claim another victim before long. The eyes in the swollen face stared up at me, and they were not only those of Silenos the satyr tutor, and of the drowned Stoll, but my own as well, as I should see them soon reflected in a mirror. They seemed to hold all knowledge in their depths, and all despair.

Thomasina Weber

The Game

Roger Clamm put the *Bolero* on low and stroked the stretching swan on the console as he listened to the first few bars. 'Lovely, isn't it?'

There was no reply from the girl sitting on the floor, back against the wall, wiry legs straight out in front of her, one hand resting on a plaid schoolbag. She stared unblinkingly at him. She had been motionless for fifteen minutes, a remarkable achievement for a child of nine. She did not seem in the least afraid.

He had parked beside the school every day for a week to confirm his initial impression of her character – the surly, inpudent kind who would grow up to be the type of woman he hated most. These were the ones who had a lesson to learn. Some of them required a lot of teaching before they understood. Others never learned at all. They were the ones Roger had to eliminate. You might call it a sort of birth control, after the fact.

'What is your name, dear?' he asked.

'Betty.'

'Betty what?'

'Just Betty.' Her voice sounded rather grim, he thought.

He smiled. 'I must apologise for tricking you into my car, Betty, but I wanted you to visit me. I like little girls.'

'You're a liar,' she said flatly.

'The first time I saw you, I said to myself, "Now, there goes a charming young lady, one I would very much like to meet." '

'Why didn't you come to my house?'

'It was you I wanted to meet, not your parents.'

'My parents would like you. They are liars, too.'

'Why, Betty, what a thing to say! But let's not talk about them. Do you like me, dear?'

'No.'

'Why not?'

'You're fat and I don't like your voice and I don't like the way you smell.'

Roger's eyebrows lifted. 'You don't like my after-shave lotion? It costs five dollars a bottle.'

'I can smell it all the way across the room.'

'Oh, I see. Too much. Well, I'm glad to know that, Betty. We are never too old to learn.'

'Your hair doesn't look real, either.'

Roger's heart skipped a beat. He had felt so secure in the new crew-cut hairpiece. As soon as this episode was over he would have to dispose of it. He had six of them in all, and each one made him look like a totally different person. He changed styles at home according to his mood, and sometimes he regretted having decided back at the beginning never to adopt one for wear at work. It was more important to maintain a supply of disguises for his hobby, and nothing was more effective than a hairpiece on a normally bald man.

The clock chimed five. 'Are you hungry, sweetheart?' The girl looked at him steadily and said nothing. He felt a twinge of annoyance. 'I have four nice lamb chops in the refrigerator. I am sure when you smell them broiling, you will realise you are very hungry indeed.'

'I won't eat with you.'

'Let's go into the kitchen.' He came toward her and put out his hand. She made no move. 'Betty dear?' Her eyes held his, unafraid. Swiftly he grabbed her long hair and yanked her off the floor. The stubborn little thing did not even whimper. Still holding her hair, he pulled her into the kitchen.

'Sit down, Betty dear,' he said grimly as he shoved her onto a chair by the table. He looked for furtive tears, but there were none. 'I was going to prepare a delicious dinner for us,' he said, turning on the broiler. 'I was going to serve a tossed salad, asparagus tips, minted pears and baked potatoes with butter and sour cream. You have spoiled all that, however, with your inexcusably rude behaviour. I will not go to all that trouble for a nasty little girl.'

'If you don't like me, why don't you let me go?'

He laughed. 'I am not yet ready to send you home, my dear.' He began to set the table. 'I often have guests like yourself. They come from all over the state. Some of them are nice little girls, but some are most unpleasant. I had an unpleasant one here last month. I spent a harrowing night before it was all over.'

Betty looked up at him. 'How did it get "all over"?'

'I'm afraid I can't tell you, Betty dear. I wouldn't want to upset you.'

669

'You won't upset me.'

'Well, she cried a lot. The more she cried, the more I hit her. And the more I hit her, the more she cried.'

'Did you kill her?'

Roger was surprised at the bluntness of her question. Then he realised she was playing a game – or rather, responding to a game she thought he was playing. He smiled down at her. 'All right, Betty, so you don't believe me. But before long you will be changing your mind. I shall certainly see to that, my dear.'

Marvin Wilson at forty-three was the youngest juvenile judge in the history of Fairview. He was also the most well-liked. He was a stranger to politics, and everyone he had contact with was treated as equal. His secretaries starred him in their bachelor-flat fantasies and his colleagues admired and respected him. He was a devoted family man, but did not burden others with his private affairs. No one ever had to gush over the latest picture of his wife and daughter.

At the moment Marvin Wilson was sitting on the couch in his living room while his wife paced back and forth before him. 'Please, Alice, it won't do any good to have hysterics.'

'Where can she be, Marvin? It's four o'clock!'

'She probably went home with one of her classmates.'

'But they all have telephones!'

'When two nine-year-old girls get together, I am sure the furthest thing from their minds is phoning home.'

'Doesn't she know how we worry?'

'Does she ever consider our feelings, Alice?'

'She's only a child.'

'You have been saying that from the day we got her.'

'Let's not go into that now, Marvin. That is an entirely different matter.'

'It is the root of everything that happens in our house, including this latest escapade.'

'It sounds as if you believe she is worrying us intentionally!'

'Would that surprise you?'

Alice covered her eyes with her hand. 'Please, Marvin, I'm going out of my mind with worry.'

'That is just what Elizabeth would like you to do.'

'But Elizabeth loves me!'

'I'm sure she does, in her own twisted way.'

Alice turned abruptly and picked up the phone. Marvin was instantly at her side. 'What are you going to do?'

'I'm calling the police.'

'The police are not going to start an all-out search simply because a child is an hour overdue from school.'

'I'll explain about Elizabeth, how headstrong she is, how independent.'

'How troubled?' Marvin took the phone from his wife's fingers. 'We can't do that, dear. Have you forgotten I am the juvenile judge in this town? How would it look it I could not handle my own child?'

'We are not the only parents in the world with an unruly child.'

'Unruly!'

'Unruly,' Alice repeated doggedly. 'She will outgrow it.'

'She will outgrow it all right, but she will become worse, not better.'

'Then what do you suggest if you don't let me call the police?'

'I suggest we calm ourselves and wait for her to come home.'

'Suppose she can't come home? Suppose she is lying in a ditch somewhere, a hit-and-run victim? Suppose she got lost?'

'Elizabeth will never get lost. She could find her way back from hell if necessary.'

Alice picked up the telephone again. 'I'll call her girl friends.' At the end of ten minutes Alice said numbly, 'She's not anywhere.'

'Has it occurred to you, Alice, that Elizabeth may have run away? Now don't look at me like that. She has done it before.'

'But that was different! She ran away after – after that bratty boy next door told her she was adopted.'

'That was the first time. She did it again after she had drawn those – detailed sketches all over our bedroom walls, and again after we found your canary smothered in a bag.'

Alice dropped to the couch and hid her face against the cushions. 'She's only a little girl.'

The telephone rang. Alice pounced on it. 'Hello?' She listened. 'Oh. I'm sorry, we can't talk to you now.'

Marvin took the phone before she could hang up. 'Marvin Wilson speaking.'

'Judge Wilson, this is Miss Brownley at Willowhaven.'

'Oh, yes. Please forgive my wife, Miss Brownley. She is – rather busy at the moment.'

'Of course. We have managed to make some readjustments in order to accommodate Elizabeth,' she said. 'You have been very patient.'

'That is good news, Miss Brownley.' He should have thought of making that sizable donation six months ago.

'You may bring the child at eleven tomorrow.'

Marvin thanked her and hung up, prepared for the icy look on his wife's face. 'Eleven o'clock tomorrow,' he said. Alice sat in stony silence. 'We agreed Willowhaven was the only answer, dear.'

'A private reform school!'

671

'Willowhaven is not a reform school,' he said wearily. 'Why do you refuse to accept the truth? Elizabeth is beyond us. She needs professional help, and they have some of the best doctors in the field on their staff.'

'Spiriting her away and telling people she has gone to visit her grandmother when all the time she will be imprisoned in that so-called estate with bars on the windows! *Bars*, Marvin. Our child behind bars!'

'Willowhaven specialises in helping people whose circumstances demand anonymity. The bars are for the patients' own protection. Some of them are seriously disturbed.' He took his wife's hand. 'She won't have to stay long, Alice. I'm sure she won't.'

Alice snatched her hand back. 'She won't even get there. She's missing, remember?'

'I'll take the car and see if I can find her.'

'A needle in the haystack! What we need is the police. They know how to search and where. We know nothing about such things.'

'We will do our best. If we can't find her, then we will see about getting help. Now, come along.'

'I'll stay here.'

'I want you with me.'

'You don't trust me, do you? You think I am going to telephone the police the minute you are out the door.'

'That's true, Alice, but I need your help. Two pairs of eyes are better than one, especially when one has to watch the traffic.'

'But what if Elizabeth calls?'

'If she hasn't called by now, she won't.'

'I suppose you expect her to come waltzing in here just as if nothing had happened?'

'That is exactly what I expect her to do.'

Betty watched the man put two lamb chops on each plate. 'You have spoiled my dinner, Betty. Lamb chops by themselves are extremely unpalatable.'

They looked rotten. Betty had never liked lamb chops. And she didn't like kidney pie or liver or pot roast. She liked hotdogs, but they never had hotdogs at home.

'Don't you have any hotdogs?'

'*Hotdogs?* It gives me indigestion just to think of them, my child. Eat your lamb chops like a good girl.'

'I don't want them.'

A funny look came over his face, as if he wanted to hit her, but when he spoke his voice was casual. 'Very well, don't eat them, then. You may go hungry.'

She watched him eat. He had good manners. He cut the meat small and chewed one piece at a time with his mouth closed, just as They said you are supposed to do. She wondered if They were worried about her, the people she lived with – the ones she had thought were her parents but who were really nobody except the world's biggest liars. She hoped They were worried; They deserved to be punished, but she knew They wouldn't be. Grownups got away with everything. They smiled and served tea and kissed you and bought you whatever you wanted and pretended to love you. But they were lying. They could say anything at all and it didn't matter if it was true or not. In a way, Betty was glad she had found out, because as long as They lied, it was all right for her to lie, and lying was sometimes much easier than telling the truth.

'Well now, shall we do the dishes, Betty? My lamb chops were delicious, but yours were even better.' He carried the dishes to the sink and put them in the dishwater.

Betty took the rinsed plate out of the drainer. It was a pretty plate and she could almost see through it. It must have cost a lot of money. She opened her fingers and let it drop to the floor.

The man looked down at the shattered plate, then at her. 'You have broken one of my best dishes, young lady.' His face was quite red. 'Are you going to apologise?'

'Why should I?'

He slapped her hard across the face, but the tears that sprang to her eyes were tears of rage rather than pain. She watched him fold the towel. Then he put out his hand. 'Come, Betty, we will go into the living room and relax. Sit in the chair by the fireplace, dear, so I can look at you.'

She ignored the chair, moving instead to the spot on the floor where she had been sitting before.

'Betty, I want you to sit in the chair.'

'I'm getting my schoolbag.' When she was settled in the chair by the fireplace, she opened her schoolbag and took out a pencil and a notebook.

'What are you doing, dear?'

'I'm drawing.'

'Ah! A budding artist.'

She began to sketch the statue on the mantel. It was a woman with a bedsheet draped over half of her. The other half was bare. Betty drew a sweatshirt reaching to her knees and gave her a bald head.

'I do believe I'm getting a slight touch of heartburn,' said the man. 'It is hardly surprising, eating an unbalanced meal like that. Oh well, by this time tomorrow it will be all over and I will celebrate with a thick steak and mushroom gravy. Perhaps snails on the side would be novel.'

She looked up at him. 'You eat snails?'

'They are delectable, my dear, once you cultivate a taste for them.'

673

She drew his face in the corner of her paper. She gave it slanted eyes and a huge garbage chute for a mouth.

'Come sit on my lap, sweetheart.'

'Why do you keep calling me sweetheart?'

'Because you are a darling little girl.'

'You're a liar.'

He moved quickly. Her notebook slid to the floor as he pulled her to her feet. His fingers were digging painfully into her arms. 'I had no idea you were such a naughty little creature,' he said quietly.

His eyes were bloodshot and his nose had lots of red lines running every which way over it. The nostrils were wide as his breath rushed noisily in and out of them. He was really mad now. 'I am trying very hard to be nice to you, Betty. One most be polite to one's guests. Manners are of the utmost importance in civilised society.'

'Drop dead.'

He hit her with a closed fist this time. She lay on the floor where she had fallen. His shoes were a few inches from her face. They were shiny brown and very wide. They looked new. She wondered how they would look with blood dripping on them.

'Now see what you made me do,' he said sadly. 'I don't like to lose my temper. Get up, Betty.'

She stayed where she was. If he wanted her to get up, he could make her. He did. She gritted her teeth and closed her eyes. It felt as if he was pulling every hair out of her head. She was almost tempted to leave right then, but that wouldn't punish Them enough. She wanted Them to get a real bellyful as They watched the hours drag by and wondered where she was. And besides, he needed to be punished, too.

'Now, shall we start all over again? Come sit on my lap, dear.' He smiled at her from the couch. She remained where she was. 'If you don't come here immediately, I am going to beat you with a strap.' She walked over to stand before him. He patted his knee. She sat and he put his arm around her. The after-shave lotion made her feel like throwing up. She wondered if anyone had ever been poisoned with after-shave lotion.

'Why did you tell me to drop dead?' he asked.

'Because you deserve to be dead.'

He smiled. His teeth were brown from smoking cigarettes. 'Let's play a game, Betty. Do you like games?'

'Sometimes.'

'This one is called Duel. Have you ever heard of it?'

'Sure.'

The man laughed. 'You are a bit of a liar yourself, Betty. You could not have heard of the game because I made it up myself just this minute.' He led her into the kitchen, took two small paring knives out of the drawer and handed one to her. 'Now, my dear, we have our weapons and we are ready to play. The object is—'

'To see who can kill the other one first.'

He laughed loudly. 'I hardly think anyone can be killed with these small knives!'

'I always win when I play Duel.'

'You have never played Duel, Betty. I told you it is my own invention.'

'I played it with the boy next door. I killed him.'

'Tut, tut, such stories! I am sure if you killed the boy next door with a knife—'

'I didn't use a knife.'

'But you can't play Duel without knives.'

'We were swimming in the river. He didn't swim too good.'

'And you drowned him, of course.'

'Of course.'

'If you say so. Now. We stand facing each other like this. You must watch for an opening and then move in and try to slash the other person like — so!' She heard her skirt rip and looked down. It was hanging in two pieces at the side. 'Head up! Head up!' he warned. 'You must never take your eyes off your opponent!'

She imitated his stance, but her eyes were on a level with his stomach and she was not crouching as he was. His belt buckle was silver and nice to look at. She would tell Them to buy her one just like it when she got back home.

He made another lunge with his knife, but she was too quick for him. He went rushing past her as she stepped aside. This was fun. She laughed. He laughed too. After three more unsuccessful attempts, he was no longer laughing. They were in the living room now. His face was red and he was sweating. He was a poor sport. It was his game and she had not wanted to play, but he made her and now she was winning and he was mad about it. But she was not winning if she wasn't stabbing him. Winning was not just keeping from getting cut yourself; winning was killing the other person. The other liar.

He was not pretending to be sweet and kind any more. His eyes were wild, just as they had been when he slapped her and when he punched her. He hated her, just as everyone else hated her despite their hugs and kisses. 'You are a little cheat!' He threw down his knife. 'I'll teach you and all those other nasty little girls—' He grasped her upper arms, hunching her shoulders together. He had no right to be mad at her, to punish her. As he pulled her to him, she thrust her knife at his body, feeling it sink into something soft.

He bellowed and released her, grabbling his side. She got in two more stabs before running to the window. She hated him even more than she hated Them now. She was going home. She threw a lamp through the glass and leaped nimbly over the low sill. She glanced back before taking off. A sudden fury flashed through her; she had not won the game after all. He was still on his feet, standing in the middle of the floor, his hands pressed to his side. He looked scared to death. She wished there had been enough blood to drip on his shiny new shoes.

The grandfather clock in the hall struck nine. 'Marvin, we have scoured this town and there is no sign of Elizabeth. I am going to call the police whether you like it or not. Your pride is certainly not more important than the safety of our child.'

'It is not my pride, Alice, it's my reputation. Don't you realise this publicity could ruin my career, and then we would not be able to afford help for Elizabeth?'

'We may not need help for Elizabeth if we don't find her soon.'

She picked up the phone. Maybe she was right, he thought wearily. Maybe in doing what he had thought best for all of them he had committed a ghastly mistake. Maybe he should have called the police sooner. Whatever he and Alice had done to bring it about, whatever the cause, what Elizabeth suffered from was a form of mental illness. If people chose to castigate him because of it, then it was no more than he deserved, had he been in any way to blame. The important thing was to restore Elizabeth to normalcy. If his career suffered, he would have to find the money somewhere else.

Alice was dialing the phone when the knock came at the door. Marvin went to answer it, telling himself after the first pang of hope that Elizabeth would not be knocking on the door of her own home.

Marvin stared incredulously at the highway patrolman standing there with Elizabeth. Her skirt was torn and her legs were covered with scratches. There was a large purple bruise below one eye.

'Elizabeth!' He dropped to his knees and took her in his arms. She stood there like a stick, not moving. 'Alice!' he called. Then, 'Where did you find her, Officer?'

'A motorist reported seeing a little girl walking along the highway in the direction of Fairview. When he tried to give her a lift, she ran into the woods. By the time I got there, she was back on the highway again.'

'*Elizabeth!*' Alice was laughing and crying at the same time. Marvin noticed how the child stared straight ahead, enduring the embrace. His heart ached for both of them.

'I'll have to make out a report, Judge Wilson.'

'Oh. Yes.' His hand went to his back pocket. 'I wonder – would you step into the other room with me for a moment?'

Betty put on the dumb act and They let her go to bed. She was glad to see how upset They had been. She felt very powerful. It was a good feeling.

The next morning She made a special breakfast of fruit juice and waffles with plenty of butter and syrup and hot chocolate with a marshmallow in it. They kept asking her all kinds of questions, just like They did when Bobby next door had drowned, but They knew she would not answer anything until she was ready.

'Aren't you going to the courthouse this morning?' Betty finally asked Him.

'Not today, Elizabeth. I have something very important to do. Besides, I want to hear all about your – adventure.'

'Why?'

'Because we're interested, dear,' She said.

'I got kidnapped.'

'You did?' She said. 'Who kidnapped you, Elizabeth?'

'A big man who smelled.'

'Oh!' She cried.

'Alice, let me talk to the child, please. Now, Elizabeth, suppose you tell us the truth. Did you go into the woods to play after school and then when you tore your skirt you were afraid to come home, so you waited until after dark, thinking we would be so glad to see you we wouldn't punish you for your carelessness?'

'I got kidnapped.'

'Elizabeth, we are not going to punish you,' He said. 'All we want is the truth.'

'He took me to a big rich house and he cooked lamb chops, only I wouldn't eat them, so he slapped me.'

'Elizabeth, we were very worried about you,' She said. 'We do not want you to do such a thing again. No matter what happens, you can always come to us and we will help you.'

'And you'll believe me?'

'Of course, dear!' She said.

'I was kidnapped. We played Duel and I stabbed him.'

His chair made a scraping noise on the floor as He pushed it back. 'Let's go into the living room, Elizabeth.'

'Marvin—'

'I'll take care of this, Alice. You'd better get ready. It is an hour's drive to Willowhaven.'

He sat beside her on the couch. 'Elizabeth, we have an appointment at eleven o'clock this morning at Willowhaven. Have you ever heard of Willowhaven?' She shook her head. 'It is a special school where children go who – don't get along too well with other people.'

677

She was not surprised. They hated her and They were going to send her away. She had known that would happen sooner or later.

'They have wonderful teachers there who will be able to spend more time with you than the teachers you have now.'

They were taking her to jail. There would be bars on the windows and bars on the doors and they would never let her out. He and She would stand safely on the other side and smile bravely at her, but all the while They would be laughing inside and congratulating each other because They had finally got rid of Their little monster.

'I want you to be polite and ladylike during our interview this morning, and if the director asks you any questions, I want you to answer them truthfully.'

Betty laughed. She could just imagine His face if she told the director that she had drowned the boy next door after he told her about the people she lived with. And she could picture His face if she told the director how she had stabbed the man and almost won the game.

'It is not funny, Elizabeth.'

She hated Him when He frowned like that. He never thought anything was funny.

'You are going to live at Willowhaven for a while. You will be happy. There are other children there and you will make friends.'

'I'm not going.'

'It has been all arranged, Elizabeth.'

'She won't let you put me away.'

'We are not "putting you away," Elizabeth. You are going for a visit—'

'You'll leave me there to die. You'll forget about me. I won't go.'

'I'm sorry, but it is all settled. The interview is only a formality.'

'I'll louse up the interview. They won't let me in.'

'If you misbehave at the interview, you will only be hurting yourself. If they think you are seriously disturbed, they will keep you there longer, that's all.'

It was a trap with no way out. There was nothing she could do. But maybe He wasn't telling the truth about the interview. Maybe it wasn't all arranged. If she made a big enough fuss, maybe they would refuse to take her. She could knock over a lamp, sweep the junk off the director's desk, kick over the chairs—

'It is time to get dressed now, Elizabeth.'

'Our director will be with you shortly,' the woman said as she led the three of them into his office, where they seated themselves facing the big desk with no one behind it.

Betty noted with satisfaction the thick glass ashtrays that would smash into a million pieces upon contact with the floor. She noticed the black desk set from which rose two shiny pens made to look like feather quills. A carved silver box that probably held cigarettes was almost within her reach. Maybe she wouldn't damage that one. She would like to have it for her own. Maybe during the commotion she could slip it into her coat pocket. She could use it for keeping poisoned arrow tips in when she could get hold of some. The carving looked sort of jungley anyway.

The door behind her opened. 'Good morning, good morning. Lovely day, is it not?'

Betty did not look around. He got up and stretched His hand out to the director. She murmured, 'Lovely day. Yes.'

'And this must be the little lady.' She felt a hand on her shoulder. She wondered exactly how big an arrow tip was and how many the silver box would hold.

The hand was removed and she could hear him moving around her to sit behind his desk. The chair creaked and he groaned. 'Had a little accident yesterday,' he said, holding his side. 'Can't get around too well.'

Betty looked up. Their eyes met and locked. Betty smiled. Starting at the top of his bald head, the director turned colour – slowly, evenly, as if a gray cloth were being deliberately dragged down over his face.

'I am sure Elizabeth will be happy here,' She was saying.

'We believe in being honest, Mr Clamm,' He was saying. 'Elizabeth may be rather difficult at first—'

But Roger Clamm was not listening. He was staring at Betty. Betty continued to smile at him, thinking of the unfinished game. She did not even hear Them when they got up to leave.

Arthur Porges

The Fanatic

They were lying on the knoll, a most incongruous couple in appearance – he so short, shaggy; untidy, and dark, with the hot intolerant eyes of a fanatic; and she, immaculate in her light summer frock, the ultimate in a cool, Nordic blonde.

The sun dipped below the horizon, allowing purple dusk to smoke up from the earth.

'Now you'll see,' he muttered.

'If I didn't know you better, I'd think you were serious.'

'I am – damned serious. Serious enough to take steps, and soon.' He gave her a puzzled scrutiny. 'I thought you understood; that you weren't like those clods in the bar.'

'But I was sure you were just seeing how much they'd swallow. I never dreamed – Jerry, you can't *mean* you really believe the things you said.'

His pale eyes flared more hotly under their heavy brows.

'I might've known,' he rasped. 'What made me think a girl you pick up in a bar might have a few brains. Look, Eunice –'

'Men in bars can have brains, no matter how much they guzzle,' she interrupted him. 'But women are different, huh? It's not my brains that are in question, but yours, if you truly believe –'

'Skip it,' he said. 'Here they come now. Watch and learn something – if that one is still in there.'

The bats were pouring out of the cave, millions of them it seemed, although an experienced observer would place that total under ten thousand. Still, as they came like dark smoke from the narrow opening the sheer bulk of their flow was overwhelming in its effect on the eye recalling the vast flights of passenger pigeons a hundred years earlier.

Jerry had his binoculars raised, and was studying the fringes of the horde. Suddenly he grasped the girl's arm, abstractedly aware of the firmness of her flesh; she's certainly quite a physical specimen, some inner part of his brain told him. Healthy as a horse – maybe a little dumber, which was disappointing, since he'd hoped there would be an ally at last . . .

'Look!' he cried. 'On the right of the main crowd – that bunch of eight – no, nine. What do you see?'

He passed her the binoculars, but she waved them aside.

'I can see,' she said calmly, her large blue eyes narrowing for a moment.

'Well?' he demanded impatiently. 'Yes or no?'

'They're just bats, I suppose.'

'Hell!' he snapped. 'Why do I waste my time. I *told* you what to look for. Now they're out of range.' He eyed her in a kind of disgust. 'You mean to tell me you couldn't see the difference?'

'For heaven's sake, Jerry, I'm no expert! What do I know about bats? They were all flying up and down –'

'Like hell they were. One was soaring – like a hawk. This is the third time I've spotted it. Just a hair bigger; maybe a bit off-colour; that doesn't matter. But bats don't soar – ever. Maybe that's because at night there aren't the updraughts day birds use; or maybe because they catch flying insects on the wing. But bats don't soar.' He took out a fat, maroon-covered notebook, and checked something off. Then he closed it with an air of finality. 'That's it. I have enough data. It's time to *do* something.'

'What *is* this data – not those little things –'

'These data – the word is plural,' he said irritably, only half-listening. Then, angrily: 'Little things! You weren't listening last night. Animals are very rigid in certain aspects of their behaviour. When you see a dog that never circles before lying down, a pigeon that forgets to bob its head; a bat that soars, instead of flitting –'

'You're too wrapped up in this wild idea,' she said. Then she put one hand on his arm in a rubbing, caressing motion, and added: 'Don't you ever want to have any fun? Just enjoy yourself?'

He moodily pushed her fingers free, and said almost to himself: 'Women are just like cats. When a guy has the time and the strongest urge, they have to wash their hair or visit their mother. But the minute he's up to his neck in something really important, then they begin to feel amorous. Once I clear up this business, Baby, you'll see –'

'I don't know why I waste so much time on you,' she said plaintively. Then, in a coaxing voice: 'Jerry, did you ever think of seeing a doctor?'

He grinned sourly.

ARTHUR PORGES

'Why don't you say it? Psychiatrist; head-shrinker.' He laughed in a harsh voice, without mirth. 'And I don't know why I bother to wake people up. Any culture, no matter how alien, would be an improvement on what we've got. Maybe I don't like being suckered. Even if nobody else is wise to Them –'

'Oh, brother!' she exclaimed. 'The old story. "Them." '

'I went at it wrong last time,' he said, ignoring the remark. 'I tried dissection, looking for different organs and things like that. But I'm not enough of a pathologist. And I couldn't get any help, damn it. I even tried sending rabbit's blood to a Public Health Office, asking for a tularemia check; I hoped they might spot something funny in the sample. But the clowns just reported negative on the tularemia. If there was something, they missed it, naturally; you have to be prepared, and not just doing a routine job, I suppose.'

'Isn't it possible,' she demanded, 'that lower animals have their morons and misfits, too?'

'Some, sure. But I've seen too many aberrations. And this time I've a better angle.'

'What is it?'

'If I tell you, you'll want to go running to the cops or something,' he said. There was a wistful tone in his voice. She sensed instantly that he still yearned for a confidant.

'I won't – I promise. Tell me.'

'Well, let's assume some of these animals are not animals at all, as I've been saying, but spies of a sort. Don't ask me from where, but very intelligent. This way they can go anywhere, and study us; wild and domestic – both. I know it's like something from the corniest old science-fiction magazines; but truth is always essentially corny. All right; they're dedicated and clever; some – maybe most – will die rather than talk. But no society is free of weaklings. With enough stress – the right threat – some will break. The minute I get a cat or dog or squirrel – or a bat – to talk – in English, their little plan is blown sky-high, that's beyond question.'

She gaped at him with those great blue eyes wide.

'You mean you're going to torture animals? Trying to make them *speak*?'

'I said you'd raise a fuss.'

'Jerry, don't you see – this is a sickness, really.'

'Sure, like Pasteur's, when he talked about germs; or Einstein's, when he said space was curved: or –'

'Those other animals – the ones you – you cut up. Where did you get them?'

'I told you I live in Redwood Canyon – in a shack, to be brutally frank. I haven't had time to make a decent living and still save the stupid human race. Anyhow, there are plenty of animals there: rabbits, gophers, deer, raccoons, ground squirrels, lizards, foxes, weasels – you name 'em. When I saw one that didn't seem normal – and I don't mean just a sick or off-coloured specimen – I tried to trap or shoot it. I didn't get too far that way, and anyhow I was careless. Some nosy neighbours reported me, and I got fined and warned. It's the old story,' he added bitterly. 'The very people you're trying to help are the ones who crucify you every damned time. But now I know how to go about it, and when I'm through, I'll have evidence on tape and film that would convince anybody.'

'And you honestly feel, now, that if you torture enough of these – these different little animals, you'll make one speak in English. And you'll get the words on tape, with pictures.'

'Yes, I do,' he said defiantly. He patted the notebook in his shirt pocket. 'This tells me I'm right. Hundreds of cases. Cats that don't wash some parts of their bodies, because they can't manage the tricky stance a real cat knows from kittenhood. Cocks that fight but never peck the ground at intervals. A mole that didn't bite off the heads of the worms it caught, I could go on for hours. Some were just different, I know; but you develop an instinct after a while – or a flair. Hundreds of biologists saw what Darwin did in his travels, but he was the only one to see the vital patterns. I see a vital pattern hidden in natural aberrations. I may be wrong, but I don't think so, and the stakes are very high. Unless the world is warned, this reconnaissance could be followed by a take-over in force. But if we're ready . . .'

She looked at him in silence, then shook her head in a pitying gesture.

'Doesn't it occur to you,' she said, 'that first of all such spies wouldn't let you trap them?'

'On the contrary. Not knowing my motives, they might hope for it – deliberately walk into the traps, in order to make inside observations on a human.'

She was taken aback for a moment, then said: 'On the other hand, if they are spies, invaders, won't they kill you if you're getting at their secret?'

'They might,' he said coolly. 'But I'm hoping that as spies, they won't carry arms; it would be risky if one were killed accidentally, by a car, say, and had some strange instrument on its body. They are here, I presume, primarily for information. I do run the risk that they can communicate over long distances; but I doubt if that's so, or I'd have had trouble with the ones I captured or shot before. They'd have tipped off the others by now.'

'You certainly have all the answers,' she said in a dry voice. 'And you mean to begin torturing all kinds of little animals.'

'Not all so little. I've seen deer that weren't deer; and a bear that passed up honey.'

'Could I come by and watch?'

He was surprised, and showed it.

'Watch? But I thought – it's an unpleasant business; I don't deny that. I *must* do it, but you . . .' He broke off, and gave her a sharp stare. 'Oh, no. Is the sadism coming out? After all those pious protests, you'd enjoy some blood and squeals. Get lost, lady; you and I don't speak the same language. Beat it – remember, I didn't pick you up; it was the other way around. Go away; you make me sick!'

She stood up, so tall, slim, and lovely, with that perfect Ice-Queen profile.

'You're very stupid and unfair; I hate you.'

She strode off, walking like an empress.

'The people you run into,' he said darkly. 'Are these the characters I'm trying to save? And she so clean-looking and all – ah, t'hell with her. It's a sickness, I suppose. She can't help it; but not in my lab; bad enough I have to do the dirty work, without making a free show of it.'

It was now quite dark. He got up stiffly, and walked to the jalopy. He half-expected her to be sitting in it; the town was a long hike away. But she was gone. He called her name a few times, being unwilling to abandon her out here; but there was no reply. Finally he shrugged, and drove off.

The next morning, Jerry steeled himself to begin what might turn out to be a long and rather revolting investigation. But just as another fanatic, John Brown, was able to slaughter innocent and guilty alike in his crusade against slavery, which to him was sufficient justification, so this one felt that the high stakes were proper enough grounds for the abuse of helpless animals.

There was just enough doubt in his own mind to make him begin with the most promising of his five captives. The mouse, somehow, however un-rodentlike its behaviour, seemed less promising as a spy, although Jerry told himself this was foolish prejudice and the power of preconceived ideas. Similarly, the rabbit, with its tradition of Disney-cuteness, was almost too endearing a creature to torment. It would be unfair, however, to suggest that the one he chose to begin on – a young raccoon – was to be sacrificed because of its bandit-like appearance, complete with black mask. In a matter like this, Jerry knew very well, it was quite preposterous to judge by look; the villainous and sly raccoon might be only a wayward member of its tribe, and the cute, bright-eyed mouse a spy-chief. Still, one had to begin somewhere.

With thick gloves, Jerry pulled the raccoon from the wire cage, and, not without considerable difficulty, tied the struggling beast to a heavy table, well fitted for the purpose with screw-eyes. It was not necessary, in the circumstances, to make the animal completely immobile as for a delicate operation, in which case an anaesthetic would be used, anyhow. It was only necessary that the raccoon be unable to escape and so frustrate the experimenter.

Then he lit the little butane welding torch, and approached the captive.

'I know you understand what I'm saying,' he told the raccoon, 'so it's no use pretending. Nothing will stop me from burning you alive, right on the table, unless you tell me, in English, just what you are, who sent you, and why – in detail. Now we understand each other, right?'

At the sound of his voice, the raccoon stopped its frantic lunges against the tough cords, and looked at him, eyes brightly feral. Then it resumed its struggles, breathing hoarsely and muttering in its throat.

'All right; it's your choice. We'll have to do it the hard way,' Jerry said tonelessly, his forehead suddenly damp. 'Maybe you don't know what fire feels like. Maybe on your planet accidents don't happen where people get burned badly. Maybe, even, in your real shape you don't feel pain – or can't feel it now. Maybe you'll pretend it hurts, but I have a way of knowing – which I don't intend to tell you. If you can't feel pain, I'll *know* I'm right, and push all the harder to break things wide open . . . But first things first.'

He adjusted the flame to a blue cone, and deftly flicked it across the raccoon's left ear. The animal snarled, and then gave a whimpering little cry. It shook its head several times; the ear wiggled feverishly.

'Hurts, doesn't it?' Jerry asked. 'That was just a tiny sample. When I hold the flame right against your body, it will be quite unbearable – if you really feel anything.'

I must remember, he told himself; don't get too excited out of pity. While burning keep feeling for increased heart-beat and pulse; he won't know about hiding those, even if he pretends to be in agony. And if they show up, I'll know he's hurting badly, and may talk.

He was about to apply the flame to the raccoon's left fore-leg, when the door opened behind him. He whirled, his heart sinking. If some damned nosy neighbour even caught him at this . . . !

'You!' he said. 'I told you –'

'I had to come,' Eunice said. She looked at the tied raccoon, her blue eyes flaming with indignation. 'Oh, the poor little thing; it's just a cub!'

She glared at Jerry. 'Why that one?'

'If it matters to you, or you know the difference,' he said, 'this raccoon didn't wash its food – except when it knew I was watching. It's my number one suspect as of now. Better get out of here; you won't like the beginning, but when he talks, you'll owe me a fat apology.'

'I won't go,' she said.

'I could throw you out.'

'The door doesn't even have a lock,' she said, giving the shack a contemptuous scrutiny.

'Stay if you like, but if you interfere, I warn you, I'll forget you're a girl, and knock you down if I have to.'

He stepped up to the raccoon, and held the flame against the animal's leg. A shrill, almost human scream burst from the tortured beast.

'Did that sound like a raccoon to you?' he asked the girl. 'By God, it was like nothing I've ever heard. What'll you bet –'

'How could it be normal, burning alive?' she demanded. 'You must stop this, Jerry.'

'No,' he said flatly. 'This should be the big break-through.' And he advanced the torch again.

Then the raccoon spoke. Its voice, in contrast with its rascally appearance, was oddly soft and well modulated, but brightly and resonantly non-human.

'It's no use,' the creature said. 'I can't bear it. And anyhow, he's bound to be a problem.'

'I agree,' Eunice said, and, gulping, Jerry spun on his heel to face the little automatic directed at his face.

'Not all of us are disguised as *lower* animals,' the girl said. 'You just had to keep pushing.' Then she fired three shots into Jerry's head.

Harlan Ellison

The Whimper of Whipped Dogs

On the night after the day she had stained the louvered window shutters of her new apartment on East 52nd Street, Beth saw a woman slowly and hideously knifed to death in the courtyard of her building. She was one of twenty-six witnesses to the ghoulish scene and, like them, she did nothing to stop it.

She saw it all, every moment of it, without break and with no impediment to her view. Quite madly, the thought crossed her mind as she watched in horrified fascination, that she had the sort of marvellous line of observation Napoleon had sought when he caused to have constructed at the *Comédie-Française* theatres, a curtained box at the rear, so he could watch the audience as well as the stage. The night was clear, the moon was full, she had just turned off the 11:30 movie on channel 2 after the second commercial break, realising she had already seen Robert Taylor in *Westward the Women*, and had disliked it the first time; and the apartment was quite dark.

She went to the window, to raise it six inches for the night's sleep, and she saw the woman stumble into the courtyard. She was sliding along the wall, clutching her left arm with her right hand. Con Ed had installed mercury vapour lamps on the poles; there had been sixteen assaults in seven months; the courtyard was illuminated with a chill purple glow that made the blood streaming down the woman's left arm look black and shiny. Beth saw every detail with utter clarity, as though magnified a thousand power under a microscope, solarised as if it had been a television commercial.

The woman threw back her head, as if she were trying to scream, but there was no sound. Only the traffic on First Avenue, late cabs foraging for singles paired for the night at Maxwell's Plum and Friday's and

687

Adam's Apple. But that was over there, beyond. Where *she* was, down there seven floors below, in the courtyard, everything seemed silently suspended in an invisible force-field.

Beth stood in the darkness of her apartment, and realised she had raised the window completely. A tiny balcony lay just over the low sill; now not even glass separated her from the sight; just the wrought iron balcony railing and seven floors to the courtyard below.

The woman staggered away from the wall, her head still thrown back, and Beth could see she was in her mid-thirties, with dark hair cut in a shag; it was impossible to tell if she was pretty: terror had contorted her features and her mouth was a twisted black slash, opened but emitting no sound. Cords stood out in her neck. She had lost one shoe, and her steps were uneven, threatening to dump her to the pavement.

The man came around the corner of the building, into the courtyard. The knife he held was enormous – or perhaps it only seemed so: Beth remembered a bone-handled fish knife her father had used one summer at the lake in Maine: it folded back on itself and locked, revealing eight inches of serrated blade. The knife in the hand of the dark man in the courtyard seemed to be similar.

The woman saw him and tried to run, but he leaped across the distance between them and grabbed her by the hair and pulled her head back as though he would slash her throat in the next reaper-motion.

Then the woman screamed.

The sound skirled up into the courtyard like bats trapped in an echo chamber, unable to find a way out, driven mad. It went on and on . . .

The man struggled with her and she drove her elbows into his sides and he tried to protect himself, spinning her around by her hair, the terrible scream going up and up and never stopping. She came loose and he was left with a fistful of hair torn out by the roots. As she spun out, he slashed straight across and opened her up just below the breasts. Blood sprayed through her clothing and the man was soaked; it seemed to drive him even more berserk. He went at her again, as she tried to hold herself together, the blood pouring down over her arms.

She tried to run, teetered against the wall, slid sideways, and the man struck the brick surface. She was away, stumbling over a flower bed, falling, getting to her knees as he threw himself on her again. The knife came up in a flashing arc that illuminated the blade strangely with purple light. And still she screamed.

Lights came on in dozens of apartments and people appeared at windows.

He drove the knife to the hilt into her back, high on the right shoulder. He used both hands.

Beth caught it all in jagged flashes – the man, the woman, the knife, the blood, the expressions on the faces of those watching from the windows. Then lights clicked off in the windows, but they still stood there, watching.

She wanted to yell, to scream, 'What are you doing to that woman?' But her throat was frozen, two iron hands that he had immersed in dry ice for ten thousand years clamped around her neck. She could feel the blade sliding into her own body.

Somehow – it seemed impossible but there it was down there, happening somehow – the woman struggled erect and *pulled* herself off the knife. Three steps, she took three steps and fell into the flower bed again. The man was howling now, like a great beast, the sound inarticulate, bubbling up from his stomach. He fell on her and the knife went up and came down, then again, and again, and finally it was all a blur of motion, and her scream of lunatic bats went on till it faded off and was gone.

Beth stood in the darkness, trembling and crying, the sight filling her eyes with horror. And when she could no longer bear to look at what he was doing down there to the unmoving piece of meat over which he worked, she looked up and around at the windows of darkness where the others still stood – even as she stood – and somehow she could see their faces, bruised purple with the dim light from the mercury lamps, and there was a universal sameness to their expressions. The women stood with their nails biting into the upper arms of their men, their tongues edging from the corners of their mouths; the men were wild-eyed and smiling. They all looked as though they were at cock fights. Breathing deeply. Drawing some sustenance from the grisly scene below. An exhalation of sound, deep, deep, as though from caverns beneath the earth. Flesh pale and moist.

And it was then that she realised the courtyard had grown foggy, as though mist off the East River had rolled up 52nd Street in a veil that would obscure the details of what the knife and the man were still doing . . . endlessly doing it . . . long after there was any joy in it . . . still doing it . . . again and again . . .

But the fog was unnatural, thick and gray and filled with tiny scintillas of light. She stared at it, rising up in the empty space of the courtyard. Bach in the cathedral, stardust in a vacuum chamber.

Beth saw eyes.

There, up there, at the ninth floor and higher, two great eyes, as surely as night and the moon, there were *eyes*. And – a face? Was that a face, could she be sure, was she imagining it . . . a face? In the rolling vapours of chill fog something lived, something brooding and patient and utterly malevolent had been summoned up to witness what was happening down there in the flower bed. Beth tried to look away, but could not. The eyes, those primal burning eyes, filled with an abysmal antiquity yet frighteningly bright and anxious like the eyes of a child; eyes filled with tomb depths, ancient and new, chasm-filled, burning, gigantic and deep as an abyss, holding her, compelling her. The shadow play was being staged not only for the tenants in their windows, watching and drinking in the scene, but for some *other*. Not on frigid tundra or waste moors, not in subterranean caverns or on some faraway world circling a dying sun, but here, in the city, here the eyes of that *other* watched.

Shaking with the effort, Beth wrenched her eyes from those burning depths up there beyond the ninth floor, only to see again the horror that had brought that *other*. And she was struck for the first time by the awfulness of what she was witnessing, she was released from the immobility that had held her like a coelacanth in shale, she was filled with the blood thunder pounding against the membranes of her mind: she had *stood* there! She had done nothing, nothing! A woman had been butchered and she had said nothing, done nothing. Tears had been useless, tremblings had been pointless, she *had done nothing*!

Then she heard hysterical sounds midway between laughter and giggling, and as she stared up into that great face rising in the fog and chimneysmoke of the night, she heard *herself* making those deranged gibbon noises and from the man below a pathetic, trapped sound, like the whimper of whipped dogs.

She was staring up into that face again. She hadn't wanted to see it again – ever. But she was locked with those smoldering eyes, overcome with the feeling that they were childlike, though she *knew* they were incalculably ancient.

Then the butcher below did an unspeakable thing and Beth reeled with dizziness and caught the edge of the window before she could tumble out onto the balcony; she steadied herself and fought for breath.

She felt herself being looked at, and for a long moment of frozen terror she feared she might have caught the attention of that face up there in the fog. She clung to the window, feeling everything growing faraway and dim, and stared straight across the court. She *was* being watched. Intently. By the young man in the seventh floor window across from her own apartment. Steadily, he was looking at her. Through the strange fog with its burning eyes fastening on the sight below, he was staring at her.

As she felt herself blacking out, in the moment before unconsciousness, the thought flickered and fled that there was something terribly familiar about his face.

It rained the next day. East 52nd Street was slick and shining with the oil rainbows. The rain washed the dog turds into the gutters and nudged them down and down to the catch-basin openings. People bent against the slanting rain, hidden beneath umbrellas, looking like enormous, scurrying black mushrooms. Beth went out to get the newspapers after the police had come and gone.

The news reports dwelled with loving emphasis on the twenty-six tenants of the building who had watched in cold interest as Leona Ciarelli, 37, of 455 Fort Washington Avenue, Manhattan, had been systematically stabbed to death by Burton H. Wells, 41, an unemployed electrician, who had been subsequently shot to death by two off-duty police officers when he burst into Michael's Pub on 55th Street, covered with blood and brandishing a knife that authorities later identified as the murder weapon.

She had thrown up twice that day. Her stomach seemed incapable of retaining anything solid, and the taste of bile lay along the back of her tongue. She could not blot the scenes of the night before from her mind; she re-ran them again and again, every movement of that reaper arm playing over and over as though on a short loop of memory. The woman's head thrown back for silent screams. The blood. Those eyes in the fog.

She was drawn again and again to the window, to stare down into the courtyard and the street. She tried to superimpose over the bleak Manhattan concrete the view from her window in Swann House at Bennington: the little yard and another white, frame dormitory; the fantastic apple trees; and from the other window the rolling hills and gorgeous Vermont countryside; her memory skittered through the change of seasons. But there was always concrete and the rain-slick streets; the rain on the pavement was black and shiny as blood.

She tried to work, rolling up the tambour closure of the old rolltop desk she had bought on Lexington Avenue and hunching over the graph sheets of choreographer's charts. But Labanotation was merely a Jackson Pollock jumble of arcane hieroglyphics to her today, instead of the careful representation of eurhythmics she had studied four years to perfect. And before that, Farmington.

The phone rang. It was the secretary from the Taylor Dance Company, asking when she would be free. She had to beg off. She looked at her hand, lying on the graph sheets of figures Laban had devised, and she saw her fingers trembling. She had to beg off. Then she called Guzman at the Downtown Ballet Company, to tell him she would be late with the charts.

'My God, lady, I have ten dancers sitting around in a rehearsal hall getting their leotards sweaty! What do you expect me to do?'

She explained what had happened the night before. And as she told him, she realised the newspapers had been justified in holding that tone

against the twenty-six witnesses to the death of Leona Ciarelli. Paschal
Guzman listened, and when he spoke again, his voice was several octaves
lower, and he spoke more slowly. He said he understood and she could
take a little longer to prepare the charts. But there was a distance in his
voice, and he hung up while she was thanking him.

She dressed in an argyle sweater vest in shades of dark purple, and a
pair of fitted khaki gaberdine trousers. She had to go out, to walk around.
To do what? To think about other things. As she pulled on the Fred
Braun chunky heels, she idly wondered if that heavy silver bracelet was
still in the window of Georg Jensen's. In the elevator, the young man
from the window across the courtyard stared at her. Beth felt her body
begin to tremble again. She went deep into the corner of the box when
he entered behind her.

Between the fifth and fourth floors, he hit the *off* switch and the
elevator jerked to a halt.

Beth stared at him and he smiled innocently.

'Hi. My name's Gleeson, Ray Gleeson, I'm in 714.'

She wanted to demand he turn the elevator back on, by what right
did he *presume* to do such a thing, what did he mean by this, turn it
on at once or suffer the consequences. That was what she *wanted* to do.
Instead, from the same place she had heard the gibbering laughter the
night before, she heard her voice, much smaller and much less possessed
than she had trained it to be, saying, 'Beth O'Neill, I live in 701.'

The thing about it was that *the elevator was stopped*. And she was
frightened. But he leaned against the panelled wall, very well-dressed,
shoes polished, hair combed and probably blown dry with a hand drier,
and he *talked* to her as if they were across a table at L'Argenteuil. 'You
just moved in, huh?'

'About two months ago.'

'Where did you go to school? Bennington or Sarah Lawrence?'

'Bennington. How did you know?'

He laughed, and it was a nice laugh. 'I'm an editor at a religious
book publisher; every year we get half a dozen Bennington, Sarah
Lawrence, Smith girls. They come hopping in like grasshoppers, ready
to revolutionise the publishing industry.'

'What's wrong with that? You sound like you don't care for them.'

'Oh, I *love* them, they're marvellous. They think they know how to
write better than the authors we publish. Had one darlin' little item who
was given galleys of three books to proof, and she rewrote all three. I
think she's working as a table-swabber in a Horn & Hardart's now.'

She didn't reply to that. She would have pegged him as an anti-
feminist, ordinarily; if it had been anyone else speaking. But the eyes.
There was something terribly familiar about his face. She was enjoying

the conversation; she rather liked him.

'What's the nearest big city to Bennington?'

'Albany, New York. About sixty miles.'

'How long does it take to drive there?'

'From Bennington? About an hour and a half.'

'Must be a nice drive, that Vermont country, really pretty. It's an all-girls' school, they haven't thought of making it co-ed? How many girls enrolled there?'

'Approximately.'

'Yes, approximately.'

'About four hundred.'

'What did you major in?'

'I was a dance major, specialising in Labanotation. That's the way you write choreography.'

'It's all electives, I gather. You don't have to take anything required, like sciences, for example.' He didn't change tone as he said, 'That was a terrible thing last night. I saw you watching. I guess a lot of us were watching. It was really a terrible thing.'

She nodded dumbly. Fear came back.

'I understand the cops got him. Some nut, they don't even know why he killed her, or why he went charging into that bar. It was really an awful thing. I'd very much like to have dinner with you one night soon, if you're not attached.'

'That would be all right.'

'Maybe Wednesday. There's an Argentinian place I know. You might like it.'

'That would be all right.'

'Why don't you turn on the elevator, and we can go,' he said, and smiled again. She did it, wondering why it was he had stopped the elevator in the first place.

On her third date with him, they had their first fight. It was at a party thrown by a director of television commercials. He lived on the ninth floor of their building. He had just done a series of spots for *Sesame Street* (the letters 'U' for Underpass, 'T' for Tunnel, lower-case 'b' for boats, 'C' for cars; the numbers 1 to 6 and the numbers 1 to 20; the words *light* and *dark*) and was celebrating his move from the arena of commercial tawdriness and its attendant $75,000 a year to the sweet fields of educational programming and its accompanying descent into low-pay respectability. There was a logic in his joy Beth could not quite understand, and when she talked with him about it, in a far corner of the kitchen, his arguments didn't seem to parse. But he seemed happy, and his girl friend, a long-legged ex-model from Philadelphia, continued to

693

drift to him and away from him, like some exquisite undersea plant, touching his hair and kissing his neck, murmuring words of pride and barely-submerged sexuality. Beth found it bewildering, though the celebrants were all bright and lively.

In the living room, Ray was sitting on the arm of the sofa, hustling a stewardess named Luanne. Beth could tell he was hustling: he was trying to look casual. When he *wasn't* hustling, he was always intense, about everything. She decided to ignore it, and wandered around the apartment, sipping at a Tanqueray and tonic.

There were framed prints of abstract shapes clipped from a calendar printed in Germany. They were in metal Crosse frames.

In the dining room a huge door from a demolished building somewhere in the city had been handsomely stripped, teaked and refinished. It was now the dinner table.

A Lightolier fixture attached to the wall over the bed swung out, levered up and down, tipped, and its burnished globe-head revolved a full three hundred and sixty degrees.

She was standing in the bedroom, looking out the window, when she realised this had been one of the rooms in which light had gone on, gone off; one of the rooms that had contained a silent watcher at the death of Leona Ciarelli.

When she returned to the living room, she looked around more carefully. With only three or four exceptions – the stewardess, a young married couple from the second floor, a stockbroker from Hemphill, Noyes – everyone at the party had been a witness to the slaying.

'I'd like to go,' she told him.

'Why, aren't you having a good time?' asked the stewardess, a mocking smile crossing her perfect little face.

'Like all Bennington ladies,' Ray said, answering for Beth, 'she is enjoying herself most by not enjoying herself at all. It's a trait of the anal retentive. Being here in someone else's apartment, she can't empty ashtrays or rewind the toilet paper roll so it doesn't hang a tongue, and being tightassed, her nature demands we go.

'All right, Beth, let's say our goodbyes and take off. The Phantom Rectum strikes again.'

She slapped him and the stewardess's eyes widened. But the smile stayed frozen where it had appeared.

He grabbed her wrist before she could do it again. 'Garbanzo beans, baby,' he said, holding her wrist tighter than necessary.

They went back to her apartment, and after sparring silently with kitchen cabinet doors slammed and the television being turned too loud, they got to her bed, and he tried to perpetuate the metaphor by fucking her in the ass. He had her on elbows and knees before she

realised what he was doing; she struggled to turn over and he rode her
bucking and tossing without a sound. And when it was clear to him that
she would never permit it, he grabbed her breast from underneath and
squeezed so hard she howled in pain. He dumped her on her back,
rubbed himself between her legs a dozen times, and came on her
stomach.

Beth lay with her eyes closed and an arm thrown across her face. She
wanted to cry, but found she could not. Ray lay on her and said nothing.
She wanted to rush to the bathroom and shower, but he did not move,
till long after his semen had dried on their bodies.

'Who did you date at college?' he asked.

'I didn't date anyone very much.'

'No heavy makeouts with wealthy lads from Williams and Dart-
mouth . . . no Rensselaer intellectuals begging you to save them from
creeping faggotry by permitting them to stick their carrots in your sticky
little slit?'

'Stop it!'

'Come on, baby, it couldn't all have been knee socks and little round
circle-pins. You don't expect me to believe you didn't get a little
mouthful of cock from time to time. It's only, what? about fifteen miles
to Williamstown? I'm sure the Williams werewolves were down burning
the highway to your cunt on weekends, you can level with old Uncle
Ray . . .'

'*Why are you like this?!*' She started to move, to get away from him,
and he grabbed her by the shoulder, forced her to lie down again. Then
he rose up over her and said, 'I'm like this because I'm a New Yorker,
baby. Because I live in this fucking city every day. Because I have to
play patty-cake with the ministers and other sanctified holy-joe assholes
who want their goodness and lightness tracts published by the Blessed
Sacrament Publishing and Storm Window Company of 277 Park
Avenue, when what I *really* want to do is toss the stupid psalm-suckers
out the thirty-seventh floor window and listen to them quote chapter-
and-worse all the way down. Because I've lived in this great big snapping
dog of a city all my life and I'm mad as a mudfly, for chrissakes!'

She lay unable to move, breathing shallowly, filled with a sudden pity
and affection for him. His face was white and strained, and she knew he
was saying things to her that only a bit too much *Almadèn* and exact
timing would have let him say.

'What do you expect from me?' he said, his voice softer now, but no
less intense, 'do you expect kindness and gentility and understanding
and a hand on *your* hand when the smog burns your eyes? I can't do it,
I haven't got it. No one has it in this cesspool of a city. Look around you;
what do you think is happening here? They take rats and they put them

in boxes and when there are too many of them, some of the little fuckers go out of their minds and start gnawing the rest to death. *It ain't no different here, baby!* It's rat time for everybody in this madhouse. You can't expect to jam as many people into this stone thing as we do, with buses and taxis and dogs shitting themselves scrawny and noise night and day and no money and not enough place to live and no place to go have a decent think . . . you can't do it without making the time right for some god-forsaken other kind of thing to be born! You can't hate everyone around you, and kick every beggar and nigger and *mestizo* shithead, you can't have cabbies stealing from you and taking tips they don't deserve, and then cursing you, you can't walk in the soot till your collar turns black, and your body stinks with the smell of flaking brick and decaying brains, you can't do it without calling up some kind of awful —'

He stopped.

His face bore the expression of a man who has just received brutal word of the death of a loved one. He suddenly lay down, rolled over, and turned off.

She lay beside him, trembling, trying desperately to remember where she had seen his face before.

He didn't call her again, after the night of the party. And when they met in the hall, he pointedly turned away, as though he had given her some obscure chance and she had refused to take it. Beth thought she understood: though Ray Gleeson had not been her first affair, he had been the first to reject her so completely. The first to put her not only out of his bed and his life, but even out of his world. It was as though she were invisible, not even beneath contempt, simply not there.

She busied herself with other things.

She took on three new charting jobs for Guzman and a new group that had formed on Staten Island, of all places. She worked furiously and they gave her new assignments; they even paid her.

She tried to decorate the apartment with a less precise touch. Huge poster blowups of Merce Cunningham and Martha Graham replaced the Brueghel prints that had reminded her of the view looking down the hill from Williams. The tiny balcony outside her window, the balcony she had steadfastly refused to stand upon since the night of the slaughter, the night of the fog with eyes, that balcony she swept and set about with little flower boxes in which she planted geraniums, petunias, dwarf zinnias and other hardy perennials. Then, closing the window, she went to give herself, to involve herself in this city to which she had brought her ordered life.

And the city responded to her overtures:

Seeing off an old friend from Bennington, at Kennedy International, she stopped at the terminal coffee shop to have a sandwich. The counter circled like a moat a centre service island that had huge advertising cubes rising above it on burnished poles. The cubes proclaimed the delights of Fun City. *New York is a Summer Festival* they said, and *Joseph Papp presents Shakespeare in Central Park* and *Visit the Bronx Zoo* and *You'll Adore our Contentious but Lovable Cabbies*. The food emerged from a window far down the service area and moved slowly on a conveyor belt through the hordes of screaming waitresses who slathered the counter with redolent washcloths. The lunchroom had all the charm and dignity of a steel rolling mill, and approximately the same noise-level. Beth ordered a cheeseburger that cost a dollar and a quarter, and a glass of milk.

When it came, it was cold, the cheese unmelted, and the patty of meat resembling nothing so much as a dirty scouring pad. The bun was cold and untoasted. There was no lettuce under the patty.

Beth managed to catch the waitress's eye. The girl approached with an annoyed look. 'Please toast the bun and may I have a piece of lettuce?' Beth said.

'We dun' do that,' the waitress said, turned half away as though she would walk in a moment.

'You don't do what?'

'We dun' toass the bun here.'

'Yes, but I *want* the bun toasted,' Beth said, firmly.

'An' you got to pay for extra lettuce.'

'If I was asking for *extra* lettuce,' Beth said, getting annoyed, 'I would pay for it, but since there's *no* lettuce here, I don't think I should be charged extra for the first piece.'

'We dun' do that.'

The waitress started to walk away. 'Hold it,' Beth said, raising her voice just enough so the assembly-line eaters on either side stared at her. 'You mean to tell me I have to pay a dollar and a quarter and I can't get a piece of lettuce or even get the bun toasted?'

'Ef you don' like it . . .'

'Take it back.'

'You gotta pay for it, you order it.'

'I said take it back, I don't want the fucking thing!'

The waitress scratched it off the check. The milk cost 27c and tasted going-sour. It was the first time in her life that Beth had said that word aloud.

At the cashier's stand, Beth said to the sweating man with the felt-tip pens in his shirt pocket, 'Just out of curiosity, are you interested in complaints?'

'No!' he said, snarling, quite-literally snarling. He did not look up as he punched out 73c and it came rolling down the chute.

The city responded to her overtures:

It was raining again. She was trying to cross Second Avenue, with the light. She stepped off the curb and a car came sliding through the red and splashed her. 'Hey!' she yelled.

'Eat shit, sister!' the driver yelled back, turning the corner.

Her boots, her legs and her overcoat were splattered with mud. She stood trembling on the curb.

The city responded to her overtures:

She emerged from the building at One Astor Place with her big briefcase full of Laban charts; she was adjusting her rain scarf about her head. A well-dressed man with an attaché case thrust the handle of his umbrella up between her legs from the rear. She gasped and dropped her case.

The city responded and responded and responded.

Her overtures altered quickly.

The old drunk with the stippled cheeks extended his hand and mumbled words. She cursed him and walked on up Broadway past the beaver film houses.

She crossed against the lights on Park Avenue, making hackies slam their brakes to avoid hitting her; she used that word frequently now.

When she found herself having a drink with a man who had elbowed up beside her in the singles' bar, she felt faint and knew she should go home.

But Vermont was so far away.

Nights later. She had come home from the Lincoln Center ballet, and gone straight to bed. She heard a sound in the bedroom. One room away, in the living room, in the dark, there was a sound. She slipped out of bed and went to the door between the rooms. She fumbled silently for the switch on the lamp just inside the living room, and found it, and clicked it on. A black man in a leather car coat was trying to get *out* of the apartment. In that first flash of light filling the room she noticed the television set beside him on the floor as he struggled with the door, she noticed the police lock and bar had been broken in a new and clever manner *New York Magazine* had not yet reported in a feature article on apartment ripoffs, she noticed that he had gotten his foot tangled in the telephone cord that she had requested be extra-long so she could carry the instrument into the bathroom, I don't want to miss any business calls when the shower is running, she noticed all things in perspective and one thing with sharpest clarity: the expression on the burglar's face.

There was something familiar in that expression.

He almost had the door open, but now he closed it, and slipped the police lock. He took a step toward her.

Beth went back, into the darkened bedroom.

The city responded to her overtures.

She backed against the wall at the head of the bed. Her hand fumbled in the shadows for the telephone. His shape filled the doorway, light, all light behind him.

In silhouette it should not have been possible to tell, but somehow she knew he was wearing gloves and the only marks he would leave would be deep bruises, very blue, almost black, with the tinge under them of blood that had been stopped in its course.

He came for her, arms hanging casually at his sides. She tried to climb over the bed, and he grabbed her from behind, ripping her nightgown. Then he had a hand around her neck and he pulled her backward. She fel off the bed, landed at his feet and his hold was broken. She scuttled across the floor and for a moment she had the respite to feel terror. She was going to die, and she was frightened.

He trapped her in the corner between the closet and the bureau and kicked her. His foot caught her in the thigh as she folded tighter, smaller, drawing her legs up. She was cold.

Then he reached down with both hands and pulled her erect by her hair. He slammed her head against the wall. Everything slid up in her sight as though running off the edge of the world. He slammed her head against the wall again, and she felt something go soft over her right ear.

When he tried to slam her a third time she reached out blindly for his face and ripped down with her nails. He howled in pain and she hurled herself forward, arms wrapping themselves around his waist. He stumbled backward and in a tangle of thrashing arms and legs they fell out onto the little balcony.

Beth landed on the bottom, feeling the window boxes jammed up against her spine and legs. She fought to get to her feet, and her nails hooked into his shirt under the open jacket, ripping. Then she was on her feet again and they struggled silently.

He whirled her around, bent her backward across the wrought iron railing. Her face was turned outward.

They were standing in their windows, watching.

Through the fog she could see them watching. Through the fog she recognised their expressions. Through the fog she heard them breathing in unison, bellows breathing of expectation and wonder. Through the fog.

And the black man punched her in the throat. She gagged and started to black out and could not draw air into her lungs. Back, back, he bent her further back and she was looking up, straight up, toward the ninth floor and higher . . .

Up there: eyes.

The words Ray Gleeson had said in a moment filled with what he had become, with the utter hopelessness and finality of the choice the city had forced on him, the words came back. *You can't live in this city and survive unless you have protection . . . you can't live this way, like rats driven mad, without making the time right for some god-forsaken other kind of thing to be born . . . you can't do it without calling up some kind of awful . . .*

God! A new God, an ancient God come again with the eyes and hunger of a child, a deranged blood God of fog and street violence. A God who needed worshippers and offered the choices of death as a victim or life as an eternal witness to the deaths of *other* chosen victims. A God to fit the times, a God of streets and people.

She tried to shriek, to appeal to Ray, to the director in the bedroom window of his ninth-floor apartment with his long-legged Philadelphia model beside him and his fingers inside her as they worshipped in their holiest of ways, to the others who had been at the party that had been Ray's offer of a chance to join their congregation. She wanted to be saved from having to make that choice.

But the black man had punched her in the throat, and now his hands were on her, one on her chest, the other in her face, the smell of leather filling her where the nausea could not. And she understood Ray had *cared*, had wanted her to take the chance offered; but she had come from a world of little white dormitories and Vermont countryside; it was not a real world. *This* was the real world and up there was the God who ruled this world, and she had rejected him, had said no to one of his priests and servitors. *Save me! Don't make me do it!*

She knew she had to call out, to make appeal, to try and win the approbation of that God. *I can't . . . save me!*

She struggled and made terrible little mewling sounds trying to summon the words to cry out, and suddenly she crossed a line, and screamed up into the echoing courtyard with a voice Leona Ciarelli had never known enough to use.

'Him! Take him! Not me! I'm yours, I love you, I'm yours! Take him, not me, please not me, take him, take him, I'm yours!'

And the black man was suddenly lifted away, wrenched off her, and off the balcony, whirled straight up into the fog-thick air in the courtyard, as Beth sank to her knees on the ruined flower boxes.

She was half-conscious, and could not be sure she saw it just that way, but up he went, end over end, whirling and spinning like a charred leaf.

And the form took firmer shape. Enormous paws with claws and shapes that no animal she had even seen had ever possessed, and the burglar, black, poor, terrified, whimpering like a whipped dog, was stripped of his flesh. His body was opened with a thin incision, and there was a rush as all the blood poured from him like a sudden cloudburst, and yet he was still alive, twitching with the involuntary horror of a frog's leg shocked with an electric current. Twitched, and twitched again as he was torn piece by piece to shreds. Pieces of flesh and bone and half a face with an eye blinking furiously, cascaded down past Beth, and hit the cement below with sodden thuds. And still he was alive, as his organs were squeezed and musculature and bile and shit and skin were rubbed, sandpapered together and let fall. It went on and on, as the death of Leona Ciarelli had gone on and on, and she understood with the blood-knowledge of survivors *at any cost* that the reason the witnesses to the death of Leona Ciarelli had done nothing was not that they had been frozen with horror, that they didn't want to get involved, or that they were inured to death by years of television slaughter.

They were worshippers at a black mass the city had demanded be staged, not once, but a thousand times a day in this insane asylum of steel and stone.

Now she was on her feet, standing half-naked in her ripped nightgown, her hands tightening on the wrought iron railing, begging to see more, to drink deeper.

Now she was one of them, as the pieces of the night's sacrifice fell past her, bleeding and screaming.

Tomorrow the police would come again, and they would question her, and she would say how terrible it had been, that burglar, and how she had fought, afraid he would rape her and kill her, and how he had fallen, and she had no idea how he had been so hideously mangled and ripped apart, but a seven-storey fall, after all . . .

Tomorrow she would not have to worry about walking in the streets, because no harm could come to her. Tomorrow she could even remove the police lock. Nothing in the city could do her any further evil, because she had made the only choice. She was now a dweller in the city, now wholly and richly a part of it. Now she was taken to the bosom of her God.

She felt Ray beside her, standing beside her, holding her, protecting her, his hand on her naked backside, and she watched the fog swirl up and fill the courtyard, fill the city, fill her eyes and her soul and her heart with its power. As Ray's naked body pressed tightly into her, she drank deeply of the night, knowing whatever voices she heard from this moment forward, they would be the voices not of whipped dogs, but those of strong, meat-eating beasts.

At last she was unafraid, and it was so good, so very good not to be afraid.

Brian M. Stableford

Judas Story

How do you feel about Jack Queen King?

You love him?

Well then, listen to me for a few minutes.

No, I'm not trying to steal a bit of the big gold rush. I'm not selling tears. This is the truth, and I'm giving it away. And besides, I – for one – think that you're wasting a hell of a lot of good tears. How many tears can Jack possibly *need*, quite apart from the question of how many he deserves?

What gives me the right to be telling you a story you don't want to hear?

Well, take a look at your photographs and posters of Jack Queen King. Have you, perchance, got one which is taken from a little further back than six feet from his fly buttons? One which shows some of what goes on *behind* Jack's pretty face and his Ace of Hearts guitar? Take that one out of the stack. There's probably a guy standing on the left of your beloved, four or five discreet paces back of him. He's tall and sleepy-faced, and he looks as if he doesn't quite belong, which is why eighty percent of the pics cut him in half with the side of the frame. That's John Joe Hope. He was Jack's bass player. Right in back, sandwiched in between Jack and John Joe, you'll be able to see a big, shiny mountain of drums. If the focus is sharp on Jack then you won't be able to see much of me. But there might be a dull grey blur, or a pair of phantom hands attached to drumsticks. Rest assured – I'm in there somewhere. My name doesn't matter, and it doesn't sound anything like what they call me, which is Clay.

John Joe and I backed Jack King for nearly two years. From the bottom rung of the ladder to the top. Whenever you heard him play, we were behind him.

Now the first thing I want to make clear is that I'm not claiming any credit for the success of Jack Queen King. There's not a shred of your affection that I want to take away from him. He can have it all. I want *none* of it. I was there, that's all. There's not a single atom of Jack Queen King's music that you can blame on me.

At the same time, I'm saying nothing about or for John Joe Hope. He can tell his own story. This is mine and mine alone.

The first time I saw Jack Queen King he made a very strong impression on me – as an untalented out-and-out bastard. It was no surprise. In our business, every guy on the road will cut your throat if you're cutting into his slice of the loaf. Which we all were. There are only so many third-rate spots for a hell of a lot of third rate outfits.

Jack was playing solo in those days – mostly common-or-garden blues, some Dylan and some lukewarm rock thrown in, to try and cater to all kinds of tastelessness. They stuck him in our dressing room because they didn't have any spare, and they figured he wouldn't take up much space.

He was on first, playing to the crowd while their minds were more on getting canned, stoned and paired-off than blowing their minds in a sweaty bop-session. We didn't want to hear him, but they had the p.a. turned up far too loud and the walls were like cardboard, so we had no option. He was pretty much of a dead loss. We didn't even notice when he deserted his pattern towards the end of the pitch and stuck in a couple of his own numbers. But he came back looking cool and far from unhappy, and he told us how well his own stuff had gone down compared to the standards. We said yeah, and great, and how were they, and he got a little uptight because we weren't even listening to what he was saying, but just making habit-noises. But we had no time for Jack Queen King in his self-elected role as God's gift to rock. We were nervy – especially Pete Candler, whose fingers hadn't worked too well since they put him on downers to break him of a speed habit and he'd got hooked on slow-time instead. He wasn't an addict, just a bit of a wreck. But he'd been part of the group since before my time, and it wasn't for me to suggest we get a new lead.

The one thing that stuck in my mind about Jack Queen King before that gig was that when he changed his jackets he took something out of the breast pocket and flipped it on the floor. It was a playing card – the Four of Clubs.

He saw me looking. 'Carry it for luck,' he said, absently. 'Never use the same one twice.' And he took out a thinned down pack, peeled the blind card off the top, and stuck it into the pocket of his working-coat.

'Don't you look to see what it is?' Marna asked him. Marna was our vocalist.

'Never,' he said. I thought even then – for no particular reason – that he was a damn liar.

We went on and did our usual performance. Solid rock with just enough bounce – lots of effort, lots of crude noise. Lots of fun for the people out front if they were simple-minded enough not to compare us too closely to what they *really* liked. Mostly, they appreciated us – if they hadn't they wouldn't book us. We were no secret by now – we seemed to have been touring the third-class circuit for the best part of our lives. We were all trading on our illusions about how good we might be, or how much we liked the life, or how long it would be before a better bandwagon rolled close by.

Up on the stage you can't hear a damn thing and you can't see much because of the fancy lighting, so you mostly concentrate on what your hands are doing and don't try to get out into the crowd. John Joe really does play gigs with his eyes shut. Occasionally, though, my mind tends to wander into the auditorium, and I try to figure what they're thinking about and what our music is doing to them. I don't try to look at them, because it's not possible. But I let myself go out there a bit, and I get this vague picture of flapping bodies and an occasional pair of staring eyes which remind me that I'm a freak in a great big goldfish bowl. I don't mind that much. A drummer has his drums to hide him. And Marna was the one who really felt the eyes – the hungry eyes and the glassy eyes.

That night, though, I caught two eyes that I knew belonged to Jack Queen King, and he wasn't busy getting a charge from Marna's sweaty legs and flopping tits. He was watching *all* of us, from *all* the angles. I don't know exactly what I saw or how I knew, but Jack Queen King was out there and he was drinking us in. And it made me shiver.

It was past closing time when we came off, but our ever-faithful manager had laid in a supply so we could drown our inadequacies to our heart's content. I was hoping that Jack Queen King might have pulled a disappearing act, but he was still hanging around in the dressing-room. After a gig, Pete and Marna like to talk, and the others humoured them. But I liked to have a quiet word with myself alone, perhaps aided by a bottle or two. So it was easy for Jack to corner me.

'I like the way you play the drums,' he said, sounding about as friendly to my buzzing ears as a rattlesnake.

'Thanks,' I said.

'Seems to me, though,' he said, 'that you could do with a little more *attack*.'

'I play drums, not machine-guns,' I told him, 'and I sure as hell don't need you to tell me how.'

He could hardly have failed to get the message, but he didn't care.

'The bass player and you,' he said, 'you got something worth keeping. The rest is rubbish. When you break up, I might be interested in making a deal. I want to change my act – switch over to my stuff and jack in the shit that everybody pulls.'

'We're all right,' I told him, emphatically. 'We aren't breaking up. We do okay.'

'Come off it,' he said. 'That lead guitar could play itself better. That guy isn't fit to cross the road. How much longer do you think he can last?'

'Pete's okay,' I said, and I stood up to move away and start packing up to leave. But he stood in my way a moment longer while he finished his say.

'You remember, brother,' he said. 'If that lead man steps under a bus, you got an interested party right here. You and the bass man and Jack Queen King. We can do something, see?'

He was a lot bigger than I was, but I grabbed his arms and I was ready to throw him out of my way. The moment I touched him, though, he moved, quick and easy, and ushered me past with a flip of his hand.

'Fuck off,' I said. He collected his gear and left.

Six days later some lunatic let Pete loose at the wheel of a car, and he ran it straight up the front of an articulated lorry. They had to scrape him off the motorway with a fish-slice.

You figure I could have steered clear of my conscience and Jack Queen King at one and the same time?

Maybe you're right, but hell, a few bitter words in a worldful os bitter facts just didn't seem that important. The business is full of guy. I can't stand the sight of. I've worked with a dozen or more in my time I like beating the skins and at my rates, I can't afford to stop for long without going back to being a milkman. I'm no man of means and the Social Security don't figure me as a worthy cause. The breaks of the business are my bread and butter, and you know how these things go.

One thing I held out for and one only, in order to try and save my pride. I insisted that Jack took Marna, along with John Joe and me. John Joe agreed that we couldn't leave her in the lurch, and between us we managed to put it over on Jack. But Jack didn't think that anyone could handle his lyrics except Jack Queen King, and the weeks we put into learning the new style and rehearsing seemed to illustrate his point perfectly. Marna could sing as well as any other cheap warbler, but Jack Queen King's songs were threaded through and through with sarcasm and accusation and plain, simple hatred, and she hadn't a cat in hell's chance of carrying things like that. They simply weren't her scene at all. But I was prepared to argue, and Jack knew it. He and I were already having our differences. He wanted *attack* in his beat, just like he'd said before, and I was slow in delivering. I'd been playing bouncy-bouncy with the sticks for a good many years, and it wasn't really in me to go at them like I was trying to beat the shit out of my ugliest enemy.

Anyhow, Jack let things go pretty easy while we were warming up to the big day when we could go back on the road. He seemed content that we were getting his foul-minded songs into our systems, and he didn't try to push too hard. I kidded myself that it would all work out okay enough for us to pay our way, and support ourselves in the miserable manner to which we'd become accustomed.

The night that we first went on stage with Jack Queen King was the night I stopped kidding. John Joe was at his turgid, fantastic best. Jack, for the first time, looked way out of the rock-bottom class. I put a lot of crash and bang into the hammers, but I could feel that my perform-ance was still short of the guts which we needed. Brute force and ignor-ance weren't enough – Jack's music needed *real* violence – viciousness and anger and hate – and I just hadn't got it.

And on top of that, Marna was a grade A catastrophe. After just one song, Jack moved in on the mike with her, and I just *couldn't* blame him. Jack had invested a lot of his time and his sweat into making those lyrics what he wanted them to be. He'd wasted a lot of words trying to make Marna understand them when he knew all the time that she couldn't get near them. He'd improved John Joe's bass beyond all recognition and he'd tried to make me into what he needed. I'd known that he was trying to make me fight, trying to set me up, and I'd resisted. He hadn't forced me – maybe because he knew that I'd catch on as soon as we started in for real.

It was deadly.

We went down like a lead-loaded lifebelt. Even with Jack singing loud and deep-throated, Marna somehow contrived to throw the whole thing away. Her weakness contaminated the whole session. So did mine. I was the foundation, she was the roof. Neither of us had what it took. I honestly hadn't realised in rehearsal that we were anything more than a second-rate rock machine. But on stage, with real people listening, I knew that we were trying to be something much bigger than that, and because we were failing we were shoving across a load of utter crap.

The audience didn't hold it against us too much. Tasteless audiences are prepared to hear tasteless music. They appreciated competence, but they don't vilify bad play – they just don't care that much. We got more than our fair share of lack-lustre applause.

Then Jack exploded. At last.

He ranted at John Joe for getting lost – which was maybe a little unfair – and he ranted at me for never getting there at all. I expected to take the big part of the hammer, but I was wrong. He wasted only a couple of minutes on me before he swung on Marna. That was a massacre.

I was very slow to react. You're always slow after a spot. The noise beats up your ears so much your brain gets numb.

Also, I thought she could make it. Marna was a hard girl. She'd jerked a good many tears in her time – including a lot of Pete Candler's, and some of mine. I knew that there was a sort of something between Marna and Jack King, and I'd suspected it was more her side than his. But that was nothing new either, and it had never hurt her before.

But this time it was different. Jack was all set to take Marna apart. It was deliberate and premeditated – the hatchet job to end all hatchet jobs, timed when she was so sick at heart she couldn't take it. It had never struck me before what kind of a man Jack would have to be inside himself, in order to write his kind of music. It struck me then.

First, I was amazed – amazed that anything could crease Marna so fast, so hard and so much. Then, I was appalled – appalled at what happened to Marna, who cracked up right in front of me, who lost her plastic-pretty face and her baby-brittle mind in the space of ten or fifteen minutes. Finally, I was frightened – frightened of what Jack had done and what Jack might one day do again. He cut Marna out. Right out.

Hours later, I realised that he had killed her.

I took her home, I tried to talk to her, I tried to listen to her, and all the time, I was getting this feeling stronger and stronger that I was in the presence of something dead. She was walking and talking, but she was dead inside. She had been written clean out of Jack Queen King's existence, but she loved him, with a horrible, total love that left her *nothing* for herself. She was dead. I thought she might recover. I was a fool.

Later still, in the very early hours of the morning, John Joe Hope showed me what he had salvaged from Jack's waste-basket. Two cards – the Ace and Queen of Spades.

He offered them to me without comment, but I knew what he meant. They were death cards. Jack Queen King had carried Marna's execution around with him all day.

We had a little talk, John Joe and I. We agreed finally to chalk it up to the breaks of the business. It's a cruel world, we said. You never can tell who's going to take the big crunch next, we said. Who could have known that Marna would fall apart at the seams like that, we said.

Poor Jack must be feeling as guilty as hell, we said.

Poor Jack!

Poor us. Marna had just ceased to be a fully paid up member of the human race. She'd be a tourist in the land of the living until the day she decided that the joke was over. And we found some sympathy for Jack Queen King. It occurs to me now that's exactly the sort of thing Jack wrote lyrics about. Blindness to the truth. Misdirected sympathy. The savage cruelty of the puppet-master which tells us the way to think and protects us from believing.

You've all heard the story of how we sprang to fame overnight.

Well, that's a lie too.

Once Jack had taken over lead vocal, we looked exactly the same as what we eventually became, nineteen months later. We did the same songs and we had the same style. We got a lot better, with practice, but the difference wasn't spectacular – not half so spectacular as the difference which we saw over our first few performances, which had nothing to do with practice, but a lot to do with attitude.

What had happened to Marna set me a fine example. I swear that it *wasn't* fear, in case the same thing happened to me, that made me into what Jack wanted. That incident was responsible, all right, but only in that it hardened me considerably. I didn't hate Jack Queen King at that point, but I was prepared to *attack* him. I was prepared to put my heart and soul into battering those drums as if I was committing murder. I was even prepared to imagine that I was getting a thrill out of the murder angle. I'd changed, you see. No more bounce and easy going. I still enjoyed playing drums, but the source of the enjoyment was new. I was *committed* – not just to hammering the skins, but also to what I hammered out – Jack King's songs and Jack King's style. The music which would sweep us to fame. Eventually.

You can still hear the music. Even now. It's immortalised in black plastic. Put one of our records on, and listen to it carefully. Now tell me: is that good rock or isn't it?

But the rock on the record isn't more than a tiny fraction of the real story. By *no* means.

Nobody leaps to stardom in ten days flat.

We were second-rate, remember? We were playing in cellars and wood huts and the cheapest of clubs. We had our musical feet six inches deep in the musical shit. Nobody *leaps* out of that. There's *no* way out except to crawl. Nobody knew us. Nobody *wanted* to know us. Each step of the ladder takes time and effort and cash. The rock which we had to offer was good, but it didn't sound so much better on black plastic than half a hundred other groups who were recently graduated from the shit-circuit. You may rave over those discs, but that's because you've been told to, or taught to. Where *we* were – the real power of Jack Queen King – was in our live performance. It was in Jack's voice and Jack's person, and the *shape* of the noise which Jack Queen King had made us produce.

I never thought that maybe the audiences were digging us just a little too much, that they were getting more out of us than had any right to be there to be gotten. What performer would think like that? They thought we were great. I thought it was great that they thought we were great. Who'd ask questions?

But as time went by, even all-out attack became simply a way of doing things. The habit was built into my system. I found myself with time to look out of the drumstack at John Joe, and at Jack King. I found myself with a little attention to spare, that I could use for thinking. I found myself wondering which card Jack was carrying. I found myself reaching out into the sound-space where the people were, just as I used to do in the old days. And I found myself beginning to pick up some of Jack's lyrics, delivered Jack's way with our help. I began to get some idea of what we sounded like.

Slowly, it began to dawn.

I never listen to lyrics. I don't suppose many other people do, either. What the words *say*, when they're written down, is usually pretty meaningless and almost invariably irrelevant. What matters in a lyric is where you put the emphasis, and which words you support with which kind of sound. The guitar obliterates some words, puts power into others. What matters about lyrics is how they *feel*. And Jack Queen King, singing *live* could give his lyrics a feel that was absolutely new.

Let's briefly review your career as a Jack Queen King fan. The first time you heard him on the radio it was just rock music, right? It took two or three times of hearing before you picked up the title of the disc and the name of the artist. *Black Star Children* by Jack Queen King. Heavy beat, words with the right hint of meaning, the right element of aggression and nastiness to appeal to your young and hungry mind. You began to listen closer, and you liked it. It didn't put your soul on ice, but it had you interested enough to want to see him.

And he was cheap and easy to see. We were on the road, playing every date we could, fighting for recognition, angling for the big time. Our price was going up in little jerks as our record climbed into the charts and began to accelerate on its way to the top. You heard that Jack was the greatest in the flesh – far better than in plastic. You caught a few tracks of the L.P. You were keen, you were really looking forward to a good time. You were just looking to be hooked, weren't you? You wanted a new idol, because the last one was developing rust. You wanted a new talking point. You wanted to get a real charge out of Jack Queen King. You were looking to love him, to be knocked out by him, to be taken over by him.

You were a pushover. A real pushover. What surprises me now is not so much that Jack Queen King stole your soul, but that you still had it to lose.

I remember Jack walking offstage, reaching into his pocket, and taking out the Jack of Diamonds. It was the first Jack I'd seen him carry. He tore it up and he was smiling all the time, like the goddamned Cheshire cat.

'*Diamonds*,' he said. 'That's *money*. We've done our time, now. The money's going to take us up from here. Up like a rocket.'

And he was right.

How could he be wrong?

We weren't in any hurry to cut a follow-up disc to *Black Star Children*. Jack's attitude to the singles market was lukewarm. He thought that we could afford to fancy ourselves and our music a little bit more than that. He knew we could sell records and he wasn't averse to making money, but he thought the records went to a totally mindless public. Their money was good, but they didn't turn him on the way that the crowds who came to watch us did.

And so we stayed on the road, hammering ourselves at a tremendous pace. The price on our heads skyrocketed, but Jack kept it down to a level which wouldn't leave us short of dates. I think he forced our ever-loving manager to make a couple of cheap deals which that worthy gentleman would never otherwise have touched in a month of Sundays.

Like I said, I knew that something was happening, because I could feel it too – not only in the lyrics, but in the whole shape of the music. But I was drunk for a while on drums and success, and I didn't really know what it felt *like*, only that it felt. I looked at the people and watched them feel, but I couldn't understand. In time, though, just as the fury had worn down to habit, so the intoxication drained away and left me a little bit cold, and made me take a sudden sharp glance around at where and what and how we were.

The night I found out there were a couple of thousand out front. It was a big crowd by any standards – there aren't a lot of places you can get that many indoors without them being stacked three deep. Before we went on, Jack was jittery with elation, shouting about how good we were going to be, and how much they'd love us. Jack always needed them to love us. John Joe was taciturn, as he always was, but I remember his making some dour comment about Jack carrying the Queen of Hearts in his top pocket, which made Jack mad. He didn't like jokes about his cards – he was still adamant that he never looked at them in advance.

And I *still* thought he was a liar.

We went out on stage.

And we played.

And they loved us. In a manner of speaking.

I was stone cold. The hatred and the violence and the bloodlust was all coming out of the drums, but it was in my hands by now. My head was a million miles away. I guess all that stuff had to be in my heart as well, or it could never have got into my hands, and for that matter I guess it's still here now, but it was so deep set there that it didn't give me any pain, or put any kind of a bite on my mind. It was cold inside my head.

And I looked at the kids who had come to see us. I reached out way beyond the cage of lights, and even tried to double back. I tried to be with them – I tried to feel what they were feeling. I got inside the expressions on their faces.

You know those expressions. You've seen them at the concerts. You've seen them on TV. Adoration, you think? Idolatory?

You're wrong.

Those faces are the faces of people whose souls are being ripped right out from inside them. Those masks of love are shaped and painted by *death*.

Jack Queen King was *killing* those people.

Killing them inside, just like he'd killed Marna. He had the power, did Jack Queen King. The power of life and death. But he'd been right. They were loving him. Genuine, tender, bloody, passionate, heartaching love. And he was teasing and tearing their lives right out of their bodies.

That's what I felt, and I know that it was true, but I didn't understand it. I knew that when we finished the last crescendo, and followed it with a silence like the grave, that those people out there would explode into applause. They would leap and scream and look as alive as anything you could ever see. And eventually, they'd get up on their legs and walk away. And someday, some of them would walk back again to go through it all for a second time, or a third. But I knew as well that what Jack Queen King was handing out in return for their love was murder, and that they were paying his price with their souls.

I hope that you know what I'm saying. Because I can't tell you any clearer than that.

Believe me, *I was there*.

And you weren't. Because inside of you, *you're dead*.

Afterwards, I asked John Joe Hope how he had known that the card Jack was carrying had been the Queen of Hearts. Jack had shown it to us briefly, with a half-smile on his face, before he tore it up and burned the pieces in an ashtray.

'Can't you tell?' said John Joe. 'Doesn't it stick out a mile which card he's carrying? The way he acts, the way he walks – everything goes with the card.'

'I don't think so,' I told him.

'I always know,' John Joe said, definitely. 'Sometimes I can only tell the suit, but usually I can pin the rank as well. Always, when it's a court card. There's always something which says "tonight, it's the Jack of Clubs", or "tonight, it's *Hearts*".'

'I always figured he was lying about not looking at them,' I said.

And John Joe said, 'I don't think he does look at them.'

That was a shock. I realised then that John Joe knew there was something more than rock guitar and fake superstition to Jack Queen King. He might play with his eyes shut, but he'd seen something, somewhere. He knew. But what? And did he care?

It struck me with sudden forcefulness that John Joe might be a part of it – with Jack. It hadn't occurred to me before that anyone but Jack was involved. You know how John Joe looks on stage – like something six weeks dead. You don't think of him as alive – just as a booming rhythm on a bass guitar. But he was a real person, all right, and an integral part of Jack Queen King's sound. And if John Joe was a killer too. . . .

What about me?

I didn't try to talk to John Joe any more just then. I wanted to think – about what Jack Queen King might be, and why; about what Jack Queen King did to the people who loved him. So I bid John Joe goodnight, and we went our separate ways. I never socialised with John Joe, much less with Jack. It was never my style. Except for the ill-fated one-time liaison with Marna, I never dragged work-time proximities into our own time.

That night I got out my own personal copy of our album – the one that was called simply JQK – and I played it for the first time.

I guess that might seem improbable to you. But I never had listened to us play. I'd heard *Black Star Children* on the radio a couple of times, and I'd listened to them hacking things up in recording studios. But I'd never sat down to feel what the music actually sounded like. Haven't you ever been too close to something to know what it's really like? How well *do* you know the back of your hand?

The record was a minor revelation to me. I already knew that we preached a dark message, but everybody and his cousin is a doom merchant these days – it's the fashion. The masses won't love you nowadays for offering them love and kisses. The going price for fame is blood and despair.

But that was the first time I realised how very full of misery and despair those lyrics were. It was the first time I ever sat on the receiving end of the blackness and the bestiality of *Doctor Faust*, *Zero Man*, *Beast Child*, *Pain Killer*, and *Down in the Hole*.

It was good. It had a lot of class and quality. But it was viciously and unrelievedly downbeat. It was purely and simply hate-music.

But it wasn't going to steal anybody's soul. The answer to all my questions wasn't in the plastic. It was in the flesh. The record, however nasty, was only a record. I guess you could claim that there's already something soulless about someone who can glory in those brutal rhythms, and bathe in thundered words that all contain ideas of death and disease and pain and no escape at all, but you couldn't claim that the record was killing people in their own sitting rooms.

All I found out that night was that you can't steal someone's soul by proxy. Murder, like love, is intimate.

I went to see Marna during the week after Jack's superstition about the playing cards became common property. I don't know who leaked it. It wasn't me. It was probably our ever-wonderful manager hunting up another publicity angle.

The market was suddenly flooded with fancy cards. In the panel they had photographs or caricatures of Jack, double-headed like picture cards in a normal pack. In each corner, instead of the denomination and suit, they bore the legend

J
Q
K

Thousands of loyal fans were carrying them around in their breast pockets. For luck. Girls clipped them onto their sweaters, or stuck them down their cleavages.

I was horror-struck when I saw that Marna had one too. I just didn't get it. But why not? Wasn't what he'd done to her exactly what he was doing to them? Why shouldn't she love him for it as well?

'You're really making waves,' she said.

'Have you seen anything of Jack?' I asked.

'No.'

'But you'd like to?'

'What do you think?'

I shook my head. 'I don't know,' I said, with some intensity, to show that I meant it. 'I'm asking.'

'Jack was right, you know,' she told me.

'About what?'

'About my singing. He had to get rid of me. It was a mistake trying to use me in the first place.'

'Sure,' I said. 'He must have been carrying the wrong card that day. Or maybe he forgot it altogether.' All the while I was staring at the thing pinned to her chest.

'I don't have to hate him,' she said.

'No,' I replied. 'Anyone else might. But you don't. That's the way the magic works. But do you really have to love him? For Christ's sake, remember what he *did* to you. Kid, it doesn't matter a damn how *right* he was. What counts is what he *did*.'

'That's right,' she said. 'I don't have to love him.' One time, she'd have hurled that line like it was a ton of bricks. She'd have had a voice like she was spitting acid. But not this time. Not any more. She said it clean and clear, right out, with no trace of anything in her voice.

'*Do* you love him?' I asked her.

'Yes,' she said.

And that was all of it. The long and the short. Yes, she loved him. It cut me up. Not because anything lingered in *my* heart for Marna – the payoff in that game had come and gone a long time ago. Because it made *her* game an out and out bummer. She was lost. Walking dead.

Jack Queen King had stolen her soul. Hers and a thousand others.

In this kind of market, old Satan wouldn't have stood a chance. Faust was the hungry millions, and Jack wasn't paying them out with any coin that they could use. He was working a massive heist.

But where was he going and why?

I just couldn't see it. What the hell *use* is a million Zombies?

I stayed with Jack. There was never any real question of my quitting. There were no long sessions of heart-searching. I didn't feel that there was any crucial dilemma. I'm not offering any excuse. I could say that I stayed because he'd have had no trouble at all replacing me, but that wasn't the way my thinking ran. The simple fact is that it didn't run at all. I stayed because I was there, and that's all there is to it.

If you believe my story, then you can blame me for being a part of it. You can call me Judas, on account of all the people who lost their souls to Jack Queen King. If you don't believe me, you'll call me Judas anyhow for betraying his beloved memory. So okay, I'm Judas – I don't know how to go about defending myself.

During the next few months, things simply went on. We played the same music the same way. Jack went on stage boasting that he was no longer the Jack that figured in his phony name, but the King. He forget to be coy about his playing cards, and he showed the audiences Kings to prove his point. Black Kings – Spades and Clubs. And still he said that he didn't know they were there until he pulled them out. I half expected him to change his name so that it was back to front.

We released the second album. *Zero Man* had been out as a single cashing in on the success of *Black Star Children*, but because it was just another track off the album it hadn't broken any new ground for us. We were off the circuit for a few weeks producing some new sounds, but we didn't find it too difficult. They weren't really new sounds at all – just more of the same. *Road to Hell*, *Desert Sky*, and *No Way Home*. . . .

Eventually, I got to talk to John Joe about it. I caught him when he was stoned, and his tongue was looser than usual. We'd both been rocked a bit by the afternoon performance. It was the day we played up to the total eclipse at the festival.

You remember it, of course. A once-in-a-lifetime occasion. It was a bright, clear day – warm, with no wind. But we all knew, didn't we, that the sun was due to be turned off? It was easy enough for Jack Queen King to drown the audience in an intimate, intangible darkness, which became a real blackout as we approached the climax of our last number.

It was *Black Star Children*. Of course.

I've never been so frightened as when I hammered out the bleak backing to those last few frantic chords of Jack's guitar, and the sky turned grey. At the same moment, the air turned cold and a single blast of wind slashed the crowd. It wasn't us. Not even Jack Queen King could command the weather. Either it was pure coincidence, or something like that always happens in an eclipse. I don't know. All I know is that it took the nerve clean out of John Joe Hope and me, and we both needed to get out of ourselves for a while. And so I got to him at last, to try and find out what he knew.

'How do you take it?' I asked him, my voice fraying a bit with the residue of the day's tension.

'I take it easy,' he said. 'I don't let it bother me the way you do.'

'I've seen their faces, John Joe,' I told him. 'I've watched what Jack does to them. You do *know*, don't you? You do know what he does?'

He looked at me, his face calm and coked-up with dope. His eyes were sleepy, like when he plays, and I could imagine his mind ticking like an atomic watch – nothing could shake his deep rhythm.

'Sure I know,' he said. 'They blow their tiny minds and scatter the pieces on the four winds.'

'Not their *minds*, John Joe,' I said, my voice cracking slightly with the pressure of the words I had to let loose. 'It's their souls. Their lives. He's stealing the souls right out of them. He's killing them inside, John Joe, and we're helping him to do it.'

John Joe shook his head.

'You've got the wrong end, Clay. So okay, that's a real something those people have to lose. But Jack isn't *stealing* anything. Far from it, brother. It *costs* him. These things – souls, you call them – they have to be paid for. Jack couldn't rip off a soul if he wanted to. It's the other way round. They come to throw their souls away. They're longing to have their lives ripped out of themselves. And Jack Queen King gives them the charge they need to do it. *They* take it from *him*. They rip it off and he lets them have it. They *want* to be dead, brother, because it's the only way they can see how to be. They're scared rigid of life, Clay. The kind of people who come to us aren't any prize for the devil. Jack Queen King is the prize – he's footing the bill.

'You say you've watched the people, brother. You always did want to be our there with the people, you poor fool. Well, just for once in your life look at Jack Queen King. Forget what's happening to them – they aren't worth it. Look at what's happening to *him*. Watch him and see if you can tell me he's killing anyone but himself. Hell, he needs their *love*, and he's paying them in the only coin they'll accept. They love him with all their hearts. Do you think they do that because he's ripping them off? Do you think a guy like Jack would rip off the souls of the people who love him?'

Yes, was my answer to that.

But I couldn't give that answer to John Joe Hope. Nor could I say: what about what happened to Marna? Because John Joe didn't care what had happened to Marna. Nor could I say: but it doesn't make sense. Because to John Joe, it did make sense.

You see, John Joe Hope *loved* Jack Queen King.

Just like all the rest.

Except me.

I watched Jack King, like John Joe had asked me to. And what I saw was Jack King, soul stealer. I watched him, and I felt the only thing that I could. I hated Jack Queen King.

You can say, if you want, that I was blinded by that hate. You can say that John Joe Hope was right, and that it's poor, deluded Clay who's wrong. But isn't it love that's reputed to be blind? Couldn't it be you that doesn't see, that doesn't understand?

And that's all I have to say, except to tell you the end of the story. It doesn't add anything. It's just an account of what happened. It didn't explain anything. It doesn't tie the whole damn argument up in a fucking pink ribbon. I can't give you any *proof* of what I say. But this is what happened at the end. . . .

They were crammed in like sardines. Far more than the safety limit. But you could see just by looking that there wasn't going to be any fire. It wouldn't stand a chance. Even fires have to breathe.

They seemed to be hysterical before we even came on stage. There was no back-up group to fill in time. They just came and they waited.

When we walked on stage, John Joe Hope came over to the drum-stack, and he stood beside me while he tuned the bass guitar. He didn't look up at me, but he said in his calm and level voice, 'You watch him tonight, Clay. He's carrying two cards tonight. They have to be the Ace and the Queen.'

He meant the Ace and Queen of Spades. The death cards. Jack had carried two cards only once before. The night he'd dispensed with Marna.

'They won't be for him,' I said. 'If they're death cards, they're for you or for me.'

He smiled a long, lazy smile. 'I'm not scared,' he said.

Strangely enough, neither was I.

John Joe moved away, and the screams of Jack's guitar jerked my hand and feet into action as we whirled away into *Zero Man*.

It was another night, like all the rest. Everybody wanted to see Jack Queen King. They didn't mind the heat and the crush and the stink. They were willing to endure it all just to be with him. And then he snatched their souls.

We played through *Cut Price Coffins* and *No Way Home* and *Down in the Hole*, and the long, long agonising crescendo of *Doctor Faust*. And we did *Sad Times*, to get a rest, and *The Alley* and an extra-long version of *Hold Me Down*. We did a couple of new numbers, for a special treat.

And then we lauched into *Black Star Children*, which was the last before they made us do our encores. Jack really belted into it. He pounded the guitar, and gave it a little bit of extra pain with the fuzzbox, and he fed it back into the speaker. The more he piled it on, the more I stacked up the attack. We were really making it, and I felt as if I'd gone way past all-out and was flying on pure adrenalin. We were taking the audience as high as a kite – I could feel the hysteria coming across the stage in waves. I could smell the high fever.

Something happened inside Jack's amp. It got hot and something gave. His mike was no longer earthed. The whole shebang was live. He came back across the stage to sing the last few words that were the final chorus, and he took hold of the mike-stand. And it struck him dead.

Somebody started pulling plugs out all over the place, and a sea of panic washed all around the hall. The crowd didn't dissolve into a fatal scramble. It was still. Nobody out front was killed.

John Joe Hope and I stood over the body, one on each side.

'I told you so,' he said.

But I still didn't figure it that way.

I looked out over the scream-strewn auditorium, and I could taste the tears. The air smelled like something was six *weeks* dead, not just six seconds.

I picked up the two cards out of Jack's breast pocket, and I showed them to John Joe Hope. Both cards were jokers.

I said to him – and I didn't just mean it for him, but for everybody: – I said: 'How do *you* feel?'

Joe Gores

You're putting me on – aren't you?

I drove into the state capital at ten o'clock on Friday morning. I could have flown, but I had some potential clients in the two states en route, and personal contact, I felt, was the best way to announce that I'd taken over Dad's business since his death three months before.

It was a big bustling city made with new money, mainly defence contracts, so I laid out extra bread for a motel on the interstate beltline around town. One of those ultramodern plastic jobs with precast ceilings, glass tops on all surfaces, indoor-outdoor carpets to make shampooing up the spilled drinks easier, and colour TV in every room.

After checking in, I went to meet the clients and to iron out the procedural details. The tension started building during the busy forenoon, increased during a numbing cafeteria luncheon, was like piano wire by two-thirty, when all the equipment had been tested. I was due back at six-thirty, and my outlying motel would spare me the evening rush hour during my return.

Back at the motel I did a few lengths of the pool, then lay on the sun-warmed cement to work on my tan and to relax. I was still Dad's untested replacement. *I* knew I was professionally competent, but the clients didn't. Not yet. Because I was turning it around in my mind, I didn't tune in the blonde at first. Then, suddenly, I did. Her wet bikini just emphasised what it covered – as it was designed to do – and the late-slanting sun caught the rounded swell of her breasts and buried provocative shadows between them. I had to deliberately switch off. Work to do.

But then she came over and sat down on the cement beside me. Up close she was even better. I dug her looks, her build, the lazy challenge in her smoky gray eyes.

719

'This place is a drag, man. You groove?' She was assessing my body as she spoke with an impudent half-smile on her face.

'Then why stay here, baby?'

She ran a delicate tongue over full lips. 'Study the animals. All the nowhere people, y'know? I mean, all you cats who always just got a haircut yesterday.' Then, without any break at all, she said, 'Want to buy me supper tonight, Mr Straight?'

'Sorry,' I said, and meant it. 'I'm just here for one day from out of state, and I have to be to work in two hours.'

She stood up with a sinuous grace. 'What kind of work can you do at night? Lizbeth Hunter, room two-oh-two. I'll wait until nine o'clock before I go eat.'

I stared regretfully after her, watching the enticing play of her taut backside under its whisp of bikini. Dammit. No matter how good-looking or well-built you are, prime stuff like that is always hard to get. And I had to work! And the job was damned important, too, since it was my first for this client. A real bummer all around.

But the job was a breeze. At 8:35 P.M. I was all finished and exactly six hundred dollars richer. And wound up tighter than a spring, crackling with tension like electricity. Well, still time to call her. A tall rangy cat named DeVille was standing around in his rather threadbare midnight-blue suit, so I asked him for a phone. He let me into an empty office.

'We'll make it the best place in town – your choice.' I told Lizbeth when she answered the phone. 'Twenty minutes. Be ready.'

'Can I drive that groovy Porsche of yours, Mr Straight?'

'We're vibing together, Miss Hip,' I told her, and hung up.

DeVille walked down to the parking lot with me, the overhead sodium lights catching the strong planes of his jaw. He was a big man with a hard taciturn face and thick blond hair graying rapidly. Guys like him turn me off; they should know better than to think in stereotypes.

'You're younger than I expected.'

'I've been voting for five years.' Then I added, 'Age isn't relevant anyway. Once you understand the physics involved, and know the mass you're dealing with, it's all mechanical.'

He rested blunt fingertips on the hand-rubbed fender of my six-cylinder Porsche, twelve coats for a sheen deep enough to dive into.

'All just a matter of mass and physics, huh?'

'That's it.'

I opened the door and he jerked back as if the fender had burned him. He hadn't realised it was my car. Stereotypes again. I rolled down the window to grin at him.

'Got to split, DeVille. I've got a heavy date with a blonde.'

Lizbeth's choice of restaurants was French and surprisingly good. I had *rognons bourguignonne en croûte* – I'm very partial to innards, well-prepared – and she, at my suggestion, had a *noisette d'agneau Montpensier* so we could share a superb Romanée Conti '59. Her red mini was cut low enough to assure me that she wore no brassiere; that, and the look in those smoky gray eyes, made me feel that the expensive wine wouldn't be wasted.

But it nearly was, at that, and for the same reason that she appeared to me in the first place – because she was such a swinging, wiggy sort of chick. Being that, she felt she had to put everything down. The establishment, the suburbs, the pigs, Vietnam, people who could afford twenty-dollar-a-day motel rooms without big monthly allowances from their parents. She'd told me about that over brandy.

'Are you trying to put *me* down too, baby? I asked lightly.

I thought she'd say I was a swinger, but instead the gray eyes were cool and appraising. 'Maybe I will at that, Mr Straight.'

Which secretly bugged me, because I pride myself on being with it. And then, while we were waiting for the car, she did it again.

'Going to fink out about letting me drive the Porsche, dad?'

I *didn't* want her driving it, actually; but the direct challenge gave me a tremendous urge to put *her* down. Hard. To crack the veneer.

'Why should I, baby? It's insured.'

She gave a joyous laugh. 'In*sured?* Beautiful! Hold that thought, man.'

The battle lines were drawn. Once behind the wheel she gave me an appraising glance, then floored it. The Porsche wound up and howled. One-twenty. One-thirty. One-forty. Oh, it was a groove, man. Doing her own thing, wild and free, like the student anarchist putting everyone down by planting his bomb in a school locker. Then it explodes prematurely and blows his hands off, and he suddenly discovers what a drag it is to type term papers with his elbows.

My hands were clenched and sweat dotted my upper lip by the time we reached the motel, but I had maintained external cool. That one was a draw. In my room she bounced down on the bed, letting her legs sprawl carelessly open to show a tempting length of inner thigh and a whisp of black lace. I was in. She was accepting my terms. The bed would be the battleground. But first, she rummaged in her handbag.

'A contribution to the evening's festivities,' she said.

I opened the twist of foil, knowing what to expect. Pot. The twice I'd tried it, maryjane hadn't shown me a thing beyond a mild disorientation, mainly spatial. Acute constipation or high blood pressure can do the same thing.

Her voice was challenging. 'Will Mr Straight smoke grass?'

What the hell, I thought, give her one. She had accepted my battleground. 'Nope. Getting busted is bad for business, baby.'

She laughed in triumph, stood up, and stripped off the dress in one quick, suddenly impatient movement. Her body was terrific. 'Leave on the lights,' she said. 'I like to watch in the mirror.'

It should have been easy: merely find a sex kick she didn't dig. Most of these ultrahip chicks, made safe by the pill, would go down for any stud who turns them on; but they're actually about as far out sexually as grandma was. But Lizbeth was different. She had a genius for corruption. The bed was where it was at for her, and by dawn we'd done everything I'd ever done or thought of doing or *dreamed* of doing with a chick. And yet neither of us had come up with anything so degrading that the other refused, so neither had been able to put the other down.

At seven-thirty she rolled off me for a final time, lit a cigarette, and stuck it between my swollen lips. In reflex action I slapped it away, then realised my tactical error even as my hand moved. She squealed like a little girl, quick to press her advantage.

'Ohhh! Is ums poor mans afraid of ums big bad cancer bugs?'

The bitch. 'I just don't like the goddamn things.'

I couldn't admit that I *was* afraid of cancer, deathly afraid, since my Dad's death; couldn't admit that I woke up sweating at night in terror of not having quit in time, of having the goddamn mushroom cells already ambushed and waiting in my body.

But that cigarette triggered in my mind a way to put her down. The smouldering black patch growing on the rug had become another contest between us; neither would admit to being concerned enough to put it out. Then, watching the fibres die, I suddenly got it.

These way-out types, they dig life without understanding where its true meaning really is at. As a result, they all want to stop war, stop pollution, stop hunting, save the little flowers by the roadside. So if I could put her on about myself, lead her on by circuitous logic to believe Mr Straight, it would be a terrible put-down for her.

I got a glass of water, dumped it on the rug, and got back into bed – all with an abstracted, busy air that made her hostile and watchful. I'd given up too easily, you see.

And then I said, 'I've been thinking, baby. About us.'

'*Us?*' Her eyes flashed. She'd caught me being uncool. 'You mean like a close personal relationship? Like *love?* Man, that's just another ego trip.'

For one minute I didn't answer. Try it some time. Sixty seconds is a long time in a conversation if no one converses. Finally I stirred myself to look over at her.

'Who said anything about love?'

'Well, like ah . . . all you straight cats think . . .'

'How do you know I'm a straight cat? All I said was that getting busted is bad for business.'

She shrugged it off scornfully. 'Another straight hypocrisy; trying to make your money-grubbing sound groovy.' She paused for a moment. 'Next you'll claim you're like outside the law or something . . .'

Beautiful. Doing my work for me, forestalling the suggestion, putting herself on. Beautiful.

'I'm not claiming anything, baby,' I said carelessly.

Silence again while our meeting yesterday churned around in her head. *I'm just here for one day from out of state, and I have to be to work in two hours.* And her: *What kind of work can you do at night?*

Finally, unwillingly, she said, 'So, like, what is it?'

She was hooked. She'd hooked herself. After waiting a second, as if undecided, I hitched myself up on an elbow to grin at her.

'Let's call this a fable, Lizbeth. Let's suppose there are a bunch of cats who don't dig another cat because of something he's done. Something like – well, maybe he's tapped one of them out, dig?'

'No,' she said flatly. But her eyes were searching my face intently now, seeming to find something there which disturbed her.

'So a dozen of them or so get together and decide they have to get rid of this other cat. Just . . . take him out. Cancel him But of course, it might be dangerous or . . . unseemly to do it themselves, dig?'

'No,' she said again. But softly this time, softly, her smoky gray eyes fixed on me with something almost frightened moving in them.

'So they naturally look around for another cat who can do the job for them. A cat from out of state, say – not from their own area at all. A specialist, dig? A sort of . . . *professional* man.'

I played for effect on the last two words, and she said again, 'No.' Her voice was still soft, but it had a sort of entreaty in it by then. 'No, no, no . . .'

'It's done all the time,' I assured her, purposely obtuse.

'No, please, you . . . you're putting me on – aren't you?'

It was a gas. She was trying to deny to herself that I could be a hit-man. That her carefully seductive supper and incredible sexual coupling afterward had been with a . . .

'You're . . . you've *got* to be putting me on. You wouldn't . . .'

But of course, I *would*, her brain told her. That's just what a pro *would* do. He'd want to pump out all the sexual arousal engendered by tapping someone out. Hell, she would have read all about it in her textbooks, she would have majored in psych or soc or lit. They all do.

'Come *on*, baby!' Time for the overkill. I used the hearty, coaxing voice that guys wearing convention buttons use on chicks they meet in hotel bars. 'It's just a story! A fable, like Faulkner won the Nobel prize with.' I stood up, very cool, very casual. 'Look, I'll catch a quick shower, a shave, then we'll eat breakfast and split.'

I was into the bathroom with the door shut before she could react. Under a hard hot shower I let out the laughter in huge whoops. Talk about a *put-on*! She'd be out there right now, trying to tell herself she *couldn't* have spent the night balling with a killer. But if she hadn't . . . why, if she hadn't, then she'd just been terribly put on by Mr Straight himself.

And she wouldn't be able to take that, either. When I went back into the room she would be gone; and the delicious part would be that she'd never know, for sure, one way or the other.

But she fooled me. When I came out of the bathroom, I saw the six one-hundred-dollar bills I'd been paid with the night before. All laid out on the bed. And she was still there, too, in her red mini once more, pressed back against the wall beside the door.

'That money was in your wallet!' she cried accusingly.

Of course. Her sort of wiggy chick had too big an ego factor not to *know* if she'd been put on. So she'd snooped for proof – and had found it. To her, those bills would be 'hit' money from the 'syndicate' or whoever she thought had hired me.

Man, it was beautiful. But before I could laugh, a heavy fist pounded the door.

'Open up in there! This is the police!'

'I called them!' she cried triumphantly. 'While you were in –'

The door burst open and a big man in a rather threadbare midnight-blue suit came through smoothly, his .38 Policeman's Special arcing the room for quarry. I froze, feeling damned silly because my towel might fall off any second. Oh, sure, for Lizbeth it was the ultimate, literal cop-out: she'd run screaming to the hated pigs. But at the moment I couldn't savour my victory. The fuzz I could do without.

At least it was one I'd met. DeVille sighed and rammed the snub-nosed revolver back into his belt holster.

'You *told* me you had a date with a blonde,' he said. 'But where did she get the idea you were a Mafia hit-man?'

Before I could answer, Lizbeth cried, 'Why are you putting your gun away? He's a hired killer! He . . . he *bragged* about it! He . . .'

'Bragged?' DeVille's cop-hard eyes raked me briefly with a sort of sick speculation, then swung back to her. 'Bragged about what?'

So she went ahead and told it, the whole fable about the hired outsider and all the rest. It should have been pretty humorous to someone with the facts, so I kept waiting for the laughter to boil up out of DeVille when he realised that she had taken me for a hired killer. But no laughter came. Instead, he started to look as if he were chewing on a mouthful of maggots.

'Dammit, DeVille, it was just a put-on,' I burst out finally. A drop of sweat was trickling down my bare spine; this clown, after all, could affect my professional future. 'A put-on, get it? A joke. I was just having a little fun with her.'

'*Fun?*' His eyes moved from her, to me, to the sweat-soaked bed, as if able to see us working grimly and lovelessly away there on each other. 'What gets me is the dozen guys who got together and hired another guy to . . . *Fun?* Jesus!'

He turned away, but Lizbeth, still not understanding any of it, seized his arm almost hysterically.

'You can't just leave!' she cried, her face distorted. 'He said . . . he talked about killing someone last night! He –'

'He did kill someone last night,' said DeVille bluntly. 'He executed him. He's a professional hangman.'

725

Tim Stout

Wake up Dead

In view of its amazing and hideous outcome, those of us involved in the Kellin experiment have agreed that an account of what we saw should be prepared at once. Dr Kellin's tragic suicide has robbed the medical world of a detailed explanation of his extraordinary dream projector. In undertaking to speak for the dead man myself, I anticipate a great deal of scoffing and incredulity. However, as my two colleagues will testify, what follows is no wild fancy but a report of plain, terrible facts. Those who cannot accept our word may care to advance their own explanation of what befell John Vanner, of whose body there now exists not the slightest trace.

For me, the affair began with a sheet of notepaper headed 'Comber Fell – Her Majesty's Prison for the Criminally Insane' and an invitation from Kellin, then and until recently the resident director of psychiatry. The letter read more like a summons than an invitation. He would be glad if I could join him and other medical guests for dinner at Comber Fell, where afterwards we would be viewers of a unique experiment. Since it could not proceed without witnesses I was urged to attend. The nature of the experiment was not mentioned, but I knew of Kellin's long-standing interest in the unconscious, and in particular of the sleeping mind. Partly out of curiosity and partly out of a sense of courtesy to an old acquaintance, I wrote back accepting.

His hospitality was very welcome after the long drive to the Warwickshire border. Our party dined alone in a large, panelled room overlooking the sweep of a dense fir plantation that ranged below the hilltop prison. The meat course was excellent, the German hock delightful and we were a merry table. Kellin's other two guests were known to each other, although not to myself.

The first, a heavily-built, short-winded man named Torry, was introduced as a specialist in nervous disorders. His companion, Hasshe, was a very pleasant American with a fund of outrageous yarns about his experiences as an army surgeon. Our conversation was buoyant, if not brilliant, and I wondered when Kellin would turn it to the subject of his experiment. It was some time since our last meeting, and I was startled to see that his hair, surprisingly white for a man of middle age, was very nearly matched in pallor by his lean, scooped-out features. He looked as though the light of day had hardly touched him. I was about to remark on this when he opened up.

Hasshe, I remember, had commented, 'Doctor, that was a real dream of a meal.'

Kellin refilled his glass with a smile.

'A dream, you say. Now there's a word that shouldn't be used lightly.'

Hasshe sipped the hock. 'Well, I was speaking figuratively.'

'Of course. But we should never forget that the word has a literal meaning too. An important one.'

He sat back and looked at us thoughtfully.

'You see, I believe that a dream is a clue.'

'A clue?' Torry's eyebrows rose. 'Hmmm.'

'A glimpse, then, if you prefer. A glimpse of a "somewhere else" just beyond our reach. It does exist, as all of us know. There's glory waiting there, a rapture – and there are nightmares, too, terrors we dare not face, sights that would blast us if we were forced to behold them.

'Most of all, don't you think, a dream is a chance to peep into a land of mystery. Just a brief look from sleep's revolving door. Before we can venture further, our bodies awaken and drag us away.'

Hasshe caught my eye, but it was Torry who voiced our reaction.

'Isn't this a bit – well, fanciful, old man?'

Kellin looked at him in astonishment.

'Fanciful? I dare say it is. What on earth does that matter? These fancies, as you call them, have gripped the minds of human beings ever since . . . well, ever since we became human beings. Think about it for a moment: dreams of prophecy, that have been handed down the centuries until the events foretold came true; visionary dreams, with the power to make a common man into a saint; dreams of supernatural intensity that haunt the sleeper nightly until they topple him into his grave.'

He paused, turned his glass between his fingers and stared at the wine.

'Where do our minds go when sleep fills them? Where do they come back from?'

He lifted his pale face and looked at me.

'I don't know. Do you?'

TIM STOUT

I shrugged and dropped my gaze. Cigar ash, I saw, had scattered over his shirt cuff.

'Of course,' said Torry, 'certain points have been established. From questioning the sleeper after he has awoken, we can state with confidence –'

'Utter rubbish!'

His vehemence startled us.

Torry bridled and turned red. Looking somewhat contrite, Kellin modified his tone.

'I'm sorry if I was a trifle sharp, but really it won't do. It's time medical men moved on from such hit and miss enquiries. You all know yourselves how easily the shreds of memory fade away. Dreams vanish with the night breeze.

'In other branches of knowledge we gather facts at first hand. We make an exception of the study of dreams? We need to see things for ourselves, as they actually are.'

I felt a thrill of excitement at the implication of his words. Torry, sitting beside me, made no effort to conceal his reaction. He took the first puff from his cigar and announced: 'Quite preposterous. Absolutely. You may want to see things for yourself, Kellin, but to want to look at a dream. . . . Well, really, old man! Nobody can.'

Kellin got to his feet and looked down across the table at the complacent neurologist.

'I think I can, Torry,' he said calmly. 'I think I can.'

More than that he would not say and, as at his suggestion we then rose to proceed on foot to where the experiment was to be held, none of us pressed him. The nature of the experiment now seemed plain, but my own attitude towards it was very largely one of scepticism, as well as a natural curiosity. I could tell from their faces that Hasshe and Torry were of the same mind. It was late in the evening and the austere prison buildings of pale brick loomed in the darkness like icebergs square-chiselled by a monster hand. Kellin's short figure strode ahead, his hands deep in the pockets of his black overcoat and his white hair stirred in the steady breeze. I fell in beside him.

'Have you been working on this line of research for long?' I asked.

'For some years.'

'A prison is a strange place to choose.'

'Not so strange, as it happens. My task here is the development and testing of psychiatric therapy for deranged prisoners. We try to eliminate, or at least to control, the criminal urge. It's a far more useful and humane treatment than locking them and their problems away together. As you can imagine, opportunities for research are endless.'

Torry, still sore from Kellin's criticism, glared at him.

'I can imagine all right. But suppose your deranged prisoners decide they'd prefer to be locked away than undergo your psychiatric therapy? What then?'

Kellin's face snapped shut.

'There is no supposing about it. That is what they do decide. But they have not been sent here to make decisions.'

His tone did not invite further conversation. None of us spoke until we reached a long, white building, splashed by the beams of two revolving floodlights set in a look-out cabin topping the nearby prison wall. Kellin mentioned us to wait. The beams played over the building and then swung away to traverse the trees beyond. Once the door was in deep shadow, we moved forward.

'There's a certain degree of secrecy about your presence here tonight,' Kellin told us.

'I'd rather we were not interrupted.'

My curiosity was as strong as ever, but as we hurried through the darkness ahead of the sweeping lights my scepticism was tinged with something close to alarm. Why, I wondered, had Kellin seen fit to behave so stealthily? What kind of medical experiment was it that required three witnesses? A hundred times since that night I have reproached myself for not having the courage of my doubts, and staying clear of the whole business. Yet I am sure that not even Kellin himself could have foreseen the frightful potential of his experiment, or guessed at its ghastly aftermath.

Once inside the building echoes of our footsteps, coughs and guarded whispers heralded us through empty corridors and past closed doors. At length Kellin halted. There was a clink as he unfastened a padlock. Then he opened a door and ushered us into the blackness beyond.

My first reaction was to fumble for a light switch, but there was none to be found. My eyes smarted for a few moments from the almost complete absence of light. Then I saw the faint glimmer of dials and the dull sheen of metal, and made out bulky shapes I took for laboratory equipment arranged against the walls like statues in a museum. My companions seemed similarly at a loss, and we stood together awkwardly. Kellin, evidently used to finding his way in the dark, brushed past us and crossed the room. There came a click, and slowly two green lamps began to make a place for themselves in the blackness.

'Over here.'

Kellin motioned us towards three steel-framed chairs. The green glow was just enough for us to see him and each other.

'Excuse the darkness,' he said. 'It is necessary, as you'll see in a few moments.'

He perched on a bench, where his white hair and pale face stood out like a huge moth amidst the shadows. The lecture began.

'As doctors, you will all know that the brain, for reasons we don't fully understand, constantly emits electrical signals. All brains do this, healthy or not. This we know.'

'It's not my own field,' Hasshe interrupted, 'but aren't these the signals measured and interpreted by the electro-encephalogram?'

'Perfectly correct. I'm certain that you, Torry, as a neurologist, will be familiar with this machine.'

'I certainly know a good deal about the electro-encephalogram,' Torry admitted. 'EEG readings are used in the treatment of many nervous disorders; epilepsy, for instance. The machine produces a series of graphs showing variations in the brain's emissions. But reading and understanding them is a matter for the expert. If you expect the EEG to give you direct evidence of a sleeper's dream, you'd better think again.'

'I expect nothing of the kind,' Kellin replied crisply. 'The apparatus you see around us – I'm sorry I can't allow you to examine it yet – receives the brain's electrical discharges. But far from producing graphs, it changes those signals into another form of energy.'

Suddenly I caught his meaning.

'You mean into light?' I asked.

He nodded. 'Although let us say rather into light patterns which, I hope, will be intelligible.'

'So what you're really telling us is that you can produce a picture of a dream,' said Hasshe. 'It sounds almost like television.'

Before Kellin could reply, Torry broke in.

'You hope the patterns will be intelligible, you say. Are we to understand that as yet you have made no test yourself?'

'That is so.'

A note of entreaty crept into his voice.

'I believe my theories are sound, and I am sure we shall see a clear image of an actual dream. But I want you to appreciate that there is a certain risk involved. Compared with the power needed to project images, the strength of the brain's emissions is weak. To compensate, I am using a recycling device. Considerable electric current will be passing through the sleeper's brain cells. I am convinced that this will do him no harm. But I felt it wrong to proceed without witnesses. That is why I have asked you all to come here tonight.'

'Who is this sleeper?' Torry asked. 'I presume you don't intend to electrocute any one of us.'

'Hardly that, Doctor. Your minds are too useful to me where they are. No, I have a volunteer available.'

He turned a knob, and one of the green lamps gleamed brighter.

'I'm sorry we have to remain in semi-darkness, but there could be no experiment at all if my volunteer awoke. Green is the most restful of colours, but even so I cannot risk more than this soft glow.'

In the small pool of light we now saw a bed on which a man lay asleep. He was hunched beneath the clothes, and we could see nothing of his face, for bolted to the head of the bed, which in turn was bolted to the floor, was something resembling a large black cowl or helmet. This seemed to encase the man's entire head, giving the passing but unnerving illusion of a decapitated body. The picture was weird enough, but what followed added a grim touch. The lighting must have seeped into the sleeper's mind, for a shudder passed through the sheeted body and his right hand fell into view with an audible clank of metal. The volunteer was manacled to his bed.

I could not tell whether Kellin noticed the distaste in our faces as he lifted the hand and slid it back under the bed clothes.

'A precaution, nothing more,' he said easily. 'The man knew he was to be restrained for his own safety.'

He peered at a dial set in the cowl.

'He is now in a deep sleep, so I can remove this. You may look at him if you wish.'

He pulled gently at the cowl.

'Remember one thing. This is not a hospital but a prison. A prison for the criminally insane.'

The cowl came free. We saw the man's face.

Even in sleep, it was repulsive. There was a greasy sheen on the broad, slab-like features. The straggle of moustache glistened unhealthily in the green light. Thick neck folds all but swallowed the chin. And for some reason it was a familiar face. I was trying to place it when Hasshe spoke.

'John Vanner. Luckily for him he was brought to trial in this country. Back home, a man like that ends up lynched.'

Then I remembered. Three years ago, I had performed post-mortems on Vanner's four victims. The prosecution had called me to the Old Bailey to give evidence.

Few murder trials can have equalled the Vanner case in gruesome detail. It aroused so much popular fury that the public gallery had to be cleared twice. The editor of a leading evening newspaper was summonsed for printing the medical evidence in its entirety, against a direction from the bench.

'Thirteen years was the sentence, wasn't it?' I asked Kellin.

He nodded. 'I believe you were connected with the case.'

'I've seen nothing so sickening since the war. Most of it was too atrocious to go to the jury. First, that old fellow in the railway sidings: his head was literally wrenched from his shoulders. Then there was the

731

flat where we found the woman. The Police took me with them. I can still remember moving aside on the stairs when the blood came dripping down to meet us. Thank God you've got him chained up.

'But the last time was the worst. Twin brothers, each nine years old. What was left of them came to the hospital in two buckets.

'I'm sorry, Kellin. If Vanner's the man whose dream you want us to watch, I don't think I'm interested.'

Kellin was unmoved.

'The killings were appalling, I agree,' he said. 'But do the man the courtesy of considering his own account.'

'What account?' asked Hasshe. 'The press said he was convicted on his own admission.'

'He admitted he killed four people. He never confessed to murder.'

Kellin pointed towards the bed.

'You saw the chains. Does it need me to tell you the poor fellow's a somnambulist? When he walks in his sleep he ceases to behave like a human being. He becomes a machine that strikes out blindly.'

Torry had been starting at Vanner's face. He turned away and looked at Kellin.

'Wasn't there some nonsense talked about during the trial of a dream being responsible for what he did?'

Kellin nodded. 'I'm surprised you should regard a recurrent nightmare as nonsense, Torry. Doubtless your lack of sympathy for my patient is matched by your obvious ignorance of the possible effects. The story's wretched enough.

'Yes, mention was made of a dream. It was the result of something that happened to Vanner while he was a young boy. He was born illegitimate. Home was an alley basement, and a screaming slut of a mother who eked out her dole money with what she could earn on the streets. One night when Vanner was about nine, there was a violent argument between her and the particular lout with whom she was living at that time. The boy was hiding under the bed, but saw the whole thing. The woman lost control completely and seized a kitchen knife. Before the man could stop her, she ripped open his cheek from eye to the mouth and rammed the blade into his chest, until jammed against the collar-bone. He dragged out the knife and grabbed her throat. Vanner says he watched him start to squeeze, but then became frightened by the noises his mother was making and looked away. When he heard the noises cease he made a dash for the door.

'In a moment the man was after him.

'Young Vanner ran for his life. He could hear the wounded killer stumbling after him, shouting out offers of money and sweets if he would hold still and wait. The knife was still in the man's hand. The boy kept running.

'The houses around were empty slums awaiting demolition. He knew no one would hear his cries for help. So he sought sanctuary among the yards and side-streets, although every moment he fancied that the murderer was upon him. Wherever he hid, the footfalls seemed to follow. Each time they came closer and closer. The boy feared that if he were caught he would be silenced for what he had seen. Finally, he could think of only one last hiding place. In his panic, he clambered over the railings of a nearby cemetery, squirmed under a tarpaulin and concealed himself in a freshly dug grave.

'He cowered there all night. His macabre refuge scared the wits out of him. But even more terrifying than the grave's dark depths was the thought that he would hear footsteps dragging towards its brink, and look up to see the tarpaulin torn aside.

'In the morning, the boy was rushed to hospital by undertakers who discovered him unconscious. Later, he was placed in a children's home until foster parents were found for him. Years afterwards, he learned that the man who murdered his mother had actually collapsed not far from the scene of his crime.'

'So he'd been running away from nothing?' said Torry.

Kellin shook his head.

'You're wrong. He was running from something all right. Running, fleeing, desperately trying to get away. Today – tonight – over twenty years later, he still hasn't escaped.'

'But you said he got away! He was safe.'

'But you never get away from your own fears,' Hasshe put in. 'That's what you're saying, isn't it?'

'Exactly that,' Kellin agreed. 'You see, what came after that little boy was a spectre of his own making, called up by all the fears and horrors that haunt a child's mind. Fear of the dark; fear of being alone. Fear of pursuit, of footsteps and of unseen padding things. Insubstantial things, yes. But to young Vanner, as real as the most dreadful monster that ever walked the earth.

'Dreams, of course, were inevitable. His childhood was tortured by them. Almost nightly, he tells me, he was visited by the same nightmare in which something huge and menacing clumped after him.'

'This dream persisted from childhood until now?' I asked in surprise.

'Not quite. It troubled him less as he grew older, and possibly would have faded altogether. No, its resurgence, and also his habit of sleep-walking, date from a bad road accident in which he received a serious head wound. It was necessary to operate to remove an extensive blood clot, but unfortunately brain damage set in before the clot could be drained. The nightmare returned.

'As you know, head injury patients often reveal a strength far greater than one would expect and Vanner was a powerful man to start with. Although at first friends controlled his wild fits and leanings towards somnambulism by locking him in at night, the time came when while still asleep he broke out and escaped into the streets. The four killings were committed during the next eleven days, while he was sleeping rough.

'Now this is the point to grasp.'

Kellin seized my arm.

'In his sleeping, dream-ridden mind anyone, even a young child who happened to come near him, was mistaken for the beast, monster, call it what you will, which he believed was hunting him down. You can see he's a heavily-built fellow. I believe he was a quarryman before his arrest.'

We looked at the still figure lying chained upon the bed. Kellin walked over to it.

'It almost goes without saying that, in common with most people, Vanner has only a sketchy memory of what he dreams. I hope that after tonight's experiment we can tell him exactly what happens. Perhaps once he knows the nature of his nightmare, it will trouble him no more.'

He tapped a bank of quietly humming equipment.

'This is the heart of the circuit. Now here –' He pointed to an arrangement of dark glass cubes – 'is what we may term the dream projector. It will cast an image upon the screen you see at the foot of the bed.

'This regulator –' He laid his fingers on a long steel lever – 'controls the strength of the current pulsing through the sleeper's brain. A weak current may show us little or nothing. A strong current will give a much clearer picture.'

He grasped a bundle of electrodes hanging from the sides of the cowl.

'I have to connect Vanner's scalp to the circuit. Perhaps you would consider the experiment.'

We watched in silence as his hands moved deftly over Vanner's head, attaching the metal pins beneath his hair and gluing them lightly into position. He plugged the leads into a grey cabinet and turned back to us.

'Unless any of you wish to raise an objection, I shall commence the experiment now.'

Hasshe glanced at Torry and myself.

'Well, how about it? I can't see any harm.'

'It seems all right,' Torry frowned. 'The fellow's an absolute brute, anyway. Let's see what you get.'

Kellin looked at me. With misgivings, I nodded.

'Very well,' he said and moved the big lever. At the same moment the lamps went out. We all stared at the vacant screen.

At first there was nothing, and with the passing of the minutes our eagerness began to evaporate. There was only the pale square before us to look at, and all that broke the silence was the hum of Kellin's electrical apparatus. Deprived of everything except my thoughts, I pondered over what young Vanner must have felt as he fled from his mother's killer. I was still trying to imagine the horrible scene when Kellin tapped my shoulder.

I looked up quickly. His rapt features were tinged with a pale blue glow. The light came from lengths of glass tubing, which had suddenly become illuminated. Within the glass, sparks flashed and sprang with an icy radiance along thick strands of copper wire. The tubes ran from all corners of the laboratory into the base of the dream projector.

Kellin stood calmly beside the projector, but his voice trembled with excitement as he announced, 'It's working! You're looking at the electrical signals from Vanner's brain. Soon they will become stronger.'

The twinkling settled into a steady pulse of blue light. The four of us could see each other quite clearly, although the rest of the laboratory remained in shadow. As far as we could make out, Vanner seemed unaffected by the experiment. Intense excitement now gripped us. We were anxious to see if all would take place as Kellin had predicted.

At length, there came a flicker upon the screen. Amazed whispers broke out amongst us. Kellin ignored them. He seemed to be juggling with a dial and a knob. The flicker returned, danced back and forth for a moment and cascaded into specks of light that patterned across the screen like snowflakes against a window. Kellin left us to busy himself amongst his transformers and other mysterious machines. Torry, Hasshe and myself were fearful lest Vanner's dreams should slither out of Kellin's grasp and vanish from the screen. Incredibly, it seemed that the experiment might succeed; and so far it had hardly begun.

Kellin's face reappeared from the darkness.

'The current is too weak,' he told us. 'I shall have to increase the flow through his brain, as I expected.'

Torry began to protest, but Kellin ignored him and tugged at the lever.

There came a troubled groan, and Vanner's body jerked as from a spasm of pain. Then he relaxed. I was about to protest myself, when a gasp from Hasshe drew my attention back to the screen.

The patterns of light were forming themselves into a picture.

I was ready for astonishment, even for marvel. But the warning shiver I actually felt took me unawares. It had not occurred to me that the experiment could be frightening, yet to look down at Vanner's sleeping face and then bypass the closed eyes into the secrets of his mind now seemed unwise and something better left alone. Nevertheless, I said nothing.

On the screen, a cloud of red flecks whirled within a square of what I can only describe as dark light. Out of the kaleidoscope appeared, in weird and shifting colours, a landscape.

An empty plain, lonely as the beginning of time, lay beneath a dusky, fire-streaked sky. Its grey wastes were dotted with patches of glowing cinders, and here and there great gouts of flame erupted from the smoking earth. As I looked I grew sick with sudden certainty that I myself had wandered dismally over this land, and would finally return to do so once more.

A movement by a mound of cinders caught my eye. In a flash, my gloom became excitement as I saw Vanner's figure come into view. He was naked from head to foot, but was otherwise identical with his sleeping self upon the bed. Moving with slow, floating steps as if the air were taking his weight he silently circled the cinder pile and halted, poised ballerina-fashion.

He was now close enough for us to see his face. Despite the easy grace of his motion, he looked badly scared. Again, I looked across to the bed. It was uncanny to compare the sleeper's calm, closed features with the wide-eyed panic of the dream-Vanner. My heart grew clammy. How would the experiment end? It was the first time I had felt sympathy for the helpless man whose mind we were dredging.

With agonised slowness Vanner turned, like a bobbing balloon. He looked behind him. Some distance back, something was snuffing out the burning embers and jets of flame as it stalked him under cover of darkness.

The projector did not reproduce the sounds of the nightmare, but we could all imagine his desperate cry. I itched to help the man. But his body was still quiet and at rest.

He tried to run, but a baby could have out-distanced him. There was no strength for motion left in his rolling, swaying body. Our viewpoint shifted, and with Vanner we saw beyond the plain to the mists and oozing dampness of a marsh, or swamp. This seemed to be his objective. Then the picture shattered into a whirlpool of broken images, which gave way to drifting smoke and tongues of flame. Whatever was following Vanner's trail passed by unseen.

The picture cleared. Again we saw the sullen plain, now barren of life and movement. There were no flickers of fire. Instead, across the dead expanse stretched a trail of gigantic tracks where flame had been smothered and stone crushed and splintered by ponderous feet.

'Great God!' whispered Hasshe. 'What does he think is after him?'

'He does not know,' said Kellin. 'To see the face of his own fear would kill him. He cannot bring himself to look upon it.'

A shriek from the bed interrupted him. The nightmare had Vanner full in its grip. His teeth were clenched and his face was contorted.

Torry was the first to protest.

'Stop this at once!' he demanded. 'Can't you see that the man's in pain?'

Kellin glanced dispassionately at the bed.

'It's nothing new,' he said calmly. 'As I've told you, Vanner and his dream are old friends. His gaoler tells me this happens almost every night when he is in his cell.'

Unwillingly, we turned back to the screen and left Vanner to toss in his sleep. During our brief inattention, the dream-Vanner had floundered into the swamp. He was making no better progress through the reeds and wet, boggy soil than he had done on land. The picture put me in mind of dreams of my own, in which I had tried to escape but could hardly move my legs. The morass seemed never-ending. We realised Vanner was trying to get away from a dense bank of mist that had rolled off the firm ground and was crawling over the marsh. Forth from behind the grey curtain slid ripples of churning water, as something plunged in his wake.

On seeing the ripples breaking around his legs, Vanner gathered new strength. He threw himself forwards to the brink of a ditch. Vomited from the unhealthy ground, the water welled up suddenly and dripped sluggishly over a rocky fall. Like a flow of thick green oil, it dropped some twenty feet into the rush and spray of the river below.

At the water's edge, Vanner hesitated. 1 ut the mist was almost upon him. Patches wafted away until only a tall, massive column remained, facing the fugitive. Still, Vanner wavered. A colossal silhouette began to appear inside the opaque, grey envelope. Tendrils of drifting greyness stole out towards him and hardened into the semblance of a clutching hand. Before the fingers could fasten upon him, Vanner spun round and toppled into the stream.

We jumped with shock as his silent scream found vent in a soul-freezing cry from the sleeper Vanner.

But it was not the shout that suddenly clogged my throat.

'Look!' cried Hasshe. 'Look at his body!'

The prisoner was drenched. I actually saw a dark waterline sweep over the bed clothes until his limbs, chest and even his hair were as sodden as if he had been swimming.

Kellin's excited voice broke in.

'Incredible! His physical, sleeping body is feeling the effects of his own dream.'

'For God's sake turn the thing off!' Torry urged him.

It was a fascinating, frightening thing to behold. Taking care not to get too close, we all examined Vanner. There was no doubt that he was soaked through. But where the water came from, or passed to, we could not understand. Meanwhile, the dream-Vanner was borne over the falls into the river below.

'There can be only one explanation,' Kellin decided. 'He's starting to live the dream. It parallels those cases of devout priests whose bodies reproduce the wounds of Christ on the cross. What if we increase the current?'

'Do you want the poor devil to die of fright?' cried Torry. 'If you're right, he thinks he's drowning.'

Kellin ignored him and moved the regulator further forward. Vanner shrieked in pain, and the incandescent light from the glass tubes overhead cast a contorting shadow of his wildly plunging body against the ceiling.

Hasshe gripped my arm.

'We'll have to stop this,' he whispered.

'He can't wake up as long as he's attached to that contraption of Kellin's. And if the dream keeps going like it's going now, pretty soon he'll be wanting to wake up real badly.'

We were rising to our feet when once more the scene changed. Vanner sought to breast the flow, but could barely keep his balance against the onrush of the river. In place of the mist, a snow blizzard raged around him. As he struggled to make headway, Vanner cast terrified glances over his shoulder. Some way back, the snow was settling upon a looming shape cloaked by the storm. Although the blizzard all but obliterated the scene, Hasshe and I were pinned to our seats.

Then, at that instant, the storm ceased. The last flakes fell away. In the stillness, we saw the river was now a strip of blue ice winding between the heights of a great canyon. Vanner was caught between its banks, held firmly by the ice sheet. He was frozen in such a position that could not but behold the monstrous pillar of snow confronting him. It was faceless and featureless and menacing.

All of a sudden a strong wind blew up. It played with the piled-up drift and began to whisk it away. Cracks appeared at the base of the pillar. I think we were all expecting to see the thing shake itself free and stride forward.

Vanner's screams had now subsided into moans. He lay huddled upon the bed. His misery was echoed in the face of the dream figure, whom the ice held almost immobile. The gusts of wind had all but bared the form of the waiting monster when the dream-Vanner made a last effort to break free. His head jerked downwards and splintered part of the ice sheet. We saw a deep gash on his forehead.

Hasshe and I gasped. Simultaneously, blood spurted from the head of the whimpering man lying at our side.

This time there was no delay. Hasshe got to Kellin first.

'Can't you see the man can't take any more? He's dreaming himself to death! Turn off the machine, or you'll make that dream come true.'

He bent over the bed.

'Unless he gets treatment right now, your patient will be a corpse.'

'Get back!'

Kellin lunged forward and dragged Hasshe away from Vanner.

'Remember what happened to the other people who got too close to him.'

'You maniac!'

There was a blow and a thud. Kellin's slight figure collapsed as the burly Torry flung him away from the projector.

'Don't you realise what's happening? First the water . . . then the blood – you're bringing his nightmare to life, not just for him but for all of us! Any moment now, the thing on that screen will come looking for him, right here in this room!'

Torry grabbed the regulator and dragged it down.

'Someone has to stop this experiment!'

Instantly, the light from the tubes became almost blinding. Scream after scream rang from the bed, as the writhing sleeper all but tore his ankles and wrists from the manacles.

'No!' Kellin gasped. 'Oh God, you've turned it to full power!'

The hum of the electrical apparatus rose to a crescendo. The brightness became an explosion, and the laboratory lights went out. So did the picture on the screen. I think we all dropped on our hands and knees. Vanner's shrieks rang out beside us, even more horrible in the sudden blackness. But this time they had a different tone. They were not the cries of a sleeping man.

We cringed together in terror.

At first faintly, but growing stronger by degrees, a new sound was borne to our shrinking ears. It came from nowhere within the laboratory: indeed, it seemed to issue from very far away. As a rail thrums from the pounding of a distant locomotive, so the room and air around us throbbed, louder and louder, with the approaching tread of mighty feet.

A presence, awful and inevitable, entered the laboratory. Footfalls trod past us in the darkness. They crossed the floor to the bed.

Vanner's shrieks came thick and fast in an avalanche of sound. We heard the clatter of chains being ripped away. Horribly, the screams rose above us as though he had been snatched up into space. There was a series of sickening crunches such as I cannot bring myself to describe, and the cries ceased abruptly.

At that moment, the presence vanished. We froze.

With courage such as I have never seen, Hasshe struck a match. The flame roamed round the dark room like a giant's candle. Our hearts in our mouths, we stepped towards the bed.

Perhaps one day many years from now I shall forget what I saw: the empty bed swimming in blood, the sheets and blankets ripped to shreds by monstrous talons.

But how can I ever forget the terrible implications of what I did not see?

For of Vanner's body we found never a trace.

David Fletcher

Corabella

It was about the middle of June when Michael first acknowledged that the children were becoming an insuperable problem. If he hadn't loved Janice so much, if he hadn't been so determined to make up to her for all the misery she must have suffered, he would have thrown in the towel there and then. But that would have caused unhappiness to both of them. In fact, it would have broken his heart. So far he had avoided making any criticism of the children because he knew how much she loved them and how they had kept her going during the worst period of her marriage and its final breakdown. And it couldn't have been easy for them, he reminded himself. No wonder they were difficult, resentful of another man entering their young lives. If their father was the only model they had to judge him by . . . But these arguments had begun to take on a hollow ring, to sound like the convenient quotes from textbooks they actually were. He had to talk to Janice about the children, even at the risk of hurting, perhaps even alienating her. He had kept quiet too long.

It was the brutal, winding kick in the stomach from Paul that finally decided it. There was a park a short walk from the small garden flat Janice had rented in South London, and Michael had taken the children there one hot, Saturday afternoon. Paul was too old, or considered himself too old to hold Michael's hand. Therefore, Melinda did so reluctantly. Michael could feel the hostility in her stiff little hand as they walked, as usual, in silence. Once in the park she broke free of him and ran after her brother.

The purpose of these outings, of course, was to give Michael and the children a chance to get to know each other. In fact, all that happened was that Michael spent his time pursuing them, trying to make sure that they came to no harm. In any open space they ran from him and quickly became absorbed in their own world. On bus rides or river trips they sat ostentatiously together and, if possible, several seats away from him. At the cinema once, they had moved seats while he was using the lavatory. Michael had tried everything to get close to them, to amuse and entertain but by that Saturday afternoon he had given up. Having located Melinda's red dress beside the paddling pool, he lay down on the dry grass and kept half an eye on them. He knew that Janice did not like them to paddle in the pool and equally that were he to cross the grass and forbid it he would certainly be greeted by open defiance. Perhaps if he didn't put the idea into their heads . . . They did not go into the water. They stayed close together, apparently deep in some game of their own. Then they turned as one and came steadily across the grass to where he lay, propped on his side.

'Hello,' he smiled at Melinda, working on the principle that being the younger and female he might make some headway with her. Besides, she hung back a little, watching him pensively. Paul stood close, however, and Michael remembered thinking, afterwards, as he had turned towards the boy that his stout shoes were quite unsuitable for this weather. The boy drew back his right leg and kicked Michael, as hard as he could, in the stomach.

By the time Michael was able to speak he had realised the futility of remonstrating with Paul. The children waited for him at the gates and, still holding his stomach which felt as though it contained a jagged rock, he joined them and led them silently home. Or rather to the corner of their road whereupon Melinda broke free of his hand and chased after her brother, leaving him to follow them in.

He spent the rest of the day with them and they were, as always in their mother's presence, polite and well-behaved to him. There was no chance to speak to Janice about them until bedtime, at which point they came to him and quietly thanked him for having taken them to the park. Paul extended his hand and Michael duly shook it. He even managed to lay his hand briefly on Melinda's flaxen head. Smiling, Janice led them out of the room.

The flat was small, all she could afford since she steadfastly refused to let Michael help her until they were married. He understood, but was frustrated by her independence. The small, square sitting room opened, by way of french doors, straight into a walled handkerchief of garden. The bedrooms were situated next to this room and the children's window faced onto the garden. He heard Janice adjusting it and the quiet murmur of her voice as she settled them.

'Janice,' he began as soon as she came back into the room. 'I must talk to you about the children. Paul kicked me in the stomach today. It's just not working.'

'Oh yes, he told me about that. I'm sorry, I hadn't realised it was anything that bothered you.'

'What do you mean, he told you?'

'About the wrestling match. He was so impressed with you, but rather afraid that his kicking you like that might mean you wouldn't do it again.'

Michael felt as though he had stepped into a nightmare, and the feeling grew as Janice steadfastly refused to believe him.

'Michael, they have never lied to me in their lives. I mean you can't expect me to believe that Paul deliberately kicked you, in cold blood.'

'But that is just what he did do. There is no way it could have been an accident, Janice. And besides, that's only the latest in a long line of incidents.'

Michael heard his voice as he recounted the catalogue of things the children had done and knew that it sounded querulous and his complaints trivial. Indeed, calmly recited in the context of their exemplary behaviour in Janice's presence, the incidents did sound trivial, and unbelievable.

'Mike,' she said gently when, out of sheer embarrassment, he had let his voice tail away. 'Perhaps the real trouble is that you aren't used to children. Even I sometimes think they are a different species. You learn to make allowances, to understand. It will be all right but, darling, you've got to get used to them as children every bit as much as they have to accept you as a step-father.'

She made it all sound so rational, so easy. He was an only child. He knew nothing about children except what he had read in books. It was very difficult for a man to take on two growing children with definite, formed personalities of their own. Janice thought the experts minimised, even ignored the vast amount a potential step-parent had to learn before he could feel at ease with children.

'I'm sorry,' he said, taking her hand. 'I suppose I have been expecting too much, and over-reacting.'

'You should have told me before.'

'I didn't want to worry you. I suppose I didn't want you to know that I'd failed with them. I so want to make a success of it.'

'You haven't failed. And you will make a success of it. You all will, all three.'

At the open window of their room Melinda smiled at Paul who grinned back.

Michael felt better, felt reassured and was determined to make greater efforts with the children. In the middle of the following week he went to dinner, played chess with Paul and snakes and ladders with Melinda. It crossed his mind that perhaps Janice had spoken to them about their behaviour for he sensed a new relaxation in them, an absence of hostility, even when he was alone with Paul while Janice was supervising Melinda's bath. Perhaps he had made the breakthrough. Perhaps that kick had been the end, the necessary, final expression of antagonism. Or perhaps the kick had been a test, a challenge to see if Michael was like their father, a man who responded violently to anything that crossed him. And when Melinda demanded that he should put her to bed and tuck her in, he knew that he had succeeded.

She slept in the lower bunk and Michael carefully arranged the single sheet over her, tucking the ends firmly in. She looked at him with her mother's frank grey eyes. He stooped to kiss her. She twisted away from him.

'Oh, I forgot to say good-night to Corabella,' she announced, jumping out of bed. Michael was so relieved that her reaction was not a violent rejection of him that he smiled and followed her across the room. Then his blood froze. He felt sick, a ringing in his ears and felt the cold sweat break out all over his body. He backed away, staring in disgusted fascination at the glass tank on the window ledge which he had not previously noticed. Melinda stood on tip-toe and peered into the case.

'Good-night, Corabella,' she said and then turned back towards the bed. Her eyes widened at the sight of Michael's face. He tried to pull himself together, but it was impossible.

'What's the matter?' she asked.

'That ... thing ...' he stammered, for he could not bring himself even to say the word. Melinda looked puzzled. He nodded desperately towards the glass case.

'That's not a thing. That's Corabella. She's the biggest and most beautiful spider in the whole world,' Melinda said proudly and trotted back to bed. Somehow, Michael managed to tuck her in again but his eagerness to get out of the room, away from that creature, prevented him even trying to kiss her.

He was shaking and knew that his face would be grey with fear. Janice thought he was ill. In her anxiety she forgot Paul, who stood in the doorway, knotting the cord of his pyjamas.

'Do you know that they've got a spider in there? An enormous one.'

Janice looked at him in disbelief, then threw back her head and laughed.

'You don't mean to tell me that you're afraid of spiders? Oh Mike, that's too ridiculous.'

'It's a phobia,' he said. 'I'm not afraid but literally terrified. Janice, you've got to get rid of that thing. I mean people don't keep them. Please, you must kill it straight away.'

'No,'

Janice shot him an angry glance and hurried to Paul who looked every bit as upset as Michael.

'Don't be silly, darling,' she said, encircling his shoulders with her arm. 'Mike wasn't serious. Nobody's going to hurt Corabella.'

'I was serious,' Michael shouted. 'Don't you understand? I can't bear the things. They terrify me. Just knowing it's there . . .'

'I hate you,' Paul shouted, and bolted from the comfort of his mother's arms into his room, slamming the door behind him.

'Now look what you've done,' Janice said, and hurried after Paul.

Michael knew that he had lost all the ground he had made that evening. He knew, too, that it was ridiculous. But he had to go and stand as far as possible from that door while his eyes searched every inch of the room for other spiders. It was always this way. Once he even suspected the presence of one he was unable to relax or even behave naturally. Summer and winter he always kept the plug in the bath and the washbasin. Throughout the warm months he sprayed his flat daily with an insecticide which killed them. It was no accident that his flat was on the top floor of a brand new building which stood in a wasteland of concrete which, Michael liked to believe, no spider would willingly enter.

When Janice returned she was too angry to say much and Michael was too frightened to stay. He fled from the flat and spent more than an hour minutely inspecting his own. He sprayed until he coughed with the scent of the insecticide and could not get to sleep for hours. Every time he closed his eyes he saw Corabella's eight horribly poised legs.

Janice tried to reason with him the next day in a long telephone call. She had, as always, taken a thoroughly practical approach to the problem. She gave him details of various cures about which she had read. Michael had read about them, too, and shuddered to think even of the first step.

'All you have to do is sit in a room with a therapist, and they have a dead spider in a sealed glass jar right on the other side of the room and . . .'

'No,' he said. 'Please, I don't even want to talk about it.'

In his turn he tried to persuade her to make the children put the creature back into the garden. No need to kill it, just get it out of the flat.

'No.' Janice was adamant. 'I've brought them up to be free of these irrational fears. Nearly all children are frightened of spiders because of the bad example of adults. I'm proud that mine are not. Besides, it's educational.'

Eventually, they agreed not to talk about it and Michael contrived not to go to the flat. He didn't ask about Corabella, nor did he allow himself to consider whether Janice realised that his sudden insistence that he should take her out, or that he should meet them all at the National Gallery, or outside the cinema was because he did not dare to go into the flat. If she did understand, she said nothing. And gradually the fear began to fade as it always did if he were not reminded of it.

And then Janice rang him at the office and, to his surprise and delight, said Melinda wanted to ask him something.

'Please will you take Paul and me to the fun fair?'

'Yes, of course. I'd love to. When would you like to go?'

Janice came back on the line full of apologies. He didn't have to take them, he wasn't to feel pressurised. It was just that she got sick on the rides.

'I love them all,' Michael told her. 'And I'd love to take the kids. I'll pick them up tomorrow.'

The whole spider incident, he felt, was behind them. He would go into the flat, collect the children and have a marvellous time. The fact that Melinda had asked touched him. He knew that Janice had been right about his having to make allowances and about letting the relationship develop at the children's speed. He felt accepted. And it was true, he did love fun fairs.

That night the children stood solemnly together in front of the glass case. Corabella had made herself a handsome, strong web, and she stood poised in its centre, her legs spread out, waiting. Paul had explained to Melinda that it might be necessary to sacrifice Corabella. She understood. In fact, she didn't mind at all. Paul did, a little, but he kept his fingers crossed. Perhaps it would not be necessary.

It transpired that the children, by some quirk of conditioning, shared between them their mother's delicate stomach at fairgrounds. Firmly they explained that Melinda got sick if she whizzed around on the whirly things, and Paul got sick if he went up high. So much, Michael thought, for Janice's claims to have brought them up without irrational fears. They must have learned these from her for such reactions were, he knew, entirely psychosomatic. However, he complimented them on their good sense in telling him and confessed himself delighted that he would get to ride on everything. He decreed a rota system. They would take it turn and turn about. He and Melinda on the helter-skelter, he and Paul on the Waltzer and so on. Neither of them wanted to go on the boating lake.

And in this way, though Michael did not realise it, Corabella was preserved from the possibly deleterious effects of any unusual motion. Paul and Melinda simply slipped her carefully prepared box to one another so that she always remained in the safe keeping of the child who waited, smiling and patient, while Michael and the other rode.

That is until the Big Wheel.

This was to be the climax of Melinda's afternoon. She insisted that they get right to the head of the queue so that they were the first to take their place in the swinging, mounting cars. That way they got a longer ride. Michael admired the logic of this and readily agreed. They got on and the bar was fastened across in front of them. Melinda was glad to see that there was plenty of room on the seat and shifted along to the end, leaving a good space between Michael and herself. Their car slowly mounted backwards with a longish pause between each jerking movement while the next car was occupied. The fun fair was busy that afternoon and they made one complete revolution of the wheel before the ride proper started. While the last car was loading, Melinda took the box out of her pocket but kept it out of sight, pressed against the wall of the bar. The timing, she knew, was all-important. Slowly the wheel turned. Michael called and waved to Paul who waved back. Melinda allowed one complete revolution to take place and the second to begin before she removed the lid of the box and deftly covered it with her hand. Corabella was anxious to get out. She could tell from the tickling against her imprisoning palm.

'Look, Michael,' she said simply as their car approached the crest of the ride, and tipped the box up on the seat between them. Probably, she thought, Corabella was confused for she paused a moment before scuttling fast towards Michael.

It is not always so that people freeze with fear. Michael didn't. He jumped to his feet, his legs trapped by the safety bar, his arms flailing, but the impetus of the car's sudden descent was made lethal by the violent rocking his sudden movement had caused. He seemed to hang for a moment, looking at Corabella, before plunging down.

Melinda hung on tight. She was far too busy to watch what happened. In fact, her car still swung sickeningly, but she was not afraid. The wheel made another one and a half revolutions before the machinery was halted. During that time Melinda retrieved Corabella, who curled up, a fat, satisfying blob in her hand. Melinda placed her gently on the floor of the car and squashed her with her foot. Then, working swiftly, she flattened the carboard box and threw it under the seat where other unremarkable litter already lay.

The rest of that day passed in a blur for the children. Everyone said they must be in a state of delayed shock. Melinda answered their questions as best she could, but there was no reason why Michael should have jumped from the car. She hadn't even been looking, and then the car swung so frighteningly . . . A doctor was called to give them both a mild sedative. Janice needed a stronger one and before she fell asleep she remembered that she had not told the children that Corabella was missing. She hoped they wouldn't be too upset.

'Paul?' Melinda whispered from the lower bunk.

'What?'

'Did his head go splat like you said it would?'

Paul giggled.

'Yes. Splat.'

'I wish I'd seen that,' Melinda said enviously, and drowsily.

'Mm. Pity about poor Corabella, though,' Paul said.

Melinda giggled in her turn. She hadn't told Paul about Corabella.

'I made her go splat,' she said proudly. 'With my foot.'

Paul felt sick.

'But that's murder,' he said.

'No. She was sacrificed. Like you said. Besides,' she added, turning over sleepily, 'she might have talked.'

Paul did not go to sleep. Ridiculous though he kept telling himself it was, he was afraid of Melinda.

Acknowledgements

The publishers wish to thank the following for permission to reprint previously published material. Every effort has been made to locate all persons having any rights in the stories appearing in this book but appropriate acknowledgment has been omitted in some cases through lack of information. Such omissions will be corrected in future printings of the book upon written notification to the publishers.

The Withered Arm by Thomas Hardy. The Trustees of the Hardy Estate and Macmillan, London and Basingstoke. From The New Wessex Edition of *Wessex Tales*, 1888.

The Bird by Thomas Burke. John Farquharson Ltd.

The Terror (1917). The Estate of the late Arthur Machen and A. M. Heath & Company Ltd

Lot No. 249 (1922). The Estate of Sir Arthur Conan Doyle, Baskervilles Investments Ltd and John Murray (Publishers) Ltd/Jonathan Cape Ltd. From *The Conan Doyle Stories*.

The Apprentice by Hilaire Belloc. A. D. Peters & Co. Ltd.

The Killers by Ernest Hemingway. The Executors of the Ernest Hemingway Estate. From *The First Forty-Nine Stories*.

Arabesque: the Mouse by A. E. Coppard. A. D. Peters & Co. Ltd.

Treasure Trove (1924 as *Thirty Pieces of Silver*) by F. Tennyson Jesse. The Public Trustee and Harwood Will Trust.

Cinci by Luigi Pirandello. The Estate of Luigi Pirandello and The International Copyright Bureau Ltd.

Suspicion by Dorothy L. Sayers. Victor Gollancz Ltd and David Higham Associates Limited. From *In the Teeth of the Evidence*, 1939.

The Last Chukka by Alec Waugh. A. D. Peters & Co. Ltd.

Dead on her Feet by Cornell Woolrich. Victor Gollancz Ltd. From *Nightwebs*.

Taboo (1940). Geoffrey Household and A. M. Heath & Company Ltd.

A Little Place off the Edgware Road. Graham Greene, The Bodley Head and William Heinemann, and Laurence Pollinger Limited. From *Collected Stories*.

ACKNOWLEDGEMENTS

The Words of Guru by C. M. Kornbluth. E. J. Carnell Literary Agency. Copyright 1941 by Albing Publications.

Yours truly, Jack the Ripper. Robert Bloch and A. M. Heath & Company Ltd.

The Glass Eye. The Estate of the late John Keir Cross and A. M. Heath & Company Ltd.

The Web by D'Arcy Niland. Curtis Brown Ltd.

The Little Black Bag by C. M. Kornbluth. E. J. Carnell Literary Agency. Copyright 1950 by Street & Smith Publications Inc.

The Physiology of Fear and *The Head and the Feet* by C. S. Forester. A. D. Peters & Co. Ltd. From *The Nightmare.*

The Veld by Ray Bradbury. A. D. Peters & Co. Ltd. From *The Golden Apples of the Sun.*

Skeleton by Ray Bradbury. A. D. Peters & Co. Ltd. From *The October Country.*

Evening Primrose by John Collier. A. D. Peters & Co. Ltd.

Back from the Grave. Robert Silverberg and A. M. Heath & Company Ltd.

A Rose for Emily. The Estate of William Faulkner and Curtis Brown Ltd.

The Island of Bright Birds. John Christopher, Victor Gollancz Ltd and David Higham Associates Ltd. From *The Golden Road,* 1974

The Comforts of Home by Flannery O'Connor. A. D. Peters & Co. Ltd.

The Skylight. Penelope Mortimer and Deborah Rogers Ltd. Copyright 1960 by Penelope Mortimer.

Pig. Roald Dahl, Michael Joseph Ltd., Penguin Books Ltd and Murray Pollinger. From *Kiss, Kiss.* Copyright 1959 by Roald Dahl.

Robert and *The Question* by Stanley Ellin. Curtis Brown Ltd.

In the Steam Room by Frank Baker. From *The Fontana Book of Great Horror Stories.* Copyright Frank Baker, 1966.

The Pencil (1953). Edmund Crispin and A. P. Watt & Son.

The Dark of the Moon. The Estate of the late Olaf Ruhen and Lawrence Pollinger Limited. Copyright 1947 by Olaf Ruhen. From *Land of Dahori.*

Falling Object. William Brittain and A. M. Heath & Company Ltd. From *Ellery Queen's Mystery Bag,* 1973.

The Terrapin. Patricia Highsmith and William Heinemann Ltd. From *Eleven.*

The Taste of Your Love. Eddy C. Bertin and A. W. Bruna & Zoons Uitgeversmij B.V., Utrecht.

Not after Midnight (1971). Daphne du Maurier and Curtis Brown Ltd.

The Game by Thomasina Weber. Victor Gollancz Ltd, Mystery Writers of America Inc. and Laurence Pollinger Ltd. From *Killers of the Mind* edited by Lucy Freeman.

The Fanatic. Arthur Porges and A. M. Heath & Company Ltd.

The Whimper of Whipped Dogs (1973). Harlan Ellison and Michael Bakewell and Associates Ltd.

ACKNOWLEDGEMENTS

Judas Story (1975). Brian M. Stableford and Michael Bakewell and Associates Ltd.

You're putting me on – aren't you? by Joe Gores. Victor Gollancz Ltd, Mystery Writers of America Inc. and Laurence Pollinger Limited. From *Killers of the Mind* edited by Lucy Freeman.

Wake up Dead (1975). Tim Stout and Michael Bakewell and Associates Ltd. From *The First Orbit Book of Horror Stories*.

Corabella. David Fletcher and Anthony Sheil Associates Limited.